To Rez

What watches you while you sleep?

KCH

THE STATION
MASTER OF
NEW BROOK WEST

THE STATION MASTER OF NEW BROOK WEST

Edited by Avril Wiese.

Published by Robert Cottreau.

Printed in Canada by Amazon.

Cover design by Jessica Cox of Jess C Design
Calgary, Alberta, Canada.

THE STATION MASTER OF NEW BROOK WEST

The oldest and strongest kind of fear is fear of the unknown.
- *H.P. Lovecraft*

Intro

This story's about destiny, fate, and choices. There's loneliness and sadness. There's love and sex. There's fear, lots of fear. There are surprises, at least many of them were to me.
The ending was never in doubt; it's the journey that makes the story.

Prophecy

Their names all in the letters lie
When the three come together, the tree will die

Prophecy

A girl from a line of boys, a boy from a line of girls.

Prologue – Christina Nicole

She watches from the edge of the road as the group stares in confusion at the accident.

The one man, perhaps their leader, looks into the car then at the stopped train as if attempting to make sense of the event, as if trying to understand what has happened and how and why. The others look on in wonder, talking amongst themselves at this most unlikely display, speculating about the cause of this horrible outcome. They shiver in the dreary fog, dusk nearly upon them.

Another man removes a pile of papers from the car and brings them to the leader who shakes his head.

"In the end, we're all alone" she hears him say as he steps away from the scene.

Yes, yes we are.

Then, he abruptly turns and spots her standing near the edge of the forest, green eyes looking out from beneath her grey cloak.

Does he see her smile? Her face?

She sees their confusion. Their sorrow.

This will be described as a tragedy.

She takes one last look at the scene then walks toward the small body with a single missing black shoe and vanishes into the forest.

1 - Funeral for a Friend

I watch from the edge of the road as my best friend's ashes are laid to rest, unwelcome as I am at his funeral. White and grey gravestones both ancient and contemporary fill the huge cemetery, its shape like a massive auditorium for the deceased. Large concentric circles of road surround a central square, a clear area accessible only by the four paths spaced evenly around it; it's inviting in its openness as if awaiting a quiet gathering, a solemn audience. Crypts and mausoleums remind visitors that even the wealthy die, their remains protected from the elements like pharaohs of old. Small tasteful fountains offer the chance for reflection, to think of deceased love ones, or to ponder life.

My place up the gently sloping hill on the fifth circle out from the center offers me the best view I can expect. My mood is both sombre and introspective, standing as close as I can be to my one true friend in the world.

This isn't how I imagined it, where our decisions would take us, what would happen along the way, or who we'd become. Or where I'd be standing today. We were supposed to grow old together. I exhale deeply knowing that this reality is now mine as well as his.

It shouldn't be a warm and sunny day; it should be dark and cloudy, overcast and gloomy to better fit this tragedy and my sadness. With rolling thunder and distant lightning strikes. With music. With friends. I wear grey clothing, not as solemn respect but to reduce my chances of being recognized. Given the choice, I'd have worn white and black; or maybe something else entirely.

A stone statue, its hands raised over its head as if about to dive, looks down on the solemn group gathered at the grave-side; most of the attendees seem to be Rick's parents' age. Had any of them even met my friend? I don't recognize any of our old friends, though he'd surely acquired some new ones during our years apart. I wonder if any of them even know he died. Do they care? Do people here care? Was he loved at the end? Will he be missed?

I wonder who will be at my funeral. Will anyone come? I hope so.

His mother kneels to place the urn in the ground, her dark knee-length skirt tightening as she does, her movements slow and deliberate. Her black outfit on the green grass under the bright sun is a striking image, almost beautiful. The small crowd is silent. His father stares into the hole in the ground as if lost in thought before casting a quick look around the cemetery, his eyes never settling on me.

Rick had tried so hard, even when he failed, which he often did. He'd tried to be good, to fit in, to do the right thing, to be the right person. Much like I had. Perhaps our faults and shortcomings were what brought us together. Some of us are more susceptible to temptation and vice, and less equipped to resist and overcome it. Some of us lose the energy to fight life's battles, to try to be good, to do the right thing; to know the right thing to do.

I refused to believe his death was a suicide, though I suppose it's possible. To be honest, I wasn't sure of the cause, assuming it was some form of overdose. I'd heard of his passing from a mutual friend who I don't see here today.

How do we become who we are? Where does it start?

His home life was as tragic as his passing, at least in my opinion.

His dad never had time for him and did an awful job at parenting, not in a 'beat-the-shit-out-of-you' way but more in an 'I-have-no-use-for-you' way. He never involved himself in Rick's life, in his successes when he wanted to celebrate, in his failures when he needed guidance, in his sadness when he needed comfort.

They spent no time together, even when he was a young child, and had no relationship to speak of.

He had definitely reached his glass ceiling professionally as an 'assistant-whatever' handling accounts of some kind as a glorified clerk. Despite his menial role in the world, he acted superior to one and all. I didn't like him and I'm quite sure he felt the same about me.

Rick had an older sister who'd moved away from home at a young age; I can't recall ever seeing her, though perhaps I did at some point and it just didn't stick with me. In any case, he never spoke of her and I never brought it up.

Rick's mom was an empty shell, like a cartoon character waiting for words to be written above her head. She had no personality, rarely contributed to the conversation, and seemed to pretty much just nod and smile. Maybe she was a vacant soul or maybe her husband had her sufficiently under his control that she had entirely lost herself in their relationship.

I may not be explaining it properly but it had a profound effect on him.

I'd always assumed that Rick was short for Richard but in time he told me that his full name was Patrick. Rick's parents had named him after the father's uncle but his dad decided early on that he would not be worthy of that name, abbreviating it to Rick. He never much liked his name anyway as far as names go. We never spoke of it again after that one time.

My home life was also a pretty empty one. Mom and Dad were just completely disconnected from reality as well as from me as if they had a child before realizing that they didn't actually want one. They'd loved me while I was an infant but I grew less likeable with age until I hit thirteen and became an absolute burden, an anchor preventing them from setting sail. My grandmother Ella, perhaps noticing this, guided me as best she could during our time together and, looking back, I'm grateful for her efforts. But the general apathy at home made my mind sad and dark, something I didn't fully realize at the time.

Rick and I met in grade ten when we were both fifteen and connected immediately. He was decidedly more popular than me, far more outgoing and rebellious, and, through his confidence, I soon found a way to channel my inner spirit into something unfocused. Seeking to make the worst of what I felt was a crappy hand, I dove into this seedy underground scene.

This came with its own set of rules, its own way of thinking, and a 'fuck-the-world' attitude which I never really understood but adopted all the same.

Girls throwing back in their parents' faces their lives of sex, drugs, and rock n roll, and 'enlightened' guys who thought they were smarter than everyone else. It all made sense at the time, at least I tried to rationalize it that way.

I rolled with this 'Scene' despite never finding my home among those with whom I associated. Everyone thought they were different, unique, and special but none of them really were. They weren't even liked-minded. It was a sad state, really. I occasionally questioned my situation but knew I didn't fit in anywhere else. The opportunities that presented themselves dragged me deeper and deeper into a dark realm where my isolation increased as I sank. I completely lost touch with what I wanted and who I wanted to be, a distance separating me from the larger whole. I thought I had friends. I used a lot of drugs, drank a lot of booze, frequently made a fool of myself, and was generally discontent with my circumstances.

I bounced from one day to the next with total disregard for my future. Sure, I got decent grades in school, but I saw no hope ahead to had no focus, no objective. It didn't feel like depression but perhaps it was. I fucked up as often as I could, drank as much as I could, took whatever drugs I thought would impress the group, and regretted it all the next day.

And then repeated my stupidity the following night.

Bad decisions got normalized as they seemed the only ones I made. Regret kept me awake at night and I went through spells of isolation where I disappeared from the Scene before running back to the only place that I felt welcome.

There's nothing romantic or glorious in hitting rock bottom but I did it again and again. Each time worse than the one before. And it all seemed so normal.

My world was grey. I'd lost the energy to fight life's battles. Nothing mattered.

Until I met Lori.

Her cutting-edge style combined with a clever intellect and tender heart bewitched me from the moment we met. She was sweet and kind and pretty with a smile that made me smile however much I didn't want to.

Her parents were well-off, her dad an executive in a large corporation, she having long ago lost any relationship she had with their lifestyle and their friends, striking out on her own. She lived alone in a small apartment several blocks away from mine and Rick's dark cavern in the basement of an old house. We met one day in the park and connected immediately.

We frequently had meaningful conversations allowing me to draw on an intelligence that I rarely revealed outside of occasional discussions with her. We always had fun when we were together, goofy playful fun. I cared for her with all my heart, protected and supported her, listened to her, talked with her, and loved her deeply. We laughed often, kissed every chance we got, and always held hands.

My world was bright and clear.

2 – Absolute love

Shortly after she turned twenty-one, she told me that she was pregnant. At twenty-two, the thought of fatherhood terrified me, but, seeing the joy in her face, I was immediately taken in by the happiness this would bring to our lives. Her parents were less than delighted, having kept me at arm's length during our year and a half together, unsure of how I fit into their social circle. I assured them of my sincerest intentions, my love for their daughter, and how thrilled I was to share a life with her and our baby. Despite their obvious displeasure with my role in all of this, they set us up in a nice two-bedroom place in a less volatile part of the city, away from a neighbourhood which held too many bad elements. My parents couldn't have cared less when I told them the news, saying things like "that's wonderful for you dear" and "she's such a sweet girl" as if they were reading from a script.

I'd had few communications with them over the previous two years with little effort on their part to take an interest in my disastrous life.

Maybe they thought I'd make a mess of this like I had with everything else. I'd successfully obtained my high school diploma but lacked the focus, desire, and income to attend university.

Lori continued to work at a local coffee shop making a decent wage plus tips, while I found a job loading trucks at a commercial delivery company, a higher-paying gig than I expected. Our relationship stayed strong, often to my surprise considering our circumstances, and we made ends meet as she worked until a week before she delivered a healthy baby girl.

I pulled myself together, focused my energies on being a good provider, a caring boyfriend, and a loving father. Lori's happiness remained the most important thing to me at all times, my heart's wish was that my smile would warm her in the same way hers lifted me.

Both sets of parents were at the hospital to be the first to see Suzie, seemingly ecstatic with their beautiful granddaughter, though rather indifferent to us. Our happiness was absolute with Suzie and with each other, confident that our family would be a strong one and that our love was timeless. We went home the next day, newborn-baby gifts from friends and family, an unmarried twenty-one-year-old couple with a child. The thought of fatherhood was still remained a terrifying one.

Suzie was amazing from the moment we walked into the apartment. She was instantly comfortable in her home, her mood jovial from day one.

We'd carefully set up a colourful room of her own for her as well as a space for her in our bedroom, to make our daughter as cozy as possible.

She slept well, interacted with others, and was generally happy. Fatherhood suited me, much to my parents' (and my) surprise, and I enjoyed every moment spent with Suzie. Perhaps I had finally found my home.

My life had changed, in a good way, and I wanted to share this new life, this new me. But my time spent with Rick became increasingly infrequent after Lori and I moved in together as he felt that I'd somehow sold out, though his mind was increasingly drug-addled so it was hard to be sure exactly what he thought. It seemed I'd officially lost my one true friend.

I didn't miss the drinking buddies, punk girls, and acquaintances from the Scene, and I doubted any of them cared I had become a father if they knew.

But that no longer mattered. My new life was filled with laughter and love and wonderful memories in the making.

Lori and I met people in our neighbourhood to hang out with giving us a sense of belonging. I had never imagined I could feel as connected to someone as I was with her, like we were parts of each other's whole.

Our love grew more powerful as if time increased our attraction, our passions and desires deepened, her smile a beacon. Lori became more beautiful every day, her smooth porcelain skin, her
raven-black hair, her shapely figure, her sparkling eyes.

The first year with Suzie was fantastic, my argument for Lori to stay home during that time sufficiently persuasive for her to agree, neither of us wanting to ask our parents for babysitting assistance. Our daughter was great, rarely fussing about, well-behaved in both public and private, allowing us to go out as a family and enjoy our time together. I loved my daughter as I hadn't thought possible, with a depth I couldn't explain. It was a beautiful revelation.

My work, though dull and mindless, came stress-free, another saving grace for a young couple with a toddler. I got a small raise, largely due to my employer's kindness, making it possible for our living arrangement to work. Though the dreariness of my job got to me at times, it paid better than anything else I could find, and I couldn't imagine relying on my in-laws any more than was already the case.

In time Suzie graduated from crawling to walking, requiring Lori be more vigilant and giving us a reason to delay buying a house with stairs.

I had every intention of asking her to marry me but we both thought it best to wait. In any case our current home, though not really 'ours', was enough for the moment.

I secretly longed for the day when I could pull myself out from under Lori's father's thumb, and provide for my family on my own.

I now had focus and motivation, and had built up some confidence and common-sense in the last few years to back me up. And had the love of an amazing woman with a wonderful daughter as my rock.

When Suzie was about eighteen months old, I started to wake from recurring nightmares. These weren't so disturbing that they needed psychoanalysis but were odd because I could never remember anything except that I was entirely alone in a dark forest and scared of the unknown around me.

I decided to keep these to myself, not wanting to upset anyone else or talk like these carried some bleak meaning. I never had much in terms of religious faith, and put little stock in the paranormal sciences, nor had any use for therapy, though in retrospect maybe I should have.

I regret a great deal about my life but never my friendship with Rick. I figured we'd be together forever, grow up and grow old, but life had its own plans and we eventually went in very different directions. Somehow, he'd managed to find me after I'd moved out, despite not really giving him my new address, and we started running into each other at random places in town. We'd chat and sometimes go for a coffee but I never invited him in to our apartment except for the first time he'd stopped by and wanted to see Suzie. Lori didn't want him in our lives in any way, knowing the potential for him to attempt to draw me back in. When we'd meet and go for a bite or stop at a café, I avoided alcohol entirely as did he, though I knew he was hoping I'd order a drink so he could as well. Coffee and lunch were my treat, though I never loaned him money which I'm sure he would have accepted. I suggested opportunities for him to get back on track, find work where he could start at the bottom but climb up, get out of the life he'd accepted. Nevertheless, he always justified his situation, saying that he took full responsibility for his mistakes, but that he'd get nowhere no matter how he tried, his efforts to re-integrate into the world consistently unsuccessful. He'd shacked up with a different girl every time I saw him, usually a young hottie who would eventually see the error of her ways, either returning to Mom and Dad or moving on to the next guy. But I saw the good in him, the kindness, the anguish, the effort he made even when it was difficult.

He soon descended further into the world of drugs and alcohol and crime, losing sight of where he was headed and beyond my reach.

Realizing I'd lost him, I moved on with my stable life, content that my place with Lori and Suzie was the best place I could be.

Life had given me a dream, one for which I was grateful every day.

Our daughter started to speak, laugh when we spoke as if she understood us, cry when she was sad not just hungry or tired. By the time she turned two, Suzie was well on her way to being a happy girl and a kind soul.

We celebrated her birthday with a few friends, Lori's brother, her cousin and husband who brought their two young daughters, and of course our parents to whom we felt beholden. It was afternoon coffee and cake, shortly after lunch but too early for supper thus removing the need to provide a meal and eliminating the possibility of someone suggesting eating at a restaurant. The day went as well as expected with presents, festivities, games, and a very happy birthday girl.

Shortly before 4:30, people began to excuse themselves, the departing guests gathering to bid farewell to Suzie. The young girls shared goodbye kisses with each other and the adults, with dwindling energy levels.

Once we were alone, the clean-up began, as simple as it was, Lori and I smiling at each other for our good fortune at the briefness of the gathering. A relatively relaxing day with the focus on Suzie not on Lori and I. Maybe a short walk before dinner would allow us to ease into the evening.

We took turns calling Suzie who neither answered nor came into the room, so it fell on me to go looking for her. Searching through the bedroom, bathroom, and living room, she was nowhere to be seen. I called, repeatedly asking her to come out, my requests increasingly frantic. Lori came to help but neither of us turned up anything. I ran down the stairs to comb the street while she phoned our visitors and knocked on neighbours' doors. This went on well into the night, our call to the police bringing four officers to assist us. But to no avail.

My heart had been pulled from my chest. What do you do when there's nothing you can do?

We carried on searching for a week, tacked a poster to everything that would hold one, spoke to anyone who would answer their door, talked to everyone we passed on the street. No one had seen her, heard her, or heard of her. We were crushed and I felt helpless.

Our search continued without result and we started to lose hope.

Our relationship rapidly soured, eventually prompting me to sleep in the living room. Though she never said so, it soon became apparent that she blamed herself for losing Suzie. I told her that simply wasn't the case and that there was no one to blame here, certainly not her as wonderful and caring a mother as she was.

I told her I still loved her as much as ever and that I'd continue to do everything I could to find our daughter. I asked her to please stay the strong woman I knew she was not just for Suzie's sake but for mine. But to no avail. She asked me to stop working so I could spend my time searching which I obviously couldn't do. I struggled to keep heart, to stay strong, to hold onto hope.

After a month, the police gave up the search, promising to keep it as an active file and stay in contact with us. My capacity to mourn the loss of my daughter, to fear for my girlfriend's health, and to keep us afloat financially had taken a huge toll on me. I had no support at home, no support from either my parents or hers, and my best friend was lost to me. There was no energy left in me to reach out to anyone else, and I felt very much alone.

Losing Suzie had destroyed me. What had happened? Was she lost and crying? Sad and lonely? Hurt? Any of these scenarios pierced my heart. She'd brought me a happiness that I tried to reflect back to her. I'd imagined her growing up, running, singing, dancing, excelling at school, finding her way, us hanging out as friends.

How had I failed so badly as a father? I couldn't even keep my daughter safe.

What hurt me the most was thinking of her somewhere scared. I dreamt of finding her and hugging her as we both laughed.

But that never happened.

Lori's depression grew, her temperament diving deeper into its abyss, her grip on reality tenuous at the best of times. She lost weight and was generally unhealthy. Once I'd even found her crouched in the corner, knees drawn up to her chest, as if simultaneously watching and hiding.

We rarely spoke, her medication depriving her of her ability to communicate anything beyond the most basic thoughts.

My fatigue worsened with time, my mood sinking like an anchor. Despite my sincere love for Lori, she was beyond my help, a vacant soul.

I'd wanted to take Lori in my arms, hold her, and tell her that I'd be with her and there for her always. Many times I did, even when it was difficult. She was my life, my heart, my soul.

But soon she was gone, first mentally, then physically, a shell of the woman I'd known and loved, lost in a world that excluded me.

Shelving my pride, I called on her parents for help, my spirits as low as they could go, my strength depleted. To their credit, they came immediately. In an instant they packed up her personal effects, promising to provide her with the best care, the most professional treatment available, and to notify me as soon as she could receive visitors.

But that never happened.

Alone for the first time in many years, my solitude comforted me, the silence soothing, the absence of responsibility a state of calm. My energy slowly returned, my work providing a distraction, my sleep peaceful as I imagined Lori recovering and eventually returning to our home. I met with friends, though rarely for long periods, unable to discuss matters other than my own despair. My soul tried to climb out from the dark caverns where it lay hidden for what seemed like forever. My Suzie was gone. I had lost my daughter to some unknown tragedy against which I was powerless. But my life slowly returned and, though it would forever be tainted with a sad reality, I would soon be reunited with my girlfriend for us to rise together.

But that never happened.

Lori's parents never called and had yet to return my attempts to reach them.

It was as if I'd ceased to exist. How could they forget me at this time?

I phoned their house, their workplaces, even went to their home, but they were either away or unable to receive visitors. I later learned that they did in fact blame me for their daughter's anxiety, her mania, her neurosis. Didn't they know that I grieved too, for both Lori and Suzie?

I endured the pain of hope for so long. Hope that Lori would be ok. That Suzie would be found. That I'd be with my family.

Hope is a horrible pain.

Sometime later, news of Lori's demise found its way to me: she'd been placed in a 'mental health facility'; an insane asylum. Perhaps that was her parents' way of washing their hands of the entire mess, solving their problems rather than hers.

The name of this institution never made it to me, its location destined to remain a mystery, the only source of information, her parents, were mute on the subject. Lori disappeared into memory for those who chose to remember her when she'd been at her best. That was how she would always live in my mind.

Lori's parents soon made it clear that I should find another place to live, the apartment would no longer be my residence. I thanked them for their kindness. All I wanted was my family planning our lives together in our own home.

I cried rivers for Lori and Suzie, locked myself away from the world for long stretches. They were all that mattered. They were my everything. To see them happy and safe was all I ever wanted. My love for them was absolute. There was no 'me' without them.

For a time, my sorrow turned to anger. How were they torn from me? What could I have done? What had I done?

But my sadness soon returned. I gasped every breath I took. My heart had died. I wanted to die. I had nothing left to live for. I was alone. So alone.

I hid from everyone. I had nothing to say, didn't want to be in anyone's company. I shivered when I saw happy couples, happy families, happy fathers and husbands together with those they loved most. Never would I hold or even see those most precious to me. What mattered now?

So many people don't appreciate what they have until it's gone. I was thankful every day for what I had in Lori and Suzie and still they were gone.

My life's dream had become a nightmare.

More than once, I contemplated taking my own life. Ending my suffering. But I didn't, perhaps lacking the courage for this final act.

I relocated to a different neighbourhood.

My new suite lacked the charm to which I'd become accustomed, the quality neighbourhood, the local amenities, the kind people.

Maybe this is home, I thought, my surroundings similar to those of my younger years. I kept my job as a stable source of income. Old habits would have been an easy outlet but that would never be my life again.

No word ever came about Suzie or even the slightest speculation as to her whereabouts. She too would live on as a distant recollection, a thought in the back of someone's mind, a name that would arise for a moment in conversation before being forgotten. I vowed to carry their names and memory in my heart with me as long as I lived.

I was still haunted by the thought of her scared, cold, and sad. Lost and alone.

Of Lori, alone in her mental and physical prison.

Of me, alone without a home.

But, in the end, I suppose we're all alone.

3 – Rick

Far too often I felt alone in a room full of people. I'd been this way as long as I could remember.

I felt very much alone in my life in my youth.

Bad decisions got normalized as they seemed the only ones I made. Regret kept me awake at night and I went through spells of depression where I disappeared from the Scene before running back to the only place that I felt welcome. Through it all, Rick stood by me. He helped me see past my mistakes, downplaying their severity. He defended me to our friends and anyone else who dissed me. He was my friend every 'next day' when I wanted to crawl into a hole, when I wanted to disappear, when I wanted to die from shame.

And every other day he was there for me and me for him. We regularly had fun, away from drinking and drugs, and supported each other at all times.

Yet, despite his loyalty and true friendship, I still felt very much alone.

Where am I? Oh, I'm in my bed; sort of.

Most of the night is a blank, after about 11:00. I was smoking something with... I'm not really sure.

It's 8:15. I feel like shit but don't think I can sleep anymore. I think I'm still drunk.

Need some juice, soda pop or something that's not alcohol. Coffee.

I stand. I'm shirtless but still wearing my pants.

Yeah, this is my room. My wallet. I don't have my wallet.

Must be in the front room or kitchen.

I hope I don't look like I feel.

Is anyone else here?

I walk with a familiar shame. Not again.

I hope Rick's not home. But when I pass his room, I see him in there asleep. I quietly pull his door closed.

A can of soda pop in the fridge will be a good start. I take a big slug which immediately makes me feel sick but not enough to throw up. I sit on the bench against the wall setting down the can.

I'm ok. I stand again.

I set to making coffee, enough for Rick to have some when he rises.

I'm having a tough time focusing.

What did I do last night? It's rarely something good. I remember feeling nervous. I remember stumbling through a room. I remember smoking up with some guys I barely knew. And then a huge black space until I woke up this morning.

Who else saw me? Did I say or do anything unforgiveable?

I must've looked like a moron.

I take a few deep breaths in the hopes it'll make me feel better which it does.

I think I knew a lot of the people last night but remember feeling horribly awkward and uncomfortable from the moment I arrived. It was all white walls and blank faces. Put back a few beers in the kitchen with some guy I'd seen a few times before. Tried to be funny and charming with some girls at the table. Drank some more and felt more relaxed.

Then things get hazy.

I remember people laughing.

I remember leaning against the wall.

I remember falling down.

Then I don't remember much at all. And that's bad.

Can I just crawl and hide? Run away? Die? I wish for the latter.

I grab a cup from the cupboard. The kitchen actually looks ok so perhaps the party didn't come back here. The sink only has a couple of plates and the counters are clear. Our dismal kitchen with its white walls and grey cupboard doors.

Maybe I just left early and came home.

Maybe I'm dead.

Adding cream to my hot coffee, I sit back down on the bench beneath the poster of a band whose music I can't place.

The caffeine gives me a jolt but I still feel drunk.

Or maybe I'm dead.

I wouldn't have the courage to take my own life but often wished I would just die.

"Hey. C-Vin" Rick enters with a smile.

"Hi"

"What happened to you last night?"

"Whatta ya mean?" I ask, also wondering what happened to me.

"You were pretty messed up" I can't tell if his face is amused or concerned.

"Yeah..." I hang my head and take another sip.

"Hey" he sits beside me "But it's okay"

I raise my head to look at him.

He puts his arm around my shoulder.

Rick had defended me both publicly and to other people when I wasn't around. He supported me when I was down and kept me grounded when I got over confident. He helped me when I needed it and I returned the favour as best I could. We were a good match intellectually and had similar world views and opinions. In short, he was a good friend. We were there for each other. Always.

"We all get that way now and then" he says "You know I've been shit-faced plenty and have my share of regrets"

"Yeah"

"Don't hang your head" he shakes his head "We can't be the best version of ourselves every day"

He puts his arm around my shoulder.

"I kinda wanna forget the whole evening"

"Then forget it" he says.

"I can't forget what I can't remember. I'm sure I was a dick. Or a joke"

"Nah. Don't be so hard on yourself" he says quietly "The people who know and love you don't think any less of you because you were drunk one night. I love you and don't think any less of you"

He pulls my body toward him with a hug then slowly lets me go and stands.

"It's a night you'd rather forget and that's fine, I get it. But don't let this one night, or any other night, define who you are. You're a great friend, a solid guy, and you make other people feel comfortable. That's who you are"

I feel a bit better, or at least not quite so alone, as I continue to sip my coffee.

"Maybe take a few nights, or weeks, off and lay low if that's how you feel, no worries" he shrugs, holding out his hands "A break can be good. Do your own thing. Go for walks, go to the park, go to a coffee shop. If you'll have me then I'd love to come with you. If you'd prefer your own company, then that's totally cool and we can catch up later"

"Yeah. Thanks"

He nods at me.

"There was a cute chick last night who was into you" his voice rises "But I think she knew you were too drunk to fuck"

"I think she was right" I hang my head.

"Yeah, there were some other cute ones there but I didn't have the patience for them" he shakes his head "And a lot of the guys there were just rude. I'm in no hurry to see most of them again. Best we all forget"

"Hmm"

"We move on, C-Vin" he says "It's one night"

"Yeah"

Rick looks back over his shoulder as if expecting to see someone but there's no one there.

"I came home alone too, you know" he frowns.

"My heart breaks" I grin.

He shoves my shoulder.

"Hey. You made coffee. Excellent"

4 – Lori

Saturday. I stayed home last night and am glad for it.

I don't much feel like doing anything but it's sunny outside, so maybe a coffee at an outdoor patio on a beautiful warm autumn day. Need to get out of this basement, get some air, get away from everything. Just get away.

A t-shirt, cargo pants, and my Doc Martens is perfect for this weather. There's a clear light blue sky, the sun hovering above the trees, the air cool without wind, everything smells fresh. It all seems so hopeful. A beautiful day to be alone.

I've always enjoyed my solo afternoon coffee Perhaps a quiet corner to put my head back against a tree away from the crowd.

I sincerely hope I see no one I know today but don't expect to. I often come to the park and have usually managed to go unnoticed which is how I hope it'll play out now.

As I approach, I see that's it's not nearly as crowded as I'd expected which suits my mood. I see small groups, families enjoying ice cream, kids playing frisbee, men and women walking about alone or in couples but my focus is on being anonymous. I hope I'll just blend in and no one will care.

I keep my head down, but not too much so, and stick to the trails, making my way toward the coffee shop across the field.

Black's Coffee makes a good strong brew that's smooth with or without milk and sugar and is worth the short wait in line. Faceless people move around and past me.

I've never thought myself particularly interesting looking and it's something I've accepted as fact. I don't find many other people interesting either so it evens out.

I try to casually scope out a place to go with my hot beverage, away from the crowd, one preferably looking into the park rather than out at the surrounding houses.

I love autumn as a season: the warm sun, the cool air, the changing leaves.

"A medium black coffee, please" I say to the teen girl in a blue skirt and white top who takes my order.

"Cool shirt, dude" a teen boy pokes his head out beside my server.

"Thanks" I nod with a smile as I hand my money to the girl.

I pass a bakery then an ice cream shop then a patio serving beer and wine; the clothing kiosks and tables with artsy wares are behind me. The park is a nice place to come and I'm lucky to live so close, one of the few benefits of my basement hovel. I should probably come more often, just to get away from it all for a moment. I rarely see anyone here that I know so it's good for a spot of solitude.

I pick out a tree a distance away from the patio's music as I regret not bringing my headphones. Passersby drift past me: quiet couples holding hands, excited children, solitary people like me passing through.

Sitting down, I turn to face the park's inner field, the shops on my left, the sun above the trees and playground to my right, the air simultaneously warm and cool. The people milling about seem to be moving more slowly now and it's quieter than before, even the distant noises muffled. It's a peaceful day. A good day to be alone.

The coffee is as smooth as I remember, strong without being bitter; the taste reflecting both the day and my mood.

I close my eyes for a moment just to breathe in the tranquility of the open air, enjoying the beauty of solitude. A few more sips and I'm at peace, an elusive state, at least for me.

I look to my right as I open my eyes where a girl around my age sways gently on a swing facing me. She's kicked off her shoes and her bare feet are dangling from the seat, purple nail polish on her toes. Black hair with purple streaks frames her fair-skinned face, a black long-sleeved shirt, and dark purple shorts hug her petite frame.

"Hi" she smiles at me, from behind her minimal make-up; thin cat eyes and shiny dark purple lipstick are all I notice.

"Hi" I smile back extending my right leg out in front of me.

"I love your shirt" she says swinging slightly.

"Thanks" I reply "I love yours. You've got wicked style"

"Thanks" she hops off the swing, grabs her coffee and her shoes, and walks over to me.

"Just getting out of my place for a bit" I say "I love autumn as a season: the warm sun, the cool air…"

"The changing leaves" she adds, finishing my thought.

"I'm Colden" I smile.

"Lori" she says, by now standing in front of me "Mind if I sit down"

"Please do" I say leaning further back against the tree.

Lori sits down and crosses her legs, shoes on her right, coffee on her left.

"I like the warm sun and cool air on my skin at the same time" she nods.

I gesture in her direction, noticing her t-shirt "I think I have that album"

"I know I have that CD" she smiles back "But do boys really not cry?"

I recall the song's name on my shirt.

"I don't think we're supposed to" I shake my head.

The next few minutes are spent talking about bands, music, and concerts. I never thought I'd meet a girl with such similar musical tastes as me; even Rick's don't come as close to mine.

Lori slides closer to me as we talk and I try to be attentive to her words distracted as I am by how pretty she is.

I get up to refresh our coffees as we chat away in autumn's afternoon sun. What happened here? How did I meet this amazing girl? What's she thinking of me? Is she even single?

Just get the coffee.

When I come back, her knees are drawn up to her chest, and she's smiling beautifully.

"This time you can have the tree" I say sitting facing my previous position.

"Thank you" she sidles across to lean against the trunk extending her legs in front of her.

"Do you live near here?" I ask "Work near here?"

"Both" she says "I've got a small apartment on Hawk St"

"Do you live alone?"

"Very much" she nods "Who could stand living with me?"

We laugh and I'm thankful that no stupid words come out of my mouth.

"What about you?" she asks.

"Small basement suite with a friend of mine on McNeil" I nod "It's not luxury but it's home"

"To the simple life" she raises her coffee cup in a toast.

"The simple life" I reply.

She smiles as she takes a sip and I think I'm smiling back.

It's already almost 3:00 but it feels like I just got here.

Lori tells me that dad works in some corporate office and her parents are very comfortable financially if not wealthy, though she pays her own way renting an apartment while working at a nearby coffee shop that I'd never visited but knew of.

She'd been at university studying English literature and history but is now trying to figure out the best way to do what she loves while actually having a job at the end of it all. She's considering journalism.

"I can read" I smile "But I won't try to impress you with my knowledge of authors"

"My English literature reading list isn't what I'd call impressive, either" she says "I just love finding the connection between history and the prevailing themes in a particular period. Who were the innovators? What topics are specific to a period and which are timeless? How has writing changed over time?"

"It sounds pretty interesting when you put it that way" I say seriously "And impressive"

"It can be" she leans forward "I was a real science nerd in high school"

"With the same style?" I ask.

"Pretty much" she nods looking at her clothes "You?"

"I got braver as I got older. Not sure it was more confident, but braver"

"But now you're confident?" she crosses her arms.

"Obviously" I gesture at myself with a laugh.

Lori giggles beautifully.

"So, what's next for you?" Lori leans back against the tree, extending her legs in front of her.

"I'm not really sure" I try not to descend into introspection "I hope something becomes obvious to me soon because I've not really been drawn to anything. I love to help people, love to read, love to learn. I'm not especially handy so the trades may not be for me"

"Music?" she asks.

"I love to listen but can't play an instrument"

"Maybe you could learn one" she shrugs.

"Maybe…"

"Maybe…"

"Do you play?" I ask her.

"No. Learn something, then you can teach me" she says.

We smile at each other.

"So, what do you do in your spare time besides play on the swings?" I ask.

"I'm new to the neighbourhood" she pulls her knees up to her chest, hands holding them "Just scoping out the area, getting a sense of where things are. This park seems like a great place to visit any day of the week. The swings are a bonus"

"It is nice here" I nod "I often come for coffee just to sit outside"

"And be one with nature?" she smiles.

"Something like that" I smile back.

Lori doesn't notice the large black bird that lands on the ground a short distance to her right.

"Cawwwww" it squawks looking up at the sky.

"Oh my gosh!" Lori jumps, then turns to look at it.

"Quoth the Raven" I laugh.

"Very clever" she wrinkles her nose pulling her knees in tight to her chest, crossing her legs at her feet.

I smile back.

"My parents considered naming me Lenore" she nods "Seriously"

"That would have suited you perfectly" I nod.

Lori leans forward to rest her chin on her knees, squinting seriously.

"So, what are your hobbies?" she asks.

"I actually spend a lot of time alone" I say "Not in a melancholy way but more in a peaceful way. Nothing special, really. I used to run, not competitively or anything, and sometimes I still do. I proudly drink too much coffee. Oh, and I suppose I do enjoy drawing"

"Like sketches?" her face shows interest in my statement.

"Mostly in black" I reply "Pencil, sometimes charcoal. An occasional splash of red to highlight a feature"

"Like, of people?" her face is inquisitive "Or still life?"

"Both" I say, feeling enthusiastic about my passion "It's fun to try to capture how someone feels not just how they look but in the end it's my interpretation"

"Sounds deep" she leans back.

"I guess" I shrug "Or maybe it's just me expressing how I feel"

"That's awesome" she smiles "And a great hobby"

"Thanks" I say "It's fun to get out and see what catches my eye"

"No drawing today?" she shakes her head.

"Not today" I say.

A moment of silence comes between us as my eyes move down from hers to focus on her lips, her porcelain skin radiant in the sun.

"You seem creative" I look back up at her eyes "What are your talents?"

"I've done some writing" she says "Wrote a couple of articles that made it into small-time magazines, a few short stories, have some ideas that might make it onto paper. It's fun to see what's in my mind, to see how it looks in print, to see what other people think. Again, maybe just self-expression on my part"

"That's wicked" I say "You've already been published"

"Haha. Yeah, I guess"

"No writing today?" I ask.

"Not today" she says extending her legs in my direction.

It feels like I'm moving closer to Lori and she isn't sliding away from me. I resist the urge to reach out and touch her bare leg, her bare foot, my eyes focused on hers.

She's a year younger than me and knows some of the bars in the area that I've been to for concerts or drinking. I avoid mentioning any names lest we have common acquaintances and she doesn't open this line of conversation either. I want her to know about me not get other people's opinion of me.

She pulls her right knee up to her body as she leans forward, her left still stretched out in front of her. Her nail polish matches her toenail polish.

"I have an idea" I say.

"Does this happen a lot?" she squints.

"Now and then" I smile "Why don't we grab a bite to eat and drink something that isn't coffee"

"Excellent" she pulls her left leg up to her body "I'll even wear my shoes"

I take her hands in mine to help her up.

"What did you have in mind?"

"It's such a beautiful day, I thought we could stay with the autumn theme at Pink's" I gesture in the direction of the outdoor patio which has several empty tables within its low fence.

"Perfect" she beams.

She still hasn't let go of my right hand so I hold onto hers and spin her beneath my arm.

She twirls effortlessly.

I release her carefully.

The clear skies have yet to cloud over, the sun moving to our left behind the stores, coffee shops, and Pink's Bistro, an outdoor patio that offers beverages, appetizers, and snacks made in the kitchen inside a small stone hut. Servers bounce about happily in their pink and black uniforms, jazz sounds echoing from the restaurant's speakers.

"I've never been here" Lori says.

"I've been a couple of times" I look in her eyes "It's decent food and drinks with a spectacular view"

We step onto the patio and take a seat against the fence dividing the sitting area from the open park. The crowd has thinned, families and couples heading off home or to their next destination. The sun still warms my skin, the multi-coloured leaves blazing like fire in its glow.

Lori has pulled her dark hair back into a ponytail, accentuating her strikingly sharp features. Her hands rest on the table in front of her.

I lean forward.

We chat about everything from world affairs to music and our travels as I continue to avoid any discussion of The Scene. I paint myself in the best light possible as I learn about my own positive qualities throughout our conversation. Lori is obviously very smart but also kind and caring.

We order two glasses of wine and a plate of mixed snacks.

The afternoon sun lights up the right side of her face, while her left remains shadowed. Her cat-eyes are that much sharper, her dark lipstick softening her lips.

A punk rock girl who doesn't take herself too seriously.

We sit on the patio until the sun begins to descend below the trees.

The bill comes and I immediately take it.

"This was my idea so I'd like to pay" I say.

"Then I'll leave the tip" she nods.

By the time we leave Pink's, afternoon has turned to evening. I try to conjure up what to say next.

"Let's walk across the grass" Lori says taking off her shoes.

"Rebel, rebel"

Lori seems to glide, her feet moving silently in the grass. I catch myself staring at her purple toenails for a moment.

"You look like you stay pretty active" I say.

"I danced when I was younger, mostly ballet" she smiles, extending her right leg and pointing her toes.

"Play any sports?" I ask.

"Some soccer and volleyball in my past life, but recently just yoga and aerobics" she says "How about you? Are you an athletic artist? I mean, apart from your non-competitive running"

"Used to run and swim but not really team sports"

Lori smiles. We slowly saunter across the field toward the darkening sky, dusk in full force behind us. Time seems to stop, as I slow to look at her.

"Thank you for a beautiful afternoon" I say.

"This was really nice" she nods.

We walk in silence for a moment, Lori carrying her shoes, our steps light in the green grass until I realize I have no plans to spend any more time with her.

"I'll walk you home" I say.

"I'd like that" she smiles.

5 – Opportunities

Lori's parents 'found her the help she needed' is how they described it as if this act on their part was more important than Lori's condition. They never told me where she was or when she went or what this place was like nor gave me updates on her health, if they even visited her. It was a catastrophic ending to her story of a wonderful, kind, and beautiful woman who just got overloaded and was no longer able to carry her life's load. Could I have done more? Should I have done more? This haunted me for months after and still does to this day. Did I abandon her when she needed me most? Did I take the easy way out by doing nothing? Was I being selfish? What could I have done? There must have been something to do. What do you do when there's nothing you can do?

I did my best to carry on with my life, feeling selfish for my inaction for years after.

Someone once told me that my name means coal mine. Or coal mining town. Something like that. It could be worse. I could have been Archimedes. Or Granite. Or maybe Lucifer.

Not sure where my parents came up with my name and I never asked them. I'm sure they had a reason.

My name's singularity had pros and cons, as so many things do but I never looked for any deeper meaning.

Things happen for a reason, or so they say. It was meant or wasn't meant to be.

But that's not how I see it. Life or circumstance, call it what you will, provides options where a choice is required. You make a decision and accept the consequences with the outcome based on your decision. Life doesn't decide for us, there is no masterplan. It's all about choices. External forces can play a part but that's chance, not destiny and not fate.

How odd, then, that life should give me an opportunity to make a life-hanging choice.

Most of my days are ordinary, my job tedious and low-paying, but my neighbourhood was both eccentric and eclectic. Artsy does have its charms when what used to be a vehicular route was blocked at either end fifteen years earlier to create a pedestrian market. The cobblestone walkway gives it an old-world feel as if you were walking down an avenue in a medieval European city. Most of the shops along the boulevard have outdoor attractions either in the form of patios or the sale of unusual wares on unusual tables. It's definitely unusual and for that I was grateful. The entire space is wide enough to accommodate many pedestrians and crossed four intersected streets, each of which were interrupted when they hit The Concourse, with foot traffic priority signals at these crossings.

The apartment I call home is the third floor of a coffee shop where I occasionally fill in when they need an extra hand. It was surprisingly quiet, given that the two floors below me were almost always occupied by customers dining on food, alcohol, and coffee. The first floor was Café Chaos, the second floor, Fantastico, an artsy restaurant with food prepared by a world-class chef whose creations were not just delicious but exotic in appearance, a space managed by the café owner but operated by the chef. The ground level patio specialized in quirky coffee concoctions crafted by Carlos Perez who had a flair for creative delights. He'd managed to create a menu devoted almost entirely to coffee.

The menu boasted catchy names like Jungle Java and Breakfast Boost but also historic or multicultural Café de Caen and Qahua Sada.

They also served beer and wine with a small menu of snacks, small meals, and desserts prepared in their own kitchen.

My walk home takes me past all manner of humanity: buskers of all talents, or lack thereof; panhandlers; punk rockers who thought they invented it; girls out to be seen; university types who either feel artsy or are looking for a cheap place to drink; the list goes on.

I pass the smoke shop selling international cigarettes and, although I don't smoke, I love the smell of the exotic tobaccos that Kamil sells. He returns my wave from outside his shop as he enjoys one of his own imports - either that or he's smoking a joint, it's difficult to tell. Sometimes the evening is quiet as is the case tonight. It's at times like these that I most enjoy my neighbourhood.

My arrival at Café Chaos sees Carlos and one of his waitresses on the patio cleaning and setting tables.

"Holà Colden. ¿Que tal?"

"Muy bien Carlos, y tù?"

"Muy bien tambien, muchacho"

"Quiet evening?" I ask.

"It is a bit cool for the patio. Still, we are ready if they come. Many people choose coffee now instead of alcohol". I like the way he says alcohol, his accent heavily favouring the last 'o'.

"I like nights a bit on the cool side with no wind" I say.

"Yes, it is much nicer without the wind", he looks to the sky as he speaks, "And the moon is bright. A good sign".

"I hope so"

"Maybe we see you later for a café?"

"Se puede. Hasta luego"

That's the extent of my Spanish.

It's just past 5:00 and the patio seems very inviting as does the new waitress, who sends a pretty smile my way a couple of times, enough to make me want to come back down later. I figure Carlos to be a good guy to work for, as far as bosses go.

He and his wife Sofia have been running the coffee shop for many years and are very friendly, even in slower periods. They'd emigrated from Venezuela several years prior. Carlos had saved some money before leaving his homeland and bought the building before the Concourse came to be. The property was surely worth ten times what he paid for it and I suppose that was his security blanket. He made the decision to take a chance and it turned out to be an excellent one.

I climb the two flights of stairs to my suite, passing the restaurant on the second floor.

A few tables are occupied by small groups, a large party at the back of the room comprised of young children right up to older folks takes up a single long table.

Occasionally I pass a smoker on the landing but no one's there today, though it smells like someone in the alley below has either visited Kamil's shop or are indulging in something a bit more flavourful.

My room isn't big but it is clean and affordable. Carlos certainly doesn't live off my $600 rent; a paltry sum considering the location. He gave me discounted meals and paid me fairly for helping out in the café when my time allowed and his circumstances required.

My home was definitely meant for one. A queen-sized bed in the left corner of the room fills a niche in the wall. Enough room for a nightstand on each side and space to get in and out of bed without walking sideways. The kitchen area to the right of the entrance is a small enclosure with the usual amenities and the added touch of a counter open on both sides with storage cabinets above this island. The living room area opposite the kitchen is more or less in front of my bed. I'd set up the seating with the couch facing the TV, and a recliner to its right. It gave the area the impression of being another room. At least I thought so.

I tried to go for a jog along the river a few times a month but it was only enough to keep me in respectable shape without the commitment or obligation of a regular gym-goer. I thought I looked OK and was strong enough to be useful.

At thirty-two, my fitness aspirations were modest. I was tall enough to appear lean, neither thin nor big; more of a swimmer's physique, or at least that's what I hoped, and not meant for heavy weightlifting. Besides, it was far more appealing to go downstairs and meet the new waitress and relax with a glass of wine and an inexpensive bite of dinner.

I throw my light jacket on a chest near the door and take off my shoes looking around my suite-for-one.

The phone rings, breaking my reverie.

"Hello."

No response.

"Hello."

Still no one.

"Hello?"

No reply on the third try and the receiver goes back in its cradle.

Very few people called my landline; it came with the suite and was included in my rent.

A soft knock at my front door catches me off-guard; a phone call and an in-person caller so close together was unprecedented. I shuffle to the door, wondering if it could possibly be someone other than my landlord.

The door slowly swings in on its hinges as I prepare to greet my visitor.

No one's there and no sound of feet leaving the scene. A few stairs lead to the roof but the door is rarely open - I have a key but seldom use it. No one down the front way either. I jog down and glance in both directions, catching sight of someone turning down an alley which is empty when I reach it. Passersby in the Concourse have increased but no one's running from the scene. The outdoor café is populated by two couples and a table of 3 older guys but I see no point in questioning them.

My laboured steps take me back to my suite as I wonder at my mysterious visitor.

A black envelope on the floor stops me at the entry and I reach to pick it up, again scanning up and down the stairs; my first name in delicate white printing across the top.

My life is less than exceptional and this type of occurrence is most unusual. My first thought goes to Lori but she and I hadn't spoken in so long that I doubted she'd even know how to find me. Or that she'd care to try. If she'd been released. In good health.

I walk to the top of the stairs but see no one on the other side of the gate and no one in the alley out back.

Who'd bother taking the time and effort to get this to me in such a clandestine manner? I wasn't interesting enough to have communications delivered to me in this way and anyone who wants could just wait at the bottom of the stairs or outside my apartment. Or even at the café.

I shut the door and sit on a barstool at the island.

The black sleeve opens easily despite being sealed.

"Dear Mr. Vintassi,

It is my pleasure to extend an offer which I hope you will accept.
We are very much in need of a Station Master to oversee and manage the train station serving our community. This highly-respect position is critical to our community's social and economic prosperity. It is vital to us that the person occupying this post is devoted to their duties and manages operations efficiently. I believe that your character makes you an ideal candidate for this position.

You will be provided with accommodation and all foods and other necessities at no charge, a lump sum payment to be provided to you in the event of your departure, should you decide to leave.
Enclosed you will find two plane tickets to London Heathrow airport and two train tickets for your furtherance to New Brook West, one for your journey here and another for your trip home should you decide that this proposal is not to your liking. The dates of the passes are open, but if you have not arrived by the end of the week, we will assume that you are declining and both will be cancelled.

I look forward to meeting you in the near future.

Respectfully, C.."

Is this for real? You know what they say about things sounding too good to be true. It seems like an amazing opportunity and there certainly isn't anything keeping me here. But how am I an *'ideal candidate'* and how did this person find out about my *'character'*?

I can only imagine this is some kind of joke, but by whom?

Sticking the letter in the pocket of my brown leather jacket, I lock the door behind me to make my way down to the café.

The new waitress flashes me another smile so I smile back from my table near the fence dividing the patio from the pedestrians.

"Hi, you must be Colden"

She knows my name?

"I am. And you are?"

"Kayla"

I stand to take her hand gently in mine. She's quite a bit shorter than me with purple streaks through the dark hair framing her fair-skinned face, a few small tattoos on her arms and chest, and several piercings in each ear. Make-up makes a thin black point out from the corner of each of her eyes, dark purple lipstick on her lips, a sharp look with the black pants and white dress shirt the waitresses wear. A cutting-edge style with a cheerful expression and sweet feminine voice.

"It's very nice to meet you, Kayla"

"The pleasure's mine, Colden" she leans in "Can I get you something to eat or drink?"

"Yes, please. A roast beef sandwich with mayonnaise and a glass of the Merlot. Please"

"Anything on the side?"

Her shoe falls off her left foot revealing purple toenail polish which temporarily distracts me.

"No thanks"

She slips her shoe back on and walks away as my thoughts stray to the idea of her in my apartment. To seeing her up close in private. To seeing how she looks out of her clothes.

I feel the letter in my pocket and am snapped back to reality.

No return address, no contact information, postal code, or telephone number. Is this some kind of joke or a scam to ambush me when I arrive at some mysterious location in the middle of nowhere?

New Brook West. What a generic name. Apparently, it can be reached by train.

I re-read the letter, turn the envelope over and look inside, even smell it. The odour is spicy, like a fancy tea shop. I put the tickets back in the envelope.

Kayla arrives with my wine.

"To beautiful evenings" I hold up my wine in a toast.

"Well said" she nods "I hope it stays this way all night"

"I hope so too" I say, deciding to stop there rather than push too hard at our first meeting.

She smiles and says "I'll bring your sandwich as soon as it's ready"

"See you soon" I smile back.

With that she goes to a couple sharing a coffee urn a few tables over, standing up on her toes when she reaches them.

I shake off my lustful thoughts.

It's been a while since I've been on a train and have never visited England. The plane arrives at Heathrow airport in London where I'd make my way to a train station bound for New Brook West which makes it sound pretty simple. But who the heck is 'C' who doesn't sign their entire name? I look around casually, hoping to catch someone watching me. No one suspicious, though it's difficult to know what to look for. I imagine a stranger in a dark suit with a top hat and cane peering from a dark alley to see my reaction to the letter. Either that or a group of people laughing at me. I see neither.

New Brook West. I grab my cell phone and do a quick on-line search. *New West Brook* and *West New Brook*. Even a *Newbrook*, but not in England. New Brook West is all that's on the train ticket to indicate the sender's address or the location of the train station. So many things don't make sense, the most striking being: why me?

As far as I know I have no connection to this place, through family, friends, or my own travels: my great-grandmother was from England, my dad's side Danish.

Kayla appears with my supper.

"Here's dinner", she nods happily.

"Thanks, Kayla."

She continues to look at me.

"Do you work the day or the night shifts?" I ask, wondering how she'll receive my flirting.

"I'll be mostly nights because I have day classes"

"Theatre student?" I lean forward with a smile.

"No that's just a hobby" she shakes her head "I'm actually studying nursing"

"I'm sure you'll be great"

"What makes you think that?" she asks skeptically.

"Instinct"

"I've been warned against men with good instincts" she squints her eyes.

"But not me specifically?"

"No. For now" a reluctant smile comes to her lips.

She turns and walks away with slow steps.

Practical jokers are the most likely culprits with this letter but the tickets look genuine and that's an expensive prank. And I can't think of anyone I know with the personality to attempt this deception.

"Hey Cold"

Only Pete calls me that.

"Hey dude, how are things?" I turn to see him coming around just outside the patio with a lit cigarette.

"Pretty good" he shrugs "How about you?"

"Good thanks"

"You look a little stunned. Like a cat staring out a window"

"I got a strange offer"

Pete thinks about it for a second.

"Is it a good offer?"

"Seems to be. But it could also be completely bogus or have some weird catch."

"Opportunities, man. They don't come along often" he shakes his head slowly.

Pete was a line cook on the main floor of the café and well-liked and occasionally assisted in Fantastico upstairs. Taller and thinner than me, he'd worked at Chaos for several years, and seemed generally happy with life. He enjoyed the job and it showed, and was someone relaxed and easy to be around, a good mood his normal state.

"I know. This will be a life-changer if I accept"

"Life needs to be changed now and then. If you stay on the same road for too long you eventually stop seeing exits. Then you're just coasting" he nods.

He's right but it's easy for him to say. Then again, it's an opportunity. There was no logic to be found in making this choice, only faith.

6 - Kayla

Faith, such as it is, takes many forms.

What do I have faith in? What do I believe? I believe that my choice now will have great consequences, good ones, I hope. I decide I'll take the chance believing that this offer is legitimate. If I decide to go, which I haven't. Nothing tied me here, nothing I couldn't leave. Such is my life.

All that being said, I do like my neighbourhood. I'd managed to fall into a pretty decent, if quiet, life. Things are ok and I'm content.

I'd had an early night so find myself awake soon after sunrise, grab a quick bite and go for a morning run, the air crisp but fresh with little wind. A long-sleeved shirt and shorts got me about an hour of exercise and I come back a little tired, a lot sweaty, and feeling good I did something productive. It looks to be a sunny and relatively warm day ahead – excellent.

Fridays off were on a rotating schedule and not optional so every second weekend was a long one.

I'll do some shopping this afternoon, maybe go for a walk by the river, and stroll through the Concourse on my way back. Then maybe take a nap and pay a visit to the café after supper and see if Kayla's working.

She seemed sweet and like a lot of fun. And smiled when we talked, which is a good thing, right?

I shower and get dressed and pore over the letter again. No way to tell where this came from because it hadn't gone through the mail. Nor to identify the 'C' who had signed it, if that matters.

The airline tickets look legit and I could easily check this out before departing. A station master. For a train station. The whole thing is downright bizarre.

I don't want to hang around downstairs too much so I'll make my own coffee up here for now. Tucking the letter in a drawer, I pour the hot water over the cheap grounds, adding a bit of milk for flavour. I sit on the steps up to my suite in jeans and a short-sleeved white t-shirt with my cup of instant brew and a muffin, the sun rising above the buildings to my left, the sky ahead of and around me a clear light blue. A beautiful day. A great day to have off.

People drift by livening up the street, the few shops I can see have just started opening for the day. Carlos got going early enough to catch the morning coffee-crowd, offering inexpensive options to those heading in to work. The patio wouldn't be open yet, probably just him and one of the servers; he did decent business in the mornings from what I saw. His location sees lots of pedestrian commuter traffic and his coffee is good.

I stare at my cup of instant and smile.

I spend the day outside as much as I can, feeling the warm sun on my skin. Other people are also enjoying the warmth on their lunch break on the benches along the river and walking through the Concourse. I've got my pencils and paper to sketch some interesting views, of which I spot a few, conceptual really, more than specific. I draw couples along the river, walking through the Concourse, smiling at each other, even though I probably have many of these already. Sometimes my subconscious adds some unexpected elements making them more interesting than they would be otherwise. I always initial my drawings at the bottom in the middle with 'CV'; maybe this is arrogant on my part but I want the world to know these are mine, even if no one else ever sees them.

The thought of seeing Kayla later lifts my mood, a pleasant image of her beautiful smile floats through my mind.

I hadn't done much dating since Lori; my heart just wasn't in it.

I notice women, especially in my neighbourhood, which attracts many pretty ones of all styles and ages. And, of course, at my job at the University. I'd met a few but nothing stuck, probably due to my lack of enthusiasm. So it is.

Around 4:00, I drift back home at a leisurely pace along the river then through the shops and patios on my street. I keep my gaze into the distance, intent on ignoring my fellow pedestrians of all styles and ages. I think of the strange letter, of New Brook West, of a journey by train, of managing trains. Of the way Kayla goes up on her toes when she stands, of the way she looks at me. I try to shelf thoughts of the bizarre offer, focusing my energies on tonight, if I do come across her at the café. I'll think on the letter tomorrow, the plane departing to England next Sunday, in a week. I'm not one to procrastinate but have a difficult time thinking on two things at once and figure I'll try to up my 'game' with Kayla. I laugh at the thought of my 'game'.

A few smiling faces emerge from workplaces, eager to beat the rush home either by car or by bus and get the weekend started. Many would go home only to find themselves back here later tonight. Yeah, I liked my neighbourhood. People had to travel from home to get here, but I live here; this is my home.

The after-work crowd now occupies some seats on the Chaos patio with wine and other drinks filling their tables. They'll soon head home for dinner or move on to a livelier atmosphere than Carlos offers. Two waitresses patrol the area outside but I don't see Kayla. It's still early so she could be starting later. One of the young servers I recognize waves to me with a smile and I wave back.

The gate to the roof is closed and no one is waiting for me on the steps up to my room. I'd never thought I had to consider the possibility of visitors to my door but, in light of recent events, decide I should stay sharp. No envelopes on the floor inside the door and all seems as I'd left it in the apartment.

The letter of offer is in the drawer where I'd put it earlier. All is well in my boring life.

I'll be in better shape tonight if I take a short nap now so lay on top of the bed to close my eyes. It's not a deep sleep, more of a twitchy catnap, but enough to make my senses sharper for tonight.

I get up at 5:15, groggy but knowing I'll feel better for it later.

Pouring a glass of juice, I take to staring at the letter once again, hoping I'll catch something I missed on previous looks.

No hidden clues on the envelope or the paper itself. It's hand-written in black pen in magnificent block printing, the paper higher quality than the regular bond common in most workplaces. No hidden clues in the writing or on the envelope, or at least none that my eyes pick up.

As much as I like where I live and am content at my job, it just didn't feel complete and I wonder at the opportunity to find my home once and for all in New Brook West. I could figure out train schedules and could help with loading and unloading but would have a more difficult time disguising my lack of mechanical skill. My character was not ideal for a position demanding these aptitudes if they know anything about me. But looking at the positives, unknown as they are, this could be an amazing gift. The location might be beautiful, the people friendly, and my expenses would be zero. Am I brave enough to go for it? Do I want to?

I veg out watching TV for a bit, frying some pork chops with a microwaved potato and some frozen broccoli for dinner. I tune into an old action movie that provides enough to keep my attention and distract me from everything else. When it's over, I read for a bit in the recliner, deciding against a cup of shitty coffee here, preferring a Chaos selection later.

At 8:30, I decide to head down, hoping I've timed it correctly so that Kayla's working but that there's room for me on the patio.

The air is still wind-free and comfortably warm with dark pants and a long-sleeved shirt, casual but not too much. Foot traffic in the street is moderate as are the customers sitting outside.

The shops across from me attract passers-by with the bright multi-coloured lights in front of their doors. I exhale a sigh of relief when I see Kayla tending to folks outside and she appears to be the only server, a handful of people inside the café eating desserts and sipping wine or coffee.

I wave to Pete and make my way onto the patio, sitting near to the barrier separating me from the pedestrians, offering me a good view in case Kayla has no interest or time for me.

Before I know it, she's standing right in front of me.

"You've come back for more" she says.

"It's another beautiful evening" I say with a smile and eye contact.

She blushes through her thin cat eyes and shiny dark purple lipstick.

"This is a really cool part of the city" she crosses her hands in front of her waist.

"I love it here" I nod.

"Can I offer you anything?" she asks.

I pause for a few seconds before answering.

"Yes. Yes, please" I say, preferring wine over coffee "A glass of the Merlot I had last night. Please"

She crosses her left leg over her right standing on her toes with her hands behind her back accentuating her tight white dress shirt, her left shoe falling off her foot. But I'm not to be distracted; well, not too much.

"You're assuming I remember"

"I'm hoping"

"I do" she smirks "Be right back"

It really is a great night to be outside, the street crowd happy to be out and about.

The moon down at the other end of the Concourse is nearly full, making the dark sky bright, the stars twinkling above and around me. The short streetlamps provide just the right amount of light for walking.

"Your wine, Monsieur" Kayla sets my glass on the table.

"Merci, Mademoiselle" I reply.

She smiles.

"It is beautiful tonight" she says.

"Yes, it is" I look in her eyes.

A brief pause ensues between us during which Kayla makes no move to leave.

"How late do you work tonight?" I ask.

"Why? What did you have in mind?" she eyes me suspiciously.

Good answer.

"I thought you might join me roof-top to look at the stars. I've got a couple of chairs up there. For a beautiful evening"

"For all the women you take to the roof?" she squirrels up her face.

"You'd be the first" I smile.

"I'm off at 12:00. Or is that too late?" Her sparkling eyes widen as she tilts her head to the left.

"That's perfect. I'm on the third floor up the stairs" I reply.

"How do you know I'll come see you?" she squints.

"Instinct" I nod.

She smiles, placing my bill next to me as she turns, walking off to one of the other tables, stopping to stand on her toes, hands in front of her, when she reaches it.

Far too many of my experiences with women were a spectacular failure, especially when the time came to open my mouth and speak. I alternated between saying nothing and something stupid. My words to Kayla sound both confident and flirty. Well done.

After the wine, I order a decaf coffee, this time from a waitress named Annie as Kayla tends to other customers. My eyes stare out blankly at the growing crowd walking by.

I don't think of myself as a happy person, not a sad one either, but not happy. But tonight, I'm happy. I might be smiling as I sip my coffee.

It's 8:15 in the morning and I haven't slept as long as I'd hoped but considering that Kayla is asleep next to me, it feels perfect. Her gentle breathing makes her chest heave slightly as she lays on her back, the bedsheet just barely covering her breasts, her left arm across her body towards me.

Her legs extend beyond the bottom of the sheets, her feet pointing out, her purple toenails twinkling in the dim light.

I lay facing the ceiling for a moment, hands behind my head not wanting to wake her. I pull the sheet back revealing her small perky boobs, run my fingers along her stomach, caress her silky skin, trace around her nipples which get hard in response to my touch. She moans softly without opening her eyes.

An amazing, if unexpected, night and she'd been as beautiful naked as clothed with perfect breasts, soft skin, and an amazing body. She slowly licks her lips without opening her eyes as my hand moves up and down her stomach from her neck to her waist and back, barely touching her skin. I move lower and draw circles around her belly button, my hand moving lower along her inner thighs. Her body shifts, her left leg bending as her foot now points in my direction. I imagine her dreams as my hands and fingers move over her skin. She still seems to be asleep, a partial smile on her lips.

The roof provided the perfect view as promised and we made our way back to my suite for ice cream and wine after about 45 minutes of chatting. We talked late into the night back in my apartment sitting on my couch as she slowly slid closer to me, touching my arm as she did before we both leaned in to kiss.

I carefully rise from the bed, rolling off it so as not to disturb the mattress. I creep into the kitchen to start a 4-cup pot of coffee. There are still a couple of muffins left which seem fresh enough to offer a guest. I can always buy us lunch somewhere, depending on how she feels.

How do I want to direct the conversation this morning? I hope to see her again and will wait to get a sense of her thoughts when she wakes up.

"You've stopped touching me so I might as well get up"

I turn to see her on her side facing toward me, the sheet pulled up to cover her breasts.

"I wanted to let you sleep" I smile sheepishly.

"That's sweet of you"

"I don't have a lot of breakfast-y things" I say.

"That's ok" she sits up, the sheet now resting in her lap "Do you have any juice?"

I pour a glass.

"Waiting here for you" I set it on the counter.

"You dehydrated me last night" she smirks.

Her bare feet with purple-painted toenails dangle off her side of the bed as she speaks.

"I assume you drink coffee working where you do"

"I do"

She gets up, pulling on her blouse without buttoning it up.

"You are stunning" I look in her eyes.

"You are naked"

I look down as she laughs.

"That's OK", she walks over, kissing me on the lips, "I like you this way"

She rises up on her toes to press her body firmly up against mine; my hands reach down to caress her upper thighs and her firm behind.

"I don't have to go yet" she whispers.

If I accept the offer, this is what I'll be leaving.

Kayla and I part ways just before lunch because she has schoolwork but I also think we both feel that we don't want to crowd the other person too much. She exits discreetly through the alley behind the café to avoid questions from her co-workers. I tell her I'll come see her during her shift the next day and we can schedule our next/first date.

My thoughts return to the letter of offer and my decision.

It seems I can't lose, even if I just make the trip to see what it's all about. Provided they don't cancel the return ticket before I get a chance to leave. If trains come through, I could just pay my own way back or call someone here to explain the situation and ask for help. It's Saturday so I have a few days yet until the plane's departure.

I call Ryan, a friend from the University, asking him to meet me at a coffee shop a few blocks away rather than hanging around Chaos again.

A quick lunch and shower refresh me and I set out for Tramps over on Barken Street.

It's another ideal autumn day, sunny with a gentle wind, a pleasant temperature. I opt for shorts and a sleeveless t-shirt.

Everyone from University students to middle aged couples fill the street people-watching, window shopping, and just being outside in the coolest neighbourhood in the city. An awesome day for a walk and I leave early so I can take my time getting to our destination.

I arrive shortly before Ryan, the letter in the envelope on the table in front of me. Ryan is more conservative in his clothing choices, showing up in jeans and a light sweater. He always looks good and has an easy manner.

"Hi Colden" I stand and we hug.

"Thanks for coming on short notice" I say.

"I'm glad you called" he smiles.

I sit down.

"Is something up?" his face turns serious "You didn't say much on the phone"

I explain the letter, its mysterious appearance, and of course my evening with Kayla.

"First of all, awesome about the waitress, you dog"

I laugh.

"It was awesome" I want to say more but don't.

"I assume she spent the night at your place"

"She did" I smile "She's an amazing woman"

"So, what's the deal with the letter?" he asks.

"That's just it. There isn't a clue why this was sent to me. But it has my name on it so it's not like I received it by mistake."

I pass him the envelope. He reads it slowly, looks over the tickets.

"The tickets look real. I assume you've been unable to find this place on a map"

I shake my head.

"A 'lump sum payment' if you leave. Sounds like you can't lose even if you just go check it out. This would be quite the adventure"

I'm glad Ryan's assessment is similar to mine; I respect his intelligence and opinion.

"But the 'why me?' part hovers over this whole thing"

"That is odd" he stares intently at the letter.

"Why is this person so intent on remaining anonymous?"

"Also odd"

"You're beginning to sound like Sherlock Holmes" I say.

"Thanks" he smiles.

"I suppose you have to decide if you believe this is real" he set the letter down "There are all kinds of reasons this person is being elusive until you meet them: long-lost relative; mutual friend; reclusive millionaire. And these days anyone can find just about anyone else. Maybe they looked you up online"

I nod at his logic.

"I'm always skeptical when something finds me without me looking for it" I shake my head.

"How'd you meet Lori?" he says quickly.

I nod slowly at his observation.

"Seriously, though, I can't guess why you were chosen" Ryan says "But they're sure going to a lot of trouble to get you out there. The money, the tickets. And if they wanted just anyone there are plenty of other people who would already be sitting on that train. I doubt they're going door to door with this offer"

"But what's so special about me?"

"You're very special" he grins.

"Thanks" I snort.

"Seriously though, it seems like a pretty good deal. Do you figure you could do it for just a few months and then check out? Is it worth paying them a visit?"

"Or maybe I can't leave. Is this some kind of cult?" I say more softly.

"'You can check out anytime you like but you can never leave'"

We both laugh at the song reference but it gets me thinking about this possibility.

"Choices are about taking chances" Ryan says, repeating Pete's thought "Would I go: no. But you're completely different in that regard, and a lot braver"

Ryan had been married for a few years to a professor at the University, a very attractive and intelligent lady. He was happy with his position as a researcher and good at his job but I suspected he'd always played it safe.

"I'm not saying go for it just to satisfy your curiosity, or mine, but it could be a great opportunity" he adds.

"Opportunities, choices, chances"

"That's what it comes down to, I guess" Ryan nods "For someone with the courage"

"It could also put some distance between me and…everything else"

"Is that what you want? A fresh start?" Ryan asks.

"I'm not sure what I want" I look around the room "I'm usually a lot better at decisiveness"

"And now this is complicated by the waitress you met"

"A bit"

We move on to other topics, talking about his work, Chaos, the Concourse, his wife Ana, the potential for seeing more of Kayla in the future. After our second coffee Mark excuses himself saying he has some errands to run.

"Please let me know when you do make your decision" his face saddens "I'm sorry I wasn't of much help"

"You were. You're the only one I've spoken to about this"

"If I don't see you again, I will miss you" Ryan hugs me.

"You're a great friend, Ryan" I say holding tightly.

I head home the long way stopping at a used music store to see if they have anything interesting, but find nothing worthwhile.

I run into the supermarket to pick up some essentials before heading home.

I don't reach my door until nearly 6:00. Hard to believe that the day has gone by so quickly, though my time with Ryan was well-spent as usual. He's a good friend, nothing fancy about it, but also someone really fun to be around and talk with.

Ryan's one of those guys that must be liked by everyone he meets. I can't imagine anyone saying a bad word about him. He occasionally got nervous in awkward social situations but that was part of his charm. He's one of the few people who knew most of my history with Lori and Suzie's tragedy. He wasn't one to pry but a good listener, intelligent without arrogance. We'd had our share of fun times both before and since he'd married Ana.

Though I was surprised by his take on the offer and his suggestion to 'go for it'.

I'll head upstairs to eat and put on some other clothes before popping in to say 'Hi' to Kayla.

I downplay it and will never bring it up but the fact is that Suzie's disappearance still burdens me, as does Lori's state, and I suppose they always will. I'll not be mentioning this to Kayla. It had been seven years but some days it still felt like yesterday. I still think about Lori but don't know what to feel beyond that. I'd sure made some horrible choices in the past.

How will history judge the decision I'm about to make?

7 – We've Got This

"That did not go well" Lori shakes her head walking into the room.

I look up from the desk to see her kicking off her sandals and dropping her light jacket on the couch.

"What happened?" I walk to her, concerned with her mood.

She'd just been to visit her parents. I'd offered to come with her but was thankful that she declined; my presence wouldn't have made things any better, anyway.

"I just wanted to say 'hi' and see how they were" she tried to hold back her tears "Tell them how I was. How we were"

I start to speak but stop, instead walking over take her in my arms. Her body nestles into me.

"I wish things were better" I whisper "You know they're not on the same page as you. You're doing great. They'll come to see that. Soon, I hope"

"Yeah" she sniffles "They should be happy for me. I've got my shit together, I'm intelligent, I've got a job. I've got you"

"And I've got you" I kiss her.

"And we've got this" she says.

"We do" I agree.

I flop onto the couch - she lies down on top of me.

"How'd the job hunt go?" Lori asks raising her head.

"Poorly" my mood falls "It's getting kinda discouraging"

I'd been laid off from my job helping on a construction job site. Not doing any of the skilled work but assisting various tradesmen and moving materials around the site. Not much to bolster a resume.

"I've talked to a bunch of people who I thought might hire but got no interest" I add.

Lori looks at me sadly as if wondering what to say.

"If I don't find something soon, I'm fucked" I go on "As dumpy as this place is, Rick can't afford it on his own and I won't ask him to pay my way"

"What else can you try?" Lori asks.

"I dunno" I shake my head, worried.

"You'll make it work" Lori smiles "You always do"

Yeah, I do.

"We fit together well" she snuggles into me again.

"We do"

"I like this" she nestles in closer.

I find a job the following week. Nothing permanent, but something to bring in a bit of coin until I can get a more regular gig.

"We could always get a place together" Lori suggests shortly after I start my new job.

8 – Rooftop

"This is your idea" she laughs.

"And a good one" I smile.

The bright sun in the clear blue sky warms the rooftop, the dark surfaces around us radiating heat. The thick blanket placed over the grey stone creates a cozy nest high above our neighbourhood. Barefoot in shorts and a tank top, Lori leans back on her elbows, legs extended in front of her, toes pointed out.

"It is a nice view" she beams "And a beautiful day"

"It's beautiful" I say, running my hand softly over her stomach.

"You should probably take off your shirt" she says sitting up "I don't want you getting too hot"

I smile as I remove my t-shirt.

Lori pulls in her legs and leans forward to kiss my chest.

"Mmmm" my stomach muscles tense.

I reach out to run my fingers over her nipple through her shirt.

She pulls her head back from me and closes her eyes.

"Ohh" she moans softly.

"You'll soon have me out of my clothes" she adds after I withdraw my hand.

The simple picnic had been perfectly...simple. I couldn't afford to wine and dine Lori in truly romantic fashion so had to improvise. Sandwiches and fresh fruit and a shared bottle of wine. I even placed a single flower on her side of the blanket. My gesture had been a complete surprise to Lori.

Our location is the rooftop of a warehouse building owned by my employer that hadn't been used in years.

She tells me about all the things on her mind, big and small, about her work, about her job applications. We talk about music. We talk about our longer-term goals and dreams. We chat about our respective apartments and how we could manage to move in together.

"So, what now?" I ask.

"Like, 'what now' at this moment" Lori smiles "Or 'what now' in our lives?"

"Either" I laugh "But I meant the first one"

"So many possibilities" she says "Now you cuddle up next with me and we lay here under the sun"

"Perfect"

We lay in silence, her head resting on my bare chest until she decides that my tan will be most unusual unless she switches sides.

A few more quiet minutes pass as I contemplate my good fortune to be holding such an amazing woman's body next to mine and the happiness she brings to my life.

"Kiss me" she raises her head.

Bringing her soft lips onto mine we slowly kiss as I pull her body closer to mine, our intensity increasing with time.

"Ahhh" Lori smiles as she raises her head.

My left hand runs up and down her sides and along the bare skin of her stomach, occasionally finding its way around her breasts and nipples which become hard at my touch through her shirt. I play with her breasts, flicking and gently squeezing her nipples as she moans her pleasure.

She eagerly pulls her shirt up over her head and I unclip her bra revealing her beautifully small fair-skinned boobs and perky pink nipples.

Lori brings her hand up to caress her bare chest.

"You're so beautiful" I whisper kissing her neck as my hands play with her nipples.

"Mmm" Lori purrs.

My hand slides down her stomach to unzip her shorts and into her panties where I caress her smoothness, my hand wandering between her legs as she spreads them.

"You're teasing me" she whispers, biting my lower lip and pulling down her shorts and underwear as quickly as she can, her bare feet kicking them aside. Her body shivers against my touch as her hands grip my arms.

Lori is now completely naked under the sun outside which is a very arousing thought.

My fingers move softly against her smooth skin, and between her legs making her body shiver and her toes point further in front of her.

"Ohh" she moans pulling away from my mouth then clenching her teeth "Nnnnn"

I love this part.

Her breathing stops as she throws her head back with closed eyes, her left hand coming up to grab her breast, her legs spreading fully apart.

She reaches her right hand down to unbutton my pants and rub me through my underwear.

I could easily relax and let myself explode but want this to last.

My hand slowly moves down between her legs as her breathing nearly stops and her legs stiffen.

Her hands now scramble to remove my pants and underwear and reveal my erection which she strokes slowly then more quickly. She moves to swing her legs under her and sit on her feet, her mouth moving down to kiss my stomach. She takes me in her mouth, sliding her lips up and down. She briefly sucks on the head bringing me close to coming.

"Yummy" she moans "I love having you in my mouth" taking me as deep as she can.

Throughout her pleasuring me orally, I rub her nipples, mindful not to let her finish me yet.

Her soft lips slowly glide over me, nearly making me release my passions.

I pull away from her for a moment to catch my breath.

"Mmmmm" she purrs turning around and rolling onto her hands and knees.

I stare at her perfect body from behind, her smooth legs, her firm heart-shaped ass.

She spreads her legs apart even wider allowing my face to press forward and lick more quickly; I love how this makes her feel.

"Ohhhh" her legs shake.

She turns back to look at me.

"Oh" she grits her teeth "Stop teasing"

I slowly slide into her as she gasps, each of my thrusts penetrating deeper than the previous one. Her body rocks back and forth, her hips dancing. I push myself as deep into her as I can causing her body and legs to tense when I do. After several minutes of moving inside her soft wet warmth, I slide in long and deep and slowly, my hands on her hips pulling her toward me, her face pressed firmly on the ground.

"Ohhh" I moan briefly, wanting her to come first.

I give a few more of my deepest thrusts, and feel her hand moving rapidly between her legs.

Each time I get deep inside her, her mouth lets out an "Uhnn" sound. I love her moaning, how her body shakes when I'm sliding in and out of her. I could stay this way forever, feeling her soft warm insides, her gasping in pleasure, building to her orgasm.

In time, her moans are longer and louder.

Her hand still rubs between her legs as I keep hold of her hips and control the speed of my thrusts.

Then: "Nnnnnnnnnn"

Her body shakes and stiffens, her legs squeezing together. I love how this feels and her orgasms are absolutely beautiful.

Her climax lasts several seconds, several wonderful seconds.

"Huhnn, huhnn, huhnn..." she moans, exhaling, eyes closed.

"Oh yes. Ohhhh" she whispers.

Her body is slowly relaxing, her legs spreading apart.

She's still on her knees, her body shaking every time she moves and I know I won't last much longer.

"Ohhhhhh" my body stiffens as my tensions are released and I vocalize my explosion, my hands firmly on her hips.

"Ahhhh" she moans.

I slowly glide out of her, looking down at her legs and her beautiful heart-shaped bum which I caress. I run my fingers over her bare foot beneath me causing her to twitch.

We fall back down next to each other.

She leans over to kiss me.

"Mmm" she smiles as our mouths meet and she enjoys her juices on my kiss. "I love how I taste on your lips"

"Do you think anyone saw us?" I ask.

"I hope so" she smiles.

We lay there for a few minutes, enjoying the afternoon sun's warmth on our naked bodies.

"Take me for a walk by the river" she stands pulling on her shorts "You can buy me a milkshake"

I stand next to her pulling up my pants.

Lori and I are compatible sexually which feels so important at times like this. Compatible in so many other ways too: in our love, in our dreams, in our character.

"I can't imagine my life without you in it" I hold her hands "Or maybe I just don't want to"

"You don't have to; I'll always be in yours and you'll always be in mine" she looks up at me with a smile.

She grabs me with a hug and I hold her as tightly as I can.

"I love the way your body feels against me" she pulls me closer "Your strength"

I never realized I was incomplete until I met Lori.

Her love makes me stronger, makes me better, makes me complete.

9 – Yellow Dress

Silvery mist fills the clearing outside the town gates, the sky hazy, the air solemn. Water trickles down the tall pillar at the plaza's center breaking the silence. A young woman emerges from a dark alley, her short blonde hair and yellow dress in sharp contrast to the dull stone buildings around her.

She stares out through the fog and into the forest, unaware of the green-eyed woman in the grey cloak watching her from inside the cemetery's iron fence.

10 – Waiting

Fog hangs in the clearing, the trees at the forest's edge obscured in the mist. All is quiet on the platform where a solitary young girl in a dirty purple dress sits on the bench facing the tracks as if waiting for a train. Her dark hair hangs forward covering her face, her thin hands rest in her lap. She waits in silence.

11 - Suzie

"Daddy. Come play"

We'd been told that Suzie was developing quickly and was very smart for her age, what every parent wants to hear. She'd acquired a small vocabulary, stringing two or three-word sentences together into short thoughts, and could identify many household items, animals, toys, and the outdoor basics. This required that I put my language in check and remove the more colourful words from my vocabulary.

I'd just returned home from an errand and am met at the door.

Lori nods and directs me to set things down and follow Suzie.

"Wow" I marvel entering her room "This is awesome"

"What 'awesome' means?" Suzie looks at me.

"It means 'really good'" I reply with a smile.

"Oh" she says "Awesome"

She'd placed her stuffed animals on her bed around a central female doll in a light blue dress.

"Is she the queen?" I ask enthusiastically.

"That's Becca" Suzie corrects me in a hushed voice. She has a fondness for whispering while playing.

"Is Becca the queen?" I ask.

My inquiry is ignored as she busies herself adjusting the blanket.

I grab two bears, marching them around the scene, mumbling rather than speaking so as not to upset whatever mood she's attempting to create.

"What they doing?" she asks curiously but softly.

"Making sure everything's ok" I reply confidently.

"Oh" she nods, picking up the blue doll and brushing her hair.

My bears march on and mumble to some of the other animals in the circle.

Whatever Suzie and I are trying to create we make it work, even if we aren't telling the same story.

Looking back, I notice Lori smiling in the doorway.

I hold up my bears, mumbling something incoherent.

Awesome.

12 – Ice Cream

I wake from a restful dream-free sleep, the sun through the curtains shining a blade of light across Lori's bare back. I know she's naked beneath the blankets and this arouses me immediately. I run my fingers along her back and kiss her neck, before gently tucking her in and quietly creeping out of the room, closing the door behind me. Suzie must still be sleeping as well since her door is open just a crack so I stealthily step into the kitchen to start a pot of coffee, hoping this'll not disturb them.

The long living room window looking out onto the street shows the promise of a beautifully sunny day, the sky clear, the sun coming up over the buildings to my right. The apartment does offer a fantastic view and I'm grateful for this despite feeling indebted to Lori's parents for their assistance in obtaining and paying for these accommodations. The suite is adequately furnished and provides a great area for Suzie to play as well as for us to enjoy family meals.

The coffee maker's beep indicates that my brew is now ready and I quietly pour a cup, putting one out for Lori for when she rises.

I place a glass of juice on the table for Suzie as she'll surely join me before long.

I really did manage to find myself a beautiful life with my girlfriend and daughter, something I would have never thought possible only a short time ago. I'm happy and relaxed, emotions I'd not thought possible.

"Daddy" Suzie steps into the room.

"Good morning, sweetie" I smile.

She shuffles across the room to join me on the couch looking out onto the city.

"Do you think we should go outside and play today after Mommy gets up?"

Suzie nods enthusiastically.

We sit on the floor, playing with a set of animals which Suzie has named and each with their own personalities as I learn when I try to animate them in my own way. I make each voice musical, the bird, cat, and rabbit all singing when it comes time for them to speak which has my daughter laughing.

Lori soon emerges in shorts and a cut-off t-shirt, padding into the kitchen.

"Good morning, everyone" she says softly.

"Hi, Mommy" Suzie yells.

I wave to her then point to the coffee.

She gives me the thumbs up.

"Looks like it'll be a nice day" Lori sits on the couch behind us.

"I thought maybe we'd eat brunch here then we could go out and I'll buy my girls ice cream"

"What do you think, Suzie?" Lori cocks her head.

"Yeah" she nods with a smile "I can wear my purple dress"

"How about pancakes and sausage for breakfast?" I say getting up.

"Yeah" Suzie nods again with her usual excitement.

"I'll finish my coffee then get things started" I say "Mommy's grumpy until she's had her coffee anyway"

Suzie nods at me without saying a word.

Lori squirrels up her face, sticking her tongue out at me which makes me smile.

My family. What a wonderful place to be.

13 – Always

I'll miss many of the things I'd be leaving behind, you always do. But remember why you decided to leave. Chances don't come often; a chance for a new life. If it turns out to be a bust, I have the return pass in my hands. Worst case scenario, I'll be in England. With no job or place to live, but in England nonetheless. And I can hold my head high for taking the chance I did.

I'm not looking forward to saying goodbye to Kayla. I decide to write Ryan a letter and mail it to him just before I leave explaining my decision, confirming what he probably expected. As unusual as it would seem to anyone else, it feels like the right way to tell him and I doubt he'll be surprised that I did it this way.

It's about choices. My choices. Hopefully, the correct choices.

There's not a lot to bring in terms of personal effects, though I still manage to fill a small trunk and a duffle bag deciding that if this turns into a long stay or a permanent residence that it's best to be prepared.

I'd made a date with Kayla, grateful she doesn't work or have university obligations that evening or the following morning. I look around my sparse room. It had been a good home and Carlos had always been kind to me. It's sad to leave it all behind but thoughts of a new beginning soon replace this emotion. The essentials already packed with the exception of last-minute items, Carlos satisfied that what's being left behind could either be disposed of humanely or left for a future tenant. He was sure to tell me that I'd always be welcome in the future if the suite was empty.

The best way to spend my afternoon would be to take a walk around the neighbourhood that had been my home for the previous three years. The sun shines without wind, the weather beckoning me to hit the streets one last time. Locking my door behind me I descend the stairs at 12:30 to a busy café. I stop in to buy a quick South American egg salad sandwich, unsure of exactly what I'll receive but determined to try something different. The waitress who brings me my bag lunch and apple juice smiles politely earning a $3 tip on a $10 order. She wishes me a great afternoon and I extend her the same as I make my way to Molly Park, a seldom crowded area along the river allowing me to eat in solitude.

Life has taught me that events rarely turn out as planned or even as hoped and I contemplate this in the context of my most recent decision to leave.

My previous life with Rick and the menagerie I called friends was littered with plans gone awry and hopes dashed. Granted this was largely due to poor choices on my part but some had genuinely been chances taken which turned out poorly despite my best efforts. I put in my earphones, thinking of Lori as I do. Is she still in the psych ward? Does she have her life back? Has she recovered from Suzie's death?

Lori had given me a life I didn't feel I deserved. I missed her constantly, and soon forgot the sadness that had become our life at the end, my mind drifting to the beautiful moments we shared. We could have lived a dream.

What had become of Suzie? Was she scared? Safe? How had I not found her? I wanted my daughter back in my arms, laughing, smiling, cuddling. To know that she was happy.

I'd lingered in my old neighbourhood for a few years longer than I'd intended, my eviction from Lori's parents' place my first new life.

I recall my last days. I hadn't told Lori's parents about my decision to start over elsewhere.

I'd thanked those close to me for their support, sold anything of value, and met Rick for a coffee.

Our awkward conversation ended sooner than I'd hoped as Rick seemed very uncomfortable throughout our time together. He drank his beverage quickly as we chatted about some of his latest adventures and I explained how I was leaving with no real plan ahead of me.

He stands and hugs me tightly.

"You're the best friend a guy could have" is he on the verge of crying? "You'll get this right. I'll love you, always"

"Always" I'd echoed.

And he was gone.

I hopped a train and left, my heart strained with mixed emotions, watching out the window until clear of the city limits. With a few personal items, a couple of changes of clothes and a small amount of cash, I contemplated what I would do when I arrived at my destination. I soon found Carlos' apartment, my job at the university, and met a couple of casual friends.

That chance turned out to be the right one.

I look forward to my next new life.

As Station Master.

And hopefully a good decision.

1872

Mother's laboratory, with all the bottles, liquids, plants, and herbs in vials and bowls around the room, many with labels, some without. Cabinets and drawers, some locked, some open. Some many elements, some visible, others hidden. So many possibilities, so many combinations, so many outcomes. So much power.

The two of them move around the room like a couple dancing, mother leading and she following, mimicking her moves, her ingredients, her mixtures. The beautiful dark-haired blue-eyed girl with the bird-like voice has charmed so many. My sister is my mother's pet, her sweet cherished child, and I am lost and forgotten in the shadows.

Shunned, apart, and alone.

The two of them giggle like children, their minds incapable of imagination. My green eyes had doomed me to a life as an outcast, my gaze instantly shunned by locals, perhaps out of fear. I could travel nowhere without feeling their distant stares, their burning looks. They showered me in their scorn, their taunts, their mockery, and I was dismissed by nearly all whom I encountered. My days were often lonely, so much time spent in solitude, unwelcome as I was.

Yet, this nurtured a strength within me, gave me purpose, instilled in me the desire to overcome to vanquish those who would make me weak.

Mother and sister limit themselves to the simplest, the most benevolent, the benign, and mundane.

Little do they know of my imagination. I've no use for anyone, none of them.

For now, I've got all I need so I'll leave them to their girlish laughter. I can return later alone.

1872

Why does she stand apart and alone. Shun us? Shun me? I love her as I can only love a sister.

I want her to join us, to be with us, to share our secrets, our laughter.

Does she not love me as I love her?

14 – My Decision

A weak man has doubts before a decision, a strong one has them afterwards. Or something like that. Does that mean I'm weak or strong?

My history with chance-taking was not a good one. Nearly every risk I'd taken had been a slowly ticking bomb. Or one that exploded immediately. Of course, this was all retrospective so easy to see. The past was just that and slows you down if you carry it. I'd spent a good part of my life like a cat left out in the rain. A series of bad choices led exactly where bad choices lead. My past was not so easily forgotten or set down like a heavy burden. Some might say that I consistently ran like a coward, afraid to face up to what I'd done and what I'd been. I didn't see it that way; it's easy for others to judge from a distance.

I want to start over, to make a life to be proud of, to find my home. But is that here or in New Brook West?

I'd moved as far away as I could afford to when I came to the Concourse, considered changing my name and it may have been a mistake not to.

I tried not to stand out financially, professionally, or socially in my new destination. The escape had been such a sudden decision there was no time to try to get a new identity.

It's been three years now in my most recent apartment and my life is good, though I'm still not sure I'm 'home'.

Lori had completely disappeared, at least from me, which was for the best. I'd heard that her parents had moved her into a halfway house for young women which seemed like a good place for her given her circumstances. She was such a sweet girl but life had hung her out to dry and so had I. Our daughter's death had been her end; there was no saving her or us after that. She sank so deeply into depression, attempting suicide on two different occasions, before I reached out for help. Perhaps it was best for her that I disappear.

Still, I often found myself hoping I'd somehow hear from her and that she was well again.

I think back to when I first met her in the park when she was sitting on the swing. A beautiful memory that I hope I'll always carry, despite how things turned out in the end.

My 'friends' from my past life were nowhere to be found and Rick's disintegration had reached its apex. And I couldn't call on my new acquaintances in our neighbourhood any more than I already had. Eventually involving her parents was the only solution. They blamed me for everything, perhaps rightly so, and never saw any of the good in me. I loved Lori absolutely. And I missed Suzie every day, the little girl I'd loved in a way I'd never thought possible.

My family.

That seemed to get lost in it all.

I sometimes felt sorry for myself; is that selfish?

But that was another life.

It seems like someone is giving me a chance to find my home or at least set me on the right path. Or the potential right path, you can never know for sure.

I like my life now but it still feels incomplete.

I really hope I'm doing the right thing.

I wake the next morning to a really bad rendition of a Bob Dylan song across the street from the café. The singer goes on to a Johnny Cash tune and it soon becomes obvious that he only knows three or four chords which form the basis of his entire repertoire, but his vocals are enthusiastic.

The sun shines brightly through the thin curtains which is always a good thing. Coffee time. That's my new addiction so finding a suite above a café turned out to be a stroke of good fortune.

Carlos had recently given me a decent sized package of an Arabian brew which is just right strength and flavour.

I open the drapes and look outside on a sunny Monday morning. It's just after 10:00 so the shops are open and some street merchants have set up their outdoor kiosks. I'd been approved for vacation for the week which feels like a deception on my part because I'm spending my time trying to decide if I'll leave town. The professor under whose direction I worked had previously told me that he didn't expect or require any real notice if I found something else. But I'd like to give him at least a couple of days as a courtesy if I decide to go to New Brook West. Perhaps he suspected something when I asked for my vacation but was too polite to say anything.

It looks like a good day for a walk, though I don't really feel like running into Kayla or the other servers right now. I'd not seen her since Saturday and did want to see her, hopefully tonight, but just not yet.

I manage to slip past the staff and into the street, hopefully without being noticed. A perfect September Sunday morning with a clear sky, a warm sun, and no wind. There isn't a heck of a lot to do in the apartment so walks became a regular part of my weekend routine. I pass a couple of interesting bistros but decide that my wallet is light enough and a luxury of that kind isn't in today's budget.

The local grocery store has surprisingly good prices, depending on what you buy. I manage to get a loaded sandwich for less than it would cost me to make it myself. Grabbing a box of granola, some milk, and a newspaper, I make my way to the market where I buy some inexpensive fruit and vegetables before heading home. Coming in the back way takes me up the stairs avoiding anyone on the café patio.

I pull my key to unlock the door, realizing after I've inserted it that it's not locked. I turn the knob and carefully push it in.

Cautious and quiet steps take me around the room but no one is here.

My first thought is that someone from my past has tracked me down but that's out of the question. Carlos is the only other person with a spare and he'd never come up here and wouldn't have given anyone else the key to do so. Still, I know the door was locked so someone had paid me a visit.

Kayla? I doubt she'd break in.

But nothing seems missing and no one's here so I dismiss it as forgetfulness on my part.

I do want to see Kayla again but have no way of contacting her other than happening upon her at the café. Maybe that's how she wants it. Or I'd been just a fun night for her. That'd be a shame.

After a bite to eat and some indecision, I walk downstairs past the patio in case I spot her. I can't recall exactly how we'd left it and if she wants me to come see her or if she's even working tonight. I'll know soon enough and hopefully be sufficiently sharp to determine if she wants to spend time with me again.

Warmer than usual with just enough wind to rustle the flags and other items on the taller buildings, I wear a dark t-shirt and light jeans skipping down the steps before strolling casually in front of the café. A full street and busy patio welcome me.

Sure enough, Kayla in her tight white shirt and dark pants hustles among the tables and into the kitchen. I lean against a lamppost waiting for her to notice me.

In time, one of the other waitresses smiles and indicates my location to her. Kayla waves softly and beams, rushing to one of her customers to take an order.

I don't want to come on too strong too soon but want to make sure she doesn't forget about me – a fine line. Because of the magnitude of accepting or declining the letter of offer, I seem to be delaying this decision. These thoughts all cause me to worry and I don't like the feeling.

I summon my confidence with Kayla, assuring myself that I've done well to this point and that her thoughts are her decision. And my decision is yet to be finalized.

A kiss on my right cheek surprises me.

Kayla.

"I'm glad you stopped by" she beams "Did you come to see me?"

"I did" I say, deciding against a witty comment.

"I'll be done in an hour. I can meet you somewhere or you can come back. Your call"

"I'll drift about a bit and come back for a coffee if there's a spot, otherwise I'll wait patiently"

"Maybe I'll make you wait" she squirrels up her face, crossing her arms in front of her with a smirk.

"It'll be worth it"

She smiles and runs off.

I walk away down the Concourse, a smile on my face; I want to turn back but don't, eventually disappearing into the crowd.

I haven't eaten much before coming out so make my way to a cheap taco stand, lacking the energy to cook but preferring to save any money I have to spend on my evening with Kayla. Despite it being a Sunday night, the streets are alive, buskers out in full force, pedestrians of all kinds, patios bustling, and outdoor kiosks selling their wares. A beautiful time for a quiet moment alone.

The sun has fully set, an amazing view of this down by the water which is where I find myself, a refreshing cold drink in hand.

The sunset makes me reflective, thinking back on all the fun times I've had here, my friends, my job, the Concourse, the time I'd spent alone which I found liberating. This is definitely the coolest part of the city; mighty good fortune to meet Carlos and score a low rent apartment that wasn't low-rent. In so many ways, this is my dream destination. Occasionally a bad memory, but I dispel it, intent on a fun night with a fantastic woman.

I haven't yet fully decided on the mysterious offer and my future here with Kayla or in parts unknown alone. Or have I?

I like it here but that doesn't mean there isn't more out there for me.

If I pass on this opportunity, will I regret my decision in the future? Will I regret my decision to leave?

Somehow, I find a bench to myself in one of my favourite locations. The crisp autumn air refreshing as it cools me. Time drifts on peacefully, my stress-free quiet contemplation watching the water flow past.

Were other things in life 'meant to be'? No way. It's about choices.

My life had been great since I'd moved here; the city was good to me; my neighbourhood was wicked; my job was, well, it was steady; my love life was…hopeful. Still, it felt like 'home' had eluded me, a concept that I understood but hadn't experienced since my life with Lori.

No. I'm happy now. I don't want to be all gloomy when I see Kayla.

Things sometimes just 'are'. Maybe that's how they're meant to be.

It's been forty-five minutes since I'd left the café so I begin my way back, a casual stroll along the well-lit cobblestone street, shadows in the dark corners. I take a turn down a dim alley filled with graffiti: some artistic, some poetic. I survey the walls for anything interesting or creative. This lane's walls have never been cleaned, the thoughts being that artists won't desecrate another's work and it's stayed true to form with no contributions being defaced by other graffiti.

Here's a strange one, in a long open space and written in beautiful type: **'Their names all in the letters lie, when the three come together the tree will die'**

A riddle? I suck at riddles. Probably means something only to the author and their inner circle. But it's something different to spice up the usual artwork.

I've grown so accustomed to the mixture of folks in this area, that rarely does anything unusual catch my eye.

It's more about the neighbourhood's vibe, the combination of activity and solitude, and the sheer variety of stores, and atmosphere within each of the restaurants and bars.

Would I be leaving my home?

In a darker and sparser area of the street, I catch a glimpse of a dark figure ducking down a darker alley but there's no one there when I walk over so I dismiss it.

I stop at the lamppost where I'd waited earlier, my location shadowed with the light at my back. I'm immediately spotted by the same server who'd seen me last time. I smile and wave at Kayla, her face lighting up when she sees me. Wow. She waves enthusiastically, holding up three fingers. I give the thumbs-up.

She scampers about gracefully, closing tabs or clearing tables, disappearing into the back after a few moments. She peeks back out onto the patio holding up two fingers this time. I give the thumbs-up again.

I casually look around without taking in anything in particular.

She throws her arms around my neck from behind me, jumping up as she does, catching me completely off-guard.

We kiss like I've been overseas for a year, her soft lips, her chest pressed against mine, her back arched.

"You move like a cat sneaking up on me" I say.

"Meow" she hisses pawing at me with her left hand.

She takes my left hand in her right one.

"I like it when you squeeze me tight" she grins "You're strong and have a buff bod"

"Ha. Thanks"

"So where are you taking me tonight?"

"You pick something" I look around "I can find most anything around here"

"How about a beer, a snack, and we decide the rest after that?"

"That sounds delicious" I kiss her.

"Rrrrrr" she purrs.

The ground-level patio where we sit is down the street from the heart of the action, an outdoor table a bonus to find.

She's wearing a black jacket over her work uniform which looks amazing on her; I feel more casual but don't look like a thug, or so I hope.

She tells me about her European travels and a road trip across the States, all of which sound amazing. I choose to talk about moving here and how awesome it is in the Concourse, and how I try to fit in. I keep it upbeat with funny stories of awkward encounters and fun times, avoiding the 'offer' for now.

We laugh, talk about her adventures in the city, her fun times in my neighbourhood, even gloss over some deeper topics including her academics and plans for future work. She giggles in a girlish way that conceals her intelligence.

Sometimes, I feel eyes on me, though I can't imagine why; this feeling still unnerves me in light of recent events. But my attention is firmly focused on my beautiful companion, watching her lips, her eyes, her chest. She places a hand on the table which I take as a sign to put mine on top of it. She smiles when I do.

After two beer each and a plate of cheesy nachos, I pay the bill, she leaving the tip.

"If you'd like to come back to my place for a bit…"

"I'd like that" she stands up as gracefully as a ballerina, holding her hands out for mine as if inviting me to dance.

"It's a wonderful night" I smile stepping into the street.

I take her hands and slowly pull her body towards me, my right hand on her lower back, her right hand in my left. I lead her through a simple dance to the orchestral music playing on the patio's speakers, moving my hips as best I can, taking short steps to avoid getting tangled in her feet.

I'm sure other people are watching but neither of us seem to notice as she looks up into my eyes the entire time.

"You are quite a charmer, Colden"

I lean down to kiss her, wrapping my arms around her as I do.

"You warm enough?" I ask as we set out.

"Yes, thanks" she says taking my hand.

And off we go through the crowd, stopping occasionally at a shop with interesting items, even briefly for her to try on a shirt that she ends up not buying. A bright moon and stars fill the clear night sky, the gentlest breeze at our backs cooling the air.

Still, a great temperature for an autumn night out. With an amazing woman.

I pick up a bottle of juice and carton of milk; I'll need both even if I spend the night alone.

We arrive at the café just past 11:30, the patio still full, the waitresses trying to pretend they don't see us climb the stairs to my apartment.

"Welcome back" I say once we're inside my place.

"You've already used your smooth moves to charm me out of my clothes once" her eyes squint.

"You're as beautiful without them as you are fully dressed" I smile.

"Still smooth" she kicks off her shoes, comes over to kiss me from up on her toes, then walks into the living room.

"Wine, juice, water, uh…" I scramble through the fridge.

"Juice, please" she removes her jacket, placing her elbows on the counter facing into the kitchen.

I pour orange juice into two tall glasses, handing one to her.

"Very sharp" she squirrels up her face looking at the glass.

"I've been saving these for someone special" I clink my glass against hers.

"More charm" she sips her juice and sets it down on the counter "You'll have me out of my clothes again"

"I hope so" I set my glass down next to hers.

She comes back for another sip of juice.

I take the glass from her hand.

"You have the most beautifully soft lips" I hold her arms at her sides and look into her eyes.

She stands on her tiptoes to kiss me.

"You're so sweet" she smiles.

I pull her close, lips together we melt into each other.

As I pull back, I notice movement on the steps outside through the space in the curtains but don't want to interrupt the moment so ignore it.

"It's warm in here" she says.

"I can turn down the heat" I reply.

"Not what I had in mind" she pulls my shirt up over my head, unbuttoning hers soon after. I throw her shirt onto the sofa, slowly unclip her bra to pull her towards me, her bare chest against mine, my hands running up and down her back.

From there, our pants soon come off, then her foot slides her underwear to the floor as our kissing leads us to the bed where she leans back. I first flick her hard nipples quickly with my tongue, taking one in my mouth and sucking it firmly, holding it gently between my teeth making her back arch. My mouth makes its way down her chest and past her stomach to her open legs as I bring my tongue against the delicate smooth skin between her legs and taste her femininity. She moans, my hands under her knees holding her legs in the air, her feet on my shoulders. I continue to pleasure her orally as her body responds to my mouth. Her back is now arching slightly off the bed and her hands are grabbing at the sheets.

"Huuh, huuh, huuh…" she exhales loudly.

I love pleasuring her this way. Is that selfish?

A few more minutes of this and her breathing becomes gasping.

"Oh, God" she yells "Oh my God"

Her back arches her off the bed, and her entire body goes stiff as she lets out a long moan through clenched teeth.

"Nnnnnnnnn"

Her hands pull at the bedsheets, her left foot pushing hard against my right shoulder as my mouth continues to pleasure her.

Her legs squeeze together as she reaches the peak of her ecstasy, her teeth still clenched as she seems to have stopped breathing.

She makes a high-pitched sound, her back still arched off the bed.

I hold her legs, my mouth still between them, her hands now gripping my hair and pushing my face between her legs.

Her climax lasts for several seconds until her body shakes and her hands push me away.

"Huhnn, huhnn, huhnn..." she moans, exhaling, eyes closed.

"Oh yes. Ohhhh" she whispers.

I love watching her orgasms. Her hands fall to the sheets, her legs squeeze together, her feet drawn up to her bum.

Then she takes a deep breath and releases the sheets as her body goes limp.

"Oh yes" she whispers "Come here"

Her orgasms are absolutely beautiful.

She sits up and I share her delicious juices in a warm kiss, her taste lingering wonderfully in my mouth and on my lips.

"Inside me" she leans back down on the bed as I climb on top of her, slowly guiding me into the tight wet embrace between her legs which are still in the air.

Her breathing stops as I enter her then turns to long moaning, her hands gripping my shoulders, her body tensing as if in pain.

"Yes" she moans.

She wraps her legs around me as if to pull me closer and deeper inside her. I thrust myself slowly and then faster, as deep as I can, her feet trying to hold me as her back arches off the bed, her legs spread wide.

Her grip on me is so tight, I can't resist any longer. I feel it begin and slowly move its way through me until it erupts. My climax is incredible, the explosion releasing my passions as I let out a low roar.

"Ohhhhhhhh"

I feel the pulsing and throbbing as this intense energy that had been building is released and I collapse.

"That was beautiful" she whispers.

"You're beautiful" I say kissing her.

We both close our eyes, me still lying on top of her. After a few minutes, she shifts beneath me.

"Can I have my juice, please" she asks with a giggle.

"I'll be right back" I say summoning the strength to rise.

Wow.

I shuffle to the counter to collect our drinks, noticing a sound again from the staircase near the door. Did someone watch us have sex? I doubt it because few people know of the suite up here.

"End of the world sex?" she says.

"I hope not" I sit next to her on the bed and hand her a glass.

"We need to do that again" she says, her naked body uncovered.

"We will" I smile taking a sip of juice.

I run my hand over her breast then up and down along her stomach.

"Mmmmm" she sighs, closing her eyes.

"Turn off the lights and come lay here beside me" she says opening her eyes.

Scurrying around the room, I shut everything off, check the door, and crawl in next to Kayla's naked body, now beneath the covers.

I fall onto my back trying to figure out her position.

"What a wonderful evening" she exhales.

"Just: wow" I say.

"Mmmmm" she exhales, bringing her head to rest on my chest, her left hand on my stomach.

I'm sure I fall asleep with a smile.

The most beautiful sight greets me the next morning, Kayla naked in the dining room area facing away from me. She rises up on her toes to do a stretch then puts on her white dress shirt, without fastening any buttons.

I lay in bed, hands behind my head watching her.

"Mmmmm" she does another stretch looking in my direction "I think you should get up and make me some coffee. I'd rather not walk downstairs like this to get two cups"

"As you wish" I pull back the covers to get up.

"You don't need your clothes" she smiles looking at me.

Fully naked, I look down at my lower half, slowly walking to the kitchen, Kayla watching me the whole way.

"I like the way you move" she purrs.

"Uh, thanks"

"And your buff bod. What keeps you strong?"

"There's a trail along the river that I occasionally run, and some apartment exercises like push-ups, sit-ups, arm stuff with heavy books. I'm low-tech. Used to run and swim but not really team sports"

"Your non-competitive running works" she comes over to stand up on her toes and wrap her arms around me from behind, squeezing my butt as she walks back to the other side of the counter.

"What keeps your body looking so amazing?" I ask setting the coffee up.

"I danced when I was younger, mostly ballet" she blushes.

"Play any sports?" I ask.

"Some soccer and volleyball when I was in school, but recently just yoga and aerobics"

"You can show off your naked body to me anytime you like" I smile.

"I just might do that" she says opening her shirt.

I walk to her, removing her shirt, pulling her bare breasts against my chest, kissing her as passionately as I can before realizing I have morning breath and hers is minty fresh. She really does have the softest lips which makes me want to kiss her even more and she doesn't seem turned off by my beast breath.

The coffee maker beeps indicating the readiness of our morning beverage but I'm distracted by the swelling between my legs which I press against her making her moan. Running my hands down to her firm bum, I lift her, carrying her back to the bed.

"Morning sex" she whispers "Mmmmm"

My hands cup her breasts making her gasp.

"Ok" she says falling onto her back on the bed.

Coffee can wait.

The next few days brought Kayla and I together often, though I knew my decision had yet to be made and she must have suspected something, having overheard a couple of short conversations I'd had with Pete. We never spoke of long-term futures or anything beyond the week. But our time together was amazing. She brought out the best in me, left me wanting to see her again, made me smile when she smiled.

Oddly, I never went to her place, though perhaps the convenience of my apartment made mine the obvious location to spend nights.

It was great when she stayed over.

There's enough to do in the Concourse that you could go out every night for a month without visiting the same place. We had fun everywhere we went.

But as the time got closer, I knew my decision had already been made.

15 – Milkshakes

Back in today's reality, there were preparations to be made before I lost my nerve and risked losing out on this opportunity. I'd always felt welcome here and had made many great memories. I'll miss Ryan. He's a great guy and fantastic friend. I'll miss Kayla, despite knowing her so briefly, our chemistry is undeniable, a feeling you can't define and one that most people look for all their lives, and I was leaving it. The professor and the other academics would soon forget me and move on to the next one, though I did appreciate the opportunity I'd been given to hold a respectable job, one that made me proud of myself. I'd even miss Carlos, a true gentleman, and Pete, a solid dude.

Still, if you don't change, you do stay the same. And I felt the need to change once again. Maybe I'd come back one day, though I suspected 'here' would be different as well if I did.

Perhaps I really will find home this time.

There's little to bring, most things I own are items I won't need, and I prefer to travel light in any case. I don't want to have to haul a ton of luggage and packages around with me and am unsure of any cargo limits or the size of the new accommodations.

Some books are easy decisions, some music as well, a lot of clothes won't make the trip but many items are my favourites and will be useful in any conditions. The large trunk which had followed me on my last move carries the heavier and the personal items, a duffle bag for short-term essentials with a couple of small things that I like to have near at hand.

The trunk could be managed by two guys but if I'm one of them the other will need to be pretty strong as this will not be possible on my own. I assume someone at the other end will assist me.

The plane departs tomorrow evening, destination: London, England. With bathroom and clothing necessities the only pieces left to pack, I decide to go for a short walk and then see Kayla at the café where I know her shift ends at 7:00. I head out the back way so as not to be seen by any of the staff who have by now figured out that we're involved and also that I've made the decision to leave. Kayla is well-liked and feels the same about most of her co-workers so there's a sense of commiseration amongst them. I don't feel like feeding into any situation which will upset Kayla nor feel the dirty or sad looks of the other waitresses. I do want to stop and see Pete before I leave and will do that tomorrow afternoon.

My steps are soft as I descend the iron staircase, creeping out the back lane like a fugitive. Another warm September day means a busy street even on a weekday, the sun bright and warming. The beautiful river makes for a great autumn walk, a light breeze playing with the multi-coloured leaves, a few stragglers hanging on to their branches, the water the colour of the darkening blue sky at sunset. I think of Lori, of Suzie, of Rick, of my previous life, how things are, how I wished they were, how I had been sad, how I'm still sad. So many bad decisions, poor choices, people who didn't give a shit masquerading as friends, lost opportunities.

I'm meant for so much more; could have been a great man, a happy man. Not who I've become. A poor turtle hiding in his shell.

I think of Kayla, of Ryan, of Pete, of Carlos, of my apartment, the fear that comes with change, leaving behind the comfort of the known for the anxiety of uncertainty. The walks through the market, international coffee with unusual names, the serenity of the university, my enjoyably dull life. There's no doubt of my connection with Kayla and it makes me sad that after all these years I was finally able to bond with someone kind and caring only to ditch her.

I welcome solitude on my own terms but want to be the one making the choices rather than dealing with circumstance.

I arrive at Chaos around 6:45.

"Hi Colden" a server I recognize comes by my table "What can I get you?"

I think her name is Melissa but it might be Melinda or Alyssa so I just say 'Hi'.

"A Turkish blend for me, please"

"Coming right up" she skips off to the bar.

A different server that I don't recognize brings my cup a few minutes later.

"Carlos told us that you're leaving Sunday" she says.

How does she know who I am?

"I'm Christi" she says, though this doesn't help me remember. What striking green eyes.

"Got an opportunity that I had to go for"

"You're leaving, like, leaving town?" her head tilts to the left.

"Like, leaving the country" I smile "I got a job overseas"

"Wow, that's great" her face seems to be trying to smile back.

"Thanks"

She smiles, curtseys, and walks away.

"Be sure you stop by tomorrow Cold", Pete emerges from the kitchen, "I'm on the day shift"

"For sure, Pete. After lunch"

"Awesome" he says with a nod.

Pete returns to his station. He's probably a great employee, both likable and hard-working. We'd never been that close but hung out a couple of times in addition to seeing each other regularly at the café.

"Hi"

Kayla's greeting sounds like a blend of hello and goodbye.

"Hi, Kayla"

I take a few steps toward her, kissing her on the lips.

In tight black jeans, a white t-shirt under a dark red leather jacket, a left-tilted black beret over her dark pony-tailed hair, with only a hint of make-up around her eyes, she's a true beauty.

"Where to?" she takes my hand.

"I thought we could start with milkshakes by the river"

"That sounds nice" she nods.

Magicians and jugglers, musicians and merchants, the streets are filled with entertainment, the performers happy to ply their trade this calm warm night, possibly for the last time before chillier weather thins pedestrian crowds. Kayla and I marvel at the diversity of people, the assortment of arts playing themselves out, the bright starry sky, and the lights of the shops.

We're both lost in the moment, my departure forgotten for the time being.

A cloaked figure stands off to the side.

"A dollar to tell your fortune" a female voice says from beneath the silver hood, her cloak extending to the ground.

"Kayla" I call her over.

"Hey" she jogs to my side.

"A dollar to tell my fortune" I say "Whatta ya think?"

She takes my hand, though seems a bit nervous.

I extend a dollar coin. The woman's right hand points to a small red jar on the ground. I drop it in.

"One a woman, one a girl. One you will kill, one will kill you" she says.

"What did you say?" I lean closer to her.

"Colden" Kayla frowns "Come on. Let's go"

I look at her, both her arms trying to pull me away.

When I turn back, the woman is no longer there, the jar empty at my feet.

"That was…" I start.

Kayla looks terrified.

"Can we not talk about that ever again, please" Kayla implores.

"Of course" I hug her tightly before leading us away to our destination.

The Riverside Dive rented boats, bicycles, and offered carriage rides, in addition to serving delicious ice cream treats. Kayla chooses a chocolate-vanilla mixture while I opt for a caramel-cream shake. Outside, a driver offers us a horse-drawn coach ride and it turns out to be an excellent idea. The clear starry sky is the perfect backdrop for an evening excursion, a cozy blanket in the back providing us warmth from the slight chill in the air. The thirty-minute ride carries us along the river bank but also through more intimate and less travelled areas. We return to our point of origin and I tip the coachman unsure of exactly where to go now.

"How about a glass of wine" Kayla reads my thoughts "There's a nice lounge a short walk from here"

I nod in agreement.

We arrive at Le Miroir, a wine bar which I knew of but had never been. We manage to find a window seat on the second floor providing a view of a street quieter than Café Chaos' location.

She orders a smooth bottle of Pinot Noir which we both enjoy very much.

"So, what's next for you?" I ask her.

"Next year's my last one in nursing and there seem to be a lot of opportunities right now at nearby hospitals. I'll hopefully be working in the neo-natal ward because that's where I'd like to be and where I'll be specializing in my last year"

"You've chosen a wonderful career" I tell her.

"I hope yours is just as wonderful" she smiles.

We spend the rest of the evening chatting about what I know and don't about being a station master. I wouldn't call myself especially handy when it came to repairs and construction but am capable enough with the basics, though I confess that aspect had me slightly concerned. There isn't much to say about where I'll be staying, how I could be reached, nor any details about the community so this topic quickly fades without Kayla giving the impression that I'm withholding information.

She tells me about her classes, about her family life - one sister - and about the small town where she grew up. My details are far less specific; Lori's demise, Suzie's death, and Rick's misery are all left out, as well as my life in 'The Scene', though I do tell her about some of the awesome bands I saw and local places I went during that time.

I avoid any mention of our awkward encounter with the strange cloaked woman by the river, though I do wonder at Kayla's anxiety at what she'd said.

When it comes time to go home, I offer she stay at my place and she readily accepts. It's been an exceptional evening with our passions released by both the wine and my impending departure. Spent and exhausted, we spoon with my naked body up against hers and fall asleep in this position.

When I wake in the morning all that's left is a note on her pillow.

I'll miss you. Be happy'

1874

They eventually drove me out with their scorn, their contempt, their anger at what I was trying to achieve, trying to be. Do none understand? Not even those closest to me? Their love is a lie.

How long did they think they could ignore me until I decided to leave?

It's better to be alone.

1874

Why is she leaving?

I want to tell her I love her in case that will make her stay but it's too late because she's already gone.

I don't want her to be alone.

16 – Chris

Clouds welcome me on my last day, the sky the colour of ash, though without rain for the moment, as I sit alone in my suite. A solitary coffee gives me time to ponder everything that's happened and all that might come to pass. I miss Kayla already; part of me wants to change my mind and see her again tonight. I don't know how to contact her to say anything that hadn't already been said. She doesn't work until this evening so we'd not see each other today, my flight leaving at 6:00 p.m. As far as my destination, there were too many possible scenarios for what awaited me and my imagination was lacking so this soon slips away. I need a walk so make my way out into the cool damp air.

I wave to the girl adjusting the patio furniture, her face a mixture of vulnerability and anger at being outside. Outdoor coffee won't entice many today and I wish it would have been nicer on my last day. Such is life.

My walk takes me up one side of the Concourse and back the other, to say goodbye to my neighbourhood. This could have been home for me, could have made me happy, could have been the end of the line, and maybe that would have been enough.

When do you stop looking for your destination, a place where you belong? Was something truly lacking here? Had I ever really had a home? I could have made one with Lori and Suzie but that was gone. For the longest time I believed that there was no 'me' without 'her', no life without her; and then without Suzie.

Kayla and I might have been forever, or maybe not and then I'd be alone here with nothing and no one. New Brook West might be what I'd searched for all along.

It's all about chances. About choices.

The return leg of my walk leads me around back and up the stairs, unseen. I round up my items, pack the last of my possessions, and set everything I don't want in boxes in the middle of the room for Carlos to dispose of or keep. My trunk and duffle bag wait for me at the door, the plane and train tickets in my pocket. My beautifully simple apartment. My life had largely been one of solitude but it wasn't lonely. It's peaceful to be alone. I've been alone here and happy about it. But it feels sad to be leaving, it always does, leaving home, such as it is.

Sneaking around back, I manage to drag Pete outside for a quick chat and a few heartfelt sentiments. Our farewell comes to an end when he butts out his cigarette and we hug.

He slips me two sandwiches, a raisin muffin, and a cup of coffee. The muffin will wait until later, the coffee will relax me now as it always does. The delicious roast beef on a bun fills me up perfectly, a hefty helping of meat and cheese and lettuce. Thanks, Pete. I will miss you.

The last of my goodbyes.

I feel like I'm about to cry.

I walk around to the small grocery store for a bottle of juice to give me some nutrients and liquid other than coffee, sitting outside against the building to drink it.

A rapid movement across the street catches my eye but whoever had been there is gone. My mysterious deliveryman? Will he follow me to the airport? All the way to New Brook West? Or is his work done? Or am I seeing things to try to make sense of this mystery?

I spend the rest of the day down by the river doing puzzles out of a book I've recently purchased with a can of apple juice. My thoughts overwhelm me. I don't feel like company or the need to interact, content to let my mind wander. Not enough attention-span to read but no desire to just roam about; the tranquility of my location suits my emotions. Alone by myself.

When my watch says 2:30, I hustle back to my apartment to collect my items and call a taxi. It arrives quickly in the back alley and I'm gone.

I check in with plenty of time, now hanging around the airport, hoping I'll not see anyone I know who'll want to know my story and tell me theirs.

More puzzles to pass the time, and a fresh coffee. I pull a sandwich from my backpack, devour it and scan the crowd. Watching people as they travel always interests me, the diversity of individuals, their idiosyncrasies, their manner, their posture. Where are they going? What adventures await them? What calamities? What obstacles? Love? Tragedy? Maybe they find me interesting, but I doubt it.

Waiting makes me groggy. I'm relieved when the plane begins to board, though it feels like a dream. My window seat has me next to a woman in her twenties with 'Chris' written on her backpack.

"Is that you?" I point at the name.

"Me" she replies.

"I'm Colden"

"Yes, it's Chris" she says.

"Is it short for something?" I ask as I buckle my belt.

"Yes" she says, her tone not harsh but friendly. When she doesn't follow up her reply, I decide not to pursue it.

I look around the airplane, a smaller one than I would have expected.

"You a nervous flyer?" Chris asks.

"I enjoy the thought of being in the air, being above the clouds" I reply with a smile.

"Where you headed?"

"I got a job offer" I say.

"Well, I hope it's a great one" she says after a brief pause.

"Where are you going?" I ask.

"I'm following someone" She smirks "Someone on this airplane. But I can't tell you who"

"Uh oh. Sounds serious" I hold up my hands "I'm not looking for any trouble"

We laugh.

The seven-hour-long direct flight departs on schedule. I'd arrive in London around eleven a.m., considering the time change, and then make my way to the train station to head to my final destination. With on-board food soon to come, I watch bits and pieces of movies before closing my eyes.

I wake to Chris looking at me.

"Good morning" she smiles. Only now do I notice her striking green eyes.

"Good morning" I collect my thoughts, recalling that I'm on a plane. My shoulder-length blonde hair probably looks like a matted mess.

Didn't one of the waitresses at Chaos have eyes like that? Christi. That's weird.

How totally odd to see two women with such a stunning feature and similar names. I hope it's a good sign.

"You had a good long nap" she says "I can never sleep on planes. The movies suck but the music's good and some TV shows have killed the last four hours for me"

"Four hours?"

"You were deep in dreams" she says "Good ones, I hope"

I now realize she's slid over to the aisle seat so there's an empty one between us.

"I figured I'd give you more room to stretch out" she says as if in response to my thought.

"Do you mind if I get up for a minute, please, to stretch a bit more?" I ask.

"Of course" she swings her legs out to let me pass.

I walk to the middle of the cabin to the First-Class seats then to the rear of the plane to the washrooms.

The plane is nearly full, a few empty spots scattered like holes punched in a piece of paper. For the most part, people sleep or try to, some opting to watch the small screen in the chair back in front of them, a few read or talk quietly. Chris seems nice and a decent neighbour for such a long flight. There to talk if I want but not chatting at me all the time. But my mind remains on Kayla.

After a brief stop to use the facilities, I return to my seat. The cabin suddenly feels cooler, as if the air conditioning has just come on, more so in the area around my row. Maybe Chris is warm and has opened the air vent above her full-force. But then why does she have her sweater on?

"Chilly?" I say scrambling past her.

"A little" she wraps her arms around her body in agreement.

A coffee and piece of cake await me.

"I took the liberty of ordering us each a coffee" she says.

"Thanks. And the cake?"

"One of the stewardesses brought that for you"

Vanilla cake with warm caramel drizzle. Few people know of my guilty pleasure, certainly no one on this flight.

"Why did she bring this?" I ask.

"Maybe you have a secret admirer" she smiles.

Had Chris requested the cake? But why? I get no vibe of her flirting with me; the opposite, if anything.

Two and a half hours until we land, the sky outside fully light, the view below us the top of thick clouds.

Chris now wears headphones so I turn my attention to drawing a sketch of the street outside of Carlos' as I remember it, trying to find the best way to portray Kayla without her photo in front of me.

Before long, the pilot's voice comes over the intercom announcing our imminent arrival, as well as the local time, describing the weather as cloudy and cool but calm. Not ideal, but such is life.

I feel groggy, perhaps the sugar in the cake sapped my energy, or just the length of travel combined with lack of sleep. Hopefully the train will be a smooth ride and I can get more rest there.

I don't want to arrive at my new home exhausted.

I disembark, immediately losing Chris in the crowd. I wade through blank faces, drift past vacant expressions, get my trunk on a trolley with another guy's help, hop in a taxi van, and show my train ticket to the driver. Much to my relief, he knows exactly where to take me, a train station some distance away which I'd never have found on my own. He even assists with the heavy chest for which I'm most grateful. I give him a nice tip and a hearty handshake.

The guy in the booth at the station arranges for my trunk to be loaded, another welcome occurrence, directing me to a waiting area. People move around me like figures in the fog, strangers in an unfamiliar venue. I drink a really bad cup of vending-machine and watch the clock.

After a short wait, a voice directs me to the platform and I board, shuffling to my seat against the window next to a well-dressed guy.

I promptly fall asleep.

1876

The town had become even more wicked with poverty and despair, anger and hatred. The people corrupt, selfish, and spiteful. Nearly all shun me, but some take my potions for which I accept a fine sum. Such is my price. Let them pay for their hypocrisy.

I avoid this place except when absolutely necessary.

My purchases made, I creep through the streets toward my cabin, noticing a handsome man as I do, sad and lost, but handsome.

His appearance and manner intrigue me.

"Where am I, please?" he asks.

"You're standing in front of me" I reply.

"I mean, in what town?" he averts his gaze from my green eyes.

"Are you afraid to look at me?" I ask.

"Only because your green eyes are so beautiful" he says "I don't mean to stare"

I try to cast my gaze around me and see that a few passersby have noticed me interacting with this unknown man. Most look for only a moment though I'm sure this produces many conversations and gossip.

"What brings you here?" I soften my tone.

"I'm a simple man" he forces a partial smile "I have no great skills or lofty aspirations, only the hope to find someplace I can call home"

He is simple, but truly kind and gentle and attractive if not elegant with a latent charm.

We sit together and talk at length before I walk him to the local inn for him to take lodgings.

In time, we become close and our time together increases as I come to see qualities in him which he denies.

"You could be so much more" I say "You could rule here. These people want a strong ruler, someone to guide them, to tell them what they need, to bring hope"

"I only hope that you'll stay by my side" he smiles "We shall celebrate together, cry together, and love together"

Clearly my elixirs are working, his charms now even affecting me.

I continue to produce the potions to keep my appearance so he will always gaze on me as his one and only beautiful love. I want his love and his touch. I need them.

He runs his hand across my bare breast and nipple, sending a shiver through my body, which continues down over my stomach and to my legs which seem to part on their own to allow his hand to touch my sex. This pleasure moves like fire through my veins from my curling toes along my legs to the heat between them and in circles out from my nipple through my breast and my entire body. I close my eyes and reach for something to hold as my body shakes.

"Mmmm" I moan as my body tenses "Mmmm"

My hand scrambles to reach down to take his thick erection and to slowly stroke it as one of his hands caresses my thighs and over my wet warmth, the other carefully playing with my nipple as my breathing stops. I'm holding him tightly in my grip as I try to keep my body still against his touch. I gasp when he slides a finger inside me. As he moves it, an energy starts between my legs, increasing with each touch as his hands explore my body. The pleasure takes over and I lose focus on the world around me, the fire burning in my veins. Ohhhh, yes.

I'm furiously stroking his rock-hard penis as I sense his stomach muscles flex.

Then he finds that most sensitive button just above my fiery hot sex and my teeth clench as my body stiffens

ready to scream, my hand holding his erection like a lifeline. His finger slowly rubs this pleasure center. My body is on fire. Oh, please, please.

The intensity, oh. The energy flowing through me is almost too much for me. I'm going to explode. Oh. Ohhhh.

I'm gasping loudly now as the world around me stops. My legs are spread as widely apart as they can, my bare feet pressed together, my toes curling uncontrollably.

I can't take much more.

"Ohhhh" I moan.

My eyes are closed.

Then the energy nears its peak. My whole body is a volcano ready to erupt. Please, it's too much.

And then I feel it, and completely lose control. I can't stop it. I don't want to. The pleasure, the heat. Ohhhhh. My back arches as my legs squeeze together over his hand and extend pointing my toes, all my muscles flexing.

I feel the scream come from deep inside me as my eyes open wide. Oh, oh, oh, ohhhhhhhhhhhh.

The pleasure, the intensity. I can't breathe as the warmth runs from my sex through my body. Ohhhhh.

The world around me is intense bliss as my body leaves the earth and I float for a moment or longer, no longer on this plane of existence. In time, I'm able to breathe again.

Eventually, my body goes limp, my legs spread wide in ecstasy and exhaustion, a tired smile on my lips.

I open my eyes to see him gazing deeply into mine.

"That was beautiful" he says.

"Yeees" is all I can reply.

This wonderful man at my side who cares only for my happiness and pleasure.

I want his seed in me, to fill me with his passions.

He makes me feel weak.

Is this the feeling of love about which so many women speak?

1876

He'd finally convinced me to abandon my modest cabin and take residence in a far more spacious home near the center of town which I graciously accepted. By now, nearly all had welcomed him as their leader. Our love grew and we were often at each other's side. He'd only ever wanted my happiness and I was ecstatic in his love and reciprocated his affections.

I didn't see his role in the community as duplicity on my part as I was merely giving the town what it needed: a charismatic leader. And allowing myself to be happy.

But all things are temporary.

It's not often that I attend funeral services and even for this ceremony I stand at the back out of view of the others. Alone.

The crowd is much larger than expected, but such is the case with a great man who is loved by so many, his voice the essence of charisma. Adoring villagers followed him wherever he went and heeded his words. He was loved by so many, that his own power got the better of him, his charms bewitching the young ladies in town who were only too eager to invite him into their homes where he cared for their happiness and pleasure as he once had for mine.

I wonder if he saw the beauty in my green eyes when I stood over him as he took his last gasps after drinking an elixir he'd thought would enhance his charisma even further.

He'd weakened me with his love and his charms.

I'll never be weak again.

17 – Hospitality

I wake to the squeal of steel on steel as the train brakes, making the first stop I've heard. Unsure of how long I've slept, I confirm my duffle bag is still at my feet. Outside, the air is clear, a few stars visible in the darkening sky, a full moon overhead. Is this my destination? I look around but there's no one else in my car, my travel companion no longer next to me, no one to ask. Is anyone else on the train? I can't recall any previous stops nor had I noticed any passenger movements within the car.

Out the window stands an old train station, a wide covered area between two grey and brown brick buildings. Two benches extend parallel to the tracks along the wall to my left; on my right, a staircase leads up to a door; the platform floor is shiny, an almost silvery-smooth. Beyond the station is a large field. Out the window on the other side of the train, a dark forest with black slender trees, low grass and dense brush a buffer between the tracks and the treeline.

It's like looking at an old black and white photograph, imagining the ghostly souls haunting this sombre station.

Is this my new home?

4:30 p.m. according to my watch, which I'd recently updated, and it's already nearly dark, the sun's final glow in the sky to my left.

A wooden sign with the black steel letters '**New Brook West**' hanging from the awning sways gently, welcoming me to town.

The railcar door slides open in one smooth motion, my eyes casting a final look to both ends of the empty car before grabbing my carry-on and stepping onto the wide stone platform, a metal corner guard against its edge. Am I to assume this is my stop? My trunk had been loaded into another part of the train, though I'm unsure which part as no ticket was given to me, which for some reason I didn't question. There's no sign of anyone else on the platform. A lonely arrival at a dark train station.

The sign above me creaks as if welcoming me.

I recall nothing of my journey by train, disappointed that I'd missed looking out on the landscape of a new country. Neither had I noticed the other folks in my car get off the train. Had there been other folks in my car, aside from the gentleman next to me? I can't recall.

I'd heard noises along the way but none made me open my eyes.

Where exactly am I?

The sky's bright colours darken as I ponder what to do. Am I expected to walk into town? In which direction? Setting my bag down at the foot of the stairs, I look out at the fringe of trees surrounding the large clearing. Many are still in leaf, some turning brown. I see no colour in the forest. And no people at the station. And no trail leading away from the station. Across the tracks, the dark forest doesn't look at all inviting, the thin trunks like skeletons at dusk waiting to come to life once darkness has fully descended.

It makes for a peaceful yet eerie scene, though I shiver as I look around myself. How could no one be here?

I sit on the wooden steps leading up to the second-floor door, feeling lost and lonely.

A licorice scent wafts toward me though I can't imagine its source.

The sign bearing my destination's name is now at rest, the black metal hooks holding it tightly.

I wish for any noise to break the crushing silence. A whistling breeze, a bird's call, a wolf's howl. But nothing comes.

I look above me.

The stone buildings on the rock platform are connected by a roof constructed of thick wood beams. Across the platform is a three-storey structure, two doors on each of its three levels, metal stairs up the middle with a small landing on both the second and third floors. The building next to me has three visible doors: one at the top of a long flight of stairs; one at my level near the tracks, providing entry into a room with a window facing the tracks; one further back past the stairs. The station appears solid, if somewhat sombre.

A light cool mist chills my bones, like being wrapped in a damp blanket, though the skies overhead are clear. A picturesque and calm beginning, though I wonder when someone will arrive to meet me.

I notice a young girl in a dirty dress at the edge of the platform by the benches.

"Hi. I'm Colden. What's your name?" I stand, walking toward her.

She slowly glides away, disappearing off the platform, perhaps a shy child losing her nerve.

"Anybody here?" I say, trying not to yell.

I receive no response.

"Mrrrow" a cat quietly announces its presence.

"Hello" I say crouching to its level.

The green-eyed white cat gives me a brief look, rubs against my leg, disappearing down the stairs and around the building.

I wonder if I'll have company at the station.

Crates of various sizes were unloaded and now sit on the platform near the track, my trunk not visible among them. The doors had all slid closed as the train slowly continued on its journey before I reacted to my missing possessions.

Movement in a dark corner of the platform beneath the staircase catches my eye. The young girl come back to talk to me? I walk closer but no one's there.

I turn back to face the tracks. I wonder how often trains come through and what exactly will be asked of me. The moonlight to my left and fading daylight to my right provide enough illumination for me to look in both directions along the rail line.

Am I the victim of some bizarre scam?

"Hello"

The deep voice behind me makes me jump because I hadn't heard footsteps or sound of any kind approaching.

I turn face-to-face with a stocky man, perhaps forty years old, in dark brown pants, a long-sleeved black pullover, with solid facial features, his form nearly rectangular. He's clean-shaven, wears no glasses, standing stock still, his face expressionless. This guy's my height and a lot bigger.

"Hi" I respond extending my hand.

He takes it with a firm grip without taking his eyes off my face. Or is he looking past me over my shoulder?

Releasing my grip, he turns to walk up the long flight of stairs I'd been sitting on. I race after him to keep up, grabbing my duffel bag as I do.

He produces two sets of keys, handing one of them to me and using one from the set he keeps to unlock the sturdy wooden door.

We enter a large open room with a small central sitting area containing a three-seater couch and a single armchair, a low table in the middle of these. Across the room, the kitchen is simple with an island, cupboards lining the far wall, three wooden stools completing the furniture. Entering further I notice a niche to my right with a large bed, to my left a bathroom, recessed into the wall. On both the right and left walls, long windows offer views outside. The room is a good size for one person and a beautiful suite.

The man turns to me.

"Please set down your bag and follow me"

He exits ahead of me, descending the stairs methodically like Frankenstein's monster, while I fumble to find the correct key to lock my room.

He stops in front of the door of the windowed room near the tracks, unlocks the door, and steps inside.

"The control room is where you'll receive the schedule", he points to a large book on a counter to the right of where we'd come in, "It will be sent by the loading station and give you the train's departure time and its expected time of arrival, as well as the weight and number of pieces to be unloaded here, in event of a delivery"

"That seems pretty straight forward" I reply confidently.

He appears to not have heard me.

"The schedule is communicated weekly, daily, and with each departure in case there are any differences in the timetable, delivery size, or cancellations"

"How will I get this information?"

"The dispatcher at the station of origin will tell you the train number, expected date of departure, expected time of departure, expected time of arrival, and expected quantity of cargo. This will happen at 9:00 a.m. each morning to indicate whether or not a train will be stopping. We have a set amount of space for the cargo we load and you will need to confirm this to us so that we know the available capacity as well as any schedule changes"

He points to a teletype unit on the counter to the right of the entrance, a kind of dot matrix printer as antiquated as a manual typewriter. Ink spools are in a small box on a shelf beneath it, an assortment of pens and pencils in a cup next to the unit.

Seriously? That's the system?

"I trust you can operate this device"

"Yes…"

"Schedule management is the Station Master's primary responsibility. The other stations have agreed to abide by our system", he tilts his head slightly downward without taking his eyes off me.

"Seems like something I can handle", I say with a smile and a nod, still stunned by the ancient gear.

"It is imperative that we know the schedule, the quantity of cargo arriving, and space available for loading. It takes time to get people and any necessary equipment in place and the train doesn't wait while we shuffle about"

"Of course" I reply with neither a smile nor a nod.

He gestures to a book.

"You fill in the details here" he hands it to me.

"Previous ledgers are in the back of the room to provide examples" he gestures to a space behind us, "We keep all historical documentation of past cargo with quantities loaded and unloaded along with the associated dates"

This system is for real.

"Do not underestimate the importance of this task. You will post information regarding deliveries on the board in front of the town hall and details will be communicated to you in this manner as well"

"You can count on me" I smile without receiving any return expression on his part.

"The people do not yet know that you are appointed but this will identify you. You will wear this while acting in your official capacity both at the station and in the village"

He hands me a thin black leather jacket with a speeding train stitched into the left side at chest height. On the right shoulder, my first name above the words 'Station Master', the former in a slightly larger text size than the latter, the left shoulder sewn with three small white dots in the shape of a triangle.

"My name is Colden"

"Yes. I'm Michael"

"Do you prefer Michael or Mike?"

"Michael"

His expression is neither threatening nor friendly but serious nonetheless.

I marvel at the simplicity of the job. Am I missing something? What was the catch?

"Your role is instrumental in our culture and economy. I expect you will take your duties most seriously"

"Absolutely"

"And there is one other matter"

Here it comes. Do I have to clean all the toilets in town or birth the cattle?

"The hotel"

Oh. That's not so bad.

I decide to go with the nagging question.

"Was it you who offered me this position Michael?" His name doesn't begin with a 'C' but I have to start somewhere.

We exit the control room, emerging on the platform.

Michael looks back at me with the same monotone look he's worn since his arrival.

"The guest rooms are over here" he says walking across the platform.

The wrought iron steps and wood landings are sturdy beneath us as we climb. The exterior brick isn't particularly inviting, its light grey colour subduing the effect of the black staircase without taking away from the eeriness of the scene.

The doors are keyed, numbered above the respective door from right to left, top to bottom, with 1 in the bottom right and 6 on the upper left on the top level. Michael stops in front of number 5, produces a keyring, and opens the door.

The room is austere yet surprisingly welcoming. The entrance faces a wall;

to the left are a bedroom and bathroom, to the right a living room with a small kitchen behind it.

"The washroom is at the rear of the bedroom" Michael says.

We enter the bedroom. A queen-sized bed on the left wall without nightstands, a low but wide mirrored dresser on the right wall, a corner desk on the same wall as the door we came through, a wooden chest at the foot of the bed, the clock above us would be visible from the bed.

"Rooms are available for occasional travelers as well as approved visitors. There is a guest in Room 6 at the moment, Mr. Schallmann" he continues.

"What's the charge per room?" I ask.

"Not everyone is welcome" he ignores my question.

"How will I know who those people are?"

"You will know."

OK. I'll try again.

"So, Michael, do you know who sent me the job offer? It's not like I applied for the job. Not that it doesn't appeal to me because it seems great but I'm just a bit curious"

He walks out the bedroom door onto the landing.

"My letter was signed with a 'C'" I add when he's slow to reply.

He sends me that same look that I'm used to by now.

A brief silence falls between us as we descend to the platform.

"There is no key for Room 1 and you will have no reason to enter it" he says "I trust that instruction is clear"

"Of course" I reply, wondering at the special treatment Room 1 requires but know better than to ask any questions considering my inquiries so far.

"You will be my supper guest this evening" he says "Your possessions will be placed in your room during this time"

Still no smile though his face does relax slightly.

I don't have a lot of options so readily accept. It also seems a good opportunity to get a sense of the people and the place. And to not be rude to my stern guide.

"It'd be my pleasure" I extend my hand which Michael accepts with a firm grip. "Where do you live?" I ask him.

"My son will come just before 6:00 and show you the way. His name is

Emerson"

Michael walks away quietly and I'm left to my thoughts.

Opportunities, man. Choices.

With some time until supper, I walk up the wooden staircase to my room's square-framed front door, a strong paneled piece set into the wall; to a passerby it would have seemed like an alcove rather than a doorway. Entering gives the impression of passing through a tunnel

 into the main living area.

A surprisingly soft square black rug covers the floor in the central sofa area, ending just before the island's stools. Finely crafted wood cabinets above smooth stone countertops, the floor a shiny hardwood as though cut from a single piece. A gas-powered stove fed by a canister underneath it next to a small cabinet that turns out to be a cooler of sorts against the far wall. A note on the counter explains that the kitchen cooler, hot water, and room temperature are controlled by a gas-powered system in the main level utility room. I'd be responsible for picking up fuel in town as well as the machine's maintenance. The bed fills nearly the entire sleeping area. The shower area and toilet are to the right of the bathroom's entry, the sink to the left, a long counter between them. It isn't stylish but simple, made entirely of sturdy wood with polished stone counters. The locals are obviously skilled craftsmen.

A long window extends the entirety of the wall between the bathroom and the corner desk, looking out onto the platform and the tracks. The glass on the other side offers a view of a large clear field between the station and a forest; the scant light reveals few details in either direction.

Looking up, I notice a transparent area in the center of the roof, maybe large enough to climb through, though I hope I'll never be asked to do this. Lanterns and oil lamps are on walls and surfaces around the room, open candles both lit and unlit are scattered throughout.

My duffle bag at the foot of the bed waits to be re-united with my trunk's less vital contents, sooner than later I hope, though Michael's vague statement as to its location and estimated time of delivery make me grateful I've come prepared.

I unpack clothes, dividing them between the dressers against the wall near the sleeping area; my light jacket I hang in a narrow closet to the left of the entry.

My toiletries are easily spread out on the long bathroom counter, some DVDs and CDs I place on the central table, their hardware still in the trunk, a couple of books and my pencils and drawing pad I place on the island.

Travel is always tiring. I sit at the foot of the bed and let my head fall back until it hits the surprisingly hard yet comfortable mattress. Closing my eyes, I let my thoughts drift, perhaps even sleep for a bit.

"Station Master"

It's a far-away whisper, softened by the windows and walls, one I barely notice. I look at my watch: 5:30, a full half hour early. Yikes. I go to the window, wave down to my guide, surprised to see what looks like a young girl in a dirty dress in the fog. I can't make out her face due to a combination of haze, dampness on the window, and the evening's darkness.

Is this the girl I'd seen earlier on the bench?

I guess Michael changed his mind about the child he'd send to be my guide. I quickly put on a white t-shirt with a plaid shirt over top and green cargo pants with my boots, my jacket on top of it all, hoping for a casual evening. Locking the door behind me I run down the stairs to the clearing.

No one there.

Give me a chance, it didn't take me that long.

The calm cool air has become damper and night has fully taken over. A thick fog hangs low to the ground, filling the area between the station and the forest, hiding whoever is out there.

"Hello" I yell.

Where did she go?

"Hello?" I try again.

Again, no answer, though I hear what sounds like a whisper whose words I can't make out, a girl's voice.

There's nothing behind me or anywhere on the platform. I walk up and down alongside the benches but see no one there nor out on the tracks.

Back in the clearing, there's still no sign of anyone in any direction, only the dark haze.

The slightest smell lingers in the air around me as if someone had just been eating licorice, my eyes scanning for its source or a glimpse of the girl.

The murkiness makes for a sombre atmosphere, the chill vapour covering the station and everything around it.

I walk back upstairs returning immediately to the window.

She's out there now, this time a less clear figure in the dark mist, a few steps further back than before.

How did I miss her?

I run down again but I'm alone when I reach where she'd been standing.

Walking around the station area, I wonder if fatigue and my new environment are causing my mind to play tricks on me. She's nowhere to be seen. Not on or around the platform or in the clearing or even on the edge of the forest that I can make out from here. For a second, I think I spot her in a dark corner of the platform but it must be my imagination because it turns out to be empty when I take a closer look.

Visions of Suzie? No way. I've had these in the past but none in years.

Maybe a local kid checking out the new stranger.

A wide wooden chair facing the clearing offers a direct view into the field and I decide to wait for Emerson, or whoever comes, outside the station despite my trepidation in the darkness. Lighting two exterior lanterns, I take my seat, deciding the covered candles will be safe to leave lit until I return.

Facing the clearing gives me a chance to look at the dense forest around me comprised mostly of deciduous trees of all ages and sizes, all types of brush and grass. The fog sits low to the ground as if held in place, the air calm around me, the field a murky soup.

The canopy reaches at least three-storeys with a few trees extending beyond that, many still green and lush. If there's any wind, I can't feel it, surrounded in my arboreal armour.

It's pleasant in the still cool air, if a little damp, the smell of the forest all around me. I expect it will take a while to get used to my new home, the eerie quiet, the faint silhouettes, the constant shadows.

I wonder if the station receives many visits from the townsfolk. And how many passengers travel by train. I have a lot to learn.

I make my way to the edge of the platform looking out onto the tracks.

Approaching the drop, I nearly lose my footing, feeling a gentle draft behind me.

Lori and Suzie still visit my dreams, standing over me, beside me, or on the ground in front of me. I'd been told that sharing my thoughts would lighten my heart but I'd never got around to it.

My eyes now catch movement ahead, a young boy emerging from the black forest, sauntering toward me, breaking my moment of introspection. He wears a long-sleeved dark green shirt and black pants, with short cropped blonde hair and inquisitive eyes.

"Hi" I say.

He nods without making a sound, his eyes turning sad as if I've just given him bad news.

"I'm Emerson" he says politely looking up at me. He looks to be about 12 years old.

"You're Michael's son?" I ask.

He nods.

"Did you see anyone else on your way here?"

He shakes his head silently.

"You didn't see a girl?"

He shakes his head again so I decide to abandon this line of questioning. His denials seem genuine, though he does avert his eyes when I ask about the child.

"Children don't come to the station" he says quietly.

"Why not?" I wonder out loud.

"Are you ready?" Emerson ignores my question.

"Lead the way" I smile.

The fog vanishes once we enter the forest, the trees tall and thin, black and brown and white, mostly deciduous, some still in leaf. Faint moonlight pierces the cloudy veil overhead outlining the trees, their slender branches pointing out in all directions, their trunks offering hiding places for silent observers. It's easy to imagine eyes on me, watching my anxious walk through the darkness.

The thought gives me a chill.

A short way in, we arrive at a fork in the road; Emerson points to his left.

"This way" he says moving along the new path.

"Where does…?" I ask trying to keep up.

"To the school" he says turning only slightly to his right as he speaks.

"Is there only one school?"

"Yes"

"Just one class?"

"Just one teacher" he replies without turning around.

"How long have you lived here, Emerson?" I ask, creating conversation to break the silence between us.

"My whole life"

"And how long is that?"

"Twelve years"

"Do you have any brothers and sisters?" I inquire.

"Two brothers and two sisters"

"So, there are five of you all together?" I ask the rhetorical question out loud.

Emerson nods.

"What's it like having so many?" I continue.

"We're a family"

"Do you have a big house?"

"Yes"

"Are you the oldest?"

"David's older than me and so is Tessa "

It would sure be easy to get lost in this forest so I'd best stay close to my guide. The moonlight provides small comfort beneath the dense foliage and cloud cover, Emerson navigating without a lantern. I haven't seen any other paths off our main trail, though they would have been easily missed, and I hope the way home will be as obvious on my own. I keep my eyes focused on Emerson, with no desire to know if I'm being watched.

Being lost and alone in this dark unfamiliar forest would be unnerving.

We walk on in silence for a moment.

"Do you have any brothers or sisters?" his question surprises me.

"No, it's just me"

"So that's why you're lonely" he says without looking back.

We emerge from the forest into a large open area of short wild grass. The dirt path we're on stops at the entry to the community between two thin stone columns, lanterns suspended from these tall posts inviting us in. The ground beyond this point is a mixture of flat rocks and hard packed earth. To the right, a low building, a fence extending out from both sides, three dimly lit oil lamps on the exterior wall facing us; although no cross or steeple identifies it as a church, I guess it to be a place of spiritual significance. At the center of a large plaza area is a beautiful fountain with water trickling from several holes around a tall central stone obelisk. Across the courtyard from us and past the fountain, a three-level structure speaks of authority, perhaps the town hall. A wide flight of stone stairs leads up to double doors, a faint lit lamp hanging on both sides of its entrance. The shutters around the upper windows catch the moonlight making them shimmer in silver.

As we near, I spot a large square panel at ground level to the left of the stairs.

"Is that where I put the train schedule information?" I ask Emerson.

"Yes" he replies without looking at it.

Emerson heads left out of the square along a wide road; we arrive at his home after about two minutes of walking in silence. Lit lampposts flank the path leading to a wide single-storey house. Its solid exterior, makes it an imposing structure.

A long window along the side to the left of the door, three small windows to the right. The door is substantial, a series of vertical planks fastened with horizontal metal strips. Emerson grasps the horizontal handle opening into a large area lit by candles on the walls around the room. In the middle of the wall across from me, a hallway leads to destinations unknown, the area in front of me a series of tables, and simple sofas.

The eating area to my right consists of a long thick light brown wooden table extending out from and connected to the wall with two chairs at the one end and benches on both sides, the kitchen beyond it an open-concept design.

"Station Master", a stone-faced Michael comes toward me.

"Thank you so much for the invitation" I say "And please call me Colden"

"The remainder of your possessions will arrive soon", he nods, "Can I offer you some wine?"

"Yes, please"

Michael grabs a metal jug from the table, offering me a metal goblet, much like a tall thin beer glass. The dark red wine is actually quite good reminding me of cherries. I take another sip as I look around the house without trying to seem too nosy.

"You have a beautiful house, Michael"

"This is my wife, Nesta"

"Hello" she comes to her husband's side bowing her head slightly, her cheery expression increasing my comfort level.

"You've met Emerson" Michael begins "David is our oldest". He motions to a boy in the far corner of the room at a writing desk who waves back without any facial expression. "Tessa is our oldest girl" a pretty blonde sitting in an armchair near David waves with a hint of a smile. "You know Emerson" he points to the boy now helping his mother set the table. "And the twins"

He quickly looks around the room.

"We eat our evening meal as a family" he continues. Nesta hustles about wiping off the benches.

"I hope I'm not intruding" I say.

"We want to welcome you on your first night with our humble hospitality" Michael answers, having yet to smile.

A young blonde boy and girl enter the room together.

"Jasmin and Jason" Michael nods at them.

Michael can't be older than 40, Nesta younger than him, a very pretty thin blonde wearing a light green dress with sleeves to her elbows. The girls are gifted with their mother's beauty, the boys cursed with their father's stoicism. Michael has a confident yet distant manner which differs only slightly from the impression I got at our initial meeting, obviously a man of strong character.

"Where do people work in the village?" I ask.

"Harvesting spices and herbs which we ship by train" Michael replies "Thus the importance of the Station Master and his role in community life"

"Are they community fields?"

"Most residents work the fields. We rely on the train for trade with outsiders"

Michael's occasional nods keep him from appearing robotic.

"How many people live in New Brook West?"

"Enough to work and provide for us"

The children remain quiet, David at his desk, Tessa in her chair reading, Emerson in the kitchen, and the twins again out of sight.

"How long have you lived here Michael?"

"All my life" he replies proudly "And my parents before me and theirs before them. Nesta's as well. We don't have a lot of outside contact. We prefer to live in traditional ways"

Communal living isn't a new concept to me and this seems a prime example. I wonder how long the area has been inhabited.

"Emerson said that there's a school"

"Yes" Nesta approaches me from on my left side.

"Is the teacher a local or were they hired like me?"

They both go stone-faced before Nesta breaks the silence.

"Dinner is ready"

Michael and Nesta sit at the head of the table, the children and I along the benches.

I anticipate a few words of grace before eating commences. All heads bow, hands are joined forming a complete circle as they hum in unison for about ten seconds, after which Tessa and David rise to bring in the food.

David carries a large bowl of boiled potatoes, Tessa a roast of some kind. Emerson goes back for fresh corn and sliced tomatoes.

"Who was that?" I ask, gesturing with my head.

"Who?" Michael looks at me.

"The girl at the window"

"You must be mistaken" Michael replies without taking even a glance in the direction I indicate.

Everyone falls still and you could have heard a pin drop.

Jasmin breaks the quiet. "I hope you stay. You seem nice"

No one speaks during the meal, though I can't decide if this surprises me or not. I compliment Nesta on the supper but she simply nods her head.

Glancing around the table everyone's eyes are focused on their plates. We eat in silence for the entire meal.

Bidding my hosts goodnight, I begin my way back to the train station alone and without a lantern. The route out the way I'd come in with Emerson leads through the quiet dark plaza, the fountain standing sentry. Beyond the three-storey square building, a number of paths lead into the heart of the community and its additional shorter structures. Across the open court, several dimly lit lanterns now hang on a tall wrought iron fence by what I presumed to be a church casting faint light into what appears to be a cemetery, the lamps on the building now extinguished.

Old gravestones emerge from the ground near the enclosure, darkness swallowing those further in, and wonder who would have lit the lamps. Two black spindly trees inside the fence keep watch over the graves, their bony branches reaching out from their narrow trunks. The stone obelisk's trickling water is the only sound in the plaza.

The sky has cleared completely, the moon and stars now shining brightly on the empty square, the lines on the buildings and shadow from the cemetery fence sharp.

My eyes search in the dark for the path which Emerson and I had taken, the overhead glow revealing little beyond the plaza. The fountain hypnotizes me with its melancholy flow, as my gaze locks onto an alley leading away from me down a dark street into town. I break my trance and turn to stare out into the silent glade between the town and the forest. The dim lanterns at the entrance to the village appear in the darkness indicating the exit from New Brook West and my return route to the station.

A glance over my shoulder and I bid goodnight to New Brook West as I enter onto the treed trail. The soft crunch of dirt and leaves under my feet is the only sound in the forest, nature's scent occasionally interrupted by the aroma of licorice.

The path I'm walking seems the same one we'd taken to the village and I hope I don't get lost on my first night. A short distance in, I look back but can no longer see any sign of the village as if the trail has closed behind me. The white moon through the treetops creates a beautiful yet sinister setting.

I'm acutely aware of the trees in the darkness, their spindly trunks and slender branches like skeletal arms. The path is only visible a short distance in front of me so I walk warily, cautious of any pitfalls. A gentle rustling in the bushes to my left sounds like the scurrying of a nocturnal creature. Or a person watching me from a safe distance. It comes and goes causing me some unease. The foliage above me has closed creating the impression of walking through a tunnel, the silence only occasionally broken by the trickling of leaves at my side. Who or what is following me?

Without a lantern or flashlight, I'm at the mercy of the night and anything else that watches.

Is it the sound of feet?

A whisper behind me makes me turn.

Is someone there?

A young girl appears in the path a short distance back; I can't make out her face in the darkness, only her dirty purple dress. Surely one of Michael's daughters wouldn't have come after me. She stands still in the middle of the trail, presumably facing me, though I can't make out her face.

I wait in silence. For several seconds she makes no sound or movement, then she begins to sway side to side. I can see black hair but not her facial features, even in the moonlight, her dress grey with dirt. She slowly raises her right arm and points at me, then takes a few short steps to the right and disappears into the forest.

I recall Emerson's comment that children never come to the station and dismiss the notion of a young girl following me through the forest at this time. After a moment of staring, I come to my senses, heading off again to my new home. Silence falls, my senses relaxing to take in the local smells and sights, as well as the fresh, if slightly damp, air.

I'm torn between walking more slowly so as not be heard and picking up speed to get back to the train station more quickly. I decide on the former lacking sufficient light to make a run for it without risking injury. Darkness and the scent of black licorice follow me to the station.

I catch a faint glow to my right like two small eyes, making me wonder if someone or something is in fact watching me. Maybe a curious animal. Or a curious child. I pick up my speed, arriving at the fork in the road after what seems like an eternity, briefly looking to my left along the path to the school. The canopy momentarily opens allowing light to break through, which is most welcome. The large clearing signals my arrival at the station, a good night's rest near at hand, damp green and brown grass between me and my new home.

I'm eager to leave the dark path.

Does someone live in the forest between here and the community?

I didn't think I was one to be easily scared but the sense of joy I feel upon reaching the station is second to none. A final look behind me before climbing the stairs onto the platform gives me another glimpse of a girlish figure standing in the dark clearing. I curse my curiosity, running to my room and locking the door tightly behind me.

18 – He Came

He came. He accepted the offer. He didn't suspect; how could he?

Should I watch him? Should I follow him? No. He'll become suspicious. I'll see him, but not so often.

19 – Dalton

She watches in silence, fingers pressed to the glass at the train station window high above the ground, her small hands leaving tiny imprints as she does. A gentle breeze rustles through the trees causing her dress to quiver, her black hair blown across her face. Her hollow eyes take in every detail of the room, of his body, of his features, of his movements. Her nails lightly scratch the pane as they move over its surface. The suite inside is warm and dry, outside is cold and damp. She slides the window open ever so slightly, her tiny silhouette entering the room without a sound. All is silent except for his breathing, his form peaceful in its stillness, dreams playing out in his mind. She opens her mouth to scream but wordless whispers are the only sound she makes.

The sound of a girl's whisper wakes me to a cold room. I hear light scratching or scraping along the wood floor like something moving quickly.

Is that breathing? Is someone at the side of the bed?

My heart stops as I wait motionless and silent for several long seconds but the brief sound has stopped and I see no movement.

The window near the bed is partially open.

My eyes adapt using what little moonlight shines through, my mind slow to take in the unfamiliar room. I look out from the bed's alcove, shadows shifting in the room, moving in the faint light. A lamp on the wall flickers and dies out, bereft of fuel.

Guess I'd forgotten to extinguish it. There's no one else in the apartment that I can see. I hold my breath listening for any sound, checking for any movements, as a chill runs down my spine but nothing comes. I slowly reach out to touch the other side of the bed which is undisturbed and cold.

I'm alone yet feel as though someone else has been here, watching.

I get up and shut the window, then make the short walk past the front door to the bathroom, stopping on the return trip for a glass of water from my cup on the coffee table. My courage emerges, allowing me to look out the large window into the clearing and toward the distant forest. Nothing. The dark army of skeletal figures sleeps, their branches reaching out, none moving. The subtle smell of licorice wafts past me.

A quick soft scratching near the entrance.

Is someone at the door at this time?

I can't be sure of the exact time and maybe late-night visits are common. But surely my evening visitor hadn't been in the room with me.

Maybe the cat's creeping about.

I walk slowly and quietly, unhook the latch, and open the door to an empty landing, no one down the stairs or on the platform. I lack the energy to investigate any further and don't want to agitate myself over something as harmless as strange nighttime noises so lock the door behind me and make my way back to bed.

A girl's voice whispers just outside the window. I run to look down into the clearing again, but no one's there. The sleepy trees, the quiet grass, the silent station. The wind's playing tricks on my senses, or perhaps just a normal night at the station with nature's creaks and groans.

The window's open; I thought I'd closed it.

I shut it and pull the covers up tightly around me.

Throughout the night, noises came and went, interrupting my restful sleep. Whispered words just outside my window, scraping against the glass, gentle rustlings in the breeze, subtle swishes near the bed as of someone quietly walking past, the cold from the open window. This will certainly take some getting used to.

The sun rises around 8:00 a.m. and I get up shortly after that, having lain in bed for a half hour. The sheets look like I've been in a wrestling match, only one of the pillows still on the bed. My hair is a tangled mess, my bleary eyes muddled from a distressed night, my body weary from the disturbances which kept me from a sound sleep.

I glance around the room noticing that all the windows are shut.

Dragging my feet to the kitchen, I locate coffee grounds and a kettle, filling the latter, setting it to boil on the gas stove. The gas-powered fridge is adequately if sparsely packed, with a metal container of white liquid, possibly milk, a bowl of butter, a chunk of cheese, a jug of red liquid, bowls of fresh fruit and vegetables. The cupboards contain two loaves of bread, jars of dried fruit, a large bag of flour, spices, jars with unknown contents, and pot, pans, and dishes, all of soft metal. The island drawers hold metal cutlery, paper and pencils, and hand tools. One is locked with no key in sight which piques my interest, though not enough to try one from my own set.

I am interested in the 'C' that had signed my letter. Why has this person not come to see me?

It's not Michael, if that's his true first name, unless people go by last name. I've yet to meet anyone in town so hopefully this person will identify themselves to me sooner rather than later so I know what's going on. New Brook West has a gloomy air, a darkness brought on by more than the fog, but the station seems quiet so that'll be enough for now. In time, I hope to find peace here.

And so begins the second day of my adventure.

Grabbing the coffee canister, adding two spoonsful of grounds to a ceramic cup, and water which is by now sufficiently hot, I sit at the island facing the open area of the suite. Had I given Michael the return ticket? How will I get my lump sum payment if I decide being station master isn't for me? How will I leave? I'll figure all that out later. I don't want to spend my first day thinking about the negative.

A sip of the coffee gives me a jolt as I make a mental note to add fewer grounds the next time.

This really is an amazing apartment and I expect the surrounding area will be just as beautiful to explore.

Unfortunately, today fog partially obscures a path across the clearing, the sun not yet high enough in the sky to dispel it. There's no way to tell if any other trails lead out from this glade. The room's a comfortable temperature having recovered from the open window. The windows can all be opened and latched from the inside, the door likewise equipped with an interior latch. They seem remarkably clean, though on closer inspection, I notice smudges on the outside of the window near the bed like small handprints. Has someone climbed up here? Why? How did they manage? Without a ladder it'd be nearly impossible to get to this height, the ledge barely wide enough to hold a small person and reaching it would require either scaling the wall or coming down from the roof. Whoever cleaned it must have been quite acrobatic.

I think on my nighttime walk back from Michael's through the forest.

Who was that girl on the path? Do I want to mention to anyone that I saw her in the forest? Best to not point out my interactions yet.

I hope to explore the village in privacy, if not total secrecy, so as not to be caught snooping. Last night's noises and voices left me uneasy and I wonder if knowing more about the community in general will calm my nerves.

Is there a theatre, a bar, a library, stores, or any of the conveniences of the city? Little hope, given the austerity of Michael's home which was entirely lacking in electronic devices or even electric light, his residence illuminated by lanterns and oil lamps just like mine.

My cell phone battery is nearly dead, cutting me off from the outside world, including Kayla, with whom I'd hoped to stay in touch for at least a while. Could I mail letters out? Receive them?

I'm glad for having brought many as yet unread books as well as my drawing supplies. The lack of distractions from modern conveniences and communication with my past might be for the best anyway, at least short-term, to launch my new life.

The rest of my things were delivered while I'd been at Michael's and I was very pleased to be reunited with them. The heavy trunk had been placed just inside the suite. In terms of gadgets other than my cell phone, I'd only brought a small DVD player and a few CDs, prepared to rely on my phone for music and now see that I'll be going without, at least until I can conjure a way to power things up. Perhaps I'll meet someone who can help or provide some advice to get me connected.

My personal effects include a small number of nostalgic mementos which would have been difficult to leave behind, though maybe starting over should have precluded keeping even these. Among them, some photos that I leaf through as they're extracted from their envelope; me with my one-time best friend Rick Noble; my cousin and buddy Daniel; Pete the cook at Café Carlos; even a couple of Kayla who made me feel stronger, kinder, even normal when we were together. Many memories are best forgotten and these reminders were deliberately left out, though I still hung onto a few of Lori and Suzie, whether or not this was healthy.

Drinking my harsh coffee, I think back to the previous evening. Michael's family avoided two subjects: the individual who hired me and the girl at the window who obviously wasn't one of Michael's. I hadn't pursued either topic so as not to offend my hosts. Perhaps there's more to this to be learned in a more discreet manner; if I'm going to stay here, even for a while, I'd like to know what to expect. Maybe the school teacher will have information to share or know of someone in the village who likes to talk. Neither Michael nor his family had given me any hints as to the schoolteacher's gender or age, nor where he or she lives and how long that person has been in New Brook West.

After four slices of bread with butter and a tasty jam and a big swig of what turns out to be fruit juice, I shower, get dressed, and venture outside. It's already 9:00 and time to check the schedule which indicates a train arriving at 3:30 today. So, do I just post this info on the board in town? Contact anyone directly? Odd that I wasn't told.

I fill in a form in the control room with the information Michael requested be shown.

I start out through the foggy clearing clad in my snappy new station master jacket.

The gloomy sky suggests it'll be a grim day, no wind and little sun to clear the murkiness. No one on the platform and the hotel doors are all closed so off I go.

I wonder if I'll see the guy staying here.

Reaching the edge of the tree line I glance back over my shoulder before stepping onto the path, the station an eerie figure in the haze. It looks lost in both time and place, as if it might disappear before I return.

The grass is wet as if from rain but I hadn't heard any in the night, the dry dirt ground in the forest's green and brown flora is clearly shielded from any precipitation under the thick canopy. The quiet walk takes about ten minutes at a slow pace, the lanterns on either side of the path welcoming me into the community. Several townsfolk mill about, talk amongst themselves or carry small parcels, none looking my way; I play it cool, deciding not to stare at anyone or anything. Grabbing one of the many large tacks, I post the scheduled arrival with the piece-count and total weight of the load on the wood board. Other closed envelopes and blank pieces of paper are affixed to it, but I don't want to seem intrusive so turn back quickly and catch several locals looking my way.

With some time before the train, I decide to head over to the school and get a lay of the land in that direction.

Arriving at the fork, I choose the path which Emerson had indicated leads to the school. Despite the time of day, the sparse light through the thick tree cover does little to illuminate my route making the mood melancholy.

Only occasionally do I spot white or purple flowers, the forest otherwise a drab green and brown. The environment does give me a strange sense of calm, though I hope I'll soon see the sun.

Occasional stirrings to my right remind me of the previous evening, like a child slowly dragging its feet through a thin layer of leaves. The rustling comes and goes, and is the only sound other than my feet on the path.

After a five-minute walk, the path curves and I exit the foliage. Ahead of me in a clearing, there's a small building with a chimney, a school straight out of the history books, the thickness of the air partially obscuring my view. I approach the dark brown wood and stone structure through the grassy moisture, its side windows high above the ground, a small wooden box connected to the back, possibly an outhouse bathroom. Stone benches, tables, and other objects of timber and rock are scattered around the field, a swing-set farther off. There's no one outside and no noise from inside the building itself, the clearing an auditorium of silence. I wonder if the teacher is present and whether or not class is in session which would account for the hush.

A four-step wood riser leads up to the front door, the only noticeable entrance. I don't want to disturb class on my first real day here, nor do I want to creep around the playground peeking in the long windows.

After ten minutes of wandering the clearing, I head back to the station to review the schedules, promising myself to come back here when my presence will be less intrusive.

I wonder at the location of the teacher's house, perhaps a kindred spirit to help me adapt to local culture.

Back at the train station, I make the control room my first stop. Today's printed notice had come with a cargo manifest listing the number of pieces arriving and the weight of each but not the goods themselves. Some pieces were heavier than I expected, others lighter given their size. I contemplate trying to connect my phone to the teletype's power source but postpone my efforts upon discovering the ancient machine's battery packs.

I have yet to be provided information on how to reach anyone in particular aside from putting up the notice in front of the town hall. I'd expected someone would come see me before the first train was scheduled to arrive at the station, perhaps a naïve assumption on my part. The time is now 1:00 so I decide to walk around the village to see if anyone knows who meets the trains.

The ten-minute walk back to the community is intensely quiet, a light breeze rustling the trees high above me, the silence following me to the village gates. Lanterns flanking the main access are now extinguished and fewer people move about the plaza than when I'd been here earlier. New Brook West strikes me as a place where no one is anonymous, however much they might try to be, and expect that the first person I meet will send me in the right direction.

In daylight, I get a better look at the impressive fountain. It has more equally-spaced spouts than I can count, the central piece reminding me of an arrow with its pointed top. The town hall is similar to Michael's house with cinder block walls and a metal-plated wooden door and roofing; the silvery glow I'd noticed around the windows last night is less evident during the day.

The stone building to my right, which I'd presumed to be a church, has large wood and metal doors that seem a deterrent rather than an invitation to visitors. The structure looks more or less square, a short tower at each corner and in the middle, the exterior entirely lacking in traditional religious symbols. The roof slopes at a low angle tapering off gradually toward the outer walls, the middle peak barely visible at its center. A dark wrought iron fence touches both side walls at the front of the building, protecting the surrounding area, a high gate on both sides of the church. Stone markers of all shapes and ages fill the enclosure, the space lacking any visible buildings or crypts.

Determined to learn more about my environment, I walk around outside the barrier, peeking in at the well-maintained gravestones rising from the ground.

The writing varies among graves as though each family claimed its preferred style, the inscriptions skillfully chiseled into the rock. Recurring last names include 'Clovinston', 'Pertwee', 'Arthurs', and several beginning with 'von' though I'm unable to make out the rest of the text.

Steering clear of the town hall, I walk around the fountain toward the main town area, those milling about paying me little attention.

Grey stone surrounds me as I stare into the heart of the community, a sombre view made more so by the grim sky overhead. All is calm and quiet. Who are the people that have chosen to make this place their home? I decide to wait until I see a friendly face to pop my question.

The narrow street's two-storey buildings connect at their side walls with very little if any space between them, and it's difficult to discern one from the next. No names or numbers serve as address markers nor have I noticed any street signs. Nameless eyes peer out from doors and windows, curious to get a look at the new stranger but they disappear once I spot them. Figures stand in narrow alleys, hidden in the shadows.

Three children run past me, one girl saying "Hi", possibly one of Michael's but I don't catch a look in time to identify her. From what I can tell, the village's colour scheme is expressed in muted earth tones: dull greens, faded browns, and soft greys. Nowhere do I see any bright or sharp colours, the only 'standout' the shiny silver shutters of the town hall.

"Station master"

A young man jumps out from an alleyway to my immediate right startling me. Embarrassed by my childish reaction, I regroup quickly.

"Hey. Hi"

"Heard you were looking for me" the young man says in a distinctly

British accent.

"You must be…"

I honestly have no idea who he is but he seems to know me. I don't want to play too dumb but hate when someone else knows me and I'm completely lost.

"Dalton" he says.

"Colden" I reply.

Is this my contact for railcar loads? How does he know I'd been looking for him? I haven't told a soul of my plan to come to town nor the news of an arrival. And how did he know where to find me? Has he already read the notice I posted in town?

"A train is arriving shortly?" he says without any facial expression.

"Yes" I reply "At 3:30"

"I'll see you then"

"Great" I nod.

He turns to walk down the street away from me without a handshake or farewell.

I watch him until he ducks down another alley and is gone without a sound.

I look around the empty street, quietly collect myself, and make my way across the plaza. I see and hear no one as I exit the village and enter the forest.

Back at the station, a child is sitting on the platform's floor against the hotel-side wall. Impossible to tell if it's a boy or a girl though the posture makes me think the latter. I'm nearly at the steps, and she has yet to look in my direction.

Is this the girl I'd seen before?

I hear a noise behind me. Is Dalton here already?

When I turn, there's no one there or in the direction of the woods.

I shake my head and turn back to the station where the space against the hotel wall is now empty.

Jogging up the stairs, I run to the tracks to look in both directions along the platform but see no one; my apartment, the control room, and the utility room are all shut.

What happened to her?

She crouches low to the ground, unseen in the shadows beneath the stairs, her small fingers sticking out the tiniest bit above the step. He'd glanced her way but has no reason to suspect she would be so close to him. He comes nearer, climbing up to his apartment, but never notices her thin frame, her inquisitive eyes behind her black hair. Her head tilts back as she watches him, her dark shape pulling back into the gloom behind her once he reaches the top stair.

20 – I screamed

I spoke but none would listen. I begged, I cried, and I screamed, but all that came out was a whisper that no one heard.

21 - The Tracks

Calm hangs over the clearing, offering unconditional serenity, and I spend much of my time near the train station enjoying this peace. It feels good to be alone without the obligations of social interaction, though I still find it odd at times. I had ventured out to explore, though cautiously so, and found amazing locations on many of my travels. Pristine beauty hidden in dark unseen places that appeared to have been unvisited in glades within the forest, small water bodies and creeks, and some rocky terrain and open spaces. These solitary adventures in my new home are special to me, a time to reflect on my surroundings and the peaceful, if gloomy, environment.

The area immediately surrounding the station is peaceful to be sure, the building and forest perfectly quiet with the exception of the occasional breeze against the exterior or nighttime rain. The foliage is a combination of deciduous and evergreen, ferns and low grasses near the treeline; I don't know a lot about botany so only the obvious is familiar.

The moon is stunning when it appears in the sky casting its light into the clearing. I can sit at the window and just stare at it. My evenings alone at the muted station, content as we are to sit together in silence the moon and I.

There's a river beyond the main community that I intend to visit when I can, and I'd been told of a library outside the village. Future adventures.

New Brook West is a quiet place to be alone and I feel a genuine sense of inner peace. Perhaps this is home.

I consider myself a fairly smart guy, though this may not be everyone's opinion. Professor Walleston valued my role as an assistant and was a great guy to work with; we became close if not friends. But opportunities at the university were limited or perhaps nonexistent, my credentials and experience precluding me from applying for most of them. He taught me logic, problem-solving, and critical thinking, all while increasing my intellectual confidence. However, I had yet to discover a way to apply any of my intelligence to the position of station master.

My morning starts with two properly prepared cups of coffee and some toast grilled on the stove with the delicious local jam. I look out the window into the clearing as I sip from my mug, the thin trees extending their bony arms in the thick grey fog.

I wonder what life's like in the Concourse and how Kayla's doing.

I think of Lori and Suzie and our beautiful life together as I stare into the mist. What could have been and what will never be.

The train's arrivals had been met with the efficiency of military maneuvers, the men unloading their cargo quickly and carefully, stacking it in the carts they'd brought, and departing quietly for the village as if time truly was of the essence, talking neither amongst themselves nor to me, disappearing into the forest pulling their burden like oxen. Loads placed into the railcars were handled with equal strength, skill, and precision.

Throughout this period, Dalton stood to the side watching, neither assisting nor speaking to them or to me.

I never notice a conductor nor any passengers or personnel in any of the cars as it pulls in, an oddity in my mind.

I suspect the incoming loads to be items not produced in the community and for which trade is necessary though I can't imagine with whom.

Today's load is handled with the same proficiency, the team loading the railcar with mathematical precision to make the best use of space.

They work tirelessly and with incredible strength if the load manifest is accurate with respect to piece weights, never pausing to rest, no individual piece requiring any noticeable exertion on their part. Again, Dalton watches from the side, only the occasional glance into the railcar, and without communicating with the men.

The cargo moved, I return to my suite, staring out the window to catch a glimpse of anything to help me orient myself both geographically and mentally. If my observations on the cloudless days are accurate, then the station is located south of the village. I scan the skies in an attempt to spot the sun but it's impossible to locate it in the clouds where the sparse light seems to have no point of origin.

Is there a New Brook East to the east of New Brook West?

A narrow path parallel and to the left of the train tracks offers the chance to do some exploring along the rail line. There's more than enough room to step aside if I hear a train even at the last minute, and the woods, although thick, would be an easy place to wait if one passed unexpectedly. The line disappears into the darkness of the forest in the direction from which the trains arrive.

I set off just before 3:00 pm to ensure I have time to return to the station before dark. I bring only a walking stick I find in the apartment.

A visual inspection of the tracks speaks to their quality. The iron is in great shape, the rails themselves seamlessly connected with almost no rust. The ties between them appear recently replaced, though not all at the same time, some slightly more worn than others but none rotted.

My knowledge of railway mechanics is limited but if I had a train of my own, I'd be fine running it along this line. The area above the rails is free of foliage and open to the sky.

It's a twenty-minute walk until I can no longer see the station behind me which is as far as I'll go for today. So many of the deciduous trees still have their leaves this late in the season though they appear brown rather than red, orange, and yellow. The forest is black, concealing anything more than a short distance from the treeline.

I stare along the railway as it extends through the tunnel created by the trees.

A patch of bush along the periphery ahead of me rustles briefly. Is someone following me? I stop, waiting to catch any more movement but none comes and all around me is now silent. I glance along the tracks heading away from the station but see nothing. I wait another moment, but, again, see and hear nothing.

Ah, well.

I zip up my jacket against a chill.

I stare into the forest's depths to my right, wondering what might inhabit the darkness. I can only see a short distance beyond the initial row of trees, try as I might to focus and squint. I look both ways along the tracks, crouching down lower as if this will help me but all is shadows.

Ah, well. As I stand, I spot a light on my left like a candle or a lantern in the black. Does someone live out here so close to the tracks? I don't want to intrude near someone's home so turn away.

In the distance ahead, nothing but darkness and trees, the sun behind me now low in the sky.

Time to head back. Taking a last look behind me, I turn toward the station, with no more rustling in the brush and nothing visible around me.

I saunter back to the platform in the quiet calm air, my pace slow, my mind clear. The absence of fog in this tunnel created by the trees is in striking contrast to the forest's obscurity and the clearing's haze.

I can't help but marvel at the station itself, the building's apparent durability, its dark corners, the absolute silence. Its presence looms in the light mist like a mighty warrior.

Approaching the station, I spot a young girl sitting on a bench facing the forest across the tracks. She looks like the same one I've seen previously in her dirty purple dress.

"Hello?" I say in a friendly tone.

I run around to come through the clearing and up the stairs but when I reach the bench on the platform, she's gone.

Odd. Where did she go? And why was she sitting here?

I glance around me and toward the forest across from the tracks but see and hear nothing.

Ah, well.

I turn to climb the stairs to the apartment and notice the control room lit from inside which was not this way when I'd left for my walk. I crouch down to move in front of it and look in through the window facing the tracks to see if someone let themselves in, my eyes peeking in through a bottom corner of the glass but no one's inside. I walk around to the door, which is closed and locked. I run to look into the clearing but see no one so come back and enter the control room.

The lantern near the back wall illuminates that part of the small room but there's no indication as to who might have done the lighting. Shadows flutter in the back of the storage area but no one's in there. I look out the window, but see only trees across the tracks. It's a mystery I'm prepared to overlook for now.

I extinguish the lantern.

Michael posted a note on the board instructing me to reinforce the station's exterior wall beneath my suite. Wood planks of various lengths lay against the base of the building. There's an abundance of hammers, saws, and nails of all sizes in the utility room. Light is definitely required for this type of work so it will be deferred until the next morning. It certainly will be a workout as the necessary thickness of the nails means a fairly large hammer, the timbers in some cases several metres long. I'll figure it out tomorrow.

Autumn's early evening weather best suits an outdoor read, a peaceful pastime in my favourite season and a windless environment. Oil lamps, lanterns, and a comfortable chair I find in the utility room that I set on the platform invite me to enjoy the fresh air, my hunger willing to wait.

Having selected my book, I confirm that anything in the apartment with a flame is extinguished with the exception of those at the entryway, exit the suite, and lock the door behind me from force of habit, unsure if this action is necessary.

The stillness of the station occasionally makes my mind wander but also provides me with the comfort of solitude, a very different environment than I'm used to. My desire to spend time alone is almost clinical. I rarely seek the company of others, preferring my own. I had always considered myself to be an outsider, someone who didn't mix well with people, even in my days in "the Scene". I had never been popular of my own merit and was only ever cool because of where I went and who I knew. Not really an identity, and as good a reason as any to retreat to solitude whenever possible.

At the station, I'm alone.

Armed with a coffee, I place the chair facing into the clearing, a lit lamp on each of the walls in anticipation of the coming night. The lanterns provide sufficient light to read but it's dull and dissipates away from the chair as if being consumed by darkness. The forest across the open field is black, the clearing itself grey, the moon above me shrouded by clouds. For a moment, I stare out into the tranquil evening, wondering what new adventures await me in New Brook West.

I lean back in the chair and am soon consumed by the story in my hands, my mind ignoring the world around me. As has always been the case, reading slowly relaxes me to the point of drowsiness carrying me into unconsciousness, the book soon resting in my lap, my head against the hard top of the chair's back, my body still.

She watches him approach the station along the tracks, his manner curious and intrigued but nervous, a fact he hides from the villagers and denies to admit to himself. He climbs onto the platform and enters the lit control room as she crawls into a dark corner on the opposite wall. When he emerges, his eyes scan the area, but don't notice her slight form. She creeps silently but swiftly on hands and feet, positioning herself under the stairs, her eyes pushed forward nearly touching the step. Soon he succumbs to fatigue in his chair, his mind drifting to places unknown.

She glides toward him with noiseless footsteps, comes alongside him, caresses his cheek.

She moves the book from his lap to the ground and perches herself on the chair's right arm to watch him in his peaceful slumber.

My groggy eyes open after a short nap, the skies darker than when I'd taken my position in the chair, so I'll head upstairs and scrounge food for dinner. I rise from the chair.

And fall hard onto a gravel base, sharp pain shooting through my ankles, my knees striking the rail, my hands scraping on smaller stones between the ties as I hit the ground. Disoriented, I'm now sitting on the train tracks. What happened?

Holy shit!

A train!!!!

I roll to the edge of the platform's base, my body flattening against the station's foundation. The train whizzes by, barely missing me, the wind throwing my hair across my face, its wheels grinding against the metal rails, clicking as they pass. My heart's pounding through my chest and I'm gasping for breath as the wheels flash past me.

The train continues on its way, disappearing around the corner in the distance as I recover my senses and catch my breath. Across the tracks, something near the treeline fades into the forest.

I climb up to the main level. The chair I'd been sitting in is now facing the tracks, my book on the ground next to it.

My eyes scan the forest across the rails but see nothing in the darkness. I turn around to look out into the clearing but there's no one there either. The control room is still dark.

Chunk. Click.

The noise startles me and can only have been made by a door latch. I stare at Room 1, the door only a few strides from me. Does someone live in there? I lack the courage to get any closer.

The haze away from the station has thickened, night now upon me and the dreary train station.

I stumble up to my apartment for a drink, hoping to shake off my recent terror and help me wake up. Or sleep. I extinguish the lamps on the platform. The lantern at the top of the stairs provides enough light for me to reach it safely. Reaching the landing, I notice light under the door as if someone were inside my suite leaving me wondering who'll be there when I walk in. Preparing myself for the worst, I bound into the room ready to attack, but no one is there, the room silent.

Had I imagined the noise?

Everything appears in place with the exception of three previously unlit oil lamps in the living room area now providing illumination.

Who managed to enter so easily and then exit without using the door? The windows are all closed.

Or is it more likely that I just forgot.

I walk around the suite, taking in any potential hiding places, hoping I won't find anyone. I methodically move around the large open room, through the kitchen, around the bed, and in the bathroom. My heart beats loudly and my breathing is short as I inspect the apartment.

But no one's here.

I look up to the high wood rafters and the skylight in the ceiling but, thankfully, see no one there either.

I stand in the center of the apartment and wait, listening. Holding my breath in total silence to catch any sounds inside or out.

Nothing.

I walk to the fridge, fill a glass with water, and stare out at the forest across the clearing. I see no one.

How did the chair get turned around so it faced the tracks?

How did someone get into my room?

How did they get out?

Who would want to hurt me?

Had this all been some horrible waking dream?

A noise downstairs shakes me back to reality as I hurry outside to hopefully catch the culprit, but again see no one. Ticking from the control room catches my attention.

Leaping into the room my ears hear the end of the typed transmission.

'Train passing through at 5:00 but will not be stopping in New Brook West'

Hopefully future notifications arrive in advance.

1876

Bad news spreads unlike good, especially when it's someone else's despair, a chance for people to be thankful they're not that poor soul. Nothing makes people so happy as knowing that another is miserable.

I'd let my guard down and been burned for it, news that travelled like wildfire through Brooks.

I'd seen how often they stopped in to say 'hello' when he was home, ignoring me once they'd entered. I'd seen how they looked at him whether or not I was in his company. I'd heard the things they said with their eyes when they saw him, when he spoke to them, when they shared words with him. I'd seen when he entered their homes to touch them the way he touched me, to whisper sweet words of seduction, to send that hot energy through their veins and overwhelm them with physical pleasure. Even those who called themselves my friends had spread their naked bodies before him.

My sister had kept her distance, though this wasn't out of respect for me but so she'd not be called on to help me, to console me, to love me. One as selfish as she would never stoop to my level and abandon her own pursuits in favour of her wretched sister. I hated her for her selfishness.

Throughout this time, mother doted on my her, laughing and smiling and sharing as I stood apart and alone. I could feel her scorn whenever she came near me even before I'd been the victim of his public infidelities. She'd always hated him, wanted to deny me the pleasure she felt I didn't deserve. Or did she covet him for herself? I hated her also, though it matters not.

This was no different than when abuse had rained on me from my classmates, only occasionally replaced by mockery, and I stood alone, fighting alone, hiding alone, crying alone. How the villagers had joined them in their ill-treatment and insults, both open and veiled as gossip spread like wildfire. Not even my family would come to me to lift me up, to encourage me, to repel the insults thrown by others. I could not fathom this attitude on their part but it soon became plain that they hoped to be rid of me sooner than later. In time, I granted them that wish and disappeared.

Still, I always hoped that they'd find me and care for me and comfort me in my time of need, of loneliness, of solitude.

But my tears fueled my rage and anger soon replaced sorrow, as the desire grew in me to strike down my enemies, those who wished me ill, who did me harm, who watched as others wounded me. A different desire entirely.

I'll never be weak again.

1876

I was deeply saddened by the news, felt my sister's pain at what I'd seen of his infidelity, angry at those who used this as a chance to gossip about another. I joyed at seeing her so happy and loved and was equally woeful when circumstances turned against her. My heart broke for her, truly it did.

I wanted to comfort her, console her, to be there with her in her time of need, of loneliness, of solitude. Why does she keep her distance?

I feel no shame and nor should she.

I love her.

22 - Time Moves Differently Here

Still shaken from the previous evening, my nerves allow me little sleep. My heart raced so fast even after I got upstairs, though I'm not sure I took a single breath until I was inside the apartment. I eventually crawled into bed where the memory replayed like a dream in my head, complete with the breeze as the cars rushed past my face. My mind couldn't shake it.

I don't know what to think. The hard fall from the platform would have been enough on its own and the dull ache in my ankles I felt for most of the evening was a constant reminder. I'm not easily scared but that train really jarred me. Hard to imagine a closer shave than that. And the chair. No way someone could have moved it with me in it. And why would they? Had I moved it myself without realizing? Why?

My mind whirled through the night and into the morning.

I'm unsure which questions to ask let alone the answers I want.

I've clearly got a lot to learn about New Brook West.

I wake early before eventually falling asleep in the armchair, jarred awake by a knock at the door. It takes a great effort to get up and make my way to open the door. I'm too groggy to wonder who might be waiting for me on the other side.

"Hi" the woman says nervously, probably due to my shocked facial expression and disheveled appearance.

"Hi..." I reply.

I almost add 'Kayla?' but am fortunate that the words get stuck in my throat. The uncanny resemblance throws me.

Shorter than me with damp shoulder-length hair, black with purple streaks, a beautiful athletic body, gorgeous mouth, and sparkling eyes; Kayla's mirror image with the exception of her hair.

I don't want to stare too long though it's difficult to miss the fact that she's wearing a close-fitting dark jacket, and silvery tights over her slim frame.

Each ear is pierced several times, the top of her left hand tattooed with a snake's head.

I stand in a trance for what seems like forever.

"I'm Cindy. Cindy Stayla" she says softly but confidently, extending her right hand "I'm the local teacher".

"I'm Colden, obviously the Station Master", I answer, "Please come in"

"Thank you", she says, and slowly passes me.

She removes her dark ankle boots and jacket, steps down from the riser in bare feet, and slowly walks toward my sitting area, her back to the door. Her short-sleeved fitted black shirt reveals that the snake on her left arm extends at least as far as the fabric of her top.

"Please, have a seat"

She sits in the armchair.

Her face seems carved in soapstone, fair skin with sharp features, thin blonde eyebrows, black eyelashes framing her dark purplish eyes, her nose narrow and slightly up-turned. Thin cat eyes and shiny dark purple lipstick are all I notice in terms of makeup.

I sit on the couch seat closest to the armchair facing her. She glances around, mostly at the walls and the few posters hanging on them as if she were at an art show. Our heads move in unison from piece to piece as I lean back in the couch.

"I like your taste in art", she says at last, "Though I admit I'm not familiar with the musicians or drawings"

"It's a good local music scene where I'm from and I loved going to the shows" I nod.

"Where are you from, Colden?"

"A bunch of different places" I drop my head. This question always made me sad, like I'd failed everywhere I'd been so far, and I never knew how to answer. Am I from where I was born or from the last place I lived? Or somewhere else entirely?

"I don't mean to pry" her eyes and mouth reveal her embarrassment.

"No, no. It's OK" I dismiss it with a wave "It's just kind of a long story. I've moved about a lot"

She slowly crosses her left leg over her right, her foot dangling as if on a string. The purple nail polish on her toes mesmerizes me and reminds me of something I can't place.

"Perhaps barefoot is a bit intimate for a first encounter" she says apologetically "I'm just more comfortable this way"

"Not at all" I look up, the spell broken "Can I offer you something to drink?"

"A cup of coffee would be great, thanks" she smiles.

"Excellent" I get up and head to the kitchen area "Two cups of coffee"

"You look like I may have caught you by surprise this morning" she reads my mind.

"I don't usually look quite this…unprepared" I shrug.

"Then I look forward to seeing you when you are prepared" she smiles.

I look myself up and down.

"I like you this way" Cindy nods.

I set to the brew, adding what I think is an appropriate ratio of water to grounds. I prefer mine on the stronger side and hope Cindy feels the same.

I consider asking her how she gets paid but decide against it, my experience suggesting that discussions about money are rarely positive, even between good friends. I keep forgetting to ask, though in truth I wouldn't know to whom I should direct my questions.

"Have you had a chance to explore the area much?" she asks.

"A bit, but I only arrived recently so haven't ventured too far" I smirk "There are some great places to walk, to run, and probably to swim, though I've not tried the latter yet"

"There are some beautiful places here" she nods.

"You look like you stay pretty active" I say hoping this isn't too forward.

"I danced when I was younger, mostly ballet" she's now standing.

"Play any sports?" I ask.

"Some soccer and volleyball when I was in school, but recently just yoga and aerobics" she says "How about you? Are you an athletic Station Master?"

"Used to run and swim when I was young, but, again, nothing recently"

"You could run here" she shifts in her seat "Keep your physique looking good"

"Maybe I will" I smile leaning against the island.

"Do you live around here?" I ask.

"Sort of" her face becomes serious "Through the forest past the school" she points in the direction of the window looking out onto the clearing.

"Do you live alone?" I inquire.

"Yes. Very much"

"How long have you lived here?"

"Not that long", she says seriously.

"How long is that?"

She tilts her head slightly to the left, "Maybe a topic for next time?"

"Next time" I reply.

I turn back to take a quick glance at the coffee and ensure I'm not messing anything up.

"What's it like teaching here?" I turn to face her "The people don't seem very expressive and I can't imagine the children are very enthusiastic"

"It's OK" she shrugs "The kids are respectful and learn extremely quickly. Laughter is rare but sometimes they find unusual things funny"

"Why is the school so far from the community?"

"It's got something to do with a location of historical significance. The building's very old with only a few upgrades over the years. Or so I'm told. Some by the Station Masters"

"I'll have to find a way to make my mark on the community" I say.

Cindy giggles.

"Did you see my cat outside?" I ask. Women like cats, right?

"No" she replies enthusiastically "You have a cat?"

"I'm not sure" I smile "I've only seen him the one time but I sometimes hear odd noises that can only be feline"

"Cats are great" she smiles back "I don't see many in town, though"

So, I'm the cat-man. That's ok. I like cats.

"Do you mind my asking what brought you here?" I ask hoping that will shed some light on my situation "I mean, to New Brook West"

"It was a good way for me to get a fresh start."

Sort of a non-committal answer, so I decide not to follow it up.

"What brought you to the station?" she asks, her voice close behind me.

This startles me because she'd crept so quietly to sit at the island, her elbows on the surface as she leans forward.

"Oh, no" she pulls back from the counter "Have I gone and asked another personal question? I'm sorry Colden"

"No, no" I assure her "But again, kind of a long answer. Maybe a topic for next time" I smile nervously.

"OK" she smiles dropping her hands to her lap "Next time"

After a moment I add "When I find my home, it'll welcome me in its arms and never let me go"

"That's a beautiful thought" she smiles.

"Coffee's ready" I say remembering what I'm doing "What do you take in yours?"

Finally, a topic I can't screw up.

"A bit of sugar please" she replies.

"Coming up" I fumble through the cupboards for the sweetener.

"How do you take your coffee Colden?"

"Usually black" I say producing a strange looking container of sugar "But I mix it up and add milk or sugar now and then"

"I've always preferred my coffee dark" she looks pensive.

She uncrosses then crosses her legs again, high up on the island's chair, her bare feet dangling to the ground. I'm staring at her body as I come around the island, at her legs, at the purple nail polish on her toes.

"Do you like my outfit Colden?"

She catches me but with admirable restraint.

"I love it" I try to recover "Did you make it?"

Did you make it?!? Really?!? That's what I come up with? What a lame-o.

"Oh no", she shakes her head with a smile, "I brought it with me to New Brook West"

"Well, it suits you perfectly"

Not 'you look very pretty' but 'it suits you perfectly'. Nice recovery.

"Thank you, sir" she stands and curtsies.

I think of the style of my current outfit; I probably looked like a thug. I haven't even showered yet.

She looks around again, as casually as she had previously, as if she were trying to solve a crime. Cindy has a way of moving as if in slow motion; it makes me feel like I'm moving too quickly, abruptly.

"It's a nice suite" she finally says.

"I can't take much credit for that" I confess "It was like this when I arrived. In some ways it feels like an old building lost in time"

"Time moves differently here" she says sipping her coffee.

Strange thing to say.

"Do you know much about the station?" I ask, "I'm still trying to figure things out"

"Not a lot. It's apparently been here since shortly after the original settlement. It's looked the same as long as I've been here, though this is my first time inside. I think there've been a lot of Station Masters over the years. Some stayed for a long time, others for only a few weeks. Or so I've heard. I'm not sure why they left, or stayed for that matter. I've only ever met one other"

"How do they pick people to work here? Why not just get locals?"

She thinks about it for a bit, biting her lower lip.

"I'm not really sure. I don't know how they choose schoolteachers or about any of my predecessors either. I didn't even meet the teacher before me. I don't know much about previous Station Masters at all"

"Do you know who offered you the job?" I ask, hoping she'll have some information to share "Or who might have offered it to me?"

"I don't recall the name on my letter" she squirrels up her face "And my inquiries here were unsuccessful if not unwelcome so I dropped it. Who sent yours?"

Cindy says all this with a seriousness that she hasn't shown until now and this causes me some concern. She seems unaccustomed to conversation despite the fact that she must be intelligent and somewhat talkative to be a teacher.

"Not a clue" I say "It arrived without a return address"

"A mystery to be solved?" she raises her eyebrows.

"Haha. Maybe" I laugh.

"It's nice to finally have someone to talk with" she smirks "I'm not very popular in town"

"I feel the same way" I smile "About having someone to talk with and not being popular"

Cindy giggles.

"I have something to confess", I say impulsively.

Cindy looks at me inquisitively.

"You've got a twin – a good friend of mine back home". It sounds better than saying 'A woman I recently had sex with'.

I go for my cell phone wondering if there will be enough battery power left to show her. It comes on slowly, letting me know that this may be the last time I use it.

I scroll through to Kayla, hoping that Cindy will find this interesting rather than dumb. In retrospect it was a new kind of stupid. Who would want to know this, let alone someone you just met?

"She must be very pretty", she plays along, smiling as she leans forward.

I find a nice photo of Kayla and turn it towards her.

Cindy gives me a confused look which turns into a scowl.

"I should go" she stands "It was nice to meet you"

"Uh…" I try to find words, surprised by her reaction.

I turn the phone to look at it myself catching a quick glimpse of a black and purple-haired zombie-girl with washed out skin, eyes half-open and mouth half-closed, sitting in what appears to be a dirty train railcar. It looks like a really bad post-mortem photo of Cindy.

The screen fades to black as I watch her leave.

23 – Caprice, the Child-Care Worker

I decide to put some time between my horrific first encounter with Cindy and our next interaction, still perplexed by the image on my phone and its origin. What the heck was it and where did it come from? I was sure it was Kayla's picture. My phone was dead so I couldn't investigate. In retrospect, it was a bad idea regardless of the photo, something I realized all too late.

Would she shun me now too, like everyone else did?

And in this place, I could use a friend. It's lonelier here than I'd expected.

The last couple of days had been dream-like, only one train receiving cargo yesterday in the form of boxes easily loaded by the beefy labourers. As previously, Dalton watched more than supervised, though perhaps his instructions were provided prior to their arrival. Or maybe he was the facilitator who arranged the pick-ups and deliveries as opposed to a worker. He never lifted a finger. The men did not look in his direction nor did they speak to him.

No arrivals are scheduled for today leaving me wondering what to do, the time now just after 10:00 a.m. Coffee in hand, I walk to the window overlooking the rail line, a light fog between me and the short trees, a gloomy day at the station. There's no wind or sun to clear the air.

I spot a small figure in the mist across the tracks. It looks like a woman or the shadow of a woman, but has yet to move. I can't make out any features in the haze. I wait for a few seconds, expecting even the slightest motion. Is she watching me? Come to visit the station?

A knock at the door startles me.

I open the door to Michael's blank gaze greets me, like a sculpture which the artist had stopped without finishing the face, his son David next to him equally deadpan.

"There will be tasks for you between trains and these will be communicated to you with postings on the board. As was the case with your work on the exterior of the station" he says heading back down the stairs at the end of his sentence.

I take this as my cue to pull on my boots and follow, meeting him on the platform.

"There is nothing for you to do at the hotel except to notify us when a room has been vacated so it can be prepared for future visitors"

"Who should I talk to about that?" I ask.

"My daughter Tessa will arrange for a cleaning team or whatever is required. Please post these requirements on the board"

"What about Room 1?" I ask hoping for some insight.

"No one goes into or comes out of Room 1" his reply especially stern.

"Does…" I begin before being quickly interrupted.

"You have no key to Room 1 and will have no need to enter it" Michael says conclusively "Is that understood?"

"Perfectly" I nod sheepishly.

"Then, farewell for now. I ask you to check the board daily, not just for train schedules but for additional tasks assigned to you. I expect this is acceptable"

I nod.

Michael and his son turn and leave, their direction taking them toward the path back to the village.

So many other questions occur to me after he's gone: How will I know which rooms are occupied? How will I know when they've been vacated? What sort of tasks should I expect? Who is the girl I see around the station?

But the conversation had not leant itself to further inquiries on my part so for now these will remain unanswered.

By now it's nearly 11:00 so I decide to walk into town if only to look around New Brook West, having overheard Michael's children talking about an outdoor market. Food has so far been provided to me in deliveries but there were surely other delicacies and curiosities.

How long have I been here? Only a few days or is it longer; I can't recall.

Opening the door sharply I nearly run into the young woman standing there. Short blonde hair, wearing a faded yellow dress with a long-sleeved white shirt beneath it, probably in her early twenties. Her clothing makes her look like a flower.

"I'm so sorry" she takes a step back.

"No, I should've been paying closer attention" I reply apologetically.

"I'm Caprice, the child-care worker" she stands up straight, a subtle citrus perfume hanging in the air.

"I'm Colden, obviously the station master. I didn't know there was a child-care in town"

"I watch over the young ones while the parents work. Playing games, eating, napping. Not very exciting, I suppose" she smirks.

"Neither is being the Station Master from what I've seen and done so far" I say "Please come in"

"Thank you kindly but, no, I should go. One of the children wanted to be sure that I gave this drawing to you. She seemed very happy to hear of your arrival. Her name is Nix. Her brother is Skitt. She's nine and he's seven"

"Thank you very much" I take the paper showing a child's rendition of a man in black pants and brown top with shoulder-length yellow hair next to a train, exactly what I'd worn when I arrived; a large green bag on his right, a rectangular box to his left. It was obviously drawn by a child but the pieces are easily identifiable, the man's only facial feature a horizontal line where the mouth would be.

"Was she at the station when I arrived?" I ask, curious how the children would have this precise information.

Caprice looks behind her and down the stairs, her expression nervous.

"That's very kind of her. And of you to bring it" I say sensing her anxiety.

"Do you plan on staying?" she asks.

"What do you mean?"

"As Station Master"

"It's a bit early to plan for the future but so far so good"

Caprice's head drops.

"How long have you lived here?" I ask after a short pause between us.

"All my life" she looks me in the eyes.

"Did you know any of the other station masters?"

"Some"

"Why did they leave?"

"This isn't a job for everyone " she says solemnly.

"How so?" I ask, as much curious as concerned.

Her face goes blank.

"I should go. I didn't intend for our conversation to be discomforting" she forces a half-smile.

"Where is the child care?" I change the subject.

"In town" she nods "I'll leave you now. It was very nice to meet you"

Caprice takes the handrail and hurries down the stairs. A scratching up near the roof draws my attention and by the time I try to spot Caprice leaving, she's vanished.

I walk a few steps down the staircase to look into the clearing but don't see her anywhere.

An unusual woman.

By the time I leave my apartment it's nearly 12:00, time once again getting away from me, a single jam sandwich my only lunch in case something at this market catches my interest. Bleak weather awaits, like most days since I'd arrived, a constant chill in the air, the dampness under my clothing. The forest isn't nearly as ominous during the day and I shake my head at my frights and nerves on my first night. The woods are silent except for my footsteps, the air still, the environment generally gloomy but calm. My eyes occasionally glance into the trees but see little beyond what's near to the path, only darkness further in.

Passing through the town's gates, I'm again surprised by the dry ground in town. There's no indication of a bazaar of any kind in the plaza around the fountain, so I walk down one of the streets in search of this place or someone who can set me in the right direction. A man up ahead spots me, stopping as he does. He looks strong but shorter than me, maybe fifty years old, fair-skinned, greying blonde haired, dark eyed, dressed all in brown.

"Can you direct me to the market, please?"

He points to my right without taking his eyes off me.

"I'm Colden. I'm the station master. What's your name?"

"Benton, sir" he bows slightly "I'll be bringing your provisions to the station"

"Great. Thanks very much, Benton"

"The pleasure is mine" he walks away.

A man of few words. Deciding not to pursue him, I walk in the direction he indicated, an assortment of wood planks and crates in the distance. As I near, I notice several booths lined up along both sides of the avenue offering different fruits, vegetables, prepared goods, and even some tools. Some people stare at me, others ignore my presence entirely as I roam about.

"These pies look great. How much are they?" I ask one of the female merchants.

She hands it to me with a nod.

"How do I pay you?" I tilt my head.

She gestures with her hands as though I'm just supposed to take it.

Another woman brings me a small wooden box filled with fresh fruit and vegetables, setting it at my feet.

"For you, sir"

"Thanks very much. I'm Colden"

"Yes sir" she smiles backing away.

"These are beautiful" I say to a woman standing next to a table of oil lamps.

"Can I offer you one?"

She looks about thirty-five, thin with short light blonde hair.

"Not right now but I'll be back if I ever need one, that's for sure"

"You're the station master" a young blonde girl in a long dress is standing on my left.

"Yes" I reply.

"Station masters don't last long" she says grimly before wandering off down an alley.

What? I watch her leave but decide against pursuit. I must have misheard and won't be running after a child.

Workers engaging in all kinds of activities mill about the market setting up tables, opening crates, moving items.

A man in his mid-forties chops wood toward the end of the line of vendors, his axe-work producing a fine pile of logs of all sizes.

"That's heavy work, man" I say.

He turns to me, his face hardened by many years of long days, his hands worn by a life of manual labour, his barrel chest a testament to his strength.

"Anything for you?"

He stops to look at me.

"No, thanks. But have a great day"

"Yes, sir"

He turns back to his task.

"Don't mind him. That's Karl"

I look down at a young blonde boy wearing a black plaid long-sleeved shirt and black pants; maybe seven or eight years old.

"Hi. I'm Colden" I smile.

Is this Skitt?

"I'm Sam" he says in a mature tone.

"Hi Sam. Do you work here at the market?"

I crouch down to his level.

"Her name's Sara" he gestures to a young woman laying out small boxes.

"That's Mica who gave you the vegetables, Piper who gave the pie, Selena with the lamps and candles, and Lexi with baked bread. And that's my sister Rissa"

He gestures with a nod of his head, my heart jumping as I turn to see a girl standing directly behind me; she'd be a couple of years older than him. She wears a dark brown jacket with a dark pink shirt beneath it and black pants similar to her brother's.

Is Rissa the girl in the fog?

No one pays us any attention, their efforts focused on their area.

"I'd better go" Sam jogs toward a woman I assume to be his mother "It was nice to meet you"

"Nice to meet you, Sam. And you too, Rissa"

The girl runs off with her brother, waving as she does.

Maybe New Brook West is a commune where everyone contributes in their own way with good and services made available to all community members. 'By each according to his ability and to each according to his need'. Or something like that. It does have its benefits in an isolated location.

I collect my items, making my way back to the fountain's peaceful flow. There are no benches in the plaza area so I sit on the centerpiece's stone edge, which is actually masonry rather than solid rock, and stare out at the clearing beyond the lanterns marking the entry path.

"Their names are in your letters"

A young blonde-haired boy in dark overalls hops up next to me on the fountain's perimeter.

"Whose names?" I wonder where this comes from.

"You know who"

"What…"

He lofts a rock over my head, the splash in the water behind me turning my head. When I look back, the little guy is gone.

I take a quick look around but he's obviously run off.

Another strange villager. They start young.

Whose names are in my letters? The letter of offer? It had no name. What other letters are there? I've not received any mail since arriving.

Do people in the village know something I don't? Something about station masters? About the station?

Fog hangs outside the gates as if it isn't welcome in the village itself, a metaphor for me since my arrival.

Why are the residents uneasy around me? Have other station masters been rude? Angry? Deviants? That would explain it but then why would they continue to offer the position to random people?

It's now 2:15 so as good a time as any to head 'home', not that there's anything in particular for me to do there but maybe not hanging about too much at first will bring people around to me. I gather up my items, arriving back at the station just before 2:30 after another quiet walk through the solemn forest.

The control room door is open a crack as though someone hasn't shut it tightly. It seems good practice to lock it so that has become habit for me. Everything seems as I left it, so business as usual. I'd already rummaged through some of my predecessor's paperwork to get a feel for the completion of the ledgers and documents. I wonder if there could be anything else of interest. A stockpile of boxes fills the back room, the large closet-sized niche seemingly added as an afterthought. These are labelled by year in different writing styles from artistic script to messy block letters and everything in between.

Local history always interested me, here that much more so given that this could provide insight into my new community and what to expect as station master.

Randomly, I grab the box marked '1920', leafing through hand-written descriptions of loads both arriving and departing, always indicating the number of pieces and their individual weight but never a mention of the contents. I don't really care if they're growing and shipping marijuana or other drugs so can't understand the big secret; though I suppose not everyone is as progressive with their views. Each sheet shows 'RC' at the bottom in proper cursive letters, matching the initials on the box, presumably the station master at that time.

Next, I find 1937, the documents much the same, though now cargo waybills are matched by entries in a small notebook. The author, Samuel Clovinston, cross-referenced the expected with the actual quantities, noting that these were not always the same. Why this person cared seemed odd, unless he didn't want it to look like a mistake on his part.

Amongst these entries, several personal thoughts:

`'Can't sleep. Relentless scratching at the windows'`
`'Someone from town is watching my movements, even observing me at night'`
`'Could I have truly done this?'`

The last entry, dated the 17th of April, simply says *'scheduled train did not arrive at 1:15'*. The tome contains many more blank pages but he'd not written anything else after that. And there's no indication he'd planned on making that his last day.

The ledger in the 1945 box, completed by C Becker, notes the quantity and weight of freight arriving and departing without cross-referencing expected with actual numbers and weights. Mr. Becker's observations focused on being watched at the station, in the forest, and in the village. Reflections on solitude and loneliness? Paranoia? Depression?

Are these guys smoking the local herb and messing up their minds?

I hope that people won't take such a profound interest in me if what my predecessors wrote about being watched is true.

Is that thunder rumbling in the distance? The noise makes me shudder. Outside is darker than I expect but I can't recall what time I arrived back at the station so have no context.

Skipping ahead to 1993, Robert V is now the station master. Robert structured his ledgers similarly to his predecessors, presumably from having read theirs. The case contains documents pulled off a prehistoric printer, black ink dots forming crude letters and numbers. The papers, filed in a plastic folder, detail the incoming and outgoing cargo.

I then come upon a book with the initials TF, that seems to be a diary beginning in August 1984.

Interspersed among his other entries and written in red pen:
'I can't sleep. Who's watching me? Someone's at the windows. In the forest'
'What did I do? How could I have done that?'
'Where do I go from here? How can I get away?'

Simple drawings accompany these below, above, or beside his text. A window. A door. A tree. The school?

Who's TF? And what is he talking about? Who was watching him? And what did he do?

Was he going crazy?

Or maybe just feeling lonely? Poor guy.

Unless someone was watching him.

I have no plans to diarize my thoughts and hope the day won't come when I feel the need to do this. And really hope I won't be watched.

I'd wanted to find the name of my immediate predecessor but am unable.

A brief noise outside stirs me back to reality. I walk to the door to look out on the empty platform. All's quiet and no one's there. My eyes make their way to Room 1 where the door looks just a touch ajar, but that isn't possible, is it?

A creaking to my left and above me as the train station sign rocks on its chains.

When I turn back to Room 1, the door is firmly closed, as it must have always been.

24 – The Photograph

I wake at 8:00 feeling pretty good.

Last night's rain lashed the windows and walls before subsiding into a light drizzle; fog and damp air seem common in New Brook West.

I light the lamp near the bed to inspire me to rise. The large window to my right offers a grim view. Outside, murky air holds the station in its grip, the treeline across the wide clearing not yet visible in the dreary dawn. The chilly suite seems more so than usual despite no open windows. I'll stoke the furnace when I go downstairs but that can wait until the sun comes up. Grabbing a long-sleeved shirt, I walk to the kitchen, lighting two candles along the way. Shadows dance as their wicks flicker.

I recall last night's unsettling moment looking out the control room door at Room 1. Was it just a trick of the shadows and flickering lights making the door appear open?

Setting the water to boil for coffee, I spot a black and white photograph on the low table in the living room. I didn't think I'd left anything out.

The photo: a man hanging by the neck from the overhead beam in this apartment. Dark hair, he's shorter and bigger than me. Viewed from the side it's impossible to make out his face but he's definitely dead and wearing the station master jacket. The paper feels old, the picture grainy. The man's hair looks wet; he wears old-style black boots that I've seen on other men in New Brook West.

Where did this come from? My eyes slowly inspect the room but of course there's no one here nor anything to remind me of this image. I check the door, which is naturally still locked. Windows all shut.

I'd have remembered this photo, wouldn't I?

I inhale and exhale deeply.

Is this for real? Had someone hanged themselves here? In this room? That wasn't mentioned. I try to get a closer look but the black and white photo shows its age, the paper faded.

Who would want to remember this person at that moment with a photo?

No way to confirm his identity or the year so no chance of cross-referencing him to any of the files in the control room. I try to make out items in the photo that might suggest a time period but everything looks pretty much the same as it does now.

It seems imprudent to show this photo around town, or to anyone at all.

A grim history for station masters.

I hope my successor doesn't find photos of my suspended body.

1878

I was overjoyed at my son's birth, so happy to have another to share my life, another to care for and to love. It was truly good news to see that he wouldn't be cursed with my green eyes, instead gifted with beautiful blue.

None were there to share in my joy, to celebrate with me, yet still I was happy. He made me feel less alone and my love for him was absolute. He was well-behaved and conducted himself quietly, serving as a distraction when we were seen in town. I knew the words in their whispers even though I couldn't hear them. I've always known.

But he soon became fascinated with the world beyond our shores and then was gone with my blessing. Why should he suffer with me?

25 - You've never travelled?

Perhaps Caprice the child-care worker could talk me through the macabre photo. I hadn't mustered the courage to go see Cindy yet.

The damp chill in the air cuts deep when I step outside, a wake-up call of sorts and a reminder of my surroundings. It's just after 10:00 when I arrive in the village square, unsure of where to go to find the child care centre. A twenty-something man sitting on the steps of what I had surmised to be the community church seems as good a source as any.

His eyes fix on me on my walk over to greet him.

"Hi, I'm Colden the new station master"

"I know" he replies indifferently. Dressed completely in black creates a stark contrast to his fair skin and dirty blonde hair making him stand out that much more.

"Do you know where I can find the child care building?"

"In the basement beneath the print shop. You'll recognize it" he points down a street to his right, my eyes following his gesture.

"And where is the print shop? Is it…"

I turn back to empty steps but it's as if he'd never been there. Obviously, a man of great stealth.

The quiet street ahead is lined with two-storey stone and mortar structures, anyone in my path quickly darting into a building or down a back alley to get out of the way. I'd never considered myself to be scary looking nor had I been impolite since my arrival. Maybe it was just the natural aversion to strangers that had been engrained after so many years of a life of isolation.

I remember the print shop once I see it, though I'd never entered it to get a look at the type of equipment they use, curious as I am to see whether it's as ancient as my own, as well as the nature of their business. My footsteps to the child care are as quiet as possible, not wanting to draw any attention to myself in the empty streets.

Tall vertical windows on the front of the building with narrow beams between each pane, a blue wooden door on the far left of the lower level. A silver mailbox hangs on the wall to the left of the door with 'C Collaston' in black letters. The sunny welcoming room has a playful appearance, in stark contrast to other buildings, the walls vibrant colours.

The door is slightly ajar as I approach, Caprice hurrying to meet me at the entrance, her bright yellow dress like a sun in the room.

"Hello, Colden. Everyone say 'Hi' to the Station Master"

"Hi, Station Master" the children say in unison, each returning to his or her activity after the greeting.

"Hi, Caprice, child-care worker"

"Not that much to see here really. It's not a very exciting job but I love the children so it's a good place for me"

"I've met Sam and Rissa. Do you look after them too?"

She gives me a confused look so I don't pursue it.

"And Skitt and Nix?" I ask.

A child calls to her, Caprice running to take care of things.

She's right that there isn't much to the room. A few long tables like those at the market; a corner with a cooler similar to mine at the station; the walls of smoother stone and occasionally decorated with child-like art. Carpet covers most of the floor, aside from the dirt entry, a wood stove in each corner of the room making it cozy and warm. The low wood-beamed ceiling suggests this was possibly a storehouse of some kind prior to its current incarnation, a musty smell lingering in the air. Despite this, it feels warm and inviting, perhaps because of the children's happiness.

"Unfortunately, you won't find people to be friendly with you, through no fault of your own. Station Masters have endured difficult times here going back many years"

"Why? Were they cruel or rude? Or just plain bad people?"

"Some were unkind, nowhere is immune. But it goes back even further than that. Folklore abounds in New Brook East and West, but some stories are best untold. The keeper of the station has had many names and I hope yours hangs on its door for many years to come" she nods.

"Thanks Caprice, that's very kind of you"

"Excuse me" she says walking over to talk to children drawing at a table.

Did she mention New Brook East?

Each wall is a different colour though I'm unable to determine the pattern, if one exists. Out the windows, rock has been placed over the dirt excavation, supporting the structure from crumbling in.

Ten children sit on the floor in the room, Caprice the only adult. On a small desk to my left several pads of paper and three quills with a jar of ink.

"I've got a lot of questions about the station and my position" I say when she returns "If you've got a moment. Please"

Her expression turns grim.

"I probably won't have many answers"

I look over at the children busying themselves with toys, paints, paper, each sitting on the floor.

"Have you always lived in West?" I ask her.

"My story is boring compared to yours, I'm sure. I was born on the island and will likely spend my last days here"

"You've never travelled?"

She shakes her head.

"Maybe they don't want to lose their best child-care worker" I laugh.

"There's no place for me to go" she smiles meekly.

"There're so many places to go" my voice returns to its previous volume attracting some short-lived attention "Rolling hills of yellow and gold, lush river valleys, awe-inspiring historical sites, breathtaking modern creations, art, music, and so much more. The world's wondrous beauty, wild escapes, magnificent mysteries to be solved"

"You make it sound like such a romantic adventure. But we have our own mysteries here"

I decide not to pursue this any further.

"This is a very different culture than I'm used to" I say.

"I imagine it is. Sometimes I feel the same despite my..." she stops herself.

Time for another subject change.

"People have been vanishing as soon as I turn my back on them. Are you gonna do that?" my head turns to the left, my right eye squinting.

"I'll still be here" she smiles.

"I may stop by to see you again if that's OK"

"I'd like that" she says before adding "As long as you know that I am promised to another"

"You mean like an arranged marriage?"

"Aren't all marriages arranged?"

"I suppose" I agree "How do you know him?"

"He was well-respected…in the community"

"Then congratulations, Caprice"

"For what?"

"Your engagement" I laugh.

"Oh, ok. Thank you" she looks confused.

I take a short step back.

"I've seen a young girl around the train station a few times but haven't met her" I ask in a light tone "Any idea who that could be?"

"I'm not sure" she answers nervously.

"You mentioned New Brook East…" I begin, thinking she might come forward with some island history.

She looks around before lowering her voice.

"East hasn't been inhabited for years. Folks gradually left the community until only a few residents remained, all of whom are now deceased, I believe. No one familiar with the community's history would return"

"What happened?" I lean in slightly, my voice softer.

She pauses, stepping closer to me and speaking even more quietly.

"Be careful Colden. This island has many secrets"

"Everyplace does" I nod "Same goes for people"

Another pause ensues between us.

"I would enjoy seeing you again" she says cheerfully.

"Even though you're promised to another?" I raise my eyebrows.

"Even though" she smiles, returning to her charges.

I exit into the street.

Caprice intrigues me in her innocence and nervousness.

Can the island's history help me figure out why I've been offered this job?

Will learning more make my life easier? It'd sure be nice to make sense of my current home. I'd like to feel more welcome and that might start with why I was picked as the next station master.

"Hey mate" a voice calls from the alley to my right, the young man's accent decidedly British.

"Hi" I walk over to him slowly and cautiously.

The guy in his twenties, his top a darker green than his pants, his black knee-high leather boots match his cap. He stands just enough off the main street to be hidden in the shadows.

"The new Station Master, yeah?" he asks in a youthful voice.

"Yes"

Could this be Caprice's boyfriend or husband? The one to whom she's promised?

He casually looks up and down the road with smooth movements.

"My name's Feryn" he takes a step back into the alley as I near him.

"Hi" I reply, unsure why he's calling me over.

"You need help getting around, I'm your man. There's no place I can't find"

His pleasant manner improves his sales pitch.

"I'll remember that. Thanks, Feryn"

He points across the street but no one's there.

When I turn back, he's gone, as expected.

For better or worse, people recognize me, something I hope will play out to my benefit once they come to realize my intentions are simple. Caprice seems well-informed though reluctant to share but perhaps that too will change in time.

I decide I'll save inquiries about the letter of offer for now.

"Good afternoon, sir" a man's voice speaks from behind me.

"Hello" I turn around abruptly.

The fellow looks more disheveled than some of the other residents, his clothes torn, his hair ragged, his face tired.

"Just wanted to offer my services if you need any help with anything around the station. I'm quite handy and a good worker"

He sounds sincere and good-natured, though I wonder why he isn't working in the fields with the other locals or off somewhere being handy.

"Good to know. What's your name?"

"Miller, sir"

"Nice to meet you Miller" I extend my hand which he shakes enthusiastically "I'll keep you in mind"

I turn to leave before realizing he might know something about my predecessor.

"Hey Miller. Did you ever meet the station master before me?"

"Only once, sir"

"Do you know anything about him? Do you remember his name?"

He thinks for a moment.

"Just that his last name began with a 'V'.

26 - The only librarian

With a 'V'. Why does that shock me so much?

Many last names begin with a 'V'. Including mine. Though it is a funny coincidence.

Interesting that he'd mention that specific detail about the previous station master. The whole idea of it being the same last name as mine is absurd. My Dad was an only child as was his father before him, though there are surely other Vintassis in the world, maybe in Denmark. But how could my family name have anything to do with events on this remote island?

I'm no good at riddles. If one exists here.

Time to get back to the station.

I wake from a fitful night's sleep, the time now 7:45.

Has it already been two weeks since I'd arrived? It's hard to keep track of time here without any TV, newspapers, or internet.

No trains are scheduled to stop in New Brook West today and I'd not been told of any loads going out. I make coffee with a quick snack then shower. The bathroom itself is a masterpiece of engineering to produce a pressurized water system without the benefit of electricity. I head out onto the platform, to walk around the station. It's an impressive structure and appears to have stood the test of time and I'm constantly in awe. The grey brick exterior of the hotel side is time-worn and faded but looks solid. The exterior of the apartment side is wood-clad, the outside walls covered with long light brown horizontal planks. These begin at the base of the platform and a short distance off the ground on the other sides of the building. Odd for such a damp environment but perhaps they prefer more traditional materials. Or they're treated boards.

It's straight out of the history books, with the exception of the long windows in the upstairs suite which give a fantastic view of the field and open up the interior space. Large square windows face out into the clearing from the second and third floors of the hotel.

On the main floor, at Room 1's position, the window is boarded-up from the inside. What mysteries does this room hold and what makes entry forbidden?

The eerie structure looms in the dreary environment as if surveying its domain. The building has an ominous presence, like an old abandoned house watching those who approach.

Something flashes past a crack in the board covering Room 1's window? I look closely but see nothing more. For a moment I'm unable to move. Am I being watched? By whatever lives in Room 1?

My trance breaks and I walk up the stone stairs onto the platform, eying the door as I take slow and careful steps to the control room. I'm relieved when I see the typed message confirming there will be no stops in New Brook West today.

Having the day to myself, it seems a good time to see if the library has anything chronicling the history of the island, the community, or the station itself. And if I can find any news of the outside world. And get away from the station for a bit.

I slip through the north side of town in the direction I'd been told by one of the markets' vendors, past shops both closed and open, past watchful eyes, past lit and extinguished lanterns, where the landscape opens into a blue field. Islands of trees surrounded by tall yellow grasses stand lonely but alert in the short blue pasture.

A few small buildings litter the damp countryside, maybe homes, maybe something else. My ears catch the sound of birds but can't determine their origin. I'd not seen any wildlife as yet, except for the rustlings and distant noises in the forest that could only be animal.

The quiet trip along the well-kept dirt path through the pale blue field suits me, the fresh air a tonic to my lungs, some separation from the community and the train station a welcome break. And my first visit to this part of the island, hesitant as I was to pass through the community while exploring. It's beautiful. Slowly the library comes into view like mountains appearing on the horizon, a monolith against the open water's background, its ancient brick exterior both welcoming and intimidating. The clear blue sky frames this colossus.

The library's non-descript exterior keeps with the austerity of the local architecture. It looks time-worn, but appears to be made entirely of stone, as though carved from a single piece of rock, with sturdy wood front doors. It's incredible to behold. For a moment I stare in awe at this massive structure.

The interior is as impressive as the exterior: a high ceiling supported by four solid columns, narrow aisles of bookshelves on every wall, a huge window taking up nearly the entire back wall looking out onto the ocean. Stone steps lead up to the main floor where a bearded man who looks a few years older than me sits at a large desk.

"Hi" I say by way of introduction to announce myself into such a striking structure.

"Hi there" his face beams.

"I'm Colden" I walk toward him all while staring about the library, its gray walls lit by oil lamps spaced around the room; the back window is the only glass making light sparse in the giant hall.

"Quite the building, isn't it" he notices me inspecting the inside "Like a piece of history. I'm Brian"

"Are you the only librarian?" I ask him.

"Just me"

Brian has a slightly different British accent, like from a hundred years ago.

"Many folks come here to be alone" he leans back in his chair "What brings you?"

"Curiosity" I reply.

"A dangerous condition" he frowns.

"Why are you so far away from the community?" I ask.

"You mean the building?" he nods, his voice serious "This is both a monument to the power of books and a deterrent to unwelcome visitors"

Wow. Ok.

"What sort of books do you have?" I decide to focus on the power of the printed word.

"Very little here in the way of contemporary popular fiction. There are some 18th and 19th century novels as well as a few newer ones and several historical works of fact and fiction. Many were written by local authors over the years, mostly of a darker nature, though there are also mysteries and even some romance novels" he describes proudly. "There's little in the way of homework brought home from school but some kids still find their way here. Very quiet when they do. Maybe they're trying to get away from the strictness in their homes or just come to explore. I'm fine with it either way, especially when I get asked a question"

He looks toward the large door.

"Make no mistake, the inhabitants are very intelligent if not worldly" he adds after a brief pause.

"What's it like being librarian?" I ask. Brian actually sounds like a pretty interesting guy.

"It's not so bad. You get tired of the usual and it's nice to meet people that actually want to learn. And that don't give a toss about posturing. I don't really miss society, the big city. It's all show without substance. Here I do my own thing at my own pace and have everything I need"

"Don't you miss anything from the outside world?"

"Some things, I suppose, but I always felt out of place 'out there' anyway" he gestures.

I glance around the reception area and at the walls, noticing paintings above bookshelves or between them when space permits; to say they're unusual would be an understatement. Each is a vivid depiction of what appears to be ancient folklore with a mix of the supernatural, each with its own eerie feel.

"I see you've found the art", Brian's eyes follow mine.

"It's certainly...interesting"

"Most are by local artists, alive or dead, some contemporary some with a longer history" he looks around the library's walls.

"Don't you find them unsettling?" I ask.

"Not really" he looks around the room "They all seem to represent the same themes: religion, fairy tales, folklore, things like that. Not that different from what you'd have found in any other culture's history. Maybe there's more to them but art interpretation isn't my strong suit"

"Mind if I look around?"

"By all means"

The bookshelves are all taller than me, an even taller one at every eighth interval. Shelves contain a mixture of hard and soft cover material. I recognize none of the titles nor how they're arranged. Each corner area has a set of three short yet comfortable looking chairs around a small square table. It takes me a few moments to notice the distinctiveness of the chairs, half dark purple and half black, split vertically down the middle. An area with three long tables is to the right of the entrance on the level below Brian's desk.

The upper level is a wide ring around the entire room except above the entry stairs where it narrows and it stops at the edge of the large rear window. A waist-high wrought iron guardrail with thin metal spindles encircles the interior edge. A spiral staircase on each side of Brian's desk leads to the upper area.

"Mind if I take a look upstairs?"

But Brian is gone.

Each staircase is secured to the ceiling by two thick steel rods beginning at the floor.

Walking around the upper level really offers an amazing view. Looking down at the main floor gives the impression of being among the clouds. The reception area is huge from this vantage point, the remainder of the room equally substantial. I can see where the stone pillars meet the roof, providing necessary support. Unlike the main floor, seating is sparse upstairs with only a single chair in each of the corners and no tables.

Paintings above the shelves up here depict scenes both natural and supernatural, their width much greater than their height.

Across the room from me, a painting of mythical creatures in battle; another with wolves howling at the moon; a third depicting a deer and her fawn in the forest; in each of these, blue, green, and purple are the dominant colours. The art is somewhat unsettling as if conjured from bad dreams.

The huge window at the rear of the room behind Brian's desk offers a spectacular view out the back of the building onto the infinite ocean. Light plays on the still water's surface; nothing discernible in the distance where the bluish-grey water meets the horizon. The building must be located at land's edge, though we appear to be a good distance above the waves. The library would look like a fortress to anyone approaching by sea.

Far off to the right I see what might have at one time been a harbour and the mouth of a river; to the left a black plateau of smooth rocks extends out into the water and farther than I can see. A young girl stands a short distance out looking toward the library. She doesn't appear dressed for the cold wet air, neither is she moving. I stare at her for a moment, unable to make out any details of her appearance nor can I think of a reason for her to be out there on the rocky wasteland.

I take a few backward steps past the staircase to take me out of her line of sight.

Turning around I bump into a partially cloaked young blonde woman who'd been directly behind me.

"Very sorry" I say, dazzled for a moment by her green eyes.

"Quite alright" she replies sternly, the hood concealing her face.

"I'm Colden, the new station master"

"I'm Tina" she nods without extending a hand so I decide not to offer mine.

She walks past me and down the stairs.

"Bye, Tina" I wave as she leaves without a glance in my direction.

Odd. Again.

Tina disappears from sight as I try to recall who else I'd seen recently with such stunning green eyes? Chris? Christi?

It doesn't come to me so my thoughts return to the library's configuration.

The arrangement of the bookcases on the main floor is almost hypnotizing when viewed from above. It seems as though a message will reveal itself if I stare long enough but after about ten seconds of investigation, I abandon the mystery. The spiral staircase winds beneath me until I come to ground beside the large desk.

The magnificent stained-glass window above the front door isn't obvious from outside. It's been cut from dark blue and purple glass; catching the sparse exterior light it creates an image I can't quite make out.

"An amazing sight from up there isn't it" Brian says.

"This really is an awesome building. It looks like a mighty solid structure"

I come around in front of the desk.

"Did you see the girl out back?"

He turns around to look out the large windows behind him.

"Way out here?" his surprise is evident.

"By herself, too" I add.

"Just one?" he pauses for a second "Not a common thing, especially for the girls"

I turn to leave before deciding this guy might be in-the-know.

"I'm kinda new here" I say.

"I gathered that" Brian smiles.

"I'm really trying to figure out how…"

"I hear what you're thinking" he sits on the edge of the desk "But be careful, my friend"

Maybe I'll save my inquiries for now.

"Ya. Ok. Thanks"

"Enjoy the rest of your day" Brian says, concluding the conversation.

Deciding I've seen enough of the library, and perhaps unintentionally offended Brian, I politely excuse myself.

I walk with the wind at my back across the blue field, with its small buildings and scattered rocks. The sky is clear though the air around the village is chilly and damp. Winding through the grey stone buildings in the streets and alleyways, I eventually finding myself in the plaza. No one's here now so perhaps it's a good time to explore the cemetery. Glancing toward the church I notice a dark figure inside the fence crouched behind a gravestone. I turn my eyes away and casually walk around the fountain allowing me to avoid any intrusion. I stop on the other side of the stone obelisk trying to avoid looking suspicious.

By the time I look back inside, the person has disappeared, though they haven't emerged through either gate.

I'd best be on my way.

Knowing that my presence is generally unwelcome in the village, I begin my journey back to the station, deciding to delay my visit to the cemetery. Despite the calm air, the lanterns' candles at the community gate flicker as I leave.

After an uneventful walk through the gloomy forest, the clearing welcomes me back to the sleepy station. I'd forgotten to extinguish a lantern on the platform but am always grateful for light at the station.

I notice clouds have begun to fill the sky as New Brook West returns to grey.

A child sits on the ground next to the staircase between hotel rooms 1 and 2 her arms resting on her bent knees. Her dirty purple dress, black shoes, and dark hair make her appearance sinister in the gathering gloom. Is she waiting for someone to arrive? Me?

There's not a sound in the clearing or on the platform.

I consider calling out to her but don't want to startle her into vanishing.

My steps are slow as I watch for any movement. Suddenly, she rises and turns toward Room 1. I stop, wondering if she'll open the door or if someone will open it for her. I don't move, can't move. I wait. Absolute silence. She doesn't move or raise a hand for several seconds. Then her head turns toward me.

Is she looking at me? Past me?

I turn around quickly to confirm I'm alone. Seeing no one behind me, I look back at the hotel but the girl is gone. No one anywhere around the station or on the platform.

My walk slows on my way to Room 1's door, my body leaning in once I reach it in the hopes of picking up a conversation.

I hear a scraping on the wood floor inside the room.

After a few seconds of courage mustering, I knock meekly at which the noises within stop. Trying to open the door is out of the question.

"I'm the station master", I say more quietly than confidently, "Anyone there?"

Silence.

"Rissa?" I say softly.

No answer. No more noises from inside the room.

Only unlocking the door remains. This requires great effort on my part. It feels like forever before I find it in me to extract the keys from my pocket. Do I even have the key to Room 1?

Does she?

The thought of someone with a key to the forbidden room makes me shiver. Am I actually considering trying to get into Room 1?

I look at the door, then side to side, then to the levels above, and finally behind me.

No. It can wait until morning. Or another time. Or never.

Turning to the apartment's stairs, I look both ways to ensure no one else is here, then check the area between where I'm standing and the steps up to the door to my room. My feet are soft, at least I hope they are, as I cross the infinite platform.

There's not a sound at the station.

I climb the stairs like a carnival-goer walking through a haunted house, withdrawing the keys to let myself in.

Before entering my apartment, I take once last glance at Room 1 where I swear someone's watching me through a crack in the door.

I hurry inside.

1908

Much time had passed and I had by now entirely renounced the community, the pariah that I was, subsisting on herbs and fruits and plants and creatures of the forest, crafting my potions from these using the skills I'd learned. I managed to retain my youthful appearance, or so I felt when I saw my reflection, and this made me happy, while also keeping my mind sharp and my body strong.

Still, I hadn't forgotten my sadness, my anger, and my hatred; the emotions that drove me remained unchanged and lived in me every day, growing stronger as I did.

When I did move about, I ensured I was hooded to hide my green eyes from those who would surely recognize me.

My sister's daughter had been blessed with her mother's looks and had many suitors in town. She led a simple life, instructed by her blue-eyed mother in the secret arts, her brother choosing a life of labour under the guidance of the town blacksmith.

The girl soon gave birth and was celebrated as a giver-of-life, even though this occurred out of wedlock. Her first child, however, did not have the gift of her mother's good looks. Soon after they were born, all agreed that her two youngest daughters would grow up to be beautiful ladies unlike the eldest.

As time passed, I wondered at the oldest, watching her withdraw, silent and dejected, ignored by her mother as I had been by mine. The younger girls wore pink and purple whereas the eldest was always clad in dark as if attempting to be unseen.

I knew well what it was to be alone.

1908

I care for all my daughters, love them all equally, want only their happiness, providing for them as I can.

I think them all beautiful. All of them.

1908

Maybe they don't care. Everyone gushing over my sisters, mother so proud of her beauties. And they adore the attention, even being so young. Always together like two cats, as I, the ugly sister, watches from the outside.

They never include me, never care, never want me with them. Why would they?

While others mock me and hurt me, my sisters shine like the sun, mother carefully doting on them. None came to my aid during my times of pain or after.

So, I sit apart and alone. Hide in the darkness. The darkness knows.

I doubt any would look for me if I disappeared. Why would they?

1908

Why does she insist on being alone?

Does she not know that I'd do anything for her? How much I love her?

She hides behind her darkness. How I wish she'd join me in the light.

I'll always help her, always be here for her, always love her.

1908

I saw her sadness and frustration and anger. I witnessed what others should have seen in me but were too self-absorbed to notice, even though I observed from afar. Her anguish, her pain. Does she want to respond, to avenge herself of those who abandoned her?

It was no surprise to me when she left them behind, fled into the forest, found a home there where none could hurt her, none could disappoint, none could mock.

She was young, but sufficiently aware of her environment to make her decision. Her home was a hovel but likely warm when a fire burned within it.

Had she been instructed in herbs and plants, elixirs and potions? Did she realize the power that existed in the forest around her?

I had no desire to invite her to live with me for I welcomed my solitude and was disinclined to draw any additional attention to myself such as this would have surely attracted. Still, I took mercy on the girl and didn't want her to lack. To that end, I regularly provided her with potions to keep her young, to restore her energies, labelled only as 'from a friend'.

When the time came, perhaps I would have an ally to call upon, one indebted to me.

1908

In the end, perhaps we're all alone. I would be away from those who hurt me, from those who neither love nor care. It was easy to leave. Better to be alone.

1908

Why? Why did she leave?
Does she not know that I love her?
She doesn't have to be alone.

27 – You Can't Pull Yourself Free?

Day quickly turns to night, the station wrapped in darkness. I stare out into the clear field, the skinny distant trees sharp under the bright moonlight. I ponder Room 1 and if I want to know what's going on inside. I don't dare ask anyone in town. Do I want to chance asking the guy at the library?

When do I reach out to Cindy again and how do I explain my stupidity?

Sigh. She seems so nice.

Are her eyes green? I don't think so.

Chris on the plane. That's who I'm thinking of. And someone at a café. What was her name? Christi, I think. Both with these amazing green eyes.

I'm sure Cindy's are blue; or at least not green. Not sure why I'm thinking of this now.

But most importantly, who is the girl hanging around the station? She's a long way from home if she lives in town.

I open the window for a brief bit of fresh air when I hear a click downstairs, as if a door is closing.

Maybe this is my chance to get a look at who's coming out of Room 1.

I quietly step outside and wait on the top landing for a moment, watching Room 1 but see no one.

I cautiously walk down the stairs looking all around me as I do.

I reach the ground but still there's no one near the hotel and no noises on the platform. I walk to look out onto the tracks and along the wall facing them.

Safely hidden, she watches. Waits in silence then scuttles across the platform and against the wall beneath the stairs. In the shadows. Alone. Her frail body is invisible in the dark. Her face had once been pretty and could have been beautiful, her life happy. She stares at the man near the tracks with anger in her eyes and sadness in her heart. The Station Master. She tries to scream but only a whisper comes from her mouth.

Is that a whisper behind me?

I turn but see no one on the platform and all around me is silent. White light from the lantern against the hotel wall fades as it flickers with the last of its fuel, eventually sputtering out entirely.

I slowly climb the stairs back to the apartment, my eyes looking down as I do, but see nothing and hear no other sounds or voices.

Closing the apartment door provides me a feeling of security like a warm blanket.

I exhale.

The shadows in my apartment don't carry a chill like those outside and are easier to ignore.

Time does move differently here, the clock above the door letting me know it's early evening, just after 6:00 and I have yet to eat lunch or dinner. Pulling some bread from the cupboard, meat and cheese from the cooler, I prepare two sandwiches, eating them faster than usual. A large glass of juice and cup of coffee later and my body feels like soft clay. My rubber legs carry me to the bed to lie down.

The last few days have taken their toll, though I can't pinpoint the reason why I'm exhausted. I've been here for long enough that my body and mind should have adapted though I can't recall exactly how long it's been.

Have too many restless nights worn me down?

My vision goes fuzzy, like wearing another person's glasses, or maybe it's a dream.

Falling on the bed and closing my weary eyes seems to shake the cobwebs. I slowly drift into a relaxed almost meditative state and slow my breathing which calms me.

I open my eyes to a light blue blur at the foot of my bed. The figure starts to take on a female form with dark hair.

I fumble for words and try to move but am unsuccessful on both counts.

Am I dreaming?

A beautiful song from a female voice trills softly in my ears as her body and face take shape. I'm unable to make out the words.

Striking blue eyes form on her face but they soothe rather than frighten me.

Who is she? How did she get in?

Am I still in my bed?

A sound from the platform like a girl crying snaps me back to reality as I sit up in bed, the woman from my dream no longer there. Throwing on my untied boots, I light the lantern at the top of the stairs outside my suite and another at the bottom facing the tracks when I reach the bottom, night now upon the station, though the air is clear. I search for something to use as a weapon but, finding nothing, quietly creep around the platform, scared of what I might find. I see no one on the main level nor outside the hotel as I move about in the silence.

The utility room door is locked. A look over my shoulder at Room 1's closed door which makes me shudder. I step down into the clearing. Nothing in either direction on this side of the station, the forest simultaneously dark and lit under the moonlight. I head back up the stone stairs past Room 1 and ahead to the tracks. The control room door is locked. A breeze rustles the branches in the forest across the tracks, though the air around me remains calm against my skin. My eyes focus on the thin trees, their skeletal branches softly clicking in the wind. And then all falls still and silent.

Movement on the platform behind me?

I turn, waiting for someone to come toward me around the corner of the building or up the stairs from the clearing. Out of Room 1.

No one comes.

From this distance, Room 1's door looks closed.

Another whisper but again I can't tell its origin, the voice too soft to identify. A girl's voice. Then it's gone. Or is this all my imagination?

The moon glows from behind the trees as I face the clearing.

Absolute silence.

Behind me, the lantern on the hotel wall comes on as if lit by an invisible hand, shadows swaying along its walls and in its corners.

I stand motionless, like a deer in the headlights who knows what's coming but can do nothing about it.

Walking back around to double-check the utility room and control room doors are locked, I return to stand in the middle of the platform, wary of what might be watching me.

Does someone live out here in the forest?

I shudder to think of it.

Train stations like this do exist outside of history books with their own mystique and secrets, their own nighttime creaks and groans. Shadows play on the walls, wind whistles through the branches.

I climb the stairs to my suite, seeking refuge for the night. I leave the lamp next to the control room lit as well as on the hotel wall in case I have reason to come outside again. I'll happily let their fuel burn out.

I close the apartment door behind me, leaving the station's mysteries on the other side.

I exhale, kicking off my boots.

Another noise downstairs, this time more distinct.

A young girl's voice crying for help, but in a whisper. I was just outside and saw no one so who is this?

I fling open the door.

No one's on the platform but I hear scuffling noises on the ground near the tracks. I run down the stairs two at a time. Reaching the edge of the platform, a young girl in a dirty dress appears to be stuck in the rails and wooden ties, though I can't see how nor make out her features. I never came this close to the rails before so must not have seen her.

A distant whistle announces a train which will not be stopping in New Brook West making the situation urgent.

I hop down, noticing the bottom of her purple dress caught on one of the spikes.

"How did you get here?" I try to smile. The whistle blows again, as I look back along the tracks.

"You can't pull yourself free?" I ask.

Does she shake her head? I can't tell with her dark hair hanging in front of her face.

"Let me try" I turn to the train's whistle, three shrieks confirming it won't be stopping.

"I'll cut it away where it's stuck and you can pull yourself free"

Does she nod? No time to care.

The train announces that its arrival is nearly upon us, my head turning once more in its direction for longer than I intend.

When I look back, the girl has vanished.

I try to stand but my pants have somehow entwined themselves onto a railway tie, its spikes, or another component of the track and it falls to me to now save myself. I quickly kick off my boots and pull my pants down and off, rolling toward the forest with my heart in my throat.

A second after I land, the train flies past without a whistle. With closed eyes I feel the wind as it passes, hear the clicking of the wheels on the rails.

I take many long breaths before I'm able to move.

I look behind me but the girl is nowhere.

Who is she and where had she come from?

And how did I get hooked onto the rails?

I catch my breath as my eyes search for her in the depths of the dark forest. There's only black space between the trees, no movement in the stillness, no sound breaks the silence.

The train disappears as it passes the minor decline in the distance and out of sight.

I stand and look onto the platform toward Room 1.

The **New Brook West** sign creaks above me.

28 – As He Sleeps

She sits cross-legged in the corner of the bedroom's darkness watching him sleep, her eyes unmoving, her hair hanging in from the sides hiding her narrow face. A slim wedge of moonlight shines into the suite cutting into the black. She's been here since he fell asleep, aware of his every breath, every movement, trying to read his thoughts, imagine his dreams. She shifts position, draws her knees up to her chest to stay warm, her gaze upon him as he sleeps.

29 – The Silver Box

I wake poorly rested in the bedroom's darkness, a single window open across the room chilling the air. I shiver thinking back to the previous evening's events and the girl on the tracks. She'd definitely been real. Had I seen her before? Who is she and where did she go? Was it a prank? An attempt to scare me off?

Should I be afraid? I am afraid.

Does she live in the forest?

Maybe I'll figure a way to ask if anyone knows of past accidents or close calls on the rails. Not many people I can talk to, though, without creating my own problems so this will be difficult.

Coffee brews while I try to remember, to think.

I'm getting used to the solitary tranquility here despite some strange goings-on, though I do have some questions.

Who are the travelers that stay in the hotel? I receive their names and arrival/departure times but never see them.

Is Room 1 reserved for special guests? Who come and go as they please?

I think of Cindy but she's surely managing fine and I don't want to seem crazy with my tales of the supernatural. And I have yet to summon the nerve to see her since our last meeting and the cell phone horror.

Are there equally odd occurrences around the school?

Through the window facing the village, a gentle rain falls on the station and in the clearing as dawn's light begins to my right. Exiting the apartment, I stand at the top of the stairs, my eyes drifting around the platform, then to the tracks.

No one that I can see, the forest across from the rail line still a black void.

A dark morning at the station.

Descending slowly, I stop to light a lamp at the bottom of the stairs and another on the hotel wall. I walk to the edge of the platform to look down on the tracks and in both directions along the line. With little wind, the rain hangs in the calm air.

Is someone behind me?

I thought I saw someone move. Guess not. I squint as I scan the platform but see no one.

Unlocking the control room, I enter without looking over my shoulder.

An early schedule waits for me on the printer indicating a 12:00 arrival with its departure forty-five minutes later. It's 7:30 now so I'll leave shortly to post this information on the board. I wonder if Dalton hangs around the plaza in the morning or if my previous encounter was by chance.

I return to my room to prepare for my walk, stopping for a moment to think on my situation. I have no money to speak of aside from the paltry sum in my bank account to keep it open and haven't inquired about any amounts payable to me should I decide to leave. Or how I go about leaving if it comes to that. I feel like I'm trapped on an island.

Perhaps today I'll seek out a tavern to see if its patrons are forthcoming with information. I'm hopeful there'll be one in the village considering Michael had given me what tasted like alcohol. Maybe I'll overhear conversations about the station or something to give me more insight into recent events.

I'd best throw on my station master jacket as I'll be acting in my official capacity, at least initially, though I'm unsure whether this will make people more or less likely to interact with me. Ensuring I lock the apartment door behind me, I check the utility room door, and head to town. The rain has passed, though the air remains cool and damp. A light breeze stirs the remaining leaves to rustle, breaking the silence. I cast a brief glance back at the tracks, wondering if I'm being watched as I leave but see no one at the quiet station.

The forest path is poorly lit and sombre, the ground dry. Even during the day, I feel the gloom in my bones, an eeriness in the air. The breeze heightens my unease because it makes it more difficult to identify sounds in the forest around me.

A branch snaps behind me. Then another.

Should I slow down or speed up? I'm not sure I do either as I continue moving forward.

The forest suddenly feels darker.

I stop.

Is someone following me? I slowly turn my head but see no one.

This is a normal forest, with cracklings and rustlings. Why would someone want to follow me?

I wait for something to move either beside or behind me but it never happens, the forest now silent.

I exhale and set out toward town. My footsteps make no sound in today's gloom.

When I happen into the clearing before the town gates, the lit lanterns at the opening are shrouded in haze, the moist air now chilling me even more. Once in the plaza, I orient myself with the church and cemetery quietly to my right, the fountain in the middle behind which four alleyways adjacent to the town hall feed off the square, the path to Michael's house on my left. I post the train's notice, as three women move about on errands the likes of which I can only guess. No sign of a tavern or bar of any kind in the square so I need to select one of the alleys quite randomly. I choose the one to the immediate left of the town hall building and make my way, vigilant of the unexpected.

The buildings on either side of the street are so similar as to appear carved from a single piece of stone; it's difficult to tell where one ends and the next begins, an occasional tunnel penetrating the smooth surface. Flickering candles in wall-mounted lanterns provide just enough light to cast shadows around me in the dismal street. Daylight has yet to shine its morning glow on New Brook West, the sun still low in the sky and behind grey clouds.

After walking the maze of streets and alleys for nearly twenty minutes without finding anything resembling a pub or tavern, I'm ready to give up and turn to find my way back to the station.

A familiar-looking young blonde green-eyed woman stands outside a shop on my left though I can't place her until she speaks.

"My manner was rude when last we met and for that I apologize" she smiles politely "Tina. From the library. You're the new Station Master"

"Yes. Hi, Tina"

She hurries into the building, emerging with a fabric pouch which she hands to me.

"Some fine herbal coffee as a welcome gift" she smiles, her bright green eyes mesmerizing me "It's also quite good as a cold beverage, sweetens the ordinary flavour of water. Better than the juice"

"Thanks very much" I reply.

"It's superior to the grounds left in your suite. I'll bring you some now and then, though it'll have to be our secret since this is meant for trade not for consumption" she pauses "Or you can stop by and visit me" she touches my arm.

Tina is taller than I remember and very thin which makes her appear more so, probably in her early twenties.

"Is this your shop?" I ask.

"Yes, it is. I prepare tea and coffee, both of which are blends handed down through generations of my family. It's quite popular, and in high demand they tell me"

"I look forward to it"

"I'll even leave some at the library in case you visit it again"

Ok. Odd, but ok.

"Wow. Uh, thanks, Tina"

She takes a single step back and curtsies.

"It's my pleasure, sir"

As I come around a corner which I assume will lead back to the station, I realize that the village is now behind me and that I've entered a clearing on the other side of town, the western entrance to New Brook West. The labyrinth of alleys is now between me as is the trail back to my apartment.

Large grey boulders are interspersed amongst the thick trunks, the ground a dark earth. Shades of green, white, and brown make the space open and bright though it feels as though the trees and rocks around me are the remnants of a once dense and prosperous environment. I wander toward a low rock as I contemplate how to find my way home to meet the train.

A branch snaps behind me, stopping me dead. Someone or something is there, and I freeze in the hopes of not being seen, cautious about being somewhere I'm not supposed to be. Turning slowly, I prepare myself for the worst as a gentle jingling sound like wind chimes sends a shiver down my spine. Then it's quiet again so I come full circle glancing around me as I do. I've got no idea where I am.

Nothing. No one. I'm alone.

I feel like I'm slogging through quicksand as I move forward.

A noise behind me like voices, as if coming from the trees themselves. Once more, my blood chills as I turn my head. Again: no one.

Taking one last look around the sparsely treed area, I decide it's time to leave this place, bidding farewell to the mysterious voices and haunting wind chimes.

I take a path which I hope will lead east and back to the village and walk this route which looks like so many others. The trail narrows and darkens as I walk, the foliage denser on both sides, a mixture of evergreens and deciduous, but my route is straighter than I'd expected, and I'm soon in the company of New Brook West's non-descript stone structures.

Back in town, confining gloom replaces the openness of the clearing, though the sun is now above the treetops and buildings, albeit behind the clouds. The silence in the streets is only occasionally broken by a voice inside a home or shop, or a creak of movement.

As if carried on the wind, a female voice speaks softly, almost sings, a single word, "Colden", but I can't see anyone.

In the road ahead of me, a woman in a light blue cloak appears then disappears down an alley or into a shop. The woman from my dream?

I walk toward where I saw her, assuming she must be the one to have spoken my name. On the ground outside a shop door, a silver rectangular box the size of a deck of playing cards, a raised black 'I' on the one side. I look up and down the street and at all the windows I can see before picking it up. As soon as it's in my hands a female voice sings softly from inside the shop with the open door.

I enter to a single lantern on the counter in front of the light blue-cloaked woman.

"Hello, Colden"

Her voice speaks the words beautifully as if sung by a bird.

I enter the shop. A hooded woman sits behind a counter.

"This must be yours" I hold it toward her.

"Thank you, Station Master" she says in her melodic tone.

Her voice hypnotizes me.

I set it down in front of her.

"I'd hoped you would come" she whispers.

"Yes…"

"You have much to learn" another musical air.

"Learn? About what?" I ask, still entranced by her voice "Who are you?"

She's either very tall or on a stool. I can't see a door at the back of the shop but it's dark so can't be sure. The faint lamp on the counter to her left provides minimal light, not enough to show me her face.

"Do I know you?" I ask.

"We are safe here"

"We are?" I stammer, my body glued to the spot "Where are we?"

"In the tree. We both are"

Is this the woman I'd dreamt of standing at the foot of my bed? Was she actually in the room with me when I woke during the night? It seemed so real but could only have been a dream.

But how did I dream of this exact woman who I'm seeing for the first time?

By now both my hands are on the cold counter, hers directly across from mine, her narrow feminine fingers visible beneath long narrow sleeves.

"What tree? Do you need help?" I say, unable to move.

Silence.

"What's in the box?" I ask.

"It's for you" she sings softly.

I inspect it closely, flip it over, twist it, push the 'I', but nothing happens. No opening for a key or any other small object to pop it open; I assume I'm looking at the top based on the marking on that side.

"And then look in the tree for the flowers" her soft voice sings, though I can't see her face or her lips beneath the hood.

"What tree?" Not this again.

Something in the forest at the station? Near the library? Somewhere I haven't been yet?

She stands up, taller than I expect, her cloak fastened with four buttons down the front, her fair skin shadowed but obviously bare above and below the clasps.

"Do you accept your fate?" she asks.

"Do I what?" my thoughts fumble at her question.

"You will have much to overcome" her gentle voice isn't threatening but soothing.

Still dazed, I try unsuccessfully to move.

She slides the silver box across the counter to me, taking a single step backwards. I stare down at it unsure what to do.

When I look up, she's no longer there and a familiar voice speaks behind me.

30 – The Nighttime Visitor

"Station Master"

Dalton's standing in the doorway; I collect myself as quickly as I can.

"Hi" is all I can muster.

My watch says 11:15.

Back over my shoulder, no sign of the woman I'd been speaking to, the room dark, the shelves empty.

The lamp on the counter is now extinguished.

"This is a long way from the station" he says leaning against the door frame.

"Yes. I went for a walk" I reply regaining my wits.

"We'd best head back to meet the train" Dalton grins.

"I'll see you there" I say.

He looks at me as if about to speak but simply turns and walks out.

Nothing around me shows any evidence of my recent conversation and I doubt it myself. Only the silver box remains on the counter.

I pocket it and exit in the direction of the plaza.

A few locals are in the town square, all doing their best to avoid me by changing direction and averting their eyes.

Hiking back to the station gives me a chance to mull over what just happened.

Who was that woman? And why give me this box that I can't open?

Or was that some kind of waking dream?

Dalton didn't seem to have seen anything out of the ordinary and maybe there was no reason he would have.

Fate. Riddles. Apparitions. Or is it all in my head, a series of disconnected hallucinations like a scrambled dream?

I'd never believed in the spirit-world or the supernatural but events are becoming difficult to explain.

The train's arrival and subsequent departure are as expected, the crew's skill and speed stunning. As before, Dalton stands to the side, though this time casting frequent glances toward the forest across the tracks, and even once at Room 1.

I look out over the tracks into the dark forest, seeing nothing but black between the trees but don't dare look at the hotel.

I need a short afternoon nap, night time sleep so hard to come by, then I can try to find Cindy's home, past the school. Maybe she knows something I don't. Climbing the steps slowly, I keep one eye on the hotel and the other on the door to my room. The air is deathly calm. The lack of any sun is starting to get to me, the clouds and mist creating a grey netherworld between day and night.

Opening the door, I notice what looks like the back of an old photograph on the floor just inside my room.

Is this the previous photo fallen on the ground?

Flipping it over sends a chill down my spine: a black and white photo of a man wearing a station master's jacket hanging by a noose from one of the rafters in my room, his arms limp at his sides. Although he's facing the photographer, his face is hidden by his drooping head, his chin touching his chest. This guy looks younger and slimmer than the fella in the other photo.

When was this taken? Who's the guy hanging?

And why is a second station master's death being shared with me now?

And who commemorates these events with a photo? Twice?

Hard to tell the age of the photo. The paper is time-worn but could be twenty or fifty or more years old.

Anger replaces fear and I run around the apartment ready to catch whoever left this for me. A single window is open across the room near the desk, to let in some fresh air during the day. But there's no one here. I flip the grim image face down on the coffee table.

A noise outside.

I hurry to the landing, immediately glancing down at Room 1 but see no one. Taking the stairs two at a time, I hit the platform, first staring into the large clearing, then across the tracks into the dark forest, but there's no one anywhere.

I spend a few seconds scanning the treeline, walking to look out in each direction from the building but there's no one anywhere.

What the hell?

I look up at the suite's open door then make my way back upstairs.

Locking the apartment door behind me, I walk to close the window and sit on the sofa.

Is someone breaking into my room? Is there another key that I don't know about? I look up at the ceiling and the clear window at its peak.

Who is getting in here and how are they doing it?

I pour a glass of juice, downing it in a single gulp.

This photo looks very real, a memory of a previous event.

My head feels dizzy. Too many restless nights have left me in a terrible state and I need to find a way to get some sleep. Ensuring all the windows are fastened, I draw the curtains and climb into bed with my clothes on. Crawling under the duvet, I'm soon overtaken by my fatigue.

My nap must have been longer than I'd expected because the time is now 5:30. I feel refreshed and lay in bed for a moment before pulling back the covers and deciding to change clothes. Out the window, darkness mixes with fog creating a dreary scene, though at least everything's quiet.

Two covered candles on the central post illuminate the suite.

I recall the photo and this rekindles my anxiety.

Starting a cup of coffee, I slowly move my eyes around the room before heading to the bathroom to brush my teeth. Despite my rest, a worn and weary face greets me in the mirror. Clearly, events are taking their toll. Shutting off the faucet, I try to shake off the bizarre incidents, convincing myself that there's a logical explanation, though I can't imagine what it would be.

I sit down to my coffee to relax a bit before venturing out into the damp veil shrouding the landscape. After a few sips I've calmed down, so go to the window facing across the tracks.

There's a figure in the haze just in front of the forest but it gradually fades into the treeline as soon as I spot it. Human or animal? The forest's mysterious resident?

I can't let shadows discourage me; I need answers or help of some kind and won't get either in this loft. I prepare a quick snack before putting on my light jacket over a t-shirt and head out into the gloom.

I don't want to wait any longer before going to see Cindy.

It's 6:30 p.m. as I step outside. An envelope is on the ground outside my door with a note inside: *'Guest Marcus Scow is in Room 3'*, suggesting he's already there. No instructions are included as to what I should do, if anything. I look across to the hotel but with no windows facing my suite and no light visible at the bottom of Room 3's door there's no way to tell if Mr. Scow currently occupies that room. Apparently, someone else stepped in to assist him with his accommodations, which suits me fine. My sincere wish is that this man will come and go without our paths crossing.

I run across the wet clearing and onto the dry dark trail, my lungs carrying me along the path to the right. The trail to the school, as with all others, is unlit and made even darker by the overhead foliage. I stop just before the clearing and walk quietly the remainder of the way.

The small school soon appears in the large glade, the wet grass shining under the grey sky, though the far away wood and stone accessories are difficult to see. Inside the building is dark. Best I leave this place.

A distant swing sways on its softly creaking chains.

Following the edge of the treeline to my left, I see a trail ahead as a narrow parting in the trees.

I turn to see how far I am from the path back to the station but it's tough to tell.

Is someone standing next to the school? A child?

A shiver runs down my spine as I quicken my steps toward the trail, hoping I'm not heading into a terrible place.

The corridor through the trees is a twisting one with no cabin or house or any lights visible from where I stand. There's really no place else to go and I figure I have farther to go back at this point so I press on. I cast a furtive glance back toward the empty clearing and see no one behind me.

I'm thankful for the quiet and calm.

It takes only a few seconds to reach a small white cabin with a red door and trim, hopefully Cindy's place. Nothing else is in the small dell. The right window is dark but the left shows light behind closed curtains so I decide to knock.

It's at least ten seconds before the door opens with Cindy on the other side wearing black tights and a short-sleeved red shirt.

"Hello" she says, surprise in her voice.

"Hi" I say softly.

"I don't get a lot of nighttime visitors" she smiles.

"I hope I didn't startle you"

And I hope you don't think I'm a jerk.

"A bit, but that's OK", she replies, "Come in"

I collect my thoughts.

"I'm really sorry about the other day" I say meekly. I'm not sure what else to say.

Apologies came easy for me.

"I sometimes get nervous talking to people, and...well... And I have no idea where that picture on my phone came from. That wasn't what I wanted to show you. The whole thing was stupid on my part. I'm so sorry"

My voice cracks as I speak.

"I'm not used to apologizing this soon" I smile timidly.

"It's OK" she closes the door behind me "I figured something had gone wrong but it still caught me off-guard. I'm not sure why I reacted the way I did. It just freaked me out"

"It was meant to be cute but was a bad idea from the start" I shake my head.

"It was a bit unusual" she frowns.

"I'm actually semi-charming" I say.

She giggles.

"You're different from everyone else here. It's not often that a guy like you comes along"

"Thanks. I think"

"You can be yourself around me. It'll be a breath of fresh air to have some comedy. And charm"

There's a sitting room to the left, an unlit room to the right, and a lit room ahead of me.

I take the liberty of removing my coat and hanging it on one of the hooks next to the door.

"I'm actually glad you came by" Cindy smiles, blushing.

No words come to me so I just smile in return.

"Do you drink tea or coffee? I've got both" we enter the kitchen.

"Coffee, please" I say quietly.

The teacher's cabin is a stark contrast to my dull earth tones with vivid colours throughout the room. The light blue table in the kitchen is surrounded by four pale green chairs, the walls a bright yellow, the cupboards bright white.

"It's so nice in here" I look around the room.

"The house is ok" she nods "Lotsa privacy way out here. And I'm near the school"

"One room schoolhouse?" I ask "Everyone in the same class?"

"Yes" she looks at me "But it's not as chaotic as I expected. The kids are really well-behaved and all know each other"

Cindy sets the water to boil.

"It's not a bad place" she says "Just takes some getting used to, I figure. I've not been here that long"

"Are people friendly with you?" I ask "They seem to avoid me entirely"

"I wouldn't say friendly" she says "They say 'hi' but that's about it. It's not like anyplace else I've been. I rarely go to town anymore. Most everything is delivered to me by a local guy"

"Same here" I nod "Probably for the best. I wouldn't know where to go anyway. Other than the market"

"It's nice around here and down by the river" she smiles "I try to see the positive"

"Good idea" I sit down at the table.

There's a window looking out the back but I can't make anything out in the dark.

"I've got a couple of silly questions" I say.

"Ok" she crosses her arms.

"I'm seeing things and I'm not sure what to think"

"What do you mean?" she sounds surprised yet part of me thinks she takes it as an offer to share.

"Do you ever catch glimpses of a figure in the fog?"

Her eyes get wide.

"The fog can really play its tricks" she says.

"Are these real or is someone following me?"

Cindy's eyes squint as though she's thinking.

"There are so many things I don't know about this place and don't really have anyone to ask" I go on.

"This doesn't sound the way I'd intended" I say "I'm not off to a good start"

"There are so many things wrong here. I sometimes feel like I should just pack up and leave" I add.

Her face turns sad.

"I think you know something that you aren't telling me" I say.

Her body falls back against the counter.

"We can't leave. We're on an island"

She Became Dark

We were young when we learned that we lived on an island. It felt so large to us with at least three other villages and what seemed like endless trails through the forest. There were no real beaches, the water much too cold, and the winds kept us away from the shore for the most part. The sun rarely shone because of the constant fog, and the fall and winter months were gloomy. But we always found ways to play in the hazy air and in the forest around us.

Sadly, some never found themselves among friends and became lost in their gloom. They were sad and lonely and cold. One girl was so unhappy that she became dark, the colour of her anguish.

She Fled

She fled the village, not seeking acceptance but to put an end to her anguish. Her solitude grew with each passing day as she found herself further and further from home. The ominous forest cast a dark cloud over her as she lived in constant fear of the unknown, the unseen, invisible eyes following her every move. On the darkest nights she found cover in darker places.

In New Brook East, her absence was immediately noted by her mother, her peers, her community, but their memories faded. If anyone came looking for her, they never found her.

Alone

In the end we're all alone, whether we want to believe it or not.
When you make a decision, when you face a challenge, when you need to be strong.
Do you not feel it? You should.
Wherever and whoever you are.
When it really matters, we're all alone, especially in the end.

31 - An island

We can't be on an island. I took the train here and trains need land; an underground tunnel is unthinkable.

"There's no way" I say, almost angrily.

"It's true" Cindy gestures as if offering me her truth.

"Did you know this when you arrived?" I ask

"Not right away" her head sags "I came through at night and never really paid attention because it was dark. I heard wind and occasionally water but thought nothing of it"

"I slept the entire journey by train" I recall.

Cindy squirrels up her face, crossing her arms.

"You've never left?" I ask.

"I've never tried"

"Why would they stop us from leaving?"

"I've always been too scared to even bring it up with anyone" her face shows a hunt of shame or guilt.

There are always ways, though in this case they might be extreme.

"Could you sneak onto a train leaving the station. It's gotta be pretty easy to hide in one of the cars or the engine or someplace"

"Do you really think we can just get on the train and say goodbye?" she implores "Are you ever alone when the train is in the station?"

I don't know. The strongmen load and unload the cargo then depart for town once finished. Dalton stands there but is he watching them or me?

"But why would they care if we left?" I shrug "I was told I could leave and there'd be a lump sum payment for me at that time"

"I don't know" Cindy says.

"Who's in charge in this village? Is there a mayor or a council? Is it Michael?" I think out loud.

"I don't know" her tone is frustrated.

Have I considered leaving? Would I? Even for just a few days? Somehow, I don't want to.

Cindy's right that it may not be that easy even though I can't imagine why not.

"So, walk along the tracks right behind a train", I say, "This way you could be sure that one won't come toward you and it's unlikely one would be behind you so quickly"

"It's been tried, or so I've heard. Unsuccessfully" she sighs.

"And it'd be a heck of a long walk over bad ground" I add. There has to be more at play here than we know. Or at least than I know. Why would these people bring us to their island only to keep us prisoner as legitimate workers? Why not let us leave?

Do I want to leave so soon? Sure, there'd been some unusual and creepy occurrences but maybe I'll figure them out and that'll be the end of that. And the people will surely come around in time and realize I'm a good guy. The island has some beautiful locations and the solitude and peace are unmatched.

Should I be sharing these thoughts with Cindy? Will this come back to haunt me? Will she communicate my comments to someone else?

Let's try this another way.

"Ever tried to find out what's going on here?" I ask.

"I wouldn't know who to ask" Cindy replies.

"Have you been to the library?"

"A couple of times but there's not much there that seems useful to me"

Not very helpful.

"Do you like it in West?" I ask her.

"I don't know. It's ok"

Yes, it's ok.

This is a paradise in so many ways with its natural beauty, its distance from so many bad memories, its promise for a fresh start, even if I'm the pariah to so many people. They might be fine folks once they get to know me.

And Cindy seems great.

But should I be careful trusting her so soon after meeting her?

Cindy. With a 'C'.

If the offer had been from her then she would have said so. Could she be a resident of New Brook West? Have some connection to the island that she hasn't shared? Is the island some sort of cult? I can't imagine this to all be part of an elaborate scam to get me here. I'm nobody.

She seems sweet and sincere, a lost soul like me. And a friend where I have few.

Hopefully I haven't put myself in a dangerous position by coming to New Brook West. And then by coming to Cindy's place in the middle of nowhere, in the darkest woods. I feel like Hansel in the witch's house.

Her words sound honest and genuine and I'm comfortable with her.

Cindy's clock says 9:30; I didn't realize I'd been here that long. Dark and murky awaits me outside. The walk back to the station won't get less eerie if I stay longer.

"Nighttime walks can be disconcerting. You could stay here tonight", she nods reading my mind.

The station is a whole mess of strange and I don't want to deal with Room 1 right now; it'll definitely be safer here or at least less unnerving. I think.

"Thanks", I reply with all the sincerity I can muster, unsure of such a swift invitation.

"On the couch, of course" she clarifies with a laugh.

"Of course" I smile.

The kettle whistles for the third time - on the previous occasions, Cindy had removed it from the stove.

"Is it time for some wine?" she asks with a smile.

"I think so" I reply, happy that I've made the decision to stay. And made the decision to trust Cindy.

She pours me a glass of red wine that smells and tastes of dark cherries, the perfect combination of sweet and tart.

"This is quite nice" I say.

"I offer only the best to my guests" she smiles.

"Your special guest" I nod.

She giggles and nods back.

"I promise…" I say.

Cindy tries to put on a serious face.

"…not to show you anymore pictures on my phone" I try to sound both apologetic and comical.

"In return" Cindy says "I promise not to poison your wine"

I pause for a second before realizing she's obviously joking.

"Very generous of you" I laugh.

She smiles back.

"Perhaps I'm the witch" she squints her eyes "In the creepy old cabin in the woods"

"And I've fallen into your trap" I widen my eyes "Whatever shall I do?"

"It's hopeless" she shakes her head "I've clearly outsmarted you and now hold you captive"

"What must I do to escape?" I continue our playful story.

"You must answer my riddle" she sneers.

She stares at me for a moment in silence.

"What is your riddle, oh wicked one?"

She pauses as if thinking.

"I don't know any" she breaks into laughter "I must rely on my wickedness to keep you"

I laugh along with her.

"Perhaps I'll offer you a poison pastry" she passes me a box filled with baked treats.

"I was kinda wondering when you'd share these" I say "I've been staring at them since I arrived"

I take what appears to be a buttertart and she grabs a chocolate cookie.

"This wine is tasty" she sips her glass.

"Delicious" I smile at her.

She tells me stories about her students and her experiences teaching; how she is generally ignored in town, polite and friendly as she tries to be; some amusing encounters with other villagers.

I tell the lighter side of my arrival and my interactions with Michael's comically stoic personality; my apprehension about what might be asked of me mechanically; joke about jumping at every sound at the station.

"It's a lot more comfortable in the living room" Cindy says.

It must be later than it feels though I can't be sure how late that is.

"Lead the way" I stand.

"I'll meet you there" she says "It's through that door. Try not to get lost"

"I'll be careful" I smile.

I walk to the large window, wine in hand, parting the curtains slightly to look outside. Night is upon us and little is visible, the trees surrounding the house calm and quiet.

I walk to sit at the far end of the couch facing the window, surveying the room. The teacher's home is even more sparsely decorated than the station, though I can't decide if this surprises me or not.

It's warm in this room, comfortable and relaxing.

Cindy enters the room wearing short dark spandex shorts below her tight red top.

"I hope you don't mind I slipped into something more comfortable" she smiles.

"It's perfect" I smile.

Wow.

She sets the wine bottle down on the table in front of me, sits at the opposite end of the couch, leans back and swings her bare feet up into my lap extending her legs, the purple toenail polish standing out sharply against her fair skin.

"This is more like it" she smiles.

My eyes scan from her delicate feet along her smooth calves to her thighs and to her shorts where I swear she's removed her underwear.

"Can I offer you anything else" she smiles.

"Everything's perfect" I say bringing my right hand up to softly caress the top of her feet then her calves.

"Hmmm" she whispers closing her eyes.

My hands continue to gently slide over the smooth skin on her calves and feet, my fingers occasionally tickling the bottom of her foot which makes her giggle without pulling them away.

Her breathing is now coming in long slow gasps.

"It's nice to have someone to enjoy a glass of wine with" she whispers opening her eyes.

"A toast" I say bringing my glass toward hers "To beautiful evenings"

"To beautiful evenings" she smiles as our glasses clink.

I sip my wine as I notice she's not wearing a bra, her hard nipples pointing out from behind her shirt. As her legs part slightly, I see she's definitely not wearing underwear either.

My hands have now moved to run along the top of her feet to just above her knees.

"Rrrrrr" she purrs again, opening her mouth slightly.

She sips her wine then reaches out to try to place it on the table.

"Let me help you with that" I say leaning in to take her glass, setting it down.

"Thank you" she swings her legs off my lap, leaning forward to kiss me.

My right hand puts my glass down, coming up to gently touch her cheek. She places her hands on my thighs as her face presses into mine. My right forearm casually swings back and forth across her breast and nipple, my left resting on her upper thigh's smooth skin.

My hand moves over her leg which has swung out wide to open her legs fully, her left still straight out on the floor.

Cindy moans softly, moving even closer to me.

My fingers play with her ear, my arm now rubbing her left nipple.

Her hands are both moving up my legs.

I take her bottom lip in my teeth, softly pulling it away from her.

She inhales with a gasp as her right hand reaches my growing erection.

She unbuttons the top button of my pants and unzips them. My excited dick bounces out. Her right thumb rubs along the shaft and tip sending a shiver down my spine.

I begin to stand lifting her up from under her arms as I do. She moves with me, sliding her hands under my shirt as she does as my pants fall to the ground.

My hands move along her sides outside her shirt.

"Mmmm" she moans looking up at me, our mouths still kissing.

I turn her around and move aside her hair to kiss the back and sides of her neck and then gently nibble around her ear.

"Ohhhh" she gasps throwing her head back.

She takes my right hand and pulls it around to her right breast.

My palm cups her boob as my fingers play with her nipple.

"Ohhhh" another moans.

I gently pinch her nipple.

"Ohhhhhhh" she leans her head back, looking up at me.

She steps forward and away from me, lifting her shirt up over her head revealing perfect small breasts with very perky pink nipples.

She takes my hands in hers and guides me into the bedroom as I kick off my pants and socks and she sits on the bed.

I pull my shirt up and off as I kneel in front of her kissing her while my hands caress her smooth skin.

She leans forward to nibble my left ear sending a shiver down my back.

My hands cup her boobs while my thumbs move back and forth over her nipples.

"You're teasing me" she smiles.

She leans back, pulling down her shorts as she does.

I lean in to kiss her stomach and around her navel then move my mouth lower to kiss her inner thighs bringing them to between her legs as I taste her femininity with my tongue.

I do this for several seconds as she moans and gasps.

"Ohhhh. Yesssss" she moans.

I move in close to her as I pull her body to the edge of the bed running my fingers between her legs before slowly sliding inside her.

"Ohhhhhhhh" she whispers like she's inhaling.

My thrusts are slow at first as she welcomes me inside her. I push deeper with each thrust, until I've gone as far as I can into her.

She stops breathing for a second as my full length is now inside her. I pause for a second enjoying the feeling of filling her completely.

I slowly pull back then slide all the way forward again.

Her legs are spread apart as wide as possible as I look over her beautiful naked body.

I'm pushing slowly then faster then slowly again as she gasps every time I do.

"Huhn, huhn, huhn…"

I put my hands under her legs and raise them until her feet are at my eye level. More thrusting as I pace myself to hold off as long as I can.

I stop for just a second before picking up speed then slow back down when I'm about to lose control.

Her eyes close and her mouth opens.

"Oh, yes, oh yesssssssssss, ohhhhhhhhhhhhhhhhhhhh"

She lets out a long loud moan as her back arches off the bed, her hands gripping at the sheets.

Her body stiffens as her muscles all seem to flex simultaneously.

"Nnnnnnnnnnn" she moans through gritted teeth.

I look down between her legs at her shaking body, then at her legs which are pointing straight up, her toes curled.

Oh, I love this part and it nearly makes me come. Her orgasm is absolutely beautiful.

"Huh, huh, huh…" she gasps as her body goes limp.

Her body twitches as I try to move my dick inside her tight grip.

She reaches her right hand down to pull me out of her. Her hand starts stroking me, the intensity building in me so quickly and I know I won't last much longer. My erection is aching.

"Oh" I'm almost there.

I feel the pulse as I explode, throwing my head back to howl, my passions released like bullets from a gun.

"Ohhhhhhhhh" my release has my breath gasping, before her hand lets me go and I look down at her.

"Wow" she smiles.

"Wow" I gasp "That was amazing"

She's still smiling.

"I made a mess" I say looking at her naked body.

"That was powerful" she replies touching her cheek then licking her finger "I liked it"

"I'll get you a towel" I stand up.

"Then come lie next to me" she says as I walk to the bathroom.

I come back to the room with a cloth where Cindy is still lying on the bed naked, legs open.

"Wow" I stop and stare at her beautiful body.

She looks at me and smiles.

"I might just stand here and stare at you naked" I say looking at her stunning form, her body still quivering.

"Throw me the towel first?" she smiles putting her hands behind her head.

"Wow" I say again, adjusting myself as desire stirs in me again.

"Come kiss me" she says propping herself up on her elbows.

I throw her the towel and walk over to kiss her soft lips and caress her smooth skin as I do.

"Mmmmm" she purrs.

We crawl under the covers and I curl up behind her pulling her naked body to mine, with my arm wrapped around her, my hand on her stomach.

I'm sure I fall asleep with a smile.

She enters silently, walks around the room, watches as they sleep. Moving around the bed, she runs her finger along his arm, then the
woman's cheek, causing both to shiver beneath the covers, their bodies shifting slightly in response to her touch. She waits, her eyes glued to the lovers in their bed, so peaceful, so vulnerable. She climbs into the window frame crunching her knees up to her chest to fit herself into the small space from which she watches them in silence.

I sleep in later than usual, or at least it feels that way. 8:00 according to the clock above the bedroom door. My nights at the train station are early ones, often due to unusual nighttime and early morning noises so I usually rise at dawn. Part of me doesn't want to get out of bed, preferring to hide from everything for just a bit longer.

Cindy's body has found its way out from under the covers, her smooth fair naked skin stirring my thoughts as she lay on her back, her bare breasts and legs fully exposed, the sheet only concealing her waist area.

I'd had no expectations of such an amazing evening or of such a stunning body beneath her clothes. And her intense passion.

She'd had such a beautiful orgasm with her moans, her body shaking and stiffening, and her desire to satisfy me afterwards. My explosion came from deep inside me and it was so hot to see her smiling and happy. By now I was nearly hard again as my thoughts build up in me as I look at her perfectly smooth skin and shapely body, the sheets beginning to slide off her completely and revealing her beautiful naked body. A partial smile seems to form on her lips as if sensing my thoughts.

I walk over to her side of the bed and reach down to softly caress her stomach, my fingers barely touching her skin. I gently move them down, pushing the sheet aside, sliding them slowly along her skin to her right breast then back down.

"Mmmm" she whispers as her legs spread, though without opening her eyes, her nipples perking at my touch. I run my finger between her legs, barely touching the soft skin, her body twitching.

I draw a circle around her pink nipple before withdrawing my hand and exiting the room.

We'd had an immediate connection, both mentally and physically.

I hate the idea of putting on the same clothes I'd worn yesterday so, for the moment, exit the room naked.

Cindy continues the slow gentle breathing of sleep so I leave her to make my way to the kitchen after pausing briefly to pull the blanket over her.

I'm already looking forward to our next evening together.

As I'm making my way to the door, I notice a photo collage on the wall on Cindy's side of the bed that I'd not seen earlier. A beautiful slim brunette in a tight orange dress; barefoot in a short orange skirt and white leather jacket; nude on her knees; and lying on the floor. She has large breasts and striking jet-black eyes, smiling in each photo.

Wow. Who is she? Cindy has no other photos that I'd seen. Interesting. Maybe I'll ask about it later. Or maybe not.

I set the kettle to boil, trying to keep quiet so as to enjoy the peace of the moment and to let Cindy sleep. I do need to get to the station soon to ensure that I check the clunky printer. My situation will not improve if I let my responsibilities slide.

I wonder how much thought or energy I should expend focusing on the station's oddities. During the day, Room 1 is less daunting. I've thought about asking Dalton for some insight but always decide against it in his presence.

I turn off the stove before the whistle blows, preparing myself a cup of coffee. Hearing no sound from the bedroom, I grab a random muffin from the closed box on the counter, sitting down at the table. It seems like a good time to read a newspaper but doubt that this amenity exists in New Brook West. I turn the chair to look out the back window offering a pleasant view of the forest, a thin fog hanging between the cabin and the trees behind the house. I don't see a path leading into the woods beyond the kitchen door but any trail could be obscured by the fog.

There's no wind in the trees outside. I spot what looks like a bird on a low branch but can't be sure; in any case, it makes no sound.

I notice a grey streak on my arm as if I've brushed against something but can't imagine what.

My mind drifts back to thoughts of Cindy's naked body fully exposed on top of the bed.

A few minutes pass before I hear her bare feet pad onto the kitchen floor.

"Good morning" she says cheerfully, wearing only a long shirt. She raises herself up onto her toes, crossing her left foot over her right, as she places a hand on the counter for balance.

"Hi", I look up and smile, "I didn't want to wake you, so…"

"Thank you" she smiles back, perhaps realizing I'm not sure about what to say next.

She walks over and bends down to kiss me, looking down between my legs, as my right hand gently grabs her to hold her near me.

"Did you sleep well?" she asks with a smile.

I notice a grey line on her cheek similar to the mark on my arm.

"I think so", I reply, "No unusual noises which is nice. A luxury that's not guaranteed at the station"

"I'm glad you didn't run off before I woke up" she's still smiling.

"I made coffee" I say quietly.

The brightly-coloured kitchen feels like a fresh breeze; blue and green and yellow lifting my spirits. I'd spent a wonderful night with a beautiful woman and have no desire to leave just yet. Nor did she seem to want me to go. I dismiss any notions of her involvement in my circumstances or my invitation to the island.

She's standing by the counter drinking her coffee, my chair now turned back into the room. She steps forward and brings a chair to sit across from me, smiling as she looks in my direction, playfully tugging at the bottom of her shirt that doesn't reach her knees.

"I'm glad I stayed" I smile, unsure of what to say or how to say it.

"So am I" her smile is beautiful, her tone sincere, which relaxes me.

She places her bare feet up on the seat of my chair, crossing them at the ankles and takes another sip, holding her cup with both hands, her shirt riding up so her bare ass is sitting on the chair and a quick glance tells me she's not wearing underwear.

"I'm still naked" I say looking in her eyes.

"And happy" she says without taking her eyes off mine and shifting in her chair making me look to see her shirt riding up showing her smoothness all the way to her belly button.

"I was thinking of you" I say, hoping this isn't too forward while trying not to stare between her legs.

"Mmmm" she smiles, her right foot sliding forward between my legs.

Her foot touches me as her toes move against my growing erection.

"Are you still thinking about me?" she says.

"Very much" I gasp.

I reach to set my coffee cup on the table then softly slide my hands along her calves moving up to her thighs, then under to caress the backs of her thighs.

"Mmmmm" she says putting her cup on the table "This is a nice start to the day"

"You're incredible" I either whisper or think.

Her legs begin to spread as my hands move toward her, her bare foot rubbing my erection.

I want to reach out and tear off her shirt so I can see her breasts.

She makes a purring sound as my hands move over her inner thighs. Her body twitches.

"You look like you need some help with that" she looks down.

"Can you help?"

"I can" she says licking her upper lip "Yummy"

I hope she's planning what I think she is. I shift my position slightly in the chair.

She giggles.

Suddenly, a musical sound echoes from Cindy's bedroom where my pants are.

She jumps, her feet falling to the floor, hands pulling down her shirt.

"What's that?" she asks with a startled expression.

"My cell phone ring tone" I say equally stunned.

Making my way to retrieve it is not a pleasant walk. Are we being watched? Who has the ability to call me out here?

It stops ringing as soon as I pick it up. No missed calls. But one message:

"*You slept well last night*"

Ice water fills my veins.

"What was it?" Cindy surprises me.

"More coffee, please" my voice wavers.

I look at the dead cell phone in my hands.

Coffee.

How did my phone ring and who sent that message? Or am I hallucinating or dreaming?

"What was that?" the fear is evident in Cindy's voice.

"I don't know" I lie "My phone was dead when I picked it up"

What is real here? Cindy is very real as is her house, right? My apartment feels real. The chill in the foggy air definitely feels real.

And my fear. My fear is real.

Now what?

I walk to the table.

"Why did you come to New Brook West?" I ask her after I've sat down, hopeful that this line of conversation will help me understand her and confirm that we're in this together.

"What do you mean?" she stands in the doorway to the living room.

Realizing my tone sounds aggressive, I soften it to take on an inquisitive manner.

"Do you know who offered you the job or why? Why did you say yes?"

Cindy takes a deep breath as if considering what to say. "I had a horrible life with a terrible husband" she drops her shoulders "I'd lost all my friends, had no income of my own. One day an envelope slid under the front door and, though I never saw who left it, I opened it immediately"

She pauses.

"It offered me a chance to start over. To get away from where I was, who I'd become, a scared little girl, a sad and lonely person." Her eyes fill with tears.

"I didn't think to question the offer" she adds composing herself.

"I'm sorry" I look for more words but none come.

"What brought you here?" she crosses her arms.

I'm ashamed of my question in light of her answer.

"I'm just trying to find my home" I say feebly, keeping my answer short.

"Not all that different from me, is it?" she wipes her eyes.

A brief pause ensues before we share details of our respective offer, noting the similarities. Our jobs here seem to be no-strings-attached deals, fresh starts for two people in need, mysterious yet exciting opportunities. Cindy was born in South Africa. Her father a doctor, her mother a teacher in a community just outside Cape Town. She married at 22 to a wealthy merchant who seemed to her a dream come true. He ran a company specializing in electronics. Carver had moved from the Netherlands in his teens, was handsome, kind, and well-liked. Until they were married.

He cut her off from the outside world, required she stay at home, kept her from her friends, belittled her, rained emotional and verbal abuse on her, and controlled her every action all while maintaining his honourable public persona. This happened over time, so smoothly that she barely noticed. Cindy gradually withered, her life no longer her own until she received the peculiar offer. She grabbed her necessities and ran without looking back.

"I got the 'ending' without the 'happy' in my marriage" she smirks "And now look where I am" she adds dejectedly.

"You're with me" I smile.

"You know what I mean" her face brightens.

"Is it so bad here?" I try to see it from the other side "Could this get better in time?"

"It could" she squirrels up her face "I hope"

"There are so many beautiful things here" I extend my arms as I look around.

"I know" she says.

"I know" I say "We don't know where we are, can't always explain events, and are shunned by the locals"

I pause.

"But we are together" I smile.

"Together" she nods without smiling.

It's just after 8:30 a.m. though outside looks more like 8:30 pm, the thicker haze enveloping the cabin has settled into the small clearing like a silver blanket. Outside, I hear no sound, no breeze, and no movements. The calm makes me uneasy as it has since my arrival. There's undoubtedly a tale to tell in New Brook West; gloom hanging like the fog. Isolation breeds dejection but so does fear. It's difficult to tell if the residents are afraid or simply reflect the dreary mood of their environment. Where are the other communities? How big is the island?

A bird caws in the distance, breaking my reflection.

"I'm going to shower" Cindy says, walking slowly out of the kitchen.

"I didn't mean to bring this up. I didn't know your circumstances. I'm sorry" I say.

"It's ok" she smiles, going into the bathroom.

"You're beautiful when you smile" I say.

"What about when I don't?" she squints.

"You're beautiful then too" I smile.

She blushes and leaves the room.

I take my coffee to the front living room window, pull on my underwear and pants, and sit in an ordinary yet surprisingly comfortable wooden chair.

Outside, gloom reigns as a hazy mesh screen blocks out the sun, obstructing all but the faintest light. Slender limbs on the bare trees extend like arms from bony demons. A shadow appears in the haze, a spectre moving in the calm shadows, its figure visible through the intense fog, like movement behind a curtain. Is someone or something watching the cabin?

Cindy's steps behind me wake me from my mental nightmare; she's wearing a green long-sleeved shirt and black jeans, her hair in a pony tail, fear in her eyes.

I want to run to comfort her, to hold her and keep her safe. I stand.

A blank envelope on the floor just inside the front door causes my heart to jump. Running to the window, I see no one so carefully approach it.

A single piece of paper is inside it: *'Meet me at the Grey Stone'*

32 - The Grey Stone

"Is that some kind of tavern?" I ask.

"Something like that"

"Maybe whoever wrote this knows something" I say.

Cindy sighs, perhaps reluctant to bring another stranger into her midst.

"Does it say when we should meet this person?"

"I assume it's right away" I look at the paper.

I remember the printer.

"I'd better hustle back to the station and check the arrivals" I stammer out my words "I'll be right back"

"Ok" she sits.

"Thank you" I say to which she exhales a quiet "See you soon"

I literally run to the train station, ignoring any of the forest's sounds.

There's no one waiting for me on the platform or the benches facing the tracks. I chance a glance at Room 1 but look away quickly when the door appears closed.

The ancient machine in the control room contains a piece of paper with a single line: 'No Trains on 16 October', the default message indicating no stops in New Brook West for that day.

A jog up the stairs to my suite to do a quick clothing change and then out for another run back to Cindy's through the green and brown forest.

By the time we leave her place, it's nearly 10:30, dreariness still hanging around her cottage, the area damp. Cindy knows where to go so I follow, next to her but not too much so, sensing her discontent with the situation. The fog makes me regret not having a superior outer garment. We walk without a word between us. Our route takes us behind her cabin and along a wide fast-flowing river, scattered boulders interrupting its course though not affecting its speed.

Cindy stops.

"What's up?" I ask.

Cindy stares down at a green plant with groups of white flowers at the ends of the many stems branching off from its central stalk.

"What's that?"

"Conium maculatum" she says.

"It's what?"

"Poison hemlock" she explains "It's deadly"

"How do you know that?" I ask.

"Herbalism" she replies starting off along the path without looking back at me.

We swing back into the trees, the forest thinner here than anywhere else I'd been, many here evergreen. She leads the way amongst the timbers along a narrow dirt track devoid of grass or brush, the fog sparser improving visibility.

Is the library off to the right?

"I think this is the best way from my place" she says looking back, her expression sad.

I catch up to walk as close beside her as the terrain will allow.

The existence of a bar in New Brook West seems almost medieval and I'm unable to conjure an image of what to expect.

Then we arrive in the clearing I'd visited previously.

Cindy walks toward two large rocks that look very similar to all the others and walks between them, beckoning me to follow. We descend a dirt staircase, pushing open the thick but light wood door, bells like wind chimes ringing as we enter The Grey Stone.

Small lanterns set on long stone tables illuminate the circular room. The dirt and rock ceiling high above is supported by crossbeams connecting a tall, thick, central metal pole to shorter ones against the walls. A large round cast iron furnace in the center of the room radiates heat but very little light due to its narrow grill openings. A stone bench along the outside wall encircles the room, wood tables set in front of these. Another circular bench on the inside of the tables provides further seating; gaps between the rock slabs and wooden tables allow for movement.

It does feel like an ancient world or a fantasy novel, this subterranean tavern. I'm glad I had no expectations because they certainly wouldn't have matched our current location.

The lanterns throughout do little to illuminate the space, as if the room consumes the light. Two inner crescent-shaped counters lit by round lanterns create a serving space for the dispensing of beverages. Six women in skirts stand between them.

Groups of men talk at the tables smiling, even laughing on occasion, though not as heartily as at other pubs I'd been to. At one table two women sit with a group talking, but otherwise it's only men, perhaps fifty patrons in total. Cindy and I look around the room but don't spot anyone sitting by themselves to hopefully identify whoever it is we're meeting; surely someone sitting alone would attract a great deal of attention here. We locate a small corner near the entrance and casually make our way, sitting side by side facing into the room.

A young woman waves at me from across the room, looking very much like Tina my 'coffee girl'; Cindy appears not to notice. I contemplate whether or not to wave back when...

"We don't see the Station Master down here very often"

I nearly jump out of my chair as a young woman now stands at my immediate left. She looks to be nineteen or twenty with bright blue eyes, short almost white blonde hair, a prettiness stolen by hardship and fatigue.

"Hi" is all I can think to say.

"What can I getcha?" she says with a partial smile.

I pause, staring at her, trying to conjure the right words.

"How about some wine?" she suggests.

"Yes, please" I smile as sincerely as I can, forgetting how early it is.

"'Please?'" she smirks, "Aren't you the charmer"

"Do you have anything else today?" Cindy asks.

"Only that and the grog, Miss Stayla" she replies.

"I'll have the wine as well then. Please"

"Coming right up"

How does she know Cindy? Or me? Maybe our identities are common knowledge.

Our waitress makes her way to the crescent counters hobbling slightly, favouring her left leg.

It seems inevitable that we'll receive alcohol of some kind though I can't guess what to expect nor how I'll pay. The Grey Stone is an unusual combination of darkness and light, warmth and cold. Upon closer examination I realize it's elliptical rather than round creating an illusion and making it difficult to discern its exact size. I wonder how this place was built partially underground and why this location was chosen.

As I'm about to ask Cindy about being recognized by our server…

"Hello Colden"

The voice to my left makes me jump since no one had been there a second ago.

"Hello…" is again all I can muster as a reply.

"It is good to see you again" she sings in a delicate bird-like voice. Wearing a light-blue cloak, her fair-skinned face and arms striking against it, her bare legs visible below the cloak which ends just below her knees. Her dark hair is an anomaly that I've rarely seen since my arrival; and with blue eyes to match. Yet no one else notices her.

"What…" I begin.

She whispers something I don't hear.

"From the shop. You gave me the box" I say sliding a little to my right and away. Her musical voice sounds distant, like a faraway song.

Cindy takes a sip of her drink, seemingly not hearing the conversation I'm having.

"Who are you?" I lean toward her.

"She cannot hear us or see me" she says answering my question.

"Why not? Who are you?"

"People are not who they seem"

My mouth opens but no sound comes out.

She continues before I have the chance to speak.

"Many have come before you but I fear none will come after" she sings.

"Many of who?" I ask quietly.

"First find yourself in the tree" she lilts "This is where you must start"

"The tree?"

What tree?

"You are at the end" she says.

"The end of what?"

Around me and in the bar, time moves in slow-motion. Who is this woman? And what is she trying to tell me?

"I will contact you again, Colden"

"Do you know who…"

For a moment, everything stops.

Her figure fades as if she'd never been there. Did that actually happen? Or is someone smoking something in here that made me see it?

"Hello" a cloaked young woman approaches, the same one who'd just spoken to me, quietly sitting on the bench across from us. Her voice is soft with the same musical lilt.

Cindy sees her immediately.

"I cannot stay long" she says.

"Who…"

"You're both in danger" she interrupts me "From each other"

"What do you mean?" Cindy asks softly.

No one else seems to notice her.

"There have been many Station Masters and many Teachers. Your destinies have brought you here to be the last"

"Last what?" I stammer.

"I will try to help you complete what must be done" the musical tone returns to her voice.

Cindy and I look at each other.

"Beware your destinies" she says "Beware the prophecy"

"What?" Cindy's voice lowers.

"You will see me again. I just wanted to meet you both together" and she disappears like smoke exhaled from a cigarette.

The room suddenly seems darker and smaller, the light dimmer. I look at Cindy whose face appears transformed by the shadows cast on it. Can we trust anyone? Can I trust anyone?

And why had she spoken to me privately? I decide to keep that to myself for the moment, assuming Cindy hadn't noticed

"What was that?" Cindy asks as I take a sip of the smooth wine our server just deposited in front of us.

Words elude me so I say nothing.

"Now what?" she says after a pause.

Back to her place or to the station by myself? While the thought of walking solo through the shadowy trees is unnerving, it also feels right to be alone.

Alone.

I can only imagine what waits outside in the cold darkness.

"Is anything wrong?" Cindy's voice expresses both concern and sadness.

"It's OK" I assure her "Now what?"

Cindy giggles.

"I just asked that"

I sigh.

"We can head back to my place" she says.

"Might look odd if we leave right after ordering a drink" I suggest.

I try to think things out as we sip our beverages for which we're assured no payment is required.

My watch says 2:30.

Have we really been here that long?

She enters the room, noting the two forms cuddled together, contentment on their faces. Her noiseless footsteps pace from the woman's side around the base of the bed to the man's side without making a sound, her feet soft against the wood floor. She pulls down the top blanket which has been hiked up to their necks causing them both to shiver, the woman tugging back the quilt, the man pulling the woman closer. She walks around to his side of the bed, brushes his cheek with her hand. She smiles at him, walks to the corner, and crouches down, her thin legs drawn up to her face, her eyes behind her hair looking up over her knees as she watches them sleep.

An odd dream wakes me or perhaps a tree branch blown into an outside wall of the house startled me from my sleep. Cindy's body releases my arm as I lay on my back, drawing the sheets and blanket up to my face. The window to my right is fully open, which hadn't been the case when I'd fallen asleep. There's nothing in the room's darkness, no sound, no movement. No breeze outside to disturb the quiet. Are we alone?

Do I really want to get up?

Without leaving the bed, I look around the room; I see nothing but feel no bolder than before. My body shivers in the cool air. I wait, listening, in the silence.

A movement to my right startles me from my trance but it's just a flutter of air near the open window.

Deciding that I won't be able to sleep with things as they are, I slowly swing my legs over the side of the bed. A light smell of licorice wafts toward me from outside the window.

Soft beams of moonlight peek through the clouds, casting a glow on Cindy's right cheek as she sleeps in silence. Watching this, it occurs to me that my cheek feels as though it's been touched, my hand reaching up to it, my fingers coming away with the slightest charcoal grey colour. Again.

I close the window.

1908

My sister had often been suspected of possessing the ability to commune with demons, to destroy them, to protect herself from them, even to summon them, though I'd never seen her invoke this talent. Had she learned this from our mother? Perhaps this was just another ability which she hid from me, to prevent me from possessing true command. Some had even suggested that father had seduced her using devilish charms, though I doubted this because father was a moron; mother held the true power.

For years, I'd attempted to devise how I might be avenged of those who had wished me ill, who had done me harm, who had ignored my pleas, who left me to suffer alone. Mostly, I wished to shame my family for their wickedness toward me in my time of torment and despair. But also to reach my full potential, to rise above my present station and know true power.

An unexpected knock at the door.

Perhaps it's chance intervening, perhaps serendipity, or just fate finally taking its course.

Who would dare visit me here?

I wait for a moment and hear nothing further outside, eventually opening the door onto a tall man dressed entirely in black.

He says nothing, merely stands smiling, his eyes piercing mine, and I freeze as if in a trance.

"Hello" I say.

"Hello" he replies in the smoothest voice I'd ever heard "It's a pleasure to finally meet you"

The aura around his person entrances me, his eyes, his smile, his body, weaken all my strength to resist anything he asks. I want this man in my home, want him near me.

"Yes" I nod "Come in"

He slowly steps inside, walks to the back of the room, then spins effortlessly to look at me. Still, he doesn't say a word.

I close the door and merely stare at him, this beautiful man.

"Yes" he squints his eyes and I melt.

With just a word, the charisma sweeps over me, like a soft whisper in my ear, like a gentle touch on my neck, like a kiss.

"I love your green eyes" he says.

I gasp.

"I would like to share something with you" he holds out his right hand which I take in my left "A prophecy"

Standing in front of him, this close to him is nearly too much for me.

He shares his prophecy and what I will come to pass – my dreams fulfilled, the power I'd always imagined. How he would give this to me I don't know or ask, as bewitched as I am by his words, his magnetism.

I know I agree, how could I not.

Again, he takes my hand in his as a delightful heat flows through my body. My breasts swell, my limbs tingle, my sex burns. How long has it been since I'd felt a man's touch against my skin, felt hands pass across my nipples, felt masculinity penetrate and fill me, the wet embrace between my legs.

My shoes drop from my feet, my clothes fall to the floor, as I tremble before him, my mind dizzy with arousal, my blood hot with passion. His lips come down to meet mine, again sending his fiery heat through my body. He holds my lower lip in his teeth as he pulls away to stand tall once more.

My mouth can resist this man's allure no more and I reach out to take his penis into my grip, a feeling both soft as silk and hard as steel. Bringing my lips over the tip of his member, I hear him groan. This feels so perfect, him in my mouth, the taste of his masculinity, my lips gliding up and down the full length of his shaft. By now he has grown so thick that I can barely fit him entirely in my mouth, though I fight to do so, eager to devour his sex.

As my lips strain over this massive erection, he begins to emit low growls, like a beast. His response to my passion arouses in me something I've never felt before. My nipples beg to be touched and pinched, my hot sex pleads for attention, for a man to fill me with all his ferocity and fury. The burning dampness between my legs, my sex is in pain as it waits. Aching. I've never felt this type of arousal before. It hurts not to have him inside me.

Before I know it, I'm straddling his body as I lower myself onto his throbbing erection. Ohh.

But it's much too big.

He grins and growls, the snarl of a beast as my arousal grows even more.

Slowly, I let it enter me and gasp. Ohhh. My body shakes as his hands come up to grab my waist. Then a bit further, stretching me in beautiful pain. I've stopped breathing, as stars flash in my eyes. Until I have him deep inside me, as deep as he'll go. I've never felt this full, this complete; he's huge, filling me with intense sensation, heat, energy. The pleasure I feel washes over me like a blanket of heat, as I struggle to keep from screaming.

Oh. Ohhhh. Bliss

His hands reach up and cup my sensitive breasts, squeezing my hard nipples in his fingers. I'm shaking. My body, which had been rising and falling on top of him to caress my insides, stops to sit on his full girth as my insides stretch again in wonderful pain. Oh no. My body's going to explode.

I feel a scream build in me, a sensation I can't resist. The pleasure I feel is so complete as to be painful. I might lose consciousness.

Then his hips thrust up and my body explodes.

"Huhhhhhhhhhhhh" I moan, the heat coming in waves, my toes curling beneath me, my hands grabbing his body, my head thrown back like a wild animal.

"Huhhhhhhhhhhhhhhh" I moan loudly as all my muscles tense at the same time.

Oh, no. Oh, yes. Ecstasy flows through my veins. Oh my God. My body fills with the most beautiful energy then releases it. I struggle not to lose consciousness.

"Ohhhhh"

My body's on fire, my sex burning in pleasure, my heart racing.

My quivering thighs sit back on his legs. My head hangs forward.

He reaches up and grabs my breasts, squeezing my sensitive nipples sending a shock through me like a bolt of lightning.

He gives one final thrust and I feel his erection pulsing within me, throbbing and the energy flows through me again, this time more powerful than the last.

"Huhhhhhhhhhhhh" I try to stifle my ecstasy.

My whole body shakes and spasms ferociously as his hands hold me in place.

"Grrrrrrrrrrrrrrrrrrr" he growls like a predator baring its teeth.

To feel this energy, this pleasure twice, is nearly too much for my trembling body to contain. I gasp with my eyes closed; where am I?

My body is so hot, so sensitive. I feel where my legs touch his, where his hands touch my waist. Ohhh.

Then I sigh and my entire body relaxes. I go limp, overwhelmed by the sensation, the perfection of the moment, still feeling him inside me, softly throbbing. This is more than bliss.

I exhale.

My lungs gasp long breaths as I collapse on top of him, no longer able to sit upright. My body and legs shake uncontrollably until I lose consciousness.

I wake, naked, to the feeling of deepest satisfaction, of unearthly contentment, of breathtaking bliss, my body perfectly warm. My eyes open and I know a smile graces my lips.

He stands near the door looking down at my naked form.

I want to pull him to me, to have him next to me, to feel his heat run through me.

He mutters words I don't understand and disappears out the door.

My exhausted body shakes then passes out again, unable to control the energy flowing through me.

1908

The black-walled cave, the stone smooth and shiny, the floor a dark red, the candles spread around the room creating the sensation of motion.

He looks different now than when last I'd seen him. I care not about this man's identity only to bathe in his power and his aura I'm barefoot and naked on my knees in front of him, my green eyes looking up at him.

White eyes stare down from his shadowed face as he whispers words I don't understand. He reaches to hand me a page that appears to have been torn from a larger book, a page with names I recognize, and years, and lines. This is the prophecy he'd told me. I take it in my hand and grip it tightly. I understand and smile.

Naked as I am, I lean forward from my knees and open my mouth to seal our contract. He looks down at me and shakes his head, his sharp white eyes piercing me. I close mine and my mind wanders. When I open them, I'm barefoot and naked kneeling on my cabin floor with the page in my hand.

33 – The island's historical

Cindy and I exchange early goodbyes the next morning, me with work to do around the station that day, her teaching at the school, our tired eyes going our separate ways. I kiss her with all my passions as she rises up on the toes of her bare feet to meet my lips with her soft mouth, to press her body against mine through her thin shirt. I hold her for as long as I can, until I slowly let her back down.

"Goodbye" I say.

"Until later" she says.

I nod.

Grabbing a cookie she'd baked the day before, I open the front door onto the clear air surrounding her house, the forest still dark.

I make my way around the back to avoid walking past the school first thing in the morning.

I welcome the peaceful walk along the river, the sun's glow just beginning to appear over the trees in the east as I leave. I'd barely slept the previous evening buried beneath the blanket like a cowardly warrior behind a shield.

Events were getting difficult to explain.

Who was the blue-cloaked woman at the Grey Stone? Why did she speak to me alone? Why had she invited us?

Is there reason for me to worry about who I trust more than I have so far?

My sombre march through the village's dry earth streets takes me past sparsely-placed lanterns providing little light, as if they prefer it dark. I meet no one walking through town, only occasionally passing a lit window, my route gloomy despite the clear air and sky.

Reaching the plaza, I look for a moment at the church on my left, the square empty in front of me.

Is someone there who might share information? Provide guidance? Surely a man of God, whichever god, will do me no harm.

Reaching the thick wooden entry, a piece even sturdier than at Michael's house, I decide it's more respectful to knock than to simply walk in. It's just before 8:00 and I wonder if I'll be welcome.

The sound of shuffling feet approaches followed by a scuffling on the other side of the door.

"Good morning" a hoarse voice speaks as if I were expected, his accent thick.

"Hi. I'm the new Station Master"

"Yes"

The priest?

"Can I speak to you for a moment, please" my request sounds plaintive. What do I have to ask this person?

The heavy door swings open quietly and closes smoothly behind me. Once inside, I wonder why I've come, what I can ask, what he might say.

The small square foyer is lit by a single covered candle on each of the three walls a short distance above me, the area itself dim. The stone interior creates a cavernous air, the ceiling a mixture of rock and mortar held in place by thick wooden beams. Ahead of me, I see what appears to be a large open area, but it's difficult to tell for sure as it's entirely bereft of light. The man who opened the door is as tall as me, slightly larger, much older, clad in a grey cloth top with black pants of the same material, and gloves which he is currently removing. He's the first person I've met to not be clean-shaven, a grey goatee matching the colour of his full head of short cropped hair. It feels as though we're standing in a mausoleum: the stale air, the darkness, the tranquility.

"Do you think I can help you?" he has yet to move from directly in front of me.

I hope so.

"Do you work here?" I ask.

"Yes"

"Like a caretaker?"

His expressionless face, wrinkled by age, betrays no emotion; his body is between mine and the dark room, my back nearly touching the door. I see no windows.

"How old is this building?" I ask, hopeful that this will initiate a dialogue.

"These halls were built here many years ago" he turns, looking around the grim vestibule "Though most lived in New Brook East at that time. It has served the community for generations"

I want to ask questions about New Brook West but now feel this may not be the right time, place, or person.

I prepare to excuse myself when he enters the room in front of us. I consider turning and leaving but follow, unsure of where we're headed. Lanterns come on along four walls in the enormous white octagonal chamber, a vertical black strip hanging from ceiling to floor against the walls without candles. I can't see the ceiling which surprises me as from outside the roof is low. The floor is plain grey stone, smoothed to perfection like the train station's platform. The black fabric on alternating walls between those with lit candles creates a mesmerizing effect.

"There are no more leaders in spiritual matters" he stops without turning back to face me, his voice echoing in the hall.

Auditorium style seating in the form of circular stone benches carved into the floor descends to a round central platform at the room's low point. Two lanterns snuff out as if by the man's suggestion, the result a shadowy solemn space with a funereal atmosphere.

We're at the topmost level. I stare down to the bottom of the room, imagining a preacher addressing the congregation. The low center area lacks a podium which seems odd to me unless this is a place for prayer rather than sermon. A voice in the chamber would have certainly been ominous, matching the sombre interior which is completely lacking in ornaments.

"Is this building a church?"

"It was when there was a God"

"What do you mean?" I ask, confused by his reply.

"When they worshipped the great Yotun"

I attempt to craft a respectful yet meaningful reply.

"They don't anymore?" I say, a stupid question.

He pauses for a moment before facing me, speaking as if to an audience.

"The will of a Supreme Being is no match for the human condition. Evil will always outweigh good. So it was here. Wicked men made decisions and preyed on the vulnerable. All that we were shattered like broken glass"

What can I possibly say to that?

"Your predecessors were most unfortunate" his voice takes on a distant tone "Many took their own lives, mad from their deeds; others succumbed to a worse fate"

"My predecessors?" I say. Or do I just think it?

I follow him around the perimeter of the room and then out a door, finding myself alone outside in the plaza. Should I knock again? Probably not. No one's around so there's no explanation required on my part.

Best to just head back to the station.

It's a quiet walk back with no one waiting for me on the platform when I arrive. Perhaps a calm morning awaits, filled with tranquil solitude.

I'd heard no previous mention of Yotun, or any God for that matter, since my arrival. Maybe he was no longer the Supreme Being worshipped by the locals. I won't feel comfortable making future inquiries of the 'caretaker'. I wonder at his role and what purpose the church serves if not to worship.

Back at the station, I see the white cat sitting at the base of the stairs up to the apartment, as if waiting for me.

"Whatcha think, kitty?" I approach him slowly "Anything strange happen here while I was gone?"

"Mrrow" he replies, green eyes looking up at me.

"This is an unusual place" I smile at him.

He turns and walks toward the tracks, heading around the corner and out of sight.

Could he be responsible for any of the nighttime noises I've been hearing?

He seems friendly without really being friendly. But that's ok with me.

I grab a snack, check the printer, and sit down to devise a plan for the day ahead.

Just after 10:00 means the streets and alleys will be sparsely peopled, residents either working in the community fields, shopping, or minding their shops. Perfect time to slink through town and hope for the best.

Putting on a dark green t-shirt, black pants, and a dark brown jacket it's time to creep into the village with absolutely no plan beyond that. Locking the door behind me and gliding past Room 1, I proceed down the path into the forest as stealthily as possible, hopeful I'm not being watched.

The walk through the forest is mercifully quiet, the clearing, and the village bathed in silence. The unoccupied streets allow me privacy, my body staying near to the alley walls. The town, now beneath cloudy skies, holds its usual gloom. I see no one but feel eyes on me.

Through the blue fields with their scattered islands of trees, past the cabins, I arrive at the colossus that is the library, as though I've been drawn here as it was not my intent to visit it. It feels like I'm at the edge of the world. The wind whistles around the stone and wood structure, the dark ocean laps at the shore below, the sky grimmer out here than in town.

Outside the library, unlit lanterns welcome me, my eyes combing the area for locals, my steps quick but not too much so. Is that a child in the distance to my left on the black rocks again? What is she doing there? Ducking into the building, my relief soars when the interior appears empty. Closing the door gently behind me, I scan the upper level, then the lower, confirming my solitude. The library is my sanctuary, a haven like a port in a storm.

Alone. I exhale.

Brian pops up from behind his counter catching me off-guard, though I am relieved to see him, hopeful that he can enlighten me in even the smallest way, and I welcome the company in the dark grey cave that is the library.

"Hello, friend" he smiles.

"Hi" I look around nervously.

"You ok?"

"I've got some questions, if you have a moment, please" I say, unsure of how to present my inquiries.

The obvious question is: why was I chosen to receive the letter? But also, why were those before me selected? The dark cloud hanging over those answers weighs heavily on me and I feel compelled to figure out how I landed here. It could help me decide between staying and leaving.
Someone knows.

But I can't just blurt this out to Brian considering his reaction to this topic on my previous visit.

"How did this island come to be settled?" seems a good starting point.

"You might find something interesting among the island's historical" he points to a large dark red chest against the wall to his left.

The lid opens easily on this ancient piece, the interior divided down the middle. On the left are dark coloured books of varying thicknesses, spine up but without writing to identify their content. On the right, thinner black volumes, also spine up and also lacking labels.

I grab a handful from the left, curious of the potential answers within.

Out the back window, the ocean's dark water reminds me of New Brook West's isolation. Clouds the colour of ash roll past the building making me happy to be inside, among the stone walls, the gothic artwork, and the unfamiliar literature. The dull colours and lack of ornamentation give the library a colder atmosphere, yet also a feeling of serenity.

Sitting at an oval table down the stairs from the main desk, I grab the top volume, pushing the others aside.

'MARIS' in the top left corner in a white block font.

At the top of the page:

'AS CHRONICLED BY ELIAS MARIS'

Beneath this, a single sentence:

'Arrived at last. Our new life begins'

A few more pages in tells me that this isn't the volume with the answers.

The tomes are all similarly bound yet must have been written at different times by different people.

I select the thinnest of them, hoping I won't have to comb through all of them to find something useful. This one has the name 'CLOVINSTON' across the top in a different script than MARIS's volume. I look back at the desk, Brian nowhere in sight to answer any additional questions, if he has any intention of doing so.

The first few pages provide a description of the area, the people that had come, and introduce a man named Jasper Colvin who was fleeing the mainland with some like-minded individuals. Colvin's group set up on the east side of the island, Maris' party having established themselves on the south coast, neither mentioning the other's presence. This went back to the

1700s, the island described as a land of opportunity with farming and fishing potential, a favourable climate, and a sufficiently secluded location to deter visitors or attract travelers. It's as if they'd found their way here completely by chance, seizing the moment to create a new community with fresh beginnings. Jasper Colvin changed his name to Caspar Clovin, for reasons never mentioned.

Clovin's community, Clovinston, started with a population of about one hundred and fifty, comprised of families and individuals of varied backgrounds, who in time mixed with residents from other island villages. The nearest had been founded by Max Brooks, as mentioned in the 'BROOKS' volume, with a smaller faction of about seventy, a mixture of families and single men, made up of craftsmen and skilled labourers. They lived a spartan existence, subsisting on garden produce and fish; there had yet to be any mention of livestock or wild game. Brooks' company had not yet christened their colony with a name; the writer referred to it simply as 'Brooks'.

In Clovinston, some adopted the town's name as their own surname, perhaps as an expression of community solidarity. Other last names were noted on occasion but never with any detail or family history. Never any mention of island natives, the land presumably uninhabited previous to the arrival of the outsiders. The Colvin and Brooks parties came from mainland England; Maris' origins aren't noted.

The reading wears me out, tires my eyes.

A noise behind me breaks my concentration, breaks the silence. I look back without getting up but no one's there; Brian in the distance reads at his desk.

I haven't heard anyone enter.

I sit still and wait for any more noises but none come.

Silence returns to the library.

The cold stone walls do nothing to lift my spirits. The plain brown bookshelves are perfectly spaced to conceal intruders, dark corners ideal hiding places for watchful eyes. The massive rear window emphasizes the infinite black water beneath the gloomy sky giving me a chill, making my heart stop if I stare for too long. Visiting the library is an experience all its own.

My right arm touches a piece of paper next to me with a scribbled drawing. Had I brought it with me? I can't recall. I take the sheet cautiously, too nervous to look around.

A child's art drawn in sharp penciled lines shows an empty noose hanging from the side of what looks like the schoolhouse. Black and grey lines against a bright white sheet create a ghostly image. Childlike and clumsy but deliberate as if the artist chose this style. Have I seen this before? Who's the artist? Rissa or Sam? Skitt or Nix?

I think of calling out their names but something keeps me from speaking. My hands grip the drawing as if keeping it from being snatched from me; my body is unable to move and I've even stopped breathing. Did someone leave this for me, someone who is now watching my reaction?

Slowly my head turns to the entrance area on my left but I see no one. I then summon the courage to look behind me, and again no one.

The room is cool and quiet and all is calm. I'm alone.

Have a couple of the lamps gone out?

I wait in silence for something that never happens.

Setting the paper down I look in Brian's direction trying to decide whether or not to get up.

"Everything OK, chum?" he asks when our gazes meet.

"Sure" I reply staying seated "Did someone else come in when I was caught up in my reading?"

He shakes his head.

Ok.

I stare at the entry area as if someone were about to enter. Waiting.

But no one does.

Silence. No sound from Brian or anywhere else in the library. I stop like an animal hiding from a predator. The walls to my right loom dismal and dreary, the balustrade above hangs overhead like someone looking down on me. The quiet among the shelves sends a shiver down my spine as though tiny fingers tickle the hairs on the back of my neck. My heart's beating echoes in my ears. I hold my breath, but nothing. A shiver begins at my neck and runs down my spine.

I inhale and exhale deeply.

I stand to take in the area around me in the dull and dark library, to free myself from the confines of the chair and desk.

"Could I trouble you for a cup of coffee, please, to settle my nerves?" I stop in front of his desk.

Brian points to a small table near his desk with a closed-top metal pitcher next to a canister; no milk or sugar in sight. I quietly pour a cup, taking in the silence around me. Out the back window, clouds hang near the island, the sky clear beyond them, the view mesmerizing.

I turn to stare on the library's entrance, the large vestibule lit by a single lamp.

Has someone come in that Brian didn't see or doesn't want to identify?

No way to know.

Mid-October, or is it already November?

Darkness comes earlier every day, the grey soupy air as thick as ever, the gloom as pervasive as a bad mood. No sign of snow which is positive, though the dampness in the air keeps the temperature reliably cool, a chill that gets into my bones, freezing me from the inside out. There's still the occasional pleasant day that allows for walking or sitting outside and I wonder what weather the coming days and weeks will bring. How is winter in New Brook West?

If I stare long enough into a corner or down an aisle, I'm certain that I spot a shadowy form or a bony figure. Are these real? I try to avoid looking but my mind can't ignore these sinister hiding places as my eyes move around despite my fear.

I want a voice to speak, to emerge from the unknown, to tell me it's not real, that there's nothing here, no one but me.

The walk back to my desk takes an eternity, each step like quicksand beneath my feet, my eyes focused on my destination and not the dark empty spaces. The room is hypnotizing, the silence oppressive, the chill under my skin. But the warm coffee soothes me and for that I'm grateful.

My empty chair welcomes me back, the books and drawing where I'd left them, my head dizzier but at the same time relaxed. Pushing the texts I've read to my left, I bring the 'BARKMAN' volume in front of me. Slightly slimmer than the others, the cover as austere as the previous ones, the community or founder's name in bold capital letters in the bottom right corner.

This story proceeds as expected. Kalvin Barkman had brought a small group comprised of his four wives and their extended families as well as twenty other individuals in the hopes of carrying on their way of life away from more prevailing customs. Barkman brought livestock, though little information elaborated on this subject or his settlement's location. According to the author, his company soon dispersed, beginning in 1802, some to Clovinston, others to nearby villages. They weren't greeted with open arms by the sounds of it but details are few and the chronicling just ends.

A succession of books mentions unfamiliar family names.

Brian has vanished to wherever he goes. Looking around me, I see no one else in the building.

All is calm and quiet and dimly lit until I pick up a smell that I can't place, followed by the soft riffling of paper in the silence, a delicate noise as if done with a gentle hand through large pages. I can't place the sound's origin nor can I determine for certain what makes this noise. I wait but all soon returns to quiet. Has someone been here this whole time? Are they near me? Upstairs waiting to come down or leap over the railing?

Should I say something?

I gently push back my chair, turning back to look down the aisles at the same time but of course no one's there, my jittery nerves again getting the better of me. I try to shake the cobwebs from my head, casting a look at the librarian's empty post.

Could someone else be here? The sound I'd heard was so quiet.

I slowly pull the chair forward, ready to resume reading.

I think I spot a quick dark movement to my right, then nothing; only unmoving bookshelves against the wall, an empty space between myself and them. An oblivious Brian has returned to his post, my voice disinclined to yell out anything to make him question my sanity, even though I'm beginning to doubt it myself.

The old clock against the library's back wall says 4:45, night having overtaken day in that direction, the view to the left out the upper-level window only slightly brighter.

The histories are interesting but not particularly insightful with respect to the present community or the train station.

I open the last thin book with illegible lettering on the cover. 'VON STELA' on the first page. Leafing through the text, it seems that it will proceed the same way as the others with descriptions of individuals within this family and their marriages, births, and deaths, the writer's thoughts on the island. A few pages in, the author mentions Martin and Katya von Stela, presumably the patriarch and matriarch of this family, and their daughters Rebecca and Christina Nicole and then Rebecca's children Hannah and Caelyn. The name Rebecca sounds familiar but is common enough so I dismiss it. Nothing to keep reading here.

I wake with my head on the desk, no memory of having fallen asleep. My mind is groggy and it takes me a moment to realize where I am and another to remember why. A single white light shines toward me as if from outside the huge window behind the empty desk, and then it's gone and all returns to black.

The stone walls, the wooden shelving, and the cool air combine to create a foreboding mood. I go from being blinded by light to recovering in obscurity. Darkness is in every corner and down every aisle around me as my eyes slowly adjust, the silence unnerving.

Am I alone? I hear nothing and see no one.

A single candle to my left in the direction of the entrance is lit by an invisible hand.

I slowly turn my head but no one's there.

I sit still and silent, waiting. My breathing slows.

There's movement to my right and then nothing.

I don't dare look. My body won't move. My eyes are locked on the desk ahead of me. It looks like a huge sacrificial altar in an underground cavern, a dark slab waiting for a wicked preacher to conduct a demonic rite. Out the back window, I see stars over the ocean, though they provide little light to the library's interior.

Outside the wind is whistling along the building.

Are the books still on the table with me; I can't look. I feel my arms shivering; did it get cold in here?

My breathing is so soft I can barely hear it.

Is someone or something in here with me? Behind me?

I still haven't moved, unsure what I should do.

I want to call for help but fear making a sound. I wait. Silence fills the empty chamber.

I want to hide but I'm petrified.

I wait to hear a noise, anything to break the quiet. My eyes nervously look side to side without moving my head and see nothing in the gathering shadows around the table.

I expect a touch on the back of my neck, on my cheek, on my ear.

But nothing comes.

A shiver starts at my neck, slowly moving down my back. Then another as the air cools even more.

My fear is now real.

What's moving? Is it me?

Wordless whispers come to my ears and then all goes silent.

I wake with my head on the pile of books, my arms hanging limply at my sides.

The lantern on my right remains lit providing just enough light to outline my reading area, the glow fading beyond the edges of the table. Only darkness ahead and behind, the other lamps now extinguished. Brian is gone from his desk and there's no sound anywhere in the library. The stillness unnerves me, its sinister calm concealing the shadows and voices I know lurk within it.

What had brought on the dream, if that's what it was?

The volumes I removed from the chest are neatly stacked forming my hard pillow, no other items on the desk. The drawing is nowhere to be seen. Had I dreamt it too?

Should I return the books to their storage or quietly exit the library? I'll never see my way to the chest so decide for the latter and abandon the histories. Carefully putting on my jacket, I slowly move in the direction of the exit, crossing the infinite lobby and entryway in the dark, too scared to look back. Pulling open the large heavy door I step out into the salty damp air. No one's visible in any direction in the evening's grey fog the moon a white orb behind the thin haze in the sky to my right.

Have I been here all day?

I don't dare look out onto the black rocks where I'd seen the girl when I arrived earlier.

I plod away from the building with heavy steps, away from the wind which blowing salty air onto the island. My head hangs low as I walk back across the blue fields to the edge of town and into the welcoming arms of the town's stone buildings.

Slinking quietly through the village's dark streets my eyes avoid every unlit alley, every dark corner. All is quiet and I don't see another soul. The air is clear in town, stars visible overhead around the small clouds passing across the sky, the moon not visible from where I am amongst the structures. It's cool and crisp and I'm glad I'm wearing a jacket, light as it is.

I wonder what residents are doing inside their homes at this time. Avoiding unlit alleys and dark corners?

I pass through the gates and onto the forest path back to the station without being seen, or so I think.

I'm so deeply entrenched in my thoughts that I'm several minutes in before I realize that I'm being followed. Short but steady steps, soft against the dirt trail, keep pace with my longer stride, their sound now apparent.

I stop and so do they. I wait for a moment in silence and all is quiet.

When I start walking again, the gentle shuffling resumes, steps that never get any closer. I pause once more, mustering the courage to look back but of course there's no one.

Evening's darkness obscures my view, the soft shambling behind me my only company. I try to look behind as I'm moving but hear no sound when I do this and find myself drifting toward the trees so don't continue. I haven't seen anyone recently who would have followed, unless whoever watched me at the library now pursues me home.

I consider turning and running back the way I'd come to catch my follower but am unsure if I want to surprise this person. Catch this person? Find out their identity? Perhaps this is best unknown.

The moon momentarily penetrates the treetops' sparse brown leaves and thin limbs casting its glow around me. The light that does make it through sharpens the foliage at ground level, shadows bouncing between the spindly trees.

I stop and wait in silence.

In the faint light, I look in all directions, even face back along the trail for several seconds. There's no sound. No movement. No one. My breathing slows in the cool air, the chill yet to breach my clothing. I wait hoping I'll hear nothing and see no one.

How long have I been stopped?

The station is close, only a minute or so away, though I also fear what might await me there. Still my pursuer seems in no hurry to overtake me if they're still behind me.

I look to my left and notice a single light blue flower a short distance off the path. Colour is scarce in these woods so this is a striking find. I'm tempted to pick it but there's so much that could go wrong with that decision; I glance around me to see if someone's watching me look at it.

No one.

The quiet calm is unnerving. I expect a voice, a rustling in the trees, the snapping of a branch. But nothing comes.

The moon disappears behind a large cloud as darkness returns, leaving me alone in the silent forest. I continue my walk, now as softly as possible, without slowing too much. There's no longer any sound behind me nor on either side so I maintain my pace for the remainder of the journey.

Emerging into the clearing's light fog, I exhale deeply, picking up speed. There's nothing out of the ordinary as I reach the platform casting a quick glance at Room 1's closed door. No sights or sounds break the gloom at the station. Two lamps illuminate the area and will remain lit.

I face the tracks and stare out into the black that is the forest before turning and walking back toward the stairs up to my suite.

The train's whistle blows loudly as if it's right next to me.

That's because I've stepped right to the edge of the platform and nearly into its path.

I fall to my knees as the railcars whip past me blowing through my hair.

I lean back and wait in this position for the train to pass.

Holy shit.

Then it's gone and I'm left staring straight ahead.

I slowly get to my feet, my body shaking. Has someone been on the platform with me? Is someone still watching me?

I turn and see nothing and no one on the platform. My imagination? An illusion in the flickering light?

The air is calm.

I exhale deeply followed by a few more long breaths.

Beginning the laboured climb to my room, I ignore the hotel entirely. My body quivers up the stairs slowly and softly, my eyes wide, my head searching for explanations. I'm not sure how long it takes me to reach the top landing but I'm grateful for the silence around me. Once inside, I close the door firmly behind me, lighting several of my many candles which flicker and dance beneath the glass and as naked flames. My dizzy mind wants to collapse like a statue that is too heavy at the top.

That can't have been real. Impossible.

Mentally exhausted from my visit to the church and library, emotionally spent from my eerie walk through the forest, anxious from what nearly happened on the platform. I undress fully, climb into bed, confident I'll be too tired for the day's events to keep me from sleeping.

Pulling back the sheets, there's a handwritten note on my pillow.

"Sweet dreams"

Sorrow

Her solitude became sorrow.

34 - Evan and Ness

I sleep like a stone, free of dreams, waking to a quiet hazy station.

The note must be from Cindy; a sweet gesture. I must have forgotten to lock the door.

The apartment is dark by my bed, the faintest of light across the room through the window overlooking the tracks. Reaching the kitchen, I'm reminded that my stock of coffee needs replenishing so perhaps a visit to Tina on my way to check the board.

I depart at 9:00 wearing the station master jacket over a long-sleeved green shirt and black cargo pants, having verified on the clunky printer that no trains will stop in New Brook West today.

My walk through the forest is a quiet one, the previous day's eeriness at the library drifting through my mind but not unnerving me. A thin fog has settled into the path and sits on top of the low bushes at my sides. I try to recall the blue flower's location but can't find it or any like it. Or any other colourful blooms at all in the murky air. It had been a pretty sight last night, a pin of blue on a dark canvas.

I step into the glade surrounding the community, the area hazy, the forest around me dark but quiet, the lit lanterns standing sentry. The sun has risen just above the trees to my right, hidden behind overcast skies. New Brook West looks cold and grey and I find myself wishing someone would pick a bunch of light blue flowers and place them in the plaza.

Nothing colourful decorates the town square to brighten the day and lift my mood. A twenty-something young man sits on the church steps looking in my direction.

His eyes fix on me on my walk over to him as I realize that I recognize this person.

"Hi, I'm Colden, the new station master" I stop in front of him "Didn't I see you in town a few days back?"

"Yes, you did. When you were looking for Caprice" he replies casually.

This guy doesn't seem afraid of me so I sit down next to him.

"Don't you work in the fields?" I ask.

"Never have. I was like you" he says without any change in expression, his eyes contemplating the thin pencil in his left hand.

"Like me?"

"Well, not exactly like you" he smirks.

"Are you waiting for someone?" I ask him.

"Have you met Rebecca?" he ignores my question, looking up at me as he speaks.

"Who?"

The name sounds familiar.

"She's not to be trusted" he scowls.

In his right hand, he holds a charcoal drawing.

The style closely mimics my own, a gothic female in beautiful grey shades, the only colour in her bright red eyes and ankle-high boots.

"Is that Rebecca?" I ask.

"Nah"

Evan stares at the drawing for a moment.

"She's a trickster casting curses and deceptions. One day she's caught and killed, but her daughter escapes"

"What happens to the daughter?"

"I didn't get that far. In another drawing, maybe"

"That doesn't sound like it'd be very popular art here but I think it's awesome" I say, marveling at the background story's fairytale.

He stares out at the man filling the lanterns marking the path out of town.

"What does 'awesome' mean?" he asks.

"It means 'really good'" I reply with a smile.

"Oh" he folds the drawing, placing it in his left pocket "Awesome"

After a moment he faces me.

"Do you believe that some people are born evil, that it's their destiny?" he looks me in the eyes.

"I think the choices we make determine who we are and where we go;

external forces always play a role but in the end it's up to each of us to decide who we want to be. Never destiny or fate"

"External forces…" he turns his head to his left, looking into the clearing.

"What's your name?" I ask him.

"Evan. Evan Pertwee"

His name also sounds familiar.

"Do you live in New Brook West?" I look at him.

"I used to live in East"

I didn't think anyone lived there anymore"

"I lived off that way for a bit, too" he points at the path to the station as he continues to look into the distance as if waiting for someone.

"Where do you live now?"

"In West"

"Right in town?"

"Just inside the gates" he sends me a sinister smile.

"Well, I hope you enjoy the rest of your day, Evan" I stand up, moving in the direction of the print shop, concerned with the tone of the conversation.

"You too, Cold"

Pete?!

I turn back quickly. No one's there. Who the heck is that guy? No one else had ever called me that, at least to my face. I look around the plaza but he's vanished. I'll not be going to the church again. No point getting freaked out over a coincidence. Or something I misheard.

I turn to keep on to…oh yeah, Tina, for coffee. I almost forgot.

A young blonde woman walks past me, with a four-wheel fully-loaded wooden trolley. She appears to be struggling with her cargo, too small to manage the load over the rough road. Is she limping?

I don't think I've met this woman but she surely knows the jacket and who wears it.

"Hi. Can I give you a hand?" I ask her.

"Thanks, that'd be great, love" she replies in a sweet voice "I'm Ness"

"I'm Colden; the station master"

"We all know you, sweetie" she smiles, lighting up her face "You're cute in person"

Her dark green jacket and black pants resemble my own, tight to her small frame. Her striking blue eyes and long dark eyelashes are that much more so against her fair skin. It's tough to tell the cart's contents without making it obvious that I'm looking.

"Where are you going?"

"To the fields. This is the workers' lunch"

I guide the cart over the rough terrain, steering it as best I can in the direction of the path to Michael's house and the fields.

"Is this your job, Ness?"

"We take turns. I used to be a server at the Grey Stone but that didn't work out for me"

"Sorry to hear that" I think I say.

Ness steps away from the wagon, satisfied that my efforts are sufficient to move it alone. The boxes making up the buggy's contents are held in place by wooden siding encircling the top. She watches both me and the cart without smiling; maybe this job left little energy for smiling. Or maybe there's more to it, as with so many things here.

"How's it like down at the station?" she asks turning back, her expression now softer.

"It's OK. Have you ever visited?"

"Twice, but only to deliver items being loaded onto the train"

"Did you know any of the other station masters?"

"You're the fourth of fifth in my life. The one before you was about your age but kept to himself. The one before that was a grumpy fellow, probably in his fifties. He came into town at first but toward the end he pretty much locked himself in his room. Nervous, always looking around. Rumour had it he'd taken some liberties with one of the local girls and then killed her; her body was found in the forest. One day he just disappeared; no one knows why"

I wonder at the station master's mysterious disappearance and any actions on his part.

"The way I heard it this girl was all over him and she was a beauty so who'd turn that away, eh?" she flashes me a playful smile.

"When was that?" my voice quavers.

Our pace slows. What will local opinion be of me helping Ness?

"A few years back. The one before him got in some trouble too, or so I've heard. Probably why they're hesitant getting to know you. It's fresh in their memory"

I want to ask about 'the one before me who was about my age' but don't, concerned about this man's character.

"The road looks better from here" I say stopping the cart "I should be getting back to the station. It was nice talking with you Ness"

"Thanks for the help, love" she replies.

I watch Ness walk away without looking back then turn my way into town.

"You'll not find it easy to leave, they're watchin' even when you don't see 'em" a voice behind me speaks.

Ness?

I watch her as she walks away in silence without turning around.

1908

No one will find me out here, none would dare look this deep in the forest. I glance around me but all is silent and calm, the forest pitch dark, the moon's light overhead obscured by the trees. The lantern is barely sufficient to see the lines connecting the names as they travel through time.

My eyes scan the names, my fingers drawing the lines connecting parents to children, a single boy born to each couple on one side, a single girl on the other.

But some information is missing, some names not shown.

"Who still lives?" I say softly to myself "And where are they?"

And how can I find them?

Wait.

Is that a movement at my side? A noise? Near the forest?

I hold up the lantern and stare into the black spaces between the trees, my eyes squinting to focus the light. But there's no one.

None would dare.

35 – Handprints

I walk back to the station in silence, the forest around me quiet and calm.

With no one to ask about my predecessors, I'm unsure where to turn for answers. Were dossiers kept on individual station masters with their personal histories? Had these people been watching me for years before extending the offer? Were my actions in New Brook West being documented? My conversation with Ness increases my unease over 'my character that made me an ideal candidate for the position of station master'. What character traits are ideal? Do I have those qualities?

And is someone watching me that I don't see? At the station? Following me as I go about my day?

Cindy expressed no concerns about being watched, spied on, or followed. Shared few of her thoughts with me in general but perhaps that's just how she is, how she became in her marriage.

She and I had spent a lot of time together over the past several days. Or had it been weeks? Time really has lost meaning. She seemed to enjoy our time together, intimate or not, and so did I. She was a stunning beauty, kind and caring and loving, intelligent in ways that I wasn't, quirky in ways that I was. Everything I wanted in a woman, but I still hadn't reconciled her involvement in the unusual events and in my coming to be station master, for reasons I couldn't explain.

It's a horrible feeling not knowing who to believe. I feel like I'm trusting too many people but at the same time that I'm suspicious of everyone.

My previous night's sleep was deep and pleasantly dream-free as so few had been for me recently. I wake early feeling well-rested, my slumber more the result of recent exhaustion than comfort. I'm sitting in bed thinking, which is a bad idea. Better to get up, get my head straight, and then assess what I can do. Sometimes you just can't do anything.

The note from Cindy, which I thought I'd placed on my bedside table, is no longer there. I hope I'll be able to find it.

I jump out of bed, ready to tackle my surroundings, unusual as they are.

Should I just dismiss the unexplained occurrences as a combination of my new environment, my lower comfort level in the village, and my lack of sleep; perhaps the ubiquitous mist even plays a part; or the mysterious herbs cultivated in the fields? The figure that keeps materializing in the shadows could be any number of things, from strange natural formations, to visions brought about by dreams or memories, even an actual person watching me for reasons I couldn't imagine. In my mind, most everything can be explained; just because I don't know why something's happening doesn't make it supernatural.

I'd been trying to convince myself of this logic since my arrival.

At the moment, all seems quiet and normal in the apartment.

A scratch at the door gets my attention and my thoughts immediately go to the cat downstairs who may finally have decided to come see me.

A small bag of coffee is on the landing accompanied by some local baked goods. I can't imagine who thought this highly of the station master given the stories I'd heard of my predecessors. Unless Tina had included the breads with her gift. Should I try to thank her? How would I? She seemed to want this transaction to be clandestine and I don't want to lose my caffeine supplier. Perhaps I'll see her bringing a future delivery to me and talk to her then.

I think back and remember enjoying excellent coffee a long time ago but can't seem to place where or when, just a distant memory. Odd. I know it happened but that's all I can recall.

Today'll be spent fixing the station roof and patching a few places up at the school, supplies for both tasks already laid outside, the tools for this work in the utility room. There's hopefully a ladder at the schoolhouse because it'll be a heck of a trek to carry the one from the station; I can't recall seeing one but will figure it out if I need to. Yesterday I'd pulled out the materials I'll need at the school and taken them there. After a basic wash-up, I head outside to get things started, accustomed to the gloom that awaits me, taking solace in melancholy air. It rarely rains despite the constant fog and humidity which has always seemed odd.

I'd ventured out in just a t-shirt on occasion, though normally opt for a light jacket to keep out the moist air and protect against the chill humidity.

Today's green cargo pants, boots, and a tight-fitting long-sleeved shirt over a plain white t-shirt will hopefully provide sufficient warmth, and mobility to do the work. The air is calm and dry today which bodes well for construction and repairs. I would have expected an island to experience at least some measure of wind, but perhaps the station is simply too far from open water and protected by the dense forest.

By now it has become customary to look around me as soon as I step outside, especially at Room 1, which at the moment appears quiet, the platform unoccupied, the control room door closed. All good signs.

A quick look at the printer confirms there'll be no trains stopping today.

First, I'll tackle the station then head to the school. I gather the necessary tools; the tar and wood sit against the back of the building. The ladder is where I'd left it, though considering recent events, I decide to stake it down more securely than previously. I make three trips to the roof with each of the hammer, nails, and other instruments, two more with the materials themselves. The low slope of the station roof will make the work relatively safe from that perspective, an important consideration in light of any potential moisture.

It's critical to place things as accessibly as possible to minimize my movement on the roof. Any minor slips will be, well, critical.

Laying some resin-coated wooden shingles in place, I reach back for the hammer but it's come off my belt. Looking back, I see it has slid away from me, though still a safe distance from the edge so I carefully make my way toward it. Reaching it, I place my right hand firmly on the driest part of the roof I can see, extending to grab it with my left. As I do, the ladder wobbles, catching me unawares and causing me to look sharply in that direction. This movement upsets my balance and my feet slowly slide down the roof's slope, a situation which nearly leads me to panic as my hands find nothing dry. I grab a rag in my right hand and use the friction from pressing it against the roof to slow my slide and bring me to a stop far too close to the edge for my liking. Though I know it a bad idea, I can't help but look down at the assorted pile of items that await me, which would have caused me great injury at best had I crashed upon them. Something moves around the corner of the building, though I don't dare look for long, knowing that I've just escaped a terrible event. No one could have deliberately shaken the ladder to scare me, could they? Was someone considering climbing up on the roof with me?

Rissa and Sam? No.

A few deep breaths and I collect myself.

Hammer in hand, I take my position and complete the repairs in good time.

"Anyone down there?" I yell. After a few seconds without a reply, I let the remainder of the items I no longer require slide off the roof's edge to the ground.

The gloom persists even at this height, the sky now hazy. From my current position, it feels like a view from a dismal castle in the clouds, looking down on the dull grass below, across the clearing at the dark forest, both within and above the fog. There's total silence up here and no mist around the station itself.

All too often, it's just too quiet.

I think of how it's been a couple of days since I visited Cindy and that I'll go to her place today. After my work at the school. I miss seeing her.

The ladder shakes with a slight rattle, snapping me out of my dream-state, reminding me that I'd taken special measures to secure it at its base. I see no one down below. Braver than previously, I hastily make my way to the top rung, grabbing hold of the sides to steady any vibrations. After a cautious yet speedy descent, I run to the front of the platform but see no one there either. A whisper echoes through the air, though the words are inaudible, if it is a voice.

Some local kids goofing around? Someone I'd inadvertently pissed off trying to scare me? Someone who figured it best to get rid of the station master before he commits any terrible acts?

It's 12:30 and as good a time as any to grab a bite of lunch before heading to the school. I eat two cheese sandwiches on breads brought to me earlier in the day, placing the tools I anticipate needing into a satchel to carry with me, locking the utility room door behind me.

After a quick stop to lock the control room, I head into the quiet eeriness of the forest, a journey which rarely holds any appeal.

A lantern has become a regular accessory on travels away from the station, even during the day. Upon reaching the treeline, I hazard a glance behind me, curious if strange goings-on occur in my absence, like a child who dreams that their toys come alive when they're away. I see no movements and hear no strange noises in the vicinity of Room 1.

I hope nothing comes alive while I'm away.

Leaving the station to enter the forest always feels like crossing into the unknown. As if confirming my anxiety, a distant movement to my right causes me to turn slowly and spot what looks like a figure wearing a station master's jacket at the treeline, but he vanishes into the fog as though he'd never been there. My mind playing tricks.

Being watched unnerves me, especially as it seems such a regular occurrence. People here don't act as though they much care what I do or who I am so it never occurs to me that they'd take any interest in my activities.

A light breeze behind me pushes me forward, a mysterious force urging me on. Whispers carry on the wind as though someone were speaking at some distance behind me, the sound fading as it reaches me. But I see no one so I try to ignore the noises.

I have yet to light the lantern, the forest sufficiently bright to see my way but not enough to look any further among the trees and shrubs, which is probably for the best. The air is cool but drier with no fog along the path itself. The canopy's green and brown leaves block out the sky as per usual.

When the school comes into view, I shiver and slowly approach it to inspect the work requested of me. There's no fog in the large clearing, the benches and swings clearly visible as is the forest across the field, though clouds persist overhead.

Is that a girl in the window staring this way?

The figure slowly disappears leaving me wondering. Perhaps a rogue student or curious child because there are no classes today and there'd be no reason for anyone, except maybe someone doing cleaning, to be in the building. But I have a job to do and can't worry about who else is lurking about.

The wood, metal, and other materials are all beneath a cover at the back end of the school where I'd placed them yesterday. The windows are too high for me to see in so I take a walk around the unlit school, investigating what needs to be done. A few exterior wall boards need replacing, as does a window which I'd brought from the station, and finally a couple of cracks on the rear stone wall demand filling to keep out the moisture. I'll look at the minor interior tasks when I'm inside.

The boards low on the side facing the path are easily replaced and the cracks in the wall take only a moment to repair. The window will be the most challenging.

Once on the school's step ladder, which I find on the ground beside the building, I pry the glass free from the cracked wooden casing. Delicate handling is necessary while removing the glass since a pair of gloves has not been included in the repair kit. I place the glass carefully against the back wall, not wanting to have to clean up shards where children will be playing.

Light will fade even earlier than yesterday, so time is of the essence, my preference to be done this job before dusk.

I replace the small pane in the casing, apply putty, and secure it in place with a new piece of wood. I descend the ladder then take a short step back to see how it looks.

It's then that I notice a child's handprints on the pane I've just installed that weren't there before. Too small to have been my hands. How did that happen? Is someone inside the school? It chills me to think so. I stand motionless for a moment, expecting to see movement through one of the windows or someone exit the building. Nothing happens. No one opens the school's front door.

Am I being watched from the forest?

I slowly turn my head to the left but no one's between me and the trees and no one's visible in the forest's obscurity. I wait a moment before looking to my right across the hazy field, and again, no one. I take a deep breath, knowing what awaits me. I hear distant creaking, like metal on metal.

I think I stop breathing for a few seconds but I'm not sure. Spinning fully around, I'm ready for someone directly behind me but no one's there, just the swings and a few tables and chairs in the distance. One of the swing's seats sways just enough to notice, its chains making the noise in the calm clearing.

The sooner I'm done, the sooner I'm gone.

I next need to secure the glass from inside and then get out of here. Opening the unlocked door, I'm not sure what to expect, but it's just a dim quiet room. An unusual layout, with rows of benches behind long tables rather than individual desks. The space could probably accommodate thirty average-sized students at full capacity, a wooden table the width of the room at the front, small openings on either side, three separate chalkboards behind it. Chalkboards. Books and papers cover the makeshift desk at the front of the room, a notebook with 'S Stela' written on it, other smaller ones marked with first names and a last name initial. New Brook West's schoolhouse.

Bringing the lantern near me, I putty the window from the inside, replacing the old wood at the bottom; tighten a table and a bench; repair a cabinet at the front of the room.

I quickly patch the cracks on the back wall and that's it. Verifying the success of my work, I pat myself on the back for a job well done and stow the tools at the back of the building.

I take a sip of my coffee, still warm in my travel mug; I'd forgotten I'd brought this.

I clean up inside and out, heading along the perimeter of the clearing to the path to Cindy's place, darkness not far off.

From the steps she watches him enter the forest.

1908

He was easily identified at the tavern, a sheepish form scuttling through the crowd. I'd followed him from town, beheld his deed, and prepared myself to enlist his reluctant assistance. I could still smell the blood on his hands.

The cocky one sits waiting for him, a smirk on his lips; he would gladly have been complicit in my plans though he would have been worthless to me, such is his ego. I allow the young blacksmith to settle in and relax, let the alcohol flow through him for a moment, embolden him. I approach him when he returns for a second drink. I whisper in his ear, whisper what I know, what I want. When it is done, I turn and leave. Although my back is to him as I walk away, I can imagine the expression on his face, the fear at what I've said and what he knows he must do.

So it begins.

36 - Preparing lessons

Cindy's place comes into view just past 3:30. The small glade surrounding it is in shadows, the air clear. There appears to be a light toward the back of the house, possibly in the kitchen.

I approach the building nervously, still wary of being watched or followed.

A note on the front door says:

'Preparing lessons. Be back soon'

I wonder where she does this, the school being the most obvious place, either that or her home, and it seems unlikely she'd do this anyplace in town, though I'd been mistaken about many things so far. With limited daylight remaining, she'd certainly come home soon, unless she's indoors. The library? I doubt it based on our previous conversations.

I knock in case she's forgotten to remove the paper but no answer. I walk around peeking into the windows but no one's in the kitchen area or the bedroom, the unlit front room covered by drapes. The colourful building looks less inviting today than usual as if it has aged. I take a step back. The light inside has gone out, the interior now dark. The sun hasn't set, yet all is grey around the house.

A shuffling in the trees behind me near the path turns my head but no one's there, the sound stopping immediately. I take a few steps toward the narrow trail.

"Cindy?" I ask.

The only reply is a gentle crunching in the brush to my right.

Maybe a route I don't know of goes around to come out the other side. Someone passing through on their way elsewhere? The crackling stops as I walk toward it. All is quiet again. I wait in silence to see if there's any movement in the forest without getting too close. My breathing slows but my heart races. Around the side of the house, I spot a crow up in a tree, its head moving back and forth as if looking around me. For a moment, I watch its movements, then follow its eyes in the direction of the noise I'd heard but see no one.

I lean against the building to rest my legs. Is Cindy outside?

Then, I hear the sound of leaves behind the house, as if rustled by someone moving through them. I walk in that direction.

"Cindy?" I say hesitantly.

"Cindy?"

I look at the path leading away from me.

Who else is here?

I stop moving and stare at the trail, then look side to side in the shadows. The clearing seems to have stolen the light from the low sun to my left. It's silence all around me. I look up at the bird who now stares into the trees to my left.

Licorice.

I freeze. Oh no.

A gentle tapping at the kitchen window turns my head back to it, faint light now illuminating the inside. Is someone in the house? I look toward the window but don't approach it. Am I being watched from inside the house?

Walking around to the large front window, I peek between the drawn curtains but again see no one, the light now appearing to originate in the kitchen. I sit, leaning against the wall beneath the window so as not to be surprised. I look at the trail and consider returning to the station. I'd make it back before dark but I'd have to pass the school and risk an encounter with whoever lurks about during my work there.

Is Cindy ok?

I head to the back of the house again and knock at the back door.

I see no one through the back window.

Have I happened on Cindy when she doesn't want to be disturbed?

"Cindy?" I speak toward the house.

No reply.

Does she have another visitor?

I wait in silence.

A weak pull at the bottom of my shirt feels like a child trying to get my attention. My head jerks back instantly but no one's there. My back falls against the wall. Is someone playing a game, watching me run around the house like an idiot?

My heart is pounding though I feel like my breathing has stopped. Who or what is here with me? Are they hiding in the forest? In the house?

What ghosts haunt the teacher's house?

"Rissa? Sam?"

I wait for an answer but get none.

Another tap on the glass but, again, no one's at the window.

I wait a few seconds longer, but there are no more sounds or movements.

I take a couple of steps backward to get a better view of my situation, the earth soft beneath my feet. I look at the rear of the building. No light inside. I haven't tried the door because I don't want to enter even if it's unlocked.

I exhale deeply to regain my senses. I close my eyes and wait.

Is something behind me?

A touch on my shoulder makes me spin in horror.

"Hi Colden" Cindy says "It's great to see you"

I hug her tightly.

"Is everything OK?" she asks letting me go after a moment, her hands on my shoulders.

My face must look as though I'm at the end of my days.

"Can we go inside?" I say.

"Of course" Cindy replies, opening the door nervously.

My eyes immediately scan the room for anyone in the kitchen and then back outside. I look in the unlit bedroom, check the bathroom, glance into the dark living room. I run to the front window and peer between the drapes. No one's outside in the dim glade, the forest dark around the house. I catch my breath, try to cast my memory back to what I'd seen.

What had I seen?

Cindy has lit a lamp in the kitchen.

"Is everything ok, Colden?" Cindy asks.

No. No, it's not.

"Who's Stela?" I ask, recalling the name in the school.

"What's wrong, Colden?"

"Had kind of a strange experience while I was waiting for you" I slump down in a green kitchen chair.

"What happened?"

I look up.

"Do your students ever come see you?"

"To my house: never" she says "They've been told not to visit unless they come with a parent. They attend school for four days then work with the family for the next four. It's not a standard week here. Why?"

"I could have sworn there was someone here" I say, trying unsuccessfully to restrain myself "And a light inside your house"

Did I imagine it? Does something lurk around the teacher's house? I shiver.

"Impossible. Both doors are locked and the windows are all bolted shut" she points to the back of the house "You saw it was dark when we entered"

"Could someone else have a key?"

"Michael might, but it's unthinkable that one of his kids would swipe it from him. There's a woman helping me clean the school but she wouldn't be here now. And she doesn't look at all like a child"

The colourful house suddenly feels grey.

"It's coffee time" Cindy says setting the water to boil, sitting next to me at the table.

"I'd ask for something stronger but that wouldn't clear my head" I try to smile.

She sighs.

I inhale deeply, exhaling just as heavily, a calmer mood slowly running through me.

"Where do you prepare your lessons?" I ask more warmly.

"There's a spot down by the river that's really pretty. Great on a warm day, or at least not a cold one. I can see the water and the library when it's clear. I lay out a blanket; it's nice sometimes to get out of the house and be in the fresh air if it's sunny. It's peaceful and one of the places here that I find beautiful"

She pauses.

"I'm glad you stopped by" she smiles leaning back in her chair, putting her bare feet on the seat between my legs.

"I was working at the school and wanted to see you again after I was done. I hope that's OK"

"It's perfect"

"I don't mean to be so weird all the time"

"You're fun when you're weird" she laughs "It's all part of you that I like. Don't apologize for being strange"

I look down, my hands on top of her feet, then into her eyes and smile back, lost for a moment. Her eyes are striking against her fair skin, almost silvery, mesmerizing me as I stare. I feel lost in them, like I'm in another world. The warm room wraps me in its arms. I feel drowsy.

I break away from the trance.

"This place could be amazing with a few changes" I say.

"I agree" she smiles sliding her feet further toward me on my seat.

I exhale looking at the stove.

"Hey, who's the naked woman on your bedroom wall?" I recall.

Her right foot moves forward between my legs.

"You're thinking of her now?"

Her foot continues to rub outside my pants making me hard.

"No" I look down at my bulge "I was just curious"

"She's my lesbian lover, Jade" Cindy smiles "Mmmm"

"Really?"

"No" she giggles "She's a good friend from years back who had those taken and wanted to share the photoshoot with me. She was nervous about how they looked. She did all kinds of modelling, some of it nude. I think this set is great"

Wow. Ok.

"Jade asked me once to join her on a shoot where we would have both been naked on our knees at a table facing each other but I chickened out"

"I would have liked to see that" I say.

The kettle whistles, Cindy hops up and removes it from the gas element, shutting it off at the same time.

She returns with two yellow mugs and a small bowl of sugar.

I sigh.

"You ok?" Cindy asks.

"It gets dark so early here" I say taking a sip, staring out the window.

"That's something I've never liked" Cindy shivers.

I get lost for a moment in the view out the back. The air looks cold and damp, dark and gloomy.

Something occurs to me.

"Come to think of it, there was also a girl inside the school today while I was doing my repairs" I cock my head in confusion.

"No way" Cindy replies shaking her head "The children are forbidden from going inside the school except for their lessons. And no one would have been cleaning today"

"But I'm sure..." my voice trails off.

There's no way in or out of her house. Not so quietly or so easily. And not right past me.

Why am I the only one seeing things that aren't there?

Is something haunting me?

I see movement out of the corner of my eye near the window, but nothing's there by the time I turn. I look back at the table and take a sip from my mug.

I'm slowly going crazy.

"Seems like you had a pretty long day" Cindy says "The air out here does get to me at times, too"

And make you see things? This is more than the air.

I lean back in the chair.

"I'll get us some supper" she opens the fridge "I made a meat and vegetable pie this morning"

"That'd be great" I try to sound grateful.

"Why don't you go lie down for a bit?"

I stand and walk to the living room, a dark space with the closed drapes. My eyes move to the window then the door. My weary body drops on the sofa.

Then everything goes black.

My mind clears as my head shakes off the cobwebs. It feels like I blacked out drunk, forgetting everything before this moment. I come around fairly quickly, in my own bed, slowly lift my head, but see and hear no one. No lamps or lanterns light the room, the air dark outside my window. I'm naked beneath the covers. I'm hazy about what's going on and what happened. Was I drinking? Smoking up? Where was I?

Ok. I'm in a bed, my bed at the station. New Brook West.

How did I get here? Who brought me? Cindy can't have done it on her own. And why would she? The way I felt now, I sure didn't have it in me to walk.

I sit up on the edge of the bed.

Was there something in Cindy's coffee?

I stand and pull on the boxers that are on the floor, walk to the shelf behind the sofa, and light a lantern.

My door is ajar, probably the cause of the moisture and chill in the air. I take a brief glance outside, see nothing, close it, and look out both large windows but, again, no one's there, only a light mist. On my way back inside, I spot a note on the coffee table.

'Train today at 8:00 a.m. Guest Max Dixon will stay in Room 4'

Odd that this arrival wasn't mentioned on the recent schedule. Or had I brought this inside myself?

I set the letter back on the coffee table. It's 6:30 a.m. now.

I need to get to town to alert Tessa and have her look after the room before Mr Dixon steps off the train. I don't have the energy to care how that'll happen. I throw on what look like clean clothes, though I'll change after I shower anyway, donning the station master jacket over my white t-shirt.

Dawn has yet to arrive, the sky still more night than morning. I stop on the platform's edge staring out into the open field. A light haze hangs low in the clearing, the black and white spindly trees around the forest's perimeter like skeletons in the fog. Stars still shine overhead in the clear sky, the moon a large white glow sharpening the trees and the station around me. The mist seems held in place by the surrounding forest like water in a bowl, the air too calm to clear it. I glance around the empty platform then across the tracks, pausing a moment to take in the silence of the train station.

I feel a sense of tranquility.

I take a deep breath and set off, not so much at a run as a fast walk, a slow jog in places, wanting to ensure that I find Michael's daughter, or maybe that she finds me, with plenty of time to make things ready. The air in the clear forest is cool and damp, though the run makes me hot and I remove the jacket. The motionless black trees watch me moving past them, wait for me to stop. No rustling follows me, none that I hear. By the time I reach the fountain, it's approaching 7:00, and of course Tessa isn't there; I expect she'll perhaps jump out in Dalton's style but that doesn't happen either. I put the jacket back on as I contemplate walking to Michael's home, instead deciding to post a notice on the board that I hope will not reflect poorly on me.

Spotting an older lady some distance ahead, I approach her.

"Excuse me, please" I come alongside her "Do you know where I can find Tessa?"

"She's at the train station" she replies softly.

What? How did she get past me? I look back to the path but can't see anyone or imagine how I missed her.

"Are you sure?" I turn to the lady but she's no longer there.

I don't have time to worry about where she's gone or how she knows. Should I retrieve the note? Doesn't seem much point leaving it here if she's already at Room 4.

The space on the board where I'd tacked the note is empty. I look at the ground around me but see nothing with no wind to carry it away. It isn't in my pockets either. Did the old lady take it?

I set out back to the station at a run, arriving in the clearing short of breath but see no one. The field is now clear of haze, the moon still glowing in the sky as the stars disappear in the coming dawn. No sign of activity on the platform, the time now 7:15, with no sound of an early train approaching. Maybe Max changed his plans and decided against his visit. A prudent choice.

A multi-coloured sunrise plays the full prism of colours, a rare but beautiful occurrence, the forest basking in morning's splendour. I climb up onto the platform, keeping my distance from Room 1. The station echoes silence.

A whistle announces the train's imminent arrival.

Staring up at Room 4, I wonder if I've been too quick to believe the woman in town about Tessa's whereabouts. Has she already cleaned Room 4? Is she in the room now?

Reaching into my right jacket pocket, I find the note I'd written advising Tessa of the guest's arrival. How did that get there?

I stare at it in my hand.

Then I'm running toward the tracks.

37 - Green sundress

The whistle blares with no time for me to stop. With one giant stride I reach the edge of the platform, pushing off with all my strength and flying past the front of the train with inches to spare, landing just before the forest. It carries on its way with no signs of stopping in New Brook West.

The train's wheels clatter along the tracks and I watch as it disappears into the forest, silence returning to the station.

Holy shit.

I gasp for air as I begin breathing again. My heart is nearly beating out of my chest. I want to stand but can't. I crawl away from the tracks close to the dark forest, too scared to look around me. I exhale deeply and sit up.

What the hell happened and why was I running at the train?

I look up onto the empty platform as I ponder what to do next. Light breaks through the trees in the east as I imagine long shadows in the clearing.

My mind won't focus and I still can't move.

A whispering from the forest behind me but it's too soft to make out the voice or the words. It sounds like a muffled or distant scream.

I turn to look but no one's there.

Mustering the courage to get to my feet, I look both ways before crossing the rails, hopping up to the main level. There's no one on the platform and the utility room's door is closed. The hotel appears quiet, though I don't look too closely at Room 1.

Although day will soon be upon me, I light a lamp at the base of the stairs up to my suite. The stars are no longer in the sky, though the moon shines to my left where it's still dark. I stare out into the clearing at the bony branches along the treeline.

My feet drag me up the stairs to my apartment, after a quick stop in the control room to ensure I haven't missed any notifications. The clicking sound of a locking door behind me. Room 1?

I don't want to know.

Max Dixon has not arrived, at least not on the most recent train; I'll check on Room 4 another time. The letter notifying me of his 8:00 arrival is no longer where I'd dropped it on the coffee table; I'll look for it later.

The time is now 8:20, the fog in the clearing slowly thinning.

A ding from the table makes me jump as I realize it's my phone receiving a text message, despite a dead battery and lack of cellular service. Now what? I look around the room, as if expecting to see someone or something before staring at the phone. Picking it up nervously, the screen indicates one unread text message.

A photo had been sent today at 5:30 a.m. Curiosity compels me to see this image, though both my heart and my head tell me not to.

A young girl in a dirty purple dress is standing at the side of my bed watching me as I sleep. Her face hidden behind her black hair, her thin hand reaching out as if to touch me. The dim light in the photo suggests a single lit candle in the apartment. I shiver as the photo disappears, the screen going blank.

Is this the girl I'd seen before?

How did she get in?

Who is the photographer?

The phone falls from my hands onto the rug as I drop into the armchair.

I need to visit Cindy, to find out about the lost time, how I got home, and what was in the coffee.

I gather my senses, too tired to change out of my white t-shirt and black jeans, grab the keys, and leave my suite, my eyes on Room 1 as I descend the staircase to enter the forest.

Touching my right cheek, my finger comes away grey.

Cindy's quiet house welcomes me into the noiseless clearing, the air calm and warm.

Do I want to tell Cindy what happened last night?

Daylight shines over the trees to my right making long shadows in the small glade. Faint light radiates from the back of the building, as if a lantern were lit in the kitchen. I peek between the front window curtains, put my ear to the front door but see and hear nothing inside. Cautiously glancing to my left and right, I move around back to look into the kitchen, unsure of what I'll see. Again, no movement through the back window, no noise to indicate anyone's home. Silence and darkness in the house. I face the path, waiting.

Where could she be?

Should I head back to the station or wait here?

I look up wondering if I'll see the crow again but it's not there. Green and brown and yellow leaves look down on me, the lower branches more sparsely leafed. The thin trees seem to be leaning forward out of the darkness between them, the sun's faint light failing to penetrate into the forest. I rest my right shoulder against the door.

A hand brushes against my lower back. My heart skips a beat.

There's no one's behind me. I stand, looking to the trail. No movement or noise in the forest, though the air is now cooler. I shiver.

What was that? I gasp, my body tense.

"Hi"

The voice is like an electric shock. I jump, and might also yell.

I turn to see Cindy looking at me from inside the open back door; her light green sun dress and black tights against her fair skin creating a striking image.

Collecting my breath, I exhale with a glare.

"Why are you at the back door?" she asks.

I place my hands on my knees as I catch my breath.

"What happened to me last night?" I stand "One minute I was in your kitchen, the next I wake up in my room this morning"

"I turned to clean up the counter but you were gone when I looked back" her tone defensive "I assumed you'd gone to the living room or bedroom to lie down. After about fifteen minutes I came out but you were nowhere to be seen. I couldn't figure it out. Why did you leave like that?"

What?!

"I didn't leave"

"Then how did you end up at home?"

We stare at each other in silence for a moment.

"Come inside" she says.

We sit at the kitchen table facing each other, her hands on my knees.

"You had a close call with the train" she says.

"How did you know that?"

"What?"

"About the train"

"What about it?"

"You asked me..."

"I asked: 'Why did you go?'" she says.

"I didn't. Or at least I don't think I did. We were in the kitchen talking next thing I know I'm on my bed with a complete blank in between"

"I was worried but wasn't going to run after you" she says softly.

What had happened? I couldn't believe that Cindy would put something in my coffee just to have me walk home. No way.

"I don't remember anything" I say meekly.

"You must have been exhausted and wandered home. Your fatigue got the better of you, I guess" she doesn't seem convinced by her reasoning either.

There's no other explanation.

"I made some cookies if you trust me to eat them" she places a container on the table and removes one, taking a bite as if she were my royal taster.

I reach for one with some kind of wild berries before changing my mind and grabbing what appears to be chocolate chip. Silence hangs over us like a dark cloud for what feels like an eternity, neither of us sure what to say. Have I gone mad? Has some 'essence' in my environment, some plant, some aroma, some food taken effect to explain my blackouts? Do I have a medical condition which finally manifested itself in New Brook West? I'm afraid to leave Cindy's but also apprehensive about staying.

It's now nearly 11:00 and my hunger makes me want more than cookies.

"How about I make us some sandwiches" she says walking to the counter "I got some things today in the village and baked bread last night"

"Yes, please. I am a bit hungry"

Cindy goes about preparations while I reflect. Trying to remember. Who had been at the station? A student from town? Someone trying to frighten me, laughing at my reaction?

I don't want to share my most recent experience with Cindy just yet.

My mind drifts to images and memories of Suzie.

"I had a daughter" I look up at Cindy, surprised to be sharing this piece of my life but also at waiting so long to do so.

Cindy sighs.

"I had no idea" she turns to me, crossing her arms.

"She disappeared when she was two. We were torn up, Lori and me. She couldn't cope with it and ultimately ended up in a psychiatric facility. Her parents blamed me, everyone did. For Suzie's disappearance, Lori's collapse, my inability to get my own life right. I still think about them, even though it's been seven years since Suzie vanished. I'm not sure how Lori is but would never have been welcome visiting her even if I knew where to go. And I'd run out of ideas to look for Suzie. Eventually I had to get away and just ran as far away as I could"

Cindy listens attentively the whole time, now sitting across from me.

"That's a lot to deal with" she says.

"Yes, it is. It was"

"Was she ever found? Your daughter?"

"She disappeared one night we had friends over. She was right there and then she was gone. We looked everywhere, spoke to everyone, but nothing. We finally gave up. But Lori never got over it. She even claimed to see her around our place. I had to ask her parents for help. We were living in an apartment they owned at the time and needless to say I wasn't welcome after that"

"What did you do?"

"Found a crappy new place and moved on as best I could. In the end I had to relocate completely to get away from the memories and the people"

Cindy doesn't seem to know what to say anymore.

"And now, visions of a little girl" I shake my head.

"Do you think it has to do with your memories?"

I shrug.

"I don't know what to think. But you never see her, do you?" I say.

"I've seen a lot of strange things here but nothing like that, no" she says.

"And no, I'm not thinking of Lori when we're together" I clarify.

"I knew what you meant when you said that" she smiles "Thanks for sharing all that with me"

Again, silence between us.

I take a deep breath, exhaling loudly.

She takes my hand and smiles.

We eat while she talks about her school day. The students are extremely attentive and, though they like her, she never feels accepted. They're intelligent and well-rounded, learning academic knowledge from her and practical skills from their parents and the community at large. New Brook West is a decent enough place to live, though she doesn't really have any friends, except the girl who helps her at the school. She'd gone to the Grey Stone a couple of times by herself to see who the customers are but almost none are women and no one ever approached her to talk. In general, women in the village are rarely alone, and seldom look her way when they're in a group or with a man, making it difficult to make any girlfriends. Men never approached her, apart from the occasional glance, and the previous station master made no effort to get to know her despite her reaching out for friendship.

Gradually my anxiety subsides, replaced by a small comfort which I often feel in Cindy's presence, my mood lightens, my mind relaxes. I suggest we sit on the couch nestled up under a blanket and maybe just take a short nap before carrying on with the day, my body exhausted from current events. It's just after 1:00 and fatigue has the better of me at this point, my intuition confident that Cindy will agree to this which she does. She grabs a soft cover from her bedroom for us to sit on her cozy green window-facing sofa. I draw the curtains together.

We speak for another ten minutes, she telling me stories of the strange looks continually cast her way, especially when she wears bright colours as she has today, the villagers preferring the neutral shades I tend to wear. I assure her that my clothing choice has not made me any more popular. I mention the oddity of Dalton, though she confesses to having neither seen him nor heard his name. I'm not sure when but we slowly drift into sleep, Cindy curled up against me like a cat.

"I like this" she nestles in closer.

A knocking at the front door wakes me, Cindy either not hearing it or deciding it doesn't matter enough to move. After several loud bangs I get up from the couch thinking it sounds more like a hammer putting a nail in the door than a hand striking it. Cindy flops down on the sofa where I'd been sitting, dopey as she opens her eyes, and I cautiously approach the front entrance, my nerves on edge, ready for just about anything, half expecting something to come crashing through.

The banging stops.

With a slow hand, I reach for the handle throwing it open forcefully once it's in my grasp, but of course no one's there.

I run around the outside of the house hoping I won't see anyone or anything but need to know who made that noise. My eyes survey the forest, but nothing. Looking back in the window, I see that Cindy is now sitting straight up, a fearful look in her eyes, her hands gripping a pillow. Casting one last look around I decide that whoever had been here is either too far away to see or is nearby motionless and silent.

Walking back to the door, there's nothing left to do but go inside and write this off.

As I prepare to re-enter, I see a drawing nailed to the door near waist height of two figures: one in a light green dress, the other in black pants and a white shirt.

1910

That terrible man, that monster.

He took everything and everyone from me and is now the town hero.

I'm powerless against him. What could I do to a Station Master?

Lost and alone in the world, I survive as I can.

Many had harmed my family, accused my mother, left me alone.

Those I could find got what they deserved and they knew it, cowards as they were to the end.

In time they all came to fear the 'grey girl' and this terror gladdened me. Let them dread what they cannot see; what watches in the dark as they sleep. My form is now frail but strong enough to do what must be done that I might be avenged.

I hide in the shadows at the train station to be away from prying eyes, to take refuge in the darkness.

And to be near the Station Master, he who committed the greatest sin. To watch him and wait for the right moment.

Whenever I see him, I feel the anger burn deep inside me. But he will be the last; let him cower in fear unaware of what watches him. I clench my teeth as I restrain myself.

But more than angry, I'm sad. I draw my knees up to my chest to keep warm in the cold shadows.

38 - Like the flower

The Grey Stone is appropriately named. Its wood and stone and dirt décor is not enhanced by the dim lighting nor the cheerfulness of the patrons, the crowd subdued, almost muted, throughout the tavern.

I've come alone this time to make a few inquiries of my own.

The corner where Cindy and I sat last time is available so I install myself there for the moment, unsure of my next steps. I'm careful not to look around too much, not wanting to draw undue attention. A few people look my way, but soon go back to their own affairs, uninterested in my doings. It somehow feels colder and darker as though we're deeper underground despite what appears to be a good number of lanterns about the oval-shaped room.

"Welcome back, Station Master"

The young woman comes out of nowhere, the same one who'd served Cindy and I on our previous visit.

"Hi. Again" I reply.

"Just you this time" she says "Lookin' to be alone?"

She puts her right hand on her hip, tilting her body slightly to the right as she puts all her weight on her good leg. She wears a long-sleeved grey top and a black knee-length skirt with black flats.

I take a quick look around ensuring that we're out of earshot of the other patrons.

"I actually came to see you" I say softly.

"To see *me*?" she tilts her head with a smile, her voice louder than I'd hoped.

"Yes" I answer quietly.

She sits down across from me crossing her right leg over her left, the shoe falling off her foot.

"Yes" my voice just above a whisper "I wanted to talk with you"

"I don't often hear that in here" her blush is visible even in our dim surroundings.

I lean in closer.

"I don't think I know your name" I say.

"Acacia. Like the flower. Or the tree"

"That's a beautiful name" I say "Please call me Colden"

"I'll do that, Colden" she places her elbows on the table, resting her chin on her interlaced fingers "Now what shall we talk about?"

Up close, Acacia has a charming playfulness. Her eyes, which had appeared dark and hardened by either poverty, abuse, or both, are now a radiant blue, made more so by her shiny platinum blonde hair. Her face, previously haggard, in this light now appears more youthful, more girlish, more innocent. It's difficult to get a read on her background from her appearance, though I suspect there's a story. There always is.

"How long have you lived here, Acacia?"

"A while. But I was born elsewhere"

Her accent becomes more evident, a higher pitch than I'd thought earlier.

"Where were you born Colden?"

"Far away"

"How far?"

"Far enough that I don't want to go back"

None of the other staff express any interest in her sitting with me which strikes me as odd. Are the women here also prostitutes?

"Is someone here making you nervous?" she says, perhaps noticing me looking around the room.

"No, I'm fine" I look back at Acacia.

"I think you're wondering if I'm a girl-for-hire but I'm not" her reply is definitive but not stern "And I'm twenty-two years old so no need to worry about that" she crosses her legs, her shoe falling off her left foot. The confidence in her words is evident.

"Do you live in New Brook West?" I decide to keep the subject matter light.

"The bar girls all have rooms in the back. It's not a lot but it's enough, and we get along fine so it works"

"Have you ever been to New Brook East?" I ask.

"And here I thought you liked me" she leans back from the table, her eyes dulled with sadness "You just have questions"

"I do like you Acacia" I assure her defensively, reaching across to touch her hands, realizing too late that this gesture may be inappropriate "If things were different, well…they might be…different"

"You are sweet" she smiles.

"I was born on the mainland" she tells me more seriously "Never met my mother. Lived in back alleys. When a man came to me one day, I thought he wanted my 'services' but he offered me a job out here and I came with him. You don't make any actual money here but things work out because everyone does what they're good at and we all share. I'm pretty sure some share less than others, but I imagine that's no different than anyplace else"

"A communal system" I nod pulling my hands back.

"Not sure what that is but I think you understand"

"So, what's in New Brook East?" I ask again.

"Never been there" she shakes her head "Don't know many that have. From what I've heard, it's just ruins. Nothing for me"

"I've heard there's a bad history" I continue.

"I've heard similar" she nods "Though I may not be the best one to tell it"

"Does anyone live there?" I ask.

"I've heard told there's a woman who still does" she says quietly "I've seen her a couple of times in the village but she doesn't seem to want to be noticed. Usually hides beneath a cloak"

A subtle honey scent hangs in the air. Acacia? I hadn't noticed it before. I feel warm.

"Why you so interested in East?" she leans in.

"I'm having a tough time making sense of some…things. Just trying to figure if it fits in with what's happening at the station"

She pauses, looking up with squinted eyes.

"I'll show you there if you promise to give me a tour of the train station"

That seems a strange request.

"I don't get about town much and rarely leave the community or even the Grey Stone. I don't remember travelling here so it'd be nice to see what it's all about. I promise to keep my hands to myself. Well, I'll try" she winks.

She smiles "Don't worry, I'd never farm another girl's crop"

"When did you want to go to East?" I ask nervously.

"If I'm leaving with the Station Master, I could go right now. Everyone knows who you are with or without the jacket"

She pauses waiting for my answer.

"Unless it's a bad time for you" she cocks her head.

"Now's perfect" I smile meekly.

"Give me a moment to get better clothes and I'll be right back" she smiles back and walks away, her limp less noticeable.

Is this a good idea? I barely know Acacia and I'm letting her take me to this unknown location where nobody ever goes to meet a mysterious woman, presumably that community's only resident. At night. And what will Cindy think if she finds out? I can't afford to make my situation any worse.

"You'll not find it easy to leave" an old man next to me says in a harsh British accent "They're watchin' even when you can't see 'em"

"What?" I turn to see him exiting the bar.

I get up to follow him.

"Scuse me, mate" two men push past me on their way in.

I step aside before hurrying outside to catch the old man but he's gone, vanished in the darkness. No way of finding him now to ask what he meant. Or if he'd even been talking to me. I feel like I've heard this before but can't recall where.

I go back inside to wait for Acacia.

No situation is so bad that it can't get worse. So how will history judge this decision?

Acacia returns wearing black pants, short boots, and a dark green jacket over her long-sleeved shirt.

We leave the same way I'd come in, a few men briefly glancing our way, the other servers all watching us leave. Climbing the stairs, we emerge into darkness, the bright half-moon visible through the branches and leaves to my right, the sky and forest around us clear. My eyes lock on the forest directly ahead of me, how the white glow sharpens the trees and the leaves in front of it, like a crowd of stick figures in the night. The clearing is well-lit, everything striking and well-defined as I watch and wait expecting a shadow to move between the rocks or trunks, but none does.

All is quiet once the door chimes go silent behind us.

I zip up my jacket in the cool night air putting my hands in my pockets. Acacia seems unbothered by the chill.

She winds gracefully among the trees, slithering like a cat, only once looking over her shoulder.

"Keep up, Colden"

"I'm coming" I hustle to stay close, my movements jagged and clipped as I navigate uneven terrain, between trunks and limbs. Moonlight hinders more than helps me with the shadows it creates on the ground in front of me.

"Do you like it in New Brook West?" I ask when I catch up to her.

"Mostly" she seems to consider her answer "I came here young and don't know much else except for living rough back home. The folks are odd and not real accepting of outsiders which is maybe how they protect themselves. I've made a few friends but have no special person in my life. I don't get noticed"

I find this hard to believe.

"Folks keep to themselves" she goes on "They don't talk much around me, even after all the time I've been here. I'm a solitary girl but it's good. Keeps me outta trouble"

"You're a smart girl" I smile.

"You're sweet" she smiles back "I try to keep my smarts a secret" she crouches down for a moment nearly disappearing when she does.

"I hear some things in the Stone" she stands up "I pick up on bits and pieces when people talk"

"Did you ever hear about who hires the station masters?" I ask "During your listening"

She thinks about her answer for a few seconds.

"There're some of you I could've done without" she says quietly "Not all good lads. But never a peep about who's picking you. I've heard that some took their own lives, others hanged by angry mobs or worse. Mind your manners in town, Station Master"

The look on my face must betray my fear.

"Don't worry" she smiles "You're safe with me. And free to talk and act as you please"

She kisses my cheek.

We enter the clearing in front of the town plaza.

Curling herself against a tree, she watches them emerge from the building, her movements more floating than walking as she follows them through the forest. Her unblinking eyes peek out from the darkness as she slithers behind them, neither too close nor too far back, creeping between the trees her body scrapes against the branches and bark.

She stays in the shadows of the forest when they go around the open grass in front of the gates into West. They pass the trail leading to the station and step onto another which she's seldom travelled. Silently, without disturbing the leaves or dirt, she keeps low to the ground watching their movements, listening.

Then her mouth gapes in terror as she realizes where they're heading. She tries to shriek, to yell, to scream at them, but all that comes out is a whisper too soft to be heard by anyone.

Is there someone whispering behind me? I turn around but no one's there. Surely nobody's following us.

I look into the village at the fountain, the cemetery, the church. All is quiet in the square, the lanterns flanking the path entering the community welcome travelers, the two lamps against the church wall remind me that there was once a great and powerful being who brought hope to New Brook West then took it away. Acacia also looks into the plaza, a melancholy expression on her face as if recalling a sad memory. We stand this way for a moment until her look turns serious as our gazes meet and she indicates with a nod that we should continue along the overgrown path that wouldn't have been seen if you didn't know it was there.

"You sure you haven't been this way before?" I whisper.

"I came with someone once but got scared and never went all the way"

"Who with?"

"I was young and impressionable" she smirks "Probably a boy. And here I go again"

The trail had clearly been a path at one time but hadn't been travelled in years, short yellow grass concealing its surprisingly level surface, foliage leans in requiring that I dodge branches and leaves both low and high. The forest is less dense here than on the way to the station, though night prevents me from seeing into it on either side. Within a minute I'm unable to make out any light from the village behind us.

Is that a crunching of leaves to my right? I take a few quick steps to be closer to Acacia, the path too narrow for us to walk side by side.

I wonder what might be watching our progress, sensing my fear.

Looking up, I spot the bright moon through the canopy, its light briefly illuminating the area around me. But then it's gone and we return to darkness.

Acacia glides ahead of me, moving silently and lithely, her body dancing through the trees.

"How far is it?" I ask after five minutes of silence between us.

"Not entirely sure" she replies "Remember: I've never actually been there"

I look over my shoulder, ensuring that no one unwelcome follows, at times sensing eyes on me, someone watching me move along this historic trail.

I'm grateful for the clear view of my surroundings, no sign of fog along the path. Overhead, the leaves and branches thin out, stars sprinkling the dark sky above me, the moon casting its light into the forest. The thin black and white trees on both sides loom ominously in their stillness, their unmoving branches haunting watchers along our walk.

We arrive at a large open area, stone buildings in various states of decay scattered about the glade. Portions of masonry have withstood time's wear, though these structures must have been unoccupied for ages; the community feels lonely. Some buildings have timber roofs, others are open to the elements. Occasionally, a single larger house sits outside the main collection of buildings, its door looking in on the community's center.

The moon shines above us casting an eerie glow on New Brook East.

"Here we are" Acacia sits on a large stone her hands on her knees "Not much to it as you can see"

She shivers slightly.

I sit on a rock of my own, unsure if I should acknowledge her chill.

Silence and solitude fill the empty village.

"You warm enough?" I ask.

"I think so" she smiles faintly "You?"

"I think so" I reply.

The ruins are an impressive sight, fragments of a once hopeful group, now a testament to a settlement long since abandoned. I feel watched, as though the eyes of the previous inhabitants either marvel at our presence or are offended by our intrusion. Their home is a memorial to a lost battle, a site long forgotten with the passage of time. Are their spirits tied to their houses, their memories locked into the land?

"There're a few other houses a ways off" Acacia says "But I suspect they'll look the same if not rougher"

The houses I can see all seem designed from the same plan, the exteriors dull earthtones or black, the doors facing inward toward the community's center. None of these homes would be fit for habitation in their present condition. It's a ghost town, the entire village a spectral entity.

"You said that a woman lives nearby" I look around unable to see any signs of recent occupation.

"I'll scour the area but no promises. This area has all manner of fables and I'd hate to become one of them"

A bird caws in the distance.

"Just preferring to keep us both safe" she adds with a brave face, disappearing into the darkness.

I'm left alone and in silence.

New Brook East feels infused by the fear and solitude the new settlers must have felt upon their arrival and for a long time after.

I'd never been afraid of the dark nor of being alone until I'd come to New

Brook West, every noise and movement now chilling me, every shadow hiding an unknown horror. I sit for a few moments listening to the silence. The occasional crackle of a branch snapping or a tree rustling breaks the quiet, hopefully from Acacia's steps.

I hear soft whispers from somewhere in the forest. Has someone followed us? Why? A gentle voice, not Acacia's, echoes lightly around me, around the small clearing, a child's pitch, a girl's voice. I stand up to look into some of the residences to occupy my thoughts and distract me from the forest's shushing. Rotten wood, broken ceramic, cracked stone from one home to the next. So many small dwellings are scattered throughout the clearing that was New Brook East. How did they live in such tiny homes? Or was this an improvement on those they left behind?

Were they afraid of the forest? Its sounds? Its silence?

When did they build the station?

After passing a few non-descript structures, I approach a larger building, the front door hanging on its frame, vines snaking through a trellis to my right. Climbing the stairs up to the narrow patio, I cautiously enter. The interior is simple yet well-built; to the right, light green walls and simple furnishings, a large window looking out on the other structures. A hallway leads to the back of the house. I spot a child partway along it.

"Wow" I jump "You scared me"

Is she still there? I faintly make out the outline of a young girl in a dress.

"Hi" I say softly "I'm sorry if I scared you"

I crouch down.

Silence all around me.

I make a slight move forward, the girl no longer there, a pile of boxes where she'd been standing.

I decide against further investigation of the house and exit.

I approach a building the size of a large shed directly in front of this structure, a few wood beams all that remain of the roof, the door entirely missing from its frame. Still, the craftsmanship seems sound, the building itself solid after all these years, the entry welcoming.

Is there a child standing in the doorway? The same one as in the other house?

Is someone else here with us? Who and why?

I stop in my tracks and wait in silence, not wanting to light one of my matches yet.

Squinting my eyes, I take a short step forward but whoever had been in the building's entryway is gone.

I wait for any movement, anything to appear, any sound, standing as still as I can. I'm still waiting when I realize there may be someone behind me, near the house I just left. I don't hear anything in any direction. My heart pounds in my chest and I'm paralyzed. I shiver.

Taking a deep breath, I slowly turn my head trying to simultaneously remain aware of what's in front of me.

I look up behind me at the larger house I'd just exited. There's no one toward or in its window. Moonlight shines over my shoulder, making the front of the building bright but keeping its interior dark.

I sigh and shiver, exhaling deeply.

Turning back to the small house, I'm prepared for anything but nothing's there, just the doorway, no one standing in it.

I slowly step toward it and inside, the interior noticeably warmer than outside, much to my relief.

Moonlight shines through the open roof onto the doorway through which I'd entered.

A short hall reaches the back of the house, three open doors along the right wall. The room to my immediate left takes up the entire side of the house, a second entry further down the hall. A rectangular table with four broken chairs around it occupies the middle of the space, a smaller table against the interior wall, a fireplace against the back one. The long exterior wall in the large room appears smooth as though cut from a single piece of rock. On it, a child's colourful stick drawings extend along the surface from the front to the rear of the house.

Lighting a match allows a better view, the flame making shadows dance in the corners and behind me. Still, I feel safe inside.

The art furthest to my left, nearest the front wall of the house, shows a tall stick-figure in a red triangular dress with the word 'Mother' beneath it; a smaller figure to her right in a light pink dress with 'Fuchsia' written beneath it; a shorter one to her left in a purple dress labelled 'Violet'; another in a black dress, trees on both sides of the dark figure with 'Sadie' above her. I don't initially see the figure in a grey dress with 'Auntie Nicole' written beneath it beside the red one.

Is this a family? The one that lived here?

To the right of this sketch, the red figure stands behind the purple one on a swing, the pink girl facing the observer, a blue book in her hands; black 'Sadie' and grey 'Auntie Nicole' are both absent from the drawing.

The simplicity of the drawings against the smooth pale surface creates a striking impression, childhood playfulness in these eerie surroundings. The moon shining through the missing roof illuminates the entry, barely reaching where I'm crouched. I look over my shoulder toward the rooms across from me as the match burns out in my fingers.

Is that a tall figure with two smaller ones standing at the back of the middle room? I see sharp outlines under the moon's glow; not enough to make out any features, though they appear female, wearing dresses.

Does someone live here? Whoever's standing there doesn't move or speak or make any sound at all. A mother and two daughters?

Moonlight comes over the back wall of the house keeping them in the shadows.

Do they see me? I wait, as still and quiet as I can be.

Does one of the shorter shapes move?

"Hello?" I say meekly.

Is this the ultimate intrusion, walking into someone's home uninvited? I take a step back then a short step toward the door as I ponder how to get out of the house.

It's too late to leave without saying something. Where's Acacia?

"I'm the new…"

I strike a match which immediately blows out in my fingers.

A creaking sound comes from somewhere in the house.

I want to run but wouldn't know where to go.

I light another match.

Three mannequins draped with partially finished dresses, a bed and a table against the room's wall. I shiver and the chill goes from my neck down my back.

I turn away from what must have been the sewing room, leaning against the wall for a moment. Catching my breath, my eyes wander back into the large room.

The moon lights up the house's interior making me notice more drawings further along the wall, their bright colours striking in the ruined structure, especially in the light.

I find myself drawn in by the art, mesmerized by its unique style.

I step forward, toward where I'd stood before my shock.

The next set includes a male form dressed in brown among the female figures, the word 'Uncle' scrawled above him, the characters standing around a fire.

Is this a story expressed in a child's drawings? What's the message? Is the artist one of those drawn on the wall?

Continuing to the right, the woman in red now hangs from a tree, a black rope around her neck, three black figures on each side of her, the purple girl behind those on the left, the other figures absent from the scene.

Although the faces lack the detail to convey emotion, I feel connected, as if observing these people and this event in real time. Had the red woman been hanged? Why? Who are the dark individuals on either side of her?

Next to it, a drawing of the girl in the purple dress sitting beside the red figure, who is now lying on the ground.

In the scene to the right of that one, a girl in a grey dress stands above six black figures laid horizontally head to toe on the ground.

The drawings are creepy, especially in the dimly lit house, the figures more lifelike than would be expected from this style of art. The black, grey, and colours stand out strikingly against the wall's white, even after what must have been many decades. I marvel at the artist's ability to convey a story that captures me though I don't fully understand it.

And the story ends there.

I shiver against the chill as I stand.

Exhaling, I lean against the wall, my heartbeat returning to normal, my mind mightily relieved that I'm alone. Dropping my lit match in the dirt, I stamp it out.

I expect to hear a whisper or a rustling of leaves or a creaking, but nothing; New Brook East is calm and quiet, the ruined village sheltered from any wind. I dare not get lost here or I'll become one of the fables.

As a cloud passes across the moon, I light another match.

I look out through the house's large crumbling rear window, giving me a glimpse of other structures near this one. The ruins beyond this small home are sharp, in their ghostly serenity, a mixture of greys and blacks and whites.

The half-moon's light comes and goes behind passing clouds, creating shadows among the buildings when it shines. Broken stone, rotted wood, and bent metal litter this collapsed melancholy site. The structures in the moonlit clearing are ravaged by time and the elements.

A sadness fills me as I think of New Brook East's residents, the debris all that remains of their homes, of their lives. How would this community have looked in its prime? Who were the people?

Through the window, a female figure stands next to a small run-down structure. I try to focus but can only discern her outline, as she disappears behind the building after a few seconds. Acacia? Who else could it be?

I take a step back.

"Find anything interesting?"

I nearly jump out of my skin, the match falling from my fingers.

Recovering from my stumble I turn to Acacia who's standing right behind me.

"Didn't scare you, did I?" she smiles.

"No" I reply as a sudden chill causes me to shiver "A little. I was looking at these illustrations on the wall"

"Children's doodles" she dismisses them without a care.

"Seems to describe a family" I say following her outside where the air has turned damp, making me shiver again "Then a hanging"

Acacia's face is serious.

"There's not a lot of talk about East" she walks past a fire pit near the center of the community with me close behind "People are generally afraid, not just of visiting but even thinking. Like there's a curse"

"What happened that was so bad?" I ask, my voice seeming to carry.

"Some say it was an ancient evil, others the result of a pact with a demon, others simply that men can be wicked" she crosses her arms "It all played out here, or so I'm told. Some situations can't be properly described. Some can't be undone. Some pasts are best forgotten"

A grim history, indeed.

"Are we going to see your friend?" I ask.

"Wouldn't call her my friend. But she's close by. I'm told she's just a lonely old lady" she turns, leading the way along a path I hadn't seen "In any case, I'll take you there. Maybe you'll get some answers"

Through the trees, we arrive in a tiny clearing with a grey tarped structure only slightly larger than the buildings we've left behind, a door at the right end of the wall facing us, a covered window on the left, light smoke escaping its chimney.

Who is this 'lonely old lady'?

Acacia stops.

"Is this it?" my voice quivers.

"I think so" she replies "If you'd rather not, I'll understand completely"

"No, it's OK. If you're fine"

"I'm fine" she says without taking her eyes from the tent, her voice betraying her fear.

I take her hand which squeezes mine in return, our faces meeting and smiling as we approach the entrance.

"Hello, Station Master. Please come in" a friendly female voice welcomes me from behind the tarp.

"Hello" I say stepping inside, surprised that she knows my identity.

"And hello to you, Acacia" to which my companion smiles and nods.

"Thank you for your hospitality" I sit on the floor next to Acacia, across from the woman, a small, four-legged metal stand over a fire between us and our hostess whose chair puts her higher than we are. She's sitting in shadow.

"Yes" she says "My hospitality"

Candles in glass jars, each flame a different colour, sit on counters and tables near the canvas walls at irregular intervals around the room, the tent much larger inside than it appeared as we approached. A narrow table is against each of the walls, a brown sack on the ground to the woman's left, several dark cups on a low wooden table to her right. The fire provides more warmth than expected though it burns low, a kettle fixed within its structure. A mix of scents fills the room making me feel high as soon as I've entered, the odour spicy.

"So, this is New Brook East" my pitiful attempt stumbles out of my mouth.

Her dark grey hooded cloak disguises her appearance and age though she appears slim, her voice and movements distinctly feminine, her tone much younger than an 'old lady'.

For a second, her eyes sparkle in the light but then disappear under the grey hood.

"Do you know why you're here, Colden?" she indicates two cups on the stand in front of us that I'd not noticed before. I take a sip out of politeness, my mind muddled from the aromas in her tent.

"What do you mean?" I say, unsure how to reply.

She looks back over her shoulder and then pokes the fire, ignoring my question.

"Do you live here?" I ask trying to bring the conversation back around.

"I like the solitude" she says.

Solitude.

A moment of awkward silence ensues. I casually look around the tent's grey cloth siding, the colourful psychedelic candles, the area a mix of colours, the lighting arranged to keep the woman's face in shadow. I can't look up at her without being noticed so eventually bring my gaze back to the center of the room.

A peppery wood aroma, like incense in a fire pit, fills the space. The increasingly warm air makes me want to remove my coat but I dismiss the thought. Acacia also looks hot, loosening her jacket and visibly affected by the heat. It feels like we're in another world.

The woman nods to me to which I take a few more sips of the sweet tea. Acacia appears to be drinking hers more quickly.

"Thank you for visiting" she says.

Is there a child in a chair at the back of the room? No way to tell in the dark corner.

"New Brook East was my home when I was a girl" she leans forward, the hood nearly falling away from her face "A happy place filled with hope"

"You have a beautiful home" I try.

"Yes" she says extinguishing two candles to her left "Some things have changed others are exactly the way they should be"

Uh-oh.

Unsure where this is going, I decide against quizzing her about East's history or previous station masters.

Candles come to light while others are snuffed out around the room making the shadows dance. Are there movements behind the woman?

Acacia hasn't said a word since we arrived and I begin to wonder if she knows more about this than she'd let on. Or if she's just terrified.

Time slows down.

"So few come to East now" her voice hisses with pride not loneliness "Perhaps they know. Perhaps they don't want to know. Some came in the past. Some wanted to know"

I look into the fire.

"You stayed in East" the idiocy of this statement occurs immediately.

"This is my home" she whispers, looking up from the fire to face me.

In my short time here, the situation has turned uncomfortable, the time due to leave, my head dizzy from the burning of incense inside the tent.

"We shouldn't have bothered you, especially for so long" I get to my feet groggy.

"I was happy to see you, Colden" she says.

"And thank you for your stories" I take Acacia's hand, turning to the door.

"I do need your help with something" she says seriously.

"What's that?" I ask turning back to face her.

"First: did you like the tea?"

I look down at the empty cup on the floor.

And then everything goes black.

39 – The tea

The witch runs from me, laughing as she does; is she leading me somewhere or running from me?

Who is she?

Through a foggy forest, only the trees right along the path are visible. I see her naked body from the back, barefoot, her hair snow white and wild. I can't make her out clearly, a combination of darkness, thick haze, and my blurry vision as her body glides through the murky air. My stride slows, like running in quicksand, yet still I seem to be gaining on her. Slender branches on either side of us line our path, watching the chase.

The thin figure ahead of me screeches, then all goes black.

My body hits a wall at full-speed.

I wake abruptly.

Where am I now? In the woman's tent? At Acacia's? Had I chased someone out and through the forest? Why? My head is spinning, my vision fuzzy, my senses awakening. I'm on the sofa in my apartment.

How did I get back here and what did I do between the time I left New Brook East and passed out on my couch? And where is Acacia?

7:00 am

I get to my feet with great difficulty, look around the room, and make my way to the window for a look out toward the path to the village. No one is visible in the clear dark air, a faint glow from the lit lanterns at the station below me. It takes me a moment to realize that I'm not wearing any clothes, my watch no longer on my wrist. Two lamps in the kitchen area illuminate the dim suite.

Had I brought Acacia back here? I don't think so.

I call out Acacia's name, walk around the room, and look in the bathroom, but she's not here. The 'lonely old lady' mentioned something she wanted me to do but I lost consciousness before she could tell me. I wouldn't have been very useful to anyone last night judging by how I feel now. What could I, of all people, do for anyone here?

Should I try to find my way back to New Brook East on my own; I doubt I'll find anyone to help me? Will Acacia be at the bar?

Do I want to talk to Cindy? Maybe not yet.

Pulling on pants and a t-shirt, I step out onto the darkness on the landing. Two oil lamps on the hotel wall illuminate the lower level. I wait, ears attuned to any break in the silence, but hear nothing. Early morning is still more night than day, the moon over the trees to my left, a sprinkling of stars in the sky. Dawn's faint orange glows just above the trees to my right.

My faculties have returned sufficiently for me to slowly move down the stairs and see if anything outside jogs my memory, if any evidence of what took place the previous evening found its way to the station, to see if I could re-trace my steps. I need the banister to descend the staircase, my eyes fixed on Room 1 as I do. Reaching the platform, I release my support, take a few careful steps toward the tracks.

In the absence of any fog, the moon's glow sharpens the lines defining the station, the stairs up to my apartment, the benches against the wall. The rails shine a bright silver, the wood ties and gravel bed striking black and white tones along the line. The dark army of trees stands in front of me, long thin blades rising from the ground. I stare into the dense growth across the tracks, darkness filling the small spaces, extending infinitely away from me.

Turning back, I notice the utility room door is open and stop.

Has someone stolen a tool? Is someone hiding in there? What should I do?

I can't just leave someone in there but don't have the energy for a struggle.

Who could have opened the door?

Approaching cautiously, I hear no sounds from inside the room, see no light. Grabbing a lit lamp off the wall I walk toward the room. Ready for anything, I step inside.

No one.

Difficult to account for missing items, though I suspect they'll all be here if I check. Closing and locking the door, I make my way across the platform.

Lamp in hand, I walk down the steps into the large clearing, hopeful that I'll not encounter anyone. Only one trail leads into the forest that I know of, with the exception of travel along the tracks. Standing at the base of the steps, I look in both directions with nothing and no one between me and the trees, the forest much nearer the station on the apartment and control room side than anywhere else. I stare up at the stars, tiny lights in the black sky, the three-quarter-moon just above the forest, dawn's first colours appearing in the east.

A calm morning.

I walk around the building below the apartment to begin my search for clues.

I'm not prepared for what I find.

40 – Why?

It takes me a moment to collect myself.

Who could have done this and why? I chill at the ghastly scene.

There are no signs of activity in any direction on this side of the station except where I'd just walked to get here. Who else would come out here?

Is someone watching right now in the silent forest behind me? My spine shivers; my teeth clench. Alone in the dark, I'm too scared to turn around.

Exhaling deeply, I walk around to the tracks, but see no one on the platform nor in the dense brush. The empty benches wait in anticipation of the train. Past the station under the hotel, I stare into the dark.

Returning to the wall beneath my apartment, I'm chilled by the terrible sight. What can I do? What should I have done? Shaking myself from a daze, I walk back onto the tracks, careful to listen for a whistle before I do. Hopping up onto the platform from the rails I notice a light inside the control room. I try the door and it's locked as it should be. Pulling the keys from my pocket, I open the door thinking someone has to be hiding here, anxious because I don't know what to do if they are.

I try to slowly and quietly open the door but am sure I fail on both counts. I enter the room wide-eyed. As with the utility room, there's no one here so secure the lock behind me as I leave.

Could someone have arrived by train and departed while I was away? None were scheduled today but perhaps one passing through had stopped allowing a passenger to get off and back on before anyone noticed.

My chest heavy, I return to my room. Could the person who brought me home be the culprit? The old woman wouldn't have had the strength to get me here on her own. Acacia certainly didn't either. There must be answers in New Brook East but I have no desire to try to find the old community on my own.

No.

41 - No one deserved this

Dusk's colours finally emerge over the treetops; faint reds, oranges, and yellows tinting the forest.

I emerge from the apartment with a heavy heart.

It's definitely her. But of course, she looks so different.

A pitchfork through her chest holding her to the wall.

Her naked body on display, her bare feet a short distance off the ground, her downward pointing toes hovering above the grass, making me wonder the reason for this pose, her clothes and shoes nowhere to be seen. Her head sags toward her chin, her face as pale as her hair.

There's just enough light from my lamp to see her arms hanging limply at her sides, palms against her thighs, her hair parted down the middle, eyes closed in beautiful innocence. The shadows sharpen the beauty of her features.

So many questions, so many terrifying thoughts, so many guilty feelings as though I should have been able to stop this horrific event. Morning will eventually increase the gloom of this tragedy. No one deserved this, certainly not someone as innocent and hopeful as her.

42 - Atrocity

Should I try to find Michael? Dalton? Feryn?

This will be difficult to explain to any of them and I'll surely be suspected by whoever I tell.

Go see Cindy? What would I tell her?

I glance down as thoughts muddy my head noticing what looks like my watch directly beneath her suspended body. How did it get here?

My mind is overwhelmed.

I pause in silence, staring at the wall, unsure of what to do next.

The pitchfork pinning her to the side of the building makes me shiver, but I know what has to be done. I stare for a moment, then drop my eyes to the ground. Inhaling then exhaling deeply, I step forward for the ghastly task. I pull gently at first, then with greater strength side to side when it doesn't immediately dislodge. With far more effort than expected, the tool eventually comes loose, her thin body slumps to the ground like a rag doll.

I jam the pitchfork's long tines into the ground, staring down at her form, recalling our talks, her sassiness of manner, the innocence in her eyes, the kindness in her heart. Could I locate any family or friends she has in New Brook West or elsewhere on the island? Who could I talk to?

I'll need to cover her body and conceal it while I consider my next steps. If she's found or someone sees me moving her to another location, I'll be convicted of a crime I didn't commit. Everyone at the Grey Stone saw us leave together.

Will taking her to a secluded location be disrespectful to her memory? It feels like disposing of a body.

Should I try to find the guilty party?

I had discovered this atrocity not committed it, right?

43 - Zack

First, I need to cover her body, out of respect.

As a short-term solution, I wrap her in a large cloth tarp from the utility room, then in a plastic sheet I found behind a crate, and put her body in a long box eerily resembling a coffin. I'd felt a special connection with Acacia, and feel horrible about this tragedy.

For the moment, I need to focus on my next steps as I'll surely be the prime suspect in her murder; had my predecessors taken their own lives to escape the wrath of the community. I had no reason to kill Acacia, but this will be difficult to explain considering the circumstances. Nothing in my apartment offers any clue as to a motive for the crime nor for how I got back here.

I lay back on the bed to close my eyes for a moment thinking about Acacia before drifting into unconsciousness.

Knock, knock.

The sound rings in my ears like an alarm clock startling me from my sleep. Where am I? I'm in the apartment. Ok.

I must have passed out. It takes a second to recover from my surprise at being in bed, my instinct telling me to hide or run because this is surely someone come to sentence me for the crime. Sparse light shines through the windows, my watch, now on the coffee table, says just after 10:00. Perhaps the angry mob come to hang me. I look at myself, then around the room, confirming that everything is in order, last night's clothes still not found. I take a good ten seconds to reach the door, my visitor is obviously patient as there's no second knock.

"Hello, Station Master" the man says, in a voice both cheerful and serious.

His black pants, dark green shirt, and grey military-style jacket make him an imposing figure, as tall as me and bigger all around. His face gives away no emotion without appearing stern, his greeting a matter-of-fact opening remark, his hands casually at his sides, his stance neither aggressive nor defensive. His hair is greying and beginning to thin, his stature that of a well-travelled man with both inner and physical strength.

Uh oh. I'm still wearing the clothes I'd worn while cleaning up.

"Hello" I look around wondering if he's alone. Doesn't seem he's here about Acacia or the previous evening's events.

"Please come in" I say hastily, eager to get him off my doorstep to avoid drawing eyes to me.

"Nice place" his eyes scan the room.

"Thanks"

Definitely not here to lynch me.

"I'm Zack", he turns to me, extending his hand.

"I'm Colden"

"You look like you could use a friend", he says.

"Why would you say that?" I'm insulted by his comment.

"Because you took a really long time to come to the door, looked around outside when you finally did, hurried me inside, your clothes are a mess, and you've had a defensive posture since I arrived. Oh, and there's blood all over the side of the building"

Shit. Did I forget to clean the wall?

"OK, so maybe I do need a friend" I sit on the two-seater couch "But who exactly are you?"

"Someone whose family has lived in the area for a long time" he removes his old-style military boots.

"But not in New Brook West or East?"

"No"

"So where do you live?" I look up at him.

"Lived in Mantiston" he leans back in the chair "About an hour walk from here along the tracks. My ancestors settled there a long while back"

He points toward the kitchen.

"I actually just heard there was a new Station Master and came by to say 'Hi'" he goes on "Thought you might be an interesting sort. Seems I'm right, but for the wrong reasons"

"This is not what I expected when I came here" I tell him "I'm not even sure what's going on half the time"

"Maybe I'll have some things to put you on the right track. So to speak"

"Do you know who selects the station master?"

"I don't, but as I recall this was not common knowledge"

"Well, I'd appreciate any information you have. I'm way off track. So to speak"

"My father was a religious man like his father before him and even further back too. My great-grandfather lived in West, after leaving East when his parents passed on. I've got no spiritual knowledge to share, only some history that may provide clarity"

He removes his jacket revealing a stocky frame; I doubt people mess with this guy.

"This goes back long before my time so keep in mind that the further back I go, the less reliable the information. Now, I'm a skeptic, but some parts defy logical explanation based on what I know - you may be more enlightened or intelligent than I am so if that's the case you can draw your own conclusions. Believe me or don't, it's up to you. I'll present what I know and you put it together how you like"

"What exactly do you do in Mantiston?" I ask "Are you a leader?"

"That's not really important to what I'll be saying" he looks at me "You have a dark past that I'm not asking about"

"How do you know that?"

"How else did you end up here?"

Fair enough.

He glances around the room as if confirming we're alone.

"I joined the local army at a pretty young age. Wanted adventure and found it travelling. I came to East regularly when I was back on the island and got to know the people and their customs.

"For a time, the communities went through an age of mutual prosperity, of plenty and happiness, life comfortable and cooperative. The island isn't that big, but large enough for six or seven villages, only two remaining today. At some point, it all changed and an illness replaced the good life to which people had become accustomed. Relations between the communities strained, inter-marriages stopped, existing ones tore apart, neighbours fought amongst themselves, brother against brother, people blaming anyone but themselves. I'm told this was very real at the time, when spiritual beliefs, social connections, knowledge of the world were all very different, especially on an island as isolated as this one.

"My grandfather and great-grandfather told me stories, fictional tales about spirits and witches, poverty and wealth, heroes and villains. About vengeance. Every place has its ghosts and its evils. Some walk among us, others lurk in the shadows and watch from a distance.

"Folks had stopped attending the church, stopped worshipping their god who had forsaken them, stopped believing entirely. Most agree that a charismatic man came and took the company of a witch, and for a time became the leader the community needed. He knew nothing of gods but had such a manner about him that confidence returned. People listened to him and he led them while. But only for a short time.

"At some point in the story, the man was found dead and his witch disappeared from the community

"I'll leave you to figure out how that part fits in to the rest of the story"

My mind searches for words but none come.

"Skip ahead a few years and things take a different turn: a woman. Always a woman" he smiles briefly.

"One thing led to another and she found herself on the wrong end of accusations against which she couldn't defend herself. No divine intervention or charismatic man came to help her. Ultimately, she was put to death, a circumstance which saddened me greatly, as she was dear to me, but was beyond my reach. East was eventually abandoned, folks wanting to distance themselves from this horrific event. Some of those responsible got what they deserved; some who were innocent got the wrong end of justice. Residents moved where they had family or could find employment; many perished, unable to support themselves and their loved ones"

He casually looks around the room again.

"There are many cemeteries, some hidden, some barely remembered, still others in which the bodies of the unwanted are supposedly interred"

He pauses as if collecting his thoughts.

"You may find some answers there if you keep an open mind" he adds.

"That's why no one lives in East anymore?" I ask, feeling I missed something in what he said.

"East was never large" he shakes his head "When a community is as small as it was, there are sure to be problems. People get too close. They know too much about each other. And there are those who covet what others have: wealth, power, beauty. And forces we can only imagine, some in the evil hearts of men and women, some outside the bounds of our understanding. Both are real"

"You mean magic, the supernatural" I roll my eyes.

"You're a skeptic, too" he nods.

"So, what happened to make you a believer?" I lean in closer.

"Spellcraft is still feared in West as it was in East. Anyone whose skills could not be explained either possessed dark magic or took counsel from demons. Believe what you want about that but I've seen events which are extremely difficult to reason.

"Now, I'm retelling tales that have been passed on through many mouths and ears and minds" he sits up straight in the chair "This can make stories inaccurate. But some of this I do know for myself. I'm not sure what you know or believe at this point"

A brief pause ensues between us as if he's waiting for me to speak.

"I think you were expecting a man of few words" he smiles "But then there wouldn't have been much point in me coming. I knew a great deal about you before I arrived and our time together has filled in the gaps for me, for what it's worth"

His clarification has taken on an unusual, if not eerie, tone.

"If you do decide you'd like to leave the island, and that's probably something you're considering, just know that I advise against it, at least right now. Boarding the train is much more difficult than it seems and attempting escape by other means is a bad idea. And I can tell that you don't have all the answers"

"Is it so different in Mantiston?" I ask, "Are you happy?"

"I've seen what else is out there and heard of even more. As far as

Mantiston goes, they relied on the train station too but never interfered with other matters. Historically, yours was a position of honour but has been offered only to outsiders for a long time now"

"What happened to the other station masters?"

"They died, I suppose" he replies seriously "Why they were chosen, you'll get different answers depending on who you ask. My opinion, for what it's worth, is that you were selected for a reason, something about you that maybe you don't even realize"

Zack stands as if to leave.

"I met a woman in the woods near East last night and things got pretty crazy after that" I rise as well, my body stiff.

"East has all manner of mysteries and relics, both physical and spiritual"

He continues after a short pause.

"You might have to change your logic to get a good grasp of things here. Things aren't always what they seem and neither are people. You'll need to figure this out for yourself in terms of how it applies in West. I've told you most everything I know. Keep an open mind and you just might find your way through"

He makes his way to the door.

"Thanks for stopping by, Zack" I extend my hand.

"Glad we could meet" he replies with a firm handshake "I keep a pretty low profile but maybe we'll see each other again. Enjoy your day"

He opens the door to exit.

"And you really should clean that up. Don't worry, I don't talk to anyone in West, at least not anymore. It is a shame. She was a sweet girl"

I wonder if he's talking about Acacia or the woman in his story.

"Do you know how I can get to East?" I step back "I'd like to take a look around"

"Best to find someone local to help you" he says without turning around "Good luck, Colden. You'll need it" he looks back at me as the door closes behind him.

I wish I had Zack's confidence.

Out the partially open window, I hear the **New Brook West** sign above the platform creak on its hinges.

1910

My sister, her daughter, her daughter's daughters. All dead or vanished.

Except for the one, the one who left so young amid the shame of her horrid looks, the mockery inflicted by her peers, the indifference imposed by her family. Only I cared for her and commiserated, in my own way and for my own reasons. I empathized with her plight, even if this empathy served my purpose.

The girl in the purple dress had succumbed to the Station Master's wickedness, a necessity to hide his misdeeds. I admired his maliciousness, his selfish intent. Again, he would have been no use to me, such was his ego.

Her purple dress now grey, I took her from their little cemetery, laying her to rest at the station, spreading a terrible tale in town to instill such fear in the villagers that they'd never dare enter Room 1. Soon, a menacing story had spread about the forbidden room, guarding it against any unwanted visitors, for simple fear would keep out any born on the island.

I place a vial of liquid next to her frail body, caressing her cold pale cheek.

I've conjured a plot to guide me, for a prophecy is not the future foretold but a destiny to be fulfilled.

The youngest may not trust me but she'll trust her sister. Her eldest sister come to be with her.

I approach the door.

Knock, knock.

"Who?" I hear a girl's nervous voice from the other side of the door.

"A friend" I reply.

I hear her slow footsteps approach then the door opens just a crack; scared eyes peek out.

"May I come in?" I ask.

She seems to consider the words as if she doesn't understand them, looks past me, then down.

"Yes"

The door opens.

Her room is pitiful; how does she live like this? There's a place for a fire in the middle of the floor, blankets next to it which much be her bed, small boxes of various sizes scattered about the space, a large bowl of water which could be either for drinking or for relieving herself.

It almost makes me sad. But I came for a reason.

"We sit down" I lower myself to a clean part of the floor.

She slowly sits down near me. She hasn't taken her eyes off me.

"I'd like to help you" I lean forward. She retreats back.

"You don't have to be alone" I say calmly.

She blinks and cocks her head inquisitively.

"You have green eyes" she says softly.

"I know someone who wants to be with you" I say "Who misses you. Who has always loved you"

She slides toward me.

"Who?" she says, her voice childlike.

I pause as I reach out and set a sweet tart on her lap.

She sniffs it then devours it greedily as her lips form a smile.

"I want to take you to someone who wants to see you, who cares for you" I say, holding out another sweet piece.

"Who?" she whispers.

"I know who's responsible for separating you from your family, for your sadness, and how you can hurt them back"

"Who?" the child whimpers.

"Go to the hotel" I say "Go to Room 1"

"Not Room 1" she shrinks away from me.

"I can help you if you'll help me" I say with a smile.

"Drink this for protection" with softly spoken words, I place a small bottle on the floor "There's someone there who loves you and is waiting for you. Then the two of you can be together"

The girl smiles, her skepticism waning.

"There's a girl in that room you need to give this drink" I continue "She's sleeping and you need to wake her. She'll help you punish the man who gave you your loneliness and pain. The bad man who kept you away from those who loved you. You need to get her to help you kill the bad man"

"Who?" her smile has turned sinister.

44 – Family trees

An entire morning spent cleaning, picking up, hiding anything on the side of the station. And remembering.

And forgetting.

How could I possibly be involved in any of this?

I feel like hiding from the world, hoping that somehow this is just a horrible nightmare.

By cleaning the area, I attempt to take away the memory of her murder because I don't want her to be remembered for her death. Her innocence, her strength, her kindness, at least inasmuch as I knew her. She seemed a good soul and would have brightened someone's life. Who and what had she loved? Where did she find beauty? I wonder if anyone will miss her, cry for her.

Will anyone notice she's missing? Was she truly alone?

She'd always wanted to visit the train station. To that end, I carve her name in a discreet location on the lower wall, in the hopes that this would have made her happy in life.

Satisfied with my efforts, I go upstairs.

Can I trust Zack's words? Be sure that he won't go to New Brook West and give me up? I have no choice but to believe him. He could have easily avoided any contact with me and kept his thoughts to himself. Probably best not to do anything suspicious right away so I decide to wait to revisit East on my own.

I'm lacking in allies and people are dying. Cindy stands with me, or so it seems, which provides some reassurance but I'll not be going to her place for the moment and I don't dare go back to the Grey Stone. Or the child care basement. Or most places except where I am right now.

Will the library offer sanctuary?

It's just after 12:00, meaning a relatively safe time to creep through town with most everyone working in the community fields. Putting on a dark green t-shirt, black pants, and a dark non-station-master jacket, I lock the door behind me, checking the control room printer much later than I should have. I creep across the clearing toward the village with absolutely no plan beyond that.

My heavy heart slows my steps.

I enter onto the path into the forest, the air clear and crisp among the sinister trees. The slender trunks rising from the ground angle closer to the trail today, the trees nearer to me, the path narrower. A few wildflowers brighten the brush and the areas between the trees though I don't want to get any closer as I'd have to leave the path.

It's a mercifully uneventful walk, my mind anxious, my hands shaking the entire way. The empty plaza is bathed in silence. Unlit lanterns welcome me, a light mist in the small glade, clouds overhead blocking out the sun. My eyes comb the area to ensure no locals are about, no one outside the church; my steps are quick but not too much so to draw attention. I take a quick look at the board which has nothing for me today. Sticking close to the walls, I slink through the alleys, hoping that no eyes are watching from the stone buildings. I don't see anyone or hear a sound on my journey through the community; even my own footsteps are silent.

Reaching the edge of town, I gaze upon the damp blue field, the trees and rocks breaking its continuity like islands in an ocean. There's no fog or mist here, though I notice darker ominous skies in the distance. Past the houses and outbuildings, past the boulders and trees and coloured grasses, my eyes focus on the road ahead.

Reaching the library, I look out at the black water, its expansiveness the closest I've come to infinity, the skies dark further out over the water. I duck into the building without passing anyone; my relief soars when the inside appears empty. Closing the door behind me, I survey the empty area, though whispers carry within the building, possibly from those I can't see. I never know when I'm alone or if I ever am. Are eyes watching me now?

Brian pops up from behind his counter catching me off-guard, though I am relieved to see him, thankful for a friendly face and hopeful that he can enlighten me in even the smallest way.

"Welcome back" he smiles.

"Hi" I look around nervously.

"Just me. At least I think so"

I approach him with soft steps.

"I'm often the only one here" I say.

"Often, but not always" he replies.

My body twitches, my eyes unsure where to look, my ears attuned to anything out of the ordinary. The grey walls feel darker today, the room dimmer. I want to look around the huge room but don't.

At this moment, I feel very much alone.

"You OK?" he cocks his head.

"I'm not sure" I reply "There's a lot going on right now and most of it is pretty frightening"

"This place can have that effect on you if you let it" he raises his eyebrows to accentuate his point.

"Are you a superstitious person?" I ask.

"Sometimes"

"I never used to be but that changed after I arrived here"

I walk toward the desk.

"Do you know anything about Mantiston?" I ask.

"Didn't think many lived there but they're fishermen so come and go I suppose. Always figured there was a divide of some kind between West and them but couldn't figure out what it was about. I've met some of them but not many. Why?"

"A guy from there named Zack dropped by my place this morning"

"What'd he say?"

"Not much that made sense, though he did share some interesting historical thoughts. Seemed like a decent guy, solitary type, rugged fella"

Brian nods.

"Mantiston was one of the original settlements, yes?" I ask.

"That's right" he says.

"Did they use the train station?"

"It's the only one on the island"

A few deep breaths on my part as I try to fill in the blanks.

I look around me but see no one in any direction, glance back at the entrance which is also unoccupied.

Brian gives me an odd look in response to my surveillance.

I take a step toward him.

"Do you know anything about Room 1 at the station hotel?" my nerves blurt this out at a lower volume.

"Just not to talk about it. You won't find any who'll tell you more than that"

"What about New Brook East?"

"Another bad topic" he frowns "Historically speaking, it's got a pretty dark past that ended in a woman's hanging from an unjust conviction. There was more than enough shame to go around and folks couldn't get outta there fast enough. Most came here, maybe some to Mantiston, a few into the woods or other places on the island. At least that's how it's told"

"Why was she hanged?" I persist, recalling the drawings in the house in East.

"Local legend says she knew things about the wrong people. This brought down the wrath of some powerful men and she was sentenced to death. Station Master at the time was involved in her conviction. One of her daughters ran away just before the hanging, the other went batty and all 'dark evil' on people afterwards for want of revenge. Some say there's a third daughter but that's another story"

"How was the station master involved?" I lean in.

"Now you know what I do" he raises his hands above the desk.

His words hang in the air for a moment. He drops his gaze to look at the papers on the desk, a sign that the conversation is over.

"Didn't mean to push" I say walking away.

I don't want to lose one of my few friends so won't pursue this topic.

"Hey, do you know anything about trees?" I turn back to ask him recalling something the woman in the Grey Stone said.

"You mean like forest trees or family trees?"

Family trees! The tree isn't a plant but genealogy.

"You have family trees?" my astonishment takes him by surprise.

"The historical includes info about the original folks who came, and then trickles down through their lineages. There's information about the different families that lived here, how they intermarried, how they lived"

"Are these on the shelves?" I lower my voice.

"No, they're in the red chest you were in last time" he nods toward it "Local history lessons are common, but at home not at school. Teachers aren't let in on much of it; but you must know about teachers" he smiles.

Apparently, my relationship with Cindy is no secret.

"Do you mind?" I point to the chest.

"By all means" he shrugs.

There's obviously something that the powerful or the superstitious or the scared want to close up for good. Are they trying to protect the innocent? The guilty? Themselves?

I wonder if there's a genealogy for each of the families that settled the island.

"There's a quiet spot over there", he points at a desk to my right against the wall, "Should give ya some privacy. And we never had any of these conversations. You'd bring down a heap o' trouble on yourself anyway with these subjects"

"Understood" I nod taking a pile of leather-bound tomes from the chest to his suggested location instead of the table from my previous visit.

The five family tree volumes I grab are similarly bound, if thinner than the family histories I'd read.

The walk back to my desk takes an eternity, each step like sand beneath my feet, reminding me of running on a soft beach. The room hypnotizing, the silence oppressive, anxiety like a black cloud over my head. The library sure does have its own atmosphere.

The empty chair welcomes me.

Grabbing the 'MARISTON' volume, I push the others aside.

A short way in I decide this isn't the volume with the answers, the genealogy incomplete with names I don't recognize. Pages beyond the first few are dedicated to individual families diverging from a single lineage beginning at what I suspect is settlement.

Brian is nowhere in sight to answer additional questions, if he had any intention of doing so.

What month is it? Darkness comes earlier every day, the grey soupy air as thick as ever, the gloom as pervasive as a bad mood. Rarely does it rain, though, which is a good thing.

'CLOVINSTON'. The first few pages provide a brief description of the original men and women who came from the mainland but this lineage doesn't seem to have lasted, at least not in name.

Mixed marriages are evident throughout, names including Pertwee, Hamilton, Smithson, and Collaston appearing throughout the genealogies.

Pushing the Clovinston tome to my left I bring the 'BARKMAN' volume in front of me. Brian Barkman is the last name in the genealogy, born in 1898. The 'BROOKS' line ends with Sophie the last individual in the family tree listed as born in 1903.

Then the thin 'VON STELA' volume, a familiar sounding name. From the historical texts?

The lettering inside the volume introducing the family is a work of art in itself, and it takes me a moment to realize that it's actual writing.

Brian has returned to his post staring down at whatever lay on the desk. No one's in the aisles behind me, at least no one I can see, and no one else has entered since I arrived. I'm presumably still alone.

The large old clock against the library's back wall says 4:45, night overtaking day in that direction. A creaking near the front door catches my attention, the small opening between door and frame closing before my eyes. My right hand clutches the book tightly, my common sense telling me to ignore these sounds.

Then, all goes quiet again.

I wait for any further noise, then look back at the entrance but no one's there.

The first page in, shows Martin and Katya's names in large print as if it were the introduction to a chapter. I recall that he'd been described in the historical volume as strong of character with a quick wit and clever mind, she a rare beauty with a keen intellect and a kind heart; or words to that effect. There is sufficient room for much more on this page but perhaps they are the patriarch and matriarch of this family or the first of their name on the island and that's how it was done to begin their family's lineage anew with their new lives. This would have presumably continued on the next page but Martin and Katya's descendancy will not be explained to me today, as this page is missing as though carefully torn out.

I wonder who would do this and why.

The few other pages are all intact but blank.

I assumed this would be the family's genealogy based on its location in the chest among the other books with similar content and hoped to see a family tree of some kind.

What a bizarre theft.

Then I remember Martin and Katya from the historical text and their children Rebecca and Christina Nicole. Rebecca's children were Hannah and an unusual boy's name I can't recall. I can't think of the names beneath them, if I'd even read them.

The name Rebecca again sounds familiar though I don't know why.

I won't be mentioning the missing page from the volume to Brian, at least not for now.

1910

It's dark in here, and quiet. I stop and look but can't see. There's only dark to my left so I turn the other way. I see a thin strip of the moon's light shining in through a crack in the wall. I move slowly across the smooth wood floor. I'm alone and I'm scared.

The woman said there's someone here who loves me, someone who will stay with me, someone I know. Where is she and why she's in here?

The woman says someone will help me hurt the man who hurt me, who sent them all away leaving me alone.

I'd almost forgot about the bad man, the Station Master, what he did. I still miss them and hoped one day they will come find me but they never came. How long has it been? So much time.

I don't want to be alone anymore.

Will this girl help me punish the man? Help me not be alone.

My eyes can see better now they are used to the dark.

I see a long box on top of some big ones near the crack in the board, near the light in the wall.

Careful, I cross the floor in the dark.

I see the small bottle that the woman said to give to the girl next to the box.

What is this box? What is in it?

I climb up and look inside the long box.

There's a young girl in the box. This must be the girl.

Does she sleep in here? Why?

I look at her closely, touch her face, move near her.

Then my eyes see her.

Oh my! It's you! In here. Oh, I've missed you so much.

Is it really you?

For a moment I stare at her, unable to believe my eyes.

1910

My eyes open, my arms slowly move at my sides. My body is stiff and weak.

Where am I? What am I wearing?

I look up but see only black.

I can't hear anything until something scrapes across the floor to my right. I look that way but there's a wall. And another on my left.

Wood boards? Am I in a box?

I taste sweet liquid on my lips.

I slowly push myself up in the box.

I look down at my dirty purple dress and the black shoes on my feet.

I pull my knees to my chest.

The room is cold and dark and I'm scared.

Where am I and how did I get here?

And who is that girl staring at me?

I feel a tear run down my cheek.

Then memories fill my mind.

The man's evil. His smile as mother was taken and shamed then hanged. Uncle tried to disguise us so we could start a new life then he left. Then my sister left too, leaving me alone again.

Most of all I remember sitting with mother as she sat alone in her cage then lying next to her on the ground after they took her life, keeping her warm and safe as she had done for me. I lay there alone as everyone else left us, lay with her. I cried for mother.

For myself. Is that selfish?

And then the anger comes. My rage. My sadness.

Why would he do that? I wipe away the tear.

No one would talk to me, listen to me.

I was helpless, a scared child.

The man was a very bad man. But what could I do to a Station Master?

I look at the other girl in the room. She looks scared but she's slowly coming towards me. My eyes can see well in the dark and I recognize a face I've not seen in a very long time.

I stand and lift myself out of the box and onto the floor, the girl backing away. Don't leave, please come to me, I think.

My hair still hangs in front of my face as it had when we left so we could hide who we were, so Uncle could hide me.

She slowly stands up, taller than me and very skinny.

We embrace and both cry as we do. It's been so long since I've held someone in my arms, since someone's held me.

We separate and look at each other. I can barely believe my eyes.

We stare at each other for a long time, remembering a time long ago.

Then she comes towards me to whisper in my ear.

I listen carefully.

What could I do to a Station Master?

Now he'll see.

45 - A girl has gone missing

Slipping out of the library, I step into a dreary scene, the wind blowing in from the ocean stronger than usual. My jacket offers just enough protection from the breeze but not the cold that comes with it. The moon looms to my left in the clear dark sky, the sun's final reds and oranges to my right as it descends into the water. Below me to my left there's a breakwater ahead of the river, potentially a harbour for the settlers before the train station; no boats are currently in the sheltered haven and I try to imagine the villagers' docked watercraft in a bygone time, a vacant space like a chalkboard that's been erased. Down on my right, the flat dark rocky terrace extends out into the water, a lonely wasteland. The library seems surrounded by emptiness.

The chill air hastens my steps across the open field and inside the village's protective shield. I stay close to the walls in the shaded alleys, quickly but quietly, vigilant of townsfolk on my way through the community. Night's arrival shrouds my presence from prying eyes but this provides little comfort given what I've already seen and heard in the dark. I wonder what watches me from the shadowed corners and black windows.

The path ahead and out of town is as desolate as ever, a sombre trek back to my accommodations. The memory of previous experiences in the forest, my spectral visions or imaginings, and the enigmatic Room 1, hang in the air as grim reminders of my circumstances.

A hushed thirty minutes after leaving the library, I climb the staircase to my suite, no bizarre drawings, children's toys, or suicidal photographs waiting for me. Another tiring day leaves little energy for food preparations, my dinner consisting of a four-egg omelet, toast, and juice. By the time I've eaten and cleaned up, it's just past 9:30, as good a time as any to pack it in, bolstered by the fact that an early train is scheduled the following morning as well as my mental and physical exhaustion.

The tranquil night combined with the day's discoveries heightens every sound in my room; I'm fortunate that the floor itself doesn't creak under my footsteps. Extinguishing all but the bedside lamps, I think back to the volumes detailing the area's history.

Who chronicled the genealogies? Why did the entries end when they did? Had the last chroniclers died without naming replacements? Did the people logging this information not keep track of people once they'd lost contact with a person or they'd left the island?

Then sleep takes me.

My body jolts upright in the darkness.

The room is cool but, despite being naked, fire flows through my veins under the blankets in the night dark. My weary legs fumble for the floor to look around the room. The oil lamps on the nightstands flicker dimly, nearly out of fuel, making shadows dance on surfaces near the bed. My eyes adapt to my dim surroundings, slowly taking in my shadowed environment, the light in the bed's alcove unable to illuminate areas in the kitchen and beyond.

Is that a head peeking up at the foot of the bed? Is someone in here with me? I steel myself for the impossible as my body tenses in fear. Then I hear something rapidly scrambling away across the living room floor. I freeze, unable to move.

Inside, the apartment is perfectly quiet; outside, the sound of rain against the window.

I stand, catching a glimpse of my reflection in the window, water drops bouncing off and sticking to the exterior pane. I stare for a moment, hypnotized by the rain hitting the window, the serenity of it.

Something moves behind me.

I turn around quickly but nothing's there. Silence. I stare into the darkness in my suite, eyes focused for any movement but see none, only the faintest light making the area around the bed glow. My heart is racing, my stomach aches, I can barely breathe. I don't think I can move and I don't dare try. Someone or something is in here with me. I wait for noise in the calm but none comes.

Is it her? The girl? Who is she?

I want to yell out but my voice is mute and all that comes out is a whisper.

The lamps behind me die.

The only sound is the rain against the window, the only light the dim white of the moon behind the clouds.

I think I can move. I have to.

I walk toward the door, looking beside the bed as I pass but no one's there or at the entrance. The rest of the room is too dark. All the corners black, the apartment in obscurity. The window facing the clearing shimmers, the raindrops visible on the glass.

I light a lantern in the living room but see nothing around the furniture or on this side of the island in the kitchen. The light in the suite prevents me from seeing outside, only my reflection visible in the windows. Far from the lantern, the corners remain too dark to see, so I look away.

I pause in silence, my eyes surveying the room. Waiting. Nothing moves, the only sounds my breathing and the rain outside.

I step into the bathroom.

The gas lantern to the right of the mirror won't light but the one to the left does, although dimly, which is sufficient to work with. Shadows dance around me as the flame flickers behind its protective glass in the dimly lit room.

It takes a few seconds for the water to turn from cold to warm as it runs through the metal piping out of the gas fired heater downstairs. The peaceful flow from the tap is soothing, a smooth soft trickle when compared to the harshness of city plumbing. Turning the lever to shut off the stream, I reach for the towel to my right touching what feels like skin as I do.

I jump back, letting out a short yelp.

I turn quickly, unsure what to expect, but as always, no one's there. The flame on the ledge plays with the darkness, silhouettes coming and going in the bathroom and beyond the doorway but nothing else.

This time I look directly at the cloth before drying my hands and face.

It's time to get back to bed for the night.

I pop up in bed to a dark empty room.

Have I been dreaming?

My heavy legs carry my body to the window looking out on the clearing between the station and the path to the village. A figure in the mist, then another some distance to the left, two others farther back near the tree line, their torches betraying their location.

At 6:00 a.m. the sun has yet to break the horizon, the yellow-orange glow yet to appear over the treetops, the fire outside that much more striking in the darkness. The figures' movements are slow, magnified by the sinister gloom, but their deliberate pace makes me think they're looking for something. Their spacing isn't as orderly as would be expected for a search party but their intentions become increasingly evident as they move about the station. Curiosity compels me to get dressed and inquire about their purpose. Are they hunting an animal or looking for something?

I gaze blankly out the window for longer than I intend, hypnotized by their movements and the pockets of light in the dark field. The cool apartment snaps me into action.

I stumble to light the two oil lamps on the coffee table. Still groggy, I take a few moments longer than usual to put on clothes suitable for both the weather and facing the villagers, a white t-shirt beneath a dark green jacket, black pants, and my hiking boots.

Two men with stoic expressions meet me on the platform.

"Good morning" I say "Can I help you?"

"A girl from the Grey Stone has gone missing"

Oh shit.

"Who?"

"She was last seen leaving the village" the taller of the two men speaks without looking at me.

"Oh no" I say trying to disguise my nervousness.

"We've searched most everywhere"

I don't dare look toward the utility room but can't decide where I should direct my eyes. I have yet to move Acacia's body.

There's another set of footsteps behind me.

"Have you seen her?" the voice approaching me asks as the other men jump down to cross the tracks.

"Who was it?"

"A working lass"

"I was at the Grey Stone the other night"

Some form of honesty seems the best policy in case we'd been seen talking at the bar.

"Yes" he says nodding as he stares me directly in the eyes.

I'm silent to keep my nervous tone to myself. My breathing has nearly stopped entirely.

"I don't suppose she got on a train" he says as if it were a question.

"There hasn't been one since I last saw her"

"She's a very pretty girl"

"Do you know her well?" I ask.

"Perhaps we'll find her yet" he nods sternly.

"I hope so" I reply.

My first thought is to walk around to the site of the pitchforking, but that seems most imprudent. I walk upstairs just fast enough to avoid any more questions without arousing suspicion. What made them come to the train station? Had someone seen us walk to East? Or back here?

We'd surely been seen leaving the bar together.

Or have they come simply to unnerve me?

The men disappear quickly and quietly, their torches no longer visible in the black as if extinguished.

Is this how it played out for previous station masters? Suspicions of guilt, regardless of the man's involvement, starting a chain of events culminating in his death either by his own hand or that of a group of locals?

Aside from being seen leaving with her, there would be no reason to suspect me of anything. I'd only spoken to her once before.

For the moment, there seems no cause for worry.

The matter at hand, as much as it saddens me, is to move Acacia's body to a safer location until I can bury it. It won't do anyone any good to have her discovered in the utility room. But where to take her? Everything I contemplate feels disrespectful.

Who can I ask for help? No one that I can think of and involving Cindy would require a great deal of explaining.

I sit on the platform reflecting on my situation.

There are countless ways for this to end poorly, including being accused and convicted of Acacia's murder.

And I'm no further ahead to solving the riddle of 'the letters'; the station masters' notes are mad ravings from guys who felt isolated; the photos a strange and creepy mystery of their own; the family trees incomplete.

Will I be the next hanging victim?

I feel very alone.

46 – Last in line

I sit alone in my apartment, processing what I've seen and what I haven't seen, what's happened and what hasn't, what I've been told and what I haven't, what might be and what couldn't possibly be. And what I'd read.

The names I'd seen in the historical volumes will surely correspond to markers in the local cemetery. But when and how can I visit it without being noticed? There's no reason for me to be among the graves so that'll definitely draw the wrong kind of attention if I get caught snooping.

First a cup of coffee, a light snack, and a fresh set of clothes; and then a moment to dispose of anything that might, incorrectly, implicate me in Acacia's demise. My mind still whirls, horrified at the scene of her death and our time in the woman's tent. What had she wanted me to do and why? Where had I gone after I blacked out? And, of course, what had happened to Acacia?

I know so little about the petite serving girl with the limp including her last name.

Maybe the librarian knows something about her. Or about the cemetery. Maybe he knows some of the names I've read in the historical documents. He seems very well-informed and friendly.

Though he must tire of my inquiries.

My concern isn't in solving some ancient mystery, but it seems the only way to find answers and escape from this nightmare, if that's how this story ends for me.

How can I face Cindy after what happened with Acacia? Should I tell her about our visit to East or keep that to myself? Will she find out anyway and stop trusting me? I don't want to hurt anyone else at this point. Or put anyone else in danger.

It's nine o'clock, so I check the clunky printer, with no news being good news. Haze hangs low to the ground in the clearing as though the clouds have fallen, the field filled with white and grey. The sun tries unsuccessfully to shine through.

Is that the outline of a young girl by the treeline?

I stop, trying to make out if she's really there and what I'll do if that's the case. I take a step forward but the figure doesn't move. It's still a good distance ahead in the forest's haze. Rissa? Someone who knew Acacia and saw us leave to East together come to take matters into their own hands? Someone ahead of the party come to give me the noose?

I begin walking again, when whatever was there vanishes.

I look behind me but see no one so carry on, my steps heavy.

The clear air in the forest comforts me, though the sombre mood prevails. I reach the village gates without any more figures in the darkness, the small clearing quietly welcoming me. The plaza is empty around the monolithic fountain, the air quiet and gloomy. Silence hangs heavy like an orchestral lull before a powerful musical climax.

The empty church cemetery to my right invites a visit later this afternoon.

The board holds no new information for me so no trains will be at the station today. A mighty relief.

Having yet to determine a schedule for the open market, I make my way down the narrow street where I'd seen it previously. The alleys aren't the most direct route to the library but allow me to go past the market, justifying my presence in town. The set-up has begun, the merchants' wares not yet fully displayed on the tables, boxes still scattered along the wall. A few merchants smile at me, others glance up only to quickly look away; most never raise a head to acknowledge my presence.

I wonder at who attends the market if everyone is working the fields but perhaps customers come at various times throughout the day if the fields are worked in shifts.

I nearly run into a woman holding out a package of buns, a nervous smile on her face.

"Fresh this morning, sir, just for you"

"Thank you"

"I'm Annie and that's my daughter Clara" she points to a blonde teenage girl with a sheepish grin, "We've met here before. But you may not recall"

This last part sounds sad.

"Yes, I remember you, Annie"

"It's very nice to see you again, Station Master" she nods with a wide grin.

"Please call me Colden"

She steps back, her head still nodding.

I smile, as I look around the area.

Annie walks farther down the line of goods, returning to her work.

A nice-looking bag of fresh fruit catches my eye, so I ask an elderly man if these are locally grown.

He rises from his chair extending his hand.

"Most definitely. Tell them Randall wishes them well"
"Pardon me?"

A younger man comes around from behind a pile of wood.

"My grandfather is not as well as in his younger days" he claps his hands in front of his face as if in prayer "I'm Tarkin"

"Colden" I reply, "Or 'Station Master' as everyone calls me"

I place extra emphasis on my title, adding a laugh, which seems to confuse the man. He extends the bag in my direction.

"Thanks very much, Tarkin" I nod when it's clear he doesn't catch the humour.

"The pleasure is mine" he replies politely.

The old man smiles heartily as I headed off.

Behind me, I hear "Be careful in Room 1"

"What was that?" I come back.

"He said 'It'll be a rainy one'" Tarkin answers for his elder before returning to his tasks.

Is there anything else I can learn at the library or do I just feel safe there? Hiding from the realities in New Brook West and my own alienation.

The general lack of interest in me or the station is astonishing. And it's extremely odd that I've been told nothing about the village or the island, never introduced to anyone unless absolutely necessary, not yet met any leadership other than Michael if that's his role in the community. No one sought me out to ask me about my home, why I'd come, what I thought of the job, the station, the town as a whole. Maybe being so insular protects their cultural identity from dilution by external influences, aloofness a means of guarding their societal values.

My social life here is limited. Cindy and I get on well, but I've always felt she's hiding something, and Caprice has mysteries of her own. Most other people either scare me or seem scared by me.

I count on Brian being there and his willingness to help me out, even if it means pushing me in another direction. Maybe now is the time to ask him about how to get off the island. There have to be boats of some kind. I wonder what these people do if something serious happens and they need to get treatment other than what exists in town.

Maybe he knows something about the cemetery.

Maybe I should keep my ideas to myself.

The alley provides a different route out of town, exits the village, and opens onto the wider road leading down to the river past the two houses and outbuildings coming back up to connect with the road to the library.

The temperature has dropped though the air is clearer now than when I'd first set out.

In the distance, smoke rises from the first small stone building; a man sits outside on its steps, the wide front door fully open. An assortment of metal tools lean against the walls and around the structure: axes, shovels, long iron bars, and an array of gardening implements. Warmth flows down the steps out into the street, the smell of dirt and fire with it. The angle of the wooden door prevents me from seeing inside but this must be a metalworker's place.

"Evan, right?" I recognize him.

"Hello, Station Master" he looks up at me.

"Are you the blacksmith?" I ask him, given his location.

"Nah"

He pulls a long knife from a leather sheath attached to the left side of his belt.

"I did make this though" he stares at the dagger.

The metal shines in the light, the blade narrower than I'd expected. An impressive piece.

"What do you think?" he asks.

"It's awesome"

"Awesome. Really good, yes?"

"That's right" I reply with a smile, recalling our previous conversation.

"A glass of beer?" he offers me an empty cup, grabbing a pitcher from a small table next to him.

"Yes, please. May I sit?" I point to a log stump turned on its end.

"Please do"

The sweet pale beer is a smooth brew and a welcome flavour.

"You said you lived just inside the gates" I say "Where exactly is that?"

"I know exactly where you live" he replies looking down at his beer "They all do?"

"All of who?"

"All of them" he takes a slug from his cup.

"Why did you call me 'Cold'?" I ask him sternly.

He sets his cup down next to him on the stairs, leaning forward to rest his hands on his knees.

"You've met Caprice"

It isn't a question.

"Yes, I have"

"She's quite a girl, yes?"

"She's very nice" I answer, wondering where this is going? Is he the 'other' to whom she's promised?

"And you know her friend Hannah?" he turns to me.

"I don't think so..."

"Hannah was a trickster"

"Who is Hannah?"

"To be honest I'm not really interested in how this all plays out" he shrugs leaning back "But I do enjoy the irony of it. Especially when she finds you like she did all the others"

"Why would Hannah be looking for me?" I wonder out loud.

"Not Hannah, you oaf. Her daughter. You're the last in line. You and the teacher"

"What?"

I set down the cup, worried about the tone of our discussion.

"I'm not here to help" he chuckles "Just to watch. To watch you. She sent me where I am, and soon you'll be joining me"

"Joining you?"

"And don't drink the coffee - she poisoned it" he smiles.

I look down at the beer.

"I need to head back now, so could you pass me that please" he points to the cup.

I reach down to grab the mug but he's gone when I turn to hand it to him.

What the hell!? I think of entering the smithy but decide against any more encounters.

My beer mug is on the ground where I'd dropped it, another one with a nearly empty jug near it on the top step. I place my cup next to it, take one final peek toward the building, and make for the library.

Evan's comments sting, because they make no sense, like he knows it all and has come to taunt me with his wisdom. Who is Hannah? It sounds familiar. And why would he say that Caprice is 'quite a girl'? Is that some kind of riddle? I hate riddles.

Just past 10:30 by my watch, though I never know what sort of schedule people keep. The beer has gone to my head, my body not used to morning alcohol, my mind dopey but not so much to discourage me from my next stop. I'll grab a coffee when I arrive.

Through the colourful field, past the islands of trees, I reach my sanctuary on the water's edge.

Three teenagers dressed in black and brown exit the building following the path to their right, without waving or glancing at me. I don't recognize them from this distance so offer no greeting of my own.

The wind is noticeable this close to the water, the waves beginning to crest, though the library's height above the ocean's surface would protect it from any turbulence.

Down to my right, the sheltered harbour guards its secrets. They must have fished before the train came into being and I wonder at their lives on the water so long ago. Were they accustomed to life on or near the water?

I've never heard mention of boats or sailors. Perhaps the train is more reliable, at least now. A dark sky approaches from the north. It makes for a grim afternoon to do my research.

Opening the door, a young girl passes me, books clutched to her chest.

"Station Master" she says without looking up.

"Hi" I reply holding the door for her.

The room seems vacated for my arrival.

I look to my right where I'd sat on my previous visit, a few sheets of blank paper on the table.

I climb the steps to Brian's desk.

"Good morning" he bellows from behind me, causing me to nearly jump to the ceiling.

"Hi" I reply, catching my breath.

"Ugly day outside" he says rounding me to sit behind the counter.

"Good day to spend in the library" I say "Is no one else here?"

"A few just left"

"Why did they all leave just now?"

"Why does anyone leave?" he shrugs "I expect they're heading home so they don't have to walk through the tempest"

I set my bag down at the table, returning to the librarian once I have.

"Do you know Acacia?" I ask him.

"Pretty one with the limp at the Grey Stone"

"That's right" I place my hands on the desktop "What do you know about her?"

"Probably as much as she knows about me" he laughs "I know where she works"

"Apparently she's gone missing. Did you hear that?"

"News hasn't made its way here"

So, I'll learn nothing about Acacia at the library.

I look around again wondering why I never see anyone else here.

"You lookin' for someone?" Brian asks.

"No"

A half-truth because I don't really know who or what I'm looking for.

"Do you have any coffee today?" I ask.

"Always. Help yourself"

Light flickers across Brian's face turning it black for just a second making me jump back.

"Everything OK, chum?"

"Yes. Yeah"

I walk to the coffee, pouring myself a cup, adding just a touch of sugar.

"I often catch a smell of licorice" the words blurt out before I realize "Is there a plant that gives off that smell?"

"Years back, that was a real treat for the kids here" he says "But it hasn't been around in a good long time. Not sure why not"

"Oh"

Through the window at the back of the room, oppressively dark and ominous clouds move across the sky from west to east. A gentle rain bounces off the glass, a reminder that precipitation comes with the windstorm. Brian seems unworried, or perhaps oblivious, unless he lives here; or doesn't mind waiting until it passes. It seems I'll be hanging around for a while after all with no desire to walk all the way back to the station in a downpour. Brian lights a small lamp at each end of his desk as I head to my position, historical tomes in hand.

In addition to those I'd read, other volumes are inscribed with 'Arthurs', 'Sanders', 'Pertwee' and others, some lighting a faint bulb in my mind, most filled with random unfamiliar names.

Where to start? Based on my previous readings, I doubt these unread pages will provide the answers I need.

A chill passes across my skin like an icy breeze, an odd sensation with the windows and door closed.

I approach the enigmatic librarian.

"Do you know anyone named Hannah or Rebecca?"

He shakes his head slowly.

"How about the name 'von Stela'?"

"Sure" he replies "But it's pronounced 'Stayla'"

47 – The blue café

The rain won't dissuade me from leaving the library now. I gather up the volumes, before walking to Brian's empty desk. I call his name but he's vanished completely so I return the thin books to their location in the chest as best I can. My light jacket will keep me dry if not warm and into it go Annie's fresh buns; I'll carry the fruit bag as best I can, less concerned with it getting wet.

Dreariness awaits outside as I prepare to head home, my stay brief, distracted as I am by Brian's revelation.

It's as if the sky has been painted black to replace the clouds. The air is thick with humidity, the horizon grim, the ocean dark. I pause for a moment on the steps of the library, looking left and right, into the desolate landscape, the shadowed fields in the distance. I shiver. Absolute gloom.

Time really does move differently here. It's now after 4:30, dusk's onset combined with the heavy cloud cover make for a dreary walk in the coming storm. Drops fall slowly at first but soon the gusting winds bring more extreme precipitation, my walk becoming a jog then a run. I soon reach the blacksmith's building but it appears closed for the day, or at least closed to unwelcome visitors, its door fully shut, no smoke escaping the chimney. From this side, it appears non-descript, a building easily forgotten. No sign of Evan on the steps, though I don't look too closely, more concerned with getting someplace dry; I won't be seeking shelter here.

Reaching the structures on the edge of town, I find none of the shops at this end of the community open. Ahead, on the left side of the street, a white glow suggests refuge. I stumble inside, much to the surprise of those already seated in the small establishment, more of an intimate café than a restaurant. Benches are fitted into the blue walls, tables equipped with armed wooden chairs face in. It's faintly lit but not dark.

Caprice is at a table to my left, looking away from me. Unsure how to approach her, I find myself a table facing the wall, remove my coat, and request a cup of tea from the young woman who greets me.

A hot beverage comes almost immediately, a chamomile blend to dispatch the cold lodged deep inside me. Lit oil lamps line the walls, a large window near where I entered showcases the dark street. The cheerful light blue walls, the navy ceiling, the bright white trim lift the mood in the dim room. The black and white tables and chairs offer a striking contrast. I wonder what inspired the owners to make their shop so stylish when the rest of the town's architecture seemed deliberately melancholy and drab. In addition to Caprice, four other groups occupy the small space, each engaged in a quiet discussion amongst themselves, no longer interested in my arrival. I don't recognize anyone but that comes as no surprise.

I see no one out the window and nobody else has entered since I arrived, just the dull grey wall across the street. It's difficult to tell if it's still raining. I stare outside past a few unoccupied tables, lost in my mind, unaware of the time, unconcerned about being recognized though I surely have been.

"Hello Colden"

Caprice is at my side.

"Hi" I reply setting down my tea "Care to join me?"

"For a moment" she sits down across from me.

"Is everything OK?" I ask, noticing her stiff posture.

"Yes, I suppose so"

"We often seem to run into each other" I say.

"I don't mean to run into you" she pulls back.

"It's a figure of speech" I smile.

Caprice always looks like she wants to get away, making me wonder if my behaviour somehow offends her, and why she keeps approaching me.

"Have I done something wrong?" I ask her.

"What do you mean?"

"You always seem uncomfortable when we speak, like you're doing it to be polite but you'd rather be someplace else"

"That's not it at all" she places her delicate hands on the table in front of her "I enjoy spending time with you Colden but am cautious for both our sakes. Things aren't as simple as they seem"

"They usually aren't"

"Dark histories persist. The Station Master's legacy is defined by the men who occupied the post before you. Their past became your present. And too often we bear the weight of the sins of our fathers"

She leans in to whisper.

"You've seen her"

Her words startle me.

"Who?" I say softly.

"But she doesn't act alone" Caprice adds.

A party at one of the tables gets up and leaves, briefly looking our way as they exit. Outside, evening's grey has found its way into town, the stone wall and the dirt street a dismal view. The young woman who'd served me earlier sets a cup down, looks at Caprice, and walks away.

"You're in danger Colden" her voice sombre.

"How? Who from?"

All my words are questions. I wonder how much her warnings should worry me.

"You've inherited the deeds of your predecessors"

"What deeds?" I ask confused by the conversation.

"How do they pick the person to offer the job of station master?" I ask before she can answer.

"You never should have accepted the offer" she turns her hands over, our palms now together.

She looks down at our hands, our connection, her body slowly withdrawing to lean against the back of the wooden chair, her eyes focused on mine.

"I wish things were different" she smiles.

I don't know how to take this comment.

I smile back.

"Excuse me" she gets up, walking to the back of the room where three young women stand in a dimly lit area as if waiting for her.

The sky is now darker than before. Outside, a lone woman walks past without stopping on the grim street or looking in the window. She seems to take no notice of the café, disappearing beyond the window.

The colourful room's corners give me a chill, the blue interior at the same time hopeful and sad.

Caprice returns so quietly it makes me jump, now sitting across from me.

"I should go"

"So soon?" I sigh.

"People talk here, which I imagine is the same everywhere, but word spreads quickly of conversations with the Station Master. And I'm considered deviant as it is"

"I had no idea it'd be such a tough gig for me doing such an ordinary job" I smile in an attempt to lighten the mood.

"It's not about you" she touches my shoulder then my arm as she stands.

"This must be a difficult place to live" I push back my chair to get up.

"I'm used to living in shadows" she bows her head.

Caprice's eyes are so sad, her shoulders sagging under her grey cloak, her hair falling straight down the sides of her head as if wet.

Words fail me though I feel I should respond. I want to reach out and hug her but decide against it.

"You'll meet many in New Brook West who wish you ill" she says "Though I am not one of them and am happy you are here"

"Thank you"

I have to ask her a question before she gets away.

"There's a guy I've run into a couple of times, early twenties, said his name was Evan Pertwee. Who is he?"

"Are you sure that was his name?" her eyes widen.

"Pretty sure. Why?"

"Perhaps you misheard" she says nervously.

"He said he used to live in East but now lives 'just inside the gates'. Where's that?"

"I'm not sure" she replies a bit too quickly.

I consider asking another question but decide against it, the conversation having taken a direction I'd not intended.

I lean in close to Caprice, lowering my voice.

"I'll see you again, I hope" I say.

"I'll make sure we run into each other" a partial smile graces her lips.

She exits into the dark as I sit down at my table alone.

Looking up, two new groups of young women now sit at tables against the wall opposite mine drinking and laughing noiselessly as if in a silent movie. Finishing my tea, I get up and walk to the back of the room.

"Thank you very much" I smile to the young woman who'd brought me my tea "It was excellent"

"I'm glad to hear it" she replies graciously in a Scottish lilt "A pleasant evening to you, sir"

I nod, making my way cautiously outside. The rain has entirely subsided, the wind no longer adding to my chill, shielded as I am by the buildings at my sides. Covered lamps against dull stone walls show the grey street ahead, the dark corners. I wind my way through the village to the plaza and the cemetery. The quiet community rests.

Am I being watched?

Can it already be 6:30?

There's no one outside that I can see which eases my mind. Willing to accept wet hair and clothing, I slide over to the dark church, eager to put my clandestine mission into action. The clouds part, the moon casting its light as it peeks through the cover, sharpening the outlines of the graves and the iron fence.

"Looking for someone?" a young man's voice from behind me nearly makes me yell.

A male figure on the unlit church steps, a dark hood covering his face and head, his clothes a dark brown, his elbows resting on his knees, his brown leather boots tightly laced above his ankles. I place him in his early twenties, having only his voice to go by.

"Maybe Rebecca?" he adds.

"Who's that?" I take a step toward him, curious about his mention of this name.

"An old name"

"Does she live in the village?" I decide to ask my question a different way.

"Not anymore"

"I'm Colden. What's your name?" I sit next to him.

"Corbin. Corbin Kapelt. My last name means 'church' in an old language. Never much liked it as far as names go"

"I'm the…"

"Station Master. I know" he interrupts me "When you came, what you've done, where you've been"

I search for words but nothing comes.

"The new school teacher's a beauty, isn't she" his cloaked face looks in my direction.

"Ok…"

"And you've met Christina more than once" he says "She goes by many names as I'm sure even you know"

Not another riddle.

"Who?"

"She's not who you think" he smiles.

"Who isn't?" I stammer.

He looks at a pouch in his hands.

"So why Rebecca?" he asks, ignoring my question.

"I don't know who that is"

"Sure, you do" he nods his head.

I have yet to get a good look at his face in the darkness.

"Do you know anything about the other station masters?" I lean toward him, my voice softer "Sounds like they were scared of something"

"Probably" he smiles throwing back his hood revealing dark eyes, shoulder length blonde hair, and a face that looks older than his voice with three small knife scars.

"This is the first time I've seen you" I say quietly "Do you live in town?"

"I've been here, but you have to know that you can't always believe what you see" he says seriously.

His pupils glow silver.

"So why should I believe in you?"

"Good point" he stares at the ground in front of him.

"You do know what she can do, don't you?" he goes on.

"What who can do?"

"She can make you see things" he ignores my question.

"Is there anything I can do?" I decide to play along.

"Not sure. Maybe. Maybe not" Corbin shakes his head.

I get to my feet, ready to part ways with my strange companion.

"Well, I'm off, Corbin" I turn away as I speak "It was nice speaking with you"

"You too C-Vin"

Rick? I quickly spin around but the young man is gone.

Where did that come from? No one had ever called me C-Vin before except Rick. Why would they?

An old woman I recognize but whose name I can't place walks toward me.

"Why are you talking to yourself, sir?" she whispers "Are you ok?"

"I'm speaking with Corbin" I look back at the empty steps.

"Who?" she says softly, concern in her face.

She stares at me for a moment, then through me as if someone were behind me.

She slowly turns away, walking back in the direction from which she came, disappearing down an alley.

Orange flames in lanterns on either side of the church entrance jar me from my thoughts, causing my heart to skip. There's no one outside the building to have lit them. I look to my left but see no one. Distant lanterns light buildings down a street leading into town, the stone gloomy despite this illumination.

There's a creaking sound as the gate to the right of the church opens but no one's there when I look. I take a step to my right to look deeper into the cemetery but only see a crooked tree further back in the enclosure, the old stone markers rising from the ground.

I wait for something to appear in the darkness, for a voice to speak. But nothing.

Taking a few steps forward to get a better look inside the fence, I stop to look up at the moon as I do. The cloud-free sky offers a beautiful view of the stars, the moon's glow making the church an imposing structure, causing me to shiver in the damp air.

I stare for a moment at the lanterns against the wall, their flames dancing behind the glass.

All is quiet as I enter the cemetery through the open gate. Stone markers throughout the area stand out sharply in the stark darkness under the white moon. The gravestones appear in better condition than when I looked previously, as though they've been cleaned and smoothed, taken back to a time when they were new. Further back among the graves, a female figure is kneeling in front of a stone, her back to me, making me consider stepping back out. I crouch next to a gravestone, watching the woman, her light blue cloak covering her lithe physique. She's not moving or making a sound, the silence making me anxious.

Should I say something and excuse myself or just get out of here? I feel like an intruder. Before I have the chance to decide, she stands and slowly turns to look at me, her fair-skinned face and striking blue eyes framed by long dark hair mesmerizing me, her light blue dress hugging her slim body.

I recognize her immediately.

She walks toward me.

I don't know what to say and am unable to move.

Before, I know it, she's directly in front of me.

She opens her lips slightly, a beautiful lilting tune coming from her mouth though I can't make out the words if she's saying any.

Her eyes remain fixed on mine.

I recognize her form and dress.

"You gave me the box in the shop in town" I mumble "And at the Grey Stone"

A chill comes upon me as if the temperature has suddenly dropped, the sky darker despite the sparse flickering light in front of the church, the silence absolute.

"The dead can tell us a lot about the living" she sings.

Voices whisper above, below, and behind me. I'm distracted as I try to locate their origin.

When I look back, the woman in front of me has vanished.

I'm alone in the moonlit cemetery, with the old grey stones, the ominous trees, the sombre air. I inhale deeply, my eyes moving side to side to spot any movement, too afraid to make any sudden moves of my own. An intense chill goes down from my neck making my shoulders arch.

I close my eyes, for how long I don't know. It seems I can't open them. I know I'm outside in the night air, sheltered from the wind. There are no sounds around me or in the distance. The moon seems to have slipped behind a cloud as only a faint glow touches my eyelids. Am I asleep?

I wake from my trance, sitting on the church steps where I'd been speaking with Corbin moments earlier, a soft warm hand on the back of my neck. My breaths are long and heavy as I try to focus.

"What..." I start, not knowing how I'll finish the sentence.

"Her name is in your letters" the blue-cloaked woman interrupts me in a sternly feminine musical voice.

"What letters?"

It feels like a waking dream.

"And you are all in the tree" she looks to the sky as she speaks.

"Which tree?"

A cloud slides over the moon, the air turning dull; my head is heavy, my body is cold.

A bird sings, a sound I'd rarely heard since my arrival in New Brook West.

Is the woman still here with me? I think so.

"Ask her for her true name" she whispers.

"Who?"

"The one who is yours"

"What is her true name?" I implore her.

"And there is another" she says.

"Another?"

Not another.

"... the three of you together" she sings sternly.

"The three of who?" my words seem to be coming from elsewhere.

Not this again.

Her song is like an enchantment and I feel spellbound.

A floral scent wafts into the air.

The woman comes toward me, then recedes, then vanishes.

Am I in the cemetery? Where is the moon? I don't think the woman is with me anymore.

My eyes are closed.

My lungs gasp for air, hands squeeze my heart.

I wake abruptly in the apartment, popping up from my bed, with no evidence of anyone else in the room.

Her true name?

Stela and Stayla.

Is it her name in my letter?

Could Cindy have sent me the letter?

A light rain falls outside as I contemplate these and other thoughts alone in the apartment's silent darkness.

1910

In the corner's darkness, she was lost in the shadows, her thin form, her dirty dress. Her eyes squinted out from behind matted black hair, watched him move across the platform, remembered how she used to watch him and others, those complicit in her mother's death and those who were silent when they should have spoken. The sweet little girl who had once been pretty and could have been beautiful, her life was now inconsolable, filled with nothing but sadness and hatred.

No more will there be a Station Master of New Brook West.
She feels the anger and the hate but also a deep sorrow, a loneliness.
Perhaps she cries, but only for a moment.
Then she hears the train's whistle and emerges from the shadow.

And he was soon replaced. And then again.
But I'd learned and became wiser and more intelligent.
I'd sworn there would never be another, never be another who could hurt me the way he had so many years ago.
I was able to hide, quietly in the dark, and none saw.
I waited. I watched. Some denied me vengeance, took their own life rather than suffer the fate I had for them, rather than wear the shame of their predecessors. The man who'd killed me so long ago soon met his own fate. The Station Master.
More came and I punished them all.
No more will there be a Station Master of New Brook West.
Never again.

48 – It's sad when people die

Clouds obscure the sky. Again. The air retains its damp chill, penetrating deep into my bones as I lay on top of the bed's blankets, my clothes both warm and cold. My jacket hangs on a wooden hook along the front wall, my boots neatly placed to the left of the door. I decide on a warm shower while pondering the evening's events.

Maybe I hadn't gone to the graveyard at all and just came back here. 2:15 am. It feels like a trance or watching a movie. Again, with the woman in the blue cloak. The letters. The tree. The flowers. Her true name. I'm lost.

For a minute or longer I enjoy the warmth of the water on my back, wrapping me in its comforting arms. I only step away because I doubt the supply of hot water.

Slowly emerging from the bathroom feels like walking in molasses, running in sand. My body won't obey my brain's commands.

Two lamps near the sofa light the large room, shadows in every corner and along every wall. Everywhere I look makes me shiver. I want to run and light more candles but also to hurry to my bed and crawl under the covers. Nothing is certain, even in the apartment. So many hiding places in the dark suite.

I step out of the bathroom, the cool air surprising me. I'll not be going outside to stoke the furnace so had best put on some clothes to sleep in.

I walk to move the one lamp nearer the bed, to spread the light throughout the room. I place it on the counter behind the couch, its light dancing on the window as I do.

Reaching down to pick up my shorts, a shadow low to the ground moves quickly through the living room. Is someone else in here with me?

I feel my eyes widen as my heart races. I can't move. All is quiet in the apartment. I crouch and raise my head, but see no one in the darkness, or in the light's glow near either lantern.

I wait for any movement, any sound, but there's nothing.

With slow steps, I walk into the sitting area to put on a fresh shirt and underwear. Now dressed, I feel better for being warmer.

I lean back on the sofa, feeling my nerves calming. Looking straight ahead at the window over the tracks, the lamp behind me flickers in reflection in front of me. I sit up stiffly.

Is something behind me?

I freeze in horror, waiting, holding my breath to better hear any noise. Nothing else moves in the window's reflection, moonlight shining in from my left.

Slowly standing and turning my head, I see nothing in the direction of my bed. The front door is closed and the windows surely are as well or it'd be freezing in here.

The room is quiet again.

Is something looking in from outside?

Scanning the room's dark walls and furniture, my head slowly moves through the apartment. The dark kitchen, the far corner's desk partially lit from outside, the shadowed bed, the windows looking onto the tracks, the window into the clearing. Nothing moves and I hear no sounds. Moonlight falls through the windows overlooking the railway, sharpening the features on that side of the room.

I'm alone in the apartment; I have to be. I decide a cup of hot tea will help me sleep and calm my nerves. Making my way to the kitchen I light another small lamp.

The flickering candles play in the dimly lit room, shine oddly on the windows, cast shadows against the walls. After a short time, I decide the water will be hot enough for my purposes and pull it from the element, taking the lid from a metal canister with sweet smelling herbs.

The candles dance to silent music making me look up into the room. I'm alone in the faint light. I pause with the loose tea in my hands, waiting, hoping I'll hear no sound in the apartment. My heart is racing despite the silence.

Clouds pass over the moon or perhaps it descended below the trees, the room now lit only from the inside.

My eyes look down to resume preparing my beverage.

I hear a creaking from out on the landing.

I stare at the door for what feels like forever, my breathing stopping, but it must have only been a second before the canister's top falls from my hand startling me into reality.

I bend my knees to grab the lid and cover the tea container without taking my eyes off the entrance. I survey the suite slowly to ensure I've checked every inch of the place, at least every inch visible from the kitchen.

I move cautiously across the room to the door where the lock is still secure. Reluctantly, I throw it open to look outside, terrified of what might be waiting but see only silence and darkness in front of me and down the stairs to the platform. There's no rain and no fog outside.

I re-enter the apartment, lacking the courage to look across to the grey hotel.

Clutching hard to the narrow ledge above the door, she watches as he exits his room, looking down to the ground, but not up into the darkness. She'd watched him from just outside the window, her hands a few feet from his sleeping body, a thin pane of glass the only thing between them. She wants to enter, to touch him as he sleeps but doesn't. Her eyes explore his face, his eyes, his hair. She wonders if he dreams and if so, is it of a thin faceless grey girl watching him?

Her slender limbs allowed her to escape to the shadows on the landing and then up when he opens the door. Once again, such a short distance between them. She could reach out or leap down, but only observes, waiting.

Taking a deep breath, I grab a fleece pull-over, the cool night air frostier than usual despite being indoors. The warm tea soothes both my body and mind as I sit on the sofa hoping to cleanse my soul.

I shiver.

I hear another creaking down on the platform; the New Brook West sign groaning on its hinges?

I exhale deeply and set down my cup, passing out from exhaustion.

When I wake, light has successfully replaced dark, though a thin fog persists, filling the space out the window facing the clearing. The time is now 8:15, with a train scheduled to arrive at 1:00 pm today, so I need to check the printer then head into town to inspect the board and discreetly scavenge for 'letters', clad in my official jacket to maintain my cover. A quick bite to eat and a change of clothes before leaving, as well as a quick survey of the platform and peek into the control room to ensure the accuracy of my information before heading into town at 9:15.

Is there something in the letter of offer that I'd been sent? Are there letters in the historical reference books? In the station masters' ledgers?

I'd never seen anything in the way of mail so it has to be something that's already here.

Or am I going about this the wrong way? Are there letters on a building or a statue or a gravestone?

Preoccupied as I am with my thoughts, I notice no unusual sounds or sights in the forest, the sun's glow, shrouded by clouds, provides sparse light among the trees.

As I near the community, I hear what sounds like the shuffling of feet accompanied by a humming like bees buzzing. Only once I reach the lanterns at the entrance to town does the procession come into view, a large group uttering a "hmmmm" sound while marching to the cemetery. Two men at the front in dark robes wheel a black wooden casket on a low cart across the plaza, the crowd falling in behind.

The low haze persists in the small glade around town but diminishes as I pass between the lit lamps at the gate. I move to my left and away from the slow-moving group in the direction of the board. I stop for a moment out of respect. Most of the men gathered wear grey cloaks, the women in similarly coloured long dresses, some with their heads down others facing forward.

"Best to watch from here"

An elderly man in a brown cloak stands unexpectedly at my side.

"Did someone pass?" I ask.

"Yes" he answers without further detail, walking to join the company of a hundred or so people of all ages.

The coffin-bearers stop at the fence, remove the small box from the carriage. Two men and a woman pass through the cemetery gates, the others waiting outside. The men who had pulled the casket grab ropes attached to its sides, carrying it behind the church and out of my view. The humming ceases as the group remains outside the cemetery.

Not wanting to be seen snooping, I make my way to the notice board, intent on keeping up appearances.

"Hello" a girl's voice speaks beside me once I've reached the board.

Rissa.

"Hi, Rissa" I stop.

"People are sad" she speaks softly "A young boy died near the river. It's sad when people die, especially children"

"Yes, it is"

I don't really know what else to say, unsure of what the locals will think of me talking with this girl given the stories I'd heard of other station masters and in light of the boy's recent death.

Sam waves enthusiastically from near a building along a street into the community.

"I should go" Rissa says "But Sam and I will come to the station later"

"Is it OK with your parents?" this concerns me on many levels.

"Don't worry, you won't get in trouble" she whispers.

I try to conjure words to abort this potentially dangerous encounter but nothing polite comes to mind.

"Bye" she trots off to her brother, adult supervision nowhere in sight.

A small figure near the fountain quickly drops below its base. I lower my head hoping this is a funeral attendee but know this isn't the case. Deciding I don't want to get a closer look, I turn away, nervous of what I might be leaving behind me.

Most of those assembled quietly disperse, many waiting near the fence and around the church.

I post a notice confirming the train's 1:00 arrival time, grab one indicating a Mr. Bitzner will occupy Room 6 this evening and that I should leave the key in that room's door. I tack a handwritten note addressed to Tessa in case any action needs to be taken to prepare his room.

No one's visible within the cemetery fence and no children are around the fountain. I glance into the hazy clearing between village and forest then to the church's closed doors.

I catch myself staring, immediately turning on my heels to the path back home, ready to be away from scrutiny, despite the fact that company would be most welcome at the moment. Perhaps I'll visit Cindy after the train's departure and school's dismissal.

It remains to be seen if my presence will be judged a sign of respect for the deceased, an insult to their culture, or a mere coincidence.

The silence of the walk in the forest's clear air is simultaneously welcome and disturbing, the only sound the light breeze rustling the treetop branches and leaves. A low mist has settled in between the trees, the pervasive gloom in the air making the day bleak, as it had with so many others. My nerves hover on the edge, prepared but not knowing whether to expect any children on the path ahead or behind me.

Is someone following me? Have they always been? Is it a child? Who is the girl I keep seeing? My head spins with questions that I can't ask. There's a soft whispering from my left, the voice so faint I can barely hear it. Then it's gone.

The scent of licorice drifts out of the forest from where I'd heard the voice, a familiar smell since my arrival that I'd not yet been able to place nor known before.

I walk nervously, feeling watched though I don't know by whom or why.

I clean and sweep the platform, lock the control room, and extinguish all lamps. I grab the key to Room 6 from the drawer in my apartment, placing it in the lock for its imminent occupant. The rest of the time I spend walking around the station, careful to stay away from the tracks, intrigued by and fearful of who or what might be watching. A movement across the clearing catches my eye but nothing comes of it so it doesn't warrant any further attention.

Just after 12:30, a solemn team of ten men emerges from the forest pulling three carts, marching like a silent army as I climb the stairs onto the platform. They stop when they reached the steps, staring straight ahead like soldiers who were told to halt and await further orders. I notice a few subtle gestures or glances within the group but even these motions are difficult to detect and I feel relieved when the 1:00 arrival pulls in to the station fifteen minutes early. They wake from their slumber and advance to the rear cars which they commence unloading with unprecedented efficiency.

It's then that I notice something missing: Dalton.

"Where's Dalton?" I address no one in particular.

I get no acknowledgement from the team. It doesn't matter that much so there seems no need to press them.

The group departs after thirty minutes of labour, some pieces requiring extra attention, other larger ones additional time to arrange, but if they harbour any feelings, they don't express them, plodding back down the path, none glancing back as they leave. They disappear into the forest, the clearing returning to silence, the area now clear of fog.

Jogging up the stairs to my room, I decide to prepare pens, pencils, paper, folders, and a snack into a backpack for my visit to the library.

At the top on the landing, a drawing of a small clearing surrounded by trees and low grass waits on the ground for me, the back bearing the title 'Little Cemetery', a sketch of sharp dark lines mixed with charcoal to shade certain features. Might as well bring it with me to the library in case it conjures a connection with a piece of information I uncover. Or the identity of the artist.

Had they been noticed, my frequent visits to the library would surely arouse suspicion or at least curiosity in the locals who I rarely observed coming or going.

Perhaps they feel safer in their homes like I do.

1960

Over time, many came but none left. Such was their fate to bear the sins of the first of their kind, the first so filled with hate, the coward that wanted my mother dead, and killed me, a little girl, out of fear.

Never again would a Station Master have that power.

But I grow weary and want to rest, in perfect peace. I'm not as angry as I am sad.

And still sometimes I cry.

For mother, for our lives.

And sometimes I cry for myself.

1960

Sometimes I'm sure that my actions are right. But sometimes I doubt, and I can see that my sister does too.

I've done all that I was asked, all that I was told, yet still I'm alone.

49 – Have you been in Room 1?

Being alone at the library always felt safe.

Though researching the chronicles laid out in the community's records has yet to uncover clues to assist with the unexplained events at the station. Or how I'd been selected for this job. Or what I should do next.

According to the documentation, New Brook East and West and the other smaller settlements initially kept their autonomy and seldom collaborated. Odd for such a small island. The rail line had come sooner than I'd expected given the logistical challenges and appeared to have been in place in the mid/late-1800s, though records on station masters are largely absent in these books.

The station served all communities, the only instance of cooperation, the apartment at the station serving as the station master's residence from the beginning, as far as I could tell. I read a few mentions of his role in community discussions and negotiations, commanding generous pay, in addition to this individual being a highly sought-after husband by women on the island. Then, about a hundred years ago, they became loners, if not pariahs, in the community. There are very few mentions of station masters in the history of the island after that, though they sometimes found their way into local folklore and occasional tales spoke of them lurking about town, without specifics. Never are they named, referred to simply as 'Station Master', so I'd need to cross-reference their tenure with the ledgers in the control room to determine who occupied the position at any particular time. If it matters.

Teachers were present from original settlement and also highly respected, though never named either. Initially, locals filled this role; the position later came to be filled by women from abroad. There's little mention of their social interactions in the community or their personal histories. I wonder if the teacher eventually succumbed to the same fate as the station master.

Although I can't tell for sure when or why they started offering the station master job to outsiders, I suspect it aligns with the changing opinion of the positions of station master and teacher. There's still nothing to hint at who makes the offers or how these individuals were selected. Or why they stopped giving these jobs to locals.

And there's no mention of the abandonment of New Brook East. Or how station masters died.

Brian isn't at his desk when I arrive at the library or at least I don't see or hear him or anyone else.

Out the back window, the grey clouds and the dark sky are the stuff of nightmares: bleak, melancholy, and ominous. A lit lantern hangs on both sides of the large window, orange flames striking against the dull stone walls and the dark exterior. It hasn't started to rain yet but appears as though it will at any moment.

I'd asked Brian about other materials in the library but he told me that most of the books are an extension of school work. The fiction is very folkloric and too far out even for him. I tried to read one story but it was almost a different language and I couldn't keep up so abandoned it.

Is that voices upstairs? I don't see anyone.

I wait in silence in case someone else is here but hear nothing else. I look around the main floor but see no one and the large door hasn't opened since I arrived.

The clock shows just past 5:00, much later than it feels, though the darkness outside soon reminds me that night has begun to set in. The assortment of candles and lanterns provides more illumination than I'd expected, only the far corners still dark. My corner of the building makes for a gloomy setting; a dull atmosphere, but a quiet one.

My thoughts drift like I'm in a dream. Drift back to my apartment with Lori, my love for her, our afternoon and evening walks in the street, smiling, talking; Suzie, playing with my daughter at the park, talking with her, laughing. Could I ever love another woman as I had Lori? I doubted it. I still loved Lori. Would I ever want more children? It'd feel like replacing Suzie.

I feel like I'm lying to Cindy, who I've come to care for very much.

Do I deserve to love again?

My eyes are closed, but I feel like I'm back in the present in New Brook West. Is this another failure? Do I really want to give up here and start over again? What am I looking for?

Candles blow out behind me as if snuffed by a light breeze. I look back expecting to see an open door or another visitor but don't spot anyone or any source of air. I decide to round up my things, shoving everything into my backpack haphazardly as a puffing sound blowing out the lights one at a time gradually makes the room darker until only the lamps nearest me remain. I turn quickly hoping to spot Brian or even Rissa and Sam but see no one and hear nothing.

Then the faint smell of licorice in the dark library.

It's time to go.

I hear a hissing overhead like wind whistling through an open window, the room now barely lit, darkness increasing away from me, shades of grey turning black against the far walls. I reach around for my flashlight, fumbling in my bag, but it's not there. I'm too far from any lanterns to try to light them. I can't stay where I am but can't make a run for it through the unknown to the exit. If someone else is in here with me, I want out. I know the door's location but can't safely make it out from my corner of the library with physical obstacles in the dark between me and the exit, in addition to anything else that might be here.

A soft scratching against the floor sounds like something small being dragged. I stop breathing to listen for any other noise but it's now gone silent. I crouch down with my backpack in hand and consider bolting for the door but don't. I scan the darkness without seeing anything. The black sky out the back window above the ominous ocean is a grim sight. A beam of moonlight pierces the window over the large door. I see the desk and items at the back of the building, the empty aisles past the door, the medieval paintings on the upstairs level, the rest of the room partially lit as I take it all in, frozen as I am by this illumination.

Then it's gone and all returns to dark.

Where is Brian? I think of yelling but decide against disturbing the silence.

I wait without moving, quietly watching and listening.

Is something moving down an aisle behind me? My eyes fear turning to stare at the darkness and shadows. I slow my breathing to allow me to better hear sudden noise in the otherwise silent chamber. Two more puffs and now just a single lit candle remains against the wall up by the red chest that held the history books. The room won't get any brighter and I hate to think that someone or something is in here extinguishing the candles. Crossing the distance from me to the door seems an impossible but necessary feat. Grabbing my bag and its contents I hurry across the open space to the exit, hoping the door will not be locked, swinging it open when I reach it. I take one last look behind, then on all sides and, seeing nothing, hustle outside into more unfamiliar darkness.

The moon behind its cloudy veil casts a weak glow, but enough for me to see the expansive black ocean, the massive library, and the path directly in front of me. One last look back at the building and I set my walking pace toward the village as quickly as I can in the darkness, followed by a five-minute jog.

My eyes scarcely spot the blacksmith's shop ahead of me, no lights within or around it, and no smoke rising from the chimney; it resembles the ruins in New Brook East in the dark. Approaching the building, the smell of metal, rubber, and wood mix with the fresh salty air. The nearby house is equally quiet and bleak. I have no desire to linger about the forge, eager to avoid any encounters or conversations. On both sides, lifeless leafless trees decorate the fields, large rocks dot the landscape, patches of low shrubs clinging to their sparse foliage.

I crouch for a moment to catch my breath, surprised at being winded after such a short run, set down my pack, and look back at the library in the distance. Lamps now illuminate the top level as if relit.

Is that a girl in the window? It's hard to tell but it's enough to make me turn tail and carry on to the village at a brisk jog.

Absolute silence amplifies the sound of my footsteps on the dirt trail and every noise to my sides. Shadows dance in the moon's intermittent light along the edge of the forest and near the rocks, a breeze whistles through the trees, the branches crackle against each other as if in conversation.

A snap behind me turns my head: is that a figure stepping across the path from left to right without a sound? A villager? An animal? The figure from the window?

Resuming my run, I make good time back to the security of the town's buildings, eyes firmly to the front the entire way, ignoring any crackling to the rear or sides in the surrounding trees and grasses, the blue-walled café my destination. My pace slows to normal as I stop for a moment to collect myself and ensure I'm not being followed.

No one's moving about in the streets, only the occasional local watching from against the walls or out a window or door. Lit lanterns hang outside, mocking my fear. The scarcity of activity makes every corner darker, every sound more menacing, every shadow longer. It's so quiet. Never before had I felt so alone in town as I do now.

Surprisingly, the café's door is closed and locked, the room unlit. I wonder if it operates on a schedule or if the owner opens when they choose. There's nothing to do here so I might as well head home for the night; I'm not in the mood to see Cindy after a rather long day and on an empty stomach nor to spend any more time trekking through the dark forest. Dropping my head, I carry on. Weaving my way through the alleys, I arrive at the town square, stopping to sit on the edge of the fountain as two women pass without looking my way.

Trickling water echoes in my ears, amplifying my solitude. The moon appears from behind a cloud, shining onto the plaza. I look up at it then at the small clearing between the village and the forest.

I sigh.

Across the plaza someone waves with a slow gesture from the church steps - Evan.

"Hi" a girl's voice speaks to my right.

I nearly jump out of my skin.

Rissa smiles at me.

"Hi Rissa. Hi Sam"

"Where were you today?" she asks.

"At the library" I try to smile "Hey do you know the guy on the steps?" I stand up pointing at the church.

"Which guy?" Sam looks at the other end of the square.

Evan is gone.

"It was Evan"

Rissa and Sam slide closer to each other, nervous looks on their faces.

Rissa is dressed in her brown jacket, dark pink shirt, and black pants; Sam in his same black plaid shirt and black pants. Their clothes are spotlessly clean and smart-looking.

"Can we come to the train station with you?" Rissa asks.

I slump back down to the fountain's ledge. I'm in no mood for company but lack the energy for a full discussion or to conjure a lie and don't feel like disappointing two of my allies. My head droops.

"If it's fine with your parents then..."

But they're gone.

If they choose to follow me or get there on their own or don't come at all will be for them to decide.

The time is now 7:15.

Reaching down to grab my bag I notice a small dim lantern at my side. Did Rissa and Sam leave it for me? If so, that's a kind gesture on their part, my heart warmed by the thought of a well-lit trail. Leaving the village behind, I enter on the path to the station across the small clearing, the tiny lantern's faint glow just enough to show the area around me.

The tunnel that is the forest blocks most of the moon's glow. I stop, staring out around me and into the eerie woods, chilled by who or what might be out there. I listen for movement but hear only silence.

I continue my journey back to the safety of my apartment, through the bleak forest, my steps quiet against the dirt. A gentle scuttling on my left disturbs the leaves like a small animal scurrying through them trying to keep up. What little light emanates from my lamp dissipates beyond the path, the darkness absolute away from the lantern's glow, filling the spaces between the trees. The rustling sound follows me, light feet at my side in the dark, the lantern producing shadows in the trees when I move it around me.

I stop again, the forest going quiet as I do, as if in response to my movements. When I carry on, the soft crunching continues close behind me. I stop one last time to listen to the stillness and calm, trying not to think about what must be watching me, safely hidden in the forest's shade.

Alone.

The scent of licorice replaces the forest's natural aroma, my pace quickening to the clearing where I feel safer.

The faint glimmer from my suite provides a beacon of light at the station, the platform dark, the tiny hotel room windows on this side also black, a relief since these aren't scheduled to be occupied tonight; Mr. Bitzner's room is on the other side of the building. I'd never laid eyes on any of the hotel guests nor hear them mentioned in town, but this secrecy seems normal in its own way. Odd how even the most unusual environments get normalized with time.

There's no light in the locked control room, the forest across the tracks as dark as ever, the moonlight creating images amongst the trees, leaves, and branches, making my tired eyes dart back and forth. There's nothing and no one in both directions along the platform and Room 1 is sufficiently quiet to satisfy my imagination. I set the lantern down against the wall and extinguish it.

Lifting the lamp from the wall at the base of the steps and striking a match, two small figures materialize halfway up; the bag falls from my hand, my heart nearly stops, my body frozen to the spot.

Shapes of a girl and a boy in the dark.

A closer look: Rissa and Sam.

"Holy sh…" I catch my breath.

"We've never been to the station before" Rissa smiles.

"Never" Sam runs down the stairs.

"We didn't mean to scare you" Rissa walks down after her brother.

"No, it's good" I say "How did you get here so quickly?"

"We've been waiting for you" Sam says "What took you so long?"

"Whatta ya mean? I came straight here"

It's 9:30. There's no way it took me that long to get here from the village.

"Did you leave me that lantern?" I ask.

"What lantern?" Rissa answers curiously.

Did Evan leave it for me? Why?

"Would you like some licorice?" Rissa looks up at me sadly.

"No, thank you" I reply.

Sam takes a piece and eats it.

"I like licorice" he smiles.

They walk to the edge of the platform. Have they been the source of the smell? But they surely weren't about every time I caught the aroma.

"It's great here" Sam grins "You're lucky to work with all the trains"

"It's not always fun" I say sitting down on the bottom step, still a bit confused.

"What do you mean?" Rissa sits next to me on my left.

"Lots of strange things happen here"

"Like what?"

"Scary things" I say, regretting my words as soon as I speak them.

"I don't like scary things" Sam sits on the ground across from us glancing around as he does.

"Some places are frightening because there were bad people there in the past; some places have bad people there now; some places have people that aren't supposed to be there; some places are scary because we don't understand them" Rissa speaks seriously.

"Those are very grown-up ideas you have, Rissa" I look at her in awe of her statement.

"Rissa's very smart" Sam nods.

"Sam's all I have" Rissa says sadly looking at her brother "But at least we're together. Some little girls have lost their family and are very lonely"

"Like who?" I ask.

"Have you been in Room 1?" she points across the platform.

My eyes slowly follow her gesture to the enigmatic suite, the door looking at me with a life of its own. A chill begins at my neck, running down my spine as my hand reaches down for my bag and the lamp from the wall.

Rissa and Sam are gone, the smell of licorice strong at first, dissipating with time.

I get up, look both ways along the platform, run out to check the path back to the village, up the stairs to my suite, and all around me but they've completely vanished. Guess they'd had their fill of the station or decided it was time to get home. Or maybe Rissa felt she'd said too much and was embarrassed. I make a point in my mind to try to find them tomorrow but have no intention of running around here now. After a quick stop to check the utility room remains locked, I make my way to my apartment, locking the door behind me, shutting all the windows once inside.

She hears the young girl's words, feels the pain in her voice, the sincerity in her tone. She's crouched in the dark corner, her thin frame invisible in the shadows, her narrow eyes unseen as she watches. She creeps on all fours across the platform under the stairs, pulling her knees up to her chest, waiting. Once the door upstairs closes, she climbs the wall, silently peering in through the window, concealed by night. Watching, waiting, wondering.

What did Rissa mean by 'some places have people that aren't supposed to be there'? And asking if I've been in Room 1. It sounds like she knows something but is too afraid to tell me.

Am I not supposed to be here?

I slump on the couch, passing out as soon as I do.

My sleep ends abruptly with a tapping at the door.

8:00. Sparse light filters through the windows in the apartment breaking the previous evening's dread, at least for a moment; my fear of the darkness is increasing daily. I recall getting up to crawl into bed at some point in the night which is where my body now lies comfortably curled beneath the covers when the disturbance comes. Wearing only boxers and a t-shirt, I open to the chill outside with no one on the landing or anywhere on the staircase or platform. It's too cool for a walk around and maybe it was just me hearing things anyway so I go back into the suite, noticing a photo on the floor behind me as I do.

An old photograph of a man in a station master's jacket with a noose around his neck hanging lifeless from the crossbeam above the coffee table, a wooden chair upended on the ground; the photo shows only his back.

Not again.

A take a quick look outside, but no one's there.

I step back inside.

How? How did this get in here? Slid under the door?

352

The guy in the photo doesn't look like me which is a relief, shorter, stockier, and older, though with blonde hair. The room looks basically the same but the photo itself looks old.

So, who is he? Why did he hang himself? Or did someone hang him?

Another photographer commemorating this event before cutting him down? Why would anyone want to remember this? This has to be more than a few years old, though more recent than the previous photos left at my door.

Who keeps leaving these for me?

And who could I ask? Probably no one. What would I say?

Is someone trying to scare me? Warn me? Ask me for help?

Maybe I should go see Cindy. Might make me feel better and I can see how she's holding up.

I'll make a quick stop in the control room then at the board in town for any train news.

Might as well bring the photo with me.

Outside, the clearing is hazy, as though it has recently stopped raining. The black and white trees visible through the haze are dark skeletons, sleeping in the early morning light. The sun's rays slowly creep above the trees providing adequate light to remind me that it's daytime but insufficient to dispel the fog. The windows behind me are all shut, the candles extinguished so I lock the door. My backpack's contents include a small lantern, a pad with some notes from the library's historical texts, a couple of granola bars, a juice-filled container, a travel mug of coffee, and the disturbing photo which is eerie to even have near me.

A quick check in the control room with the printer's message confirms that no trains will be stopping today in New Brook West.

My quiet departure from the train station takes me into the solemn clearing; the spindly trees, some still in leaf, watch me enter the forest. The air is clear once I'm on the path, the hazy station behind me. Thankfully the only sound on my way into the community is my feet rustling the debris along the trail. Today feels gloomier than usual, a sense of melancholy hanging in the air, or perhaps it's simply the combination of so many sinister events with the sombre atmosphere and isolation affecting my mood.

I reach town, creep stealthily to the board which contains no information for me, and slink back out and into the forest between the lit lanterns at the gate. I don't think anyone sees me, at least I don't see anyone else.

Silence follows me, the trees carefully watching my quiet movements, no motion or sound among them to startle me. My pace is steady, fast but not too much so to ensure that I remain vigilant of the woods around me with all their potential for concealing. I arrive at the school after an uneventful walk. Clear air accompanied by occasional sun gives the area a playful feel, though the field's emptiness keeps it slightly lonely. Total silence lies in the large clearing, the unoccupied benches and swings making it look like an abandoned village.

Keeping on track, I follow the path along the treeline to my left and around the twisting path to Cindy's, arriving at her house just before 9:30.

How will I start this conversation?

How will she react?

Do I really want to do this?

A gulp of coffee and warmth flows through me.

A light low mist encircles her house, thinnest at the building, thickening progressively toward the trees at the glade's perimeter, dusk's darkness still very much in place here, the area sombre despite the building's bright white walls and red trim. There are no lights in the front windows but the inside seems to be lit from the back, possibly the kitchen.

I consider walking up to the front door but while pondering what to do, a quick dark movement to my right gets my attention.

Cindy?

No one's there.

Slowly, my legs carry me to the wall to look around the corner. Again no one. Who or what is here?

"Cindy" I say softly but get no answer so don't speak a second time.

I see nothing in the forest, hear no noise. I wait for any sound or movement but none comes. I glance up to my right where the sun is attempting to break through the cloud cover and to my left where the skies are grey and ominous.

I lean forward against the wall, looking around the side of the building, exhaling.

A soft tug at the bottom of my shirt spins me around.

My eyes are immediately drawn down expecting to catch a child but there's empty space all around me. Rissa? Sam? Couldn't be.

A scuttling sound moves away from me but I can't see into the forest, the sinister trees offering hiding to whatever is here with me. By now I'm around the back of the house.

A take another sip of coffee.

I sense movement, but can't see or hear anyone. Is there someone else in the fog with me? Do I dare move? I'm petrified, unsure what to do next. I force myself to breathe as I stand both alert and terrified.

Anyone could surprise me or watch me and wait as I stand helplessly on display. I stop, my eyes scanning side to side, my back against the house's wall.

Silence.

Perhaps this is the wrong time to visit.

"Colden. I didn't expect you"

My heart stops.

Cindy is in the doorway wearing a long t-shirt ending just above her knees.

Her face is different somehow, her movements more clipped.

I hesitate.

"What's wrong?" her tone changes from happiness to concern as she returns to form.

The bag drops from my hand; or had this happened earlier?

Should I walk toward her or turn and run?

There's nowhere to go.

"Come inside" she holds out her hand.

Her face flickers for a fraction of a second like static on a TV.

I couldn't have run if I'd tried. I pick up my sack and move toward the door.

"I made enough coffee for both of us"

"OK" I whisper.

Two lanterns hang from hooks on the wall opposite the back window casting the slightest of shadows in the room illuminating it with a subtle glow.

I sit in the chair nearest the door, adjusting it with the exit at my side, and take a sip of the coffee I'd brought, setting it down on the table.

Cindy brings a cup, sugar already on the table.

She sits facing me, her feet up on my seat as she leans in pulling her chest toward her knees.

"I'm super-happy to see you, but you look like you just saw a ghost" she smirks.

Is the room spinning?

"Here's your coffee" she says as if reading my mind, sliding the cup across the table.

My hands slide down from her knees to her ankles, her smiling eyes following them, her legs moving the tiniest bit apart. I pick her feet up from the seat of my chair, placing them on the ground, sliding my chair away as I do, her face scowling.

"So, your name's Cindy?" I blurt out, surprised at my tone.

"What?" her eyes squint.

"How long have you lived here?"

She seems about to speak but says nothing, simply pulls her shirt down past her knees.

"And why aren't you scared of what's going on here?"

"I'm terrified" she shakes her head with angry eyes "Is this really you speaking?"

My legs push my chair back further.

"What's your real name?" I ask.

"My what?"

"Your true name?" I repeat recalling what I'd been told to ask "Is it really Cindy?"

"It is" she replies impatiently.

"With a 'C'"

"Colden" her tone changes to concern "What's wrong?"

Do I push with the Stayla and Stela and von Stela?

What am I saying? What's wrong with me? My head is spinning.

"I keep seeing…"

"Seeing what?" she leans closer.

I decide I'll keep the discovery of the 'von Stela' name to myself for now.

She slowly brings one foot up to rest on the seat of my chair.

"We're both pretty scared" she says "You can drink the coffee. I didn't poison it"

She smiles.

I reach for the cup she set out for me and take a sip.

"Things are starting to get to me" I suddenly feel apologetic "I'm really sorry, Cindy"

What is real? Who should I trust?

I reach out my hands which she takes in hers.

"It's fine" she exhales deeply, taking a sip from her own cup "I'm on your side, you know"

I know that, right?

"Now what?" I ask.

"Now we stand up" she whispers.

My body and mind feel comfortable in her presence and my mood relaxes.

Getting to my feet, I slowly glide my hands up from her knees up her thighs to her waist, the shirt with them. She shivers as my fingers caress her thighs and then the sides of her stomach, as the thin white garment comes up to her chest.

Her arms wrap around me holding me tightly; for a moment I hold her close as well.

"I just stepped out of the shower" she says, no clothing beneath her top.

I lift the shirt higher, revealing perky pink nipples and beautiful smooth breasts. She gasps as my hands cup her boobs and rub her nipples. Rising on her toes, she meets my lips with the softest kiss.

"I'm glad you came" she whispers.

"You are so pretty" I say, my hands falling to grab her bum.

"Mmmmmm" she moans pushing away my jacket and removing my shirt.

"I love the way your body feels against me" she pulls me closer, her bare breasts against my chest "Your strength"

As we remove our clothing and shuffle toward the bedroom my eyes catch a glimpse of something dark in the far corner of the living room but it had disappeared when I looked more closely so must have been my imagination.

50 – A group of men are on their way

The cool air wakes me earlier than I want, the window on my side of the room partially open allowing a chilly dampness into the room. That was definitely closed last night, wasn't it? Unlikely I'd get up to let the night air lower the bedroom's temperature given that I'd fallen asleep without any clothes on. Cindy faces away from me curled up tightly, her naked body warm to the touch.

7:30

I get up, pull the window down, and climb back under the covers until sleep takes me again.

8:15

It's later than usual, but there's still time to check the board in the town square to make sure I stay on top of things.

I swing my legs out of bed, sitting on the edge for a moment before standing up.

Cindy stands in the doorway in shorts and a crop-top shirt.

I kiss her, grabbing my boxers and shuffling to the bathroom with a groggy smile. Strange that my feet are dirty.

Coffee waits on the stove, fruit and bread on the table. I could get used to this. I have a distant memory of the previous evening causing me anxiety but can't recall why.

"Thanks" I kiss her again, pouring a cup and walking to look out the back window.

"Did you get hot last night and open the window?" I ask her without turning around.

"No way. It's cold in here at the best of times"

Ok.

"I should head to town soon and then check the schedules. And the control room at the station. I don't think any arrivals are expected but prefer not to be surprised"

"I've got a class shortly too so I'd be throwing you out anyway" she smiles.

I sit in my usual chair.

"So, what do we know now that we didn't know before?"

"That I'm not lying to you" she replies.

"And that we still don't know our employer"

"Until we figure things out, I'd best continue teaching. Regardless of what we decide to do"

"And there's not much else for me to do being that my home is at the station"

"Do we really want to leave?" she says "I've not got anyplace else to go"

"I think so. I don't know"

I try to conjure something confident.

"How about a dinner date at my place?" I suggest "To help us refresh a bit. Come by after class and I'll prepare a meal for us. Maybe with some candles"

"Sounds romantic" she smiles "I've got a little black dress"

She walks over, hugs and kisses me, and walks to the bedroom.

"I'm done in there" she points to the bathroom "So you're welcome to get ready here if you like"

"I'll get ready at my place, thanks" I say.

The peace of Cindy's home relaxes me, the calm, the colour, the quiet.

"A woman as stunning as you must get a lot of attention in town" I watch her from the doorway "I'm sure lucky"

"You are"

"Your ex-boyfriends aren't gonna come after me when they find out, are they?" I laugh.

"The men in town ignore me completely" she shakes her head.

"I find that hard to believe" I smile.

"Some are decent looking but absolutely vacant from what I can tell"

"How do you mean?"

"The married men show no affection to their wives or girlfriends" she says "I've never seen them kiss, hold hands, smile at each other. They're like empty shells. Emotionless. And when they look at me their faces are like blank canvases waiting to be painted

"The ones who aren't married either act completely aloof or like they've always got someplace serious to be" she goes on "I rarely get a glance, even out of curiosity. I've thought about bathing nude in the forest but probably wouldn't have been noticed there either"

"I never came upon you bathing nude in the forest" I try to look serious.

"You're missing the point" she smiles.

"Hang on" I close my eyes "Still working on the picture of you nude in the forest"

Cindy crosses her arms.

"Still, I bet some of them would like to...see inside the teacher's house" I smile.

"I'm not sure they'd know what to do if they saw inside the teacher's house" she smiles back.

"You're more handsome, anyway" she nods "And have a better body"

"Well, I am the station master"

We both laugh.

Still time for a cup of coffee at the apartment after a stop in town so I decide against a second one here. But the pastries on the table look yummy so I help myself. Chocolate is OK but caramel has no equal and the perfect sweetness in this fluffy treat makes me think of a flavoured croissant. Delicious. And another one for the road.

I'll shower when I get back to the station, with nothing clean to wear here anyway. I'm about to call out my departure when I feel a chill coming from the kitchen.

Cool air meets me as I near the back of the house with the door ajar. I shut it without mentioning it to Cindy.

"Until tonight" I call out.

"Tonight" she replies.

My jacket is nowhere to be seen so I have no choice but to leave without it and hope Cindy brings it later. A t-shirt will do for now. I'll be running if it's cold outside.

There's no mist today which suits me fine but the customary damp chill follows me to the school's clearing. The open area makes for fresher surroundings, though the sun seems unable to pierce the clouds, the setting a gloomy one.

Then I realize my backpack must still be at Cindy's along with my jacket. Should I turn back?

I stand on the fringe of the forest contemplating a minor decision in the bleakness of the open glade.

She'll either bring it or I'll get it another time; I don't feel like going back. I still have to check the board in town.

Is that a young girl at the side of the school? Not again.

Has she seen me? Is she facing toward me or away?

I approach slowly, hoping to speak with her and learn her identity. Or find out if she's actually there at all. My ghost girl.

She runs off behind the school, so I hustle in pursuit, coming around the side of the building. I'm sure there was a girl there.

Oh no.

My backpack is on the ground beneath Benton, his body suspended by a noose secured below the roof's edge, his feet just off the ground.

The school children are nowhere in sight, no one else visible from where I stand. The girl from the side of the building is gone making me doubt she'd ever been there.

Cindy has class here soon so this has to be taken care of. But how? Should I go to town for help? Should I go back to Cindy's place?

Then I realize he's wearing my station master jacket.

Is someone watching me? Watching me take in another ghastly scene? I freeze like an animal on display.

Should I walk around the school? I don't dare look behind me or into the forest, fear rooting me to the spot. Slowly turning my head without moving my body, I look toward the treeline behind the building, seeing nothing but skeletal trunks and bony limbs with dead leaves and yellow grass. The empty field is scattered with empty wood and stone tables and benches.

No wind. No sound.

I touch Benton's body, his form swinging slightly until I stop him. The thought of laying a hand on him feels disrespectful.

His eyes are closed, his skin gaunt and drawn. I'm thankful he's clothed.

I try the school door but of course it's locked.

I run fully around the building without seeing anyone or anything out of the ordinary.

Then I'm back in front of Benton's limp corpse.

I see a figure in the window next to where the body hangs, like a shadow or an outline, a mannequin, a short distance back from the glass inside the school. And then it's gone, whatever it is. If it was ever there.

I fall to a crouching position, gasping for breath.

Benton.

Not again.

Why?

Had he taken his own life? In my jacket?

I have to get him down. And then what?

Should I go to town and find someone to help? I'd obviously had no involvement in his death. Except he's wearing my jacket.

I panic.

The crawl space beneath the building can hold his body for now until a better option presents itself. There's no way to take him back to the station. And I won't be going into the forest here.

Plastic sheeting left over from my recent repairs will serve as a wrap, a temporary measure to keep away forest critters. I secure the clasp on the door under the school as a final safeguard.

Picking up my backpack, I stagger out of the clearing in the direction of the community, vigilant of any spectators. My jacket draped over the back of my bag – it's too big to fit inside it and inappropriate to wear just yet.

How the hell did my jacket find its way to the schoolhouse or to Benton or even out of Cindy's place? And why was he out here this morning? He had no reason to come this way that I can think of. There's nothing out here but the school and the teacher's house. He was a good guy in an ordinary way, nice to me and probably the same to everyone else. Who would want him dead?

I can't tell his family because how would I know he'd died, and there's no way I'm going to describe how he'd been found.

I make a quick stop at the station to drop off my bag, and check for notes on the printer, then head straight into town to check the board. I quickly survey the suite from the entry and back out I go after dropping my pack safely within. There's no one visible and no sounds around the platform. I pull on the station master jacket to avoid any suspicion while in my 'acting' capacity.

My thought burden me on the quiet walk to town, the sun slowly rising above the trees, my chest heavy, my lungs struggling to draw breath. The low fog in the field doesn't follow me into the forest, the air clear and crisp and cool. My solitary journey ends at the village gates, haze neither in the plaza nor in the glade surrounding it as if kept out by unseen forces.

Those milling about the town square pay me little attention which suits me fine, given recent events. I approach the board cautiously, wary of what might wait or who might be watching my movements. A note tacked to the board indicates an arrival tomorrow at 1:15 pm; it's well-timed to have today to contemplate alone.

Furtively glancing around me, I see no eyes looking my way but no one seems to be avoiding me either so I finish checking the board. A small pouch with my name on it is tied to the panel, some fragrant loose coffee inside; a piece of paper reads simply: 'Enjoy. T'.

Distant voices and noises of activity make the world seem so far away.

I wish the day could remain this peaceful.

I inhale and exhale deeply.

"Hello, Station Master"

The voice above me makes me jump.

Osterman, a friendly enough man with too much time on his hands.

"Oh, hello, sir" I reply.

"Rather foggy today. Not a good day in the fields, I'm sure"

"Hopefully we'll clear up before the end of the day"

"What will you do about Benton?" he says.

"Pardon me?" I stammer.

"I said it'd be nice if the fog lifted"

"Maybe it will later" I regain my composure.

"Perhaps" he looks around from his position up on the steps of the city hall building, arms crossed in front of him "Are your days well-spent?"

"I think so" I answer eager to get away but careful not to let it show "The work is getting done and when it's quiet I enjoy the time alone"

"Yes, time to oneself is good. Well, I'll leave you to it"

He saunters back into the building.

I pocket the coffee pouch, anxious to get back to the station.

Head down, I walk back the way I came, my footsteps soft. Passing the gate, the lanterns extinguish behind me as if by an invisible hand. I stop, turning as I do.

A grey-cloaked man nods to me "Good day, Station Master" his sinister eyes glaring into mine.

Dropping my head once again, I breathe a sigh of relief once I reach the treeline, eager to put New Brook West behind me for the day.

Despite the bleak green and grey among the trees, I welcome this familiar environment. The sun rarely finds its way in and I sometimes wonder how things would look if it did, if I'd see more of the colourful flowers. The sound of birds chirping in the distance to the right of the path as I enter the forest breaks the silence. A light breeze rustles the leaves high in the canopy, the birdsongs in the foliage accompanying me back to the station's clearing, the area now free of fog.

Thankfully no one waits for me on the platform or in the vicinity that I can see; I don't have the energy for encounters right now. I jog up the stairs and into the suite to get away from any potentially prying eyes. The station master jacket has no stains or unusual markings, no rips, no dirt. It didn't fit Benton properly given that he's smaller than me but otherwise nothing strange is visible to suggest a struggle. Who had a grudge against this guy? What's the point of killing him then putting the jacket on him? Or putting it on him before his death?

The jacket must have been to send some kind of message, but what do I have to do with any of this? And who would have sent me this message?

I prepare a cup with my new coffee grounds and sit down to regroup.

Poor Benton. I liked him. And now have another secret to keep.

Why would he enter Cindy's place? And how?

Had Cindy gone out in the night?

I stretch out on the couch and am asleep before I know it.

A knock at the door makes me jump. Who now?

I consider laying in quiet until my visitor goes away but decide against it in case this person knows I'm inside, making my actions suspicious given recent crimes. Opening the door, Rissa and Sam are standing on the landing.

"Hi" Rissa smiles.

"Hi Rissa. Hi Sam" I exhale deeply.

Best I step outside; if people see me inviting these two children in it'll be curtains for me.

"You look sad" Sam says.

"No. I'm fine"

"A group of men are on their way" Rissa tells me as we walk down to the platform.

"Here? Why?"

"A man in town disappeared and people are concerned" she says "Perhaps they're interested to see what you know. Some of the Station Masters before you weren't nice men. But you're nice. I hope nothing bad happens to you"

"Me too" I say "How do you know about this?"

I hear voices and footsteps from out in the clearing.

When I turn back to the stairs, the children have vanished.

Walking to the top of the stone steps, I spot the group of men approaching the station, their leader the same man who'd visited me after Acacia's death.

Were disappearances common? Or will this be pinned on me and my arrival?

"Hello, Station Master" the man faces me on the platform.

"Hello. Is everything OK?"

Playing dumb seems the best strategy because how would I know anything about Benton.

"We're looking for a man from the village. He didn't come home last night and remains unaccounted for"

"Who's that?"

"Have you seen anyone in these parts?"

"Not since yesterday's train's arrival"

"Mind if we look around a bit?"

"By all means" I say, eager to get away.

What if he asks to look in the utility room? That'll be the end of me.

He points across the tracks by way of instruction to his companions.

"I'll check the hotel rooms" he says.

"I'll come with you"

One by one he examines each room, starting at the top floor. It's obvious Room 5, has been recently occupied though not cleaned since the guest's departure.

"Who stayed in here?" he asks.

"Mr. Hanson" I answer, fully nervous about this inspection "I haven't been in touch with Tessa yet to arrange for it to be re-made. I'm heading to town after this"

He looks in Room 2 but never makes a move toward Room 1.

One of the men looks up from the ground next to the platform shaking his head.

The man next to me nods in reply.

"Good day, sir" he then nods to me as the group disappears into the forest.

My heart races like I'd run a marathon. A deep breath.

Back up to my room to collect my thoughts. What now? Do people think that I've played a role in the deaths of Benton and Acacia? Why would they even suspect me - I have no reason to kill anyone. Had previous station masters been subject to this level of scrutiny? Had they been guilty?

Benton and Acacia both had connections to me, so the obvious suspicion. I wonder if there's a police force in the community and the form of any judicial proceeding. I hope I never learn of either.

I quickly make a coffee and pour a glass of wine, unsure of which I want. Taking a sip of first the cool then the hot beverage, I sit on the window's edge staring into the room.

I consider my next steps. Acacia's body has to be moved and Benton's as well at some point. But not just yet.

The quiet room eases my mood. The silence and peace of the moment cause me to inhale and exhale intensely several times. The coffee calms my nerves, relaxing my thoughts.

A knock at the door. Do I answer? Expecting to see the guy from before, I now see a beautiful brunette woman about Cindy's age, slightly shorter than her.

I open the door before realizing I'm wearing only my t-shirt and boxers.

"Hi Colden" the pretty brunette says "Can I come in?"

"Sure. Who are you?"

"I'm Jade"

She may have said more but for now I'm too distracted.

She wears a fitted orange dress over her slim figure and large bust, her raven black eyes and smile hypnotizing. I recognize her from somewhere but can't place it. Did Cindy say this is the girl who cleans the school? I can't remember. She looks to be about twenty and I've definitely seen her somewhere before.

She steps in, removing her shoes.

"I've been wanting to meet you for a while now" she says "I hope that's OK"

She approaches me, as I sit on the sofa. She lifts a leg, placing her bare left foot on my thigh, before sliding down next to me to face me and crossing her legs at the ankles, both feet up on the couch, her dress is riding up almost to her waist. I stare at her bare feet and legs noticing that she seems to not be wearing underwear.

"I'm so happy to see you" Jade whispers, leaning forward to put her hand between my legs giving me an instant erection, "And you're glad to see me too"

"I hope you don't mind if I take this off" she says, pulling her dress up over her head revealing a tanned body with huge bare breasts. And no underwear.

Is this really happening? She's gorgeous, naked, and all over me. I stare at her thin athletic body, her smooth skin, her tanned breasts, and down between her legs.

"First you can take this off" she lifts my shirt over my head smiling "Then let's get this out" Jade says pulling down my underwear as she gets on her knees in front of me.

I have no control, as if watching myself in a dream.

Jade runs her fingers across her breasts making her nipples hard with a moan.

"Mmmm"

She tucks her bare feet beneath her, leaning in towards me.

"Wow" she says taking my erection in her warm mouth, sliding her lips several times over the tip making me gasp.

I close my eyes, not sure what to make of my current situation. Her soft lips make my breathing stop, my arms useless at my sides. How long does this go on, her lips sliding up and down?

Ohhh. I'm close.

2:30 pm

Another knock snaps me from my 'dream', because what else can it be. Looking down I notice I'm naked and...very much aroused, my clothes on the floor in front of me, an orange dress near the sofa.

Quickly looking around the room, I see no one, but can't imagine Jade having left my apartment naked.

I pull on what clothes I can find as quickly as I can, throw the orange garment under a couch cushion, and find my way to the door. Cindy smiles at me.

"You look happy to see me" she looks down.

"I was...dreaming"

"Hopefully about me" she steps inside, wearing a fitted black dress beneath a longer dark coat, kissing me on the cheek as she walks past me.

"Of course" I smile back, pulling her toward me to kiss her on the lips.

I guide her in the direction of the kitchen.

"How about a glass of wine?" I ask "I could use a drink"

"Sounds good to me"

There are two full and one half-filled bottles in the fridge so the latter comes out and is emptied.

"I like the outfit" she smiles "Very sharp"

I'm wearing only a t-shirt and my underwear. With an erection.

"Everything OK?" she asks.

"I think so. It's been an odd day, especially since I got back here"

"How so?"

"A group of guys came out here looking for someone who went missing yesterday" I come clean about the visit without providing details "Not sure why they'd think I was involved"

"Are you involved?" Cindy says, her question surprising me.

"No way" I say sternly.

"Then no reason to worry"

Pulling on dark pants, I casually button up a nicer short sleeved dress shirt; I wish I had a tie but wouldn't know where to find it if I did.

"Oh, this was outside your door" she puts something on the island.

"What is it?" I ask.

"An envelope" she sips her wine "I didn't open it"

Do I even want to know what's in the envelope? I suppose it could have some bearing on activities at the station, or loads, or arrivals and departures. Or be something entirely creepy.

"I found some of the Station Masters' ledgers" I say "And there're books on community history at the library. Nothing specifically with the stations masters' biographies but I think some of the guys before me weren't pillars of the community. If people think I'm like them then it's no wonder they avoid me. Or suspect me. Or both"

"The original New Brook West families" I say as I put on pants and a dress shirt "Clovinston, Brooks, Barkman, Maris. Family trees for each of them. Jasper Colvin first reached the east of the island but there's no name anywhere for the island itself just the communities named for the leaders of the groups of settlers. Jasper later changed his name but it doesn't say why. The other families came after him though there seems to be no connection among any of these groups. The von Stela's arrived at John's Cape, wherever that is. Have you ever heard of it?"

"No. I didn't know any of this"

"You don't know the name von Stela?"

"It sounds like a predecessor to mine"

"That's it?"

"What did you think I'd say?" she scowls.

The page showing the von Stela family tree was missing from their genealogical volume, I think but don't say.

I adjust my shirt as I come around, by now looking presentable.

"Very sharp" Cindy smiles.

"You look fantastic" I say looking her up and down.

"Thank you" she blushes.

I sip my sweet wine, smoother and more flavourful than I remember the last time I drank it.

I pick up the envelope with 'Colden' written on it in simple cursive, surprised at seeing my first name as I'm usually simply referred to as 'Station Master'.

This would seem official were it not for my name on the plain envelope.

I wonder who would bring me this clandestine note. Attempting to imagine the contents, I shudder at the possibilities as it occurs to me that this could be just about anything.

A threat? A photo of a dead station master? A senseless riddle?

It's better to know than to wonder, right?

The process seems to take forever, as if I'm moving in slow motion for theatrical effect, the plain light brown envelope thicker than I expect. Carefully removing the paper from inside takes an eternity and even longer for me to place it on the island in front of me.

It's a twice-folded piece of ordinary paper. A family tree written in perfect block letters descends down five or six generations.

Von Stela.

Martin and Katya at the top then their children Rebecca and Christina Nicole.

Weren't Martin and Katya's names at the beginning of one of the tomes at the library with the next page obviously torn from the book.

I wonder at that page's importance and look more closely at the paper.

Rebecca's children are Caelyn and Hannah.

Hannah's children: Fuchsia and Violet.

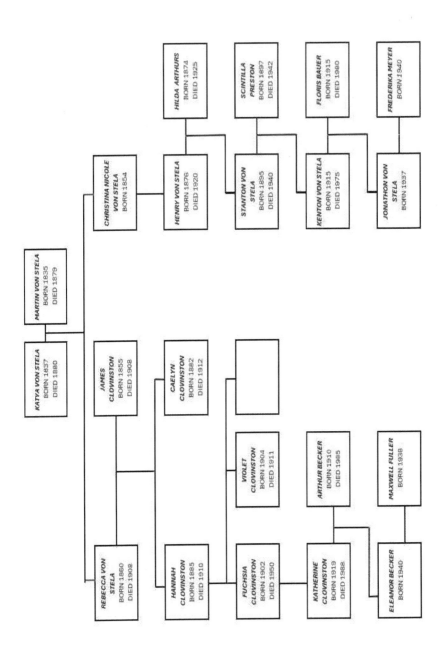

Fuchsia's daughter: Katherine.

Katherine's daughter Eleanor is the last name on that side of the tree.

On the other side Christina Nicole's son Henry then Stanton then Kenton then Jonathan where it stops, each of the men's wives listed by name as had been the case with the women's husbands on the other side with years of birth and death beneath the respective names. Christina Nicole's year of death is missing. But she'd be long dead now according to her sister's dates so maybe the person who wrote this out simply couldn't remember.

The von Stela name survived on the one side with the male children carrying the name forward, at least up until Jonathan. The lineage beneath Rebecca loses the von Stela name when she marries James Clovinston, though I can't recall if this marriage is documented in his genealogy.

Hannah's children, Fuchsia and Violet, show no father and there's a third blank box next to the girls which strikes me as odd; perhaps the person who transcribed this forgot that detail. Fuchsia is only one who had children, and from that point a single girl is born to each couple, the surname changing frequently as a result of a new male marrying into the family each time.

There would certainly be a lot of overlapping family trees and duplication of descendancy, assuming everyone recorded family history.

The text is in sharp block letters, not the same florid script I'd seen in the other tomes at the library. Still, someone went to a lot of trouble to copy this all out and get this to me and either has an excellent memory ore went to great efforts to reproduce the original.

I wonder who'd bother and what this is supposed to mean to me. I can't see how this helps.

I return it to the envelope to keep it safe.

Clearly there's more to this than meets the eye, a condition I should be used to by now. There's nothing inherently sinister or mysterious about any of the genealogical information, at least nothing I can see but every place has its secrets and perhaps some of them are contained in the family tree that was torn from its volume at the library.

I'm disinclined to ask Brian about this detail or even share the fact that a page is missing from one of the books.

Have I met any von Stela's since I arrived? I don't think so but can't be sure because people rarely provide their last name.

Cindy's looking over my shoulder.

"What exactly is this?" she asks.

"The von Stela family tree" I say softly "The island's original settlers it seems"

"Who gave this to you?"

"No idea" I push the sheet away "Someone clearly wants me to know all this, but why? What does it tell me? And why bring it in secret?"

"Then they obviously aren't supposed to be sharing this with you"

Obviously.

Is there a name here that answers one of my questions? That helps me figure out what's going on here? That gives a clue to getting away?

I hate riddles.

"What do you make of it?" I ask.

She pulls the sheet toward her, eyes scanning the page.

"This is all news to me" she says without looking up.

"What do you know about family trees?" I ask her.

"About mine? Almost nothing. Why?"

I search for the right words, words that won't seem crazy.

"There's something about a tree, but I haven't a clue what it could be"

"What about a tree?"

"I'm serious" I say seriously "I've been having dreams, or something, someone telling me about a tree, 'the end of the branches' and 'I am in the tree', things like that. Maybe a family tree"

"Dreams?"

"Like a vision. Like someone talking to me ..."

"From the 'other side'?" her face squirrels up.

"Maybe" I say "I don't know. What I do know is that I have to get out of here because I think I'll end up dead if I don't go crazy first. It seems like someone's been eliminating station masters over the years but that many of them lost their minds working here before that. These guys kept ledgers of arrivals and departures but then a guy's entries will suddenly stop, a new station master showing up a few months later. They wrote about strange goings-on, mysterious voices, odd occurrences, and how they're going mad, sometimes a girl around the station; and then they're gone"

"Maybe they got scared like you" Cindy shrugs her shoulders "Or just decided to cash out and move on, who knows. Or died; everyone dies somewhere. Some things don't have an explanation"

"You think this is all normal?"

"No way" her eyes widen "But you're talking about visits from the grave"

"So why am I seeing all these things and you aren't? No one's killing off school teachers"

A blank look.

"The guy at the library's got all kinds of info about the community; we should go see him" I add.

"What guy?"

"The librarian. Brian"

"There's no librarian, Colden" Cindy shakes her head with a worried look on her face.

"Not true. I've spoken to him. He's told me local stories, showed me where to look for information, offered me coffee"

"There hasn't been anyone there in several years, at least from what I've been told. I've been twice and there wasn't anyone working there. The children go regularly but have never mentioned a librarian"

"Then who the hell am I talking to?" I can't be sure if my voice is a whisper or a yell? The question is partly directed at Cindy and partly rhetorical.

"Are you feeling ok, Colden?"

"I think so. But turns out I'm conjuring up ghostly conversations, imaginary advisors. What the hell is this place? I'm a pretty ordinary person who can't commune with the dead or levitate objects off the table"

My mind still struggles to wrap itself around my time at the library. I slide the tomes away without looking up.

There's no way I'd imagined all my conversations with Brian.

"This is interesting but nothing jumps off the pages" she says "Family trees, text about where people settled and why, but no obvious mention of station masters or school teachers"

I stare down at the names in the boxes.

Rebecca and James Clovinston who lived here over a hundred years ago.

Several levels down on the left side of the tree: Eleanor.   My grandmother's name. But it isn't an uncommon one.

"Recognize anything?" I point at the names.

Her eyes widen as she tries unsuccessfully to speak.

"Those are my grandmother's and great-grandmother's names" I point at 'Eleanor' and 'Katherine'.

"My grandma is 'Rika'" she says, her eyes landing on 'Frederika'.

"There can't be many of those" I add pointing at several unique names.

"No" her voice is just above a whisper.

It takes a few seconds for the pieces to come together for me.

"So, we're related?" I say.

"Hardly" she frowns "There's barely a connection going that far back"

"It's messed up" I say loudly, contemplating the significance of this discovery.

"Barely" Cindy assures me "How many degrees of separation is that? That's if she's even your ancestor. And mine. Lotsa people have had the same name over the years. And names that sound odd now might have been common a hundred years ago"

"Maybe" I reply filled with false confidence that the answers are now clear to me.

51 - The son of Rebecca and the daughter of Nicole

A glass of wine and some genealogical investigations and it's already 7:30 pm.

Am I really a descendant of previous inhabitants of New Brook West? This would have been an interesting detail to know before I came.

It occurs to me how little I know about my ancestry.

Is Cindy related to the folks on the other side of this family tree?

Neither of us recognizes any of the distant ancestors, but who would. We each pore over our respective genealogies without it conjuring any practical thoughts about our origins, our backgrounds, or if we're reading into scenarios that don't exist.

There isn't a lot here that means much to me and certainly nothing that gives me an epiphany about my situation or what to do next. Judging by Cindy's expression, she's had no more luck than me with her reading material.

Evening's descent comes quickly. I ponder my questions as we eat bread and meat dipped in a cheese fondue, which I'd managed to assemble faster than expected.

We manage to have light-hearted dinner conversation about the food, about New Brook West, about what we might be missing in the outside world both good and bad. Could we really make a life here? Do we want to? Would we do this together?

"There might be better men than me who want to see inside the school teacher's house" I say with a smirk.

"Haha" she chuckles "No, no I don't think there are"

"Better men than me? Or that want to see your house?"

"There's no one I'd rather be with than you, Colden" Cindy takes my hand and stands to kiss me.

Wow. That was unexpected.

"You're amazing" I say as we stand together.

I hold her body close to me for a long moment.

"I do like this" I say.

"So do I" Cindy replies softly, head resting against my chest.

My eyes scan the room for anything out of the ordinary or out of place, look to the window for any ghostly girls watching from outside, look up to satisfy my curiosity and ease my anxiety.

I'm beginning to understand how my predecessors felt about being watched.

"So, did you prepare any dessert?" she separates herself from me looking around behind me.

Uh, no. I was lucky to come up with what we ate for dinner.

No, wait. I have some muffins or cupcakes or something from someone. Ha.

"Of course" I say confidently walking to the other side of the island. If I can find them.

A short search turns up exactly what I was looking for, or at least what I'd hoped I'd find. A small box of small lightly iced cupcakes.

"Voila" I lay them out on a plate and place them on the coffee table.

"Impressive" she raises her eyebrows "Where did you get these?"

"Forever a mystery" I cross my arms seriously walking to set water to boil for coffee.

We leave after our sweet treat and cup of coffee, as I'm eager to get away from the station before anyone comes with news of more missing residents. Maybe tomorrow I'll go to town to find answers but for tonight I only want to get away from the station for a night. Even if I'm not entirely sure of how Cindy fits in, we stand together or at least I feel we do. I think.

"You just want to see inside the school teacher's house" Cindy smiles.

"Every chance I get" I take her hand.

There's no one outside waiting for me so we hurry across the clearing to the path, the dark forest hopefully masking our departure. We slow our pace, mostly to avoid attracting attention. No sounds on the trail ahead or following us and none on either side, a good sign for the moment, my ears keenly attuned to our environment. Not a word is spoken between us; I wouldn't have known what to say and am thankful for Cindy's silence despite what turned out to be a wonderful evening.

But I am happy.

Who can I trust in the village to help me? My friends were few, and some of them are now dead. People seem either indifferent to me or wary of me. Are the apparitions around the station real or is my mind playing tricks on me in my new herb-and-incense environment clouded by my own ghosts? What is happening here and what does it all mean? And am I any closer to an explanation for Acacia's and Benton's deaths?

A short distance ahead and off the trail to our right, a slim female figure in a long silver cloak stands outside a small dimly lit shack. A friend come to assist me in my time of need? A resident I've not yet met? A meeting best avoided? Something tells me this visit is not optional and the invitation is best accepted. Cindy and I glance at each other before moving into the trees and toward the woman as if drawn to her.

Experience has taught me to be cautious and, too late, I fear I've encountered a woman I'd rather I hadn't met.

"The son of Rebecca and the daughter of Nicole. Together" she says as we enter the structure's door.

Her smooth movements, youthful appearance, and an inexplicable aura give her a charisma which puts me at ease, at least for the moment. Platinum blonde hair frames a sharp-featured face, her black fitted dress hugging her body and extending to the ground.

The round interior forms a large circle. A fire, encased in an iron stove, burns at the center providing a comfortable warmth; blankets cover the ground prompting me to remove my footwear out of politeness. The small space is dimly-lit by the central hearth, complemented by a single lantern behind the woman.

"Thank you" I say "I'm the new station master"

"You both came"

Uh-oh. This sounds familiar.

"Is it warm enough?" she asks politely.

"Yes, thank you" Cindy replies removing her boots, tucking her feet beneath her.

"Do you live here?" I ask "I've never seen you before on my walks to town"

She smiles and nods several times slowly as if answering a question I haven't asked. Still, her manner relaxes me and I feel no anxiety.

"The forest is beautiful" I add.

"Yes" she replies drawing out the 's' "It is"

I'm trying to place her but don't recognize her from any of my visits to the community. Does she work at the market? I don't think so.

"I'm rather new here in New Brook West" I cross my legs in front of me "So still getting used to life at the train station"

Cindy seems to have gone mute. I look to her and can't tell if she's feeling sleepy, nervous, or is just preferring to be quiet.

I try to calmly survey the room, to take in our surroundings but only see the stove, a crate on both sides of the space, and the blankets beneath us. The woman is standing and I can't see anything past her because of the lantern behind her.

A shiver runs down my back like cool air has just blown into the room.

I look up at the woman.

"I don't believe we've met" I say, hoping this will elicit an introduction on her part. I consider standing but don't.

"I don't know many people" I add sheepishly.

"You've met Tina. Green-eyed Tina" she replies sitting on a pile of cushions to our left.

"You're a friend of hers?" I ask.

"No, not a friend" she looks at the fire.

Cindy brings her legs in front and up to her chest of her wrapping her arms around them.

"Do you live here?" Cindy sounds confused, repeating my question from earlier.

"It's the way I'd expected, and events will soon come to their climax" the woman shakes her head.

"What you expected?" I ask, concerned with this cryptic conversation.

"Did you think this your story, son of Rebecca?" she says softly with a smile.

My story? Huh? Son of who?

I don't think I say any of this. I'm too stunned to say anything.

She looks at Cindy and seems to say something but no sound comes out of her mouth. Then she turns around and flips a hood up over her head, picking something up from the ground at her side.

Cindy gives me a worried look though I'm unsure of how to politely and safely exit our current situation.

The woman is now facing us again, poking a long metal rod into the stove's fire making it spark.

I look around the tent, making sure it's only the three of us. How do we get out of here?

"One a woman, one a girl" she mutters under her breath.

A burst of orange flares up behind the iron grate shining on her fair-skinned face.

"One you will kill, one will kill you?" she smiles at me.

This sounds familiar but I can't imagine why.

"We really should go" I say to no one in particular.

Her face has lost all its features, now just a pale and white surface. She stands up gracefully, turning her back to us as Cindy and I frantically grab our footwear, scrambling for the exit.

I take Cindy's hand and we jog as quickly as we can safely.

Once we're back on the trail, we stop, wary of anyone else in the forest.

I catch my breath as I try to make sense of what just happened.

All is quiet behind us, no hut visible in the darkness. Of course.

"That happened, right?" I ask Cindy.

"I think so" she says, obviously flustered.

"Let's go, yes?" I say.

"Yes" she replies hurrying along the path to the school.

"What was she saying about killing you?" Cindy stops me.

"I don't wanna know" I say, trying to remember where I'd heard this before.

The calm forest has me on edge, and I'm unsure of what watches or waits, but there's no sound in any direction or farther ahead along the path. I'm grateful to not hear any rustling of dirt and leaves following me though anxious because I know what the silence conceals.

Cindy leads the way

"So far so good" she says quietly, although it sounds like a question.

"We're not there yet" I say "And who's to say there isn't a posse waiting for us at your house"

"Think positive" she smiles nervously.

"And I don't even know what to think about that woman in the forest" I shiver.

"Can we just not talk about that ever again, please" Cindy says seriously looking back.

"Of course" I say, though wonder why she wouldn't want to discuss our most recent encounter.

I come to her side and take her hand and off we go at a steady jog, the forest dark and misty on both sides.

Reaching the large clearing, a small figure appears at the window of the school, or at least I think it does. I scream at Cindy to look but no sound comes out of my mouth. I watch but it vanishes out of sight. I hear a sound like a whispered voice ahead of me toward the school.

No longer holding Cindy's hand but with her at my side, I run to the treeline, which will hopefully provide greater cover than out in the open field, the air cold under my light jacket. I look back at the school but can't see the windows from here which is probably for the best. I dismiss the figure in the window as my imagination.

It takes an eternity to reach the trail to Cindy's place, the forest's gloom slowing my progress. The time is now 9:15. A chill has set in enveloping me like a shroud and making me want to stop as if that will warm me up but I won't be resting here.

Cindy waits for me before heading off down the path toward her place, my legs moving as if in deep sand, the air around me pushing me back.

"What's taking you so long?" she asks.

"I feel like I'm in molasses" I reply "Is there anyone behind us?"

"Not that I can see"

"Did you see the girl?" I ask.

"What girl?" Cindy says.

"Never mind"

Soon we'll be in darkness and all that it brings.

"I just want to get to your place"

"Same here" she smiles "Let's go"

Taking my hand, she leads me, drags me, along the gradually narrowing trail. The moon appears overhead to my left, shining through the mist.

After jogging a short distance, I hear a noise behind us so turn without stopping, but see only black.

I shake off my anxiety as I slow my pace and face forward again.

Cindy is now far ahead of me, nearly disappearing on the winding path, her dark clothing barely discernible. I try to yell out to her but only a whisper comes out of my mouth. I make to run but my legs will barely move.

Looking around, I see nothing but the forest shrouded in night, the trees hiding whatever lies between them, the moon overhead sharpening the trunks and branches but not helping me see my companion. I look behind me but the trail has closed and I see more of the same.

I force my body to move forward, to gather speed, to keep going but Cindy's still not in sight.

What's going on? And where did she go? And what's wrong with me?

Suddenly she's right in front of me as though I ran into a brick wall.

"What's wrong?" she asks.

"I couldn't see you" I say shaking my head "Where were you? You were so far ahead"

"I was right in front of you" she replies.

She gives me the confused look that I know well.

"Let's go" I say taking her hand.

"Ok" she turns and we set off at a fast walk.

We navigate the dreary path, our feet crunching along the dirt trail, branches crackling to our right. I try to pinpoint the sound but can't locate it, can't see anyone in the dark forest. I curse not bringing a lantern. My skin tingles as I shiver in the cool air. A light appears in the distance, possibly near her house, though I'm unsure if this comforts me or not.

We slow our pace as we get nearer. Who or what waits at her house? Inside her house? Is this the end of the line for me in cold darkness?

We approach the building cautiously, the light I'd seen before no longer visible in the glade or inside. The red trim and white exterior walls stand out in the dim clearing as we walk around to the other side of the house. Cindy slowly opens the back door, entering the kitchen as I keep watch for anyone outside. She touches the table, then the chairs, then moves toward the hall and I lose her from my sight in the darkness. A few seconds go by, more than I'd like, and I still haven't heard from Cindy.

I stare into the black interior but can't make anything out beyond the table and chairs, the counter across the room too far away. I try to think where I might find a lamp but can't recall anything and certainly not in the dark.

Then there's a faint whisper in my ear but I see no one near me and don't hear any other sound.

A light appears in the living room, glowing around the corner and into the hall. But still Cindy doesn't come to the door or call me in. I wait with no sound inside or out. Should I call out for her? Keep waiting? Run inside? Has she lit a lantern?

The moon's light shines into the trees to my left, the branches and leaves standing out sharply, though I'm unable to see past the treeline, the white glow only illuminating the area around the back door.

"Cindy?" I yell but it only comes out as a loud whisper.

With one final look behind me, I enter the house.

My movements are slow and deliberate as I feel my way toward the partially lit hall, the entrance to her bedroom visible on my left. Something feels off, like someone else is here, watching, waiting for us to arrive. There's a scent of incense in the air, a spicy aroma that I've smelled before but can't place. Ahead of me, a light flickers on the hallway wall.

I stop and listen for any sound, watch for any movement but nothing.

I look behind me and out the door but see only the dark forest under the moon's glow.

I shiver from my neck down my back, my shoulders stiffening in the process, before resuming my gradual walk into the room, stopping at the kitchen counter, wary of what might be in the room. Dropping my head, I take a deep breath and look up as I step into the lit living room.

"Now what?" Cindy's sitting on the couch.

Words fail me. I don't know whether to be angry or scared.

"What are you…"

"I found a lantern" she smiles, pointing at the lit lamp.

"I see that"

"Now what" she says again "Where do we go from here?"

I sit next to her on the couch, look at her face, her eyes, try make sure everything's ok, that it's actually her. Is someone looking in the front window between the part in the drapes? Is something in the room with us?

The room's colours are dull and grey; it's cold and feels unfamiliar, uncomfortable. But I'm here with Cindy and that's good, my mind at ease as I try to settle in and put my arm around her as she nestles in to me.

Despite my misgivings at the environment, I reveal my thoughts and the information I've gathered.

"The guy at the library shared some local history with me. About New Brook East. Something happened that led to a hanging, or maybe more than one. Shortly afterward, people left the community. The story is that one of the girls of a hanged woman plotted revenge, though I'm not sure how or against whom. Apparently, station masters disappeared pretty quickly there for a while"

My mood sinks as I recount the story, my eyes trying not to wander to the front window.

"So where does that leave us?" Cindy asks.

A deep breath on my part.

"I've been to the old settlement" I say softly.

"Really…"

Uh-oh

"When?" Cindy squints.

"Let's not get off track" I divert the question "I keep thinking about a Hanging Tree"

"I've never heard any of this" Cindy thinks about it.

"Maybe Feryn'll know where to find it. He said he knows how to get anywhere and kinda appears and disappears at will"

"How do you know him?" she asks.

"He just found me one day. A local guy. I'm still trying to figure out the nature of our relationship"

She looks outside. My eyes follow hers.

"Doesn't seem to be anyone out there" she says.

"What?"

I lean back in the couch, Cindy's still looking outside.

'The son of Rebecca and the daughter of Nicole'. What was that?

I'll go to town in the morning to find Caprice and ask her for help. And maybe Feryn will find me. No way I'm going for a walk now.

"Come here" I say to Cindy who leans in to me.

We curl up together, falling asleep on the sofa.

I get up from the couch, gently laying Cindy's head on a cushion. I step quietly into the kitchen so as not to disturb her. The lamp in the living room is still burning making it impossible to see out the front window. I haven't the energy to look through the house to confirm we're alone, instead slumping into a chair near the back door.

It's 11:00 pm.

I hear her feet walk into the room.

"Hi" she says.

"Hi"

We sip juice in the kitchen, only occasionally looking at each other, my body bereft of energy, my spirit sagging. The lantern she lit on the counter illuminates the room and its corners, the living room lamp still burning in the hallway. My eyes fix on the back window, waiting for eyes to appear, for scratching, for whispers. But none come. Will they come later? Is someone or something waiting outside? Do I want to know?

I make my way to the bedroom and remove my clothes, crawling weakly into bed.

"I'm exhausted" I yell out "I'd better call it quits for the day"

"No energy?" Cindy stands in the doorway completely nude, her skin silky smooth from head to toe. But I know what will likely await me tomorrow.

"Wow" I say "I just don't think I'd be at my best"

"Well, I'll come to bed now in case you change your mind" she extinguishes the last of the lights, crawling in next to me.

Her bare skin next to mine stirs my arousal, my right hand running along her side as I pull her body towards mine but in the end, I kiss her goodnight and close my eyes. I'm too scared to think of anything else.

She hates the love they share, hates how they touch each other, how they care for one another. She's been denied these emotions, these feelings. Would she one day have loved? Felt loved? Their bodies lie quietly side by side in the darkness, their breathing relaxed as they sleep. Her frail form sits in the window watching them, wondering if they dream, and of what. Are their thoughts of a young girl so close to them as they lie peacefully in bed?

She clenches her teeth as she reaches toward him without touching him.

She screams but all that comes out is a whisper.

I wake with a start, shivering, a soft voice next to me jarring me from my sleep. My heart races as I slowly raise my head, my eyes scanning the walls, corners, and near the door but no one's here in the dark bedroom. I exhale and lie back down pulling the blanket over Cindy's naked body in the cold room. Moonlight shines in the window beside me. Is someone at the open window frame? I jump as the form vanishes.

Then there's a scratching noise on the ground outside. I get up to shut the window without looking out.

I cover us both in blankets and pull Cindy's body tightly to me, closing my eyes.

Adjusting the blankets, I hear a voice whisper my name and pull Cindy closer.

52 – Feryn

I'm standing on Cindy's side of the bed, the temperature in the bedroom much hotter than it should be. I'm naked and it's nighttime. A lantern shines weakly from the hallway providing just enough light for me to take in the scene.

The yellow sheets around Cindy are red with blood, a knife on the bed in front of me.

My hands are the same colour as the sheets.

Oh no. What happened?

I look around quickly but no one else is here.

Did I do this?

Who can I go to for help? Is Cindy ok?

My body is unable to move.

A whisper in my left ear speaks words that I don't understand. I turn but no one's there.

I can't remember anything since I'd gone back to sleep after closing the window. Cindy lies motionless, her mouth and eyes partly open, her body uncovered and naked. No one else is in the room.

Am I covered in blood from trying to save her?

I touch her then try to wake her. I touch her neck, her wrist but she's gone.

What happened? My mind is a complete blank. How did I get on this side of the bed?

Has someone else been in here? I look around the room, the window on my side of the bed is closed, nothing and no one else in the room.

I'm frozen to the spot, paralyzed by what I might have done. My heart races as I gasp for breath.

What do I do?

"Colden"

I hear Cindy's voice but her body doesn't move, her skin pale beneath the blood.

Is this the madness that afflicts station masters, a dementia that makes them kill? Have I become like my predecessors?

I drop to my knees, holding Cindy's hand in mine and closing my eyes.

"Colden"

I open my eyes.

Morning.

I'm lying in bed and Cindy's not with me.

My lungs gasp for breath.

The bed sheets are black and there's no blood on my hands.

Daylight peeks through the window on my side of the bed.

"Is that you getting up?" Cindy's voice rings out from somewhere outside the bedroom, confirming that all is well.

"Yes" I reply weakly.

"It's already 9:30" she says.

Whoops. Didn't mean to sleep in so late but it was obviously needed.

Better hustle to check the printer at the station and into town to check the board, then try to catch Caprice or Feryn or someone who will talk to me.

I stop and stare at the woman in the photo collage on the wall; in the orange dress; naked on her knees; in an orange skirt. Why is she so familiar? But when would I have met her? I just can't shake the feeling that I've seen her before.

But, then, I have to keep my thoughts straight and stay focused.

Looking around the room for some clothes, I check the window next to me which is closed tightly.

Outside looks bright, more so than usual.

The empty room as a metaphor for my life. It sure is easy to feel alone here.

"Colden" a voice whispers.

But no one is behind me when I turn.

"Cindy?" I call out.

Walking into the living room, I again say her name again without a response. It isn't like her to play a game like this but still I walk around without seeing or hearing her. Then I spot movement at the kitchen window. She must have gone outside and tried to get my attention before she left.

I open the back door but she isn't there. I step around the corner to the right catching a glimpse of movement but there's no one in front of the house when I get there, my eyes glancing toward the forest.

Are there eyes in the trees?

I decide to go back inside for now. Cindy must be leading me around somehow.

Shutting the door behind me, I notice her step out of the bathroom.

"Where were you?" she asks me.

"Outside" I stammer.

"Why?"

"I thought you were outside"

"I told you I was going into the bathroom" she looks at me quizzically.

"I'm gonna make some coffee" I light the stove as she walks to the bedroom.

Where are the things I'm thinking coming from? Where are the things I'm seeing coming from?

The water boils and I pour it into the urn, grab two cups, and wait by the table. A sound behind me as a face flashes past the back window.

I don't go outside this time. No one will be there anyway.

A knock at the front door.

I really don't want company.

"Someone here to see you. Says you're expecting him"

"Him?" I ask.

"Him. Sharp looking guy. Dressed for a walk in the woods"

At least it isn't Acacia.

Feryn leans up against the wall next to the closed door. He's taller than I recall.

"You looking for me?" he asks.

"Uh" is this guy psychic "I was thinking about you last night and hoping you might be able to help me"

"Maybe I can" he answers.

Feryn's green, brown, and grey attire make him seem ready for a camouflage maneuver.

Cindy walks to the kitchen "I'll leave you boys to talk"

"How did you find me?" I ask.

"Everyone knows where to find you, Colden" he smiles sitting on the bench next to him.

I crouch down, my back against the wall.

"Where do you want to go?" he asks.

"I assume you know how to get to the 'Hanging Tree'"

"I do. How do you know about this?"

"I'm not sure" I say sheepishly.

"You might be remembering this conversation" he says.

"But I thought of it before we had this conversation" I put my hands on my knees for balance.

"Time moves differently here" he looks away with a half-smile.

I drop my head.

"You sure you want to go there?" his question surprises me.

"Yes. I think so"

"It's not what you think" he says, his face serious.

"What do I think?"

"You tell me"

"I'm not really sure. What should I expect?" I ask.

"Best to have no expectations" he replies "What have you heard?"

"Not much. People don't talk to me"

"And you're wondering why" he says as if he'll share something insightful.

"Does it have to do with me being station master?" I ask standing up.

"Probably"

"But that's not my fault" I plead.

"Probably not, it's hard to be sure"

"What?"

"My Mother probably explains it better than I do"

"Your Mother?" my head drops.

"She's better at that sort of thing"

"So how does…"

Feryn holds up his hand, then checks his belt.

"Shoot" he grunts "I forgot them"

"Were they important?" I ask softly.

"Nah" he lifts his head with a smile "We're fine"

"I've got a bunch of questions for you"

"I like you, Colden" he nods "You're a good guy"

"And so are you" Cindy enters the room "You try to come across aloof and indifferent but it's all an act. All you really want to do is help. Help people that need it"

"You've unmasked me" Feryn throws up his arms with a smile "So what now?"

"Now you take me to the Hanging Tree" I say.

"Just you" he nods once.

"Just me" I agree.

I set down my coffee and get up to go shower and change my clothes. When I come out of the bedroom, Feryn and Cindy are sitting in the kitchen laughing.

They spot me.

"He's telling me some funny stories about New Brook West" Cindy smiles.

"I didn't think there'd be many of those" I pour a cup of coffee, grabbing a cookie.

"Even the darkest cave occasionally sees the light" Feryn says taking a sip of his drink.

"I suppose it does"

"I'll let you boys go be boys" Cindy puts away the uneaten items.

"All set?" he looks at me.

"Ready" I reply, unsure if it's true.

"Let's be off" he gets up, putting a cookie in his jacket pocket and setting down his cup.

"And, thank you" he smiles at Cindy, bowing his head.

"You're most welcome" she nods.

I walk over to Cindy.

"Do you know what you're doing?" she says.

"Nope" I reply with a smile "Sort of"

"Good luck" she hugs me.

I try to think of things I should bring but can't come up with anything so grab my jacket with a knife in an outside pocket and a short length of rope in an inside one and head outside to meet my guide. Feryn's leaning against the trunk of an overturned tree on the edge of the forest, his head down. The clear sky bodes well, the sun just above the treetops in the south. A light breeze blows in from across the clearing, the temperature ideal for a hike, cool without the damp chill that dominates most days.

"You probably won't need your knife but you never know" Feryn stands.

I nod, wondering how he's always a step ahead of me.

He turns to walk in the direction of the trail behind Cindy's house without saying a word. He lifts a dark green cap to his head.

I follow him until he takes a right turn a short distance along our route down a path I hadn't noticed on my previous trips.

"Never saw this way before" I tell him.

"It's always been here" he replies without turning around "You just have to know where to look"

We march the narrow trail for about ten minutes until we reach a three-way fork in the road. Feryn calmly turns left.

"You really do know the area" I say, trying to make conversation.

"It's amazing what you see when you look in the right place" he says, again without looking back.

"Do you know much about the Hanging Tree?" I ask.

"Do you?" he answers my question with a question.

"An old community came upon hard times and made an example of a woman which resulted in a mass exodus from the community. The Hanging Tree must be where she was put to death. At least that's how I understand it"

"More or less" he says "The ending played out a bit differently. New Brook East was the original settlement back when it was just called Brooks. Many small houses and a close-knit community. Then things went wrong. The last woman to be killed there had three daughters, who went in three different directions, none of them ever seen again"

"Where'd they go?"

"Legend has it the youngest wanted to avenge the wrong done to her mother"

"Did she?" I ask "Get revenge for her mother's execution?"

"I think so but perhaps she's not so sure" he says.

Huh?

Is this the tree referred to in my riddle not the genealogies?

I wonder if Feryn knows who might have brought me that family tree page. Or if I should mention the page torn from the von Stela volume at the library.

He's been so kind and helpful to this point I don't want to somehow offend him or make it look like I'm up to something.

But the words come out of my mouth anyway.

"Someone brought me a version of a family tree, and I'm not sure why or what it means"

I pause.

Feryn stops and seems to be thinking on his answer.

"That does seem odd" he slowly turns to me "Do you know anything about your background? I mean, your family tree?"

"Almost nothing" I say, after a moment of thinking. It occurs to me how little I know of my family history and that I've never seen any genealogy from either of my parents' sides.

"So many of us know nothing or nearly nothing about our past or about ourselves" Feryn crosses his arms.

"Is there something I'm supposed to do with this?" I ask "With this information?"

"One of the things I was fortunate to learn early in life is that some things can't be explained" he shrugs with a half-smile "We're taught to find answers, to understand 'Why', to want an explanation, but often there isn't one or at least not one that satisfies us. Or we find something out that we wish we hadn't but it's too late because now we know"

I don't expect my companion's serious side and I'm lost for words.

"Do you really want to know how something is possible?" he adds softly "What lives in the dark corners? What watches you while you sleep?"

All I can do is look in his eyes which seem to have lit up and now sparkle.

"Let life have its secrets" he says scanning the forest around us "It's often better that way"

Colden repeats this as he thinks back on East.

I wonder at the wisdom in his words.

"It's sometimes better not to know" he smiles leaning forward.

I nod.

I decide against asking him about the photographs I've received. I don't want him to think I'm only spending time with him so he can answer my questions.

I hear a rustling in the leaves behind us.

"Do you hear that?" I ask "Back there"

"All kinds of noises in the forest. Spirits, some say"

"Spirits?" I ask.

"Places with a history of death have a negative energy. Sadness, anger, evil: they get stored in a person or a place and then released when visited. You never hear of someplace being haunted for no reason"

"So, the Hanging Tree is haunted?" I shudder.

"It is"

"Is the train station haunted?"

"Absolutely" he stops for a moment "After what happened"

"What happened?"

Feryn sniffs the air.

"Hate to interrupt our discussion, but from here we go in silence" he says turning back to me.

"Ok"

The sky's colour has gradually changed from blue to grey, clouds shielding us from the sun's light. The spindly branches on the sparsely-leafed overhead reach out like bony arms. Is there wind higher up that I don't feel at ground level?

We move along the poorly-lit path without a lantern, my senses aware of even the slightest movement at my sides, every faint snap of a twig and every rustle in the bushes. Shadows move silently in the forest around us. Trees on both sides monitor the progress of our journey. Their branches reach out to point the direction but never interfere in our advance, never obstruct our way. I look into the darkness, ponder what might be watching, what might be hiding, careful to not let my companion get too far ahead; the thought of losing him and being alone in here makes me shiver.

I hear distant crackling in the forest, though perhaps too far away for concern. I dare not look too closely lest I spot something I don't want to see. I prepare myself for the scent of licorice which never comes.

As I'm beginning to doubt myself and this journey, Feryn comes to a stop.

"From here you're on your own" he says stepping aside to let me pass.

"What do you mean?"

"I brought you here. I'm not going in"

"Why not?"

"It's not my place"

"Your place?" I say "What does that mean?"

"You'll see. Remember this is your visit not mine" he casually sits down on the nearest log.

"My visit" I sigh "Where do I go?"

"You'll see" he points.

Unsure that I want to carry on, I take a deep breath and head off in the direction he pointed, without a look back, no idea what to expect along or at the end of this trail. The chill air gets under my skin along my silent walk. All around me is quiet, no rustling of leaves or rattling of branches in the calm air, sound ahead or behind me. Overhead, the dark grey sky towers over the trees. With every step, I brace myself for a sudden noise or unexpected movement but none comes.

A few steps ahead, the forest opens into a wide clearing with two large trees, each extending strong thick branches out from the main trunk. Two trails are visible across the glade from where I'm standing. Is there also a path leading off to the left? It's hard to tell.

A strong negative energy hangs in the air, like a sickness, a sadness.

At the stockier of the trees, a woman in a red dress hangs from a noose attached to a large limb, her body shaking, a silent group staring in her direction. Oh my God.

What's going on? Is this happening now? Why didn't Feryn warn me?

I look around but see no one else to come to her aid.

"Wait" I yell "I'm coming" as I run toward them unsure why the group isn't helping her.

But I can't move and am of no help at all.

As I'm trying to will myself to hurry in her direction, a young dark-haired girl in a light-purple dress steps out of the forest, looking up at the now unmoving suspended woman as the others recede into the forest. The girl remains, the last person at the tree, alone to contemplate this event.

The woman is obviously dead and I was too late, useless as I was.

Why couldn't I move?

Why did no one help her? Was she being hanged by those watching her?

The girl doesn't say a word or make a sound, just stares up at the lifeless woman.

Is that her mother?

How did I get here? And what the hell is this?

"Help" I yell trying to turn back to call my companion but am unable to look away from the scene, my voice nothing but a whisper in the eerie forest.

Why was I sent to see this?

The woman falls to the ground, the girl standing over her as if waiting for help, but none comes and she simply stares at the woman lying in front of her. She looks around the clearing but there's no one else. She now appears to be crying, wiping her eyes with her hand. After a moment, she lies down next to the woman's body, curling up against it as if for warmth, and closes her eyes.

The detail of this scene is now much clearer even if its meaning isn't.

I try to go to her but still can't move. What's going on?

It's not yet dark but the overcast sky makes for an ominous environment.

"Feryn" I yell but no sound comes out of my mouth.

A take a few breaths to collect myself.

It feels so real. I try to watch attentively wondering what will happen next as I'm still unable to move.

A man wearing the station master jacket runs across the clearing behind them, disappearing into the forest to my right, unseen by the young girl.

Back at the tree, the woman and girl have vanished and I find myself alone, staring at the forest, confused and afraid.

Is someone else here with me? Many people? Is there a drug of some kind in the air?

Did that really just happen in front of me?

Or is this somehow a re-telling of past events through some sort of vision or hallucination?

What does it mean? And who were the people I saw?

I catch my breath like I've been running. I feel nauseous.

The trees and grass are turning a dull grey, not rotting but actually changing colour. There's no movement and there are no sound anywhere in the clearing or in the forest around me and when I look back, the large glade is empty. My body moves and my legs wake from their slumber as I step forward. I consider walking toward the tree or around the circle or looking at the other paths but decide against it, partly out of fear but also worried that Feryn might leave without me.

Turning, I slowly retrace my steps back to where my companion waits, a sweet smell coming from a lit incense stick in his fingers. A darkness fills me, my heart, my head; I feel sick. My feet drag, my body burdened by an invisible weight.

"What was that?" I try to yell but my words are soft.

Feryn's head is down and looking away from me.

He speaks without turning in my direction.

"Some things are difficult to describe" he says quietly "And can't be explained"

The smoke wafts toward me and I can't help but inhale some of it.

"What was it?" I stammer "How…"

I stop, unsure how I want to finish my sentence or what I want to ask.

My head spins. Was that real? Or is Feryn smoking something that brought on an illusion?

"What…?"

Again, I can't find the words to finish what I want to say.

"Is it what you hoped for?" Feryn asks, still staring at the smoke coming from his stick, a smoke that hangs in the air around me.

How…? What did I just see?

The fumes from the incense relax me.

"Not sure what I expected" I say quietly as I try to recall the scene.

"I told you about expectations"

"Ya" I sit down next to him, enjoying the burning scent.

"Have you ever been in there?" I ask him as my mind calms.

"Never want to. It's one thing to know how to get here…"

"I saw a scene" I say "Like a story. Looked like a …"

"It's for your eyes and ears" Feryn interrupts "I don't even want to know. Not being rude, only trying to keep what's mine and what's yours with their rightful owners"

"Oh, ok" I say, though I don't understand why he doesn't want to hear or if I actually said it at all. I was kinda hoping he'd help me make sense of it.

"You'll be wondering where the cemetery is" Feryn says after a few seconds.

"Which cemetery?" I ask.

"That one" he points to a trail in the distance, beyond the path I'd just taken.

"Go on" he says moving to a large rock "I'll wait here"

Off I go along a trail that appears well-groomed, the ground clear, branches well back from the path's edge. After a minute or two, it opens up and widens. Up ahead, an owl's hoot encourages me to press on, that there's life, that I'm not absolutely alone. Despite the clear path in front of me, the forest itself darkens, the air thick but without the gloom I'd felt at the hanging scene.

My journey ends in a square clearing surrounded by low golden brush. It appears to have been recently tended, the grass cut low, the treeline trimmed, no loose leaves or blemishes on the earth or ground. Seven flat worn stones are embedded into the ground, each with a crudely written letter as if carved in haste: 'M', 'K' in a row above 'J', 'R', 'H', 'S', 'F', 'V' each a good distance from the one next to it. Do these mark graves? A family plot? Something more sinister? Nothing indicates to whom this area belongs or what it might be and I see no other markings on the ground, in the trees, nor any signs.

I walk toward the plaques but remain a respectful distance back, unsure what to do. I stare at the ground then look up at the forest – was the clearing this large when I'd arrived?

What's gonna happen here?

I take a deep breath as I wait for something that never comes.

It feels oddly peaceful here, nothing like the other clearing; not happy but serene.

Dusk will soon be upon the little cemetery but I don't feel anxious or unnerved or worried about who might be watching. My mind seems to float out and away from my body as I try to focus my thoughts.

A rustling in the forest to my right makes me jump.

Then a soft lilting song fills the air, though I can't make out the words or its origin. The soothing tune is sung by a human voice though it has a bird-like quality to it.

The song stops and my mind snaps back to reality and my location. I look into the trees around me, down at the plaques, up at the clouds.

It's getting late; time to go.

Back along the path, the brush is increasingly dense closer to the main trail and I keep my attention on my surroundings because I'll be sunk if I get lost. It occurs to me that as bright and blue as the sky had been earlier in the day it's now an equally oppressive dark grey.

"You ever been in there?" I ask when I'm next to Feryn.

"Never. Not interested either" he shakes his head.

"Good call" I assure him.

"Anything helpful?" he looks at me.

"I'm not sure" I think about the day's events "I'm exhausted"

"I can imagine" Feryn stands, the incense no longer in his hands "Let's get back before dark"

We head off along the path that only he can find because he knows where to look as I ensure I stay close.

Does Feryn know more than he shares? He must but doesn't seem to feel comfortable talking about where we've just been so I don't want to press.

Does Cindy know any of this? Hard to know for sure but I like to think she'd have mentioned it by now. Then again, this would be difficult to put into words.

We reach the trail back to Cindy's in what seems like seconds. This time I have no conversation to make, no friendly banter to exchange, no small talk. What could I say after that? The scenes play over in my head, melancholy still weighing me down.

Somehow, we bypass Cindy's place entirely arriving at the train station's clearing, much to my surprise.

"How'd we get here?" I ask.

"Took a different route" he replies "Thought you should spend tonight alone at home, maybe work through what you saw or heard or felt. You looked pretty heavy back there"

"Yes. It was heavy" I begin walking toward the platform.

"Enjoy the rest of your evening. As best you can" he says with an awkward smile.

"Thanks" I reply as our eyes meet "And thank you for all your help today"

"Of course" he nods "Bye"

"Bye" I turn and walk away.

"Do you…" I start to ask but turning back realize he's vanished. Of course. I'm too tired to care.

Perhaps some things are best unexplained.

Night descends rapidly, the orange and red in the east slowly being replaced by purple and black as the sun dips below the horizon in a sky much clearer than where we'd just been.

Arriving at the steps, a young girl in a dirty dress sits on the platform's edge facing the tracks, her legs hanging over the edge. Is this that same girl I've seen in the past?

Who the heck is she? Is she actually waiting for someone to arrive in New Brook West?

A train isn't expected tonight but that doesn't mean one won't pass through without stopping.

"Hey" I shout running up the stairs.

Does she look back at me? I think so.

Then she jumps down onto the tracks.

Not again.

I jog to where she'd been sitting but see no one when I get there and there's no way to pick her out in the obscure dusk.

Until a pair of small hands on my lower back pushes me forward.

Then everything goes black as my body hits the ground with a thud.

53 – Rissa

What happened? Ohhh. Owww.

I can't move. I can't get up or turn my head or raise my arms or even speak. I try to orient myself; where am I? My eyes slowly come into focus. Then I hear a whistle.

I'm at the train station.

I look up to my left and see a small figure's up on the platform above me but no words come out of my mouth when I try to speak.

"Help me" or do I just think this.

Does she say something to me? Is she really there or is it my imagination? The whistle blows again in the dark.

I'm on the ground.

I call out for help but again my voice is silent.

The ground and rails shake as the train's engine comes into view.

In my dazed state and the dark evening, my mind can't convince my body to move. I stare down one direction of the tracks but can't be sure which one. Is a train coming?

As I prepare for a collision, my body is pulled toward the forest onto the rocks and grass as the cars speed past creating a breeze against my skin.

"No" a combination of voices yells out.

I see a blurry flash of pink and black as two small figures disappear into the trees. My breathing slows and my vision comes into focus.

I'm in the grass at the train station in New Brook West.

I raise my body to a seated position facing the station as the train disappears to my left. No one's on the platform or in either direction along the tracks. The clear crisp air spurs me into action. I turn around but there's no one between me and the trees, no one visible within the forest's darkness. And I have no desire to enter the woods here.

Who pulled me off the tracks?

The air is calm, the moon shining high in the dark sky to my right. Wearing only a light jacket, the cold has crept inside my clothes and I'm eager to get upstairs.

Hauling myself up onto the platform and crouching low to the ground, I crawl to the base of the stairs leading up to the apartment where I sit and clear my head.

I'm alone. Alone and afraid.

I hazard a look in the direction of Room 1 and am grateful that I see nothing and that the door is closed.

I stagger up the stairs and into the suite. Kicking off my boots and tossing my jacket on the chair, a see black and white drawing on the island.

There's no one in the apartment so I run to the door but see no one on the platform either.

How did this get here? Was it here before I went out? Did I bring it in? Where did I get it?

The windows are shut and will remain that way, at least for the night, the door locked behind me.

The drawing shows a man wearing a brown jacket with a shovel facing away from the camera, two long boxes on the ground next to him.

Written on the back: 'Her flowers'

I don't see any flowers in the photo. Is the man planting flowers?

Scratching at the door sounds like something trying to get in. This freezes me sending ice through my veins.

The unpredictable cat?

Or whoever brought the drawing coming back?

I open the door but no one's there, so I walk down to the empty platform again, the lanterns on the walls providing a measure of comfort but giving no clue as to the sound at the door.

No trains are expected tonight or in the morning, at least none that will be stopping here, and unexpected arrivals are rare, though passing trains are more common than I'd like. Night has fallen early as usual, the sky already black, though the sky is star-filled with a beautiful moon. I walk past the benches to the far end of the platform, hop down, coming all the way around the station through the clearing and up the stairs onto the platform.

I'm still alone. I take a deep breath as I stare out across the tracks.

My courage surprises me; or is my bravery stupidity in disguise.

The quiet evening is most welcome, but I know this hides its own secrets. My mind wanders, my eyes lost in the dark forest around me.

I feel a gentle brushing on my leg, like a cat rubbing against me. Looking down I see nothing but hear scuttling toward the staircase. Time to head back inside. Enough happens in the daylight, there's no need for any additional time alone in the dark.

I hustle up the stairs and into my room without looking back.

Locking the door behind me and again taking inventory of the windows, I pour a glass of wine, sitting at the island to contemplate the drawing.

Who's the man? Where is he? What's he doing? Why?

Too many questions to even consider.

And, of course, who is the girl visiting the station? Does she want me to leave? Or is she trying to make me stay?

I sit on the couch and close my eyes for a second in the hopes of finding a distraction in the recesses of my brain and my mind thinks back on Lori and Suzie. Our lives, our future, our happiness. I still feel what must have been Suzie's fear and Lori's sadness. I gave up on consciously trying to solve the mystery of my daughter's disappearance years ago but there'll always be a place for them in my heart and my thoughts. I think of what could have been, what should have been, what I didn't do, how I wished things were. What will never be.

I dispel my recollections from my mind.

And then I arrive at Cindy's without even realizing I'd left the station, the time now 6:30 pm.

"Didn't think I'd see you so soon" she says unenthusiastically, wearing black yoga pants and a yellow t-shirt.

"No, me neither" I take a few steps into the living room.

"Ok" she leans up against the wall in the hall.

Something's different about the atmosphere in the house. It's bleak and weary. Everything looks the same, though only a single lantern lights each of the front and rear rooms which is unlike Cindy.

Her blank expression reveals no emotion at my being here, at the surprise of my evening visit, at how she feels at all.

Then, a sound like my cell phone ringing. What?!? When I find it on a chair around the kitchen table, the screen flashes with no incoming phone number on it. I look at it then at Cindy then slowly move toward it.

This can't be good. It rings four times before I answer.

"Hello?" I fall to sit in a green chair.

"Hi, Colden. Just wanted to make sure everything's okay"

"Fine, thanks. Who is this?"

"Feryn"

"How did you…"

"If you need me again, just come to town and I'll find you"

"How?"

This call confuses me in every way.

"Sounds like you could use a rest" I can imagine his smirk as he says this.

"Ok"

"Enjoy your evening, my friend"

He hangs up. Or whatever he does to end the call from wherever he is.

"Who was that?" Cindy asks, now sitting in the kitchen with me.

"Feryn. The guide"

"How did he…"

"I didn't get a chance to ask"

"Are you sure it was him?"

"Yes"

Ok.

I set the phone down on the table and look around the room though I'm not sure why I do this.

I stand up "I could use a nap"

Cindy rises slowly, concern on her face "Why did you come out here?"

"I'm not entirely sure"

"Then, I'll see you later" she smiles half-heartedly.

"Yeah, ok"

I make my way to the front door, unsure of what else to say. I think of looking back as I leave but don't. My head hangs, exhausted. My steps are automatic, like someone else is controlling them.

Odd that she'd sent me on my way so abruptly like I'd interrupted her. She's probably tired herself and working through everything that's happened in her head. Maybe she doubts my role in it all.

It's an uneventful walk back to the station that seems to take only a few seconds, though I'm grateful for this.

Upon my arrival, I collapse on the bed, too tired to care about witches, curses, destinies, or ghost girls. Or Cindy's unusual behaviour.

I crawl into bed and sleep takes me almost immediately as rain begins to fall in the clearing and on the roof.

A bang against the window wakes me, like someone striking it.

Looking up from bed, I see what looks like the face of a young girl but then it's gone.

I stare for a moment then scramble back away from her, my lungs gasping. I try to speak but I can't. I look into the room but see nothing in the darkness. When I look back at the window whatever had been there is gone.

Who…

And then I'm asleep again.

Scratch, scratch.

I wake to the sound of a branch scraping against the window or wall near the bed. The flickering flame of a single lantern in the kitchen creates dancing shadows in the corners of the room; I was sure I'd extinguished everything. The apartment is cooler than I expect, colder than when I arrived. I look to the door and across to the windows over the tracks but everything appears normal.

Maybe a bird pecking for food? Sand blown up against the building?

The elusive cat?

My mystery girl?

I get up slowly, peeking out the window into the clearing in all directions with no one in sight.

Ok. 9:00 pm.

The same questions every time. Who? What? Why? Had I dreamt the young girl at the window earlier? And I'm sure it's much later than it is.

I stand, putting on pants and a long-sleeved shirt, exhaling deeply as I do.

Knock, knock.

Shit. Now who?

I walk to the door fully prepared for there to be no one there.

"Hi, Colden"

Rissa looks up at me inquisitively.

"Hi, Rissa"

I hold the door open a bit wider assuming she'll come in, hoping she won't.

"I can't stay" she says in response to my gesture.

"What brings you all the way out here?" I ask.

"I like visiting you Colden" she replies with a sad smile.

Her eyes survey the room.

"But I really should go" Rissa turns.

I look back to the table, eager to ask her about the photographs and the drawings.

"Do you…"

But she's gone.

Alone again, I crouch down on the landing to look down on the platform and into the clearing near the station, but see nothing and no one. A gentle breeze whistles through.

Turning to my left, I notice the control room door is open a crack. Rissa?

"You in here, Rissa?" I push it all the way in, lighting a lantern as I do.

Silence. The room is empty.

I step inside and see an open box against the back wall labeled 1910. Confirming no one's in here, I step toward it curious as to its contents and perhaps some history of the island and the station. Cargo manifests, load weights, arrival times, departures with 'EP' at the bottom of each of them. Who or what is that? Leafing through the box, I find more of the same, each with a date. The last document in this collection is dated '17 November 1910'. Is 'EP' someone's initials? The station master at the time?

A black and white photo of a young man and woman falls to the ground. He's proudly wearing the station master's jacket, she in a light-shaded dress, a sombre look on her face as if trying unsuccessfully to smile. On the back, in the bottom right corner, a date: 12 May 1910.

Is that his wife? The resemblance to Caprice is uncanny; must be a distant relative. The guy looks familiar too, now that I think of it, but I can't imagine why. Probably an ancestor of someone I've seen in town. This is fascinating in its own way but a hundred-year-old photo of people from families I don't know doesn't help me. I return the photo to the folder I'm guessing contained it and return the other documents to the box.

I put out the lamp and shut the control room door, finished with nighttime investigations.

Cool damp air, the moon behind a haze of clouds and fog, the forest calm.

Then: smell of licorice.

I hear a moaning, almost a whisper as I climb the steps to the suite.

Out of the corner of my eye, I spot movement at the edge of the platform, like someone hopping onto the tracks.

A distant whistle blows. This train must be going straight through because nothing's scheduled.

I turn back to confirm everything ok when, halfway down the stairs, my right foot catches something and my body reels forward, crashing against each step until it thuds against the stone at the bottom.

I think I lose consciousness for a moment, but the train hasn't yet passed so I stumble to my feet like a drunk to orient myself and look down on the tracks. No one's there but I nearly fall off the platform myself, my head spinning from the tumble.

I stagger backwards, sitting down at the bottom of the steps leading up to the apartment, as the train speeds by. Another close call on my part and where's whoever I saw earlier?

My eyes strain to focus as a figure appears at the edge of the platform.

"Rissa?"

She's too dark to make out, my head not yet clear, as I try to take stock of the situation.

"Step back, sweetie. It's dangerous here" I say my vision now clear as I rub my eyes.

But whatever was there has vanished.

I drop my head forward into my hands, gathering my strength and recovering my senses. I feel drunk.

When I'm able to confidently stand, I grab and hold the handrail on the climb to my room.

Setting the photo of the couple on the coffee table, I shuffle past to get a glass of juice, which I drink greedily. I thought I'd put the photo back. I'll figure that out tomorrow.

Dropping onto the couch, I lean my head back and pass out.

Cautiously creeping in through the partially open door, eyes peering through the dark hair falling around her face, her dress fades into the shadows. She approaches him crawling on all fours, scared to get too close, afraid to touch him. Flickering candles make shadows dance in the corners and in reflections on the windows. Staying out of the dim light, she hugs the walls, stays low to the ground. It's so quiet in here. Her eyes scan the room, look him over. His arm twitches. She skitters out the door to find solace and safety in the darkness.

"Cindy?" I say feebly, lifting my head.

It's freezing in here.

Has someone been in here? I thought I'd heard steps or scratching but can't be sure. A dream?

The door's open a crack.

I'm still on the couch.

I stand up, look around slowly, and shut the door before walking to bed and crawling under the covers, too tired to look around the room.

Outside, morning has yet to bring its faint glow in the eastern sky. My sleep was restless, the whole evening was bizarre; how much of it, if any, was a dream? I try to recall last night's events from visiting Cindy's to someone coming to the door to the train coming through. I can't seem to keep reality straight. Or maybe I am and all these strange occurrences are real and my current home truly is that unusual and preternatural.

I wonder when or if Cindy will come to the station. She wasn't very welcoming at our most recent encounter and I'm not inclined to visit at the moment. Maybe she just wanted some time to herself which is fine or was simply tired. Or maybe that was all in my head, in my dreams. But I don't think so. I may have just misread the situation because I've certainly done that before, especially here.

Staggering to the kitchen, I begin making coffee and toast. It must be early but I can't be sure with the days getting shorter. I know it's morning because I can see the slightest amount of light beginning to emerge in the east.

My coffee cools as I bite at my breakfast and look around the room. This really is a beautiful suite and for that I've been most fortunate. And working at the train station has been great in many respects and I love the serenity and tranquility that comes with living away from the community.

I wonder if it was always this way and how my predecessors lived, if they enjoyed the calm atmosphere, the quiet station.

I spot the photo I'd brought from the control room; so that part of the evening was definitely real. I remember a black and white shot of a man and woman; were they at the station? I look more closely at the photo of the couple. My impressions from the previous evening remain and I'm thankful for the date on this print which may be a clue to these peoples' identities.

Would anyone in town be able to help me figure this out?

Caprice? If I can find her. How will she react to me putting an image in front of her which must have been lost for decades? One that surely shows one of her ancestors. I'd come to learn that West's past wasn't always proud and inquiries are often unwelcome.

Rissa? Like Caprice, she knows more than I've been able to figure out. And also speaks in riddles. Wisdom beyond her years but still just a little girl. And I'd do well not to spend too much time with her, especially at the station.

Feryn? Unless he contacts me, his assistance seems unlikely.

I could go to the blue café and hope for a friendly face but this is kind of a shot in the dark and might end up backfiring on me.

Will Cindy come while I'm gone? There's no way to know or plan for this.

Heading out after a quick wash-up, I jog across the clearing, the sun's glow visible just above the treeline, and walk down the path to the village. Nothing moves and I hear no sounds around me nor do I see anything out of the ordinary. A sliver of moonlight pierces into the forest, making shadows all around me; a breeze high above whistles through the branches.

Then there's a far-away whisper, words that I can't make out, like someone trying to tell me something, coming from all around me in the calm air. I look for the source of the voice but see no one in the black forest or on the path. Evening is still very much upon New Brook West, the glow from the lantern I've brought stopping at the treeline. The moon does little to light the path, the forest absorbing its glow, cancelling it out with darkness in the spaces between the trees.

The whisper is nearer now, like someone standing very close. I stop but no one's there in any direction, at least that I can see. I wait for several more seconds like a deer stuck in the headlights. Or maybe I can't move. All is quiet in the dark when the ghostly voice stops.

I quicken my walk to a jog.

The clearing between the trees and the gates is a dim expanse as usual, the covered torches on both sides of the entry the only illumination before I see a single light on the church, and another on the town hall. The moon has now vanished behind a cloud, a faint aura overhead and to my right indicating its place in the sky.

I'm alone in the plaza.

I check my watch.

7:30 am

Making my way through the back alleys and on to the café, I hope I'm avoiding any prying eyes. I'd worn my green jacket to blend in as best I can but probably still stand out like a beacon to anyone spotting me; I'll check the board on the way back. Few buildings have any lit lamps outside, most with dark interiors to match, shutters and doors and windows all closed as far as I can tell. The few candles conjure dark figures which could be villagers or worse. The dark alleys seem more so today, shadows in every corner. The grey stone walls radiate a damp chill, their surface shinier than I recall in the quiet streets.

A chill goes down my spine.

The silence is unnerving but also peaceful.

I arrive at the blue café, its interior lit, wondering if I've made the right decision or if I should turn back. I pause outside, looking around me, then try to get a glimpse inside but am unable to see anything through the large window.

I'd better get out of the street.

As I muster the courage to enter, two young women emerge so I slip in before the door shuts behind them. They seem uninterested in my presence.

The faint interior lighting provides little insight into the room's occupants, the illumination from covered candles extending only a short distance from their source. My entrance prompts one of the servers I recognize to come from behind the bar to greet me, her light blue and white outfit a welcome mix of colours.

How is it already 8:30?

"She's been waiting for you, sir" Comet says, gesturing to a table to my left where a cloaked figure faces away from me.

54 - Be careful, sir

There are few friendly faces in New Brook West. People avoid me, whether they know who I am or not. They either stare or do everything they can to neither look my way nor cross my path. But mostly they ignore me. Probably no different than in my 'other lives', and I'd grown accustomed to this condition to a certain extent, though somehow hoped it'd be different here. I'd be accepted, even welcomed. Find a place where I belong. Not so alone. But it was not so.

Despite being the perpetual stranger here, the blue café feels safe, comfortable, and welcoming, where all are accepted, including me. Perhaps I'm anonymous or perhaps not but people neither avoid me nor pay me undue attention. It feels nice. Although I can't be sure of the identity of the other patrons at this enigmatic location, here I feel normal and relaxed; myself. Not so alone.

Soft music is in the air, violins coming from everywhere and nowhere as I see neither speakers nor musicians. Muted conversations whisper around the room, the serving girls standing happily and patiently at the back wall, as if waiting to be summoned. A quick look around the room, though I'm not sure why, perhaps just force of habit. I ponder whether or not I want to know the identity of my hooded companion, whether I've made a mistake and should turn and leave.

This person obviously knows I'm here so knows where to find me if I leave.

The grey-hooded figure lifts a right hand, and, without turning around, waves me over.

Why is she waiting for me and how did she know I'd come?

Comet places two tea cups on the table. I survey the room again with no one looking my way. This is my last chance to leave.

"I was hoping you'd come, Colden" a female voice speaks as I near the table. A faint citrus aroma wafting through the air causing me to pause. It's an alluring smell that distracts me for a moment.

"Yes" is all I can muster as I take my seat, glancing back at the window to see if the young girl is outside.

"She can't hear us" the woman says.

"Ok"

I feel like adding "Who?" but don't think I do.

A woman's fair-skinned petite hand comes out from under the cloak's sleeve to bring the tea to her face, revealing nothing of my companion's identity. I look at my tea, contemplating the potential contents of my beverage. The room seems darker, the walls less cheerful, the mood not sombre but more serious. I glance toward the window again but see nothing of the outside, just a reflection of the interior in the glass.

I look without staring, hoping to catch a glimpse of my cloaked lady, though I honestly can't imagine who would have been waiting for me at this time. I didn't expect I'd be here; who else would? The muted colour of the woman's garment seems out of place in the café.

Do I know who this is?

A long silence ensues between us.

Should I blurt out requesting her identity? Play it cool? Stand up?

Only two other occupied tables, both with two blonde fair-skinned women in long dark dresses. I worry that eyes watch me through the window, eyes that wish me harm. I shift nervously in my seat. The music's volume lowers to a nearly inaudible level, as my companion inhales deeply.

I take a sip of my tea, not wanting to appear rude; it's sweeter than I expect.

"I'm glad you came" she says softly.

'You seemed to know I would" I reply.

"I hoped"

I know this voice, don't I? But it sounds different now.

"I know you have questions" she says.

I nod.

"I'm not sure I'll be much help" she throws back the hood.

"Not as dramatic as I expected" I cock my head, relieved.

"It wasn't meant to be a surprise" a partial smile crosses her lips, her voice slightly off from how I remember.

"It is comfortable in here, isn't it?" she adds while I'm considering what to say "You look relaxed"

Do I? I don't feel that way as much anymore.

"What do I do now?" I interlock my fingers, placing my hands on the table in front of me.

"You leave" she says seriously "And hope that's enough"

"Why wouldn't it be?" my tone surely betrays my anxiety.

"There's more going on here than you realize, Colden" her voice wavers slightly.

"That much I know" I shake my head.

The room gets darker, several candles now extinguished, and the air feels cooler. I shiver even more as I try to see out the large front window without looking in that direction.

"Is she there?" my companion asks.

"I don't know" I say.

"Do you see her often?"

I stare at Caprice as I take a deep breath.

She waits in silence for my answer.

"Who is she?" I whisper.

"She'll follow you as long as you stay"

"So how do I leave?" I ask.

"Get on the train on its return to the mainland"

"It's that easy?"

"No" she replies.

"'No'. That's it?"

"No, that's not it"

"So..."

"She won't come in here"

"Is that Hannah?" I gesture toward the window with a nod.

"No"

"Who is it?" I plead.

Caprice seems to think about what to say, looks at the wall behind me, and drops her head.

"I was engaged to be married" she says "He was a handsome man, a fine man, a Station Master. I was good and kind, loving and devoted. I'd be taken care of all my life, never want for anything, live happily forever. But that's not how it plays out, is it?"

"Not always" I say, surprised by the unexpected insight into her life.

"We were to be wed in East, in our home. I'd only ever wanted to be loved, to have someone to love. It sounds boring, I'm sure, empty, to live only for another person like a dutiful wife, a kept woman. It didn't feel that way to me. Life with a person you love is twice lived"

She looks up for a moment before lowering her head again.

"How could I know the level of his betrayal, his cowardice? I was sure he wanted me for himself. Or had he always wanted her instead? She was a true beauty and good and kind. I didn't hate her for it. I'd always loved her and that could never change. But I wouldn't choose"

She pauses for a moment as if collecting her thoughts.

"Perhaps it was inevitable. Destiny always wins"

She speaks as though recounting the tale to herself.

I don't want to interrupt her reminiscence, her emotional reflection.

"Did you find the photo? Of the couple?" she asks.

My reaction is slow, words eluding me to express my thoughts. I want to console her, to comfort her, to hold her.

I honestly don't know what to do.

"Yes" I answer.

"You're wondering who they are?" her voice falters again.

"Yes" I say, wondering if this knowledge will improve or worsen my situation.

"I think you know"

She seems on the verge of tears.

"No, I don't"

"You don't want to believe"

Believe what? Why won't she just tell me?

"She looks like…" I begin, then stop as I look at Caprice.

"Yes, she does"

But, that's not possible.

"Hopefully this answers one of your questions"

I lack the words, the ability to express myself.

"You've seen him as well" she adds. It isn't a question "He's more dangerous than you realize"

"Who?"

A hand on my left shoulder from behind me turns my head.

"You should probably go, sir" Comet tries unsuccessfully to force a smile.

"Why?"

I look back at the empty chair where Caprice had been.

"Where did she go?" I turn behind me to see that Comet has also vanished.

I scan the dimly-lit room as best I can, seeing neither of them. Perhaps ten lamps illuminate the entire café, the blue wall visible in patches at these locations, an island of colour in a sea of grey.

Now it's time to leave.

I look at the window to the street, the café reflected in its glass.

"I'd better go" I stand up.

"Be careful, sir. On your walk home" Comet's back at my side. Her hands come together in front of her face as though in prayer for me.

"Yes. Thank you, Comet" I turn to leave without looking back.

I open the door carefully, stepping outside like a cat, a few lit lanterns now on the walls up and down the street keep it in shadows, the air cool and crisp. No one's in front of the café, the only sound a background whispering which gives me a chill and the impetus to move. I look behind me but see only the closed door.

Enough looking around, it's time to go.

Overhead, the sky is lit by the moon behind the clouds, dulling the alley's shadows for the moment.

That can't have been Caprice in the photo, can it? And her Station Master husband? The 'other' to whom she was promised? My head spins with this new information. Is this for real?

Despite my anxiety, I choose the Grey Stone as my destination, rather than the train station, preferring company to solitude. And perhaps some conversation with a server to find out more about Acacia. In retrospect, it may have been better to just stay away and simply head back on my own but such is hindsight.

Hopefully it's open at 9:00 am.

It takes me a moment to orient myself to the correct direction without passing through the plaza. I stay to narrow streets and alleys, my steps soft. I pass no one but always feel the gaze of invisible eyes watching me from dark corners and windows. Gloomy alleyways make me shiver, whispers entice me into poorly lit crooks, alluring smells distract me from my route. A gentle breeze rustles loose objects higher up on the buildings.

An ordinary walk through New Brook West.

Now and then I get confused about my location and the correct route to my destination but in time arrive in the tavern's clearing.

My eyes dart all around me, hoping not to catch sight of any movements or unusual sights or hear noises of any kind. The darkness doesn't seem as absolute here in the sparsely-treed rock-filled clearing as it does in other parts of the forest. All is still and calm and almost peaceful, but not quite enough for me to linger. Seeing and hearing nothing, I descend into the bar.

The place is active but not crowded, my head down as I move to the wall immediately left of the door.

"Hi" a young female voice welcomes me "I'm Tasha. What can I getcha?"

Tasha is tiny, probably twenty, blonde hair in pigtails; her enthusiastic smile lifts my spirits. Her white top and knee-length blue skirt make her look even smaller, like a flower, making her blue eyes even brighter, though the left side of her face has a slight twitch.

"Hi Tasha. I'll have a…a coffee of some kind would be super, please. Are you able to add something stronger to it?" I say changing my mind about my choice of beverage.

"I know exactly whatcha need" she skips to the bar area "Be right back"

Do they serve alcohol this early? I don't smell marijuana nor do I see any food so I wonder what people are doing here.

The clientele is similar to my previous visits in both number and character, again with very few women. Several men on the other side of the elliptical area are engaged in an animated discussion, though I can't tell if they've been drinking. I make a special note to avoid looking in their direction. I see no familiar faces.

Perhaps this is the night shift in the fields that comes for a drink at the end of their day.

"Here it is" Tasha springs to the table with a tall thin mug "Enjoy your drink, Station Master"

She bounds away, smiling as she goes.

Hard to keep a low profile here.

'Just get on the train when it's heading back to the mainland' - is it that easy? Maybe it is.

Did Station Masters before me leave?

"Hi, Colden" a female voice rouses me from my thoughts.

Next to me sits a beautiful blonde woman, bare legs and arms beneath an orange dress: Is she Cindy's friend Jade? I'm unsure how to react given her previous visit to my apartment, if it hadn't been just a dream.

The dress sure looks familiar.

"Mind if I join you?" she asks, though the point is moot as she's already next to me on the bench.

"Of course" I smile, sliding away from her.

"What brings you here?" she smiles, her black eyes piercing me.

"I was in town on some business and stopped in before heading back"

"Same here" she says kicking off her shoes and crossing her legs in her lap "Not a lot of places to have fun here"

I laugh at this remark. She's right.

"Where do you go for fun?" I ask her.

"I meet strange men in strange places" she slides closer "Sometimes"

"Lots of strange men here" I inch away "Any of these guys your type?"

"Just one" she smiles.

"I've been meaning to ask you…" I begin.

"Drinking alone?"

I turn to my right where a tall man looks down at me.

"What?"

I am in fact alone, Jade nowhere to be seen.

"Best be careful on the walk home, Station Master"

The man disappears into the crowd, his appearance and manner nondescript, like any average guy from West.

Who the heck is he? And what does he know?

Tasha walks by gleefully.

"Hey, Tasha"

"Hi" she stops, turning to face me with a smile.

But I don't know what to say.

"Thanks" I nod, finishing the contents of my cup, getting up to leave.

"Bye" she says sadly.

"Bye" I wave without looking back.

I'd lost my nerve to try to learn anymore about Acacia or perhaps I'd come to my senses by not saying anything.

Will I just draw more attention to myself if I make unsolicited inquiries around town about a woman who was last seen with me and then turned up dead at the train station? Something else I need to be careful about.

I've learned that when in doubt, it's best to keep your mouth shut.

Outside, sunlight tries to break through the cloud cover, casting a faint glow in the soupy air. I doesn't look like anyone has followed me out and I see no one in the haze waiting for me.

What now?

Would Caprice be at her child-care building? Is there any value in seeing her again? Should I try to avoid her?

She seems to be one of my few allies.

Winding through town, I stay close to the buildings, careful of flickering shadows and shimmering figures in the dim corners, past closed and boarded up doors, dark windows, and stone walls. Wary of watchful eyes but careful not to look too closely at anyone. Day has arrived but the sky is still mostly dark grey and the air itself feels solemn. Halos radiate from the lamps on the exterior walls, candles sputter behind lantern glass despite protection from the gentle breeze. I try to keep my bearings to avoid taking what could be a wrong turn.

"Station Master" comes a whisper from down an alley.

I stop but don't dare look.

"Here" the female voice speaks soothingly, one I don't recognize but which draws me to it.

What am I doing?

I take a few steps forward, without entering too far into the shadowed lane

where a female figure stands, visible only in outline. She isn't moving though I'm pretty sure she's facing me. And it's not Caprice. A moment of silence passes until I take a deep breath and exhale as quietly as I can.

"The potion mistress will assist but you'll have to help her first. Find her flowers" she says, her words gentle "And mind the letters are correct"

And then she fades smoothly backwards into the darkness, as though on rails and I'm left alone.

A shiver runs down my neck as I stand at the mouth of the obscured lane wondering at the identity of the young woman who just vanished, what to make of her cryptic advice, and how to get away from here.

Is anyone else here?

I step away backwards out of the alley, find myself alone in the street, and jog away, stopping as I approach Caprice's workplace.

The interior is dark, unlike on my previous visit, a single unlit lamp to the left of the door. I move down the stairs after a cautious glance in all directions to confirm no one's watching me, the steps creaking gently beneath me. Wooden benches, both under and across from the window, offer a resting place for weary legs, their surfaces worn by time. The blue door doesn't look as inviting as before.

And no one's here.

Just silence and darkness and shadow.

"Hi, Colden" the voice speaks from above and behind me.

55 – Where were you?

Dark and gangly, she crouches in the corner beyond the wooden bench, chin resting on the knees drawn up to her chest, watching through squinted eyes.

He doesn't know she's here. She pulls her legs tightly to her body to stay warm.

A woman's voice from up in the street.

"Hi. Didn't expect to see you here" I stammer, leaning back against the door.

"Thought I'd follow to make sure you were ok"

"Uh, thanks"

"Looking for Caprice?" she comes to the top of the stairs, standing up on her toes as she holds the railing.

Unsure of what to say, I say nothing.

She crosses her arms "So where are you headed now?"

"Probably back to the station; it's getting late" I check my watch, worried about how long I've been gone.

"She'll be back there by now"

"Huh?" I pretend I haven't heard her though my surprise may have escaped my mouth.

"It's a shame. We could have a lot of fun" she smiles.

Yes, that much I know.

"Where did you go in the Stone? Suddenly you were gone" I say, unsure how to get away from where I am.

"I was there" she squints her jet-black eyes.

Was she? Is she here now? Sure looks like it, though I now notice she's wearing a white leather jacket over her body-hugging orange dress. The orange dress I've already disposed of.

"Are you eying me, Station Master?" she does a partial curtsy, hands at her sides.

"I should go, Jade" I walk past her, surprised to be saying her name aloud.

I hear nothing and hope that means she's gone and won't be following me.

"What did you call me?" she says softly from behind me.

I should ignore her but turn around anyway – she's vanished.

I keep seeing her in person here but feel like I've seen her somewhere else as well – I can't put my finger on it. Ah, well.

No one else is in the street, down by the child care door, or near any building that I can see.

A gentle rain begins to fall which does not improve my situation.

I'm alone to ponder this mess. Am I going crazy somehow? What part of my time in West has been real? All of it? None of it? Who are my allies? My enemies? Where am I, really?

Have I asked these questions before?

Glancing behind myself and down, I spot the silver mailbox with 'C Collaston' on it.

'C' for Caprice.

'C'

Could she have sent me the letter? Why? To help her somehow? Why not tell me? Or is there more at play here than I realize? Caprice told me so before.

I consider looking in the mailbox but am afraid I might find something.

It's sometimes better not to know.

I wander away from the child care centre, lost in thought. I hardly know what to think anymore.

"Hi, Station Master" the male voice speaks from behind me.

I turn like I've been struck.

"It's me: Evan" he's leaning up against a building "Haven't seen you in a while"

Another puzzling individual who pops up inexplicably only to speak in riddles.

Evan.

"Who are you, anyway?" I ask, a hint of irritation in my voice.

"No one, anymore. But a long time ago, I was the same as you"

I try to conjure words to ask a question but find none.

"I don't have a part anymore. Not like you do" he shakes his head.

"Are you real?" I say bravely, taking a step toward him.

"Absolutely. Not much longer, though. Not once she finds out"

"Who? The girl?"

"You should get going. Tick, tick, tick" he says tapping his wrist.

I check my watch confirming the time is 11:45 and when I look up, he's gone.

My light jacket won't keep me dry for long in the gentle rain, and there's nothing else to do in town.

I wait, the child care centre at my back, wondering what will come next. Raising my head, I look as far down the street as I can in both directions and see no one.

I'm alone. I shake my head.

Back to the station.

My surroundings are now unfamiliar, the child care centre and print shop no longer near at hand. The grey two-storey buildings on my sides are identical in this alley, like walls in a maze, two windows on the lower level and another two on the second floor, an extinguished oil lamp on both sides of a closed door. I'm not sure where to go or what awaits me down any street, my sense of direction completely off track. There's no one in sight and not a sound.

Which direction do I take? I can see intersecting streets and alleys both ahead and behind me but nothing to help me decide my course. What part of the village is this? Does anyone live here?

"This way" Dalton appears in the distance ahead so I take off in pursuit of his swift form.

He disappears, lost in the shadows and winding streets. At least I'm on the right track. I hope.

Why am I following this guy that I barely know? And where am I going?

Hustling to find my way out and back to more familiar territory, I arrive at a four-way intersection with nothing but faith to guide me in my decision.

Selecting the path to my right, I take off at a jog, eventually emerging in the plaza along a street I'd never travelled before now. I leave the community and enter the forest, eager to get back to my suite though dreading the walk. Leaves and branches that have accumulated in this shelter, now rattle and crunch softly at my sides.

I should know the woods by now but every journey feels like the first time.

It's always so dark in here, regardless of conditions in the open, like its own world.

I run through the clear forest air for what feels like a long time, nothing familiar along the trail; overhead the sky's the colour of steel. I smell wood and leaves and dirt for what feels like the first time since I arrived, the scent reassuring. I hear no movements at my sides, the forest now silent. Then the path widens but my feet keep carrying me forward as if they know where to go. Then the terrain angles up and I climb for a short distance before the ground levels off.

My vision is clouded, my head dizzy.

I stop at a flat stone block when my body demands a rest.

How long have I been running?

Dropping my head as I sit, I slowly regain my energy only to realize that I'm sitting on the edge of the platform, legs dangling over the side.

What?!? The station?

I lose my balance as I stand, succumbing to gravity as if being pulled off the edge before a hand grabs the back of my jacket.

"Watch your step, Colden"

Caprice helps me to the bench along the wall.

"What happened?" I ask as I take a seat, my head groggy.

"You nearly fell" she replies sitting next to me.

"Thank you. Thanks" I mutter looking around.

"What are you looking for?" she asks with her head cocked to the side.

What?

"Just getting my balance" I say avoiding the question.

My senses are returning, my head clearer as I take in my surroundings.

What now?

"Now you need to leave, as much as I'd like you to stay" Caprice reads my thoughts.

"But…"

"Colden" she says sharply.

"Just get on the train, right?" I exhale, dejected and confused.

"That's right"

"Tonight?"

"There's no train until tomorrow night" she replies casually.

"And how do I get on that train?"

I look toward the tracks as if a train were in the station.

"Who are you talking to?" Cindy speaks from the top of the stairs behind me.

"What?"

I feel like a trance has been broken.

"I heard you talking to someone. Where have you been?"

I look all around. No sign of Caprice.

"I'm coming" I change the subject, struggling up the stairs.

"Have you been drinking?" she asks as I enter the room.

"No" I reply collapsing onto the couch.

I have no desire to explain everything to Cindy; not now. The apartment is warm and bright, lit lanterns arranged around the suite giving it a sunny air even on this cloudy day.

I close my eyes, head tilted back.

I want so badly to trust Cindy, to be with her, but part of my mind feels something isn't right and that I should stay vigilant. My mind doesn't know what to think, what to make of the people, the forest, the station. Who and what am I seeing and is it all real?

"The next train's due soon" I say "I'll check the schedule to figure out exactly when"

"And then what?" she sits on the table in front of me.

"And then we leave" I say.

And then everything goes black.

There's no one on the platform, a few oil lamps lighting the area around me, those I leave lit until I pack it in for the night. A light breeze blows a chill across me, but my body isn't cold even in just a t-shirt and shorts. I'm sitting on the bench facing the tracks, facing the forest. It's nighttime.

How did I get outside?

I take a sip of the cup of coffee at my side which is, thankfully, nice and warm. It's nearly empty so must have brought it down with me

The moon shines brightly in the clear sky, the illumination most welcome, if uncommon. The silence is heavy, like my ears are plugged or covered, my head dizzy, my body off-balance, I don't dare try to stand.

Is Cindy out here with me? I don't see or hear her. I say her name or maybe I just think it, I'm not sure.

Upstairs, a sliver of light is visible under the apartment's closed door.

To my right and on the bench farther away from me, there's a young girl in a dirty purple dress, or is it grey, her face hidden behind her dark matted hair. She seems to be looking past me down the tracks as if expecting a train. She approaches me hesitantly like an underfed mangy dog who's been alone too long to remember the company of others.

My head vibrates like a church bell as I put my hands on my knees for balance, attempting to get up.

I look back at the girl.

She appears ready to reach out and touch me as a voice speaks to my left.

"Where the hell were you?" Cindy says.

"Hi" I say turning to her.

"Hi?!?"

Looking back to my right, the girl is gone.

"My head is killing me" I mumble.

"What's going on here?" Cindy's eyes are wide, a combination of confusion and anger.

What is going on?

"I'm not sure" I reply as I try unsuccessfully to stand, my body falling back to the bench.

"Where'd you run off to this time?" her head shakes.

I can't think of anything intelligent to say so slowly walk to sit on the steps up to the apartment.

"You disappeared in the time it took me to walk to the kitchen" she adds angrily.

My watch says 9:15.

Where did the time go?

Have I been drugged? How did it get so late?

I stagger upstairs into the empty apartment. The warm air draws me in, the door closing behind me. I'm hunched over, still trying to regain my balance.

There's a scratch at the window behind me but I'm too afraid to turn, scared of what might be there. I drop to the floor in weakness and despair, leaning against the wall and fall backwards closing my eyes.

"Where were you?"

Her voice wakes me from my dream.

Looking up, Lori's standing over me in our apartment.

"Eh?"

"Deep in thought, or exhausted?" she asks.

"Where are we?"

Yes, where are we, or at least where am I?

"What?" Lori cocks her head. Beautiful Lori with her quirky smile, her sharp eyes, her lean body.

"Uh, yes, where?"

"Do you mean, like, where are we in life or where are geographically?" she smiles.

"The second one"

"Well, we're at home, I'm a bit tipsy, and you're about to make wild love to me"

"At home…"

"That's the part of the sentence you heard?"

"I just meant…"

"That's ok, loverboy. I'll make myself pretty while you think things over" she smirks.

"Yeah…"

"Yeah"

I rub my disoriented eyes.

Opening them, I see an unexpected scene.

I look around my familiar surroundings – the furniture; the windows; the smell; Lori in our good years. The band posters on the wall, toys on the floor, soft carpet under my feet.

The open kitchen and living room; the windows looking out on the city; the front door; the hallway to my right.

It had been a dream. All of it.

What were 'New Brook West' and 'East' and ghost girls and Caprice and Cindy? How did I conjure those images? I wasn't high.

What the heck does it mean?

Had Lori's madness been a dream too? A nightmare?

What was true of the rest of my life?

I don't dare ask more questions about where we are. But I'm most certainly in our apartment now, where I want to be. It's nighttime.

What about Suzie? She must be here.

"Is Suzie here?" I yell to the bedroom.

"She's likely asleep by now"

"Sure" I walk in the direction of her room.

"Your name is in their letters" she says from behind me.

"What did you say?" I yell back.

"I didn't say anything" Lori says in a confused tone.

Where did that come from? I feel like I remember that sentence but can't place it. Ugh. I'll figure it out tomorrow.

Opening the door slowly, a small figure is tucked up beneath the covers, eyes closed, mouth partially open. I smile inside like I've just received the most beautiful gift and walk to kiss her and ruffle the blankets around her. I stare for a moment then exit, shutting the door quietly.

I step into the bathroom to check the mirror and I look more or less as I expect. A little tired, maybe, but it's me.

Lori has shut off all but the bedroom lights and leans against the doorway wearing only a long shirt.

"I have some ideas" she smiles.

"Me too" I remove my shirt and pants, throwing them into the room.

Walking toward her, I pull her head to mine, kissing her like I haven't seen a woman in years. My hands run up and down her body through her thin shirt before I lift it over her head and pull her body to me, her perfect bare breasts pressing up against my chest. Her beautiful body, her smooth skin, her soft lips, her moans.

My hands run over her round ass, her thigh muscles tightening as she stands on her toes. We devour each other like it's our first time. I love Lori more than anything and figure she'll be my last love. There's no one else like her. There could be no one else.

I don't know what could have summoned that horrible and detailed dream but for now it doesn't matter.

Before I crawl in next to Lori for the night, I go to take one more look at Suzie, to touch her, to kiss her cheek.

I pull on shorts and stand up.

I wished it and I was brought back to the life I longed for, to the people I care for.

These things don't happen.

Lori has already curled up in bed, calling me to cuddle up with her.

"I'll be right there" I promise.

The clock in the hall reads 12:15, well past Suzie's bedtime, and mine as well, but tonight has been exceptional.

My daughter sleeps soundly, her face nestled in the blankets, her tiny body wrapped up tight and warm.

I go down on one knee beside her bed to pull back the sheet and kiss her goodnight.

"No, these things don't happen" the voice beneath the covers speaks.

56 – No, these things don't happen

The words must have come from her mouth but the sound came from everywhere. I pull back the blankets and her body is like a corpse on display.

I leap back.

"Lori!" I yell.

"What?"

Lori's figure appears in the doorway, her face drawn and pale, her eyes glazed, her body emaciated. Not the woman I'd been with earlier this evening.

"Lori…" I whimper.

"Sweetie; what is it?" her voice grates.

I try to call out for my family, scream their names, but no sound comes out of my mouth. My eyes close as I fall to my knees.

The room goes dark and quiet around me. I wonder if Lori and Suzie are still in the room with me.

What's happening? Where am I? Are Lori and Suzie safe?

My eyes open and cold dark air surrounds me. I'm utterly disoriented. I can't see the doorway. Again, I try to yell but again, make no sound. A whispering voice behind me speaks my name.

Who? Help me. Please.

A fire crackles in the distance, the ground hisses at my feet, I feel a light touch like a feather on the back of my neck and my ears.

I struggle to find my way from this dream, to wake up, to get back to Lori. The black room has no visible exits. How have I conjured this place?

Then a song, like a bird's, fills my ears.

I wake on top of my bed at the station, Cindy on the couch in the living room drinking something, the oil lamps lighting the apartment, the outside skies hazy. The gloom is again real.

How did I get to the bed? How am I back here? Had I ever left?

Had my return to Lori been real? Is that my real life?

Is Cindy real?

Is this place real?

It's daytime but of what day?

I'm exhausted but can't imagine sleeping.

I'm horribly confused and nearly shaking but my body seems fine.

I need to get some air.

Getting to my feet is surprisingly easy, my body strong, my senses awake. I'd have preferred not to disturb Cindy or alert her to my departure. Rising slowly and without a sound, I make my way to the door where my boots slide on quietly as I contemplate sneaking out.

10:30 pm

"Going somewhere?" she asks without moving.

"Need to check the schedules for the next train heading out" I mumble.

"Now?"

"Yes"

"Should I come with you?" she sips her beverage.

"Better if you stay here in case something goes wrong" I reply "If we're both down there, then we're fu…in trouble"

"Well put" she says.

I cast a brief glance her way but she keeps her eyes down, so I make my way out without another word.

A light mist has descended, the air calm and cold, the night quiet.

The lantern between Room 1 and 2 flickers helplessly, the oil nearly consumed.

It's time to muster my courage and take action, in whatever form.

Striking the lamp in the control room, I notice a recently printed sheet. A scraping noise near the bottom of the stairs turns my head, my eyes peering out the door, but no one's there or anywhere else on the platform. I wait to see if I'll spot anyone moving but abandon this after a few seconds. The air is clearer which is either good or bad for me; I have no desire to see whatever's in the shadows.

The boxes lay in varying states of order in the back closet, my mind utterly uninterested in research.

Blowing out the candle, I shut the door, making my way back up the stairs, the unread paper in my hand.

Watching from the shadows, she can feel his heartbeat from beneath the stairs, his breathing. She draws her knees up to her chest, dark hair hanging across her lifeless face, her form nearly disappearing in absolute silence. She waits, invisible.

Emerging from her hiding place, and with no place else to go, she scuttles across the platform, close to the ground. Extinguishing the flickering flame on the wall, she turns the handle to Room 1.

Cindy hasn't moved. Still holding her cup, which appears to be filled with something other than tea, she doesn't lift her head to welcome me back to the apartment.

The time is now 10:45 pm.

"I brought the schedule" I exclaim triumphantly.

"Great" she mutters.

To confirm it is in fact the schedule, I set the paper down on the island, poring over the transmission.

The next train's arrival is in two days at 5:00 in the evening, the cargo, pieces, and weight listed for reference. This information needs to go up on the board to avoid suspicion. That mean still two full days until our attempted escape. Has Cindy vacated her residence in favour of mine? I worry about the audacity of this move on her part. I doubt our relationship is a secret to anyone in the village.

"So, now what?" I ask.

"Now I go to sleep" she stands without looking at me, places her cup near the sink, and heads to the bathroom.

"In the bathroom?" my attempt at levity is poorly timed, judging by her reaction.

"I'm considering it" she closes the door.

I strip to my underwear, extinguish all but the two candles near the bed, check the windows and door, and sit on the edge of the bed awaiting

Cindy's return. Outside, the wind has picked up, dispelling the fog and making the station howl as air passes through small cracks in the structure and rattles loose items around the building. My eyes drift along the windows, light reflecting off them just enough to keep me from seeing through them, which is probably for the best. Shadows play in the corners of the apartment and along the wall, hiding things I'd probably rather not know are there.

After about five minutes, Cindy steps out of the bathroom wearing a long shirt.

"Everything OK?" I ask.

"Sure" she sits next to me "There's a lot I'm trying to understand, now more than ever. I'm frustrated by everything, including you. I don't know how I fit into all this or how you do. Am I cursed by associating with you? I'm kinda scared and confused, you know"

"A bad combination" I put my arm around her.

She nestles in close.

"And what happens after we leave?"

"We're getting out of here" I enunciate distinctly "We put this all behind us, then we'll worry about what comes next once we're gone"

"Ok" she kisses me on the cheek.

"Together" I say, without realizing it.

"Together" she smiles.

I put my watch down on the bed, noticing it says 10:20.

My body is tired, my mind dopey. I extinguish the lanterns.

"How can it be 10:20?" I ask Cindy, my voice panicked.

"It isn't. It's five after eleven"

I set my watch on the nightstand without looking at it.

Time to sleep.

"Time to sleep" I think I say out loud.

"Goodnight"

"Goodnight"

I wake with a start to a knock at the door.

Cindy doesn't budge.

How late is it? Who comes to the station now? I can only imagine what awaits me. Should I get up or lie quietly until whoever it is goes away?

I don't hear anyone outside.

The wind has let up, only a light breeze now whistling around the station. Not sure if it's foggy or clear, though I can't see any stars or the moon out the window.

I consider waking Cindy but decide against it.

My watch isn't on the nightstand.

I sit up in bed, look around the sleeping area and then into the larger room but can't make out much in the dark. I see no movements and hear no noises in the suite.

I swing my legs off the side of the bed and pull on my pants. Slowly making my way to the door, I'm unsure if I should open it even as I grab the handle.

There's no sound on the landing and no odd smells, both good signs.

I pause, look around the room, and open the door with a swift pull.

There's nothing and no one down the stairs nor out on the platform from my vantage point so I head back inside.

"Whatcha doin'? a female voice speaks behind me.

Lori?!?

I'm still in the station's apartment but Lori now stands near the bed.

"Lori?" I whisper.

"Uh, yes" she replies reaching out for me.

I pull back much to her surprise.

Has it always been Lori here with me at the station? My mind aches as I try to work out what's going on.

"What's wrong?" she says taking a step back herself "And why were you looking outside?"

"Thought I heard something. Guess I was wrong"

I don't know where to stand or what to say.

Where I am? Do I run to her or away? Has everything been a dream?

"Come on back to bed" she gestures me toward her.

"Uh..." I mumble, trying to find words to express my thoughts.

"Uh?"

The voice is Cindy's.

"Cindy?" I look at her.

"Me" she's sitting on the edge of the bed.

"Yeah" I go around to my side "Bad dream"

"Ok" she tucks back under the covers.

"Goodnight" I say.

"Goodnight" she replies.

57 – United in eternal love

I wake before Cindy, my watch telling me it's 7:50, the clock on the wall a matching time, much to my relief. The room is dimly lit, the morning sun just above the trees in the east. I ease out of bed, careful to not jostle anything and wake her, walking to the fridge to grab a glass for juice. Coffee can wait for her to sleep a bit longer as I ponder my nightmare. Another vision of Lori that seemed so vivid, so real.

Why am I suddenly having these reflections? Is something here causing these memories to emerge now? Why?

I shake my head and convince myself that I won't succumb to the madness that afflicted my predecessors. A shiver runs across my neck and down my back reminding me of where I am.

The air outside looks clear and it's not raining so I'll wait outside for Cindy to sleep a bit longer.

Throwing on my cargo pants and a white t-shirt, I step out the door to survey the platform in the surprisingly warm air. All is quiet and there's no wind to disturb the calm. To my surprise, a short-haired blonde woman sits on the bench facing the tracks, wearing a yellow skirt and a long-sleeved grey sweater.

I close the door softly and creep down the stairs, fully prepared for her to vanish.

"Hi, Colden" Caprice turns to me.

"Hi, Caprice" I stop a short distance from her.

"I am very sorry" she says dejectedly "For everything"

"What do you mean?" I ask.

Here it comes.

"There's so much I should have told you"

"Who are you?" I sit next to her.

"I didn't lie about that"

"But you lied about other things?"

"No. I just didn't tell you the whole truth"

"Can we really leave New Brook West?" I ask.

"Yes" she continues staring straight ahead "At least, I hope so"

"How?"

"You'll see in the end, I suppose. Some things I cannot change"

"But some things you can?"

"Some" she looks at me "But for now I must go. We will see each other again soon. I only wanted to make sure you were ok"

Caprice walks across the platform away from the tracks and down the stairs toward the village, her form fading in the distance, and I'm left alone to ponder what she said. What should she have told me? Will she before my attempt to leave? This, combined with my unease about my recent dreams.

I stare across the tracks into the dark forest, then in each direction along the line. The crisp air feels good, makes me feel alive. A gentle breeze breaks the stillness, the silence. Perhaps the sun will shine on New Brook West today.

"How long have you been up?"

Cindy looks down from the top of the stairs in shorts and a long-sleeved shirt.

"Hi" I stand up.

"What're you doing down there?" she asks.

"Letting you sleep a bit longer" I walk to the bottom of the staircase, looking up at her.

"Well, I have a reward for you up here" she smiles.

"I like the sound of that" I walk cautiously.

When I reached the top, she kisses me sweetly on the cheek.

"I made coffee" she smiles.

10:10

How can that be? I'd only spoken with Caprice for a minute or two. I sit at the island, sipping my hot beverage.

"I'll be back after a shower" Cindy closes the bathroom door behind her.

"Sure"

My head is overwhelmed by thoughts, too many to focus on one thing. It all seems out of my control.

Destiny.

I sit facing into the room.

My mind turns to my library visit and the family trees. Something in the genealogies isn't connecting and I can't put my finger on it. Some of the names don't fit. A missing piece of information.

Or maybe something is familiar and I can't figure out why.

I feel myself increasingly absorbed in life here in West and in trying to solve the ages-old mystery of ghostly girls and station masters. But why? How did I get so caught up in this? And what's keeping me from putting it together into something meaningful?

There's no one to ask for help so I'll be figuring this out on my own, if at all.

I finish my coffee as Cindy walks out of the bathroom, dropping her towel to the floor as she does, revealing her beautiful smooth naked skin.

"Whoops" she smiles.

I calmly walk over, running my hands softly up and down her sides as she pulls my shirt up over my head. I caress her bare bum with my fingers then firmly grab it to lift her onto her toes. I kiss her softly, her delicate lips, then run my tongue over them before I grab her bottom lip in my teeth. Her hands squeeze my arms then grab my back, sliding down to undo my shorts and pull them and my underwear to the floor and off me with her foot. Her mouth moves down my body, kissing my stomach, making my muscles flex. She gets on her knees and takes me in her mouth, her soft lips sliding up and down my length as I gasp.

Before I let her finish me, I get her to her feet, cupping her breasts when she's standing, making her body shiver. I guide her body to the ground onto her hands and knees and kneel behind her, caressing the backs of her thighs, her bare feet beneath me.

She gasps as I enter her from behind and my thrusts inside here eventually make her breathing stop and her muscles tense.

"Nnnnnnnnn" she moans loudly with her cheek pressed against the ground and her eyes closed, her hands in fists. Her orgasms are absolutely beautiful.

"Huhhhhhhh" she exhales pressing back against me again so I'm fully inside her for a moment, her body's muscles still flexed.

I hold onto her hips firmly, pulling her towards me, and continue to push inside her until I reach the point of no return and my passions explode.

My eyes are closed, my teeth clenched until I'm ultimately spent.

"Huh, huh…" I catch my breath.

She continues to moan with a giggle, her legs twitching, the side of her face on the floor.

"Wow" she says, her body shivering.

"Wow" I echo her sentiment in a soft voice.

She raises her body up onto her hands, still on her knees.

My arms wrap around her body from behind her, my hands on her breasts making her twitch. I caress her stomach.

I pull away as her body shakes, running my fingers over her bare foot as I do. I straighten my back, and she turns to face me, tilting her head so I kiss her.

"Mmmmm" she purrs.

I hold her as she leans in against my chest and we catch our breath, her soft breasts pressing in to me, her feet kicking playfully behind her.

I hold her like this for several seconds or more then inhale deeply.

"Should we get up?" I smile.

"You first, then help me" she whispers.

After assisting her, I walk to the sofa, still naked.

Relieved as I am that Cindy hasn't transformed into anything or anyone else, I catch my breath and try to calm my unsteady legs.

Cindy sits naked in the armchair, bare legs extended in front of her, toes pointed straight out as she exhales deeply, her body still twitching.

"End of the world sex?" she smiles.

"I hope not" I say kissing her "I wanna do that again"

"Yesssss" she hisses.

As amazing as that sex was with Cindy, my mind drifts to our circumstances in New Brook West. And I'm tired.

"Lunchtime" I rise from the couch to walk to the kitchen "You tire me out"

I set to making coffee.

"So, you fuck me but you don't trust me?"

"What?" I spin around.

"I'm thinking things but didn't say them" she smiles.

I turn back to the fridge, my mind spinning.

We eat sandwiches and fruit and pastries. My mind wanders amid thoughts of escape, of Caprice, of Acacia, of Benton, of the ghostly grey girl.

"If you have your strength back..." Cindy slouches in the armchair opening her legs, still naked.

"You look delicious..." I contemplate the possibilities.

"But..." she sighs.

"I need to pay a visit to the librarian...the library" I put my clothes on "But I will be back"

"You don't sound sure" she watches my every move.

"I'm sure"

Once dressed, I kneel down to kiss her long on the lips, pulling her face toward mine, my hand cupping her breast. Standing, I put on my jacket.

"I'll be back real soon" I say smiling.

"Bye, loverboy" she waves, curling up in the chair.

I exit, closing the door behind me. As I descend the stairs, I take a slow look around the platform, across the tracks, and along the wall then hurry across the hazy clearing into the calm forest. I've brought the paper schedule from the control room printer with me as a pretense for coming inside the gates, a task which needs to be performed anyway.

After tacking the notice to the board, I slip through back alleys to come out the other side of the village, careful to avoid the blue café. The long walk seems to take only a few seconds.

It's 12:20 when I reach the large wooden doors, Brian behind the desk, his face cheery as I enter.

"Hi friend!" he smiles "Didn't think I'd see you again so soon"

"Got a favour to ask - well another one I guess"

"Whatcha need?" he sets his hands on the desk.

"Do you know anything about the church cemetery?"

"Not much other than what you can see by wandering around it yourself" he leans back in his chair "Someone specific you're lookin' for?"

"Maybe. I don't know. Can I grab those genealogy books again, please?"

He points to his left where several tomes that I'd inspected previously are piled on his desk as well as a couple that I either haven't looked at or weren't included on my previous visits

'Mariston', 'Brooks', 'Clovinston'.

I step to the side recalling the strange woman Cindy and I met in the forest who seemed to know us.

"Do you know…" I start but then decide against asking.

Brian looks up.

"Sorry. Just thinking out loud" I say.

I pull the Von Stela genealogy from my pocket and stare at Katya and Martin at the top of the page.

Beneath them: Rebecca and Christina Nicole. Sisters.

I've heard Rebecca's name several times and met an unusual woman who may or may not be her incarnation. So, now I know where she fits in the family tree but still don't know how she fits in with what's happening.

Christina Nicole. It's odd that she's mentioned using both names, the only person that I've come across in any family tree with this appellation. I wonder at the reason for this but dismiss it as unimportant.

I've met a few variations on the name Christina recently: Christi back home at the café, Chris on the plane, Tina the coffee girl. It's a weird coincidence but not helpful.

And I've heard the name Nicole somewhere since I arrived in New Brook West. But who would have said it to me? Who ever speaks to me? Almost no one. At the Grey Stone? No. A person I met? Not likely. The library? No, Brian never uses names when we speak. Neither does Feryn.

Rebecca and Christina Nicole. Rebecca and Nicole.

'The son of Rebecca and the daughter of Nicole'. The strange woman in the woods said that to Cindy and I.

But I've also seen the name Nicole before. In a book? I don't think so. At Cindy's? No. Written somewhere? Maybe.

Where have I been where things were written?

Some place in town? No. The library? All I've seen there is the strange art and her name wasn't in any book except the genealogy.

Where else have I been?

The school? No, there's never been anything written there.

My visit to East. That house in East.

'Auntie Nicole' was on the wall in that ruined house in East with the drawings of that family.

According to the genealogy, Hannah is Rebecca's daughter and Violet and Fuchsia are her daughters. And another child was drawn on the wall whose name I can't remember and is also missing from the paper family tree I was given.

Assuming one of Hannah's daughters is the artist, then Christina Nicole would be her great-aunt.

Could Christina Nicole and Nicole be the same person?

Christina Nicole had a son Henry but there's no husband shown for her in my family tree.

This sure is confusing.

For a small community the connections sure are confusing and there must be a lot of overlap, genealogically speaking.

"Is there a definitive record anywhere of all the town's residents?" I speak in Brian's direction.

"Far as I know, everyone's history is recorded somewhere in one of those books" he says "There's no comprehensive document with the entire population. These folks are pretty particular about chronicling history but do it by family or groups of families; births, marriages, deaths. Haven't heard of many departures so not sure what that'd look like"

"I haven't found any of the station masters' names in the history books"

"Station masters' records might be at the station. At first, they were community folks but later came from abroad, like yourself"

"And their children?"

"Probably with the father's family, if he was from the community. After that, I can't say"

"Have there been any female station masters?"

"Never" he replies definitively.

No secrets in this town and everyone's a descendant of another resident.

"Thanks, Brian"

"You're most welcome"

I turn to leave, stopping as I reached the door.

"Are there any gates in the area?" I ask.

"I suppose there's the gates coming into town if that's what you'd call 'em"

"Where would I go if someone said they 'lived just inside the gates'?"

"The cemetery" he says seriously.

"Oh, thanks"

Ok, so that's weird. And creepy. Still, I can only imagine that guy's messing with me. Based on our conversations, it seems a real possibility. And Caprice's comment about him 'trying to unnerve me'.

I'll make a quick stop at the church if I can manage to sneak into the graveyard unobserved, a tall order considering its location. The names I saw on the markers when I looked in the first time must be the families in the genealogical tomes. Overcast skies loom, the weak breeze insufficient to refresh the damp air. I cast a silent wish for it not to rain beneath the charcoal sky.

What will I find in the cemetery? Be careful what you look for because you just might find it.

I hustle back to the community without seeing a soul and am happy there's no one in the streets either nor in the town plaza, at least no one visible.

I walk to the board to discourage any curious looks before making my way across to the church building. I still see no one so casually carry on. Reaching the iron gate on the right side, I scan the area inside the gates and behind me to confirm my privacy, then step into the enclosure.

Where to begin? This place is a lot bigger than I expected.

There are two trees farther back, both taller than me but compressed like someone pushed them down from the top, branches beginning high up the trunk, frail as they are, dark and spindly and leafless. The stone markers are in varying states of decay, worn down by time. Wandering the well-kept grounds, I notice many of the historical names I'd seen at the library: Clovinston, Brooks, Mariston, von Stela. Nothing stands out.

I move slowly to hopefully draw less attention to myself. It's hard to imagine who acted as groundskeeper unless it was the guy I'd met before.

Was everyone who'd died in East and West buried here?

It feels odd to be amongst the old graves in such an unusual community. Yet it all is somehow appropriate: the ghostly atmosphere, the eerie silence. The peaceful setting.

Family surnames seem grouped by area; some more recent deaths popping up randomly, presumably due to space limits in the fenced area.

After about ten minutes I find several 'Collaston' markers. Caprice's family?

I comb this section but don't really know what I'm looking for considering I don't know any of her relatives or predecessors. Or if I want to know more about her.

Who is she anyway?

"Come here and I'll show you"

Caprice is standing a short distance behind me.

"Caprice" is all that comes out of my mouth. Or do I just think it?

Holding out her hand she takes mine, guiding me to the 'Pertwee' part of the cemetery.

"That's who I am" she points at the grave.

'Evan Pertwee' on the left plaque and 'Caprice Collaston' on the right; Evan deceased in 1912, Caprice in 1913.

"But…" I start but don't know what to say next.

"I tried to tell you" she says, her head hanging.

What the hell is this? This can't be real. No one lives forever, certainly not staying and looking that young. I look around to see if anyone else is watching and to remind myself where I am. I close my eyes and wonder how it'll look when I open them.

I'm still in the cemetery, Caprice in front of me.

"But you're not dead" I say, stating the obvious, concerned about the direction of our conversation, unable to conjure anything more intelligent.

"No" she says sadly "I learned the art of potion making"

It sounds more like a confession than an explanation.

"Magic…"

"Herbalism. Residents thought it witchcraft, though many still requested elixirs anonymously from those who practiced this art"

"How?"

"I've tried to help you and regret that I've failed. The teacher is fortunate to have spent the time with you that she did. My life was not so happy"

"What happened?"

"My husband was not a good man"

"What did he do?"

"I must go" she ignores my question.

"Was it you who sent..." I begin.

Caprice vanishes behind the church.

So, Caprice had been married to Evan Pertwee. How is he still alive? How is she?

There's no one else to ask if I can't ask her. I don't dare bring this up with anyone else and really hope I don't see Evan again to hear his thoughts.

So what records are at the station that aren't at the library?

It's time to take a closer look in those boxes in the control room.

4:10

Time has become something I can't rely on; it passes at its own speed regardless of how I feel it should. It's always either later or earlier than I expect. And everything's a surprise. What should I be doing differently?

Leaving the cemetery and exiting the village, I notice a few people moving about the plaza. There's no need to play at the board; the schedule is posted for anyone who cares. No arrivals or departures are expected tonight which means fewer people and situations to avoid. Enough happens at the station as it is. I walk past the board casting a cursory glance at it as I do.

Rustling in the trees and bushes follows me to the station's clearing where it stops. No longer do I fear these disturbances and wonder at having normalized this. There's no one behind or to my sides that I can see on my walk through the forest; I never stop looking, though I know this is in vain.

I wonder what Cindy has done today, if she's been expecting me, if I'm Late or early, or if it matters. I approach the station slowly, watchful of the area around the building, my senses attuned to any sudden movements, noises, or smells, of which there are none.

The platform is dark, though light shines from inside apartment. The sun casts the last of its glow for the day, the sky in the west and just above the treetops a muted red. Carefully up the steps onto the stone floor, my eyes alternate between Room 1's closed door and the ground.

I walk to the edge of the platform to scan in both directions along the tracks and at the benches, confirming there are no visitors which is a mighty relief.

My eyes again go to Room 1 whose door appears shut. Thankfully.

The cat? Haven't seen much of him since the first day. I wonder what became of him or maybe he lives in the forest and only comes around on occasion since I don't feed him. I enjoyed the few times that I saw him.

I unlock the control room door, closing it behind me, and light the lamp in the back room.

So many boxes with so much history.

Most are labelled by year which gives me a starting point but only vaguely since I'm not sure what I'm looking for.

I grab the box labelled 1850. Brian Brooks seems to have been the original station master, overseeing the construction of the first station. He mentions his previous position as town librarian, overseeing a small collection he'd hoped to expand upon in a larger building at a new location but that's all I gather of his life, the first station master of New Brook West. Trains were few and most carried little cargo, the most common items listed show tools and building supplies. There's no mention of any exports from New Brook West. I next look at 1855, 1856, 1857, and 1858. Mr. Brooks must have passed away in 1858 because beginning in September of that year, Paul Barkman started making notes, his first entry on the 19th of the month.

He was the first to take up residence at the train station having designed a small suite where the hotel is now located. I wonder how much the station master's lodgings have changed over time and how the station has evolved. How many have visited, how many have stayed, how many have left?

The box marked 1860, contains more of Barkman's ledgers. Nothing noteworthy jumps at me, though it's impossible to look through every document, cargo manifest, and notebook.

Then on to 1865. Kristopher Clovinston. I'm hopeful, but again no real clues, with the exception of some notes on a woman from the village. She'd given

Kristopher a tonic to help him sleep; he made a note in a calendar

reminding him to speak with her again. The woman isn't named. Kristopher

speaks of an illness he'd contracted which worsened with time, possibly leading to his demise as his entries stop in 1869 when Braun Wallace assumed the position.

Evidently Mr. Wallace was enamoured of a local girl and felt wronged because his advances had been spurned while the woman gave birth to a child later that year. Seems he only held the post for a few months leaving for reasons not documented but I assume to be related to his love for this girl.

I wonder how long most people held the post of station master. Why some stayed for longer than others? How many declined the offer? I guess it really isn't for everyone.

I pore through several others until I come upon 1909 and the one I've been searching for.

Mr. Evan Pertwee was station master that year. His records are accurate, though he does note a number of personal entries in a journal I also find in the box. He wrote a great deal about himself and the admiration he felt women had for him. He considered himself good-looking and intelligent which apparently drew a lot of attention from women in the village. His family were of modest means and he felt he was a self-made man, if such was the achievement of rising to the rank of Station Master. He met and felt he'd attracted the earnest attentions of a young lady who'd sought him out on several occasions. Mr. Pertwee felt he was entitled to Hannah, and was wronged and embarrassed by her rejection, though there's no mention of him actually loving or courting her. The language is more anger than heartbreak. He later tells of his engagement to an unnamed woman, who he fails to describe in any detail but to mention her blonde beauty.

A paper falls from the binder, a photo.

Evan and Caprice in front of the station at the time, presumably on the day of their engagement, with a caption: 'to be united in eternal love'.

So, Evan was… And Caprice is…

I set the folder down, catching my breath.

So, it is real. How am I talking to these people? How are they talking to me?

I sit on the floor and pick up what I'd been reading.

I skim over Evan's notes leading up to his marriage until he mentions a

hanging as an act of justice, the righting of a wrong, though provides little detail of the actual event or the circumstances leading to it. A woman had been accused of crimes of which she was surely guilty and committed to the noose. His words carry a sense of pride as though he played a role in this episode, though this is not explicitly mentioned. He goes on to describe life as folks move to New Brook West in increasing numbers, surprised as he is by this mass exodus from Brooks, which is what New Brook East was initially called, if I remember correctly.

The Station Master's residence is now above the control room, though I miss the sequence of events leading to this relocation. The hotel's six rooms are also in place by that time.

His next entry is of a dark girl lurking about the station, haunting locals and travelers alike, disappearing into shadows, emerging from places she couldn't have been. Those who come to the station report that she creeps about silently, watches from corners, and on occasion lights or extinguishes lamps. He sometimes sees her, but only briefly as she vanishes before he can get close enough to identify her. Evan felt she'd surely been involved in several killings in the area but no one could catch her and none could prove it. Men were found hanged in their homes or in public places in the village over a period of time in New Brook East and West. East had by now been vacated by all but a few residents and been renamed.

The lamp on the counter behind me flickers.

I look around the room but am too afraid to look up at the windows. The door is still closed which eases my mind.

Sightings were infrequent but the young girl's presence was 'felt' by many in the community and especially at the station, including by Evan himself. This went on for some time and seemed to anger the station master as he wished to be the one to rid the community of this menace. One day he spotted her out in the open, unaware of his presence, unconcealed. This time it was him who stood alone in the shadows. She casually surveyed the platform, unconcerned with the train passing through at full speed. He ran up behind her and used their momentum to throw her onto the tracks as the train steamed through the station, killing her instantly, or so he assumed.

And that was the end of her lurking at the station, or so he wrote.

Shortly after her demise, he spotted a grey figure skulking in the shadows, the dark corners, disappearing seemingly at will. He saw it at his windows, heard scratches at the door, and woke to a small female figure sitting in his apartment watching him sleep. But always, she vanished. For two weeks this continued, Evan's ravings like those of a madman, no longer making mention of his beautiful fiancée, obsessed as he was with this predator. He was unable to sleep for fear of this devilish girl's actions while he slept and grew increasingly afraid to be at the station or in the forest.

Could this be the girl who had previously lurked about the station? Impossible, since she'd surely died that day, no one could have survived that.

It also sure sounded like the things I heard and saw but anyone from that time would be long dead. I shake my head and continue my reading.

Then his writings stop. For no reason he'd mentioned. They just stop.

I rummage for the next box 1912. Then 1913. But I find neither. 1914 lists Colin Clovinston. Colin also wrote about strange movements, scratching at the windows and door, comings and goings from Room 1, or so he believed. Then his writings stop.

Sam Clovinston assumed the position later that year, though it doesn't mention if he and Colin were related. His journal's notes express his doubt of the myth of the 'grey girl' with the power to vanish at will, to make men do her bidding, to make them kill themselves. But Sam stopped writing after only a few weeks, Richard Clovinston replacing him, or at least his is the next name I come across. Richard held the post for about eight months, slowly descending into madness and becoming a recluse, according to his own journal. His last entry is dated 17 November 1916.

That's a lot of station masters in a short time. And all with the same last name, but perhaps that wasn't considered unusual at the time.

Several more years of boxes filled with cargo manifests, some containing personal notes; diaries of hauntings and visions and madness.

Arthur Becker was the station master between 1929 and 1932. His notes are objective and without opinion, straight to the point. He wrote about the station and occasional 'odd noises about the platform' but never expressed any fear at his circumstances. He carried on for two years after his marriage but quit the position and moved into town after the birth of his daughter to do carpentry and construction.

John Becker came next, serving for five years, his writing increasingly illegible with the passage of time until I could barely read his notes, professional or personal. Another Becker followed him, Peter, invited from the mainland to New Brook West to start a new life away from his activities which had caught up with him. After only 6 months, his entries stop. His last few days were filled with horrible drawings of what could only have been the girl he saw: her mangled hair, her mottled dress, her blank face. The art had such an effect on me, the drawings so true to life. I wonder if Mr. Becker was scared, if he felt alone. If he went mad.

Again, the candle in the control room shivers as if someone were blowing on it. This sends a chill over me as I again confirm the door is closed and that I'm alone in the room. And avoid looking at the windows.

Were any of these men related? Their relationship, if one existed, is never mentioned, neither is the reason for their selection.

I'm unable to establish a seamless timeline either because boxes are missing or I can't locate the next station master.

Outside, darkness is overtaking the station, a faint glimmer of light through the window and to my right out the door brings an end to the day's sun.

In 1954, Fuller, Arthur Fuller, assumes the position for several years, or so it seems, then his notes just end without any notice he'd be leaving. Then another Fuller, then a couple of Beckers, then a Clovinston. There sure have been a lot of station masters of the years. Truly not a job for everyone.

I notice a name I didn't expect to see again – Pertwee. John Pertwee's notes and ledger entries are lucid and ordered, though his origins and background story are not in his ledgers, nor are his years of service as his records indicate day and month but not year. He makes frequent mention of oddities at the station in the form of a girl who watches from outside his windows. She is often on the platform and the benches, vanishing before he can approach her. He hears scratching and knocking at the door but the landing is always empty when he opens it.

This sounds all too familiar.

John doesn't appear to have been station master for long, his ledgers lasting only a few weeks.

It seems as though most people didn't occupy this post for very long, many only for a few months. Did they leave? Did they die here? Were any of them the men in the photos of hanged station masters that I'd received?

Soft breath on my neck sends a shiver across my back. I cautiously look around the small room again but no one's here nor at the windows where I finally summon the courage to glance.

All's quiet in the control room and there's no noise out on the platform.

I see a box marked 1974, ten years before my birth. The station master that year: Andrew Vintassi.

Who's he? No one I know though a probable relation. The temperature drops in the control room, the candle flickering behind its glass cover.

Amongst his documents: a letter inviting him to the island. With similar if not exactly the same wording as mine, if I recall it. And had I seen another one earlier as well?

I look around me and my nerves are relieved I'm alone in the room. I decide against looking outside in case something outside indicates the contrary.

It's difficult to tell how long Andrew held the position due to his disorganized notes. His successor is John Fuller followed by Matthew Fuller. Both wrote of rustlings in the forest as they walked to town, figures looking up at the window from the clearing at night, a girl sitting on the benches facing the tracks.

And they all stop writing within six months after they began.

This couldn't be the same girl now as it had been throughout time, could it? Is there a family living in the forest?

There's never a mention of Room 1.

1980 saw Marcus Vintassi come to the island from somewhere in Europe to get away from the anxiety he felt in the big city. Marcus was succeeded eight months later by Larson Fuller, then Eric Vintassi six months after that.

Who are all these guys with my last name?

"Hello"

I nearly hit the ceiling when I see Caprice standing in the open doorway wearing black tights beneath a dark yellow dress.

"How did you..." I begin but don't finish.

"I came to see you, Colden" she hangs her head as she speaks.

"What's wrong?" I look up at her face.

"I need to tell you more of the story I started. Or try to"

"Ok" I turn my body toward her.

"Evan committed a terrible sin out of arrogance and superiority" she crouches down to my level "A horrible crime of passion"

"Oh" I don't know what else to say.

"He was responsible"

"He was?" I ask, wondering what exactly we're talking about.

"I lost my fiancé to a tragic accident and a blessed event"

"That's horrible" I say, still confused.

"Yes"

"So, what does he want from me?"

"He seeks to put you on edge"

"Why me? I'm nobody"

"Not true"

I pause, contemplating my next words.

"Are you the one that invited me to New Brook West, Caprice?" I say softly.

"Why would you think that?"

"It was signed with a 'C'" my words are hesitant.

"A common initial" she says seriously "The first letter of your name, in fact"

"And yours. Did you send me the letter offering me this job?"

"No"

That was direct.

"So, who did?" I ask leaning back.

"You should go to the school teacher. She's nervous"

"Where is she?"

"Upstairs"

Cindy with a 'C'. Oh no.

I walk past her out the door, looking up the steps to the apartment.

"Did Cindy sign the letter?" I ask turning back.

Caprice is gone, a faint hint of citrus lingering in the air, a reminder of her presence.

I scan the area by force of habit, climb the stairs, and enter the apartment, closing the door behind me.

Never

I watch from the forest, hiding in the trees. I don't think he sees me. Sometimes I follow. Watching him.
Sometimes I watch the woman in the house with red doors. Watch her as she walks to and from the school, to and from the station.
I never go into the village. Never.

58 – I didn't poison it

"Welcome back" Cindy's frustration is evident in her tone.

"Thanks" I smile.

"In case you didn't know, it's now 10:30 pm. You left almost twelve hours ago"

"I'm trying to get answers" I walk toward her "There's a heck of a lot going on here"

"You don't say" she takes a step back "Care to share anything. I'm in the dark. Remember we're trying to figure out how the school teacher fits into all of this too"

I look at my watch then toward the window, the apartment's interior reflected in the glass.

"Who signed your letter?" I blurt out, tired of being on the defensive.

"What letter?" she crosses her arms.

"The letter of offer for the teacher position"

"Haven't we had this conversation?"

"The letter inviting me to come here was signed with a 'C'" I fix my gaze on hers.

"Ok…"

"You've already lied about your last name" I say with more sadness than anger.

"I never lied. I'm sorry you didn't get the spelling from its pronunciation"

"So, who wanted me to come here? You?" I say louder than I intend.

"I didn't know you until I met you at the station. Why would I send you a letter inviting you here?" she holds her hands in front of her as she speaks.

"I never gave mine a second thought" she regains her composure "The offer gave me a second chance. It couldn't be worse than where I was"

I take a sip from the glass of wine on the table.

"Help yourself" Cindy grins.

"Whoops" I set it down quickly.

"My first name doesn't even begin with a 'C'" she says "It's Scindi with an 'S'. I was named for Scintilla, a long-ago relative. You saw her name in the family tree"

A pause ensues between us as I collect my thoughts and wonder where to go from here.

"You do know that your name begins with a 'C', right?" Scindi smirks.

"I'm aware"

I walk over and hug her.

"Ok. So, I'm done with the paranoia" I say "But I could use some wine"

"You don't want to just drink mine?" she steps back to look at me.

"I'd prefer my own" I smile.

She pours a glass, passing it to me.

I pause before slowly reaching out for it.

"Don't worry, I didn't poison it" she shakes her head.

I sit on the couch hoping she'll do the same which she does. She leans up against me and we sit in silence for a moment sipping our wine.

"After the library, I was in the control room looking through old records" I say.

"Who were you talking to earlier?" she asks.

"Myself, I think"

She stands and walks into the kitchen.

"What do you know about the previous school teachers?" I ask when we're sitting at the island.

"Not much really. I saw a few of their names from finding past lessons. Why?"

"Do you remember the names?"

"Several von Stela's..."

"Did any of them keep personal notes, like a diary?"

"All of them. Mostly their personal thoughts, some notes about the students. Angelina von Stela wrote about life in the village; Layla Brooks about beautiful places she found in the forest; Winter von Stela wrote about the kind and handsome station master; another said what an ass he was.

Dear diary..."

"Were any of them haunted by anything or anyone? Specifically, a young girl. Strange noises and so forth"

"Don't think so" Scindi recoils from me "Some mentioned being shunned by locals. I remember Layla Brooks was teacher for four years; Winter seemed to only be here for a few months; one von Stela teacher from overseas married here but her husband took a liking to another girl. Her notes stop soon after she mentions that"

No clues there.

"What's this about?" Scindi's voice softens.

"Do you know where that family tree I brought back is?" I ask.

"Sure" she gets up, bringing it from the kitchen counter.

"Notice the difference between the two sides" I point at it.

Scindi looks for a moment.

"Ok" she says without taking her eyes of the page "Small families. Lotsa name changes on the left with couples giving birth to a single girl every time. On the right, the von Stela name carries on through Christina's line with male children, again only one to each couple"

She pauses.

"You don't have any kids, right?" I ask Scindi a question I may have asked before.

"None"

"Me neither" I say.

"Other than Suzie" I recall sadly, pausing to collect myself.

Scindi waits for a moment before speaking.

"So..."

"So, we're the last ones"

"Of who?" her face squirrels up.

"Of our families. We die and our lineage dies with us" I lower my voice.

"So, we're assuming that this genealogy shows our grandparents on the last line?" her head tilts to the right.

I try to think of something to say but nothing comes.

"Then there's something else" Scindi goes on "On my side, every couple had one boy so the family name carries on. Until me"

I nod.

"On your side, it's the opposite" she squirrels up her face "All girls, until you"

"Ok" I nod "So, now we know this"

She raises her left hand.

"All the station masters are men, right?" she asks enthusiastically.

"That's right"

"And all the teachers were women from what I've seen and most are von Stela's" she speaks slowly, her hands on the island "What are your predecessors' last names? I mean, your station master predecessors"

"Clovinston, Becker, Fuller, then a couple of Vintassi's..." my voice trails off as I finish my thought.

"Ok" I say, trying to follow her line of thinking "Lotsa similar last names"

I stare at the genealogy.

"Seems the station masters' last names match the names in your family tree" Scindi smiles.

Yes, they do. I'd noticed this, right?

"So, who picks the station masters?" Scindi cocks her head.

I think for a second, think back to my letter signed only with a 'C', the questions I'd asked.

"No one seems to know" I shake my head "Or if they do, they aren't telling me"

"I eventually stopped asking" I add after Scindi doesn't respond.

"Is it a secret cult group or something?" she asks.

"I get the impression it's something that isn't asked" I raise my eyebrows "Or that is better not to ask"

Scindi squints her eyes.

"Where the hell are we?" she shakes her head.

Yes, where are we. Despite my best efforts, I did get entangled in the ages-old mystery and trying to solve a massive creepy riddle.

I love history. I hate riddles.

"And what does this all mean?" Scindi says softly but impatiently.

"I don't know" my voice is quiet.

I shake my confusion to bring my mind back to the moment.

"And where are the female teachers coming from if it's all boys born on the other side?" I lean over the family tree.

"You're the first boy in a long line of girls" she smiles.

"After Hannah's brother Caelyn"

"True, but he didn't have any children, if this is the definitive source"

"Interesting" I look up at her "Whatta ya figure it means?"

"I didn't get that far" she shrugs.

Predecessors

"Does someone want me dead?" I think out loud "Because of something my ancestors did?"

But who would care about me? Does this even make sense? Why would someone care if I died? Clearly there are other Vintassis in the world, judging by previous station masters. It's not like my name wouldn't carry on. And who cared if it did or didn't?

And why Scindi? How are we connected?

"So now what?" I ask.

"Do you realize how often you say that?" she smiles.

I smile back.

After a brief pause, I begin "So now..."

"Ok" she interrupts "Who wants to kill you?"

"I can't imagine anyone here would? Why invite me here to kill me? I was an easy target where I lived before coming here"

"Seems like I'm guilty by my association with you" Scindi says.

"Yes" I reply sheepishly.

"It's almost midnight" she says leaning up against the island.

"Ya"

She sighs, walking to the fridge.

"I'm gonna sit outside for a bit" I say getting up.

"Ok" she heads to the bed.

"Goodnight, Scindi with an 'S'"

Down the stairs, I walk to sit on the bench facing the tracks.

A clear sky, clean air, and bright moon welcome me outside. A pleasant evening. So far.

Too many riddles, macabre photos, mysterious residents.

Perhaps it is easier to believe in fate.

"Who the hell is going to tell me anything?" I say out loud.

"I'll try to"

Feryn's voice speaks from the platform to my left.

"You have a habit of popping up unexpectedly"

"I've been told" he smiles his boyish grin.

"Sit with me, please" I point next to me on the bench.

"What has Caprice told you?" he sits, turning to face me.

"About her and her creepy fiancé. How he committed a terrible sin out of arrogance and was generally a bad man. Probably other things I'm not smart enough to pick up on"

"Ah" he says knowingly.

"Ah?"

"It's interesting the way she told it"

"How so?"

"It's just interesting" he leans back, crosses his arms, staring into the distance.

"Are you alive?" I point at him "Or did you die years ago?"

"I'm alive" he replies confidently "But my story's a different one"

"I'm afraid to ask"

Feryn seems lost in his thoughts, his eyes focused on the forest.

"Sometimes it's better not to know?" I smile.

He turns to me with a wink.

I'll try something more direct.

"What's going on with station masters coming from a limited set of families? Do they only offer the job to you if you have a particular last name?"

"So it seems"

"Care to elaborate?" I glare at him.

"Remember: I know the 'where' not the 'why'"

"So, who is Caprice?"

"I think she already answered that question?"

"Not very well"

"I'd best leave that to her"

"What about Michael?" I reach into my brain for another name.

"What about him?"

"Who is he?"

"He's an attendant of sorts for the Station Master; his family have played that part for generations, since long before my time"

"What's his last name?"

"You know, I'm not entirely sure"

"Is it von Stela? Vintassi?"

"Neither of those" he shakes his head.

"Does he pick who gets offered the job?"

"Definitely not. But my mother knows more about those things than I do"

I stare at him waiting for more details.

"And what happened to the station masters before me?" I feel my eyes widen "Why did so many kill themselves?"

"Some Station Masters took their own life whether out of despair and loneliness or guilt for some committed sin" he says seriously "Some were bad people who did bad things, others were just unfortunate victims. Or so I've heard"

I feel like I've heard this before, or something similar.

"Best not to waste time on this subject" Feryn shakes his head.

"What's in Room 1?"

"Room 1?"

"Here at the hotel"

"You're a smart guy" he cocks his head.

"Obviously not"

I sure don't feel smart.

I don't want to spend my time with Feryn constantly pelting him with questions but he seems my best resource and someone I can trust.

"Who's Hannah?" I keep hoping I'll get an answer.

"Really?" he looks stunned.

"Really" I assure him.

"That I'll have to leave you to"

"Really?" I glare again.

"Really" he replies.

"So, what do I do now?" I ask, exasperated.

"You already know what you want to do"

"But will it matter?"

"Everything we do matters"

"Come on…"

Really?!

"Seriously. Do what feels right to you" he looks at me "You may never know if your choice was the correct one but be satisfied you made a decision. So many leave their fate in the hands of chance"

"That sounds nice" I sigh.

He smiles his boyish grin.

"I just get on the train and leave?" I ask.

"That is your plan, isn't it? Your friend is expecting you to bring her with you"

"Maybe not anymore" I smirk.

"Yes, she still does"

"How do you know these things?" I ask him.

"I'm good at reading people"

"I used to think I was" I drop my head in to my hands.

Feryn's standing somewhere near me.

"What's all this about 'fate'?" I stare off across the tracks into the forest "It seems to come up a lot here"

"Fate and destiny are words we use to explain something we can't otherwise. It's an easy reverse logic to follow but a faulty one. Make your own luck. It's you making the decision, whether you realize it or not"

I turn to look in his direction but he's gone. As usual.

I sit alone for a moment, wondering what to do next. What to do at all.

Back upstairs to Cindy and to bed.

Closing the apartment door, I think about Caprice and Evan united in eternal love.

The bad man

This man looks different than the one I knew as a child with my mother and sisters. That one, I remember, had a fake smile and cared only for himself. This one seems kind and caring and confused. Could he really be the bad man the woman told me about?

Still, I'm alone

I'd thought I'd be loved, have a home, have someone. But still I'm alone.

59 – Bring Her Flowers

I wake up sitting just outside the cemetery fence at Acacia's service. The majority in attendance are women but too many to be just the other servers. I know nothing of her friends in the village; was she truly a loner? Do they perform large ceremonies for everyone who passes?

And why is this taking place at night?

How did I get here in the dark? And what time is it?

I stand up. Moonlight shines down on the scene, stars speckle the sky, the air is dry and crisp and calm.

Absolute silence. Most of the attendees are outside the fence like me but with none of the buzzing like at the ceremony I'd witnessed previously. Everyone stares up at the sky. Acacia is in a vertical casket wearing a dark-coloured dress, her socks burgundy and white horizontal stripes, her eyelids crimson, her shoes dark red, her hair in pigtails with black bows, all striking against her fair skin. The coffin's white interior contrasts sharply with her clothing and the dark wood exterior.

Several lanterns hang from the iron fence illuminating the area.

A man clothed entirely in grey rises from the ground beside her, his hands over his head in a diving position, his eyes closed. His lips are moving but I hear no words. Still, the crowd stares up.

The box slowly lowers until it is horizontal and on the ground.

The man near the coffin lowers his hands until he is pointing at the crowd and speaks in a language I don't understand. His eyes open looking directly into mine.

"Destiny" he says in a deep voice.

Over my shoulder I feel breath on my neck causing me to shiver. I can't see anything around me and am unable to turn to look or to move.

I close my eyes and scream but make no sound.

I wake with a jump next to Scindi, her mouth breathing against my neck. I gently move her away and fall onto my back.

3:50 am

Am I really here? Or will I suddenly appear in my old apartment? Is it really Scindi next to me? Is New Brook West my dream?

"Whatcha doin'?" she mumbles.

"Bad dream" I reply.

"Mmm" she rolls away from me onto her other side.

I walk to the fridge for a glass of water, checking the windows and door as I do, all of which are closed. There's no reason to light candles as that will only create shadows.

I look out the window down onto the tracks. A child is on the rails facing the direction from which the trains come.

The child of whoever lives in the forest? The ghost girl?

The scene feels like a photograph, a painting.

Then she turns her head to me, her featureless face.

I leap back from the pane, setting down my water after nearly dropping it.

Whoa. I catch my breath as my heart races. Ok.

Do I want to look back down there again? What will I see?

My eyes scan the apartment, my ears perked to any noise; Scindi's breathing from across the room is the only sound. Moonlight shines in, creating shadows as it does in the dark corners, bringing my imagination to life. But no one's in here with me, right?

What does it matter who's outside or on the tracks or in Room 1? What does it have to do with me?

And then I slowly approach the window, as if my body is not my own. My feet slide along the floor, not lifting off the ground. Time stands still as I move.

In the reflection in the window, there's a girl with wiry dark black hair in the room behind me. I fall to the floor as I turn to look back, my heart pounding through my chest, my body shaking.

No one's there.

Holy shit.

But there's nobody in the room. I was sure I'd seen a girl.

What is this?

I try to lift my head to look back at the window but my terror keeps me from doing this.

Did I dream that?

I can't just sit here wondering what's in the room with me. There's still no sound in the apartment or outside.

Getting to my feet, I feel groggy, unsteady like I've been drugged.

Was someone at the window? In the room? Nothing's there now.

I shuffle back to bed and pull the covers up tight to my neck. Surprisingly, it doesn't take me long to fall asleep.

This time, there are no dreams.

I wake to a quiet apartment.

Scindi is already up and out of the room when I open my eyes, the smell of fresh coffee and warm pastry wafting through the air. There's a chill in the air, not a great incentive to get up and it's still dark outside, the clearing misty through the window to my right.

I throw on a t-shirt and stagger to the kitchen for a hot beverage and warm muffin. I slowly go to the window, seeing only the empty tracks. I have a distant recollection of looking out here last night but can't remember why.

I shiver looking outside, sipping the coffee to warm my body.

Wondering where Scindi might be, I walk around the apartment peeking out the other windows but see no one. There's no reason to call out for her or go downstairs yet so for now I'll just enjoy the quiet. During the day, the suite is peaceful, free from scratching, shadows, whispers, dark figures. Despite the social and cultural differences, New Brook West could have really been a paradise, a home away from home. Or at least an escape even if only for a time.

I put on shorts and a long-sleeved shirt, walk downstairs with my coffee, and sit on the stone steps facing the clearing in the calm damp air. It's warmer out here than yesterday. So far, so good.

The silent station eases my mind, though I'm careful to take the occasional glance over my shoulder onto the platform. I see no movements in the forest ahead of me or behind me. No figures in the fog. An enjoyable start to the day. The muffin is delicious; was this from Annie? Piper? I'll be sure to thank them both if I see them today.

9:00

Setting down my empty coffee cup, I stand up and take a few steps forward to look back at the station. Had I sketched the building? The tracks? The benches along the wall? I couldn't remember. I should. There's a goldmine of drawing potential here.

I turn back to face into the large open area, a thin fog close to the ground but otherwise a clear view across the clearing to the forest in the distance.

Odd that Scindi'd be up and gone so early.

"Scindi" I call out into the clearing and then again in the direction of the tracks but get no response.

I look up and down the platform and along the tracks but can only muster the courage to peek at Room 1 from a distance. No need to get any closer. I make my way back into the apartment, checking around from the top landing before closing the door behind me.

A refreshing shower then I'll walk into town

It's 10:00 as I leave, locking the door behind me and giving the platform the once-over. A quick stop in the control room confirms what I already know about the train schedule.

The mist has almost entirely lifted, the air crisper than before. It's quiet. I welcome the silence.

Only once I reach the town gates does it occur to me that I'm late to check the board for any scheduled adjustments. A quick visit indicates no news for me so I carry on.

Maybe the blue café will welcome me.

My walk takes me past the market, a route I seldom travel to stay away from prying eyes in general. I wonder if I'll see Sam and Rissa or any of the merchants I recognize, the few villagers who don't want to hex me on sight.

I first catch sight of Mica arranging her produce on tables.

"Hello, Mica" I smile. Mica has a pretty smile and is usually in high spirits.

"Hello, sir" she returns my smile with a beautiful lilt in her voice.

"I would love some of your wonderful fruit, please"

"By all means. Please help yourself"

She hands me a small tightly woven wicker bag, surprisingly soft to the touch.

I pick a few apples, pears, plums, a handful of carrots, and 2 cucumbers.

"I'd like to give you something for this" I ponder what I have of value.

"Not at all, sir. It's a pleasure to see you"

I think of what I have on me, which is nothing, really. I suppose I could offer her a service of some kind in return. I'd offer to help her set up but don't want to intrude into community custom nor get too friendly with women in town, having read and heard of my predecessors.

"Thank you very much" I say walking away, happy from this pleasant encounter.

Piper has an assortment of pies and other delicacies on the back of two wooden carts, bowing when I reach her.

"Good morning, Piper"

"Good morning, sir. Beautiful day, isn't it"

"Yes, it is"

"Any pastries for you or your lady?" she smiles coyly.

Clearly news of my relationship with Scindi has spread.

"I really enjoy your muffins and small cakes"

"Then this'll be just right" she hands me a tray of medium and large buns of all kinds, seemingly covered in plastic wrap.

"Your goods are delicious" I smile.

She notices me touching the protective coat, something I have yet to see on the island.

"I save it for my special customers" she holds my hand for a moment before pulling away with a blush.

"Thank you, Piper. You're very sweet. Thank you for everything"

"Good day, sir"

"Goodbye"

Passing Selena with her array of lamps and lanterns, I spot a small girl in a dark corner behind the vendors.

"Rissa?" I call softly.

"Who's Rissa?" Selena asks me.

"Just a young girl I sometimes see around town"

Selena looks puzzled, returning to her work without another word. I carry on to the café, goods in hand, wishing Selena a nice day.

Past the market, the streets are quieter, the air cooler.

I'd not intended to pick up items until my return trip but am now saddled with all kinds of food which I lug to the café.

Comet greets me as if I've been expected, bringing me juice and coffee a few seconds after I've seated myself, my foodstuffs on the ground at my feet.

I walk to the large pane to look out into the street.

"Everything alright, sir?" Comet stands behind me in a beautiful sky-blue skirt.

"Sure, yes"

"Are you expecting someone?"

"No"

I glance outside but see no one.

"It's odd that…" I begin.

But Comet is gone.

I slink back to the table in the inviting well-lit shop, the bleak skies outside requiring interior illumination in the form of candles placed around the room.

Looking back to the entrance, two women enter without looking my way.

"Mind if I join you?"

Caprice now sits at my left, wearing a white shirt with a yellow skirt.

"Of course" I stammer.

Caprice looks at me with sad eyes.

"What's wrong?" her voice pleads.

"A few things" I'm not sure if I'm confused or angry "You neglect to tell me your fiancé was a station master. You won't tell me why I'm here despite the fact that I think you know. You keep the little girl's identity a secret. You tell me to leave town but not how I should do it. And why wouldn't you tell me you're…"

"You need to make your own decision to stay or to leave. I'd like it very much if you remained in New Brook West but understand if you're not happy here"

She pauses for a second to lean forward.

"There are some secrets that I dare not share in case my voice reaches the wrong ears. I've been elusive to protect us both" her voice becomes softer as she speaks.

"Protect me from what?"

"It is not so easy to get away from New Brook West" she moves closer to me "And you'll not find any help here. The local townsfolk are wary of strangers, especially new Station Masters. In any case, they don't want you to leave"

"Why not?"

"Our history is not a proud one. And it hasn't been kind to Station Masters. Some were wicked men, but most were innocent of all but their thoughts"

"Then why are they invited?" I lean in "Why was I invited?"

"There are reasons which I don't fully understand or even know" she whispers "But there is a reason, a reason for most things, and in this instance for sure"

I can see this is getting me nowhere.

"I heard there were some really bad guys" I say in a quieter voice.

"That's how history will remember them but they too were manipulated, at times. Many were convicted of crimes they perhaps didn't commit. Things aren't always as they appear"

She pauses.

"Yes, I know"

"But, yes, some were bad men" she whispers.

Caprice looks over my shoulder.

"Excuse me, please" she stands "I'll be right back"

"Sure"

I suppress the urge to follow her with my eyes.

None of the customers at the occupied tables look in my direction, and I'm grateful for their lack of interest in me. Despite the bright air inside the café today, the patrons remain obscured, their faces shadowed. A subtle floral scent fills the air, a pleasant aroma.

A thin young woman in a white shirt and pastel blue skirt takes Caprice's seat.

"We just want you to be safe, Colden"

"Who does?"

"We do" she points to the street "We'll do what we can"

I look toward the large front window.

"I just want you to be safe, Colden"

"Ok"

Caprice has returned and now sits across from me.

"Sometimes forces work their way to provoke us to commit acts we wouldn't have otherwise. Sometimes the power of suggestion can nearly move our hands"

Ok.

"But there are, of course, those who are absolutely guilty of their actions and intentions" she adds.

Yes.

"Be mindful of what you see or hear" she goes on.

"Is that what's happening here?" I ask "Am I seeing things that aren't really there?"

She gets up to leave, walking toward the door.

"Caprice. Wait..."

"Sir" Comet says to my right "A note came for you"

She sets a small piece of paper on the table.

I look at the tiny blank document.

"Caprice..."

But she's gone. Of course.

On the back of the paper: 'Meet me at the fountain'

Presumably now.

"Are you leaving, sir?"

"Yes. Goodbye, Comet"

"We're watching you"

"What did you say?" I turn back to Comet.

"I said 'See you soon'"

"Oh. Yes"

Off to the fountain.

The sky is clear, scattered patches of cloud rolling slowly across the sky in the calm air. A few townsfolk go about their business in the street as I exit. I bypass the market, choosing instead to take a series of side alleys I've travelled previously.

I look around me as I walk, wondering at the mysterious note's author, hoping to spot anyone following or watching me, but see no one. How does everyone always seem to know where I am?

I arrive at an empty town square. There's no one at the church, near the cemetery, or in front of the administrative building. And no one at the fountain.

I take a deep breath as I ponder the situation.

Should I have come? Is someone here watching me?

"Just me"

Feryn approaches from behind me.

"Why the note? Why not just come in?"

"I didn't want to interrupt"

"So, why'd you want to meet me?"

"I didn't. But it didn't feel safe for you to be talking with Caprice. I'm surprised she didn't notice"

"Let's come clean shall we. How do you know so much?"

"I'm connected to places and events in ways that even I don't understand. My name means 'compass' in an ancient language, allows me to find places and things that others can't, see things that others don't"

He pauses for a moment.

"My mother watches over events" he goes one "Like a timekeeper or chronicler. Never influencing outcomes but playing an important role nonetheless. I'm sometimes not as good at being impartial"

"What does your mother do?" my voice betrays my fear.

"She bears witness"

"Again..."

"Maybe I'm the wrong person to explain it. I've never been very good at this sort of thing"

I'm envious of Feryn's relaxed manner. Nothing ever seems to phase or upset or confuse him. He always seems ready for the next question, even if he can't answer it.

"So, she writes it down, like in a journal?" my voice is either confused or angry or scared.

"No, not like that"

"Ok" is all I can say, shaking my head.

"We should go to the library" Feryn says.

"What?"

"You heard me" he says sternly.

"Why?" I follow him like a dog as he walks away.

"You need answers"

"I'll say" I hang my head as we set forth.

"The school teacher is very nice" he says.

"Yes. Yes, she is" I try enthusiasm, but fail.

He looks back and smiles, possibly with a wink.

The blue fields, the open spaces, the blacksmith's cottage where I'd met Evan, are all unoccupied. We pass no one which is fine with me, but apparently no surprise to my companion who skips and hums for the duration of our walk. I feel safer in his presence, less concerned of the unknown, of being watched.

Behind the library, the open sea invites long introspective gazes, for which there is no time. The overcast sky has no intention of clearing, murkiness hanging over the dark water like an old coat. Waves crash against the rocks below, breaking the silence, though the wind is light around the structure.

I look down to my left at the rock plateau where I'd seen the girl standing on a previous visit but no one's there this time.

Feryn enters the library without looking back and I follow him in.

There's no one inside the building, which is a mighty relief.

"Are we here to see Brian?" I ask.

"Who?" he stops.

"The librarian"

"There hasn't been a librarian in years, not in my lifetime"

Uh, what?

"So, who've I been talking to?" I raise my voice, looking around as I do.

"I'm not sure. I don't know anyone named Brian" he replies walking away from me.

"I'll be right back" he says, trotting up the stairs to the second level.

There's no one on the main floor that I can see, the library stuffier than I recall. I spot an open book on the table where I'd spent much of my time, so wander over to see if anyone is back in that area.

No one.

"Over here" a young woman's voice whispers down an empty aisle.

"I didn't mean to intrude…"

"Not at all, Colden" her lilt is soft and delicate.

"Do I know you?"

A young fair-skinned woman wearing a light blue dress with white trim standing near the back wall approaches me. Her feet glide toward me as if she were floating instead of walking.

"You're nearly there" she whispers.

My body freezes, my eyes like a deer in the headlights.

"Bring her flowers, Colden"

"Her flowers? To who?"

"Her flowers are in the tree" she replies calmly.

Not the tree again.

"But the letters have to be correct" her smooth voice goes on.

"The letters?" I try to think of a question.

More letters.

"Who ya talking to, son?"

Brian's voice behind me.

I turn to him then quickly realize I've taken my eyes off the woman who has vanished when I face where she'd been standing.

"Hello?" I say meekly but get no reply.

"Hello?" I try even more softly this time; again nothing.

I catch my breath as I glance around me hoping to spot the woman in white and blue but see no one. She looked similar to but not exactly like the one I've seen before, that I saw at the Grey Stone and who gave me that small box.

Silence in the library.

A shiver runs down my spine as I consider who or what might be watching me. A deep breath as I collect myself, my head drooping forward.

"You ok, friend?" Brian's voice sounds genuinely concerned.

Who is this guy, anyway?

"Who are you, really" I ask him sternly, immediately regretting my reaction.

"Whatta ya mean?" he leans back in his chair, crossing his arms.

"There's been no librarian for years, so who exactly are you?"

"A friend" he leans forward.

"Ok, friend. What's my next step?"

"Seems like you want to leave, and I can't say that's a bad move"

"Ok. So how?"

"Good luck, friend" Brian nods.

I gather my items, turning to look upstairs for Feryn but don't see or hear him.

When I look back to the desk, Brian has vanished.

For a moment, my eyes lock on the scene out the large back window's view of the water. The never-ending emptiness beyond the island seen through the building's eyes. The vast ocean, an ominous yet calm dark blue expanse, grey clouds above it. An infinite barrier surrounding me like walls around a fortress, trapping me in this prison.

I pause as I take in a view that I seldom acknowledge during my library visits, the ocean like fear all around me. My vision gets lost as I fall into a daze, hypnotized by the dark water and sombre sky. My mind is hazy staring at the solemn scene.

A bright flash in the distance of what must be lightning breaks my trance, a faraway rumble following a few seconds after.

"How'd it go?"

Feryn's voice behind me.

Brian's still nowhere in sight.

"More of the same" I say, dejected.

"It'll all make sense soon enough" he smiles.

"I hope so"

"Ready to go?" he says cheerily.

"Sure" I stretch and we walk out the door.

"How did you know I'd get answers?" I ask once we're outside.

"I didn't but I hoped you would" he replies confidently.

"Where are we going?"

"Home. At least I am" Feryn says.

"I still haven't found Scindi"

"She's likely at her house" Feryn says walking ahead.

"How do you know that?" I ask.

"I don't, for sure, but it's likely"

We walk in silence away from the library until we reach a path heading off to the left which I hadn't noticed on my previous trips.

"You'll get to her place faster along there" Feryn points.

"Where did this come from?" I ask, stunned at its sudden appearance.

"It's always been there. Remember what I said about knowing where to look" his face is either serious or smiling, I can't tell which.

"Yeah" I say "Thanks, Feryn"

"Of course" he replies trotting off toward town.

"Of course..." I mumble to myself.

Mid-afternoon and hunger hits me so I sit for a moment to scarf down some of the food I'm carrying. Not an ideal lunch but enough to get me to Scindi's. For a few minutes I wander the trail through the tall wild grass. Birds fly about, landing on branches or pecking at whatever they fancy in the meadow. I enter a sparse forest, the trees here shorter than those around the station, shrubs interspersed amongst them. The river meets me on my left, surely the one running behind Scindi's place; staring out, I can see where it meets the sea at a narrow estuary. Water flows past alternately rapidly and slowly, the water clear. The narrow path I'm on is not well-travelled.

I soon meet up with the trail to Scindi's that I've walked before and I'm happy I'll be seeing her now. My pace slows as I take in my surroundings.

Is that movement up ahead among the trees? I hope not. I never know if the sounds are a product of my imagination or actual noises nor if these should concern me if they are the real thing.

Scanning the landscape, I'm unable to pick up what I thought I'd seen.

Getting down on my knees, I look around near the base of the plants and trees for any motion but see none. Concerned about standing and revealing my location, I wait, concealed, hoping nothing will appear.

There's no noise and no movement for several seconds as I stare ahead and around me and all is quiet.

In any case, I can't stay here.

I get up and make for Scindi's house.

It's 4:00 and the sun's descent carries it just below the top of the tallest trees casting long shadows. I'd not planned to be out so late as to need artificial light; I recall Selena's lamps which would be most welcome now.

I can't be far from Scindi's, the landscape by this time taking on a more familiar appearance.

A few moments more and I'm on the path behind her place. Within a minute or two I reach the unlit house, the small clearing by now fully in the shade. There appears to be no one home so I knock without getting a response.

I see no one in the forest and have no intention of yelling out.

The smell of pine and wood and grass.

No lights, no breeze, no noises. I wait in silence catching my breath.

I'm simultaneously fearless and terrified of the unknown that surrounds me. Am I being watched? Have I been followed?

Should I wait for Scindi? If so, where?

I'm still in front of the house. Dusk will soon be replaced by dark and I'll be sitting here alone waiting on Feryn's hunch that Scindi will come here. A chill creeps under my clothes, under my skin. I lean against the wall near the corner.

A tug at the back of my shirt makes me jump.

No one's there. Maybe it got stuck on something loose along the wall.

Or maybe not.

I set off to try the school, hoping to find her and get back here or to the station.

A short walk, without any sights or sounds brings me to the vast clearing, my destination across the open area.

The door to the school itself is closed so I walk around to catch sight of any light through the windows. As I circle the building, a faint glow emerges from inside, light flickering off the glass and the interior walls like a candle or a match. I slowly made my way back around to the front, unsure if I want to go inside or just keep on back to the station.

I see movement in the trees: what looks like a tall woman. Gradually, she recedes into the thick foliage, disappearing, as if she'd never been there. A villager who doesn't want to be seen lurking about the school? The forest's mysterious resident?

I'm sure I not iced her green eyes.

I shake my head and carry on.

Night's fall continues, the moon not visible from where I'm standing.

And I don't dare scan the forest around me in case I spot someone.

The light inside the school is now gone, a window partially open above me. Do I want to wait and see or just get out of here? My mind can't decide. Will I find Scindi inside if I enter or something else entirely?

I press my back up against the wall, to the right of the door. Silence. Then I hear a scratching on the floor inside, like something being dragged across the wood.

And the sound of the door opening.

I hurry off to the side, peering around the corner. The door is ajar, but no further motion in or out, no noises. No light.

I creep up the steps to poke my head into the school and, seeing no one, step inside.

The desks are neatly arranged in a single circle around the teacher's larger table at its center. There are two piles of paper, neatly positioned to one side of the teacher's table, an envelope on the other.

I look around the room, above me, and under the desks but see no one so grab the envelope and leave out the door, closing it behind me.

Outside darkness is upon me, faint moonlight casting a glow around the building and clearing, just enough to get my imagination racing. I jog for a bit away from the school and into the forest, turning left at the fork in the trail to arrive in the station's clearing in short order.

Light glows inside the apartment windows, several lamps on the platform also lit offering me a warm welcome. I see no one around the station, though I can never be sure. My approach is slow in the hopes of not being caught unawares. The last of the day's light makes a murky blend of reds and purples behind a thin cloud cover in the west.

Nearing the station, I look both ways along the building for any silent visitors in the shadows. Despite being in a well-lit area, my anxiety rises with thoughts of hidden eyes and grey girls but I see neither so climb the stairs to the platform level. I take a furtive glance at Room 1's closed door, as I keep a maximum distance crossing the stone floor. I stop to take it all in with no sounds coming from the hotel or the rooms beneath my suite.

I walk to the benches facing the tracks.

The lamps along the wall are all lit, but there's no one in either direction or across the tracks that I can see. I snuff the candles lighting the wall facing the tracks. The stillness is oppressive, the silence like an aching in my heart. No lights are on in the control room and the door is locked. Up the stairs to the apartment, the envelope I collected at the schoolhouse still in my hand.

Scindi, lying on the sofa, stirs as I enter.

"Welcome back" she says in a sleepy voice.

"Thanks"

"You look like…" she says.

"Ya"

"How was your day?" she comes to sit at the island.

"Ok, I guess. More of the same. You?"

"Went to my place for a bit, then the school, then back here"

"When were you at the school?" I set down my juice glass louder than I'd intended.

"This afternoon. Why?"

"No reason. I was in the area and didn't see you"

I glance towards the door hoping I won't hear a knock.

"It's interesting" Scindi says without looking up "Our names have exactly the same letters rearranged"

"Yours has no 'V'"

"It does if I include 'von' in my last name" she says proudly.

I think for a moment.

She's right.

"Well done" I say.

"Thank you" she nods.

Looking outside, I see that night has arrived at the train station.

"Is everything ok?" she asks from across the island.

"Sure" I look around the room as I speak, scanning the windows for unwelcome visitors, ghostly eyes.

"I'm bagged" I say, a true statement.

"Ok" she walks back to the couch with some juice of her own.

I slowly undress in the warm apartment, throwing my clothes on a chair near the bed.

"Oh" I say walking over to her "I almost forgot. I found this at the school"

I drop the envelope next to her on the couch and make my way to bed.

I'm woken in the dark by movement on the bed. It's night inside and out, no lit lamps or candles in the apartment, Scindi asleep next to me. I'm facing the window as my eyes adjust to the darkness. The moon shines far off to the left and away from me allowing me to see outside it closer to the bed but creating a reflection near the foot.

The room is perfectly quiet.

I raise my head without sitting up entirely.

Holy shit. Someone's sitting at the foot of the bed facing away from me. A girl? My body freezes. She's totally still. I hope she's facing away from me or else she knows I'm awake. Long jet-black hair hangs down her back; her arms must be in her lap because they're not at her sides. She's not making a sound and I can't even hear her breathing. Whatever she's wearing is dirty, a dress, I think.

I wait, hoping I haven't made a sound.

How long has she been there?

Her head turns toward the window. She's a child. I barely feel her weight on the bed. Have I moved? I hope not. Did I move the blankets when I saw her? She hasn't looked in my direction yet so I stay as still as I can without closing my eyes.

I wait for her to move or speak, but neither happens. For a sound, but all is silent.

I want to call for help, but who would come.

Scindi's asleep and I wish for her to stay that way.

My heart races as I try not to breathe, not to blink, not to twitch.

Hopefully she doesn't know I'm awake and terrified.

Who the hell is she?

She stares outside for a few seconds before turning her gaze forward once again to look away from me. There's nothing for me to do and no place to go so I sit silent and still. Watching her and wonder if she knows I'm awake and afraid.

An eternity passes before I hear another sound, like wind blowing across the station. She looks outside and I look to the window but see nothing. When I look back, the girl is gone.

60 – On the edge of the bed

Silent and still, her body creeps inside so she can be closer to see his movements, hear his breathing, watch him. Her body is frail, weak, and tired; her spirit weary, longing for rest; her heart heavy; her thoughts melancholy. Her movements are slow and crude.

She sits on the edge of the bed facing into the room. The sleeping woman doesn't move. He's awake behind her, though he doesn't think she knows.

61 – Sanya

I wake at sunrise, stiff from an uncomfortable sleep. A dream of someone in the room that I try to recall but can't piece together the details.

It's become difficult to tell the difference between imagination and reality.

I sit up and slowly scan the areas of the apartment that I can see.

The quiet suite makes me melancholy though I'm not sure why, the warmth filling me with sadness. So much has happened since my arrival in New Brook West, a town not on any map nor in any reference book. I exhale and walk to the kitchen as I think on what my time at the station.

It's 8:00 and Scindi is sleeping so I start coffee, the smell filling the air.

A knock at the door.

I hurry to get there before my visitor disappears but don't make it in time, finding only an envelope on the landing at the top of the steps.

'Change to train schedule. Details on the board'

Ok. I'd better get there quickly in case this is relevant to this morning's events. Damn. I relaxed morning would have been most welcome.

I hustle into some clean-ish clothes and make my way into the clearing through the clear cool air. Darkness still hangs over the station, the multi-coloured sky taking shape in the east. There's no one outside, at least not on this side of the building. The open space looks so different without the murky fog, like a field waiting to celebrate a festival on a sunny afternoon and a star-filled evening. But even now, I know what might be hiding in the black forest or out of sight much closer to me and shiver at this thought.

The path across from me is evident even in dusk's obscurity, a quick jog from where I am. I keep this pace through the trees until I reach the small clearing outside the town gates. If any noises had accompanied me through the forest, I hadn't noticed, focused as I was on my run and covered by the sound of my steps and breathing.

I pause just before the lit lanterns to glance around the square, the fountain, the cemetery. It's all so quiet.

A couple walking through the plaza ignores me as they turn down a street and out of sight. There's no one else here.

An envelope is tacked up on the board addressed to the Station Master.

'Come to East' reads the note inside.

I'm not keen on this and it obviously has nothing to do with the train. Right? Or maybe it has something to do with my planned escape on the train. Shit.

I scour the board for any other notes but find none.

I consider my options. I'd best go see what this is about to ensure I've not been found out.

Off I go to New Brook East with a chill in my bones.

I glide through the alleys to the far northeast corner of town with the softest movements possible. Few people are out and about at this time, allowing me to slip past discretely. Doors and windows are shut, exterior lights extinguished or not yet lit, streets and back roads clear of any debris or trash or people. I often wonder at boarded-up doors and windows of presumably vacant spaces and what they once held or now hide. I hope no prying or wicked eyes watch me from the dark recesses but know that this isn't guaranteed. I stay close to the walls, avoiding the corners.

The trail beyond West's buildings winds about and I wonder how I'd remembered to come this way, how I'd been able to spot the paths I took, if someone was helping me. Feryn?

No movement or noises break the calm during my ten minutes of labyrinthine wandering through the forest, when I emerge in a clearing which can only be what was once New Brook East

The charcoal grey sky overhead casts gloom onto the vacant community, even as night turns to day. Rubble and waste fill what would have once been streets and alleys. Some buildings lack a roof, others walls, others windows or doors, some all of these. It's sad to behold what had once been a home to so many be reduced to this state. I wonder how it looked at its most beautiful.

I don't recognize anything from my visit with Acacia, alone in the quiet ruins.

The sun has risen but hides behind the dismal cloud cover, its glow muted. But there's no fog in the glade that is East, the clear air sharpening the tragic ruins. Even the trees surrounding the scene are grave, their branches stiff and solemn.

A sombre sight.

"You came" a soft voice speaks, but I see no one.

"Yes" I say out loud.

Behind me, a woman sits inside the remnants of four low walls on an uneven makeshift bench comprised of a wood plank and two rocks, the left side higher than the right. A fire burns in a raised pit in front of her.

A small black hat on her perfectly combed jet-black hair, a sleek white shirt, and tight black pants on her slim legs. She looks at me with black pupils and a flawlessly white smile. A striking figure.

"Who…"

"I'm Sanya" she says, her voice sad but stern, "You've met my son"

"Who…" I start again, but don't finish my sentence.

"I kept you a seat, Colden" she waits on her crooked bench.

Who is this woman? She's seated but looks as though she'd be very tall if she stood up, and very slim. A most unusual character.

Have I made a mistake by coming? Should I get the hell out of here?

I wait a safe distance back from her for a moment as I try to think things through. Where would I go if I ran? And would I get away?

Is this Feryn's mother?

"You're quite safe with me" she says poking the fire.

Part of me believes her and the other part doesn't know what else to do so I sit next to her on the higher end of the board.

"You've not understood everything you need to" her voice lowers "I can't tell you anything but can perhaps show you the past. And hope that's enough"

"Show me?" I lean towards the fire's warmth.

"You've seen some already" she says without looking up.

I have?

"There was a prophecy" her dark eyes fix on me "A prophecy told to another"

"What prophecy?"

"One that I can only observe. My role is impartial, detached, a spectator"

"I just want to leave" my voice rises unintentionally.

"I know you do"

"But you won't tell me if that's the right choice or how to do it?"

"Correct" she nods, her face is expressionless, her pupils smaller than before.

Is one of my ancestors or a previous station master involved in what's happening now? I'm not sure if I say this or just think it.

I forget my seat is backless and nearly fall off the bench.

"You've met her, many times"

"So, who…"

"The story is a long one to tell" she pokes the fire again with the metal rod in her hand.

What is this? And who is this woman? What's she gonna tell me?

"Remember, Colden: I observe. I don't influence outcomes"

"So, what exactly do you do?" I ask out of frustration.

"I perform a role you wouldn't understand" she looks at me sadly.

The fire is warm and I lean in closer, sliding nearer to the woman as I do. I can't imagine what role this unusual woman performs or why I wouldn't understand but won't pursue these topics.

My eyes wander around the community, wondering what could have made the residents leave and what kept people from coming back. Maybe she'll tell me that.

"Perhaps there's wisdom to be found. See in the fire"

I look into the flames, as red sparks explode inside them. The fire flashes brightly, my eyes wincing at the burst of orange light.

The flash shocks me; when my eyes adjust, I'm standing inside a small house; not just looking at it but actually there.

"What am I looking at?" I turn to ask my companion but she's no longer with me and I'm alone in this home.

How did I get here? The last thing I remember is sitting next to her.

I'm now standing so take a slow step forward.

The room looks familiar.

The sun shines in through a large window but I can't see through it to the outside. The room's light green walls, the simple yet stylish furniture, the cozy and warm atmosphere. A man, a woman, and two young girls sit around a table eating, each of them dressed nicely but not overly so. They seem happy to be together, the girls talking and giggling, the adults smiling at them and each other.

I'm actually standing in this room with them. How do they not see me near the wall?

How do I explain why I'm in their home?

"I'm sorry, I..." I start to say holding out my hands but they don't move to look my way or seem to notice or hear me at all. How can they not? I want to yell out, to wave my arms, to formally announce myself but decide against any of these actions. I choose instead to quietly creep out of the room backwards along the wall and notice a door to my right leading outside onto a small patio.

I stop at the top of the stairs leading to the ground to look out at a small community of familiar buildings though I can't recall or imagine why I recognize them.

Where the hell am I and how did I get here? Am I high from something the woman put in the fire?

Then I realize I'm still holding open the door into the house.

The inside has become a small circular laboratory, bottles lining the walls, liquids and herbs in vials and bowls on a round central table. The woman I'd seen in the previous room moves about looking at the coloured waters, plants, and seeds, muttering to herself. The area is poorly lit though still has a warm quality.

How did I get from the house to here? The woman hasn't noticed me. Am I actually here with her now? Where is this? I shake my head and focus my eyes but my location doesn't change.

'I'm really sorry" I start "I don't know..."

But the woman doesn't react to my words at all. I step back against a wall to be as unobtrusive as I can, though there's no place to really be out of sight. My vision remains focused on my surroundings as well as on her. She stares intently at several items and papers in front of her, mixes two liquids together, adds a yellow powder, and stirs the blend, satisfied with her creation. A candle extinguishes behind her though the area seems no darker. She carries on examining items around her while I'm keeping as quiet as I can without making a move.

Two teenage girls enter and stand next to the woman. She shows them plants, herbs, and liquids, talking as she does, as if providing instruction, though I can't hear the words. The younger dark-haired blue-eyed girl eagerly follows her mother's instructions, talking to her as she mixes these together, focused as she is on her task. The older blonde green-eyed girl creates concoctions using a different blend of ingredients than her sibling, away from the other girl and the woman. Her clandestine activities seem to go unnoticed by both of them, the green-eyed girl squinting as she creates combinations unbeknownst to her companions. She hides her potions beneath her shirt as she leaves.

I move around and as far away from them as I can, careful not to knock anything over. I feel like I'm watching a movie or that I'm high. Or both.

The girl and the woman hug tightly, the woman gently weeping, the girl muttering something softly. A small light blue songbird flies in through an open window and perches on the ledge to watch them.

I try not to listen and am grateful I can't make out the words between them, intruding as I am on their private moment.

I decide this is my opportunity to leave so I quietly back out the door nearest to me and I'm outside in the dark in a small clearing surrounded by trees.

Whoa. I'm dizzy. I put my hands on my knees to keep from falling over.

I'm facing a young blue-eyed woman in a light blue cloak crouching next to what must be an open grave.

The scene is bathed in moonlight and I can clearly see her outline and features. I kneel in the tall grass to do my best to not be seen.

Now where am I? For a moment, I watch not wanting to disturb such a solemn occasion.

The young woman raises her head and stares into the forest, singing softly in a beautiful lilted voice as I realize it's the young daughter, now older. Her mournful tune fills the air as I realize the woman in the previous room must have been her mother and the girl her sister. After a moment, she quietly leaves.

My body is still bent low to remain out of sight. Was she alone here? Wherever 'here' is.

This place looks familiar though I can't imagine why. I creep toward the opening in the ground. Inside is a woman's body, arms at her sides, eyes closed. Her mother?

I close my eyes out of respect for the scene. When I open them, I'm standing in what must be a schoolyard.

Again, I drop to the ground to quickly get out of sight, unsure of where I am or how to explain my presence here if I'm seen, too scared to make a run for it; where would I go?

The older girl from the laboratory, her green eyes betraying her identity, is speaking with two other girls, showing them vials of liquid. Each of them takes a small tube from her, drinking the potion in a single swallow. The girls return to the building as a group.

When everyone's back inside, or at least not in the yard, I turn around, still sitting on the ground.

I'm in a cemetery, a large one surrounded by a black iron fence, with a sombre crowd dressed in black.

The church cemetery in West? I kneel behind a gravestone.

What the hell is this?

I recognize the two girls from the schoolyard who'd consumed the liquid, their bodies displayed vertically against the fence. I spot the older girl, her green eyes watching from a distance as their bodies are laid to rest.

I focus my eyes and turn to my left where my companion calmly looks into the fire.

"What am I…"

"Look" she interrupts without moving.

Is this playing out like it had with Feryn, where I'm watching yet unable to interact with those in the scenes in front of me? The irony occurs to me as I remember what the woman had said about the observer role she performs. The air clears. I'm in a house or a laboratory in the corner of a larger room, shelves and tables filled with liquids, powders, plants, and instruments. The room is dim, without windows and lit only by two candles.

A man walks into town, speaking timidly to anyone he sees.

I step away from the building I just left and sit on the ground near a patch of bush.

The green-eyed young woman from the forest, watches him from a distance, following his movements. The man shyly leaves the small crowd around him and, noticing the woman, approaches her. She whispers in his ear to which he smiles timidly. She brings him to her cabin, removing her clothing.

I walk away, knowing what will come next.

These must somehow be scenes from the past that the strange woman who invited me to East can conjure in the fire.

A noise behind me makes me turn back to the house from the previous scene. The woman is outside, returning to her home, bringing herbs and liquids of various colours in vials.

I walk to the window to get a closer look, braver now that I feel a spectator rather than a participant. At least that's what I hope.

She's combining components into an elixir which she offers to the man whom she'd invited into her home earlier. He drinks the potion, gets dressed, and leaves the cabin, heading into the center of town where he is surrounded by a great crowd. He speaks passionately to a group who cheer as he waves. The man walks past me into the woman's house. He exits, her hand in his, bringing her with him to a larger house in the center of town. The woman smiles lovingly.

Scenes speed past me, like time on fast-forward, stopping when I'm standing a short distance from the man I'd just seen.

These sights feel like hallucinations and I struggle to stay focused.

Is there some kind of drug in the fire that is making me see this, like visions?

The man walks about town in the presence of enthusiastic villagers, always with a charisma I can sense even as an observer. Events flash past and then slow as he follows a young woman into her home, then a different one, then another one. These events have obviously occurred over a period of time.

Night falls.

The sun rises on the man's funeral. The green-eyed woman who had initially invited him into her home and given him the flask stands well back, her arms crossed, her expression stern.

The crowd disperses and the scene fades to night.

I step back and away from everything to sit and rest for a minute, putting my hands on my knees and dropping my head.

When I look up, I'm in a black cave, the walls shiny smooth stone, the floor dark red, flickering candles spread around the room creating the sensation of motion.

This place doesn't look friendly.

I'm no longer sure I'm just an observer.

I do not want to be here.

I try to back away to stand near a wall, behind something but no matter how I move I'm still in the same place. I don't want to make too many moves to draw attention to myself so crouch close to the ground as still as I can be.

Now I'm afraid, with no place to hide and no visible exit.

A naked woman is kneeling in front of a statue? A man? A demon? The woman's naked body must be frozen in this temperature; sitting on her bare feet, her head is angled up, looking at the creature's black face, its white eyes staring down at her. I can't make out the standing figure's features, just that he seems much larger than the woman in front of him. Her head moves toward him. He either nods or shakes his head; I can't tell which. He hands her a piece of paper that she looks at first with surprise then curiosity.

He speaks words to her that I don't hear and she replies.

He nods as he speaks again.

I really don't want to be here.

Please let me go back.

I close my eyes and my wish is granted as I'm now standing in a dark forest, disoriented once more.

Where is this, now?

The woman from the cave, sits on a rock alone, a lantern at her side, looking at a piece of paper that appears to have been torn from a book, tracing lines with her fingers on the pages. The lamp's light barely extends beyond her as if unable to shine out. She mutters words I don't hear as she pores over the document.

I'm standing behind her but closer than I'd like and no longer feel invisible so try to slowly back away into the forest.

Her head turns and her bright green eyes look right at me, squinting as if trying to make me out. I'm standing as still as a stone and no longer breathing as she relaxes her gaze, returning to her documents.

She drops a potion which explodes bright green on the ground creating a thick cloud of smoke and I'm once again in front of the house from the initial scene.

Am I back where I started?

I'm drawn to the building, as if I'm being called to come inside and I can't resist, though I wish I could.

The house's interior is simple yet pleasant and welcoming. To the right, the same light green walls and simple furnishings I recall from when I'd first been here moment ago, a large window looking out on the other buildings; to the left, a closed door. A hallway leads to the back of the house.

I quietly enter the room.

On my right where a woman in a light-blue cloak and a clean-cut man in sharp attire sit with a young girl and a younger boy.

I crouch down, which is all I can think of doing. They never seem to see me but I'd still rather not be standing in plain sight.

Am I still a spectator?

I'm as quiet and still as I can be, anxious, yet hopeful that they don't know I'm here, as seems to be the case.

They're smiling and appear happy. The man rises, poking the fireplace, mesmerizing me, stunning me.

"No"

Where's that coming from?

"They cannot see" I hear the woman I can't see speak in my ears "Just watch"

A bright flash causes the embers to spark.

This is absolutely surreal and I'm beginning to wonder if I'm high.

Although reassured by my companion's words, I'm still more than confused by what I'm seeing and where I am; my head is dizzy, as if drug-addled, and my movements are slow.

Outside it's daytime. The red-cloaked daughter, now in her early teens, stands before a kneeling older man in the green-walled room; he takes her by the hand into a side room. The girl emerges from the room showing early signs of pregnancy as the man leaves out the front door toward a carriage. She returns to the room, exiting it a moment later with an infant girl, the older man no longer in the house. Although this has clearly taken place over a longer period, the series of events is plain to me.

I back away to lean against the wall.

A boy a few years younger than the young mother walks out of the house with the girl and her toddler daughter, an older couple close behind them. The girl and the child enter a small cabin in front of the larger home, closing the door behind them.

"And then…"

I think it's my companion's voice, but I can't be sure.

The scene swirls around me like a whirlpool of white and black, stopping in front of a building with an open front.

Inside what appears to be a blacksmith's shop, the boy from the previous scene, now a young man, works with an older man.

I back away, leaning against a nearby building as I do.

A third man, wearing the station master's jacket, enters and talks to the young blacksmith. The men leave the smithy and I follow them to a bar on the other side of the forest. After a moment, they come out laughing, heading off in the direction of the young man's home.

"Turn…"

I turn around to see the man in the station master's jacket. He's speaking with the young mother in the red dress, on the edge of the forest. He's smiling, leaning in to kiss her.

I step behind a tree.

She pulls away, holding up her hand as he begins talking.

He's noticeably angry. The girl looks scared and runs away quickly leaving the man to seethe alone.

He lets out a loud yell that causes me to cover my ears and close my eyes.

When I open them, I'm outside at night in front of the house with the green living room.

This is like a carnival ride that won't end. But I always feel compelled to keep up with the characters I see, to stay close and observe their actions.

As anxious as I am, I also want to see where this leads, how it all ends.

I follow the young blacksmith to the other side of town.

He enters the smithy where the older man is working and goes to the back of the shop out of my sight. He appears a short while later with blood on his hands.

I step around the corner of a building and out of sight.

He cleans himself in a water barrel outside the shop before heading off through the forest and arriving at a bar. I follow quietly behind, standing against a wall after entering.

He's greeted by his friend with a drink. They talk as other patrons come and go. The young blacksmith appears nervous, hanging back from the others and not revelling as heartily as on his previous visit. A green-eyed woman I recognize, who'd been standing against the wall, approaches him and whispers in his ear before leaving the bar.

I follow the young man and his friend when they exit the tavern, staggering toward the young blacksmith's house.

He bids his friend farewell and enters his house. The man in the station master's jacket seems ready to leave before changing his mind and entering the girl's cabin.

I want to warn her but my mouth makes no sound, my feet rooted to the ground.

I yell for help but no words come out.

He emerges from the small house, adjusting his clothes as he does; it's obvious to me what has taken place. He vanishes into the darkness.

My eyes don't follow him.

I want to go to the girl but am unable to move.

I try to yell out but my voice is mute.

No.

I close my eyes.

When I open them, I'm standing outside the house with the green living room at dusk. I step to the side and around the corner of the patio, hopefully out of sight, if such a move on my part is necessary.

The sun rises and the parents exit their house, heading off in separate directions. A girl in a red dress comes out of her small cabin with her young daughter and an infant. She greets another girl wearing a yellow dress with a warm hug and they talk on their way into the main house.

Is that...?

The girl who'd been wearing the red dress emerges shortly after, wearing a knee-length grey skirt and a tight-fitting long-sleeved white shirt, heading toward the forest.

I follow her to an establishment in a small clearing, a location far more welcoming than where her brother and his friend had been drinking.

The outside is constructed entirely of stone and mortar with windows of metal and wood, a chimney on both the back and left side wall.

I walk in and am soon lost in the crowd, positioning myself near a wood pillar.

The young mother, obviously a serving girl, joins two similarly clad ones, making her way to the bar where a tall man dispenses alcohol. The crowd includes men of all ages, some military, some merchants, some general labourers, some regular townsfolk. She scurries about distributing beverages to her clients, many of whom become increasingly intoxicated.

One fellow grabs her by the waist, setting her in his lap to her mild protests. He laughs, running a hand up and down her back as she squirms unsuccessfully to break free.

I'm not sure I'm the right one to step in here even if I could.

Fortunately, one of the military men rises from his seat, walks to the man, grabs his shoulder, and pulls him backwards onto the ground, allowing the serving girl to stand. The drunk customer gets up in a fury and rushes his aggressor but the soldier is too quick for this lame attack and soon the man is on his knees with an arm behind his back. The soldier whispers something in his ear then allows him to get to his feet. He speaks quickly to the waitress and sits back down in his seat, the soldier returning to his place. She runs to express her gratitude to the heroic man who simply nods in acknowledgment. The soldier looks familiar though I can't imagine why.

The young woman exits the building and I follow her through the forest presumably back to her home. She collects her two children from the main house, hugging the woman in the yellow dress who disappears into the maze of buildings. The young mother extinguishes the interior lights on the larger house and enters her smaller cabin, a single oil lamp remaining lit on the main building.

I sit for a moment on a piece of wood large enough to accommodate me.

Her brother and his friend arrive in the clearing and talk briefly, the brother heading into the larger house, dousing the outside lamp as he does. His friend decides once more to enter the young woman's cabin, my voice mute, my body paralyzed, and I'm unable to rise from my seat or to shout my warning.

I watch the moon move across the sky until he comes out heading off down the path.

The young woman emerges in the morning, now with a third daughter.

Not again.

The scenes are so vivid, playing out before me alternately at great speed and then slowly, making me dizzy. It's difficult to follow.

I sit at one end of a wooden bench.

I'm back in front of the fire with my companion, the ruined village around me. I only have a moment before an invisible hand grabs my shoulder spinning me around.

I'm now outside the large house. Breathless, I step to the side out of sight.

The green-eyed woman who'd previously whispered to the young blacksmith in the bar, knocks at the door, glancing my way for a moment as she does.

Oh, no.

The young man answers, and she hands him a vial of dark red liquid then turns and leaves without looking back.

Darkness falls on the house as I sit on a rock, exhausted, like running a marathon high.

The sun rises on a group of men, official in appearance, arriving at the house. One of them points behind the building, calling the husband and wife outside.

I walk around the house from the other side to watch the scene unfold.

Three other men come forward with shovels, digging near a tree where a man's dead body is removed from the earth. The couple's hands are bound. The group's leader holds up a vial with a small amount of dark red liquid in the bottom, following the others into the center of the community.

My body spins several times like on a carnival ride, making me dizzy.

I stop abruptly in front of the couples' house.

Now what?

The young mother emerges from her small cabin and meets her friend who takes the children back inside. I follow her across the settlement to a circular building.

She enters and I make my way to a window to look in, careful to check that no one's outside watching me.

Her parents are standing inside a circle created by six men evenly spaced around them. The men take turns speaking, and gesturing at the couple and at the crowd assembled inside. The group stands back from the scene, silent and still, their faces sombre.

I hear quiet voices from people inside and out but never does the couple make a sound.

Either no one sees me or they're ignoring me which is fine by me.

When all six men are seated, they point in unison to the pair, and then stand as a group, exiting the building. The silent couple are escorted out, their hands bound with rope in front of them.

I watch them leave as the groups inside and outside quietly disperse.

"And then..."

Is that my companion's voice? I don't see her.

Another bright light flashes blinding me for a moment.

When I open them, I'm at the edge of a small clearing at dusk. I step back into the forest's cover to watch the scene.

Through the trees, a young woman in a red cloak and two young girls wearing pink and purple dresses respectively, are all kneeling. The woman places a plaque flat on the ground above a fresh pile of dirt, another pile adjacent to it. The young blacksmith, his face solemn, stands with his head bowed. The green-eyed woman who'd visited him at the house earlier is in the forest across the clearing from me, watching the gathering, the setting sun behind her. A girl dressed in black steps out from the trees for a second, then disappears into them, vanishing.

Is this the young mother with her daughters and her brother?

I don't hear any words or sounds of any kind so keep still.

The man nods at the ground, turning to leave along a narrow path behind him.

The green-eyed woman who'd stood in the trees is no longer there.

The sun rapidly sets and darkness sets in, the only light the stars in the sky above me.

I look up as the sun rises to my right.

I'm now in front of the home of the deceased couple.

How did I get here?

I step away and crouch low to watch, unsure what else to do.

The young mother brings two girls into the main house, the children now nearly ten.

Where's the third one?

I follow her as she sets off walking to the tavern where I'd seen her working as a server. Time rolls by quickly as I sit alone and undisturbed at a table.

At the end of the night, her soldier waits for her outside the bar, walking her home when she exits. Upon reaching her cabin, he makes no attempt to express any affections, though it appears she wants him to. He heads off into the forest once she enters her home.

I wonder if I should be learning something from what can only be historical scenes? What does this all mean?

I feel my companion's presence near me.

"What is..." I try to form a question.

"Keep looking" she says, without looking at me.

In a flash, I'm standing in the main house's laboratory watching. The young mother in a red dress from the little cemetery makes tonics, a regular stream of visitors, mostly women, collecting these mixtures over a period of time that speeds past.

I try to follow but am confused.

In time, she creeps stealthily out of the house with a vial and I follow almost against my will. She enters a house on the village's periphery. I watch through a main floor window as she and an older woman talk, the young potion-maker pulling the bottle from her pocket, the other woman drinking it in a single gulp. The older woman hugs the younger one, before stepping into another room. While the young woman packs up her items, an older man enters the house, speaks to the young woman, hugs her. She is unsuccessful in pushing him away and he grabs her roughly. As he is forcing himself on her, the older woman returns, aghast at the scene. The man pushes the young woman away, pointing at her and yelling. He bends down to pick up the vial that his wife had dropped earlier.

Loud voices speak behind me and I turn, dropping to the ground as I do.

When I stand up, I'm looking through the same window as on my previous visit.

The young woman sits at the center of the same circle in which her parents had stood, her hands bound, the man who had previously grabbed her now pointing at her and speaking words I can't hear. He holds up an empty bottle. Those forming the circle all stand and the young woman is taken away and placed in a barred cell.

I sit near the woman's small prison, unsure if I should interfere even if I could.

Her youngest daughter, perhaps nine years old, arrives and sits outside the barred cell as day turns to night.

I close my eyes to get a moment's rest but am soon woken by the sound of men approaching.

A group removes the woman from her prison, escorting her to a large tree in a large clearing, a place I recognize. Townsfolk silently gather around it in a semi-circle. She is bound with a noose and hanged, though her death takes longer than I would have expected it to from this method of execution, and her body thrashes about helplessly as her life is taken. When she finally goes still, the crowd slowly disperses without a sound.

The woman's body falls to the ground in the forest's empty clearing. Her youngest daughter walks to her, sits beside her, and curls up on the ground next to her mother's dead body.

I stand helpless. The air seems to have turned cold and I shiver, wrapping my arms around myself and looking at the ground.

When I look up, I'm now facing the executed older couple's home.

Here, again. When will this end?

The blacksmith, leads the two young girls into the home. When they emerge, all are dressed in vastly different clothing, the youngest now with jet-black hair hanging in front of and concealing her face, the older girl's blonde hair cut short. He hustles them away from the house, each with a single bag.

The sun sets in front of me and rises behind me. I turn and see the older sister with a large fabric bag disappearing into the forest to my left with a young man. Shortly after they're gone, the blacksmith appears, vanishing to my right with a large sack of his own, gone down a narrow path.

Are they leaving town for good?

I wait for something else to happen, someone else to come, but I'm alone in silence in the dark forest.

My world spins around me furiously, like clouds in a tornado, stopping as I fall onto the bench in front of the fire, my enigmatic companion once more at my side.

It takes me a moment to catch my breath.

"I just watch" she says.

"Yes…"

"Yes" she nods.

"So what do …"

I try to stand up but it doesn't happen, dizzy as my head is.

"It's sad to be alone, isn't it" the woman says without looking up.

"Yes…" I say as I contemplate the scenes that have flashed before my eyes.

These images must represent past events considering they appear to have taken place in East, and not recently, if I'm correct about the figures in them. And about the places I visited with Feryn. But why show me this?

Somehow, this woman has conjured these scenes.

Is there something psychedelic burning in the fire, something that made me suggestible to this story, made me see the things I did.

How did I see all that?

"Knowing helps with understanding, even if we don't realize it" she says without looking at me.

It'll take time to process all that I saw.

I stand and look out on the ruins that were once New Brook East, the homes of so many, the lives of so many, the beginning and end of so many. Was there love? Hope? Happiness? All that remains now are its shadows, its history, and its ghosts. So still, so calm.

It's 11:30 by my watch, the sun above the trees to my left.

"Is this where I turn around and you disappear?" I say without looking back.

When I hear only silence, I look behind me.

"I thought I'd stay for a while. I like it in East" she pokes the fire with a sturdy branch.

"Ok. Thanks"

I don't know what else to say.

She stands, reminding me of her height. Wow. I think she's taller than me, the sharp lines of her clothing distracting. She isn't looking at me but I feel like she can read my mind.

Time to head back. The cool morning air has yet to warm, the stillness causing me both peace and anxiety.

What now?

"I just watch" she repeats with a partial smile. I wonder at how much she's watched. At how I've been shown what I've seen.

She sits in the rubble that was once a home, content by her fire, contemplating whatever it is she reflects upon. I never got to ask who she is.

I consider my options. I could go back the way I came through the village, a route which I feel I could retrace without too much difficulty, or I could attempt to find my way back along the tracks and perhaps gather my thoughts, avoiding any townsfolk.

Without realizing, I wander a few steps in the direction from which I'd arrived, despite the benefits of the alternate path.

I cast one final look back at East and step onto the trail.

Will someone one day watch me as station master in historical visions? What will my history show?

East certainly had a history, one marked by tragic events, at least inasmuch as I saw them.

A weight lifts from me with each step away from the ruins. I try to imagine the inhabitants' emotions as they left their homes for parts unknown and arrived on this island as newcomers or in other established settlements on the island. Then as they departed once again to rebuild in a new location.

I can barely make sense of my thoughts, of the things I saw today, if they were real. How was I able to see these things? Who or what is Sanya? What was that place, really?

Some stories are best untold and I wonder if this was one of them. I wish it had stayed that way.

The journey back to New Brook West happens in an instant, as though I've simply passed through a door between the neighbouring communities. I have no recollection of the forest or the fields, just my arrival in the tunneled streets, West's imposing maze of stone buildings. Waves of memories rush over me like the tide, soaking me with emotion, with joy, with anger, with sadness, all at once, too quickly to take it all in. Such was my time with

Sanya.

I avoid passing near the blue café, not wanting to see Caprice, instead choosing a less familiar route I hope will lead back to the plaza. A small group of women stop their conversation as I pass, my head hanging low to hopefully dissuade any curiosity on their part. A man repairing a door seems engrossed in his work, not turning to notice me. Otherwise, I see no one as I pass through a web of streets as I struggle to keep my bearings hopeful that there are no eyes peering out from behind windows or in dark corners.

Now I'm in unfamiliar territory of narrow alleys, dark corners, and ominous silence. All too often, everything looks the same to me here.

"Colden" a female voice whispers.

Glancing around, I see no one so dismiss it as my imagination or anxiety in this part of town.

"Colden"

Again, the same voice.

The empty street; the closed windows; the gloomy buildings.

I inch forward, checking down each narrow lane as I do. I see no one down any of these passageways, all of which end in darkness that discourages further investigation. Looking up, the sky overhead clouds over, the dreary grey increasing as it does. A window on the level above me to my left closes softly but noticeably, my observer protecting him or herself from whatever follows me through the dark streets.

"Hi, Station Master"

My heart nearly bursts from my chest.

Rissa.

"Huh…" I stammer.

"You ok?" she asks, her expression one of genuine concern.

"What are you doing here?" I ask as I collect myself.

"Where?"

"Here" I gesture around me.

"I live here"

"On this street?"

"No, silly", she shakes her head, "Not here"

"Then where do you live?"

"What are you doing here?" she asks sternly, crossing her arms.

"On my way back to the station"

"You took the long way" she squints her eyes.

"Yes" I look around, feeling eyes upon me, the chill under my skin like cool breath on the back of my neck.

I turn back but she's gone.

"Rissa? Rissa?" I call softly.

No reply.

Time to get out of here. I look up. Things won't get better if I'm caught in the rain, though the clouds look more woeful than waterlogged.

I set off at a slow jog, arriving at the plaza in a few seconds, by sheer chance as far as I'm concerned, considering I have no idea where I'm going. The empty square welcomes me. I walk to the board in case I've been seen. Several items are posted, none pertaining to me or the station. Until I notice an envelope with my name, not addressed to the Station Master. I look around slowly, figuring whoever left this will surely be watching me take it, but see no one.

I stare at the item in my hands.

Should I open it here or take it back to the station?

I look inside in case the contents are relevant to my current location, wary of anyone watching.

A charcoal drawing. A small girl in a grey dress from the back, wiry black hair down past her shoulders, thin legs, arms at her sides, facing a brick wall similar to the hotel's exterior; a lantern on both sides of her. There's a ghostly feel to the childlike style, sharp lines detailing her body, a faint, almost invisible halo making her appearance that much more menacing. And the eerie mystery of her facing away from the artist so close to the wall.

Written on the back 'Room 1'. Oh no.

Do I dare look around me? Is someone watching from a distance? Nearby? Shivers run across my neck and down my spine.

The sky grows darker still, though without fog or haze.

A lantern lights to my right in the direction of the church. I don't turn. No one will be there anyway.

What does this sketch mean? Who would leave this for me? What do I do with it?

The small girl in the drawing faces the wall, the colours entirely black and grey with the exception of the bright orange candles in the lanterns.

I return the paper to the envelope.

I don't want to move but need to leave the village.

I wait, as if help might arrive, but know I'm alone.

Is someone close to me?

"Colden" the voice whispers in my ear as if the person is directly behind me.

Splash.

I spin in terror in the direction of the fountain.

Water trickles down the stone colossus into the pool below, the sound unmistakable, its origin certain. But there's no one at the base or in the plaza. No one I can see. The water is calm.

Rissa again? Do I want to know?

No one's in front of the church, its doors closed, the gates into the cemetery also shut.

Better to know what's there than wonder all the way back to the station what might be following me.

I approach cautiously, reaching the obelisk in silence. Taking a deep breath, I lean over to look into the clear water, the dark clouds overhead reflected in its surface. I walk the circumference of the fountain observing the same calm conditions in the pool everywhere.

I'm alone, the area quiet.

I expect shadowed motion near the cemetery or in a dark corner or alley but see none. A breeze scatters debris across the courtyard, shakes fixtures in windows and against buildings. And a drawing of the 'grey girl' in an envelope with my name.

Only now do I realize I'm sitting on the edge of the fountain, my mind filled with possibilities, with questions, with fear. As I carefully place the folded sketch in my pocket, my eyes wander to the unlit lanterns at the town's gate.

Soft fingers touch my left hand, waking me from my dream.

I jump, staring back into the pool and the stone bench where I've been sitting but no one's there. Maybe it's just leaves blowing across the top of the riser enclosing the water. Or a light breeze. Or maybe not.

There's not a soul in the plaza, the only sound from the fountain behind me.

"Rissa?" I say softly, looking first to my left then my right.

I get no answer which is partly relieving, partly unnerving.

Two lamps are lit along the church wall with no one outside the building or along the cemetery fence. I stare at the gravestones inside the enclosure, mesmerized, my head heavy. The gentle trickling of water echoes in my ears, a light breeze blowing across my face. The silence is unbearable. I feel like screaming to the shadows, yelling at the houses, but it would probably come out like a whisper.

I had taken the long way back to the station.

62 – Who are you talking to?

I look out on the plaza, the sky above the trees purple and red as dusk descends. The dark forest sharpens the outline of the white trees, the trail across the clearing leaving New Brook West a tunnel or both protection and terror.

A light breeze blows dried leaves across the plaza floor breaking the quiet.

Have the lanterns at the town gate been lit this whole time? It's as though they came to light on their own in response to nightfall.

Out the corner of my eye, I notice light in the direction of the church, a sign to get away from here.

I take a deep breath and summon the courage to rise, crossing the plaza's flat stone and dirt surface and walk out the village gate, unwilling to look back to see who's there or if anyone's watching me. My time here has taught me to stifle my curiosity.

I hear no sound behind me or in the dark forest ahead; the trail is clear, the trees skeletal onlookers concealing whatever hides among them. I hustle away from the community and onto the path. Above me, the canopy blocks out any moonlight or view of the stars, if there are any. The chill under my clothes making me shiver, though my mind tries to stay focused on the route ahead, my ears piqued for any noise at my sides. My pace is steady but quick, my footsteps the only sound.

I'm alone which is both worrying and comforting as I consider my journey to the station and doubt creeps into my mind.

Is the path getting narrower?

How long have I been walking?

Am I going the right way?

I wait for movements, for noises, for smells, but none come. The darkness n here is now absolute, no light overhead, no lanterns in the distance, a dreary mood in the air.

I breathe a sigh of relief upon reaching the large clearing, the station in sight as I exit the forest. A single lamp at the base of the stairs up to the apartment illuminates the platform. I see a glow from within the suite, the clearing bathed in faint moonlight shining through the thin grey clouds. All is both dark and light. My steps are laboured and slow as I cross the open area feeling exposed and vulnerable.

I climb the stone steps, walk to the edge of the platform, and sit facing across the tracks, my legs hanging over the side as my thoughts take on a different form. I will miss the peaceful solitude of New Brook West, the tranquility of isolation, the beauty of the natural environment. It's a true escape from society and its social apprehensions. It was a new beginning in a new world. But another world I can't handle, this time for reasons beyond my control.

There's nothing and no one in either direction along the tracks nor into the foliage. At least nothing I can see. And the absence of noises around the station and in the trees is most welcome. The thinning cloud allows the moon and stars above to share their light with the dark earth below. My mind drifts to a quiet place free from stress, fatigue, anxiety.

The air is calm, the evening tranquil. I enjoy this moment of peace.

The **New Brook West** sign above me creaks on its hinges, swaying briefly in the invisible breeze.

I'm alone in the increasing darkness.

A candle flickers behind me, making my heart race. I stand and turn, unsure if I want to know what waits.

Jade.

"Hi, Colden" her black eyes pierce me like daggers. She's barefoot in a short orange skirt and white leather jacket.

One of the rare individuals who addresses me by name.

"Hi, Jade"

Something about her always catches me off-guard.

She must be cold in that outfit.

Who is this woman that seems to know me but that I just can't place?

She's so familiar and so are her clothes.

"You here to see Scindi?" I ask, hoping she'll say yes, unsure of how to approach interactions with her after our previous encounters.

"To see you" she replies taking a few steps forward "Mind if I sit with you?"

"Of course" I return to the edge of the platform. Jade's skirt ends just above her knee, the white leather jacket at her waist, her bare feet dangling off the edge with no shoes in sight. Her dark hair is tied back in a pony tail. An exceptional style in such a conservative community.

We sit in silence, for how long I'm not sure, as I try to keep from looking at her. How do I proceed with this woman? I don't want Scindi to misunderstand any intentions on my part, of which there are none.

"I've missed not seeing you" she breaks the silence between us, crossing her feet at the ankles, her legs swaying.

"Just look for the awkward guy in the station master jacket" I reply with a smile.

She giggles.

"I like you, Colden" she looks at me "You're so different from everyone here. It's not often that a man like you comes along"

"Lucky for New Brook West" I say turning to face her.

She giggles again.

"Do you think you'll stay?" she asks in a serious tone.

Uh oh. Does she know something? I can't imagine Scindi having said anything.

"Haven't decided my future yet" I answer evasively "There are lots of strange goings-on here"

"I suppose that's true" her voice softens "But I'm here"

"Yes" is all I can think of saying.

I hear the sound of a door closing behind me.

"Who are you talking to?" Scindi's voice asks from the top of the stairs.

I turn to see her then back to my right where Jade no longer sits.

"Just thinking out loud" I lie, getting up.

Scindi hadn't mentioned seeing Jade leaving nor of suspecting her of having been in the apartment at all so I don't bring up these encounters.

Some things are best left unsaid. We spend a quiet night: her reading and writing; me reading and drawing, with little said between us in comfortable silence.

This is what I need and she seems content to keep her thoughts to herself.

Sleep comes easily for me, Scindi crawling in next to me shortly after I'd packed it in. I think I kissed her goodnight. I think she smiled.

I wake unexpectedly in a quiet dark apartment, the candle in the lantern against the room's central post snuffed out, its wick still glowing dimly orange. I scan the suite out of habit, then look up to the small skylight in the ceiling's center, then out the window to my right at the bright moon.

Tranquility. I exhale happily.

I hear nothing inside or out and wonder what woke me. I don't see anyone in the apartment nor at the windows, though it's hard to be sure in the dark. I'm sitting up but wait without moving for several seconds.

I carefully get out of bed and shuffle in the direction of the kitchen for a glass of juice, moonlight through the window guiding my walk. My eyes are focused on my path across the suite.

With my back to the room, I hear a soft creaking behind me.

Turning around, I nervously survey the darkness, the moon's glow creating shadows in the corners and near the furniture but I don't see anyone but this only unnerves me more. Now I don't dare move. I slowly sink lower next to the island, though my concealment does little to calm my nerves. I suddenly feel cold as if a window is open.

Then the apartment is quiet again.

I see no one from where I'm hidden.

Oh no. Above me.

An icy shiver runs across my neck as my breathing stops.

Is that a noise near the ceiling? Is something in here with me? Looking down on me?

I'm petrified.

Slowly I tilt my head back to look up at the darkness.

I see and hear nothing, though the ceiling overhead is obscured by black.

I stare for longer than I intend at the candle on the room's central post.

I look down expecting to see Scindi near it but she's not there.

A poorly extinguished wick coming to life?

I stand, mesmerized by the yellow and orange glow above the thin white taper. Scindi's still in bed. The room is quiet.

How long do I stare at the flame?

I muster the courage to look around me but, again, see no one, the areas of the room away from the candle darker than before.

I look to the window overlooking the clearing, white light shining in faintly through the glass, the trees near the tracks through the other window sharply outlined in the moon's glow.

Why did I get up? What woke me?

A cloud passes over the moon turning the room black.

I look around quickly, fearless.

I see no one in the darkness.

Is someone watching me now? I wait in silence.

Then all goes black.

63 – Safety in the dark

Curled up in the corner near the bed, she pulls her body as far back into the darkness as she can. She'd been quietly watching him sleeping and imagining his thoughts when she accidentally made a sound that woke him. Terrified, she'd scrambled away, her thin frame hidden in the room's shadows.

She watches him walk away but fears her location will be revealed as he returns. Then he disappears and she crawls away to safety in the dark.

64 – Lineage

I wake at 7:30, my mind in its perpetual haze, my head filled with cobwebs. Climbing out of bed gently to avoid waking Scindi, I inadvertently caress her naked body; she moans softly but doesn't open her eyes. She's kind and generous and supportive, intelligent and insightful. How could I suspect this amazing woman of any wickedness?

I don't, do I?

I creep to the kitchen to prepare coffee. The apartment looks like someone has cleaned and organized while we slept. Scindi must have taken action the day before that I hadn't noticed last night. Odd behaviour on her part but I'll not be questioning it.

I have a distant recollection of getting up in the night but don't remember why or what I did. Or perhaps it was all a dream.

Tonight: the great escape, the silent departure.

But something still feels missing like a door I haven't unlocked yet. My only interest in mystery-solving at this point is its role in my departure. I feel for Caprice but there's little I can do to help her. My leaving might be for the best for her.

A train is scheduled for this afternoon at 1:15 and another at 10:30 tonight, the latter our transportation. I'd better check the control room for any updates and head to town to post my notices to keep up appearances. I can only hope that Scindi has made any necessary preparations at her end with respect to her teaching responsibilities.

A cup of coffee, a glass of juice, and a day-old bun and I'm out the door. A shower can wait. Without mist, the temperature is comfortable with the station master jacket unzipped. The treetop branches sway under a light breeze, the effect barely noticeable once I reach the forest path. Nothing's visible along the trail in the direction of the school, as I make my way to the village gates.

The lanterns marking the gate have yet to be extinguished, the sun only now casting its glow above the trees in the east.

A few faceless townsfolk mill about the plaza as I post my notes on the board, some glancing in my direction, others ignoring or lacking interest if they do see me. I nod at one older fellow who passes me effortlessly carrying a closed basket the size of a small box, sparing me the shame of not offering assistance. The fountain trickles as quietly as ever the church doors are closed, the cemetery gates open. Neither Rissa nor Sam is about the area so I casually make my way down the street in the direction of the Grey Stone, intending to deflect my route toward the blue café once I've left potentially inquisitive eyes.

A short distance along the street, I look around and above me, but see only closed doors and windows, so veer in the direction of my true destination, cutting down a narrow alley. Grey walls and black windows tower ominously above me, more imposing than on previous visits among the closed windows and doors, the empty streets. The air is calm in the shelter of the buildings. Winding my way, I eventually arrive just down from the cafe.

Will it even be open?

What do I want at the café? Is there some final wisdom I hope to gather? Am I saying goodbye? To Caprice?

I approach tentatively, unsure of what to expect when I get near or what I'll see inside. The quiet street simultaneously puts me at ease and unnerves me. There's no living soul in the street or watching from a window or door that I can see. No movement or noise of any kind. So quiet. Too quiet.

Two lit lamps against the exterior café wall, and another two across the street, glow a faint yellow.

Two small open windows above the café look down on me like a giant's eyes. A door is ajar to the right of the large main floor window, though I can't be sure if it belongs to the café or a neighbour.

I pause, unsure of myself, the silence distressing.

"I hoped I'd run into you one last time before you left"

Caprice's soft voice behind me.

"Hello. Hi" I stutter.

"Hi" she smiles meekly "Do you have time to come inside for a moment?"

"Sure. Yes"

She leads me to a table against the front wall to the side of the large window.

"It's a shame you have to leave" she says softly when we're sitting.

"Yes, it is…"

"But you want to" she adds.

"Yes"

"Yes"

A girl with a bright smile brings us each a cup of coffee, a rich fragrance filling the air.

I hesitate for a moment, cup in hand.

"You can drink the coffee; I didn't poison it" Caprice smiles.

Of course not. Right?

"Of course not" I force a smile, taking a sip. It tastes normal, a dark smooth flavour.

Two other tables are occupied, each by two young women, our server the only attendant I can see. The inside walls shine bright blue, warming the interior without over-lighting it, though the room's corners remain obscured. Dark and light green furniture, the floor pure white as though made of glass. Is this how it's always been? I can't recall.

Caprice wears a dark yellow skirt, a long-sleeved white top, and white knee-high socks with black flats. Yet despite the colour of her clothing, it seems a perfect match to the décor.

She sips her coffee, her actions mirroring my own.

"When do you leave?" she asks, setting down her cup.

"What do you mean?"

"I mean what I said" she replies calmly.

The other two couples speak intently in their own conversations, oblivious to ours, my ears unable to pick up any of their words from where we sit.

"Too many things are happening here" I say "It's not normal. I'm being stalked by someone or something"

"A girl?" she asks without expression.

"A girl" I say "Or maybe something else entirely. Something I don't understand and don't want to. I'm still not sure why I'm here. I can't stop asking 'Why me?'"

"Yes"

"Yes" I echo, taking another sip.

"I am sad that you're leaving. It was good to know you, Colden" she says with a sad smile.

"It was good to know you, Caprice. Perhaps in another life..."

"Perhaps"

I surreptitiously look in our waitress' direction, but don't see her. I don't want to get caught glancing about, want to give Caprice my full attention.

"Where will you go?" she asks.

"I'm not sure. I don't have much money. But I'll find my way if I can get a fresh start"

"Isn't that why you came here?"

"Yes, it is"

The thought makes me sad.

Caprice sips from her cup.

Outside the window, a group of men pass pulling several large trees on a cart. Focused on their task, they ignore the café entirely. It makes me think of the team who come collect and deliver freight to the station, a group I'd see at least one more time today.

Caprice looks at me, her beauty tinged by a latent sadness.

"I'm much older than I appear" she says setting her elbows on the table and leaning towards me "My potions keep me young but take their toll on my body and my spirit"

She pauses, lowering her voice.

"Evan forbade me practising alchemy but Hannah and I still met to experiment and I learned from her" she goes on "Our elixirs were effective for their users. Some, however, had harsh negative side effects causing memory loss, dementia, or depression in those who consumed them. Still, people came to us, discreetly of course, for help with their ailments. We warned of potential side effects but few were dissuaded. Some came with requests we could not fulfil and wouldn't try to"

That can't be.

"You're probably wondering why I'm telling you this" her voice is stern.

"Hannah?" is all that comes out of my mouth.

"Yes" her eyes pierce me.

"So how old are you?" my thoughts are simultaneously skeptical and curious.

"I was Evan's fiancé and Hannah's best friend. Hannah, whose beauty betrayed her"

Not possible. I'd dismissed it before, or tried to.

"Seriously" she adds as though reading my mind "I've told you all this before"

I don't smile, unsure where this is heading.

"I'm dying painfully" she says leaning in closer "My potions have allowed me to deceive townsfolk so as to avoid suspicion but nothing I do at this point will change me. I leave behind all my friends every time I have to re-invent myself and start over"

"But you…"

"I've been careful with what I say, and what I don't, because I know who might be listening"

"Who?"

"Saying a person's name draws their attention, makes them aware of a conversation, makes them take notice. I want none of these things for either you or myself. I was strong in body and mind but have weakened with time, the price of longevity. I fear that I could not withstand her wrath nor protect you. There's more at work here than you realize" her pensive eyes seem to disappear for a moment.

"Then why won't someone fill me in?"

"For just that reason" she smiles.

"I'm not trying to interfere or get in the way. I don't even know why I'm here"

"I think you do" she nods.

"Really, I don't"

I really don't.

"You've seen the tree. The answer is in the tree"

"Again, with the damned tree" I fall against the chair's back.

"Sorry" I say after a short pause.

"You've seen your lineage? And the schoolteacher's"

"Sure"

Wait a second.

"Did you leave me that family tree?" I raise my head.

"Did you notice anything about previous Station Masters?" she ignores my question.

I had noticed, hadn't I?

"Well, I saw a couple of Vintassis that I didn't even know existed who preceded me in the position, which is completely strange"

"How far back did you go in your ancestry?" she asks.

"The family tree went all the way to Katya and Martin" I answer.

"And their children. And their children's children"

"Yes"

"And you saw your name in this history?"

"No"

"Your great-grandmother, your great-great-grandmother, your great-great-great..."

"I'm a descendant of Hannah's" I conclude "And Rebecca's"

She smiles.

Whoa. Is this for real?

"So now what?" I ask.

"That's up to you, of course" she smiles weakly.

"Of course"

She sips from her cup.

"Am I supposed to 'do' something here?" I ask softly, leaning forward.

"You've already done something here"

"You know what I mean"

"No, I don't. Everything you do and many things you don't have an impact on those around you. We're defined by our decisions. No one expects you to do anything in particular and I wouldn't know what to tell you to do if you asked. You want to leave and that's where your heart lies. I think you've made your decision. This choice will change the course of your life as well as that of those around you. Especially the schoolteacher"

"Especially her?" I ask.

"She's leaving with you, isn't she?" she cocks her head.

"You know she is"

I'm not getting much out of this.

Caprice sighs.

"I'd hoped that you'd find me when you arrived, free me, fill my heart" she says "You are the last living relative of my best and only real friend. And I hoped that you were my destiny. But perhaps there's no such thing"

Perhaps.

"My time here is like a dream" I say quietly "Is any of this real?"

"It's real to me" Caprice replies "You here. Your mood, your courage, our fear. My lives, my homes, my fears. So much has happened over the years, so many memories"

Her words sound both beautiful and terrifying.

I can't think of anything intelligent to say.

"I already miss you, Colden. You did find me. And filled my heart. And I will soon be free. So perhaps my destiny was fulfilled in its own way"

"Destiny" I sigh.

"I need to go" she stands "This is my last goodbye. It has been a true pleasure to know you, even so briefly. I wish you happiness for all your days"

"I'll always remember you" I smile as sincerely as I can.

She smiles as if about to come toward me, but stops herself and gently bows, before walking out the front door without looking back.

Looking around, I notice two more tables now occupied, though I hadn't seen anyone else enter. I smile at our server and leave, Caprice nowhere in the street. Maybe Brian has some final knowledge to share relative to my departure, so off to the library: my sanctuary, my haven, my school. He'd been good to me, kind and supportive and generous with information. I'll never know his true identity, his reason for helping, his connection to my story.

I want to get back to the station sooner than later to at least check in on Scindi and take a final look around.

It's 9:45 as I step out into the street.

Past familiar houses and buildings, around which I'd never seen any residents, nor any activity. No open windows or doors this time. Sunlight breaks through the clouds, brightening the grey stone walls, dispelling the shadows from the dark corners, and lifting my spirits. The air feels entirely different under the sun. A short distance along the dirt streets, I find myself on the path outside the village toward the blacksmith's and the library.

The clear sky persists, a welcome sight in this dismal environment, small patches of clouds interrupting the otherwise azure ceiling. The blue fields, sparse trees and rocks, a couple of buildings in the distance, and the blacksmith's home and workshop up ahead. I have no desire to converse with any version of Evan Pertwee. The structures appear unoccupied, no sign anyone had lived here in ages.

My steps hasten as I approach the smithy and carry me past it quickly with no movement, sound, or smell around the building. Ahead, the library looms, the waves lapping against the rocky shore below in the light wind.

I climb the stone steps slowly, pausing at the entrance before opening the door.

There's rustling upstairs, as I catch a glimpse of two teenagers on the second level, and an adult to my left reading, or perhaps sleeping, in an armchair.

"Hi, friend" Brian welcomes me enthusiastically.

"Hi" my tone is less animated, and quieter than his.

"You've come with more questions, I assume" he says from behind the desk.

"How do you know that?" I ask.

"That's usually why you visit" he smiles.

"Actually, you're right" I say moving closer to the large desk "What do you know about potions?"

"Very little" he says.

"Any herbalists or alchemists in town?"

"Not anymore, that I know of" he replies softly.

"Was this a common occupation in New Brook West, or East?"

"Not a public one" his voice lowers "It wasn't considered witchcraft or sorcery but had the reputation of invoking dark arts and spellcraft and such. You didn't walk around saying you could cure this or that or make something happen. Few women knew this art and even fewer practised it. Or so I'm told"

"What did they do?"

"Like I said, there was no actual magic, just smarts about nature combined with some arcane knowledge. Didn't think they could raise the dead but I've heard they could make you see things that weren't there, make other people see you differently, even make some folks stronger"

"Is there any history of devil-worship on the island?" I ask, recalling the visions the woman had shown me.

He ponders for a moment.

"There were rumours in a previous age. Still some today, I imagine. Rumours have a way of transcending time. Best not to discuss invoking demons"

The heavy front door falls shut, startling me. Must have been someone leaving because no one has come in. The solitary guy is still in his chair near the door, but the teenagers are no longer upstairs or visible from where I stand.

"You've had your fill and been tested in ways you never imagined" he says seriously "It's a lonely place and can break the strongest person. You've stood taller than many"

"New Brook West certainly has an air to it" I say.

"Well put"

"I'd best be off, Brian" I say "It was a real pleasure meeting you and my sincere appreciation for all your help"

"The pleasure's mine" he stands "Not sure how much I helped but I hope this all works out for you"

We shake hands firmly and Brian sits down.

I walk slowly to the door, discreetly looking around the library as I do, but hear nothing. I pause at the exit for a moment, then pull it open in a single motion, leaving without looking back. I'll miss it here: the library has been good to me.

Brian will remain a mystery, one I'd expended no effort attempting to solve. He seemed to want to be helpful and any hidden agenda on his part wasn't obvious to me, if one existed. Who is he? Is he or had he ever been librarian? Why did he try to help?

Doesn't matter much at this point.

He seems happy. Should we all be so lucky in life.

The air is warmer than previously, more so than I could remember since I'd arrived, and it's November. I think.

I remove my jacket, eager to take in the sun's rays, however briefly. Water laps against the shore, low whitecaps visible in the distance. It's a spectacular view from the library, the immensity of the ocean spread out before me, the vast blue sky above adding to the expansive feel.

10:45

I stand for a moment, taking in the infinite ocean, the boundless sky, my anxieties literally behind me.

Am I being watched? Followed?

I pause for a moment, but with few options carry on to Scindi's and the school.

65 – This, I do not expect to see

I'm alone.

The air is warm, the sky clear, the area calm. I close my eyes for a moment, inhaling deeply. This could have been home.

A touch grazes my right hand, like fingers caressing my palm, and I freeze.

Then summon the courage to look to my right but no one's there.

My eyes turn ahead of me for any motion but, seeing none, look behind me, where I see only the water and the open area back to the library.

A cool breeze catches my hair making me curse my fears. Surely the wind is playing tricks with me alone on the path. Maybe Brian had been smoking something in the library that got into my head.

It's time to move.

A bird calls out ahead of me, away from the water, causing me to stop again. A surprise in this environment where animal sounds are so rare. It caws one more time, then silence falls as the trail moves inland.

I hear feminine voices in the direction of the bird's declaration. No reason to investigate but I feel myself drawn like Odysseus to the Sirens, their voices a song to my ears.

Near the water, Comet sits on a bench, opposite a strawberry blonde of similar build and age seated on a flat rock. Our eyes meet across the distance and it seems we'll be forced to acknowledge each other.

I approach the young women; cautiously.

"Hi, Comet" I say.

"Hi" she attempts a smile "This is Fresa. We were just talking"

"Hi, Fresa" I nod my head rather than extending my hand.

"Hi" she beams enthusiastically.

They smile at each other without saying anything.

Fresa's striking fair skin and red pupils, combined with her short sky-blue skirt and white long-sleeved top remind me of a flower. Comet wears a long dark blue skirt and white long-sleeved shirt giving her blue eyes a mesmerizing appeal and a more delicate floral appearance. Fresa is barefoot facing her friend, her legs extended out in front of her.

"It's a beautiful day" I attempt conversation.

"I like the sun on my skin" Fresa says pointing her right foot in my direction "We're going swimming and it'll feel wonderful when I come out"

"The river's pretty cold, isn't it?" I ask unaware of a beach.

"We know a private spot where the water's warm" Fresa lowers her voice "Where we don't need bathing suits"

Comet blushes at her friend's comment.

"Sounds fun" I stammer.

"You should join us" Fresa extends her right leg in Comet's direction.

"I've got station master things to do today" I manage to sputter, turning to continue on my way.

All I can think is: Wow.

"Bye, Station Master" Fresa smiles.

"Bye" Comet hasn't stopped blushing.

What is with the women in New Brook West? I haven't had this much attention since…ever.

How had I not met Fresa before? She's obviously a good friend of Comet's if they skinny-dip together. But I don't know Comet that well and never really thought about it with her being so aloof at the café. Clearly there's more to her.

Does Fresa work at the café?

Turning back, they're gone with no one else visible.

Back to the station. Hopefully I'll not have any more distractions.

It's already 11:30.

Time really does move differently here. I quicken my pace to outrun whatever mysteries or strange encounters pursue me.

The walk past Scindi's place will allow me to check on it and the school while avoiding the townsfolk. The narrow dirt path follows the river, alternately at the top of the banks and much further inland, short beige grasses on both sides giving it dimension. The stream, in some places narrow enough to step across and at others extremely wide, flows over shallow rocks and deeper boulders, rushing and swirling more dramatically in sharp curves and steeper inclines. The water's gurgling accompanies me on my quiet walk. A beautiful area on a sunny day, alone in nature's splendour.

Scindi's house eventually appears through the trees, its colourful red and white in stark contrast to the sparse foliage. Why is the teacher's home so bright while dull and muted earthtones dominate in town?

Long shadows cast by the tallest trees fill the clearing, the blue sky's glow bathing me and the house in its tenderness.

A lantern's light inside?

I hear no sounds or movements in the building. I hazard a peek in the kitchen window at the rear but see nothing and no light, likewise at the bedroom. I look to my left at the large window and see the source of the light.

There's a familiar sounding female voice inside, one that I can't quite place. My body tenses as I approach, my eyes scanning everywhere so as not to be caught unawares. Creeping to the front window, I lay low beneath it for a moment before summoning the courage to raise my head to peek inside between the closed curtains.

This, I do not expect to see.

Jade, nude on her knees, her bare feet tucked beneath her. No one else is in the room. A small lantern on each side of her provides light. What's she doing? And what's she doing here?

Then, another female voice from further back in the house.

Scindi?

Can she be here too? Dropping back below the window, I regroup my thoughts. What is this? I try to remain silent, my breathing echoing all around me, my blood pumping loudly in my ears, my movements clunky and loud.

I hear voices, though I don't catch the words.

Scindi enters the room, also naked, and sits across from her friend, tucking her feet beneath her, placing her hands in front of her reflecting her companion's pose. They smile at each other before Scindi starts giggling.

I quickly drop out of sight.

How did I not know this about Scindi? Is this real? What are they doing?

I cautiously peek back in the window and they're still naked, now expressionless and unmoving like statues. I watch for several seconds during which time neither shows evidence of breathing, blinks an eye, or betrays even the slightest motion to break their pose. Then Jade's hand twitches. And Scindi turns ever so slightly to look in my direction.

I crawl away from the building, breaking into a run as I get to my feet. I reach the edge of the schoolyard clearing in seconds, no one visible around the school. A quick glance over my shoulder tells me I haven't been followed so my pace slows to a jog then a walk.

What the hell had that been? Is that how Scindi spends our time apart? No way. That can't have been real. I'm seeing things, right?

I stop when I reach the school, crouching down to lean against the side wall, facing the path to the train station. Clouds have rolled across the sky, eclipsing the sun, and creating dull grey shadows against the treeline. The temperature has dropped, my clothing no longer suited to the current conditions, the moisture chilling me to the bone.

I could have sworn I'd worn my watch but it isn't on my wrist, so obviously not. I need to rest for a bit, even here. I close my eyes for a brief respite and am surprised when I open my eyes to be on the other side of the building. It has to be after 12:00 by now. How long have I been here?

I have no desire to make the journey back to the station but won't be staying here either so rise to head out into the dark forest.

It'll soon be the 1:15 pm train.

The lack of any haze among the trees allows some visibility on either side of the path, a lack of wind keeps the branches and sparse leaves still.

My head swirls with thoughts of Scindi. What is really going on with her? Do I know her and her intentions? Am I right to be wary?

Could what I just saw have possibly been real? There's no way. Something's messing with my head.

There's rustling ahead of me, like someone trying to beat me back to the station. Do I want to get there before this person? Better than them arriving first, so I jog to the intersection by which time I've lost the sound.

Could it be Scindi?

The fog-filled clearing between me and the station conceals the identity of a figure standing on the platform. Scindi? Caprice? It's too early for the men unloading the train and there'd be many of them in any case.

Approaching cautiously has become common practice on my part and this time is no different. Careful to survey in all directions, I slowly cross the open space, eager to reach the suite but also to determine the identity of my visitor. There's light inside the apartment, though whether or not Scindi is there remains to be seen.

As I near the station, the figure on the platform recedes, moving backward toward the tracks. I pick up my pace in an attempt to catch this person but the form fades before I get there. I break into a full run, reaching the steps in a few seconds but find no one around the building or across the tracks in the trees. I look up the stairs to my apartment, seeing only the closed door; the control room and utility room doors are both locked.

What about Room 1? I consider the possibility that my intruder is now hiding in there.

Is that a scratching of metal on wood from inside the room?

The faint smell of licorice hangs in the air. I back away from the hotel.

As I make my way up the stairs, I wonder what awaits me inside the apartment.

She focuses on his movements, her skin chilled, her heart aching. Watches in silence. Hidden in the shadows.

The apartment's door opens smoothly into the quiet room, Scindi not in the living room area. Two lamps light the wall to my left past the bathroom, one on my right next to the entrance, a small lantern in the kitchen. I take three steps into the room, watching all around me as I do, unsure of what to expect or what I might see. No one's here, Scindi or otherwise.

Setting hot water to boil, I add grounds to my cup when it's sufficiently warm, its smooth flavour relaxing me. I've really been fortunate to have befriended Tina.

A female voice behind me nearly shocks me into a scream.

I spin ready to defend myself.

"Hi" Scindi's in the entryway in jeans and a dark jacket, her hair tied back.

"Hi" I breathe deeply.

"Everything OK?" she asks, her face squirreled up.

How'd she get back here so quickly? Unless she was never at her house and what I saw was some sort of vision conjured in my mind, some hallucination.

Am I going crazy with all these scenes playing out around me or in my mind?

"Where were you?" I set my empty cup in the sink, stepping around from behind the island.

I shake off my thoughts.

"In town. I went to pick up some food items to bring with us. Bread. Cheese. Fruit. Been here for a while now"

She sets down a bag.

"Oh. Sure"

"'Oh, sure'?" she crosses her arms "Care to elaborate?"

"I was in town for a bit too. Then by your house on my way back"

"Why go past my place?" she asks.

"No reason. Just curious if anything was going on. And at the school"

"Was anything going on?" her tone is serious.

"Uh, no"

There can't have been anything going on – it's not possible.

"You don't sound too sure" she cocks her head.

"Nothing out of the ordinary" I try to back out of the subject, unsure if I want to share what I saw or imagined I saw.

"Hmm"

"Hmmm? Care to elaborate" I say in an attempt to lighten the mood.

Scindi smiles.

"When does the train come?" she asks removing her coat.

"There's one at 1:15 pm and another tonight that I'll confirm later"

"It's 12:30 pm now" she says stepping into the room.

"I'll head downstairs right away to meet the men" I say, my eyes still scanning the room.

"Do you plan on packing anything to bring with you?" she asks, taking off her shoes.

I walk to the kitchen.

"Not just yet" I think about it "I'll check the control room for confirmation of tonight's arrival and post notice in town before I do any of that"

"Whatcha doing now?"

"Making coffee" I light the gas stove, noticing a coffee up in the sink.

"Me too, please" she places a large cloth bag on the floor, takes off her shirt, shoes, pants, and socks, and pads into the bathroom.

Setting the water on the element, I walk to the window to look out onto the tracks and platform below.

The calm cloudy air persists, the chill penetrating the glass and creeping under the doors. Grey gloom hangs over the station, the air thick, the army of black spindly trees surrounding us.

The constant murkiness feels heavy but has never made me sad or lonely until now.

New Brook West exists in a state of perpetual obscurity, a home to chills, and shadows, and darkness. The black rails, visible against the white gravel, break me out of my trance.

A candle flickers behind me causing me to turn expecting to see Scindi, but she must be in the bathroom. There's no air movement inside to disturb the shielded oil lamps, the candle flames are calm.

I look around at my possessions, sad that such a small number of them will be coming with me when we hop the train tonight. Photos and memorabilia? Or more practical things? How long will it be until I'm able to resupply myself? Where will I be and what'll be most useful to me there?

I'll not likely see anything I leave behind in New Brook West ever again.

Do I dare mention the scene from her house? What would I say? Am I sure it was Scindi? Was it some sort of vision? I already feel it fading from my memory.

"Whatcha doing?" she walks across the room in a long thin white shirt.

"Coffee's ready" I reply placing her cup on the island.

"Great" she kisses me.

Scindi goes around to the other side of the counter, facing me and leaning forward.

"I'm actually a bit nervous about tonight" she says "How exactly do we get on the train with all those guys standing right there? Which part of the train do we get on? Where do we get off?"

"I don't really know" I lean back against the counter behind me "I'm hoping it's more obvious when the time comes"

"Is there anyone you can talk to?"

"I don't think it's a good idea to share our plan" I shake my head.

"No" she sips her drink "Just please don't kill me"

"What?" I jump.

"I said 'You're probably right" Scindi replies with a shocked expression.

I set my unfinished cup next to the sink.

"I'd better get outside to wait for the team" I say "They never seem to show up in the same way"

"Ok"

I lace my boots, grab my jacket, and make my way down the stairs, vigilant of any presences on the platform.

Passing as far away as I can from Room 1, I sit on the platform facing the clearing, my legs hanging off the edge.

It's 12:40. Any second now the silent band of brothers will emerge from the forest, carts in tow, led by Dalton.

Are these the same men who will come tonight? Will Dalton be with them? Is he the lookout watching to ensure I don't try to escape?

Too many thoughts in my head.

What else is gonna happen today? Is leaving now the right thing? Am I right to trust Scindi?

How did I end up here?

I think about destiny and those who came before me, how they felt, what they thought. If they left.

The party comes into view through the fog, twelve men in total, Dalton nowhere to be seen. Their gait seems more laboured than usual, their lumbering pace slower than I recall. By the time they reach my position, it's just before 1:00, their faces as stoic as ever.

"Hey, guys" I get to my feet with a friendly wave.

None of them even look at me. I have no desire to offend this group of burly dudes, but also wish I could get one of them alone to see what they know. There's no way that'll be possible.

"Station Master" the man's voice speaks behind me.

Dalton.

"Hi, Dalton" I reply with a nod "Train should be here any second"

As if on cue, a whistle through the trees signals its proximity.

Six men climb onto the platform like soldiers, standing a short distance back from the edge, facing the tracks. This process always makes me nervous.

I sit at the bottom of the steps up to the apartment to watch their movements, hoping for some insight into an escape route.

"It's not easy, you know" Dalton says from my side.

"What isn't?" I panic.

Dalton smiles, walking to sit on the bench against the wall, facing the train.

With robotic precision, the group unloads the train, fills the carts, and disappears into the forest.

Dalton is no longer on the platform or among them, which I write off as inattentiveness on my part.

'It's not easy'!?!

I hope to never find out what he meant by that.

I check on the printer in the control room but nothing has come. I lock it behind me, extinguish the candles and lamps, and verify the latch on the utility room.

"Hey"

Scindi's voice behind me.

"Hey" I reply, mildly startled.

"I might walk into town again, look around a bit" she says.

She's dressed for the weather in dark jeans, boots, and her brown jacket over a long-sleeved purple shirt.

"What're you looking for?"

"Just looking" she smiles "One last time"

"Ya" I reply heading toward the stairs to the apartment.

"Everything OK?" she asks.

"Sure. I might take a nap. Feels like a long day already"

"Bye" she trots off into the clearing.

"Bye" I reply, climbing the steps.

It's 1:40 now, so there's plenty of time before anything needs to be done.

What would Scindi want to look for in town? My distrust for everything to do with this situation increases with each new interaction.

Or perhaps it's just my confusion, the not knowing that scares me.

Box

As I lie in my box, I think on the man I've seen, but he looks so different from the one I'd known as a child with my mother and sisters. The one I remember had a wicked smile and cared only for himself. This one seems kind. Could he really be the bad man the woman told me he is?

I'm confused; angry, sad, and confused.

And tired.

65 – The Prophecy

Now comes the worst part: waiting.

The apartment feels dim despite the two lit lamps against the wall, the kitchen lantern now extinguished. Shadows dance in the corners under the flickering light, sparse daylight seeping through the windows. I'm not sleepy but definitely tired so lay down on the couch, closing my eyes to escape my surroundings for a moment. I never fully drift off, which is probably just as well because nothing good ever seems to come of it.

I try to just blank out my mind to give me a break from the madness. A few long breaths, meditation-style. I stretch my body to its full length.

A knock brings me back to reality, such as it is.

Who is this now?

I look out the window onto the tracks, then into the clearing, before walking to the door and opening it with false cheerfulness.

Oh. Feryn.

"Hi, there" he smiles.

"Hi, Feryn" I open the door wider to invite him in.

"Hey, coffee" he says walking into the kitchen without removing his boots.

"Please do" I sit at the island facing him.

"Actually, I'd better not" he shakes his head.

He comes around to sit next to me.

"How are things?" he asks.

"OK, I suppose"

"Just OK?"

"Just OK" I assure him.

"What're you up to today?" he cocks his head.

"Nothing special…"

"Besides…" he pauses.

"Besides..." I repeat.

"So, I imagine you've said goodbye to Caprice" he says.

"Whatta ya mean?"

"Come on. You're a smart guy. And so am I"

"OK" I try to conclude this part of the conversation.

"So, where'd your lady friend go?"

"Not too sure. Into town somewhere"

"But you don't believe her" he suggests.

"What makes you say that?"

"You don't hide it well" he says.

"Thanks" I say.

"It's nice in here" he changes the subject, suddenly across the room looking out the window into the clearing.

"It's OK" I agree standing up.

"Just OK?" he smiles.

I approach him.

"So, what's up with all the attention I'm getting from women in town?" I ask "Comet and her friend were the most recent to fall under my spell"

"Is that a bad thing?" he crosses his arms.

"Just unusual" I shake my head "Is Comet real?"

"Very much" he replies nodding.

"So, when did I acquire this charm?" I ask.

He pauses for a moment and looks down then out the window.

"You know about the prophecy" he says without looking at me.

"The what?"

"You know what happens when the last of your line dies?" he turns to face me.

"What?"

"It's bad"

"How bad?"

Feryn's head tilts to the right.

"It's a fairy tale, a myth handed down over time" he speaks slowly "Folklore, if you will"

"OK"

"I'm pretty observant but don't catch everything" he leans against the wall.

"An ancient story about a woman and a Demon. It's played on people's minds here for generations and likely still does today, at least to some"

"When was this?"

"Before my time"

"And how old are you?" I ask.

"Older than Comet" he replies.

So, now what?

"Hard to say what comes next for sure" he goes on "There's talk of a small coven of witch...of women devoted to protecting you and keeping the prophecy from being fulfilled. You're the last of your line, Colden. Unless you have a child. Or children"

"The last of my line?"

What does that mean?

"Years back, a woman tried to cast an enchantment to render future women in her family infertile so that her family's legacy would die. But something happened, the result being that each woman was only capable of bearing a single child and each man only fathering one of his own" he pauses "Or so I've heard"

This guy knows more than he lets on.

"So, where does that leave me?"

"As the last of your line. Unless you create some children. Do you have any?"

"Not anymore"

This makes me sad for a moment.

"Your school teacher's the last leaf on her branch too, so if you both die here then that's it"

"Then what happens?"

"I hope I don't find out"

"So that's how it ends? My dying childless opens an age-old curse upon the world? That's why the women all want to be with me? So, I'll get them pregnant?"

"Either that or they're just really excited by the hot new stranger" he smiles "It's up to you what you want to believe"

"It's up to me?"

"Contrary to what you might think, I don't have all the answers" he says seriously "Or maybe I've got it completely wrong. You've decided to leave and I hope you succeed"

So do I. Why wouldn't I? I'm not sure if I say this or think it.

Feryn sighs deeply, looking down as he does.

"You will be offered help to get you going on your trip" he says after a heavy breath.

"From who?" I frown.

"I thought you knew"

"How would I know?"

"You're a smart guy"

"Obviously not"

I haven't felt smart in a while.

"I think my mother told you all that she could"

"Your mother?" I ask.

"Sanya" he says "Tall woman with a black hat"

"She's your mother?"

"Yes"

"She's good with 'when', I'm good with 'where'" he shakes his head "Neither of us is good with 'how' or 'why'"

I try to recall the scenes she played out for me in New Brook East.

I exhale deeply.

"What do I do?" I say "I'm not trying to get involved in a hundred-years-old folktale"

"Too late" he shakes his head.

"So, what do I…"

"You put too much faith in my knowledge"

"And you in mine"

"And I should be going" he skips forward a step.

"Going where?"

"Just going" his face betrays no emotion nor hints at any ulterior motive.

"Am I on my own now?"

"Yes and no" he walks to the entrance "You're not alone. Never. I've just done all I can for now"

"Ya"

"I do hope we'll see each other again" he smiles as he opens the door "I think we will"

"Ok"

I like Feryn. For all his cryptic language and aloof attitude, he's a good guy and a helpful sort. One of the few people I can trust. Almost a friend.

"Farewell, friend. For now" he says, exiting and closing the door behind him.

"Bye"

And he's gone.

I don't bother walking to the window, knowing he'll have vanished by whatever stealth or magic he possesses.

Outside, wind whistles past the station, the nearby trees rattling like a wicked musical ensemble. There's no fog in the clearing, though grey clouds keep out the sunshine, the temperature cool even in the apartment. The chill in the air makes it seem darker outside.

I glance around the room at the lit lamps, the inanimate candles, the thick rafters, the wood walls that had surely seen many faces. I wonder if New Brook West is cheery and clear in summer or if gloom reigns all year. Who had come before me? Had they felt alone? How were things on the island in years past? So much history.

I stare at the door as if expecting someone, waiting for a sound: a knock, a tap at the window, a whisper in my ear. But nothing comes. I'm alone in silence. Alone.

The dimly lit room does nothing positive for my mood so I walk around to light four more candles. Despite not wearing boots, my footsteps echo in the large room in a way I've never noticed before.

Sitting on the couch, I look up to the small skylight at the ceiling's central peak as clouds roll past against the sombre sky.

How long has it been since Feryn left? It's difficult to remember.

I contemplate closing my eyes but decide against it. Too weary to get up and do anything productive, I lean back, exhaling deeply.

"Hello, Station Master" the soft feminine voice speaks as I open the door.

My coffee-friend is wearing a long dark jacket and carrying a small purse. She stands sheepishly in the doorway.

"Please, come in" I offer.

"Thank you" she steps inside, taking off her boots and opening her jacket as if preparing to stay.

"How are you?" I ask, trying to make conversation.

"Really good, yes, thanks" she seems surprised by my question "You?"

"I'm doing well, thank you"

Her green eyes scan the room and up to the ceiling.

"It's much bigger in here than I expected" she says slowly.

"It's a nice apartment" I say cheerfully.

She pulls a pouch from her bag. She's wearing make-up, unlike previous encounters, which makes her looks strikingly pretty, if slightly wicked.

"Is this..." I ask, hoping she'll finish my sentence.

"Is this...?" her voice squeaks.

A brief pause ensues.

She sets the pouch down on the island.

"Well, I hope you like it" she tries to smile "You are my special guest"

She closes her jacket over her grey outfit.

"I really do appreciate it"

"Well, you enjoy your day, sir" she stops in front of me, curtsying "It's been a pleasure"

"Yes. Thanks. You too"

It feels like she's slowly moving toward me or maybe it's me moving toward her.

Time stops for a few seconds as she looks at me.

"Ya. I should be station master-ing. Got a couple of things to do downstairs" I take a short step back.

"Of course" she smiles, turning to leave "Goodbye"

"Goodbye" I sigh in relief as the door closes behind her.

I walk to the window to watch her walk across the clearing but see no one. I wait but see nothing and hear no sounds from the platform.

Putting on a light jacket, I step out and walk around the building. No one's here or walking away from the station. Control room locked. Utility room shut. Room 1 quiet, as far as I can see.

There's still no one crossing the clearing. Maybe she walked back along the tracks for some reason, though I don't see her there either. At least she's gone. Another unusual woman whose motives I can only imagine.

It's 3:00 and still no Scindi. What is she doing?

I plod back upstairs for coffee. The water heats in no time and I sit to try the latest batch. Such a treat to have delicious brew delivered directly.

On a small card: 'Enjoy Ti'

Tina is her name, I think.

She'd certainly come around since our unfriendly encounter at the library. She seems nice, even though we rarely speak beyond the subject of coffee. Her name sounds familiar but is common enough. But those amazing green eyes can't be common.

I recall other girls with green eyes. Who?

Christi was a waitress somewhere; a café? Chris on the plane. And a woman I'd seen in those visions, or whatever they were, with Sanya. How could I forget those stunning eyes. So sharp and piercing.

The sweet coffee feels smooth on my tongue, a pleasant sensation and a tasty blend. I enjoy a few sips as I look out the window onto the tracks.

I'd figured today would go somewhat smoothly, or at least bring fewer visitors. Seems not.

I welcome my moment of escape as I enjoy the delicious, if strong, roast. I wonder where coffee beans are grown in this environment.

I turn around with my cup of coffee to see Jade sitting at the island with a cup of her own.

Holy…

How did she get in? While I was outside?

"Hi" she smiles bringing her cup to her lips, her dark eyes watching me as she sips.

Wearing the same short orange skirt and white leather jacket as on our previous encounter, one bare foot hanging off the chair, the other tucked beneath her.

"Hi" I reply setting down my beverage.

"Leaving so soon?" she asks.

"What do you mean?"

I try to ask how she got in but the words don't come out.

"We barely got to know each other" she says pulling her foot from under her to cross it at the ankles with the other, her skirt shorter than I recall.

I know you well enough, I think, whoever you are.

"That's too bad" I say, hoping this will conclude the conversation but realize immediately that it won't.

"I've known men, but never one like you"

Ok.

"So where do you live?" I ask to change the subject.

"It's nice in here" she replies evasively "You live alone?"

"I should probably get to work" I say taking a gulp of my hot drink "Lots of station master-ing to be done"

She stands up "You're with the wrong girl, you know"

"Huh?"

"I'd take care of you, Colden. Make a great home for you"

"Yes, I'm sure…"

She walks toward me.

I bring the coffee cup to my lips as if this will discourage her from coming closer.

What is going on today?

"Take care of you…in every way" Jade leans in to kiss me.

I turn my head then my body to face away from her.

I wait a second before turning back, to see the door swing in as if pushed by the wind.

I run to the window, a light fog in the clearing below. No Jade. No Tina. No Scindi.

Just me.

Who is Jade and why do I keep seeing her? She seems real.

I need to get outside.

Grabbing a light jacket and boots, I head down the stairs, hop off the platform, and am standing in front of the huge building at land's end. Looking back, the path leads across the blue field and back to town. Ahead, the library.

How…?

With slow deliberate steps, I approach the door, ready for the unexpected. I look around me, shake my head, close my eyes and open them but I'm still outside the library.

I try to get a closer look in the windows but they're high and lightly tinted such that I can't see the interior. In a slow smooth motion, I pull open the door as a boy emerges without noticing me. With no one in sight, I walk up the steps to the large unoccupied desk.

The ocean's gloom looms out the large windows against the back wall, a grim view. An army of sturdy glass-walled lanterns illuminate the expansive room, though it feels cold and dark, as if the candles' light can't penetrate the obscurity, the library darker in the chill air. I shiver. Shadows shimmer in partially lit corners and down each aisle, whispers echo off the bookshelves, faint spicy aromas hang in the air.

"Good day" Brian's voice to my right brings me back to reality, his tone less enthusiastic than usual, his words almost a question.

"Hi, Brian"

His perplexed look catches me off-guard.

"Everything ok?" I ask.

"I should ask you" he walks behind the desk.

My eyes scan both levels of the library.

"Looking for someone?" he asks in response to my examination of the room.

"Eh? No. Just curious if there's anyone else here"

"The last fellas just left" he says "These latest must have been educated folk. Did their own thing and I didn't pay much attention?"

"There are some strange folk here" I say.

"You bet there are" he smiles.

"Do you know a Jade in town?" I go straight for it.

"Can't say as I do. What'd she do?"

What did she do, really? Nothing that unusual except show up all over the place whenever I'm alone and then disappear.

"So, who've I been seeing?" I ask.

"Could be anyone. Or no one"

Odd answer, or perhaps it's his intention to conclude that line of conversation.

"Do you know Dalton?" I try another name.

"Not a popular name"

"What do you mean?"

"Dalton Vintassi was the last Station Master who tried to escape the island"

"What happened?" I ask, though I already know the answer.

"He failed"

67 – The key

Dalton preceded me by about fifty years, kept to himself for the five or six months he lived in New Brook West, and was hanged for attempting to board the train with the cargo one November evening. No one knew how long he'd been planning this or what made him finally decide he couldn't stay any longer. Brian shares this reluctantly, and nervously. I'm both grateful and anxious about what he says.

I shudder to think about his punishment.

I now know 'DV' from the control room's ledgers. And why Dalton never talks to or helps the men at the station – he's not really there.

It's 3:45 now, though it feels much later. Out the back window, darkness hangs over the water, the clouds moving about as a reminder of the dreary hours ahead.

"No one's left since?"

"No one's tried" he leans back in his chair "Only they know if they wanted to and what stopped them from trying if they did"

"So, what…" I start a sentence not knowing where it will go.

"You should get back to the station" he interrupts "Be with your friend. She needs you now"

"Should I trust her?" my head droops.

"Who do you trust?" he asks.

"Yeah…"

"You've got some work to do yet" he stands "Best get on with it"

"Thanks, Brian. I'm still not really sure who you are but you've been good to me and I'm grateful"

"Be well, friend" he nods.

I turn to leave.

"So, I…" I begin.

I look back but he's gone. I don't bother calling his name, knowing I'll get no answer, which is fine. I guess I'll never know who, or what, Brian is.

Fewer candles now light the library, the room darker than when I'd arrived; I wonder how they got extinguished but try not to think on this. I look around the main floor, the tall bookshelves, the grey walls, the mystical art, the mysterious yet impressive library.

Looking out at the expansive ocean, I feel small and alone.

Silence fills the library as I stare outside pondering life, what's happened, and what comes next.

A movement upstairs is my cue to leave.

Without hesitating, I walk to the door and out into the gloom, dusk turning the sky to my left orange and red.

A strong wind blows in from the ocean filling the air with salty moisture. The blue field is laid out in front of me, New Brook West's buildings beyond the horizon. To my left, the river flows toward Scindi's house. I take a quick glance around and begin my journey back to the station.

The blacksmith's cabin and workshop no longer feel welcoming. No smoke rises from the chimney, no warmth from the building, no light in any of the windows. What had happened on my previous visits couldn't be explained, nor will I look for answers, knowing I probably don't want to know them. Despite my curiosity, I decide against taking a look behind me once I've passed the smithy, unsure if I want to see who or what might be watching.

My courage and fear force occasional looks to the sides into the field but I see nothing in the falling dusk.

The structures on the village periphery soon come into view, inviting me into the comfort of their familiarity.

Reaching the first buildings, ominous and grey, I turn back to see the boulders dotting the fields, the dark trees and branches, the tall grass swaying in the breeze. Viewed looking back from a distance, the area between the community and the library appears peaceful and cheery, like reflecting on an old memory. I ponder this thought for a moment, before entering the grey road into New Brook West. The still air among the village's stone and wood structures fills me with a strange feeling. A cold blanket wraps itself around me, alone on the edge of town.

Walking through the hard dirt streets, the only sounds are my steps and my breathing, the wind unable to penetrate the outer circle of buildings and any mist that's gathered hanging outside the city limits. Drab walls, dark windows, closed doors. Silence around every corner as if I were in a deserted village. The occasional lit oil lamp along an exterior wall reassures me that I've not been abandoned.

Reaching the fountain, a destination I'd not intended, provides both solace and discomfort, the massive form reminding me how small I am just as the ocean had. The church door is closed, the cemetery gate open, no one in the fenced area that I can see. Two lamps light the church's exterior, one each on either side of the large door. The town hall is dark. Along the streets behind it, the occasional lantern casts a yellow or orange glow on a grey wall. It's calm in every direction.

The quiet, broken only by the trickling water, freezes me like a tranquilizer, mesmerized as I am by my solitude and the monotonous drizzling. I try to turn my head to look around the plaza but can't, my body petrified, but my mind aware. I can't afford to be caught by surprise nor do I want unsolicited conversation from a passerby so had best be moving along.

Am I staring at the fountain? Or does my mind see something my eyes don't?

"Are you looking for someone?" a distant woman's musical lilt breaks the silence.

There's only one person with that voice.

Standing against the cemetery fence in dusk's dim light, a light blue full-length dress hugging her slim body, blue eyes behind thin-rimmed glasses resting on a delicate nose, black pointed boots visible beneath the folds of the skirt, dark hair hanging straight down a feminine face.

I approach, not wanting to ignore her, partly out of politeness, partly out of fear, partly because I'm drawn to her, stopping a respectful distance from her.

"I'm not sure"

I can almost make out her striking features.

"Where is everyone?" I ask.

Mist hangs low in the clearing, stopping at the village's gates.

A beautiful whistle fills the air, as if nature itself were singing.

"I'm Colden" I decide to say something simple.

"I know"

"Do I know you?" I ask, hoping to elicit more information.

"Yes" her blue eyes look down at her fair-skinned hands.

"Have we met before?"

"Yes"

"Are you Rebecca?" I ask quietly.

Her voice sings something I don't understand as she stares up at the sky then stops.

What is she doing? Am I hallucinating?

"Are you real?"

I'm still rooted to the spot, try as I might to step backwards.

My eyes furtively scan around the cemetery but see only the grey stone markers and iron fence, a tree farther off in the distance.

I try to speak again but the words don't come out.

"She was so sad" she says without looking up.

"Who was?" my voice is now softer.

I feel at ease in this woman's calming presence. She seems to be looking not just at me but into me. Still, it feels soothing, even in the fading light outside the cemetery. She opens her mouth as if to speak but says nothing.

"I wish I could have done more" her voice is musical, though she isn't singing.

"About what?" I ask "Do you need help?"

"You're a kind man" she looks at me, her voice a beautiful lilt.

I try to think of what I could ask her to help me understand everything but nothing comes.

"I must go" she sings as she hangs her head and floats across the plaza and clearing and into the forest toward East.

Was she Rebecca? Her ghost? A vision?

Behind me the fountain's water trickles down into the pool below. The cemetery gate creaks shut, then opens again.

I stand and wait for a moment, staring at the church, wondering what I should do.

Back to the station.

The deepening darkness slowly turns the murky grey into dreary black, the air chilling me beneath my thin jacket, like low clouds come to earth. The dull plaza holds no appeal for me now.

Overhead, a bright moon penetrates the clouds, casting a soft white glow on the square, dull shadows appearing against the walls and in the corners. Subtle movements catch my eye, candles flicker against exterior walls, a gentle breeze carries faint voices, whispers on the air that send a shiver down my neck and back. Is someone near me? Close enough to touch me? I lack the courage to look behind me toward the church and cemetery. And the tranquility I'd felt in the woman's presence has now abandoned me.

Serenity becomes anxiety.

The sky darkens returning me to dim solitude. And silence. The quiet feels unnatural. No longer does the fountain trickle into the pool below. The sputtering and dancing candles stop their flickering motion. I can't move in the stillness. The large open plaza feels like a straight-jacket around my chest. My eyes move side to side but see nothing and no one; my neck refuses to turn as I prepare for the worst.

Alone but watched. I know there must be someone behind me near the fountain or near the dark cemetery. Have I stopped breathing?

I wait for a whisper, a smell, a movement. Am I once more part of the scene rather than a participant?

A soft touch grazes the back of my neck. Then again like a feather on my cheek. Oh, no; my eyes water.

I'm afraid to turn.

I watch the sun's final dark colours sink below the buildings, then close my eyes in the hopes that I'll reappear someplace safe. I wait in silence. I fear opening my eyes, fear that something or someone will be directly in front of me when I do.

I hear no sound, feel no more gentle touches. Nothing.

Many seconds pass before a creaking of metal breaks my trance, allowing me to move once again.

My eyes look at the lit lanterns marking the exit from town but see no one. I wait, simultaneously enjoying and fearing the quiet.

The unknown surrounds me; in the cemetery; outside the church; down the alleys; in the forest; in the mist.

My tired feet drag me out of the plaza and through the gate, the suspended lamps signaling my departure from town life. Far-off voices speckle the quiet air, breaking the silence of my solitude.

Wind stirs the branches and lonely leaves high above me. It's a quiet calm walk as I focus on breathing deeply.

Emerging into the open, the well-lit station welcomes me home like a lighthouse beacon greeting a lonely ship. Candles and lamps sparkle on the platform and outer walls, the upstairs windows beaming like a lover receiving a long-awaited adventurer.

Up onto the platform, I step toward the tracks to look along the benches facing the forest, happy to see no one. I consider sitting but quickly decide I'm in no mood for encounters with any of the station's mysterious visitors.

Turning toward the apartment stairs, I notice small narrow footprints on the stone floor, like a child's or a small woman's. Scindi?

I shuffle up the stairs into the apartment with a sigh of relief.

"Welcome home" Scindi smiles from the island.

She's barefoot in shorts and a tanktop, her hair tied back, the apartment almost too hot.

"Hi" I said unenthusiastically "Things are good?"

"Things are good. You?" she smiles meekly.

"Good"

"Were you outside barefoot on the platform?" I ask.

"No. Why?"

"Thought I saw footprints outside and I wondered" I shrug "My mistake"

I stagger to the chair next to her.

"Say goodbye to Caprice?" she says.

"Eh?" I say, the shock evident in my voice.

"I said 'at least it's a nice evening'"

"Oh. Yes, it is" I exhale "I'm exhausted"

"I see that" Scindi walks to put her arm around me.

I take a sip of coffee. Did I just make this?

I look around the room as I enjoy the warm beverage.

"Is this yours?" I ask looking at Scindi.

"No, it's yours" she squints her eyes.

"I'm making cheese sandwiches and more coffee. Anything for you?"

"Yes please" I get up "I'm gonna check the schedule so we're ready on time. We don't wanna be surprised by any last-minute changes. Be right back"

I walk out without my jacket but can't be bothered going back once I realize. By 5:00, darkness has normally set in and tonight is no different. A single guest, whose name I can't recall, occupies Room 6 on the top level of the hotel but it's impossible to tell if he's in his room at the moment or not. His departure tomorrow evening won't conflict with my activities tonight. Still, I need to be vigilant of his movements to ensure he has no interest in my nocturnal plans.

The quiet unlit control room has always been a simple place for me, a microcosm of the mysterious community.

A fresh schedule waits on the ancient printing device, the paper indicating a revised arrival time of 1:00 a.m. with space in a railcar allocated for the fourteen pieces the men here will load into it. This unexpected change concerns me, if only because it will appear odd for Scindi and I to be up and about on the platform at that time. Still, there's nothing to be done about it and the men who come don't seem the inquisitive types. They can ponder it to their heart's content once the train has left the station with us inside it.

Will there be room for us in the car with all the cargo? Will there be other cars with space? Will there be passengers?

Stuffing the notice into my pocket, I prepare to extinguish the lamp when I spot a small book on the counter in front of the piles of paper manifests and schedules. The black leather cover and silver metal clasp are in excellent shape, giving no indication as to its age.

The door hasn't been locked this time, so to whom does this belong?

Rissa? Caprice? Feryn?

Do I want to find out? I'm not a curious person by nature and this feels like a violation of someone's privacy, not intended for my viewing.

Still, I decide to at least look inside the front cover to determine its owner, with no markings of any kind on the outside to indicate its contents. I glance at a few of the words, the dark ink from a fine-tipped instrument have created a dull and faded script. The penmanship definitely that of a young girl, elegant but unrefined, a mixture of block and script.

This is a journal or a diary of some kind.

'Why did she leave? Does she not know that I love her?' is written on the first page.

'That horrid man'

'I cried again today. Alone'

'It's so dark'

'I'm all alone'

More writing follows beneath these initial entries but I already feel ashamed at my intrusion, my violation of someone's private thoughts.

This book looks a hundred years old.

As I close the cover, I notice a 'V' written in the upper left corner of the inside cover. 'V' for Vintassi? Or for someone else?

I set the diary down as I'd found it on the counter and exit the control room, shutting the door behind me, leaving it unlocked for whomever might come to retrieve their journal.

There's no one on the platform, no sound in the forest, and the clearing's empty.

Had someone watched me look at the diary?

I walk down the steps into the field, around under the control room, then hop back up to the platform to sit on the long bench. I stare into the trees across the tracks but see nothing in the dark void. No one's in either direction along the rail line. All is calm at the quiet station.

I try to think about tonight but can only conjure images of the dark forest, figures in the fog, and faces at the window. I shake my head in an attempt to dispel these memories, or whatever they are.

I wait for a movement, a noise, a smell. But none comes.

I take slow steps up the stairs to the door with a quick look back before entering the apartment.

I'm happy to see the room is brightly lit.

Scindi sits facing me, her back against the island, in red shorts and a white sports bra, a cup of coffee in one hand, a pastry in the other.

"Welcome back" she says after swallowing a bite of her cake.

"Ya"

"Ya?"

"Just worn out"

"Not just you" her voice is sharp.

"I know. Sorry"

"So, you and Jade are pretty close, eh?"

I've said it before I realize.

"Jade?"

"The girl who helps you at the school"

"Where's this coming from?" her look turns serious as she sets down her tart.

"Did you go back to your house earlier today?" I continue.

"Yeah, briefly, to make sure I'd not left anything behind" she replies.

"Was she there?"

"Who?" the tone in her voice is now verging on anger.

This isn't going anywhere.

"So why were you at my place and the school this morning?" she presses.

"Looking around. Strange things are happening lately"

"Lately?" she squints.

"I keep seeing that girl you introduced me to who helps you at the school"

"Milena helps me at the school"

"And what does she look like?"

"*What does she look like*?" she squirrels up her face "Early twenties, slim, blonde, taller than me"

"Oh" No resemblance to Jade.

"*Oh?*"

"I must have been confused" I try, unsuccessfully, to sound apologetic.

Who have I been seeing? Another vision?

"With what?" she stands "Is there something you'd like to tell me?"

"Not really"

I struggle to recall what I'd seen at her place with Scindi and Jade but it doesn't come to mind. And who is Jade that I've been seeing everywhere? That, I do remember.

Her eyes fix on me, her arms crossed in front of her.

What does she want me to say? Have I already said too much? Likely.

Scindi's expression becomes increasingly stern as I formulate my thoughts.

"Jade is an old friend of mine" she says "Remember, the poster in my room"

No, that can't be. This woman was real.

A tap at the window facing the clearing catches our attention.

We both turn but nothing's there.

Scindi starts toward it but stops after a few steps. I go right up to the glass and peek out. Nothing.

My eyes linger for a moment but eventually I turn and make my way back to the island.

Then, a noise at the door, like someone setting down a bag of coins.

Scindi looks but doesn't move.

I look to the window again but, seeing nothing, make a move to the door.

Is that scratching? Feet running down the stairs?

I hesitate before slowly pulling it open.

No one. And no bag of coins.

The only light on the platform is from the lanterns facing the tracks.

I turn to head back inside and spot my key ring in the door's lock. That had never happened before.

I pull them loose and shut the door behind me as I return to my seat.

"Bad place to leave your keys" Scindi says.

"I don't know how they got there. They're always in my pocket"

"Guess not" she turns away from me.

I walk to the window looking onto the clearing.

Does one of my keys open Room? What's in there? Does it matter? Do I want to know?

It's so dark. It's always dark in the shadows.

Who cares about her? Waits for her? Wants her to be safe? Loves her? No one. Alone. Forever, alone. She reaches the man's door only to flee back to her room once she does.

Does she cry? Maybe.

Out the window, the moon peeks through the spaces between the clouds against evening's dark background. Black and white branches and trunks extend up from the ground like a skeletal audience come to see this final performance.

The path to town does not seem inviting tonight.

I go downstairs to light a lantern between the main floor hotel rooms, the quiet platform now glowing with soft light from the gently flickering candles in the lamps along the walls.

Still no sign of the man in Room 6.

The keys play in the palm of my left hand.

I walk into the kitchen for coffee or wine. I open the wrong drawer while looking for a spoon and see the box I'd been given in the shop by the blue-cloaked woman. I'd never spent the time to try to open it and discover its contents.

The heavy silver box seems shinier now, the thin black 'I', disproportionate in its elongated shape, straight down the middle, but somehow beautiful. I hold it gently in my hands looking at it, turn it over, examine it for an opening, a slit into which I might insert something, push and turn it, caress it gently, rub it, grab it firmly. Nothing.

I set it down on its side to look at it from a distance, then grasp it to focus my touches on the 'I', press lightly then firmer, rotate the box, push and pull at the raised mark. In the motion of pressing it, I feel a click as a piece of the dark metal lifts slightly from the rest, enough for me to turn it until it clicks a second time, then moans as the top spins away from the bottom.

Its plain white interior contains a shiny silver key, similar to those provided to the hotel guests, nestled in the center of the box. What does it open? And why did that woman give it to me?

Was that really Rebecca?

The hotel doors are much older than the rooms' interiors, which had undergone upgrades in recent years, the keys dating back possibly to the original construction.

I can't think of anything in town that begins with an "I", no place, no person, no one in the historical texts, no book at the library, nothing at the school or station, no cargo received or shipped out, not even an object.

Was there a previous station master? I don't recall seeing any names beginning with "I", either first or last.

It has to be something at the station but what?

I stare at the key, then at the box.

What if it isn't an "I" but a "1"?

68 – Room 1

"Whatcha doin'?" Scindi comes toward me.

"Just want to check on something" I say, carefully slipping the key into my pocket, unsure of my intentions.

She walks to curl up on the couch.

I put on my jacket and walk out the door alone, the air pleasantly cool.

There's no one outside and no sound other than a soft breeze in my ears in the calm darkness.

The platform is empty in every direction, across the tracks just trees and grasses and rocks, the clearing dark yet mostly clear of haze. The moon above and to my right provides veiled light.

I cross the infinite distance between the steps to the apartment and Room 1, my eyes and ears attuned to any break in the quiet night.

I stop near the lantern between Rooms 1 and 2, then look at each door in turn.

A covered candle along the utility room's wall combines with the lamp in front of me to break the darkness and cast spectral shadows in poorly lit areas. Facing Room 1, I dispel my instinct to knock, waiting several seconds before withdrawing the key from my pocket. I examine it, check the lock in the door, look at the key, and stare at the door. There's no light visible beneath it.

Again, I wait. I look side to side, then stare at the door some more as if waiting for it to open on its own.

Only now do I notice the lock and handle are shinier than on the other rooms.

Exhaling, I realize I've been holding my breath. Petrified, I wait for something I hope won't come. For a second. Or is it a minute? Or is it longer?

Absolute silence everywhere.

I inhale deeply, place the key in its hole, and spin it until it clicks. Do I want this? It seems somehow worse to wonder than to know, or so I tell myself.

Does the key unlock the door?

Now what? Do I have it in me to actually open it? What could possibly be in there that opening it is forbidden? And that I've been given a key in this most unusual fashion?

I turn to take in my surroundings, content to still be alone. No sound, no movement, no smells. I face the door again. Withdrawing the key from the hole, I return it to my pocket. A few seconds pass as I stand mesmerized by my circumstances.

The cool damp air finds its way under my jacket. My heartbeat quickens.

There's still no sound from inside Room 1.

I take a deep breath.

The station's sign behind me creaks on its hinges giving me a chill.

Before I realize it, my left hand has reached down and turned the knob, the door slowly swinging inward to the left on its own weight. I hadn't thought to bring a light of my own and so stare blankly into the room waiting for my eyes to adjust.

The smell of licorice.

I find myself unable to move, staring into the abyss that is Room 1.

It's 6:15 and darkness is fully upon the station.

The moon's scant light, with help from the exterior candles, reveals just enough of the interior for my vision to take in some of the room's contents. Scattered crates against the far wall, I think; to my immediate right, an empty lamp on the wall next to the door; farther to the right, a boarded-up window above two smaller crates, a long box on top of them; to my left a corridor, presumably to the bedroom. The floor appears to be uncarpeted wood, but it's difficult to tell further into the room. My legs step into Room 1 as if moving on their own.

Dusty air hangs in the bleakness, the sparse items spread throughout giving the impression of it having been unvisited for many years. The intact wooden crates against the wall opposite me look similar in appearance to those which the men load and unload from the trains, though I can't be sure of details in this light. I walk in the direction of the wall to my right where slivers of moonlight penetrate the aging planks covering the window, carving white lines on the floor further into the room. The box atop the crates resembles a small coffin, its size befitting a child. I stop a short distance from it, take a deep dust-filled breath and step forward.

I hear a soft noise behind me. Scindi?

But no one's there when I turn.

The room is quiet and calm, almost peaceful in its tranquility, despite the shabby interior. I spot what looks like small footprints on the dusty ground like those of a child sending a chill across my neck and down my back.

Does someone live here?

My eyes struggle but are unable to see farther back into the room, as I try not to imagine what might be watching me.

My eyes revert to the boarded-up window, knife-like blades of light slashing through razor thin cracks in the old wood.

Stepping forward, I reach the crates beneath the window and lean forward.

Oh my God.

There's a child's body in the box; her skin pale; her dress a dirty purple, almost grey; hands folded across her chest. Surely a recently deceased person to appear so life-like, she looks as though she'll open her eyes at any moment and rise from her slumber. I freeze, ashamed of my intrusion, worried I've entered a solemn chamber. The box looks old, the wood thick and untreated yet smooth and hard, the boards even and solid.

The girl's skin looks both dead and alive, her face and hands unwrinkled but colourless, her body frail and thin but lifelike. Her slender fingers, her tiny legs, her skeletal black stockings, her charcoal shoes. Her dirty clothing is from a time-gone-by, odd for a child so recently dead. Tangled jet-black hair frames her fair skin and covers her face. Judging by her body, she can't be older than 10.

I wonder why she's here.

Behind me, the door swings shut.

I turn, unsure what to expect but see nothing, though the diminished light makes me shiver at the unknown. The door is in fact closed, no more light shining in that way. Again, I curse the fact that I've brought no lamp, my eyes unable to adjust in the darkness. I attempt to focus my gaze and channel the sparse moonlight to reveal anything new in the room but to no avail. I'm alone.

Or so I hope.

A shifting noise, as of wood on wood brings my attention back to the box but it's as I left it, the girl still in repose in her casket. I have no desire to take a closer look at her body.

Will my path to the exit be blocked by persons or objects?

My eyes have adjusted as much as they will, just enough to make out a thin crack of light at the bottom of the door leading out onto the platform. Most of the floor between me and the exit remains obscured in darkness, making me nervous about what might wait in that direction.

Could I pry the boards off the window and scramble out that way? It would mean climbing over the girl's body, a grim thought.

Should I yell for Scindi? Will she hear me?

Does someone or something know I'm in here? Is that person or thing in here with me?

I struggle to make out any detail but am unable. Darkness in every direction, like floating in infinite space.

Again, a scratch from behind me, gentle but deliberate like a nail drawing on wood. I wait for several seconds for any other noise or movement, hoping I won't be touched. I can't turn around; the thought of seeing the girl sitting up in her coffin is nearly too much for me.

But nothing happens.

The clouds momentarily part outside as a bright white sliver slices through the cracks in the window's covering providing a brief glimpse of the area in front of me and then the illumination is gone as I return to darkness and the unknown.

Is that more scraping from inside the long box?

I drop to my knees, hoping this will make me less visible, my heartbeat echoing in my ears. I try to slow my breathing and gather my senses.

The view from so low is no improvement as I feel in my pockets and on the ground for anything that could be used as a weapon, though I fear physical objects will be of no use against whatever occupies this room with me now.

I shuffle around in front of the crates, breathless and shaking.

There's no scratching or creaking or footsteps for the moment, all is quiet but for the sound of the gentle breeze outside.

It feels like an eternity since I'd entered, though it has probably only been a minute or two. Will Scindi know where to look for me if she becomes worried? Unlikely.

I'm alone in Room 1.

I stand up in the obscurity. A sensation of helplessness and solitude.

As ghastly as it sounds, perhaps there's an item in the girl's coffin; a candle; a lamp; matches. I turn to see if I can conjure the courage to inspect the box.

The girl is in her funereal pose, arms at her sides.

Who is she? I hadn't heard of the recent passing of a child. This would have certainly been news in a town this size, or at least warrant conversation among the townsfolk and a ceremony, such as it is.

I pause staring into the box.

Considerations of climbing over the girl's coffin come and go. Even if I summoned the bravery to attempt it, it's a storey-high drop to the ground. And I'll have to move the long box so as not to step inside it to even get to the point of dismantling the covering with my bare hands.

Another desperate check of my pockets which contain exactly what they did on the previous inspection: nothing.

No way to examine any more of the room. I've seen more than I expected and just want out.

I hear a noise outside the door. I consider whether or not to yell. I decide against it, recalling Michael's explicit instructions to not enter this room. Part of me hopes someone will open the door but part of me realizes that will just make everything worse.

I wait alone. In darkness. In silence.

Time passes, though how much I don't know.

I summon the courage to take a single step in the direction of the door. I inhale deeply before my next step. No obstacles at ground level, though I wonder whether I should protect my head as well as my lower body. I look to my right to spot anything further into the room but see nothing in the darkness. The light previously visible beneath the door has disappeared, its location a guess on my part based on my recollection of the number of steps into the room.

How long have I been in here?

Another slow step toward my exit comes with a deep breath.

I pause after each step, as if this will make my movements a secret to anyone else in the room with me.

The smell of licorice wafts over me as it had when I'd first entered, though I can't imagine its origin. I hear a soft scratching near the coffin.

My heart stops. I freeze.

I take another quiet step to the door. My next steps are small quick jogs to the door which I throw open, stepping out into the night air. I immediately close Room 1 behind me and run to the bench alongside the tracks to catch my breath.

"What are you doing?"

I nearly scream. Again.

Rissa on my right

"What are you doing out so late?" I ask.

"We're out and about a lot" she replies casually.

"You and Sam?" I say.

"Us too"

"As well as who?" I wonder who else is here.

"As well as you" she smiles hopping down onto the tracks.

"Hang on…" I say but she disappears along the tracks to my left.

Was she in Room 1 with me? Does she know about the body? Will anyone else find out about my intrusion? Does anyone else already know?

Anxious and shivering, I feel no less terrified and no more informed for having entered Room 1, the unknown dead girl weighing on my mind. Her tiny life-like body, her pale skin, her stringy black hair.

I stand alone on the platform in the night's silence and the station's stillness. Time pauses. I stare into the forest across the tracks, walk to the platform's edge, and look in each direction as the rails trail off into the unknown. My body stops, my mind freezes. I'm held in place by mystical forces unable to move.

I'm truly afraid; cold and afraid.

I take a deep breath and make my way back upstairs. In the apartment, Scindi stands looking out into the clearing, wearing only a long t-shirt. The apartment is bright from the many lit lamps.

The room's warmth holds me in its embrace, my body free from the chilly grip of the damp outside air. It feels wonderful.

"Hi" I say.

"Hi" she replies without turning around.

Unable to think of anything else to say, I walk to the kitchen but stop before I reach it.

Should I tell her I've been in Room 1?

"What time is it?" Scindi asks.

"Now? Almost 7:00" I reply.

"We should eat" she walks toward me, kisses me, and goes on to the fridge.

While she opens and closes doors and boxes, I walk to the window overlooking the platform and train tracks but see nothing. There's still a lot of time before we need to be ready, but what crucial preparation is missing? We can't just walk out and step onto the train as the men load it. I'm never alone when it's in the station and who knows if someone is actually there out of sight watching or if this is part of the team's role. I don't want to succumb to whatever fate had befallen Dalton. What did he neglect to do?

"Come and get it" Scindi says quietly.

She's laid out an assortment of breads and meats and fruit. This is most welcome.

"Thanks"

She sits at the island.

"An interesting discovery" she says "I can make 'Clovinston' from the letters in your name"

"Ok" I think of the letters in my name.

"With the remaining letters and I can spell 'Dasie' or 'Sadie'"

"Sadie" I think out loud.

"Who's Sadie?" she asks.

I stop, dumbfounded.

"I don't know…" I whisper.

"You don't know?"

"'Their names are in your letters'" I mumble.

"What about your letters?" Scindi asks quietly.

"There's always been a riddle with letters but I never thought it'd be the letters in my name" I say "How did you come up with that?"

"I'm smart too, you know" she smirks, hands on her hips.

The letters. Who is Sadie?

If she's a Clovinston, is she related to Hannah? I don't recall her name in the genealogy but I've seen it somewhere.

"So, your name, my name, and Sadie's name all have exactly the same letters" Scindi says "Weird, eh? Is there a Sadie Clovinston?"

The plaques in the little cemetery. 'S' for Sadie?

My head hurts as I sip a cup of coffee.

"So, what now?" she asks after we've snacked in silence for a minute or two.

"I'm not sure" I say.

"Not very reassuring" she shakes her head.

No, it isn't. But what should I do? There's no one left to ask.

I finish eating and stand, looking around the room.

"It might be just us now" I say.

"That's ok, right?" she says softly.

I could have made a home here, or so I thought when I'd accepted the offer. Everything was provided. Exploring the island would've been a blast and the outdoor potential here is endless. The blue café provides an escape as does the library. And Scindi is great. Or so I think.

Where will I go now? If I get out of here.

"I was in Room 1" I say without realizing.

"You were where?" Scindi jumps up.

"I know. It's not like I even planned it. It just happened"

"It just happened?" she looks stunned.

"What I mean is…"

"What you mean is…"

"That I went in there without telling you" I finish for her.

She sits back down as if out of breath.

Scindi stares at her hands on the counter in front of her.

I want to tell her about the dead girl's body but don't, unsure where that will lead and how much I want to share. It would be difficult to put my experience into words.

Two candles to my left go out, another on my right flickers behind its glass.

The shadowy apartment seems to be closing in around me, the room smaller, the corners darker, the scant light weaker. Scindi has almost faded away completely, her motionless form nearly transparent.

"So, what was in there?" she asks without looking up.

"Just a dusty old room. Creepy and dark" I lie.

"That's it"

"And a bunch of old crap, some of which has been there for a mighty long time, I'm sure"

Like the dead body that looked both recent and old.

Did I do the right thing by entering Room 1 or will that come back to haunt me? I wish Feryn would show up but it doesn't happen despite my most earnest desire. We sit in silence. Scindi is even more muted recently than usual, to the point where I sometimes forget she's here.

Clock-watching. Lotsa time to do that with the train not due until 1:00 am. What am I supposed to do now? I don't really want to sit outside. Certainly not go to town. I do want to be with Scindi. Don't I?

I'll never be the same after this adventure. What could possibly match my time as station master?

Scindi stares out the window into the clearing.

"Did…" my sentence hangs in the air as I consider how to finish it.

"Eh?" Scindi looks my way.

"Nothing" I say "Just thinking out loud"

"Oh" she turns back to looking outside.

Is the train really coming at 1:00 a.m.? That seems a bizarre time.

"I'm gonna check at the control room again" I ponder out loud "That arrival time seems mighty strange"

"Ok" she whispers without turning.

I walk out the door and down the stairs, the platform clear and quiet, the forest calm, Room 1 closed. Clouds fan the moon, revealing then interrupting its light, though the sky is clearer now than earlier; the fog in the clearing is now just a thin mist; the gentle breeze rustles the trees around the station. I look along the tracks and the benches facing them. No one's here. No smells. No sounds. Quiet and tranquil.

Inside the unlocked control room, everything seems as I'd left it. No new papers or documents. No mysterious notes or packages. Nothing on the printer so I check the ledger where I store the printed schedules and note the records: 1:00 am arrival with goods to be loaded. I'd already forwarded the cargo list which had been left for me on the board in town describing the quantity, size, and weight of the load to destinations unknown via the ancient machinery.

I'm not looking forward to the robotic army.

I notice that the diary is gone.

Did its owner come to retrieve their thoughts put to paper? 'V' for Violet?

Back up the stairs, I expect to see or hear motion from Room 1 but nothing.

I enter the suite, Scindi now on the sofa in pajamas as if waiting for me.

"Where ya been?" her smooth accent rolls off her tongue.

"Control room" I say "Train's still at 1:00"

"One in the morning?" her eyes widen.

"One in the morning. We knew that" I throw off my jacket and boots, surprised at her surprise "And we won't be alone. The men will be here loading up whatever it is they load up"

"So that's it?" she says, impatience in her voice.

"What do you mean?"

"We just walk out and step onto the train at 1:00 am with everyone watching?"

"I hope so"

"Can't one of your friends help us?" she asks.

She swings her feet off the couch to look at me.

"I thought you had connections in town" her voice softens "Did anyone give you any ideas for us to make this work?"

"Not really"

"I thought you saw things. Saw people" she squirrels up her face.

"Sometimes, but it's not like that. It's hard to explain"

She seems aggressive but I'm sure it's only her nerves so I try to remain calm.

Do I offer further explanation into my actions?

What does Scindi think? Is she waiting for me to ask?

We're alone at the station. Or so I believe.

I drag myself to the kitchen.

Lanterns and candles light the apartment more than usual; perhaps the brightness calms Scindi.

She gets up, as if about to speak but just stares at me.

With nothing to say, I stare back.

She must be scared; I am.

What am I missing?

I ponder another coffee but don't want to feel jittery or have to relieve myself during our escape. Wine? I need to stay sharp. I'm not hungry, though I contemplate eating to pass the time.

Scindi sits back down facing away from me, feet beneath her body and underneath a blanket on the sofa. Should I share what I know? What I suspect? My concerns?

Too many thoughts in my head, too much uncertainty, too much time until the train arrives.

The time on my watch says 7:25. The clock over the door shows the same time. I check my watch again then look at Scindi curled up like a cat. I'll leave her be alone a bit to get her mind straight.

I'm sitting with my back to the island facing into the room. Is Scindi sleeping? I don't want to speak or make any noise to disturb her.

I get up slowly and without a sound. Scindi doesn't move. I turn in the direction of the window looking into the clearing, the moon's faint light illuminating the field. Reaching the window, I stare out at the thin black and white tree limbs on the forest's perimeter, motionless in the dark.

I stare up at the moon, its three-quarter shape outlined behind the small cloud passing across its surface.

I exhale deeply, turning back into the room, sitting on the window ledge.

How will this play out, my attempted escape from New Brook West?

Never again

One by one they fell, none who came left. Such was their fate to carry the name of their ancestors. And to further my plan, the prophecy. Yet two still remain.

Few had seen my green-eyed stare, fewer still knew that I watched.
I've been thought weak, been forgotten.
I'll never be weak again.

69 – Violet and Fuchsia

I notice the purple flowers in a vase on the island.

"I picked them today" Scindi says standing in front of the couch with a smile "I'd never noticed them before but they're really pretty" The flowers are nice: soft purple petals that almost look like small butterfly wings with a tiny yellow dot at the center off a large stem. I'd seen them in the forest maybe once or twice but never thought anything of it, never thought to bring any to Scindi.

"They are pretty" I say "Pretty like you"

Scindi smiles.

"Then you should have picked me some a long time ago" she walks over to kiss me on the cheek "Maybe I'll bring these with me when we leave. I've always loved flowers"

"Flowers are nice"

Flowers. Caprice said that someone wanted flowers. And I'd heard it from someone else as well. Her flowers. I can't think of anyone in town to give flowers. Do these flowers belong to someone? Should I be giving these to a woman in town? To any woman? But how do I do that? Knock on someone's door and give them flowers? That can't be the answer.

"What kind of flowers are those?" I ask pointing to the vase.

"Violets" Scindi decides after a moment's thought "I've seen a few of them, mostly in patches in damp areas"

"I've also seen some fuchsia" she goes on "Mostly as bushes but a couple of times like bells or lanterns hanging from stems. They're a really pretty colour: mostly pink-ish. They're even rarer and farther from the community"

I'm trying to recall a memory, something in the back of my mind.

"I don't know a lot about flowers" she says softly.

"Violet. Fuchsia" I lower my head in thought.

Flowers as well as names in the family tree.

"The 'mother wants her flowers'" I lift my head "Hannah wants her daughters"

"Who are they?" Scindi starts toward me but stops.

"Violet and Fuchsia" I yell triumphantly.

"The plants…" Scindi says.

"Hannah's flowers. Her flowers are her daughters"

"Ok"

"I think I know where Hannah is and how to give her flowers to her" I try to contain my elation.

"Ok…" Scindi's eyes squint.

The letters 'V' and 'F' on the plaques in the cemetery I visited with Feryn.

'V' and 'F' from the drawings in the house in East.

"I think I've seen Rebecca's grave" I shudder as my enthusiasm wanes "And Hannah's too. The women in the family tree"

"And…" Scindi says.

"And I might know about Violet too, though I wish I didn't" I cringe.

"What about her?"

"We have to go into Room 1" I say quietly.

"What?" Scindi's face lights with terror.

"To get Violet" I cringe "At least I think it's Violet"

"What's she doing in there?" Scindi takes a step back.

"She's dead?"

"Dead Violet?"

"Yes" I shiver. It occurs to me what I'm suggesting.

"Is Fuchsia in there too?" Scindi looks at me woefully.

"No" I reply meekly "I don't think so"

"So, where is she?"

"I don't know" my head sags in despair "This is all I can come up with"

"Ok…" her arms sag to her sides.

Hannah was Violet and Fuchsia's mother and Rebecca's daughter. Their names are in the tree. The family tree.

Am I seriously contemplating entering Room 1 to find a dead girl's body to take to the cemetery? Bury the girls next to their mother? Is this the correct answer?

What about Fuchsia? How do I find her?

"Grab your coat" I say gently "Please"

Scindi stares at the floor for a moment before taking a deep breath and walking toward me.

"Do you know what you're doing?" she asks softly.

"Yes" I assure her.

Light jackets and boots on, we walk out the door, locking it behind us. It's so calm around the station, unnaturally quiet, like I've gone deaf. Is Scindi behind me? I feel like I'm moving in slow motion in the stillness. Moonlight comes and goes in the spaces between the clouds, casts its glow onto the station's grey stone floor and dull brick walls, into the field's short green and brown grass. I scan the area across the tracks for any signs of movement, check both ways past the benches along the wall, look across the clearing, and open the door to the utility room. I recoil at the thought of entering this room again, remembering poor Acacia, but need a lantern, a tarp, a shovel, and two carts. I place one cart just outside the room. The other I slowly walk down the stone stairs, its wood wheels striking each step loudly, shattering the silence.

The fog in the clearing is gone, though the damp chill remains.

I place the cart in the short grass to the right of the steps leading up to the platform.

"I'm really not looking forward to going in here" Scindi shivers.

"I know" I set the shovel on the cart at the bottom of the stairs "But this might be the missing piece"

"Burying a dead girl?" Scindi raises her voice.

"I'm doing my best. This is morbid for me too. I've already seen her body"

A lantern?

"It's pitch dark in here" I say "But I don't think a lantern is a good idea"

"Seriously?"

"Trust me. Please"

I set the lantern down outside the door.

"Ok. After you" Scindi steps back, gesturing for me to take the lead.

"After me" I say taking a deep breath.

The door swings open slowly but quietly, as I pause to remind myself what I'm doing. Will everything be where it was before? Is someone else in here?

It's so dark.

Will removing the dead girl's body make things worse? It's too late to reconsider.

I wonder if anyone in town has ever entered Room 1.

I freeze in dread, the effect of the room coming over me. It's as solemn as before and just as dusty, a few slivers of white light slicing onto the floor to my right through the cracks in the window covering. My adjusting eyes tell me that objects are in more or less the same place. The door opens fully and we wait in silence. From behind me, Scindi takes my hand. At least I hope it's Scindi.

I take a short step forward until I'm standing just inside the room. I hear Scindi's feet shuffle against the wood floor. I force my lungs to breathe.

I hear no sound in the room, though I wonder if this is good or bad.

How long have I been waiting? My eyes look to the coffin on top of the crates under the boarded-up window so we can begin our cheerless task. I'm thankful for the thin shards of light through the cracked planks to guide me.

The **New Brook West** sign near the tracks creaks as if warning us of what lies ahead.

I pull Scindi's hand and slowly make my way across the room to the window.

I pause as we reach the crates and release Scindi's hand, sending her a half-smile that she may not see in the dark. I peer over the side at the white light shining on the small girl in her dirty dress peacefully at rest, arms crossed over her chest. Scindi leans in next to me and takes a quick glance at the body before pulling back sharply.

"Ok" I whisper.

"Ok" she replies.

"Wait here" I say walking back to the door.

"What?" panic in her voice.

"I have to get the cart" I reassure her.

"Hurry" she shivers.

I return with the narrow four-wheeled buggy, a surface barely sufficient to hold the coffin but enough to get it to the larger one to haul into the woods. The cart's width allows it to barely pass through the door. I turn it to the right in the darkness.

"Scindi" I say quietly.

No answer. I try to pick out her figure in the black room.

"Scindi" I say louder.

Still no answer.

I push the cart forward in small steps until it touches the crates. The door swings shut behind me, a thin line of yellow light visible at the bottom.

"Where are you?" I whisper anxiously. My eyes haven't adjusted to the darkness.

Where did she go?

My hands reach into the darkness in all directions, my heart beating loudly in my chest, my breathing gasps. Oh no.

Silence all around. I'm alone.

"Scindi" I say again weakly.

A hand touches my shoulder.

"I'm right here" she says "Why do you keep calling my name? And what the hell took you so long?"

"I was gone for ten seconds at most. Where were you?"

"I thought you'd ditched me" she says, her figure barely visible "From now on we stay together"

"Together" I repeat.

I take a moment to collect myself and walk around to the head of the coffin to confirm the body is still inside. Serene and grey, the pale young girl lies in perfect peace as though merely taking a nap. I'd better make sure she's dead - I can't bury someone alive just because they look creepy. And sleep in a coffin in a locked and abandoned hotel room.

I just want to be out of here. Please.

First, I'll get her onto the cart, then take a closer look when we're outside.

"Gimme a hand" I say to Scindi.

"By doing what?"

"Stand on the other side of the deck" I gesture in the darkness to the other end of the buggy "To hold it in place"

"I can barely see it" she slides around.

We move the cart's surface parallel to the crates which sits slightly lower, allowing me to slide the box onto it a bit at a time. I climb up and ease it down with a few gentle pushes, placing it in the center of the narrow deck.

Thin knives of light pierce the window, shining into the casket.

I cover the coffin with the tarp both out of respect and fear of the coffin's contents.

"There must be a lid" Scindi says.

"I wouldn't even know where to look" I hop down and walk around to pull the cart out of the room "Let's get out of here"

I reach for Scindi's hand "Together"

"Together" she repeats softly, taking my hand.

The cart rolls slowly across the floor ahead of me, its wheels scratching the wood surface, the sound echoing in the room. I remain vigilant of my surroundings despite being unable to see anything but the sliver of yellow at the bottom of the door. I try not to look around, focused on leaving with my gruesome cargo. I release Scindi's hand when we reach the door, casting her a half-smile that she probably doesn't see in the dark. With her a step ahead of me, we exit Room 1, and step onto the platform, me pulling the cart with both hands.

Moonlight shines brightly as it emerges from behind cloud cover combining with the lit candles to dispel the gloom, the area around me bright yellow and white. The walls are fresh, the stone floor smooth, the utility room door a sharp blue colour. The stairs up to my apartment appear solid and new in the moon's glow, the station reborn, the building taking on its former glory. The New Brook West sign hangs from shiny silver chains, swaying ever so slightly but noiselessly. The clearing is a vibrant green, the distant trees vivid. The station is calm and quiet, the air cool and light.

The scene in front of my eyes is a stark contrast to the train station I've come to know.

Is it still night? It feels so different, like I've stepped back in time.

A noise like a branch breaking snaps me back to the present, as a cloud passes across the moon.

Is someone else here? I can't even think about that.

I try to regain my senses.

The station is solemn as if in mournful sadness, the two lit lamps creating shadows under the stairs and against the walls. The trees across the tracks offer no solace, the spaces between them filled with deep darkness, the large clearing lit by occasional moonlight.

We made it out of Room 1.

I turn to look back at the coffin on the cart's deck beneath the tarp, and send Scindi a confident glance.

Is anyone watching our macabre undertaking?

The sinister black and white trees loom across the clearing, the path to the village and the school barely discernible despite the clear air.

"Are we really doing this?" Scindi asks walking down the steps.

"I think so" I say, following her then turning back to slowly guide the cart down the stairs, the sound of wood on stone quieter than I'd expected.

"Burying a girl in the middle of the night" she shivers, lowering the lantern to her side.

"Yes" I nod.

The moon now lights our grim endeavour, the sky mostly clear, the air cool. We slide the decks together as I carefully move the box to the new carriage, Scindi holding them together as best she can. I try not to think about the long box's contents, covered as the girl is with the tarp. After transferring the coffin to the larger cart, I stop to catch my breath. My blood feels like cold water running through my veins, my head a hazy mess, my movements slow and deliberate.

I encourage Scindi with a brave front, my fear hidden behind this mask, though I do feel that this action is both beneficial to our departure and well-intentioned if not compassionate.

I pull back the tarp to see the grey girl, her frail body, her lifeless form both dead and alive in the lamps' yellow glow. I touch her cheek behind her hair, cold but fresh like she's just walked in the outside but not like stone or glass or how I imagine a dead body, more like skin that has merely been exposed to cool air. Her arm flops weakly when I raise it. Her body is unresponsive when I prod it, her dirty dress flaps helplessly during my examination. She's been laid on several white sheets, separating her from the wood beneath. I press her wrist and feel no pulse; press her neck and again nothing. She must be dead.

"She's very much dead" Feryn steps around the corner.

"Where did you come from?" Scindi jumps.

"She's been dead a long time" he continues.

"So, what…" I begin but stop, not knowing what I'll ask.

"You seem to know where you're going" he nods.

"Not really" I say "Bringing a mother her flowers. At least this one. I don't know where I'll find her other daughter"

"I do wish you luck, Colden" he looks out across the field "This is very brave on your part"

Scindi comes to my side and we look toward the wide dark trail across the clearing.

Waiting for Feryn to add a piece of wisdom, it takes me a moment to realize he's gone.

I wonder how the rest of the evening will unfold.

The empty clearing ahead, the moon and stars above, the station behind me. I look around the building and out toward the treeline but see and hear no one. Perhaps we are alone. With dead Violet. I nod to Scindi and grab the cart to carry on to our destination. I hear no sounds on either side as we creep through the melancholy woods. Moonlight from above gives the slender trees a knife-like appearance, slim and sharp, their branches clearly defined; darkness fills the voids between their trunks. All is calm.

We move quickly across the open area to reach the shelter of the trees. The path welcomes us, the forest even darker off the trail than in the clearing, the treetops overhead blocking out most of the light.

Scindi steps to my left, her right hand on the cart, the lantern on the deck in front of me, lighting the way ahead.

Silence around us is both relieving and unnerving without any rustling in the trees or crunching of leaves and branches, no sounds of any kind around us or in the distance. We turn right at the fork leading to Scindi's place.

In a moment, we reach the school's clearing, the glade larger than I recall.

"Where are we going?" Scindi asks.

"Trust me" I say.

High above to the right, the moon slips behind a thin layer of cloud, though its light still illuminates much of the clearing. I stop the buggy to check under the tarp, the girl resting peacefully in her death pose.

There's no one on the benches, near the school, or in the shadows of the forest's fringe. That I can see. The only sound is an orchestra of leafless branches and limbs gently snapping against each other, a single owl's low hoot in the distance, like the singer of a ghostly band.

Scindi shuffles up behind me.

"So now where?" she looks around the clearing "Past my place?"

"There's another way" I try to recall my trip with Feryn "Across the field"

"And you know how to find this?" she whispers "You do realize we're pulling the body of a dead little girl. I don't need to tell you I'm more than a little scared"

"We're almost there" I say, trying to reassure her.

I hope the moonlight will reveal any inconsistencies along the edge of the forest, show me the path to the little cemetery. I can't spot the mysterious route from where we're standing; there's not enough light and I'm too far away. The lantern in Scindi's hand seems to be impeding rather than assisting with my locating the hidden trail so it'll be of no use.

"I'll be right back" I say "I need to walk around the perimeter"

"You're leaving me here with her?" Scindi's arms drop to her sides, her eyes wide "Again?"

"I'll be right back" I head off without waiting for her response.

I leave her the lamp as cold consolation.

I start to my right and come around at the back of the schoolhouse. I immediately spot what appears to be an old overgrown trail, but not the one I need as it heads in the direction of the tracks rather than past Scindi's place. Approaching the building, my pace slows, my eyes lingering on the window to catch sight of any light inside the building, any figures moving within, any movements outside along the walls. Moonlight illuminates the area around me, sharpening the structure's details. The interior is unlit, only the moon's reflection visible in the dark windows. No one's toward the front of the school nor on this side, the windows striking against the building's walls.

I pause, waiting for any sudden sound or movement either in or outside the building. The clearing is eerily quiet.

I glance back at Scindi and the cart with its cadaverous cargo. She looks in my direction, her right hand still touching the cart, the lantern on the ground at her side. I want to yell some encouragement but don't want to break the silence.

I carry on past the school, eyes focused on the forest to catch sight of the trail.

The moon comes and goes behind thin cover making the area around me even more difficult to survey. A crackling of the branches in the forest to my right makes me stop, then shudder, as a gentle wind through the grass creates a whispering sound. The thought of looking in the direction of any sound is too chilling to consider. I want to look back to Scindi but feel compelled to keep my eyes on my objective, eerie as it is to stare into the forest's eternal darkness. Like looking into a bottomless pit. The trees come to life when the moon fades, their spindly arms reaching out to me, their voices talking amongst themselves, the black space between them concealing the unknown.

I take a look back and notice I've reached the point directly across the clearing from where Scindi's standing, my steps a safe distance out from the tree limbs. I look up, pleading the moon to keep its glow on me for a few moments longer so I can feel safe while searching.

Feryn said 'it's easy to find if you know where to look'. But I'm sure I don't know where to look. It's all just sinister darkness between the skeletal branches.

By now, the lantern's orange glow is all I can see of Scindi's location.

I shiver at the dark forest, the open clearing, the cool air. Clouds have tucked the moon behind them, the dim illumination of little help.

I've inspected half the clearing with still no sign of a concealed path or potential route wide enough to accommodate the cart. Was it ever here?

My mind ponders what might be happening at the station or in the village right now and if anyone has a reason to want to pay me a visit tonight. I think of Rissa and Sam, whose nuisance would be a welcome presence right now; of Caprice who was always so sad but kind and caring and who I would miss; of Acacia who had been so confident and sweet; of Comet who was so much more than she seemed; of Scindi who I want to protect and who wants to protect me but who I haven't fully figured out. For a moment I forget about my clandestine actions with a dead young girl in a dark forest on a moonlit night.

To my right, an outline appears in the darkness between the trees, the figure vanishing as soon as I spot it. An animal? The mysterious forest resident?

I exhale then stop breathing to stand as still as I can in the silence. I'm frozen. What had been there is now gone, no more movements in the forest. Were we followed?

For a moment, I stare blankly at the trees ahead of me, discouraged as I am by my lack of success. I'm afraid to look behind me, scared to move at all.

I take a deep breath and look to my sides. The moon's faint glow makes the trees more distinct, the darkness between them blacker.

'If you know where to look'

I relax my mind and drop my shoulders. I don't have Feryn's 'compass' abilities but perhaps if I slow everything down my mind will be sharper and more aware.

I slow my breathing and stare at the trees, trying not to try so hard like looking at those pictures with hidden images. I scan next to me and further along as I slowly advance.

Around me all is quiet, the moonlight overhead breaking the darkness.

A few steps ahead the trees part, a trail only visible if I look directly at it.

That has to be it.

I can't call for Scindi to bring the cart so reluctantly step into the forest and grab a rock to mark my place, staring at the path before I turn around. I'm at a full run across the middle of the clearing as clouds drift past the moon.

I'm elated to see Scindi still with the cart and our ghastly cargo; she leaps and nearly yells out when I arrive.

I hug her tightly.

"What the fu... What were you doing?" she glares at me.

"What do you mean?" I'm confused.

"Where have you been?"

"Obviously, looking around the forest for the path. I found it" I smile triumphantly.

Scindi doesn't look like she wants to celebrate.

"What took you so long? I thought you'd left me here with..." her voice softens as she speaks.

"No way" I check my watch "I've been gone five minutes, ten tops"

"That's a long time"

"I found it" I say again.

"It's easy if you know where to look"

"What?" I recoil.

"This is how long it took?" she says.

"Ya"

"So now where?" she looks across the clearing.

"I placed a rock marker in front of the opening. Let's go"

Scindi picks up the lantern as I glance around behind us and into the forest, my breathing slow and deliberate. We seem to be alone.

I come alongside the cart and lean in as I carefully pull back the tarp. Arms at the sides of her faded purple dress, her peaceful form sends a shiver along my neck and down my spine.

Did her eye just twitch?

I shake my head to dispel the thought.

I replace the tarp and take the back of the cart to push it straight across the field. Ever vigilant, I keep an eye on Scindi at
my left as well as the surrounding obscurity, the sinister trees
watching our every move. The lantern now rests on the deck, its glow lighting us up but making it more difficult to see in the distance. We pass the swings and benches on our right, the cart's wheels surprisingly quiet throughout the journey.

We arrive at where I remember the breach in the forest but I see no rock and nothing in either direction. I walk a short distance each way but still nothing.

"I'm sure this is where it is" I think out loud.

"How do you know?"

"Because I was just here"

My eyes survey the trees in front of me as I side-step first to my right then to my left but it all looks the same.

"It's easy to find if you know where to look" I whisper to myself.

"What?" Scindi's muffled voice speaks.

"Step back with the lantern for a second" I say.

Scindi takes the lamp and cautiously walks a few paces backward.

And then I see the gap, the track curving as it enters the woods, the ground greyish-brown.

"Let's go" I say grabbing the cart to pull it.

One last look behind me, and we take our leap of faith into the unknown.

As soon as we're safely past the first curve, I glance back but see no entry or opening or thin area of trees; no clearing as if it had never been there. The path seems to have begun exactly where we are.

I lift the tarp to check on the grey girl rekindling my fear and I quickly cover her with a shiver.

No light in any direction, the moon's glow barely penetrating the canopy. Scindi walks next to me, her hand on top of mine.

The trees are mostly leafless thick-trunked deciduous, branches of all sizes reaching out to the edge of the path; thinner, slender limbs higher up. Between these, skeletal arms from smaller trees extend out in all directions. A cacophony of rattling echoes high above us, the breeze causing the high limbs to clatter like a dissonant symphony. The wide trail is a mixture of scattered

stones and hard black dirt; the branches hanging into our path make us duck and dodge their grasp. No birds or animals call, sing, or move in the forest.

"It's been ten minutes" Scindi speaks at last "How far is this place?"

"I can't really remember" I say "I came at it from the other side and was with Feryn in both directions so it seemed shorter. I'm sure we're near"

"Who is Feryn, anyway?" her voice frustrated "Why does he keep popping up?"

"It's totally odd to me as well. He seems to come when I need him or have a question"

"I've got a few right now" she frowns looking around nervously.

"I know" I say "So do I"

The path ahead is difficult to discern, the forest dark in all directions. The moon suddenly appears above us, bright white behind the dark branches, an eerie image that casts little light down onto the area around us. I slow for a moment to look into the trees but see nothing, the forest quiet in every direction. The lantern's light doesn't extend to our sides nor for a great distance in front of us. I look over my shoulder, the trail seeming to have closed behind us.

I slow, then stop to check on the girl.

"What are you doing?" Scindi asks.

"I need to know that everything's ok with Violet"

"Why wouldn't it be?" her arms clutch her body for protection and warmth.

"It'll soon be over" I hug her tightly "Things are gonna be fine"

"Just go check your…girl" Scindi says taking a step backwards.

I carefully remove the tarp from the top of the wooden coffin. The skinny grey girl lies in the same restful position as when we'd left, her dark hair concealing her face, her arms crossed over her chest. I have no desire to reach in for a closer inspection so leave things be.

The trail that previously seemed to be taking us in a straight line away from the school's clearing now turns gradually to the left, narrowing slightly. The timbers around us thin in density
and size, larger rocks in the clear areas with fewer and smaller trees. During the day, it would have been possible to see a fair distance into the forest, but in the dark, visibility is limited.

I look up to the bright moon through the treetop branches high above us, silently wishing for it to send us its light. The air is crisp and fresh as we progress along our route but dry and I'm grateful that there appears little chance of rain.

"Will it…" Scindi starts but at that moment the trail widens, opening into a clearing with two large trees.

I stop abruptly, look over my shoulder and around me, then stare at the larger tree.

I recall the images Sanya had shown me as well as on my visit with Feryn: the hanging; the crowd; the young girl dragging the woman's body across the clearing.

"You ok?" I say softly.

"Sure. You?" she tries to smile.

"I've been here before, but it's no easier this time"

"Where to now?" she glances around.

"This way" I haul the cart, taking a quick look at the coffin to ensure that it remains undisturbed.

I take the more circuitous route around the perimeter to our left where I'd stood on my visit with Feryn, maintaining a safe distance from the surrounding trees, rather than cutting right across the clearing. Scindi's left hand holds onto my jacket.

I try to avoid looking into the clearing to prevent any potential visions of past events.

"Sorry, but I've got to ask you to wait here again, for just a quick moment" I implore an anxious Scindi "I'm not sure the cart will make it on the next portion of trail and I can't recall how far it is to the graves themselves"

She shudders.

"Go" she says crossing her arms and taking a step backwards.

I take a quick full view of the clearing to confirm we're alone and head out along the path, which is in fact too narrow for the cart.

The well-groomed square glade opens before me, larger than I remember. The cool air beneath the star-filled sky creates an oddly peaceful mood. Despite the darkness, I'm able to make out
all the details. The moon, visible behind the tallest trees, illuminates the area, its white glow in sharp contrast to the spindly branches in front of it, the stars making the night sky appear darker than usual. Tall grasses buffer the area from the forest, thin white trunks nearest the treeline, taller and thicker evergreens and deciduous further into the woods. Low-hanging black and white branches reach across the shrubs into the clearing. Ahead, I

see the flat stone markers, and on my left a dark coffin, slightly longer than the one waiting on the cart.

Shadows among the trees and grasses remind me that I might not be alone.

Is there a breeze? I can't tell for sure.

I stand alone, a terrified benevolent intruder in this most scared of places, in full view of anyone concealed in the dark.

The silence is deafening, oppressive, the calm before the storm.

I shake my head to remind myself where I am.

Nervously looking at the large casket from what seems a safe distance, I know someone or something watches me; how else could this be explained? I wait in silence, wait for someone to appear, something to move. A voice to speak.

But nothing.

The quiet cemetery.

The little cemetery.

The craftsmanship of the fine ebony casket is in stark contrast to the one I've transported. The polished black exterior is of smooth treated wood with a closed lid, and two silver handles extending out from the side facing me. A silvery glow emanates from it, like an aura shrouding it.

How did this get here?

And who is inside?

A chill goes down the back of my neck.

I approach the coffin, unsure what to do when I reach it. A soft whistling sound from a gentle wind rustles the grass.

Two holes have been dug near the markers, both sized to accommodate a long box, a dirt pile next to each. I kneel beside the ebony box and, in a moment of courage, slowly remove the lid. Inside: a slim pale girl, taller and a few years older than the girl on my cart, fair skin, short light hair, a beautiful pink dress and dark pink knee-high socks inside shiny black shoes, the girl's face smooth with soft features, her hands set upon her upper thighs. Her clothing is immaculate, her skin faded but delicate, her short blonde hair is combed beautifully straight. The box's interior is lined with finely-stitched padded white linens, to the sides of and beneath the body.

I look around again, more deliberately this time.

Feryn? I want to call out his name but decide against it.

I carefully replace the coffin's lid.

I look out on the moonlit little cemetery, the golden grasses, the sharply lined trees, the long box and the mounds of earth near the flat markers. Who created this place? Who else knows about this place?

"Colden"

A female voice from where I've left Scindi shakes me back to reality.

Time to head back to where I've left her alone. I slowly back away from the scene, my mind at ease. I'm not sure what I expected but recall what Feryn told me about expectations. The small clearing has an air of serenity, a lightness that is rare in New Brook West.

With cautious steps, I return the way I came, slowly and carefully, listening for any sounds. Is someone watching me complete what I've begun? My slow-paced walk takes an eternity, my anxiety increasing. I look back over my shoulder but see only darkness.

I emerge from the trail with a gasp of relief.

Scindi stands wrapped in her arms as if trying to keep herself warm.

"It's freezing out here" she says as if in response to my observation.

I look around the clearing, at the two large trees, the air colder here than when I'd left. I pause, staring up at the stars, to catch my breath.

"I found it" I say "And there's another coffin"

"What?" her face drops.

"Come on. You can help me carry her" I say walking toward her "She won't fit on the cart"

There's not a sound in the forest around us, the silence absolute. I stare for a moment at the nearest of the large trees, assuming this is the one where the hanging took place. It chills me as I recall the images with Sanya in East as well as the drawings in the ruined house and my visit with Feryn. I shiver, shaking off the grim memories, as a breeze blows through the glade, the branches above us rattling in the wind.

"You're serious" Scindi shudders.

"I can't drag her in there alone" I shake my head.

Scindi steps toward the cart.

The open graves await.

I check on Violet, hoping that's who she is, her slender purple-ish grey and black form at rest, though it appears she could rise at any moment. Replacing the tarp, I look to Scindi who hasn't moved. By now, I've slid the box to the edge of the deck.

"Please" I plead "We have to do this"

"I know" she exhales, coming around to where I'm standing.

"This shouldn't be very heavy" I say.

We manage to pull it off the surface into our hands without setting it on the ground, the girl and her casket even lighter than I expected.

I spin around to carry the weight behind me so I can face the path.

"This way" I spot the trail's opening "Slowly and smoothly"

"Right" Scindi says confidently.

A light up ahead, like a small candle, catches my attention, guiding me directly toward the graves and their markers, the route much straighter than I recall. I slow my steps, allowing Scindi to set the pace.

Is there movement in the trees? Ugh. I can't be jumping at every noise now. I'm past the point of being scared.

The walk along the narrow track to the small clearing takes only a few seconds, the moon and stars casting just enough light to shine on the little cemetery I'd visited on my trip with Feryn, this

time with two open graves. We set the coffin next to the nearest of the dug holes. Plaques at the head of the open graves are carved with 'F' and 'V' respectively, four other plaques extending away from us and two more above this row of six. The soil below each shows evidence of a small mound; the ground below the 'S' appears undisturbed.

"What the heck is this?" Scindi's eyes scan the area.

"Must be a private cemetery of some kind" I think about what I've learned of the community "A long time ago a woman was hanged here for a crime she didn't commit. Maybe they wouldn't allow her body in the village cemetery"

"So, there are several people buried here?"

"I think 'H' is for Hannah, the woman who was hanged; 'R' for Rebecca, her mother. 'V' and 'F' must be Hannah's daughters, her flowers: Violet and Fuchsia. The 'S' could be Sadie, who I suspect is her oldest daughter, but there's not much about her. I heard she left East very young. Maybe she's the Sadie Clovinston we were wondering about"

"This place has a strange history" Scindi shivers.

"There's more to it. I gave you the short version"

The finer casket is as I'd left it, though I thought I'd closed the lid and it's now open. I walk over, look inside at the pink girl, glance around the clearing, and shut the solid top.

"Why is it open?" Scindi asks, sensing my confusion.

"Guess I was nervous or just forgot when I heard you call me"

"I didn't call you" she says timidly.

Oh. Maybe I'm not remembering correctly.

I pause to look around the perimeter of the little cemetery, but see and hear no one.

"Let's get this done" I say decisively "And get away from here"

"Ok" she walks over to look into the two holes "Did you dig these?"

"No"

"Who did?" she asks.

Yes, who did? Who would?

"Not sure" I reply softly "Maybe I've got a friend"

"I hope so"

Two open graves and two coffins.

We agree to place the older sister in the pink dress in first; based on the drawings in the house in East, I'm guessing she's Fuchsia. I drag the box to the grave, look into the hole, then at the coffin. The only way to get it down there will be to drop it in somehow.

"Do we have any rope?" I ask Scindi.

"Don't think so" she looks around and back at the cart.

"No. There isn't any there" I say, then have an idea "Wait here a second"

"Not again" Scindi shakes her head.

I run back to the cart and manage with some difficulty, and a lot of noise, to pull it through the brush along the narrow footpath, the wooden deck tearing at the plants and trees, the back wheels falling off before I reach Scindi.

"What's this for?" she stands shivering next to the smaller coffin.

Without answering her, I begin to dismantle the cart, removing the axles until only the deck's flat surface remains, comprised of several smaller boards held together by three cross pieces.

I position the deck on top of a small rock such that I'm able to break off the cross-pieces one at a time, separating it into four boards.

"So..." Scindi begins.

"So, now we can slide them in" I state with pride.

Maybe we can do this.

Pulling back the tarp, the grey girl lies peacefully. I touch her cold cheek, but feel no sign of anything but a long-ago death and no sign of movement inside or outside the coffin. Her face behind the long dark hair: her tranquil form; her once-purple dress; her body in final repose, ready for the grave. I feel a sense of peace looking at her.

I sigh as I walk to the older sister's dark casket. I place a board beneath it and drag it to the end of the open pit.

"So, what's your plan?" Scindi shudders against the chill air.

"The hole is longer than the coffin so, now that it's on this piece of the deck, I can slowly slide it down. You'll receive it at the bottom. Then I'll pull out the board and it'll fall into place on the ground"

"Really? That'll control it on the way down?"

"I hope so. It's all I can come up with"

"How about I pull it back while you're down there lowering it into place" she points into the hole.

"There's more room for you" I observe with a faint smile.

Scindi stares into the open grave for a few seconds before crouching on the edge of the hole.

The moon and stars light the scene of our gruesome task.

"Gimme a hand" she says.

I grab her left hand then the right and lower her to the bottom, her head just below ground level.

She looks up at me mournfully.

"Let's hurry" she says.

I place the board into the hole at a steep enough angle to allow the casket to slide in.

"Here it comes" I hold the end of the box at the top of the slide "You ready?"

"Less talk more action" she says.

Scindi stands at the far end, one foot against the back wall of the grave as she leans forward to lower the sliding coffin down the ramp. After a few tense moments, the casket is in place and I pull up the wood plank, lowering the box into position.

Moonlight from above the trees illuminates our endeavour and shines on the girl's coffin. Although I knew neither of these girls, I somehow feel close to them. I'm happy to be bringing Hannah her flowers.

"I'm ready to come out now"

I pull Scindi out to move on to the grey girl's box, figuring to tuck the tarp under the coffin once it's at the bottom so the earth that fills the grave will be on top of it not directly on her body. Scindi shuffles around behind me, presumably trying to stay warm, as I adjust the tarp as best I can for now to provide the girl with a respectful interment.

A cloudy cover drifts across the moon diminishing its light behind me. A shadow of Scindi appears to my left, a club raised over her head. I spin back as the moon emerges, seeing her shivering, arms again wrapped around her body.

"We're almost done" I head to the other side to face her.

We work in silence. Alone in the moonlight in the little cemetery.

I slide the makeshift casket to the edge of the grave's opening, facing Scindi as I do.

"In you go" I say coming around to her end of the opening as she clambers in.

Extending her arms up as I push it, she catches the coffin and together we lower it to the bottom, she tucking the tarp in all around beneath the wooden box, Violet under the sheet.

I turn back to help Scindi out of the hole. She sits crouched at the foot of the grave looking down.

"It's kinda sad" she says.

"What is?"

"That no one has buried these girls" she stands up "They have no one. Did anyone cry when they died?"

"I suppose we're all alone in the end" I say.

"That's a grim thought" Scindi looks to the sky "I hope we're giving them a proud resting place"

"I think we are" I hold her hand in mine.

Scindi seems lost in thought, her eyes fixed on the pile of dirt at the head of Fuchsia's grave.

"I'll get to work" I say grabbing the shovel, gesturing to the shorter grave.

"I'll push some of it in over here with this board" she says "Won't be as quick as you but it's something to get us out of here faster"

Scindi walks over to what was previously the cart as I begin the task of covering the grey girl's body with dirt from the adjacent pile. The lamp we've brought casts a pretty thin light due to low fuel, but I don't dare play with it or we'll be walking back in the dark.

Scindi gets low to push dirt into the grave as best she can while I set to it at my end. The earth makes a harsh noise as it hits the tarp. I think back on what I know, of a scared young girl living alone surrounded by a population who either hated or feared her, mourning the loss of her only parent, filling her mother's grave by herself in the dark forest and wonder how she managed to do this

alone. Where was her sister? And where did Sadie go? Rustles behind me sound more like slow deliberate movements rather than the spirited noises I've heard over the past weeks. Like someone walking rather than running. A crunching comes from a single location that I can't place, the noise subdued as of someone not concerned if they're heard. Whoever or whatever watches remains unseen in the darkness.

I move to get better access to the dirt and double my speed, pushing the dirt as much as shoveling it. I'm grateful that the dirt is so close to the grave. In doing so, I turn away from Scindi, who has been pushing the soil from her knees.

A few minutes and I've completed my task, happy with my efforts, and in much faster time than expected. I stare briefly at the low mound trying to conjure appropriate words of solemn respect but find none so feel satisfied with the value of my silence.

Turning around, Scindi is gone.

I want to yell out but the words get stuck in my throat. I spin to survey the forest but see and hear nothing and there's no one in the direction of the path out. I drop the shovel and run to the grave she'd been filling, my voice mute.

Light from the moon and stars does little to assist me.

Then I turn and look into the darkness of the as-yet-unfilled hole, unable to focus my vision.

"Scindi" I hear the whisper from my lips.

I drop to my hands and knees to get a better look but my vision has blurred. At the same time, I catch the smell of herbal spice, like someone burning incense.

"Scindi" I whisper again.

No response.

Has she left me? Been taken?

I stagger to my feet, reach out to keep my balance, and fall against the small pile of dirt next to the grave. I feel drunk, dizzy. What's happening? Am I alone?

I stare up at the moon and stars, the scattered clouds in the sky.

A voice.

"Colden. You ok?"

Scindi. Where is she?

"Hey. What's wrong?" she speaks.

I look toward to grave, imagining her at the bottom.

"We can rest for a second if you like" she says.

My vision clears enough to see her crouched next to me.

"Yes. For a second"

The small mound covering the younger girl is as I'd left it. I hear no noises in the forest and smell no more mysterious aromas to confuse me. That strange odour must have made me dizzy.

"Let's finish this and get out of here" I stand up.

Our lamp is fading fast so I pick the speed up and, between the two of us, the dirt is moved in a few minutes. I set down the shovel and brush clear the markers at the head of the graves.

'V' and 'F'. Are these really Violet and Fuchsia? Hopefully.

I take Scindi's hand.

"I wish I could think of something nice to say" I think out loud.

"Finally they can rest; the Mother has her flowers" Scindi says.

"Eh?"

"I said 'Finally they can rest, their family is together'. I assume this is their family cemetery"

"Must be" I say picking up the shovel and lamp.

I feel like some distant musical with ethereal vocals should be playing, though I'm glad this isn't the case. For a moment, I lose myself in thought.

I wonder how many have visited this little cemetery and what they did when they came, who they came to see, and does anyone still come. Will anyone ever come again? Or is being alone not necessarily lonely and if all are at rest perhaps that's enough.

Regaining my focus, I contemplate the best way back to the station. Is it better to go back the same way or take the alternate route past the teacher's house which comes with its own mysteries?

"We have two options" I look around the clearing "And it's probably best for us to not go out the way we came in"

"Where's the other way out?" Scindi tries to follow my gaze.

"Over there" I motion with my head "We're going past your old place"

"Not what I expected" she shivers.

"Let's go"

Scindi follows me onto the narrow path that leads out, both of us taking one last look at the girls' final resting places as we leave. We proceed single-file, Scindi ahead of me, the trail too narrow to do otherwise, the foliage here comprised primarily of short thin-trunked trees, the ground softer than I remember. In a minute we reach the wider trail which leads to the house in one direction and the river in the other. High above us, branches from taller trees break the modest moonlight illuminating our walk, the lamp light in my hand running on fumes.

"You ready?" I say turning in the direction of her one-time residence.

"Ready"

I take her hand and we slowly make our way toward the small glade and the house.

"Try not to be distracted by any sounds in the forest" I say "There can be lots out here"

She nods.

The canopy above us gradually parts allowing the moon's glow to reach the dirt path ahead of us. I catch an occasional crackling in the forest to my right, as if someone's walking alongside us, cautious of the noise caused by their steps. Scindi doesn't seem to notice so I do my best to focus on the path ahead, that being most important anyway.

Up ahead, her house comes into view.

"Home sweet home" Scindi whispers.

I stop for a moment to inspect around us and take in as much as I can gather from the area near the house. Sounds no longer follows us.

"We're almost there" I say, reassuring myself as much as her.

Releasing her hand, I take a few steps to the right to look behind the building but, seeing nothing of interest, come around to the front. It doesn't appear as if anyone has been here recently, until I spot a light inside, like a dim lantern.

"What's that?" Scindi says, seeing the same light.

"That's our cue to leave" I hasten my steps away from the house "Come on"

She catches up and we make our way out into the larger clearing, stopping as we reach the edge of the open area. In the distance ahead: the school; behind us: the unsettling cabin. Moonlight glows dimly through a thin cloudy veil, like a lantern behind a blanket, providing just enough light to create dull shadows in the trees.

I think of the girl from Room 1, her body now at the bottom of a grave. Her emaciated form, her tangled black hair, her dirty purple dress.

70 - Vials

Eager to put the school behind us, we hurry out of the clearing. Moonlight through the branches above the trail allows us to see the ground ahead of us and the trees' edge on our sides. We're alone in the lit obscurity. If shadows or sounds dance alongside us, I don't notice them, too immersed in the experience of the girls' burials in the little cemetery and our exit from the forest.

Scindi's head hangs low, her eyes firmly on the ground at her feet, her body exhausted, her steps short and laboured. I, on the other hand, feel free, like a weight has been lifted, happy to have been able to bring the flowers to their mother, if such was our achievement. The mysteries of Violet and Fuchsia remained about their life in East both before and after their mother's death.

The faint light cast by the dying lamp does little to improve my view of our surroundings and relieve my anxiety so I extinguish it.

A voice whispers my name.

"Did you hear that?" I stop.

"I heard, like, a bird or something"

I wait for a moment without moving. The voice is gone.

"Must have been" I say quietly taking Scindi's hand in mine.

We pass the fork in the road and soon arrive at the train station's clearing.

There's still lots of time before we need to ready ourselves for the journey by train. I have yet to figure how to get on the train in the company of the group of the men and any other eyes that might be watching. I remember Dalton, the station master who tried unsuccessfully to escape. This piece of information will not reassure Scindi so I'll keep it to myself.

The moon, larger than before, fully emerges from behind its fog blanket to brighten the opening as if heralding our return. No movements play in the forest around us or near the station itself, a most welcome sight. With Scindi's hand in mine, I pick up the pace to the building and relative safety of the apartment. We reach the steps in short order, take a cursory look at the hotel doors, along the platform, and across the tracks.

"Come with me for a sec" I drag her to the control room.

There are no lights on inside but I open the door anyway to check for any new printouts and inspect the counters, which are as clean as I'd left them. I tentatively poke my head into the back room filled with boxes wondering if one day my notes and ledgers will be read by a successor or curious villager. Had I made any notes? I can't recall.

It's too dark to see anything and I don't feel like creating any light, but nothing moves or makes a sound which satisfies me so I exit, locking the door behind me.

I step out toward the tracks, where the empty benches face the forest across from them. Grabbing a lighter from beneath one of the lanterns, I put flame to two of the four near the benches, the illumination sufficient to light the narrow platform but not enough to shine into the area across the tracks.

Scindi faces the forest across the tracks as if hypnotized, as if watching something.

"Do you see someone?" I ask looking in the same direction.

"No, just really tired" she mumbles.

"Here's the key" I hand her my loop "I'll be up right away. Try to take a nap. We've got some time to kill yet"

"Ok" she says, keys in hand.

I'm undecided about napping since missing the train would be the end of us.

I walk across the platform to face the quiet clearing. My eyes move through it, watching for the unusual or any inquisitive eyes who might suspect our imminent departure but see neither.

There's no light beneath Room 6 or any sign of a guest's presence inside this room. I leave the lantern next to Room 2 lit, stepping back a bit when I realize I've approached Room 1. For all the courage I'd summoned previously to enter that sinister space, I can't bring myself to even be near it now. I'm confident that I've not learned all the mysteries contained within it but have no desire to do so now. I can't get the image of the grey girl's coffin out of my mind, her frail body, her dirty purple dress, the wild dark hair covering her face.

Returning the lighter to its place on the wall, I climb the stairs to the suite, my eyes looking down onto the platform.

The door is locked when I reach it.

Knock knock.

"Hello?" Scindi's voice from inside calls out.

"Let me in, please" I say.

"Colden?"

"Yes"

The shuffling of feet precedes the click and opening of the door. Scindi is barefoot wearing only a long t-shirt of mine, her face exhausted.

"I'm gonna lay down here for a bit" she says walking toward the bed. All the windows are closed, the room well-lit, the lanterns casting a bright glow. I extinguish the two nearest the sleeping area.

"Good idea" I kiss her as she curls beneath the covers.

I walk to the kitchen to set the water to boil, and grab a cup, grounds, and powdered milk. The coffee has an odd smell, almost like the incense from the forest, and I feel dizzy for a moment. This is my most recent batch from Tina and I wonder what ingredient gives it that peculiar scent? I pull out a pear I'd been given by Sara and take to eating it.

I walk to each of the windows in turn, looking outside for anyone or anything. There's no motion in the forest nor sparks of light in the darkness and no scratching at the glass or doors.

It feels good to be alone, though I can't help thinking of the girls in their new graves in the little cemetery.

I stand in the center of the room and take a deep breath.

Two light knocks at the door make me jump.

Oh, shit. Is this it for us?

I look to Scindi fast asleep, curled like a cat beneath the blankets. I walk to the door. There's been no second set of knocks and no sound outside on the landing. Has someone uncovered our plan and come to confront us?

I open the door confidently, but see no one. I stare down the stairs and out onto the platform but, again, there's nothing and no one.

Just outside the apartment door, there's a small square silver box. It looks vaguely familiar but I can't place it. One last look around, even down at Room 1, and I bring it in, closing and locking the door behind me.

I stare at it in silence as I walk to the kitchen, wondering who would have left it and what's inside. I examine the light metal piece, turn it over to see the bottom and all its sides without finding any clues.

Do I want to open this?

I take a sip of the coffee.

"Whatcha got?"

Scindi's voice behind me.

"Not sure. A box"

"What's in it?"

I ignore her question and set it on the island.

"There's something about it…" I say.

"Looks like another one I've seen around here somewhere" Scindi looks around the room.

"What do you mean?" I ask.

"I'm sure I've seen a similar box"

Yes. The box that held the key to Room 1. But it had a "1" or an "I" on the lid. Could this be another key? What would it unlock?

Unlike the other box, the lid here is evident.

I slowly lift the lid, unsure what to expect, and find a note written in beautiful script and two small vials of green liquid.

'To help. R..'

To help with what?

And 'R'. Not an 'S' or a 'C' or a number designating a room number.

The most obvious assistance would come from Feryn but he wouldn't put an 'R', would he?

Rissa?

I run to a window out into the clearing and then the one over the tracks but see no one. Moonlight illuminates the area around the station making the black forest a striking sight. Am I still alone? Have I ever been?

"What are you looking for?" I bark at Scindi. Did she really know about the other box?

"Pastries for our trip" she says surprised at my tone.

"Oh. Yes"

I need to take a quick walk to the board in town and make sure the arrival is correctly posted to avoid suspicion.

"I've gotta take a trip to town and make sure the train's itinerary is posted" I walk to the door.

"Who are you anyway?"

"What?"

"I said 'OK, be safe'" her face squirrels up.

I shake my head as if to clear it.

"I'll have the keys so lock up behind me" I say closing the door and dragging my feet down the stairs.

"Definitely" I hear from behind the closed door.

My feet hustle across the clearing and onto the path to town, light from the station behind me fading as I enter the sinister forest. I move quickly along the trail, an occasional glance to either side, but see and hear nothing. My movements are silent, my feet barely touching the ground or making any noise when they do. I reach the town gates in short order and run straight to the board. I attach the arrival time of 1:00 as well as the number of pieces and weight which the train expects to be loaded. There's no one around the square. Water trickling from the fountain breaks the silence, causing me to jump a couple of times when I imagine splashes but there's no one here with me, no one I see.

I wait for the smell of licorice but it never comes.

I take a deep breath before making my way back across the plaza toward the lanterns at the gate. This'll be my last time in town and I briefly think back on the happy memories I had coming to town and smile.

"Goodbye, Colden" the female voice whispers.

"Rissa?" I say softly.

No reply. No one's around the watery obelisk nor the church nor the cemetery, its gate closed. I do the only thing I can think of.

"Goodbye" I say, before jogging into the forest.

The journey back to the station's clearing takes even less time than the trip to town, and without any sound along the way. Moonlight welcomes me back casting twisted shadows in the dark corners around the building and sharpening the details in the forest and on the station.

The candles illuminate the platform more than I expect. The distant treeline with its black and white bony limbs and branches stands out sharply in the light. With its sturdy grey building, solid black rail line, and bright orange lamps, the old station stands proudly.

After a quick look along the tracks, I scamper up the stairs to the apartment.

"What took you so long?" Scindi roars.

"I ran both ways" I say taking off my boots and jacket.

"You've been gone almost an hour" she points at the clock.

"I've been gone fifteen minutes" I point at the clock myself.

"You left an hour ago" she pleads.

No, I left at 11:00. But this is the wrong time to pursue these details.

I'm at a loss for words.

"Your hair looks different" I notice. Now it's black streaked with purple. Like Lori's had been.

"Different, how?" she squints.

"Did you dye it?" I ask "Add purple to it?"

"It's always been this way" she takes a step either backward or toward me, I can't tell which "Are you ok?"

"No" I try to collect my thoughts "Yes, yes I'm fine. Just tired. You look really great"

She forces a smile.

When did she change her hair and why? Why now?

I take a deep breath and look around the room. The room that had been home for a time. The room that could have been home. The thought of leaving makes me melancholy, pensive, as I think back on the beautiful peace and quiet solitude that is New Brook West.

I open my eyes to Scindi looking at me from the living room.

"Are we ready to go?" she drops her shoulders.

"There's not much to do but wait" I say.

"So how do we do this?" she asks.

"I guess we hang about outside when the men are here and then sneak into an open car when they aren't looking"

"Simple as that?" she cocks her head.

"I hope so" I sigh.

"You don't figure there's someone out of sight watching?" she grimaces.

"I sure hope not" I scowl.

"What about that box you got tonight?" she walks toward me.

"It's got two small bottles of green liquid"

"What's the liquid?" she walks to the island.

"Good question" I face her across the island, the vials in front of me.

"You figure it's a poison we give to the men?" she asks.

"They've never asked for anything before. They don't even look at me, and I'm not going to offer them a drink"

"Throw it on the ground?" she guesses.

"That's a big chance. If nothing happens then it's gone"

Scindi squirrels up her face as she appears to be thinking.

"Didn't you say women in the past were potion-makers?" she gazes at the vials.

"Yes"

"Maybe this is a potion, one bottle for each of us" she points at them.

"Could be" I say "But who's it from?"

Feryn? Comet? Caprice?

None of these explain the 'R'.

"There was an 'R' on a marker at the cemetery tonight" Scindi says "Maybe it's got something to do with her. We did a good thing for her family, right?"

"We did"

I think for a moment.

"Rebecca" I whisper to myself.

Scindi doesn't seem to have heard.

"What do you figure it does?" she looks closely.

"Hopefully not kill us" I say.

"And if it does, then we'll never know the difference" she shrugs.

I close the box, placing it in the middle of the island. Stuffing my essential items in a small bag, I drop it by the door next to Scindi's, checking the lock as I do.

Walking to the windows in turn, I look out onto the tracks, then across into the clearing, the only things I can think of doing. Each time I see no one and hear no noise. The station is quiet and calm, the apartment bright and cheery, the sky moonlit and starry; a pleasant night for the Station Master of New Brook West.

I walk to my fresh cup of coffee, placing Scindi's on the island. Now we wait.

I look at Scindi as she sits on the couch.

"Come cuddle up next to me" she pats the seat.

For the next hour, I alternate between sitting next to Scindi, pacing the room, and looking out the windows to make sure we have no unexpected visitors.

Suddenly, I find myself out on the landing looking down on Room 1, wondering at its mysteries and if I want to know them. The real story of the grey girl in her coffin.

Does it matter?

My time here has taught me that not knowing is sometimes best.

Scindi breaks the silence.

"So, who did you charm into bringing you coffee all this time?" she smiles.

I didn't realize I was drinking a cup until she said something. I really have become addicted to this delicious brew.

"A woman I met at the library" I recall "She runs a coffee shop of some kind in town and took it upon herself to get me some. She seems nice"

"Is her name Tina?"

"What?"

"I said 'She's got a station-master-crush'"

"Haha. Yeah, maybe"

Tina. Green-eyed Tina.

My mind can't process all the details and assemble the pieces of the puzzle. We'd assumed the grey girl in the dirty purple dress in Room 1 is Violet. She must be the girl in the purple dress on the wall in East.

"Whatcha thinking?" Scindi stands over my shoulder.

"Just looking at these family trees and trying to figure out how we fit in" I say.

"Does it matter?" she says.

"No, I suppose not"

"I'll be happy when we're safely away from here" she leans into me.

I fumble through the documents for the next twenty minutes, occasionally getting up to look out the windows. No answers come to me, no clues hidden within the genealogies. So many names, so many riddles.

I hate riddles.

Some of the lanterns in the room have gone out, the apartment behind me noticeably darker, the air more sombre. Scindi's lying on the couch, possibly sleeping, still wearing only my long shirt, her bare feet and purple painted toenails catching my eye as she extends her legs. My thoughts are a mess. Have I missed something that needs to be done before we leave? What'll happen if we're caught? I don't want to be the next Dalton.

"Are we ready?" Scindi gets up.

"I think so" my face doesn't feel like it expresses much confidence "Let's get ourselves together. I'll put the bags down on the platform next to the bench while you finish up in here"

I finish my coffee.

Grabbing the bags, my gait takes me down the steps and out across the platform, my eyes careful to scan the area for any of the loading party. Seeing and hearing no one in any direction, I look out across the tracks and up and down the waiting area before placing the small bags out of sight but easily accessible between the benches. I hope the men will have no reason to come over this way.

The moon shines brightly; the stars sharp points in the sky; the air cool, crisp, and dry; the station lonely as if it knows I'm leaving.

It feels sad, despite the terrifying events, as it does with all departures. I've still not found 'home'. Each time it ends with me leaving.

Directly above me, I spot metal brackets which I'd not noticed in my previous passes down this portion of the platform. The absence of a clock had always struck me as odd but perhaps this was its previous location. I hadn't seen one anywhere around the station that would fit this assembly and would have certainly tried to repair this deficiency had I known. For whatever reason, the town's decision-makers deemed it unnecessary.

I stare out into the empty clearing, hands in my pockets, contemplating the moment, nothing and no one in the empty darkness. Silence all around me.

I turn around to look across the tracks.

Is someone watching from the forest? I see and hear no one. My nerves are on high alert doing nothing but waiting. This isn't like anyplace else I've left. I'm not even sure where I am. Or if we'll be nabbed trying to sneak away in the night. Or if a worse fate awaits us.

And there should be no more reason to doubt Scindi's role but I can't help but shake the suspicious corner of my mind.

Is there a destiny that I'm about to fulfil? Has Fate been pulling the strings all along?

A quick walk around the station will calm me. Going past the control room, I hop down to the ground around the back of the apartment, hopefully out of sight if Scindi happens to be looking down, recalling poor Acacia's demise. My eyes aren't particularly keen at night but I casually check the area around me as best I can nonetheless. Coming around into the clear field, the openness instantly overwhelms me, the moon's glow lighting the clearing but ending at the treeline, only darkness in the forest. Casting a sideways glance up onto the platform, I proceed around the back of the hotel, careful not to look at Room 1's covered window, though finding my eyes drawn to it.

Is anything else in that room? I hope I don't find out tonight.

Around to the tracks and alongside the platform behind the hotel, I peer into the forest, my efforts to see futile at best. Jumping up onto the stone floor, I take a quick look behind me but no one's there. That I can see. I look up at the hotel and up at the apartment. I'm still alone. Alone.

Back upstairs to Scindi and our final preparations.

Once in the apartment, I immediately walk to the windows to confirm everything looks as I want and hope that everything within my control is in order. I wonder if I could be better prepared but can't imagine how. I wonder what to expect prior to the train's arrival; as we attempt to board; as the train leaves the station. It's hopeless to try to anticipate what might happen given my history in New Brook West since my arrival.

Is anyone or anything watching from a distance?

My experiences here in the dark defy explanation and won't easily be shared with others and would be difficult to put into words, though I somehow don't regret coming to New Brook West.

I stare out the window for a moment, mesmerized by the vast openness.

"We should probably get downstairs" Scindi emerges from the bathroom wearing black tights with a dark blue long-sleeved shirt, her hair hanging in a ponytail out from the back of a dark baseball hat. It makes the features of her fair skin that much sharper.

"You're very pretty" the thought escapes my lips.

"Haha. Thanks" she smiles.

She really is a beautiful woman and does bear a striking resemblance to Lori, reminding me of her.

She pulls on her black hoodie while I grab my station master jacket; a souvenir I could do without but a necessity if for some reason I'm spotted in the presence of a train. Black pants and a green shirt complete my outfit, dark boots over my wool socks.

Scindi produces two travel-cups of coffee and a small box of pastries.

"Snacks while we wait" she says.

"Perfect" I open the door for her to pass.

For all its oddities, I will miss it here. In another life, this could have been home. Now, it's just another destination from which I fled. History truly does repeat itself. Goodbye, New Brook West.

Stuffing the keys in my pocket, I walk down to meet Scindi.

A single lantern lights the hotel wall.

I look at Room 1 and wonder at what I saw in there, at what else might be in there, and what other mysteries lurk at the station.

"How about we sit facing the road to town for now" I point into the clearing "I've had my fill of being taken by surprise"

"Sounds good" she hands me a cup and we sit on the edge of the stone floor facing the open glade. There's no fog in the clearing tonight.

I look to the sky as the partial moon appears from behind a cloud sharpening my view of the clearing and the distant trees without actually providing light to the area. The lanterns and lamps behind us illuminate only the platform. The distant path is only discernible because I know where to look. The sinister forest surrounding us is simultaneously beautiful and chilling, spindly trunks winding their way up from the ground, skinny limbs pointing up and out like statuesque skeletons. A soft breeze swirls in patches around the building catching loose items, leaves, and grasses, but never intrudes on our quiet moment. The same tranquility I'd felt when I first arrived.

"I used to love autumn as a season: the warm sun, the cool air…"

"The changing leaves" she adds, finishing my thought.

I smile at her.

I can't think of anything to say and Scindi doesn't initiate any more conversation so I remain silent, choosing instead to sip my coffee and enjoy the serenity of the moment.

A tiny crack of light to my right turns my head.

For just a second, a spark like a lit match appears in the trees, then disappears. No sound or motion in that direction, no one visible in the forest.

I wait but nothing comes. So much the better.

Still the team does not arrive causing me to wonder if they know something I don't and if their absence carries more meaning.

The train's whistle in the distance announces its imminent arrival, the time just before 12:45. I look around behind me but there's no one on the platform.

"I'll just be a second" I stand up.

There's no one in either direction along the wall, nothing visible across the tracks, our bags still in place. I walk past the benches to the end of the station without seeing anyone or anything. I stare in the direction of the arriving train, its light yet to appear. I look up at the now clear sky, the glowing moon, and twinkling stars.

A caw far to my right breaks my trance. A single noise, faint and distant.

'Quoth the Raven' I think.

I join Scindi who's sitting where I'd left her.

"Anything unusual? Any bad news?" she asks without looking at me.

"Nothing to report" I sit.

"Good" she forces a smile.

The men appear, their presence too prominent to go unnoticed, their movements quiet and rhythmic, as though marching to music only they can hear.

"Let's get out of their way" I suggest, taking the cups and remaining pastries, setting them on a crate next to the control room.

"Do we want them to see us at all?" Scindi whispers "Is there any value in them seeing you when they load the cargo? Do they care? Why don't we just hide and make them think we're upstairs, then they'll be less wary of our presence on the platform?"

"Good idea" I say "I left a couple of lights on to make it look like I'm home"

We casually walk around to sit on the bench near our bags, the group having yet to give any indication they've noticed us.

I don't see Dalton or the vision of him I've been seeing.

I extinguish the lanterns near the benches, lighting the lamp outside the control room instead.

"When do we drink these?" Scindi asks.

When indeed? What will happen when we do? Will something happen to them? To us?

"If something horrible happens, it's been wonderful to know you, Colden" Scindi leans in and kisses me.

"Nothing bad's gonna happen" I reassure her "But let's wait until the train arrives before we commit ourselves"

We sit for a moment in silence on the far bench waiting for whatever's next.

The train comes into view to our left, gradually decelerating into the station; the engine pulls ten or twelve freight cars and two passenger coaches, stopping with the last three freight cars open onto the platform. No silhouettes in the passenger cars reveal any travelers in the darkness, the conductor not visible in the lit cab, no personnel evident anywhere. Our position allows us to see in all directions but remain out of sight to hopefully time our escape.

The burly zombies appear to our left and move as one, placing the small and large boxes in the rear-most car without looking in our direction.

Scindi produces the vials which we consume in a single gulp.

The last man pulls the sliding door on the now loaded car, latching it.

Grabbing Scindi's bag and taking her hand, I run to the nearest open car, but as I do, two pairs of eyes turn our way. Should I stop? Hurry?

I choose the latter and we hop across the small space between platform and train, duck around the open door and into the car, and freeze. Peeking around the door at its lowest point, I notice the men staring briefly at the train before turning back and trudging toward the steps down into the clearing.

Are we caught?

I freeze, too scared to look back outside lest I should be noticed, too nervous to celebrate our successful escape. My breathing stops completely as if this will keep me hidden.

Did one of us alert them with our movements or make a slight noise?

I fall into the corner where I'll be out of sight to anyone outside the car.

Why isn't the train moving?

I can't hear anything on the platform but don't dare look again.

Where's Scindi?

My heart stops.

Then, the engine groans and we move a short distance before coming to a stop.

I have yet to close the door, not wanting to give away our location.

I look to my left but still don't see Scindi and don't dare call out her name. She must be in here somewhere out of sight.

I wait without breathing, without moving.

In time, I dare to look outside, my head at the bottom of the door. We're directly across from the benches with no one on the platform that I can see. Unless they're right against the train. Or checking inside the other cars. I pull my head back in, slowly sliding toward the corner and the safety of the darkness.

For the next minute or more, I take long deep breaths to calm myself. I reach out and touch Scindi's backpack, pulling it closer to the wall, hearing her sigh as I do this. I'm relieved to hear she's next to me.

More time passes as I wait, knees drawn up to my chest as much as I can. I spot Scindi against the wall to my left, her head sagging between her knees to hide her face behind her dark cap.

I press the side of my face against the wall. Waiting.

How long has it been?

My pounding heart slows as the train labours out of the station, eventually reaching full speed. I look throughout the car as best I can, given the lack of light, and we're alone, at least in this car.

Silence and solitude.

"We made it" I whisper.

Scindi gasps for air next to me, her mind hopefully at ease.

Had we been seen and will there be repercussions at some point along the journey? How far will we travel and when should we get off? Where will I go after I get off?

I slide the heavy door partially closed to conceal our presence in case we make other stops. The door shows no signs of moving any further once I stop pulling it, partly due to its age and rust, partly due to its sheer weight. Just enough light comes in for me to make out Scindi's form next to me but since she's curled up in the corner, her features are in shadow. She doesn't budge and I consider reaching out to touch her but something prevents me, perhaps my desire to leave her to process the day's events or even just collapse from exhaustion. My senses remain alert, my mind racing with elusive thoughts that come and go, my body aching from fatigue.

I find the travel coffee mug at my side and take a sip from its pleasantly warm contents.

As I set it down, I catch movement across the car in the opposite corner from where we're sitting, hear what sounds like breathing.

Is someone else in the car with us? I feel like I can see a form in the darkness. The door on the opposite side of the railcar open is just the narrowest crack allowing the slightest amount of moonlight. Had that been shut before? I try to focus my eyes, all the while convinced at the impossibility of anyone else being in the car. I sit in silence, my body shaking, as I watch and listen. Waiting. And then the figure's gone as if it had never been there.

The mesmerizing clicking of the wheels across the rails numbs my weary mind into a suspended state and I briefly zone-out. A cool damp breeze finds its way into the car keeping me awake and chilling me. My bag contains nothing to help me and I don't want to use my change of clothes so soon, not knowing what obstacles surely lay ahead, nor am I hungry for the pastries we've brought. I struggle to slide the door closed just a bit more to keep out the cold as much as possible without drawing any attention in case we stop. The journey by train has so far had very few noticeable curves, though it can't be described as smooth, the seams increasingly pronounced with distance from New Brook West.

Thinking the community's name sends a chill down my spine, like the memory of a bad nightmare. I no longer miss my one-time home.

Scindi lies beside me quietly, either asleep or too agitated to move. I decide I'll not disturb her, holding her hand instead.

The coffee cup in my hand is most welcome.

I take another small sip before setting it out of the way. Soon, the hypnotic rhythm beneath me makes my eyes heavy and I lose consciousness as thoughts of Scindi and Jade in the teacher's house play through my head.

I wake to noises outside the railcar mixed with a buzz of distant voices.

I was dreaming, entirely alone in a dark forest and scared of the unknown around me but can't recall any details. So much the better.

A thin blade of orange light slices through the crack in the door next to me. Creeping to the slim opening, I peek out onto a rail yard. I look to Scindi but she's not in the car. Her bag is next to mine but otherwise there's no sign of her.

I reflexively reach to take a sip from the still warm coffee cup next to me. This can't be the same one but it tastes familiar and I'm happy to have it.

71 – She's gone

The railcar is dark and dirty, smells rusty and wooden. My watch says 7:30 but without knowing which way the door faces, I can't hazard a guess as to our location nor confirm my watch's accuracy. We're no longer moving. I sit up and lean toward the narrow space between the sliding doors careful to stay low and hopefully out of sight. The air tastes dusty and metallic.

It's too dark outside to make out our current environment, though I see a small building in the distance, lights farther away to my left, and other railcars scattered across a large area. The ground is either gravel or rock.

I don't recall any other stops but can't be sure I didn't just sleep through them. I'm thankful the car I'm in wasn't intended to hold a load and it's just us.

But there is no 'us' at the moment, just 'me'. I'm alone in the car and don't know how long we've been stopped.

Is the door on the other side of the car open more widely than before? Could be from the bumps and bounces along the ride, I suppose. It'd only be enough space for a child to fit out of on that side.

I scan outside for Scindi but don't see her in dusk's dim light.

Why would she get out? Surely not to ditch me.

Had she slipped out through the gap? Maybe her slim body could have squeezed through on our side; mine will require that I widen it.

I stand and pull the door as slowly and silently as I can, making it possible for me to exit the car should I decide to do so. The sky is dark, orange and yellow light coming from my right suggesting that's east. My eyes adjust and I now see figures moving about between black and brown railcars, noisy metal sounds crashing in the distance.

I can't decide if the railyard is loud or not. I've been away from activity and volume for so long, the noise seems distant; perhaps it is.

Peering out the opening in the door, I spot two men near some other trains, their backs to me. After pulling the door, I immediately realize the noise levels outside are not as extreme as I'd initially believed, which makes the sliding of metal on metal more distinct.

I stop, withdrawing inside and dropping to the ground. Neither of the men I see appears to have noticed. I wait without moving, barely breathing. What consequences await if they do hear or see me? Is this the end of my escape or just the beginning? Where the hell am I and where do I go from here? Is this another creepy village?

But most importantly, where has Scindi got to? Has she really ditched me?

I look at her bag next to me, deciding I'll snack on a pastry while I wait for her eventual hopeful return. What else can I do? I nestle into the corner of the poorly lit car to stay as much in the shadows as I can.

The air is dry, but remains cool. The inside of the car, or perhaps the rail yard in general, reeks of rust and metal and oil and dirt. Outside, the activity has subsided making things much quieter, simultaneously peaceful and unnerving.

After a few minutes pass, I decide I can't wait any longer and exit the car to look for Scindi.

Grabbing her bag and mine, I crawl to the opening, jumping out feet first and rolling under the car. I see no one between me and the building, a chainlink fence to the right of this structure. I can't be too stealthy or I'll not find Scindi.

Is that someone else creeping among the railcars a short distance over? Too small to be Scindi so I can't worry about it. Maybe an animal.

I wait for a moment, ensuring that no one's looking this way and that any other train hopper is out of sight.

Standing up, I casually walk toward the fence. It'll all be for nothing if I get caught wandering about in here. And if I abandon Scindi.

Unless her plan was to abandon me.

Finding a safe stop next to an old railcar, I set things down to look around for my companion. But I'm alone. She's gone.

72 – You've done this before

Sunrise is upon me, the sky to my right a beautiful array of colours, a stark contrast to the dirty metal of the rail yard. The cloudless sky remains dark to my left and ahead of me in the morning air. I'm leaning up against a rusted railcar with its doors closed, scared to move, a feeling I recall all too well.

It's quiet here, the activity now in remission in the railyard.

I don't dare ask these men for help, as much as I'd like to.

I look at Scindi's bag. Where will I look for her?

Am I near a town?

Am I alone? I am for the moment.

Ahead of me, a road runs parallel to the train tracks, rolling hills in the distance to the right, trees to the left and across the street, the air not yet clear enough to take it all in.

The piece of chainlink fence in front of me extends a short distance to my right, a lonely barricade disconnected from the rest of the yard's enclosure.

The small single-storey building to my left must be an office, a structure much smaller than New Brook West's solid wood and brick construction, three cars parked in front of it, one of them running; the building's interior is dimly lit.

Has Scindi found someplace to hide? Someone to help us?

Why not come back for me?

A slow sad instrumental song plays in my head. My body feels heavy, my eyes tired, my heart defeated.

I look off to my left, hoping I'll spot her in the yard, but see only brown and grey railcars in the dust and gravel.

"You thought I'd ditched you?" a female voice speaks to my right.

Scindi.

"Uhh…" I stammer.

"Well put" she smiles.

"So, what now?" I say.

"Now we get in that running car and get the heck out of here before we're found out" she points at a four-door dark sedan.

"Steal someone's vehicle?" I say sternly "That won't draw any attention"

"Do you wanna ask for a ride?" she scowls.

We could. Maybe. No.

"There's gotta be another way" I shake my head.

"Let's hear it" she crosses her arms squatting next to me.

Ok, so I have no other ideas.

"The driver went inside that shack and he's talking to someone" Scindi points at the building "Not sure why he left his car running. No one else is in it"

Wait. I do have an idea.

"Do we have any tools?" I ask.

"I don't" she shrugs.

"I have a knife but that's not what I need" I think out loud.

"For what?"

I survey the parking lot.

"We're in England" Scindi says.

"How do you know?" I ask.

"Steering wheels are on the right side of the car" she smiles.

"Gotcha" I say "Grab our bags. I've got an idea"

I spot the same small figure I'd seen earlier duck behind the building. Surely not the car's owner. Probably just my tired mind playing tricks.

I run to a nearby pickup truck with a covered cab, scrounge inside the back and soon find a wrench. Removing the licence plate from its rear bumper I quickly swap it with the one from the vehicle we're about to thieve, screwing the bolts in loosely. I'd done this before so manage fairly quickly.

"Let's go" I hop into the running car on the right side.

We close both front doors as quietly as possible and I slowly back into the road, pulling away gently. When I'm a safe distance from the building, I pick up a normal speed and we're off.

"Now if they report it stolen, the plates are on someone else's car" I say "Might buy us some more time"

"Good thinking" she smiles "You've done this before?"

I smile back.

Scindi pulls out a pastry, which I decline, having enjoyed one earlier.

"So, now what?" she sighs.

"Drive until we find something we recognize or that might have some answers" I say "I've never done *this* before"

"We're alone again" she leans her seat back.

"I'm used to it" I sigh.

73 – Together

"That happened, right?" Scindi speaks after a moment of driving in silence "We got away?"

"I think so" I exhale deeply "But we'll only really know when we're someplace we recognize"

"Yes" she says.

"Yes" I adjust my grip on the steering wheel.

"Together" Scindi places a hand on my right knee.

"Together" I take her hand in mine.

The two-lane road we're on leads us toward the sunrise and whatever awaits us in that direction.

"Guess I'm still looking for home" I say.

"Home" Scindi says softly.

Our dark blue four-door seems sufficiently non-descript, though I hadn't caught the make and model.

The coffee keeps me going and I drink it generously.

"Where'd you get the coffee refill?" I ask Scindi.

"I didn't" her eyes squint at me.

"This is warm"

"Hmm?" she says in a sleepy voice.

"Nevermind" I whisper "Just rest"

"Hmm" she mumbles.

I set the coffee down between the seats where it rustles against a tarp or blanket.

The winding road takes us up and down small slopes, like a rollercoaster for small children. I keep a safe slow speed unsure of the limit, though not too much so to draw attention that way.

In time the road levels off and looks to be straight ahead for a stretch, green and yellow fields on both sides.

The sun rises ahead and slightly to the right of the direction I'm facing.

Scindi has fallen asleep, shoes off, and I let her rest feeling sufficiently awake myself to manage for the moment, my trusty travel mug filled with coffee at my side. Scindi must have refreshed it because yesterday's brew would be ice cold. I take a sip for a quick boost and set it down between the seats as I look at Scindi. She looks so peaceful. I feel partially responsible for putting her in this situation, plotting the escape from New Brook West.

We've driven for about twenty minutes when Scindi shifts in her seat. She still has our bags in her lap. I take them from her, tossing them into the back seat.

"Uhn"

What was that? I turn to look behind me but see only a pile of blankets on the floor and our bags on the seat.

Scindi moans with a smile, curling up tightly.

By now the sun appears to have risen to my right behind a cloudy veil. The countryside is pretty, if flat, patches of trees spread throughout the colourful fields.

Considering the steering wheel's on the right, I've been driving on the left side of the road, hopefully a correct assumption. I have yet to see any road signs indicating our location or what lies ahead.

Scindi hasn't moved, her breathing short. I occasionally touch her to reassure both of us that we're not alone and our flight from one nightmare will hopefully not land us in another one.

My eyes tire as I stare out onto the monotonous landscape on this dim morning. I sip on and off from the warm mug setting it on the blanket between the seats when it's not in my hand. My mind wanders in and out of sleep, at times feeling as though Scindi is no longer next to me. It'll soon be necessary to stop and actually rest.

Are the fields blue? Impossible. Am I dreaming? My exhaustion forces me to pull off the road, nearly onto the wrong side.

I close my eyes for what feels like a few seconds.

I regain consciousness in a panic, Scindi now in the back seat.

I reach for the coffee which has fallen further into the back, taking a welcome sip.

"Come cuddle up next to me" she says patting the seat.

I look out the front window quickly, ensuring I keep my eyes on the unfamiliar road.

"That sounds great but we're in a pretty conspicuous location if anyone passes by" I bring myself back into the moment, the correct one, I hope.

"So now what?" she asks.

"Now we keep going" I reply putting the vehicle into drive and moving forward.

I could have sworn I'd worn my watch but it isn't on my wrist. Perhaps it had fallen off or it's in my bag. I can only guess at the time, maybe 800 or 900.

"Drive safe" Scindi says, now in the seat next to me in the front.

I take a small slug of the hot beverage, setting it down on my left.

Wow. Time for a nap. Soon.

74 – So now what?

Odd that we've passed no vehicles since we left the rail yard. The road is paved and has yet to take a substantial curve, the ride relatively smooth. What day of the week is it? Where exactly are we? Is this area remote? I have as many questions now as before.

The cloud-obscured sun and bleak atmosphere are reminiscent of New Brook West, though the road itself remains clear as does the view on either side.

Still a half tank of gas, according to the gauge, with no idea where the next station could be or what I'll do to pay for refueling. I don't want to leave a crime trail to follow us all the way to our destination, wherever that is. I wonder how far behind us the owner of our stolen ride pursues us. Has New Brook West made contact with anyone in the area to report us missing? Will punishment be enforced by locals or has a party departed West to seek us out?

I've not seen a single person and no houses in the fields on our sides. I roll down the window for some fresh air. Silence. The car makes little noise. I shake myself to ensure I'm still awake, the endless supply of coffee in my mug keeping me on the road. Scindi's asleep next to me, her breathing so shallow as to barely be noticeable.

I pull over briefly to reach for any food or drink in either of our bags in the back seat. I find an apple which will be perfect to give me some energy as well as something to do other than stare out at the fields.

I hear a thud from the back seat as one of the bags settles on the floor.

I take a quick glance but, seeing nothing and hearing no more sounds, focus on the road ahead.

We're obviously alone in the car so I need to keep my attention forward.

It seems an eternity that we've been driving this mundane route to nowhere with few exits, no signs, no thought as to what awaits at the end of the line. More of the unknown.

Suddenly, the skies go dark, as if thunderclouds have rolled in or night has fallen, visibility limited in all directions, rain falling hard enough to require the wiper blades. It's a solemn scene around me, no longer the colourful countryside, the land now rocky and sparsely forested, thin trunks with long spindly branches. A dreary air far too similar to the environment I've left behind.

Is there movement among the trees? Figures watching me? Impossible.

"So now what?" Scindi speaks.

"You ask that a lot"

She smiles.

"Now we find someplace to rest or eat and get out of this car into something not stolen" I say.

"You'll make it work. You always do" she says seriously "You're the Station Master"

Not anymore.

75 – The gloom

The rain continues, the overcast sky persists, and the sombre view out the windows stays with us. How had it turned this ash colour so quickly? I'd barely noticed the weather's transition. Now it appears a thunderstorm is imminent.

I thought for sure I'd left the bleak and dreary days when we got on the train but some memories can't be forgotten.

Still Scindi sleeps, barely stirring. She's stripped down, now barefoot in shorts and a t-shirt, the car comfortably warm, her head resting against the window, her body curled away from me, her feet tucked beneath her. She reminds more and more of Lori the more I look at her.

We'll eventually need fuel and food to keep us going; I need more than coffee.

How long have we been driving? It's hard to say.

Mist hangs low to the ground combining with the small drops bouncing off the windshield to keep the environment outside the car damp and dismal. The forest is now denser on the left side of the road than the right, skinny branches extending up and out from slender white trunks. The sun's light barely penetrates the haze as though it's early evening rather than late morning. On the right, low shrubs and grasses buffer the road from the trees, waving in the wind, the noise of the gusts against the car the only sound. On the left, the trees come up to the edge of the shoulder.

The gloom fills me, recalling memories I'd rather forget.

Up ahead, a woman on the left side of the road stands at the edge of the treeline. Tall and lean and wearing a grey cloak, she must be cold and wet. I slow down to offer aid, though I see no car and become wary.

But I decide I have to stop, so pull onto the narrow gravel shoulder as she steps into the forest and vanishes. I park the car where she'd been and stare into the trees, into the darkness between and around the thin limbs but see no one. Just darkness. Perhaps she lives nearby along a path I can't see.

I re-enter the road, eager to reach someplace to rest. In the rearview mirror, I spot her slowly stepping out of the forest as if she'd been watching and waiting for me, her hood now pulled back, though I can't make out her facial features. I'm happy I didn't get a closer look at her. I lack the courage for mysterious encounters.

Another fifteen minutes of driving and the haze has yet to clear, the sky as dark as ever. I hope we're travelling inland and toward a populated centre. Someplace with food and coffee and a bus station. And sunshine.

I take a sip of what remains, surprised at how much is still in the cup and how warm it is.

I spot a light up ahead on the left side of the road, an invitation to take shelter from the dreariness and maybe ask questions of some locals. I slow down carefully as I get closer to the small yellow beacon. I see no path into the forest and no buildings as I get closer. I come to a full stop next to a lamp and look into the forest as much as I can without getting out of the car. I see nothing but darkness and the lone lantern. I pause for a moment as I take in the scene around the car. This no longer looks inviting.

As I pull away, I see a tall lean woman in a grey cloak in the rearview mirror step out of the trees and pick up the lantern, her hood pulled back.

I press the gas pedal more firmly, leaving this eerie scene behind me.

The rain still falls, mist covering the land in every direction.

Conversation with Scindi would be most welcome but I decide not to wake her and drive alone in the gloom.

76 – A shadow up ahead

In the distance ahead, the skies clear enough to hopefully break the gloom of my current drive. But they're so far away and have been for some time now. Fog shrouds the car, limiting visibility, the dark forest on my left reminiscent of the one surrounding the train station, though I can't tell if the haze here creeps in among the trees.

My foot releases the gas pedal slightly as I stretch.

"Deep thoughts?" Scindi says, extending her legs.

"Always" I smile.

Nothing's visible on the right apart from the occasional thick-trunked tree, a stocky sentry watching us pass. The murky air makes me melancholy, the drive more sombre than I'd hoped.

I glance in the rearview mirror happy to have had no further glimpses of grey-cloaked women at the side of the road.

"It's good?" Scindi asks.

"It's good" I reply, though driving on the left side of the road sets me off balance at times. I almost add 'Lori' to the end of my sentence and hope this thought stays in my mind.

Brighter skies remain just out of reach in the distance, like a prisoner seeing the end of his escape tunnel but never quite reaching it. It feels discouraging to not reach the clear blue skies but gives me a goal.

The rain has stopped, the fog has not. A dismal mood hangs around us, like a terminally ill hospital ward where patients know there will be no cure to their ills. The ominous trees on the left continue to distress me, the consistent illusion of movement among them as I pass.

A chill runs through me as I reach for the coffee, which has again fallen onto the back seat floor.

A quick sip of the familiar warm brew lifts me.

Ahead of us, a figure walks across the road from right to left. The shape moves slowly and deliberately; the stride appears female but I can't be sure, the form obscured in the haze. It vanishes into the dark skeletal trees as if it had never been there.

"Did I see that?" I say awaiting confirmation from Scindi.

"See what?" she turns.

"A shadow up ahead" I shake it off "Just my imagination"

"The fog can really play its tricks" she nods, curling her feet up under her.

My eyes scan as far ahead as they can, hoping I'll see no more shadowy pedestrians.

What watches from the forest, waiting for me to pull over and step out of the car?

I'll soon need to stop to relieve myself from the coffee I've been drinking and would prefer to do so without the company of cloaked women.

The grey is now absolute, the skies as dark as they could possibly be during the day, the fog nearly black and just thick enough to make the gloom complete. No clear sky looms ahead of us. A chill runs down my spine.

Something rustles and settles in the backseat, probably some tools or other items on and around the blankets.

Rain hits the windshield rhythmically, the wiper blades keeping time in their monotone fashion.

I can't tell if Scindi has gone back to sleep or staring out the window.

"Hey" I blurt out "Have you seen my watch?"

"Yes" she looks at my hands "It's on your wrist"

No way. I know it wasn't there before.

12:30 which is impossible so it must have stopped. Would be nice to know the time as some frame of reference.

My back has bothered me for the last while and, as loathe as I am to get out in the dreary forest, it can't be helped.

I pull over.

"What're ya doin'?" Scindi looks stunned.

"Have to stretch out for a few seconds. And pee"

"In the rain?"

"Can't help it" I open the door, stepping out into the dark fog, careful on the edge of the road.

It feels good to be up and moving again, even in the chill, damp air. I move my waist around, twist high and low, take a few deep breaths in the light rain.

I step so I'm out of sight from the road but on this side of the forest.

Am I being watched? I slowly turn my head to look into the forest, as my peripheral vision catches movement among the trees. One final stretch and I return to the car, only to realize I'm several paces away from it, the headlights guiding me back.

Movement behind me?

I nervously look over my shoulder but see no one.

I shiver, enter the car, and lock the door.

"Brrr" I sip from the mug to warm myself up.

"Better?" Scindi asks.

"Better" I reply, throwing my jacket into the back seat.

"Uhn"

"Pardon me" I look at her.

"I didn't say anything" she says.

"You look comfortable" I smile.

"I can take more clothes off if you like" she grins.

"Best to not get distracted" I say, shaking off the possibilities of a naked Scindi next to me.

"It'd be like bathing nude in the forest" she winks.

"Make sure you let me know when you plan on doing that" I pull into the road.

"I'm doing it in my mind right now" she closes her eyes.

I look at her over the travel mug pressed to my lips. If she goes any further with this fantasy, we'll be off the road. Then I realize we're stopped on the tracks.

The wipers keep the rhythm; the rain the background music; the mist the curtain; the trees the performers. A ghastly orchestra on a gloomy drive.

77 – Who are those two?

The scene is horrible. How did this happen?

Who stops on a level crossing?

Granted, this one is old and unattended. No signal box or signalman here. But the lights should have alerted the driver.

"Sir, we've got a single casualty in the car" Sergeant Bradley says "Man probably thirty or so. Foreign identification"

Inspector Robinson walks back to the wreckage.

"Two backpacks in the back seat" Detective Inspector Robinson observes "But only the driver in the car. Could anyone have fled this disaster?"

"No one could have survived that, sir" Bradley replies "Not and walked away, at least"

No. Then why two backpacks? One of them with women's clothing?

Not often does fog settle in this area as it had today, thought Robinson. The sky has darkened considerably, the air murky and dreary to match the damp chill. Fortunately, the road is quiet. The train has been shuffled onto a siderail as a formality because the motorman certainly isn't at fault and there seems no doubt as to the cause of death.

"I found a pile of drawings" Bradley brings the papers "All with the initials 'CV'"

"'Little Cemetery'; 'Beneath the Steps'; 'Her Flowers'; 'Room 1' with a girl in a grey dress from the back, wiry black hair down past her shoulders, facing a brick wall" Robinson shudders "Perhaps our friend here is 'CV'"

"His driver's permit says Colden Vintassi"

Cool air settles in on the men, the haze heavy and damp.

"Does he have a mobile?" the Detective Inspector asks to one in particular.

The officers look around and at each other.

"Well, someone go check" Bradley barks as the men scatter.

A few moments later, one of the constables hands a cell phone to Sergeant

Bradley.

"Check his calls, his texts, his photos" Robinson says quietly "Let's try to figure out who he is. And if there was anyone else with him"

Bradley clicks through the phone swiping screens and looking over the information stored in the device.

"This is interesting, sir" he passes the phone to the detective.

Robinson looks at the photo of the woman, a dead woman, in what appears to be a dirty train railcar. Very pretty, athletic physique, messy purple-streaked black hair, a dark blue top.

"Why would someone take this photo?" Bradley thinks out loud.

"Why, indeed?" the Detective Inspector replies.

"And where was it taken?"

"Impossible to tell"

A cool breeze blows across the road.

"Maybe this is the owner of the second backpack" Robinson looks back at the car "But why not get rid of it once she's dead. Assuming he killed her, why'd he keep the pack?"

The constable looks to the ground.

"Anything noteworthy in with the woman's items?" the inspector goes on "Like something he was transporting for her?"

"No, sir" Bradley shakes his head.

"Sir" a constable approaches the two men "I found a child's black shoe in the back seat"

"Just one?" Robinson asks.

"Just one"

A momentary breeze passes across the scene without disturbing the fog.

A chill runs down Robinson's back causing him to shiver.

"Maybe the driver wasn't alone" Bradley suggests.

The Detective looks back at the wreckage then at the forest around him.

"In the end we're all alone" he replies with a sigh.

He tries not to look in the direction of the green-eyed woman in the grey cloak, watching the scene from a distance.

She soon vanishes, gliding into the forest and out of sight.

78 - Violet

They left me alone in the dark, with only a whisper for a voice.

But now I can rest. With those I love.

I'm no longer cold in the shadows.

No longer alone.

Violet..

79 – Christina Nicole

My green eyes survey the scene one last time before vanishing into the forest with the pitiful child in tow. She'll soon expire and the tree will be dead.

I am the last and the scroll's prophecy is fulfilled.

Gone are the son of Rebecca and the daughter of Nicole.

Blue-eyed Rebecca failed as she always would.

Now it is my time.

I'll never be weak again.

Christina Nicole von Stela..

ACKNOWLEDGEMENTS

This took me much longer than I expected/hoped/wanted as I vastly underestimated the magnitude of effort involved in writing a story. I hope this book was entertaining and that perhaps some of you noticed the underlying themes. Or have a favourite character.

But I couldn't have done this alone and so many people inspired me, whether directly or indirectly, and I owe them all a debt of gratitude.

Firstly, Avril, not just for your constant inspiration and encouragement but also for reading this story on several occasions, which was no small task. But you did so much more than the editing. 'Thank you' isn't enough to express my gratitude.

Jessi – I've already acknowledged your beautiful cover design that captures the essence of the story so well but wanted to do so again. It was a true pleasure to work with you and to see your talents create something better than I thought possible.

Amber – I thought it would be cool for you to tell your friends that your dad wrote a book and to maybe one day see it on the shelves of a bookstore. I hoped it would make you proud of me.

Loki – My feline companion. Your likeness appears briefly in the story to commemorate our friendship.

My parents Joe and Billie – I wanted to make you proud and regret that you aren't here to read my story and to see my success, however small, in finally completing my creation.

Manufactured by Amazon.ca
Bolton, ON